ALSO BY E L JAMES

Fifty Shades of Grey

Fifty Shades Darker

Fifty Shades Freed

Grey

Darker

The Mister

FREED

E L James

Bloom books

Published by Bloom Books, an imprint of Sourcebooks
P.O. Box 4410, Naperville, Illinois 60567-4410
(630) 961-3900
sourcebooks.com

Library of Congress Cataloging-in-Publication Data is on file with the publisher.

Printed and bound in the United States of America.
WOZ 10 9 8 7 6 5 4 3 2 1

For Eva and Sue.
Thank you, thank you, thank you
for all that you do.

And for Catherine.
We are a woman down.

Sunday, June 19, 2011

We lie in postcoital bliss beneath pink paper lanterns, meadow flowers, and fairy lights that twinkle in the rafters. As my breathing slows, I hold Anastasia close. She's sprawled all over me, her cheek against my chest, her hand resting on my racing heart. The darkness is absent, driven out by my dream catcher…my fiancée. My love. My light.

Could I be happier than I am right now?

I commit the scene to memory: the boathouse, the soothing rhythm of the lapping waters, the flora, the lights. Closing my eyes, I memorize the feel of the woman in my arms, her weight on top of me, the slow rise and fall of her back as she breathes, her legs entwined with mine. The scent of her hair fills my nostrils soothing all my corners and jagged edges. This is my happy place. Dr. Flynn would be proud. This beautiful woman has consented to be mine. In every way. Again.

"Can we marry tomorrow?" I whisper near her ear.

"Hmm." The sound in her throat reverberates with a soft strum across my skin.

"Is that a yes?"

"Hmm."

"A no?"

"Hmm."

I grin. She's spent. "Miss Steele, are you incoherent?" I sense her answering smile and my joy erupts in a laugh, as I tighten my arms around her and kiss her hair. "Vegas, tomorrow, it is then." She raises her head, eyes half closed in the soft light from the lanterns—she looks sleepy yet sated.

"I don't think my parents would be very happy with that." She lowers her head and I skim my fingertips across her naked back, enjoying the warmth of her sleek skin.

"What do you want, Anastasia? Vegas? A big wedding with all the trimmings? Tell me."

"Not big. Just friends and family."

"Okay. Where?"

She shrugs, and I'm guessing she hasn't thought about it.

"Could we do it here?" I ask.

"Your folks' place? Would they mind?"

I laugh. Grace would leap at the chance. "My mother would be in seventh heaven."

"Okay, here. I'm sure my mom and dad would prefer that."

So would I.

For once we're in agreement. No arguing.

Is this a first?

Gently, I stroke her hair, that's a little mussed from our spent passion. "So, we've established where, now the when."

"Surely you should ask your mother?"

"Hmm. She can have a month, that's it. I want you too much to wait any longer."

"Christian, you have me. You've had me for a while. But okay, a month it is." She plants a tender kiss on my chest and I'm grateful that the darkness remains quiet. Her presence is keeping it at bay.

"We'd better head back. I don't want Mia interrupting us like she did that time."

Ana laughs. "Ah, yes. That was close. My first punishment fuck." She grazes my jaw with her fingertips and I roll over, taking her with me, and pressing her into the deep-pile rug on the floor.

"Don't remind me. Not one of my finest moments."

Her lips lift in a coy smile, her eyes sparkling with humor. "As punishment fucks go, it was okay. And I won back my panties."

"You did. Fair and square." Chuckling at the recollection, I kiss her quickly and rise. "Come, put your panties on and let's get back to what's left of the party."

I ZIP UP HER emerald dress and drape my jacket over her shoulders. "Ready?" She laces her fingers with mine and we walk to the top of the stairs of the boathouse. Pausing, she looks back at our floral haven as if *she's* memorizing the setting. "What about all the lights and these flowers?"

"It's okay. The florist is returning tomorrow to dismantle this bower. They've done a great job. And the flowers will go to a local seniors' home."

She squeezes my hand. "You're a good man, Christian Grey."

I hope I'm good enough for you.

MY FAMILY IS IN the den, abusing the karaoke machine. Kate and Mia are up dancing, and singing "We Are Family," with my parents as their audience. I think they're all a little tipsy. Elliot is slumped on the couch, sipping his beer and mouthing the lyrics.

Kate spots Ana and beckons her toward the mic. "OMG!" squeals Mia, drowning out the song. "Look at that rock!" She grabs Ana's hand and whistles. "Christian Grey, you delivered."

Ana gives her a shy smile while Kate and my mother gather round to inspect her ring, making the appropriate admiring noises. Inside I feel ten feet tall.

Yeah. She likes it. They like it.

You did good, Grey.

"Christian, could I talk to you?" Carrick asks as he stands up, his expression grim.

Now?

His stare is unwavering as he directs me out of the room.

"Um. Sure." I glance at Grace, but she's studiously avoiding my gaze.

Has she told him about Elena?

Fuck. I hope not.

I follow him to his study, and he ushers me in, closing the door behind him.

"Your mother told me," he says with no preamble whatsoever.

I glance at the clock—it's 12:28. It's too late in the day for this talk…in every sense. "Dad, I'm tired—"

"No. You are not avoiding this conversation." His voice is stern and his eyes narrow to pinpricks as he peers at me over his glasses. He's mad. Really mad.

"Dad—"

"Quiet, son. You need to listen." He sits on the edge of his desk, removes his glasses, and begins to clean them with the lint cloth he pulls from his pocket. I stand before him, as I often have, feeling like I did when I was fourteen years old and I'd just been expelled from school—again. Resigned, I take a deep breath and, sighing as loudly as I can, place my hands on my hips and wait for the onslaught.

"To say I'm disappointed is an understatement. What Elena did was criminal—"

"Dad—"

"No, Christian. You don't get to speak right now." He glares at me. "She deserves to be locked up."

Dad!

He pauses and slides his glasses back into place. "But I think it's your deception that disappoints me the most. Every time you left this house with some lie that you were studying with your friends— friends we never got to meet—you were fucking that woman."

Christ!

"How am I to believe anything you've ever said to us?" he continues.

Oh, for fuck's sake. This is a complete overreaction. "Can I speak now?"

"No. You can't. Of course, I blame myself. I thought I'd given you some semblance of a moral compass. And now I'm wondering if I've taught you anything at all."

"Are you asking a rhetorical question?"

He ignores me. "She was a married woman and you had no respect for that, and you're shortly to become a married man—"

"This has nothing to do with Anastasia!"

"Don't you dare shout at me," he says, with such quiet venom that I'm silenced immediately. I don't think I've ever seen or heard him this angry. It's sobering. "It has everything to do with her. You are about to make a huge commitment to a young woman." His tone softens. "It's a surprise to all of us. And I'm happy for you. But we are talking about the sanctity of marriage. And if you have no respect for that, then you have no business being married."

"Dad—"

"And if you're that cavalier about the sacred vows that you will soon be affirming, you seriously need to consider a prenuptial agreement."

What? I raise my hands to stop him. He's gone too far. I'm an adult, for heaven's sake. "Don't bring Ana into this. She's not some grubby gold-digger."

"This is not about her." He stands and steps toward me. "It's about you. You living up to your responsibilities. You being a trustworthy and decent human being. You being husband material!"

"For fuck's sake, Dad, I was fifteen years old!" I shout, and we're nose to nose, glowering at each other.

Why is he reacting so badly to this? I know I've always been a huge disappointment to him, but he's never spelled it out so plainly.

He shuts his eyes and pinches the bridge of his nose, and I realize that in my moments of stress I do the same. This habit comes from him, but in my case the apple has fallen far, far from the tree.

"You're right. You were a vulnerable child. But what you fail to see is that what she did was wrong, and clearly you still can't see it because you've continued to associate with her, not only as a family friend, but in business. Both of you have been lying to us for all these years. And that's what hurts the most." His voice drops. "She was your mother's friend. We thought she was a good friend. She's the opposite. You *will* cut all financial ties with her."

Fuck off, Carrick.

I want to tell him that Elena was a force for good, and that I wouldn't have continued my association with her if I thought anything else. But I know this will fall on deaf ears. He didn't want to listen when I was fourteen and struggling in school, and it appears he doesn't want to listen now.

"Have you quite finished?" The words hiss with bitterness through my gritted teeth.

"Think about what I've said."

I turn to go. I've heard enough.

"Think about the prenup. It will save you a great deal of grief in the future."

Ignoring him, I stalk out of his office and slam the door.

Fuck him!

Grace is standing in the hallway.

"Why did you tell him?" I spit at her, but Carrick has followed me out of the study so she doesn't answer. Her frosty glare is directed at him.

I'm going to fetch Ana. We're going home.

My mood savage, I follow the sound of caterwauling into the den and find Elliot and Ana at the mic strangling "Ain't No Mountain High Enough." If I wasn't so angry I'd laugh. Elliot's tuneless rumbling can't really be classed as singing, and he's drowning out Ana's sweet voice. Fortunately, the song is nearly over so I'm spared the worst of it.

"I think Marvin Gaye and Tammi Terrell are spinning in their graves," I observe dryly when they finish.

"I thought that was a pretty good rendition." Elliot bows theatrically to Mia and Kate, who are laughing and applauding with exaggerated gusto. They're definitely all inebriated. Ana giggles, looking flushed and lovely.

"We're going home," I tell her.

Her face falls. "I told your mother we'd stay."

"You did? Just now?"

"Yes. She brought down a change of clothes for us. I was looking forward to sleeping in your bedroom."

"Darling, I was really hoping you'd stay." It's a plea from my mother, who stands in the doorway, Carrick behind her. "Kate and Elliot are, too. I like having all my chicks under one roof." She reaches out and clasps my hand. "And we thought we'd lost you this week."

Muttering an expletive beneath my breath, I keep my temper in check. My siblings seem to be completely oblivious to the drama that is unfolding in front of them. I expect this cluelessness from Elliot but not from Mia.

"Stay, son. Please." My father's eyes bore into me, but he appears genial enough. It's not like he's just told me that I'm a complete and utter disappointment.

Again.

I ignore him and respond to my mother. "Okay." But it's only because Ana's giving me such an imploring look, and I know that if I leave in my present mood it will be a blight on what has been a wonderful day.

Ana wraps her arms around me. "Thank you," she whispers. I smile down at her and the dark cloud that hangs over me begins to dissipate.

"Come on, Dad." Mia thrusts the mic into his hand and drags him in front of the screen. "Last song!" she says.

"Bed." It's not a request to Ana. I've had enough of my family for one night. She nods in agreement and I knit her fingers with mine. "Good night, all. Thanks for the party, Mother."

Grace hugs me. "You know we love you. We only want the best for you. I am so happy with your news. And so happy that you're here."

"Yeah, Mom. Thanks." I give her a swift peck on the cheek. "We're tired. We're going to bed. Good night."

"Good night, Ana. Thank you," she says and gives her a swift hug. I tug Ana's hand to leave as Mia puts on "Wild Thing" for Carrick to sing.

That I do not want to see.

SWITCHING ON THE LIGHT, I close my bedroom door and pull Ana into my arms, seeking her warmth and trying to put Carrick's blistering rebuke out of my mind.

"Hey, are you okay?" she murmurs. "You're brooding."

"I'm just mad at my dad. But that's nothing new. He still treats me like I'm an adolescent."

Ana hugs me tighter. "Your father loves you."

"Well, tonight he's very disappointed in me. Again. But I don't want to discuss that right now." I kiss the top of her head and she tilts her face up, focusing on me, compassion and understanding shining in her eyes, and I know neither of us wants to raise the specter of Elena…*Mrs. Robinson*.

I'm reminded of earlier this evening, when Grace, in all her avenging glory, threw Elena out of the house. I wonder what my mother would have said, back in the day, if she'd caught me with a girl in my room. Suddenly I'm energized by the same teenage thrill I had when Ana and I snuck up here last weekend during the masquerade ball.

"I've got a girl in my room." I grin.

"What are you going to do with her?" Ana's answering smile is seductive.

"Hmm. All the things I wanted to do with girls when I was an adolescent." But couldn't. Because I couldn't bear to be touched. "Unless you're too tired." I trace the soft curve of her cheek with my knuckle.

"Christian. I'm exhausted. But thrilled, too."

Oh, baby. I kiss her quickly and take pity on her. "Maybe we should just sleep. It's been a long day. Come. I'll put you to bed. Turn around."

She complies and I reach for the zipper on her dress.

WHILE MY FIANCÉE SLUMBERS beside me, I text Taylor and ask him to bring us a change of clothes from Escala in the morning. Scooting down beside Ana, I focus on her profile, marveling that she's asleep already…and that she's agreed to be mine.

Will I ever be good enough for her?

Am I husband material?

My father seems to doubt it.

I sigh and lie on my back, staring up at the ceiling.

I'm going to prove him wrong.

He's always been strict with me. More so than with Elliot or Mia.

Fucker. He knows I'm a bad seed. As I replay his earlier tirade in my head, I drift until sleep claims me.

Arms up, Christian. Daddy has a serious face. He is teaching diving into the pool. *That's right. Now curl your toes around the edge of the pool. Good. Arch your back. That's right. Now push off.* I fall. And fall. And fall. Splash. Into the cool, clear water. Into the blue. Into the calm. Into the quiet. But my water wings push me back to the air. And I look for Daddy. *Look, Daddy, look.* But Elliot jumps on him. And they fall on the ground. Daddy tickles Elliot. Elliot laughs. And laughs. And laughs. And Daddy kisses his tummy. Daddy doesn't do that to me. I don't like it. I'm in the water. I want to be up there. With them. With Daddy. And I'm standing in the trees. Watching Daddy and Mia. She shrieks with joy as he tickles her. And he laughs. And she wriggles free and jumps on him. He swings her around and catches her. And

I stand in the trees alone. Watching. Wanting. The air smells good. Of apples.

"Good morning, Mr. Grey," Ana whispers as I open my eyes. The morning sun glimmers through the windows and I'm curled around her like a vine. The knot of homesickness and heartache—evoked by a dream, surely—unravels at the sight of her. I'm smitten and aroused, my body rising to greet her.

"Good morning, Miss Steele." She looks impossibly beautiful in spite of the fact that she's wearing Mia's I ♥ Paris T-shirt. She cups my face, her eyes sparkling and her hair wild and glossy in the morning light. She runs a thumb along my chin, tickling the stubble.

"I was watching you sleep."

"Were you now?"

"And looking at my beautiful engagement ring." She stretches out her hand and wiggles her fingers. The diamond captures the light and throws tiny rainbows across my old movie and kickboxing posters on the walls.

"Ooh!" she coos. "It's a sign."

A good sign, Grey. Hopefully.

"I'm never going to take it off."

"Good!" I move so that I'm covering her. "Watching me for how long?" I run my nose down hers and press my lips to hers.

"Oh, no." She pushes at my shoulders and my stab of disappointment is real, but she rolls me onto my back and straddles my hips. Sitting up, she sweeps her T-shirt off in one swift move, and throws it to the floor. "I was thinking about giving you a wake-up call."

"Oh?" My cock and I rejoice.

Before I can steel myself against her touch, she leans down and places a soft kiss on my chest, her hair tumbling around us both, creating a chestnut haven. Bright blue eyes peek at me.

"Starting here." She kisses me again.

I inhale sharply.

"Then moving down to here." She runs her tongue in a wayward line down my sternum.

Yes.

The darkness stays quiet, subdued by the goddess on top of me or by my bursting libido. I don't know which.

"You taste mighty fine, Mr. Grey," she breathes against my skin.

"I'm glad to hear it." The words are hoarse in my throat.

She licks and nips me along the base of my rib cage as her breasts graze over my lower belly.

Ah!

Once, twice, three times.

"Ana!" I clutch her knees as my breathing accelerates, and squeeze. But she squirms on top of my groin, so I let go, and she rises up, leaving me waiting and wanting. I think she's going to take me. She's ready.

I'm ready.

Fuck, I'm so ready.

But she moves down my body, kissing my stomach and my belly, her tongue slipping into my navel, then grazing through my happy trail. She nips me once more and I feel the bite right through my cock.

"Ah!"

"There you are," she whispers and she stares greedily at my eager dick and then peeps up at me with a coquettish grin. Slowly, her eyes on mine, she takes me in her mouth.

Sweet Jesus.

Her head bobs up and down, her teeth sheathed behind her lips, as she pulls me farther into her mouth each time. My fingers find her hair and sweep it out of the way so I can enjoy an uninterrupted view of my future wife with her lips around my cock. I tighten my buttocks, pushing up my hips, seeking more depth, and she takes it, clamping her mouth around me.

Harder.

Harder still.

Ah. Ana. You fucking goddess.

She picks up the rhythm. And, closing my eyes, I fist my hand in her hair.

She is so good at this.

"Yes," I hiss through my teeth and I lose myself in the rise and fall of her exquisite mouth. I'm going to come.

All of a sudden, she stops.

Damn. No! I open my eyes and watch her move above me, then sink oh-so-slowly onto my bursting dick. I groan, relishing every precious inch. Her hair tumbles to her naked breasts and, reaching up, I caress each one, running my thumbs across her hardening nipples, over and over and over.

She lets out a lengthy moan, thrusting her tits into my hands.

Oh, baby.

Then she pitches forward, kissing me, her tongue invading my mouth, and I taste and savor my saltiness in her sweet mouth.

Ana.

I move my hands to her hips and ease her up off me and then pull her down, thrusting up at the same time.

She cries out, grabbing on to my wrists.

And I do it again.

And again.

"Christian," she calls to the ceiling in a quiet plea as she matches my tempo and we move together. In time. As one. Until she falls apart on top of me, taking me with her and triggering my own release.

I NUZZLE HER HAIR and thrum my fingers down her back.

She takes my breath away.

This is still new. Ana in charge. Ana initiating. I like it.

"Now that's my idea of Sunday worship," I whisper.

"Christian!" She whips her head to mine, eyes round with disapproval.

I laugh out loud.

Will this ever get old? Shocking Miss Steele?

I hug her hard and roll us both over so she's beneath me.

"Good morning, Miss Steele. It's always a treat to wake up to you."

She strokes my cheek. "And you, Mr. Grey." Her tone is soft. "Do we have to get up? I like being here in your room."

"No." I glance at my watch on the nightstand. It's 9:15. "My parents will be at Mass." I shift to her side.

"I didn't know they were churchgoers."

I grimace. "Yes. They are. Catholic."

"Are you?"

"No, Anastasia."

God and I went our separate ways a long time ago.

"Are you?" I ask, recalling that Welch could find no religious affiliations during her background check.

She shakes her head. "No. Neither of my parents practice a faith. But I would like to go to church today. I need to thank…someone for bringing you back alive from the helicopter accident."

I sigh, visualizing a bolt of lightning burning me to a cinder if I step onto the hallowed grounds of a church, but for her, I'll go.

"Okay. I'll see what we can do." I kiss her quickly. "Come, shower with me."

THERE'S A SMALL LEATHER duffel outside my bedroom door— Taylor has delivered clean clothes. I scoop up the bag and shut the door. Ana is wrapped in a towel, beads of water glistening on her shoulders. Her attention is focused on my bulletin board, paused at the photograph of the crack whore. She turns her head toward me, a question on her beautiful face…a question I don't want to answer. "You still have it," she says.

Yeah. I still have the photo. What of it?

As her question hangs in the air between us, her eyes grow luminous in the morning sunshine, drinking me in, begging me to say something. But I can't. This is not somewhere I want to go. For a moment, I'm reminded of the gut punch I felt when Carrick handed me the photograph so many years ago.

Hell. Don't go there, Grey.

"Taylor brought a change of clothes for us," I whisper as I sling the duffel onto the bed. There's an impossibly long silence before she responds.

"Okay," she says, and she walks toward the bed and unzips the bag.

I'VE EATEN MY FILL. My parents have returned from Mass and my mother has cooked her traditional brunch: a delicious, coronary-inducing plate of bacon, sausage, hash browns, eggs, and English muffins. Grace is a little quiet, and I suspect that she might have a hangover.

Throughout the morning I have avoided my father.

I haven't forgiven him for last night.

Ana, Elliot, and Kate are in a heated debate—about bacon, of all things—and arguing over who should have the last sausage. I half listen with amusement while I read an article about the failure rate of local banks in the Sunday edition of *The Seattle Times*.

Mia shrieks and reclaims her place at the table, holding her laptop. "Look at this. There's a gossipy item on the *Seattle Nooz* website about you being engaged, Christian."

"Already?" Mom says, surprised.

Don't these assholes have anything better to do?

Mia reads the column out loud. "'Word has reached us here at the *Nooz* that Seattle's most eligible bachelor, *the* Christian Grey, has finally been snapped up, and wedding bells are in the air.'"

I glance at Ana, who pales as she stares, doe-eyed, from Mia to me.

"'But who is the lucky, lucky lady?'" Mia continues. "'The *Nooz* is on the hunt. Bet she's reading one helluva prenup.'" Mia starts giggling.

I glare at her. *Shut the fuck up, Mia.*

She stops and presses her lips together. Ignoring her, and all the anxious looks exchanged at the table, I turn my attention to Ana, who blanches even more.

"No," I mouth, trying to reassure her.

"Christian," Dad says.

"I'm not discussing this again," I snarl at him. He opens his mouth to say something. "No prenup!" I snap with such vehemence that he closes his mouth.

Shut up, Carrick!

Picking up the paper, I find myself rereading the same sentence in the banking article over and over while I fume.

"Christian," Ana murmurs. "I'll sign anything you and Mr. Grey want."

I look up and she's beseeching me, a sheen of unshed tears reflecting in her eyes.

Ana. Stop.

"No!" I exclaim, imploring her to drop this subject.

"It's to protect you."

"Christian, Ana—I think you should discuss this in private," Grace chastises us and scowls at Carrick and Mia.

"Ana, this is not about you," Dad mumbles. "And please call me Carrick."

Don't try and make it up to her now. I seethe, inwardly, and suddenly there's a burst of activity. Kate and Mia get up to clear the table and Elliot quickly stabs the last remaining sausage with his fork.

"I definitely prefer sausage," he roars with forced levity.

Ana is staring at her hands. She looks crestfallen.

Jesus. Dad. Look what you've done.

I reach over and grasp both her hands in mine, and whisper so only she can hear me, "Stop it. Ignore my dad. He's really pissed about Elena. That stuff was all aimed at me. I wish my mom had kept her mouth shut."

"He has a point, Christian. You're very wealthy, and I'm bringing nothing to our marriage but my student loans."

Baby, I'll have you any way I can get you. You know this!

"Anastasia, if you leave me, you might as well take everything. You left me once before. I know how that feels."

"That was different," she mumbles. And she frowns once more. "But, you might want to leave me."

Now she's being ridiculous.

"Christian, you know I might do something exceptionally stupid—and you…" She stops.

Ana, I think that's highly unlikely. "Stop. Stop now. This subject is closed. We're not discussing it anymore. No prenup. Not now—not ever."

I scramble through my thoughts, trying to find safer ground, and inspiration hits me. Turning to Grace, who's wringing her hands and looking anxiously at me, I ask, "Mom, can we have the wedding here?"

Her expression shifts from alarm to joy and gratitude. "Darling. That would be wonderful." And she adds as an afterthought, "You don't want a church wedding?"

I give her a sideways look and she capitulates immediately.

"We'd love to host your wedding. Wouldn't we, Cary?"

"Yes. Yes, of course." My father smiles benignly at both Ana and me, but I can't look at him.

"Have you a date in mind?" Grace asks.

"Four weeks."

"Christian. That's not enough time!"

"It's plenty of time."

"I need at least eight!"

"Mom. Please."

"Six?" she pleads.

"That would be wonderful. Thank you, Mrs. Grey," Ana pipes up, and shoots a warning glance at me, daring me to contradict her.

"Six it is," I state. "Thanks, Mom."

ANA IS QUIET ON the drive back to Seattle. She's probably thinking about my outburst at Carrick this morning. Our argument from last night still rankles—his disapproval a burr chafing at my skin. Deep down, I'm worried that he's right; maybe I'm not husband material.

Damn, I'm going to prove him wrong.

I'm not the adolescent he thinks I am.

I stare at the road ahead, deflated. My girl is beside me, we have a date for our wedding, and I should feel on top of the world, but I'm picking over the remains of my father's angry tirade about Elena and the prenup. On the plus side, I think he knows he fucked up. He tried to make it up to me when we parted earlier but his fumbling, inadequate attempt to make amends still smarts.

Christian, I've always done everything in my power to protect you. And I failed. I should have been there for you.

But I didn't want to hear him. He should have said this last night. He did not.

I shake my head. I want out of this funk.

"Hey, I have an idea." I reach over and squeeze Ana's knee.

PERHAPS MY LUCK IS turning—there's a parking space outside St. James Cathedral. Ana peers through the trees at the majestic building that dominates a whole block on Ninth Avenue, then turns to me, a question in her eyes.

"Church," I offer, by way of explanation.

"This is big for a church, Christian."

"True."

She smiles. "It's perfect."

Hand in hand, we head through one of the front doors into the antechamber, then proceed onward into the nave. Out of instinct I reach toward the stoup for Holy Water to bless myself, but I stop just in time, knowing that if a bolt of lightning is going to strike, it will be now. I catch Ana's openmouthed surprise, but look away to admire the impressive ceiling as I wait for God's judgment.

No. No thunderbolt today.

"Old habits," I mutter, feeling a little embarrassed, but relieved that I've not been rendered into a pile of ashes on the grand threshold. Ana turns her attention to the magnificent interior: the lofty ornate ceilings, the rust-colored marble columns, the intricate stained glass. Sunlight streams in a steady beam through the oculus in the transept's dome, as if God were smiling down on the place. There's a whispered hush that fills the nave, enveloping us in a spiritual calm that's disturbed only by the occasional echoing cough from one of the few visitors. It's quiet, a refuge from the hustle and bustle of Seattle. I'd forgotten just how tranquil and beautiful it is in here, but then I've not been inside for years. I'd always loved the pomp and ceremony of a Catholic Mass. The ritual. The responses. The smell of burning incense. Grace made sure her three children were well versed in all things Catholic, and there was a time when I would have done anything to please my new mother.

But puberty arrived and all that went to shit. My relationship with God never recovered, and it changed the relationship with my family, especially my father. We were always at odds with each other from the time I hit thirteen. I brush off the memory. It's painful.

Now standing in the hushed splendor of the nave, I'm overwhelmed by a familiar sense of peace. "Come. I want to show you something." We walk down the side aisle, the sound of Ana's heels ringing over the flagstones, until we reach a small chapel. Its golden walls and dark floor are the perfect setting for the exquisite statue of Our Lady, surrounded by flickering candles.

Ana gasps when she sees her.

Without a doubt this is still one of the most beautiful shrines I've ever seen. The Virgin, eyes cast down at the floor in modesty, holds her child aloft. Her gold-and-blue robes shimmer in the light from the burning candles.

It's stunning.

"My mother used to bring us here sometimes for Mass. This was my favorite place. The Shrine of the Blessed Virgin Mary," I whisper.

Ana stands and soaks up the scene, the statue, the walls, the dark ceiling covered in gold stars. "Is this what inspired your collection? Your Madonnas?" she asks, and there's wonder in her voice.

"Yes."

"Motherhood," she murmurs, and she peeks up at me.

I shrug. "I've seen it done well and done badly."

"Your birth mom?" she asks.

I nod, and her eyes grow impossibly large, revealing some deep emotion that I don't want to acknowledge.

I look away. It's too raw.

I place a fifty-dollar bill in the offertory box and hand her a candle. Ana clasps my hand briefly in gratitude, then lights the wick from one of the tapers and places her candle in an iron sconce on the wall. It flickers brightly among its companions. "Thank you," she says quietly to Mary, and wraps an arm around my middle, placing her head on my shoulder. Together we stand in quiet contemplation in this most exquisite of sanctuaries in the heart of the city.

The peace, the beauty, and being with Ana restores my good humor. To hell with work this afternoon. It's Sunday. I want some fun with my girl. "Shall we go to the game?" I ask.

"Game?"

"The Phillies are playing the M's at Safeco Field. GEH has a suite there."

"Sure. Sounds like fun. Let's go." Ana beams.

Hand in hand, we head back to the R8.

This morning has been extremely aggravating, and I'm ready to rip someone limb from limb. There were hordes of reporters, including a couple of TV crews, camped outside Escala and Seattle Independent Publishing.

Have they nothing better to do?

It was easy to avoid them at home because we arrived and left through the underground garage. At SIP it's another issue. I'm confounded and appalled that these vultures have managed to track Ana down so quickly.

How?

We dodged them by skirting the SIP building and going to the rear loading doors. But now Ana's trapped inside her office and I'm ambivalent about that. At least she's safe there, but I'm sure she's not going to tolerate confinement for long.

My heart sinks. Of course the Seattle media are curious about my fiancée. It's part of the Christian Grey *bonus*. I just hope to God this attention doesn't drive her away.

Sawyer pulls up outside Grey House, where another couple of hacks are lurking, but with Taylor beside me I storm past them, ignoring their shouted questions.

What a fucking start to the morning!

Still aggravated, I wait for the elevator. I have a to-do list longer than my dick and I have to deal with the fallout from the weekend: missed calls from my dad, my mom, and Elena Lincoln.

Why the hell she's calling me I don't know. We're done. I made that clear on Saturday night.

I'd rather be at home with my girl.

In the elevator I check my phone. There's an e-mail from Ana.

From: Anastasia Steele
Subject: Showing A Fiancée A Good Time
Date: June 20 2011 09:25
To: Christian Grey

My dearest husband-to-be
I feel it would be remiss of me not to thank you for
a) surviving a helicopter crash
b) an exemplary hearts-and-flowers proposal
c) a wonderful weekend
d) a return to the Red Room
e) a very pretty rock, which everyone has noticed!
f) my wake-up call this morning (especially this! ;))
Ax

Anastasia Steele
Acting-Editor, Fiction, SIP

PS: Do you have a strategy for dealing with the press?

From: Christian Grey
Subject: Showing a man a good time
Date: June 20 2011 09:36
To: Anastasia Steele

My darling Ana
You are entirely welcome.
Thank you for a wonderful weekend.
I love you.
I'll come back to you about a strategy for the f****** press.

Christian Grey
CEO, Grey Enterprises Holdings, Inc.

PS: I think wake-up calls are underrated.
PPS: F****** BLACKBERRY!!!!!!!!!!!

How many times do I have to tell you, woman!

Amused and mollified by our e-mail exchange, I charge out of the elevator. Andrea is at her desk in my outer office. "Good morning, Mr. Grey," she says. "I…um…I'm glad you're still with us."

"Thank you, Andrea. I appreciate that. And thank you for all your help on Friday night. It was invaluable."

She flushes, embarrassed, I think, by my gratitude. "Where's the new girl?" I ask.

"Sarah? She's on an errand. Coffee?"

"Please. Black. Strong. I have a great deal to do."

She gets to her feet.

"If my father, mother, or Mrs. Lincoln call, take a message. Refer all press inquiries to Sam. But if the FAA, Eurocopter, or Welch call, put them through."

"Yes, sir."

"And, of course, Anastasia Steele."

Andrea's face softens with one of her rare smiles. "Congratulations, Mr. Grey."

"You know?"

"Everyone knows, sir."

I laugh. "Thank you, Andrea."

"I'll get your coffee."

"Great, thanks."

At my desk, I wake my iMac. There's another e-mail from Ana.

From: Anastasia Steele
Subject: The Limitations of Language
Date: June 20 2011 09:38
To: Christian Grey

```
**.****, **** *******!
*** ***** ** **********.
* **** ***, ***.
```
Ax

I laugh out loud even though I have no idea what she's written. Andrea enters with my coffee and sits down so we can run through the day's schedule ahead of my first call.

I'VE BEEN ON THE phone for what feels like three solid hours. When I finally hang up, stand, and stretch, it's 1:15. *Charlie Tango* is being recovered today and should be back at Boeing Field tonight. The Federal Aviation Administration has handed the inquiry into the emergency landing over to the National Transportation Safety Board.

The Eurocopter engineer who was one of the first on-site says it's incredibly fortunate that I put the fire out with the extinguishers. It will help to speed up theirs and the NTSB's investigation. I'm hoping to have their initial report tomorrow.

Welch has informed me that as a precaution, he's secured all of last week's CCTV footage from the helipad in Portland, and from in and around *Charlie Tango*'s private hangar at Boeing Field. A shiver skates up my spine. Welch thinks it might be sabotage, and I have to admit the possibility has been at the back of my mind since *both* engines caught fire.

Sabotage.

But why?

I've asked him to have his team comb through all the recordings and see if they find anything suspicious.

After much wheedling from Sam, my VP for publicity, I've agreed to a brief press conference later this afternoon. Sam's nagging voice rings in my head. *"You need to get in front of this, Christian. Your miraculous escape is still all over the news cycle. They have aerial footage of the recovery operation."*

Frankly, I think Sam just loves the drama. I hope that a press briefing will stop them from hounding Ana and me.

Andrea buzzes my phone.

"What?"

"Dr. Grey is on the line again."

"Fuck," I whisper under my breath. I guess I can't avoid her forever. "Okay, put her through." Leaning against my desk, I wait for her dulcet tones.

"Christian. I know you're busy, but two things."

"Yes, Mother."

"I've found a wedding planner I want to use. Her name is Alondra Gutierrez. She organized this year's Coping Together Ball. I think you and Ana should meet her."

I roll my eyes. "Sure."

"Good. I'll arrange a meeting later this week. Secondly, your father really wants to talk to you."

"I spoke to my father at length on the night I announced my

engagement. We were also celebrating my twenty-eighth year in the world and, as you know, I'm always reluctant to mark these milestones." I'm on a roll. "And I'd just survived a hair-raising crash-landing." My voice is rising. "Dad really rained on my parade. I think he said enough then. I don't want to talk to him now."

He's a pompous prick.

"Christian. Stop sulking. Talk to your dad."

Sulking! I'm fucking pissed, Grace.

My mother's silence stretches between us, laced with her censure.

I sigh. "Okay, I'll think about it." The other line on my phone flashes. "I've got to go."

"Very well, darling. I'll let you know about the meeting with Alondra."

"Good-bye, Mom."

My phone buzzes again. "Mr. Grey, I have Anastasia Steele for you."

My rancor disappears. "Great. Thanks, Andrea."

"Christian?" Her voice is small, and uneven. She sounds scared.

My breath catches in my throat. "Ana, is everything all right?"

"Um…I went out for some fresh air. I thought they'd be gone. And, well…"

"The reporters and photographers?"

"Yes."

Fuckers.

"I didn't comment on anything. I just turned around and ran back into the building."

Damn. I should have sent Sawyer to watch over her, and I'm grateful once more that Taylor persuaded me to keep him on after the Leila Williams incident. "Ana, it's going to be fine. I was going to call you. I've just agreed to give a press conference later this afternoon about *Charlie Tango*. They'll ask about our engagement. I'll give them the barest of details. Hopefully that will be enough to satisfy them."

"Good."

I chance my luck. "Would you like me to send Sawyer to watch over you?"

"Yes," she says immediately.

Whoa. That was easy. She must be more shaken than I thought. "Are you sure you're okay? You're not normally so amenable."

"I have my moments, Mr. Grey. They usually occur after I've been pursued by the media through the streets of Seattle. It was quite the workout. I was breathless when I got back to the office." She's making light of the situation.

"Really, Miss Steele? You have such great stamina, normally."

"Why, Mr. Grey, what on earth are you referring to?" I hear the smile in her voice.

"I think you know," I whisper.

Her breath hitches and the sound travels straight to my groin.

"Are you flirting with me?" she asks.

"I hope so."

"Will you test my stamina later?" Her voice is low and sultry.

Oh, Ana. Desire streaks through my body like lightning.

"Nothing would give me greater pleasure."

"I'm so glad to hear that, Christian Grey."

She's far too good at this game. "I'm so happy you called me," I say. "Made my day."

"I aim to please." She giggles. "I must call your personal trainer, so I can keep up with you!"

I laugh. "Bastille will be delighted."

She's silent for a moment. "Thank you for making me feel better."

"Isn't that what I'm supposed to do?"

"It is. And you do it well."

I bask in her loving words. *Ana, you make me feel whole.*

There's a knock on my door, and I know it's either Andrea or Sarah with my lunch.

"I've got to go."

"Thank you, Christian," she says.

"For what?"

"Being you. Oh, one more thing. The news of you buying SIP is still embargoed, isn't it?"

"Yes, for another three weeks."

"Okay. I'll try and remember that."

"Do. Laters, baby."

"Okay. Laters, Christian."

ANDREA AND SARAH HAVE gone all out today. I have my favorite sandwich—turkey club with a pickle on the side—a sprinkling of salad, and some potato chips, all served on a tray with GEH linen, a cut crystal highball glass with sparkling water, and a matching vase sporting a perky pink rose.

"Thanks," I mutter, bemused, as they both fuss setting up the tray.

"Pleasure, Mr. Grey," Andrea says with a smile that is becoming less rare. They both seem strangely distracted and a little skittish today. *What are they up to?*

While I tuck into lunch I check my messages. There's another one from Elena.

Shit.

> ELENA
> Call me. Please.
>
> ELENA
> Call me. I'm going crazy.
>
> ELENA
> I don't know what to say. I've been thinking about what happened all weekend. And I don't know why things got so out of control. I'm sorry. Call me.
>
> ELENA
> Please answer my calls.

I have to deal with her. My parents want me to cut ties with Mrs. Lincoln, and frankly I don't know how we come back from all that we spewed at each other on Saturday evening.

I said some pretty awful things.

So did she.

It's time to end it.

I told Ana I would gift Elena the company.

I scroll through my contacts and find the number of my personal lawyer. Ironically, it was Elena who first put us in touch. Debra Kingston is a commercial lawyer who also happens to enjoy the same lifestyle that I do. She's drafted all my D/s contracts and NDAs, and handled my dealings with Mrs. Lincoln and our joint business.

I press call.

"Christian, good afternoon. Long time no speak. I understand congratulations are in order."

"Thanks, Debra."

Jesus! She knows, too.

"What can I do for you?"

"I want to gift the salon business to Elena Lincoln."

"Excuse me?" Her voice rings with disbelief.

"You heard me right. I want to gift the business to Elena. I'd like you to draw up a contract. Everything. Loans. Property. Assets. All of it. It's all hers."

"Are you sure?"

"Yes."

"You're cutting ties?"

"I am. I want nothing to do with it. No liabilities."

"Christian, as your lawyer I have to ask, are you sure you want to do this? This is an incredibly generous gift. You stand to lose hundreds of thousands of dollars."

"Debra, I'm well aware of that."

She huffs into the phone. "Okay, if you insist. I'll send over a draft in the next couple of days."

"Thank you. And I want to conduct all correspondence with her through you."

"You two have really fallen out."

I am not going to discuss my private life with Debra. Well, not this aspect of my private life.

"I get it," she adds. "Keeping the ball and chain happy?"

What. The. Hell?

"Debra, just do the fucking contract."

Her response is tight-lipped. "Very well, Christian. And I'll let Mrs. Lincoln know."

"Good. Thank you."

That should get Elena off my back.

I hang up.

Whoa. I've done it.

And it feels good. A relief. I've just kissed good-bye to a small fortune by GEH standards, but I owe her that much. Without her there
would be no GEH.

"I've been thinking about our recent conversation, Christian."

"Yes, Ma'am?"

*"You, leaving Harvard. I'll lend you $100,000 to start your
business."*

"You'd do that?"

*"Christian, I have every faith in you. You are destined to be
a master of the universe. It will be a loan and you can pay me
back."*

"Elena... I..."

*"You can thank me by showing me what you learned earlier
today. You top. I'll bottom. Don't mark me."*

I shake my head; so began my training as a Dominant. My success as a businessman is tied to my lifestyle choice. I smirk at the
pun and then frown. I can't believe I've never consciously made the
connection before.

Shit. I can't cower behind my desk. I owe her a call.

Showtime, Grey.

Reluctantly, I press her contact on my phone.

She answers on the first ring. "Christian, why haven't you called
me?"

"I'm calling you now."

"What the hell is wrong with your mother and your...fiancée?"
she sneers over that final word.

"Elena, this is a courtesy call. I'm gifting you the business. I've
been in touch with Debra Kingston; she's drawing up the paperwork.
It's over. We can't do this anymore."

"What? What are you talking about?"

"I mean it. I no longer have the energy for your bullshit. I asked
you to leave Ana alone and you ignored my request. We reap what we
sow, Mrs. Lincoln. It's over. Don't call me."

"Chris—" I hear the alarm in her voice as I hang up.

My phone buzzes immediately, her name flashing on my screen. I switch it off and look over my to-do list.

I have about an hour before the press conference, so to take my mind off Elena, I pick up my office phone and call my brother.

"Hey, hotshot. Having second thoughts?"

"Fuck off, Elliot."

"*She's* having second thoughts?" He snickers.

"Could you silence your inner asshole for two minutes?"

"That long? Dubious."

"I'm buying a house."

"Whoa. For you and the future Mrs. Grey? That was quick. You knocked her up?"

"No!" *For fuck's sake.*

He cackles on his end of the phone. "Don't tell me. It's in Denny-Blaine or Laurelhurst?"

Ah, the tech millionaires' suburbs of choice.

"No."

"Medina?"

I laugh. "That's far too near Mom and Dad. It's on the water just north of Broadview."

"You're kidding."

"No. I want to watch the sun sink into the Sound, not rise above a lake."

Elliot laughs. "Man. Who knew you were such a romantic?"

I scoff. I certainly didn't. "It needs gutting."

"It does?" That has Elliot's interest. "You want me to recommend someone?"

"No, dude. I want you to do it. I want something sustainable and environmentally friendly. You know, all the shit you champion at family meals."

"Oh. Wow." He sounds surprised. "Can I see the place?"

"Yes, of course. I've not gone to contract yet, but we're going ahead with surveys over the next week or so."

"Sure. This is rad. But you'll need an architect. I can only do so much."

"What was the name of the woman who oversaw the renovations in Aspen?"

"Um…Gia Matteo. She's cool. She's now at some fancy downtown firm."

"She did a great job at the house in Aspen. And I seem to remember she had an impressive and imaginative portfolio. Do you recommend her?"

"Yeah. Um… Sure."

"You sound hesitant."

"Well, you know. She's the kind of woman who doesn't take no for an answer."

"What do you mean?"

"She's…ambitious. Hungry. Driven to get what she wants."

"I've got no problem with that."

"Neither have I," says Elliot. "In fact, I rather like a predatory female."

"You do?" *Well, Kavanagh fits that bill.*

"She and I…" Elliot trails off.

I can't help my eye roll. My brother suffers from sexual incontinence. "Will that be awkward?"

"No. Of course not. She knows her shit."

"I'll call her. And take a look at her updated portfolio." I scribble down her name.

"Cool. Let me know when we can scout the place."

"Will do. Laters."

"Dude."

I hang up, wondering how many women he's fucked. I shake my head. Does he know that Katherine Kavanagh has designs on him? Could he not see that over the weekend? I hope he doesn't end up with her. She is possibly the most annoying woman I know.

Sam has e-mailed the statement for the press conference, which is in half an hour. I review it and make some changes; as usual, his prose is overwrought and pretentious. Sometimes I don't know why I hired him.

Twenty minutes later he's knocking on my door.

"Christian. Are you ready?"

"SO, MR. GREY, ARE you suggesting that this could be sabotage?" the journalist from *The Seattle Times* asks.

"I'm not saying that at all. We are keeping an open mind and waiting for the accident report."

"Congratulations on your engagement, Mr. Grey. How did you meet Anastasia Steele?" I think this woman is from *Seattle Metropolitan*.

"I'm not answering any specific questions about my private life. I'll just reiterate, I'm thrilled she's consented to be my wife."

"That's the last question, thank you, ladies and gentlemen." Sam comes to my rescue and ushers me out of the GEH conference room.

Thank God that's over.

"You did well," Sam says, as if I need his approval. "I'm sure the press are going to want a picture of you and Anastasia together. I don't think they'll stop hounding you until they have one."

"I'll think about it. Right now I just want to go back to my office."

Sam smirks. "Of course, Christian. I'll send you a compilation of the conference press coverage when we get it."

"Thanks." *Why is he smirking?*

I step into the elevator and I'm delighted to find that I have it to myself. I check my phone. There are missed calls from Elena.

For heaven's sake, Mrs. Lincoln. We're done.

There's also an e-mail from Ana.

From: Anastasia Steele
Subject: The News!
Date: June 20 2011 16:55
To: Christian Grey

Mr. Grey
You give good press conference.
Why does that not surprise me?
You looked hot.
Loved your tie.
Ax

PS: Sabotage?

My hand strays to my tie. *That Brioni tie. My favorite.*

I looked hot. These words give me more pleasure than they should. I like to look hot for Ana, and her e-mail gives me an idea.

From: Christian Grey
Subject: I'll Show You Hot
Date: June 20 2011 17:08
To: Anastasia Steele

My darling wife-to-be
Maybe I can use the tie this evening, when I test your stamina.

Christian Grey
Impatient CEO, Grey Enterprises Holdings, Inc.

PS: The sabotage is just conjecture. Don't worry about it. This is not a request.

THE ELEVATOR DOORS OPEN.

"Happy birthday, Mr. Grey!" There's a cacophony of voices. Andrea is standing by the doors, holding a large frosted cake with *Happy Birthday and Congratulations, Mr. Grey* written in blue icing across the top. There's a solitary gold candle burning on top.

What the fuck.

This has never happened.

Ever.

The throng—which includes Ros, Barney, Fred, Marco, Vanessa, and all the VPs of their departments—breaks into a rousing chorus of "Happy Birthday." I fix a smile on my face to hide my surprise and, when they finish, blow out the candle. They all cheer and start applauding, as if I've done something worthy of celebration.

Sarah offers me a champagne flute.

There are shouts of "Speech. Speech."

"Well, this is a surprise." I turn to Andrea, who gives me a slight shrug. "But thank you."

Ros pipes up, "We're all grateful you're still here, Christian, especially me, because it means I'm still here, too." There's a smattering of polite laughter and applause. "So we wanted to express our gratitude in some way. All of us." She extends an arm to our colleagues. "We also want to wish you a happy birthday and congratulations on your good news. Let's raise a glass." She does. "To Christian Grey."

My name echoes through the office.

I raise my glass to salute her and take a large swig.

There's more applause.

I really don't understand what has gotten into my staff. Why now? What gives?

"Was this your idea?" I ask Andrea when she hands me a slice of cake.

"No, sir. It was Ros's."

"But you got all this together."

"Sarah and I did, sir."

"Well, thank you. I appreciate it."

"You're welcome, Mr. Grey."

Ros gives me a warm smile and tips her glass toward me, and I remember I owe her a pair of navy Manolos.

IT TAKES ME THIRTY-FIVE minutes to extricate myself from the little gathering in my office. I'm touched, and I'm surprised that I'm touched. I must be going soft in my old age. But as ever, I'm anxious to return home…anxious to see Ana.

She comes dashing out of the rear entrance to SIP and my heart flips to see her. Sawyer is by her side; he opens the Audi door and she slides in beside me while Sawyer climbs in front with Taylor.

"Hi." Her smile is dazzling.

"Hi." Taking her hand, I kiss her knuckles. "How was your day?"

Elena's eyes are like flint. Cold. Hard. She's in my face. Angry. *I was the best thing that ever happened to you. Look at you now. One of the richest, most successful entrepreneurs in the United States. Controlled, driven, you need nothing. You are master of your universe.* Now she's on her knees. In front of me. Bowed. Naked. Her forehead pressed to the basement floor. Her hair a shining coronet of lightning against the dark wooden boards. Her hand is stretched out. Splayed. Tipped with scarlet nails. She's begging. *Keep your head on the floor.* My voice echoes off the concrete walls. She wants me to stop. She's had enough. My grip tightens on the crop. *Enough, Grey.* I wrap my fingers around my cock, hard from her mouth, covered in crimson smears from her lipstick. My palm moves up and down. Faster. Faster. Faster. *Yes.* I come and come. With a loud guttural cry. Painting her back with my cum. I stand over her. Panting. Heady. Sated. There's a crash. The door flies open. His frame fills the doorway. He roars, and the blood-curdling sound fills the room. *No.* Elena screams. *Fuck. No. No. No.* He's here. He knows. Elena stands between me and him. *No,* she cries, and he hits her so hard she falls to the floor. She screams. And screams. *Leave him. Leave him.* I'm in shock. And he hits me. A right hook to my chin. I fall. And fall. My head spins. I'm faint. *No. Stop the screaming. Stop.* It goes on. And on. I'm under the kitchen table. My hands on my ears. But they don't shut out the noise. He's here. I hear his boots. Big boots. With buckles. She's screaming. And screaming. What did he do? Where is she? I smell his stench before I see him and he peers under the table, a lit cigarette in his hand. *There you are, you little shit.*

I wake instantly, gasping for air and doused in a sheen of sweat with fear streaking through my veins.

Where am I?

My eyes adjust to the light. I'm at home. Escala. The coming dawn casts a faint rosy glow over Ana's sleeping form, and relief rushes through me like a cool autumn breeze.

Thank fuck.

She's here. With me.

I blow out a long, steadying breath as I try to clear my head.

What the hell was that about?

I rarely dream about Elena, much less about *that* horrific moment in our shared history. I shudder as I lie staring at the ceiling, and I know I'm too wired to get back to sleep. I contemplate waking Ana—wanting to lose myself in her once more—but I know that's not fair. Last night she more than proved her stamina; she has to work later today and she needs her sleep. Besides, I'm ill at ease, my skin's crawling, and the nightmare has left a sour taste in my mouth. It must be the severing of my friendship and business relationship with Elena that's haunting my psyche. After all, Mrs. Lincoln has been my lodestar for over a decade.

Shit.

It had to be done.

It's over. *All of that is over.*

Sitting up I run my hand through my hair, careful not to disturb Ana. It's early—5:05—and right now, I need a glass of water.

I swivel out of bed and find I'm standing on my tie, discarded after last night's diverting shenanigans. A delicious memory of Ana invades my senses, her hands bound above her head, her body rigid, her head tipped back in ecstasy as she clutches the pale gray slats of the headboard, while I lavish my attention on her clitoris with my tongue. It's a much more pleasing recollection than the remnants of my nightmare. I pick up my tie, fold it, and place it on the nightstand.

It's unusual for me to have nightmares when Ana is sleeping beside me. I hope it's a one-off. I'm grateful that I have an appointment with Flynn later today so I can dissect this new development with him.

Pulling on my PJ pants, I grab my phone and exit the bedroom. Perhaps some Chopin or Bach will soothe me.

As I sit down at the piano, I check my messages, and there's one from Welch, left at midnight, that catches my eye.

> WELCH
> Sabotage suspected. Initial
> report first thing this morning.

Fuck. My scalp tingles as the blood drains from my head.

My fears have been confirmed. Someone wants me dead.

Who?

My mind rolls through the few business associates I've outplayed over the years.

Woods? Stevens? Carver? Who else? Waring?

Would they stoop to this?

They all made money; lots of money. They just lost their companies. I can't believe this could be connected to my commercial activities.

Perhaps it's personal?

There's only one person who looms large in that regard and it's Linc. But Elena's ex-husband already took his revenge on her, and that was years ago. Why would he act now?

Perhaps it's someone else. A disgruntled employee? An ex? I can't think of anyone who would do this. Apart from Leila, they're all doing well.

I need to process this.

Ana! Shit!

If they're coming after me, they could hurt her. Fear steals through me like a ghost, leaving goose bumps in its wake. I have to protect Ana at all costs. I text Welch.

> Meet this morning.
> 8 am Grey House

> WELCH
> Copy

I text Andrea so she can clear any meetings I may have, then e-mail Taylor.

From: Christian Grey
Subject: Sabotage
Date: June 21 2011 05:18
To: J B Taylor

Welch has informed me that *Charlie Tango* may have been sabotaged. The initial report will be with us later this morning. We're meeting at Grey House at 8 am.
Reinstate Reynolds and Ryan if they're still available. I want Ana accompanied at all times. Sawyer can stay with her today.
Thanks.

Christian Grey
CEO, Grey Enterprises Holdings, Inc.

I need to release all my pent-up nervous energy and decide on a workout. Sneaking into my closet, I change quickly and quietly, not wanting to wake Ana.

While I run on the treadmill, I watch the markets on TV, listen to the Foo Fighters, and wonder who the hell wants to kill me.

ANA SMELLS OF SLEEP and sex and a fragrant orchard in the fall. For a moment I'm transported to a happier time, when I'm hassle free, and it's just me and my girl. "Hey, baby, wake up." I nuzzle her ear.

She opens her eyes, and her face, already soft from sleep, glows like a golden dawn. "Good morning," she says, and runs her thumb across my lips, then gives me a chaste kiss.

"Sleep well?" I ask.

"Hmm…you smell so good. You look so good."

I grin. It's just a well-tailored suit. "I have to go into the office early." She sits up. "Already?" She glances at the radio alarm. It's 7:08.

"Something's come up. Sawyer will stick close today and keep the press at bay. You okay with that?"

She nods.

Good. I don't want to frighten her with the news about *Charlie Tango.*

"I'll see you later." I kiss her forehead and leave before I'm tempted to stay.

THE REPORT IS BRIEF.

FAA Accident and Incident Reporting System (AIRS)

GENERAL INFORMATION
Data Source: ACCIDENT AND INCIDENT DATABASE
Report Number: 20110453923
Local Date: 17-JUN-11
City: CASTLE ROCK   State: WA
Airport Name: PORTLAND HELIPORT
Event Type: INCIDENT
Mid Air Collision: NOT A MIDAIR

AIRCRAFT INFORMATION
Aircraft Damage: SUBSTANTIAL
Aircraft Make: EURCPT   Aircraft Model: EC-135
Aircraft Series: EC-135-P2
Airframe Hrs: 1470
Operator: GEH INC
Type of Operation: AIR TAXI/COMMUTER
Registration Nbr: N124CT
Total Aboard: 2   Fatalities: 0   Injuries: 0
Aircraft Weight Class: UNDER 12501 LBS
Number of Engines: 2
Engine Make: TURBOM   Engine Model: ARRIUS 2B2

ENVIRONMENTAL/OPERATIONS INFO
Primary Fight Conditions: VISUAL FLIGHT RULES
Secondary Flight Conditions: WEATHER NOT A FACTOR
Flight Plan Filed: YES

PILOT IN COMMAND
Pilot Certificate: COMMERCIAL PILOT
Pilot Rating: ROTORCRAFT/HELICOPTER
Pilot Qualification: QUALIFIED
Flight Time Total Hours: 1180
Total in Make/Model: 860   Total in Last 90 Days: 28

EVENT REMARKS
ON JUNE 17, 2011, AT APPROXIMATELY 14:20 PT, AN EC-135,
N124CT, OWNED AND OPERATED BY GREY ENTERPRISES HOLDINGS
INC, HAD A MAJOR INCIDENT. THE AIRCRAFT WAS STABLE WHEN
THE AIRCRAFT SUDDENLY PITCHED AND THE #1 ENGINE FIRE-LIGHT
ILLUMINATED. THE PILOT SECURED THE #1 ENGINE WITH THE FIRE

BOTTLE AND ATTEMPTED TO RETURN TO SEA-TAC ON THE REMAINING
ENGINE. #2 ENGINE FIRE-LIGHT ILLUMINATED. THE PILOT MADE
AN EMERGENCY LANDING AT THE SOUTH-EAST CORNER OF SILVER
LAKE. ON LANDING THE PILOT DEPLOYED THE SECOND FIRE BOTTLE
AND SHUTDOWN AND EVACUATED THE AIRCRAFT. NO INJURIES WERE
REPORTED. THE PILOT DEPLOYED THE ONBOARD PORTABLE FIRE
EXTINGUISHER. THE AIRCRAFT MANUFACTURER IS EXAMINING THE
AIRCRAFT ENGINES AND THE INITIAL ASSESSMENT IS THAT THE
DAMAGE IS SUSPICIOUS AND MAY BE A RESULT OF MALICIOUS
INTERFERENCE. THE NTSB WILL REQUIRE FURTHER REVIEW.

In my office, Welch, Taylor, and I pore over the report. Welch's griz-
zled face is craggier than ever in the harsh morning light, his expression grim. "At the moment, the NTSB only suspects sabotage, but we
should proceed as if there was malicious interference. To that end, we've
checked through all the CCTV footage at the helipad in Portland and
found no suspicious activity." He shuffles in his chair and clears his
throat. "However, there's an issue in the GEH hangar at Boeing Field."

Oh?

"Two of the cameras were inoperative, so we don't have complete
coverage."

"What! How did that happen?" *What the fuck do I pay these people for?*

"We're endeavoring to find out," Welch answers, his voice deep
and gravelly like an old car exhaust. "It's a major breach."

No shit, Sherlock. "Who's responsible?"

"There's a rolling shift system. So, it's down to four or five people."

"If they're found to be negligent, they're fired. All of them."

"Sir." He glances at Taylor.

"At present, we have no leads as to who's behind this," Taylor says.

"There's going to be a forensic examination of the aircraft," Welch
adds. "My hope is that they'll turn something up."

"I want more than fucking hope!" I raise my voice.

"Yes, sir." Both men speak at the same time. Each of them looks
contrite.

Hell. It's not their fault. *Grey. Get a grip.*

I continue in a more measured tone. "Find out who fucked up
at the hangar. Fire them. And as soon as we have an idea of what

occurred, I want to know. In the meantime, make sure the jet's secured and it's safe."

"Yes, sir," Taylor says.

"We're on it," Welch growls. He's pissed. He should be, this has happened on his watch. "The National Transportation Safety Board is all over this and I expect they'll brief law enforcement as their inquiries continue and, if appropriate, invite them to investigate in parallel. I'll circle back with the NTSB to confirm this."

"The police?" I ask.

"No. It'll be the FBI."

"Okay. Maybe they'll find something. Where are we with backup close protection?" I ask Taylor.

"Both Reynolds and Ryan are available and will start today."

"I want to keep Anastasia out of this. She doesn't need the worry. And I want to see the shortlist of who might be behind this. I have to say I'm at a loss."

"My team is compiling a list of potential suspects," Welch says.

"I'll do the same."

"Sir, now that this is on the FAA site, the press may pick it up and start asking questions," Taylor says.

Shit. "You're right. You can brief Sam now. I'll get him up here."

"Will do," he responds.

If this is going public, I have to tell Ana, too.

How the hell did we come to this?

Sabotage!

I do not need this shit right now.

I leave the two men discussing likely suspects and poke my head out of the door. Andrea looks up from her computer. "Mr. Grey?"

"Ask Sam and Ros to join us."

"Will do."

THERE'S A KNOCK ON my office door. It's Andrea. "Would you like more coffee?" she asks.

"Please."

On my computer screen is a list of all the acquisitions I've made since I started my company. I'm going through each one to see if I can find any potential suspects. So far I've drawn a blank; it's depressing. Deep down I'm worried about Ana—if someone wants to hurt me, she could end up as collateral damage. How could I live with myself if that was the case?

"Latte?"

"No. Black. Strong."

"Yes, sir." She closes the door and an e-mail pops up from my girl.

From: Anastasia Steele
Subject: Quiet Before/After the Storm?
Date: June 21 2011 14:18
To: Christian Grey

My dearest Mr. Grey
You are most quiet today. This concerns me.
I hope all is well in the land of high finance and business dealings.
Thank you for last night. You are quite the mouthful. ;)
Axx
PS: I see Mr. Bastille late this afternoon.

Ana! A warm flush spreads under my collar and I loosen my tie. She is quite the wanton with her choice of words. I type my response.

From: Christian Grey
Subject: Storm is here
Date: June 21 2011 14:25
To: Anastasia Steele

My darling fiancée
I must congratulate you on remembering your BlackBerry.
The storm clouds are gathering here and I will apprise you of the
weather report and coming deluge when home.
In the meantime, I hope Bastille is not too hard on you. That's my job. ;)
Thank YOU for last night. Your stamina and your mouth continue to
amaze me in the best of ways. ;) ;) :)

Christian Grey
Meteorologist & CEO, Grey Enterprises Holdings, Inc.

PS: I'd like to collect your remaining belongings from your apartment
this week. You're never there…

From: Anastasia Steele
Subject: Weather Predictions
Date: June 21 2011 14:29
To: Christian Grey

Your e-mail has done little to assuage my concerns. I comfort myself
in knowing that should it be needed, you own a shipyard and can no
doubt build an ark. You are, after all, the most competent man I know.
Your loving Ana xxx
PS: Let's talk this evening about when I move in.
PPS: Is meteorology really your thing?

Her e-mail makes me smile and I run my index finger over the *x*'s.

From: Christian Grey
Subject: You Are My Thing.
Date: June 21 2011 14:32
To: Anastasia Steele

Always.

Christian Grey
Madly in Love CEO, Grey Enterprises Holdings, Inc.

IT'S 5:30 WHEN DR. FLYNN waves me into his office. "Good afternoon, Christian."

"John." I amble over to the couch, sit down, and wait for him to
take his chair.

"So, big weekend for you," he says, sounding affable.

I look away. I don't know where to start.

"What is it?" he asks.

"Someone's trying to kill me."

Flynn pales—a first, I think. "The crash?" he asks.

I nod.

"I'm sorry to hear that." He frowns.

"My people are all over it. But I'm at a loss as to who it might be."

"You have no inkling?"

I shake my head.

"Well," he says, "I hope the police are involved and that you find
the culprit."

"It will be the FBI. But my main concern is Ana."

John nods. "Her safety?"

"Yes. I've put additional security in place, but I don't know if it'll be enough." I swallow my rising anxiety.

"We've talked about this," he replies. "I know you loathe feeling out of control. I know you're panicked about Ana, and I understand why you feel that way. But you have the resources and you've put measures in place to keep her safe. That's all anyone can do." His gaze is level and sincere, and his words are reassuring. He smiles and adds, "You can't lock her up."

My laugh is cathartic. "I know."

"I also know you'd like to but put yourself in her shoes."

"Yeah. I know. I get it. I don't want to drive her away."

"Exactly. Good."

"That's not all I want to talk about."

"There's more?"

I let out a long sigh and recount in the briefest of terms the argument with Elena at my birthday party, and the subsequent rows with each of my parents.

"I have to say, Christian, it's never a dull moment with you." Flynn rubs his chin in response to my resigned smile. "We only have an hour—what do you want to talk about?"

"I had a nightmare last night. About Elena."

"I see."

"I've cut ties with her, as per my parents' requests. Gifted her the business."

"That's generous."

I shrug. "It is. But I'm okay with that, I think. Of course, she's still calling, but it was only twice today."

"She's been a huge influence in your life."

"She has. But it's time for me to move on."

He looks thoughtful. "Which did you find more upsetting, the argument with Elena or your parents?"

"Elena's was awkward, because Ana was in the room. We were spiteful to each other." My regret is clear in my tone, and deep down I wish we'd parted on better terms. "And Grace was so mad at me. I've never heard her curse before. But the argument with my dad was the worst. He was an asshole."

"He was angry?"

"Very." I ignore the stab of guilt in my guts at my disloyalty to Carrick.

"I wonder if he's projecting his anger at himself onto you. You can understand why he felt that way, can't you?"

No. Yes. Maybe.

Flynn continues, "Whether you agree or not, your father probably thinks Elena took advantage of a vulnerable adolescent. It was his job to protect you. He failed. That's probably how he sees it."

"She didn't take advantage. I was more than willing." My frustration echoes in my words.

I am so done with that argument.

John sighs. "We've discussed this many, many times, and I don't want to get into a debate with you about it again, but you might want to try and look at the situation from your father's point of view."

"He said I might not be husband material."

Flynn seems taken aback. "Oh. How did you feel about that?"

"Angry. Worried that he might be right." *Ashamed.*

"In what context did he say it?"

I wave my hand dismissively. "He was lecturing me about the sanctity of marriage. He said if I had no respect for that, I had no business being married."

John's brows draw together.

"Since Elena was married." I clarify for him.

"I see." Flynn purses his lips. "Christian," he says gently. "Your father may have a point."

What?

"Either you were a willing participant in a relationship with a married woman, a relationship that cost her her marriage—and much more, considering what happened to her—or you were a vulnerable adolescent who was taken advantage of. Which is it? You cannot have it both ways."

I glare at him. *What. The. Hell?*

"Marriage is a serious business," he says.

"Fuck it, John, I know that. You sound just like him!"

"Do I? That's not my intention. I'm just here to give you some perspective."

Perspective? Fuck.

I glare at him, then down at my hands, as the silence grows between us.

Perspective, my ass. "I think Carrick's wrong," I mumble eventually, and I realize that I sound like the surly teen my father still thinks I am.

"Of course he is. No matter what my views are on your relationship with Mrs. Lincoln, over the years you've demonstrated a constant commitment to her. I think it's your regret at terminating all contact with her that is wearing on your conscience."

"There's no regret!" I snap. "I've done this willingly."

"Guilt, then?"

I sigh. "Guilt? I don't feel guilty." *Do I?*

John remains impassive.

"Hence the nightmares?" I ask.

"Maybe." He taps his lip with his index finger. "You're giving up a long-standing pivotal relationship to please your parents."

"It's not for my parents. It's for Ana."

He nods. "You are rejecting everything you know for Anastasia, the woman you love. It's a huge step." He smiles once more. "In the right direction, if you ask me."

I gaze at him, not knowing what to say.

"Think about all I've said. Time's up," he says. "We can continue talking about this when I see you next."

I get up, feeling somewhat bemused. Flynn, as ever, has given me a great deal to chew on. But until we speak again, I have one outstanding question. "How's Leila?"

"Making good progress."

"Well, that's a relief."

"It is. I'll see you next week."

TAYLOR IS WAITING OUTSIDE in the Q7.

"I'm going to walk home," I inform him. I need some time to think. "I'll see you back at Escala."

He gives me a pained look.

"What?"

"Sir, I'd be much more comfortable if you rode in the car."

Oh, yes. Someone's trying to kill me.

I scowl as Taylor opens the rear door, but resigned, I climb inside.

Am I no longer master of my own universe?

My dark mood worsens.

"WHERE'S ANA?" I ASK Mrs. Jones when I enter the living room.

"Good evening, Mr. Grey. I believe she's in the shower."

"Thanks."

"Dinner in twenty minutes?" she asks as she stirs a pot on the stove. The aroma is tantalizing.

"Make it thirty." Ana in the shower has possibilities. Mrs. Jones tries to hide her smile, but I see it and ignore it. I go in search of my girl. She's not in the bathroom but the bedroom, standing at the window, wrapped in a towel and dewy from her shower.

"Hi," she says with a huge smile that vanishes as I approach. "What's wrong?"

Before I can reply, I wrap her in my arms and hold her tight, inhaling her sweet, just-showered fragrance. It soothes my soul.

"Christian. What is it?" She runs her hands up my back, pressing me close.

"I just want to hold you." I bury my face in her hair that's twisted into a chaotic topknot.

"I'm here. I'm not going anywhere." Her voice is tinged with tension. I hate it when she's anxious. I bring my hand up to cradle her head, tip it back, then press my lips to hers and kiss her, pouring my anxiety into our kiss. She responds immediately, caressing my face, opening up to me, her tongue sparring with mine.

Oh, Ana.

When she pulls away we're both winded, and I'm hard.

Fucking hard. For her.

"What's wrong?" she asks, gently cajoling me and scrutinizing my face for clues.

"Later," I murmur against her lips, and start walking her backward to the bed. She grabs at my lapels and tries to divest me of my jacket while her towel falls to the floor, leaving her naked in my arms.

Reaching up, I tug on the elastic holding her precarious bun and release her hair so that it tumbles down around her shoulders and breasts. My hands skim down her back and I cup her backside, pulling her against me. "I want you."

"I can tell." She wriggles against my erection.

Fuck. I grin and gently push her onto the bed so that she sprawls across it in all her naked glory, while I stand over her, my legs between her knees.

"That's better," I whisper, my earlier pique forgotten.

"Mr. Grey, as much as I like you in a suit, you seem to be over-dressed." Gone is her anxiety—her eyes shine up at me, full of teasing desire. It's arousing.

"Well, I'll have to see what I can do about that, Miss Steele."

She bites down on her lower lip and runs her fingers down between her breasts. Her nipples are rosy, erect and ready. For my mouth.

It takes all my willpower not to rip off my clothes and bury myself in her. Instead, I grab the knot of my tie and gently tug it so it slowly unravels. Once it's loose, I toss it on the floor and undo the top button on my shirt.

Ana's mouth opens in a sexy, appreciative gasp.

Next, I shrug off my jacket and let it fall to floor, where it lands with a soft thud. I think that's my phone. But I ignore the sound and yank the hem of my shirt from my pants.

"Off or on?" I ask.

"Off. Now. Please." Ana doesn't hesitate.

I grin and ease my left cuff link from its place, then repeat the process with the right cuff.

Ana squirms on the bed.

"Keep still, baby," I whisper while I undo the lowest button on my shirt, then move my fingers up to the next, and the next, my eyes not leaving hers. When my shirt is undone, it follows the way of my jacket, and I grasp my belt. Ana's eyes widen and we drink each other in. I drag the end through the belt loop and undo the buckle, and as slow as I can I tug my belt free.

Ana angles her head slightly, watching me, and I notice the rise and fall of her breasts increases as her breathing accelerates.

I fold the belt in half and let it slide between my fingers.

Oh, Ana...what I'd like to do with this.

Her hips rise and fall, too.

I tug both ends of my belt so it snaps against itself, with a sharp crack. She doesn't flinch, but I know she hasn't signed up for this, so I drop it on the floor. She forces out a shallow breath, looking both relieved and maybe a little disappointed—I don't know. But now's not the time to think about that. I step out of my shoes and dispense with my socks, then undo the button on my pants and slide down the fly.

"Ready?" I ask.

"And waiting." Her voice is husky with lust. "But I'm enjoying the floor show."

I grin and drop my pants and boxer briefs, freeing my straining cock. Kneeling on the floor, I trail kisses up the inside of her calf, to her thigh, along the line of her pubic hair, up to her navel, to each of her breasts, until I'm hovering over her, poised and ready.

"I love you," I whisper, and ease into her, kissing her at the same time.

She groans. "Christian."

And I start to move. Slowly. Savoring her. My sweet, sweet Ana. My love.

She wraps her legs around me, her fingers diving into my hair and tugging hard.

"I love you, too," she purrs in my ear and moves with me, so we're in sync.

Together.

Us.

As one.

And when she falls apart in my arms, she takes me with her.

"Ana!"

SHE NUZZLES MY CHEST and I tense, waiting for the darkness, so she stops and raises her head. "As much as I liked your impromptu striptease and its aftermath, are you going to give me the weather report that you mentioned in your missives, and tell me what's wrong?"

I trail my fingertips up and down her back. "Can we eat first?"

She smiles. "Yes. I'm hungry. And maybe I need another shower."

I grin. "I like making you dirty." I sit up and slap her backside. "Up! I told Gail we'd be half an hour."

"You did?" Ana is scandalized.

"I did." I grin.

MRS. JONES'S THAI GREEN CURRY is delicious, as is the glass of Chablis we're enjoying with it. "So, the initial report came back from the FAA, and it will go public at some point."

"Oh?" Ana looks up from her meal.

"It appears that *Charlie Tango* was tampered with."

"Sabotage?"

"Exactly. I've upped our security arrangements until we nail who's responsible. And I think it's better if you stay here for now."

She nods, her eyes round with alarm.

"We have to be vigilant."

"Okay."

I arch a brow.

"I can do that," she adds hastily.

Good. That was easy.

But she looks stricken.

"Hey, don't worry," I murmur. "I'll do everything in my power to protect you."

"It's not me I'm worried about, it's you."

"Taylor and his people are all over this. Don't worry."

She frowns and places her fork on her plate.

"And don't stop eating."

Ana toys with her bottom lip and I reach across to clutch her hand. "Ana. It's going to be okay. Trust me. I won't let anything happen to you." I change the subject, hoping to move us to a safer topic. "How was Bastille?"

Her expression lightens, with her fond smile. "He was good. Thorough. I think I'm going to enjoy my sessions with him."

"I look forward to sparring with you."

"I thought we did that already, Christian."

I laugh. *Ah, touché, Anastasia…touché.*

The morning sun is streaming through my office window as Ros enters, and we sit down at my small conference table. "How are you feeling?" I ask.

"Good, thanks, Christian. I think I've fully recovered from last week's crash-landing helicopter escapade."

"Your feet?"

She laughs. "Yes. Blisters are under control. You?"

"Yes, thanks. I think so. Though knowing it's sabotage is a bitch."

"Who would do such a thing?"

"I've no idea."

"Have you considered a disgruntled employee?"

"Welch's team is scrutinizing all the employee and ex-employee files to see if they can turn up any likely suspects. We've only identified Jack Hyde, the guy I fired at SIP."

"The book editor?" Ros's disbelief is obvious from her high-pitched exclamation. Her shocked expression almost makes me laugh.

"Yes."

"Seems unlikely."

"It does. Welch is trying to track him down, as it appears he's not been to his apartment since I fired him. He's following up on that."

"Woods?" she offers, as if suddenly inspired.

"He's definitely a suspect. Again, Welch is investigating."

"Whoever it is, I hope you catch the bastard."

"I hope so, too." Sooner rather than later. "What's first on your agenda this morning?"

"Kavanagh Media. We need to crack on with this deal. Have you approved the costs?"

"I know. I know. I have a couple of queries, which I'll discuss with Fred. But once I've done that, our final proposal can go. If their people approve the cost per foot, we can start on the fiber optic surveys."

"Okay. I'll hold off until you've checked with Fred."

"I'm seeing him later. I'll discuss it then. He's showing me his latest iteration of the tablet. I think we're ready for the next prototype."

"That's good news. Have you thought about the next step with Taiwan?"

"I read the reports. They're interesting. It's obvious their shipyard is thriving, and I understand why they want to expand. But what I can't get a handle on is why they're looking to the U.S. for investment."

"Uncle Sam is on our side," Ros asserts.

"True. I'm sure there will be tax advantages, but it's a big step to move some of our construction effort out of Seattle. I need to know they're solid, and that it works for GEH."

"Christian, it'll be cheaper in the long run. You know this."

"Undoubtedly, and with the price of steel climbing as it is right now, it might be the only way to keep the GEH shipyard open long term and retain jobs here."

"I think we should do a full impact assessment on what this will mean for our shipyard and the workforce."

"Yes." I respond. "That's a smart idea."

"Okay. I'll talk to Marco and get his team on it. But I don't think we can stall for too long. They'll go elsewhere."

"I get it. What's next?"

"The plant. Detroit. Bill has identified three potential brownfield sites and we're waiting for you to make a decision." She gives me a pointed look; she knows I've been procrastinating.

Why the fuck does it have to be Detroit?

I sigh. "Okay. I know Detroit is offering the best incentives. Let's do a comparative cost analysis, then talk through the pros and cons of each site. Let's try and get that done by next week."

"Okay. Good."

We move on to discuss Woods once more, and what legal recourse we're going to take, if any, for his disregard of our NDA.

"I think he's hung himself," I mutter with disdain. "The press has not been kind to him."

"I've drafted a letter and threatened legal action."

"And expressed our disappointment?"

She laughs. "Yes."

"Let's see if that shuts him up. Asshole," I mumble under my breath, but Ros frowns in disapproval at my epithet.

"He *is* an asshole," I exclaim in my defense. "And he's a suspect."

Ever the professional, Ros ignores my rudeness. "On a personal note—we're on track for your house purchase. You'll need to put the money in escrow. I'll send you the details and we can proceed with the surveys."

"I told my contractor that we'll start them next week, though I'm not sure I need them. I'll be making changes to the house."

"It can't do any harm. It would be good for your contractor to know what they're up against."

I nod. "You're right."

Her brows knit together once more. "You know, I've been thinking." She pauses.

"What?"

"Given the threat to your life, have you thought about installing a panic room in your apartment?"

I'm taken aback. "No, it's never occurred to me. I live in a penthouse. But you're right, maybe I should now."

Her smile is grim. "My work here is done."

"Not quite." From under the table I grab the Nordstrom bag that Taylor delivered earlier this morning. "These are for you. As promised."

"What?" Ros frowns, puzzled, as she takes the bag and peeks inside.

"Manolos," I say. "Your size, hopefully."

"Christian, you—" she protests.

I hold up my hands. "I gave you my word. I hope they fit."

She inclines her head and regards me with what looks like affection. It's unnerving. "Thank you," she says. "And for the record, in spite of what happened, I would fly with you again, anytime."

Wow. That is the greatest compliment.

AFTER SHE'S LEFT, I sit down at my desk and call Vanessa Conway in Procurement. I've been meaning to do this for a couple of days.

"Mr. Grey," she answers.

"Hi, Vanessa, this is a tall order, but here goes: after my helicopter went down Ros and I were rescued by a guy named Seb, who drove a semi. He's a one-man operation. I don't know if we could use him— he drives a huge rig."

"You want me to contact him?"

"I do. But you'll need to find him first. I don't have his details."

"Hmm. I'll see what I can do."

"He travels mostly between Portland and Seattle. I think."

"Okay. Leave it with me."

"Thanks, Vanessa." I hang up and wish once more that Seb had given me a card. At least he has mine, if he hasn't thrown it away. I'd like to repay him somehow.

I turn to my computer to check my e-mails. There's one from Ana.

From: Anastasia Steele
Subject: Missing you
Date: June 23 2011 11:03
To: Christian Grey

That is all.
Axx

From: Christian Grey
Subject: Missing you more
Date: June 23 2011 11:33
To: Anastasia Steele

I wish you'd change your mind and move the rest of your things to
Escala this weekend.
You're with me every night as it is and what's the point in paying rent
for a place that you never stay in?

Christian Grey
CEO, Grey Enterprises Holdings, Inc.

I've been subtly trying to persuade Ana to move in full-time. But as of yet, she refuses. Why is she hesitating over this? Since she arrived in Seattle, she's hardly lived in her own apartment. She's agreed to marry me…but not to this? I don't get it. It's irritating.

Move in with me, Ana.

From: Anastasia Steele
Subject: Stay With Me
Date: June 23 2011 11:39
To: Christian Grey

Nice try, Grey.
I have some wonderful memories of you in my apartment.
I told you. I want more.
I always want more.
Stay with me there.
Axx

Oh, Ana, Ana, Ana. You always want more. And I would, if we were safe.

From: Christian Grey
Subject: Your Safety
Date: June 23 2011 11:42
To: Anastasia Steele

Means more to me right now than making memories.
I can keep you safe in my Ivory Tower.
Please reconsider.

Christian Grey
CEO, Grey Enterprises Holdings, Inc.

PS: I hope you like the wedding planner.

My mother is meeting us tonight at Escala with The Wedding Planner. This is not how I would like to spend the evening. Why couldn't we just go to Vegas and get married? We'd be husband and wife by now. I might feel happier about it if Ana would stop procrastinating about moving in.

Why is she reluctant?

Does she need her apartment as a bolt hole, just in case she changes her mind?

Fuck.

Doubt is an ugly word, for an ugly feeling.

Why won't she fully commit?

Enough, Grey.

She's agreed to marry you!

To distract myself from these unsettling thoughts, I pick up the phone to call Welch for an update on the investigation into the crash, to ask if he's located Jack Hyde, and to inquire about panic rooms.

TAYLOR WILL NOT LET me walk to or from the mayor's office, so after a long lunch with the mayor, I reluctantly climb into the back of the Audi for the short drive back to Grey House. I'm not sure I appreciate him flapping around me like a mother hen. It's suffocating. I let out a long, slow breath, remembering Ana accusing me of doing precisely that.

Hell. I hope she's tolerating Sawyer's watchful eye.

On the plus side, Taylor has advised me to stop playing golf. Apparently there are too many trees surrounding the golf course where an assassin could find cover. I'm not a fan of the sport, so it's no hardship to give it up, though I believe Taylor is being a tad dramatic.

Glancing up through the panoramic sunroof, I catch a glimpse of brilliant summer blue above the steel and glass of downtown Seattle. For a moment I wish I was up there.

The freedom of walking on air.

I need to get back up there with Ana. We'd be safe in a sailplane, soaring the skies. And no longer under the ever-present vigilance of our security. The idea is extremely appealing. Only thing is, if I want to take Ana, I need a new sailplane, a model made for two. I rub my hands with glee, as this presents my kind of shopping opportunity. I fish my phone out of my pocket and start scouring the Alexander Schleicher website for their latest aircraft designs.

"THANK YOU SO MUCH, Christian, Ana. It has been wonderful to meet you, and you're going to have the most magical wedding."

"Thank you, Alondra," Grace coos. "I love your ideas." My mother claps her hands in uncharacteristic enthusiasm while I make a supreme effort to keep my smile fixed and not roll my eyes. I am on my best behavior. Ms. Gutierrez's ideas are great. I just want them done, and quickly, so we can get married.

"I'll see you out," Ana says, and leads her to the foyer.

"What do you think?" Grace asks.

"She's fine."

"Oh, Christian." Mom sounds irritated. "She's much more than fine."

"Okay. She's God's gift to wedding planning." My sarcasm bleeds into my words. Grace's lips thin and I think she's about to scold me, but Ana reenters the room.

"What did you think?" Ana asks, her gaze searching my face for answers.

"I thought she was fine. Did you like her?" That's the important question.

"Of course. I thought she was full of imaginative ideas. Dr. Gre—"

"Ana, *please*. Call me Grace."

"Grace," Ana says with an embarrassed smile. "So, we need to do a save-the-date note to all our guests?" Ana blinks rapidly, suddenly looking shell-shocked. "We don't even have a guest list," she whispers.

"That's easily done," I reassure her. Apart from the family, I think I have two guests: Ros and Dr. Flynn and their respective partners. Maybe Bastille…and Mac.

"There is one more thing," Grace says.

"What?"

"I know you don't want a Catholic ceremony, but would you consider asking Reverend Michael Walsh to officiate?"

Reverend Walsh. The name rings a bell.

"He's the chaplain at my hospital. He's such a dear friend, and I know you never saw eye to eye with any of the priests we know."

"Oh, yes. I remember him. He was always kind to me. I don't want a religious ceremony, but I'm fine with him conducting it, if that's okay with Ana."

Ana nods, a little pale; she looks overwhelmed.

"That's great. I'll talk to him tomorrow. In the meantime, I'll leave you two to get on with a list." Grace raises her cheek to me and I give her a quick peck. "Good-bye, darling," she says. "Ana, good-bye. I'll call."

"Great," Ana replies, though I think she lacks conviction. Is she not happy with the wedding planner? Is she as bewildered as I feel? I give her hand a reassuring squeeze, and together we walk my mother out to the foyer. Grace turns to me as we wait for the elevator.

"Please call your father, Christian."

I sigh. "I'll think about it."

"Stop sulking," she warns, quietly.

"Grace!" *Back off.*

Ana glances at the two of us, but wisely holds her tongue and says nothing. I'm saved by the ping of the elevator and its opening doors. I reach for Ana's hand as Grace steps inside. "Good night," she says, and the doors close.

"You're not talking to your father?" Ana asks.

I shrug. "I wouldn't go as far as to say that."

"Is this from last weekend? Your fight with him?"

I return her curious gaze, but say nothing. This is between him and me.

"Christian, he's your dad. He's only looking out for you."

I hold up my hand in the hope that she'll stop. "I don't want to discuss this." She folds her arms and raises that stubborn Steele chin. "Anastasia. Drop it."

Her eyes flash cobalt blue, but she sighs and lowers her arms, regarding me with what I think is a mixture of frustration and compassion.

Fifty Shades, baby.

"We have another issue," she says. "My dad wants to pay for the wedding."

"Does he, now?"

No way. It will cost a fortune, which he doesn't have. I'm not bankrupting my father-in-law. "I think that's out of the question."

"What? Why?" Ana's hackles are up.

"Baby, you know why." I don't want to debate this. "The answer's no."

"But—"

"No."

Her mouth forms that mulish line I know so well.

"Ana, you have carte blanche on this wedding. Whatever you

want. But not that. You know it's not fair to your father. It's 2011, not 1911."

She sighs. "I don't know what I'll say to him."

"Tell him my heart is set on providing everything for us. Tell him it's a deep-seated need that I have."

Because that's the truth.

She sighs again, resigned, I think.

"Now, shall we work on the guest list?" I ask, in the hope that starting this process will relieve her anxiety and also distract her from Ray.

"Sure," she acquiesces, and I know I've avoided a fight.

I NUZZLE HER EAR as she gasps for breath, fresh from her orgasm. Sweat beads on her forehead and her fingers still grip my hair.

"How was that, Anastasia?"

She garbles my name and I think she says "fantastic."

I grin. "Please move in with me."

"Yes. But not this weekend. Please. Christian." She's breathless. Her eyes flutter open and she implores me. "Please," she mouths.

Damn.

"Okay," I whisper. "My turn." I nip her earlobe and flip her onto her front.

Leila wants to talk to you," Flynn says, and I know from the narrowing of his eyes that he's focusing on my reaction. I *think* this is a test, but I'm not sure.

"About what?" I ask, cautiously.

"I would guess that she wants to thank you."

"Should I?"

John leans back in his chair. "Talk to her? I don't think it's a good idea."

"What harm could it do?"

"Christian, she has strong feelings for you. She's displaced all that she felt for her deceased lover onto you. She thinks she's in love with you."

My scalp tingles and anxiety grips my heart.

No! How can she love me?

The thought is intolerable.

It will only ever be Ana. The sun, the moon, the stars—they rise and set with her.

"I think for Leila's sake you'll need to establish clear boundaries if you're going to engage with her," Flynn says.

Probably for my sake, too. "Can we keep all communication between Leila and me through you? She has my e-mail address, but she hasn't been in touch."

"I suspect that's because she's afraid you won't answer."

"She's right. I'll never forgive her for holding Ana at gunpoint."

"If it's any consolation, she's full of remorse."

I blow out a breath in exasperation; I'm not interested in her remorse. I want her healed and gone. "But doing well?" I ask.

"Yes. Very much so. The art therapy is working wonders; I think she wants to return to her hometown and pursue a fine-arts program."

"Has she found a school?"

"She has."

"If she stays away from Ana—and me, for that matter—I'll fund her studies."

"That's very generous of you." Flynn frowns, and I suspect he might be about to object.

"I can afford to be generous. I'm just glad she's recovering," I add quickly.

"She'll be discharged this week. She's going back to her folks."

"In Connecticut?"

He nods.

"Good." She'll be on the other side of the country.

"I've recommended a psychiatrist for her in New Haven, so she doesn't have to travel too far. She'll be well looked after." He pauses, then changes the subject. "Have the nightmares ceased?"

"For now."

"And Elena?"

"I've avoided all contact, but I signed the contracts yesterday. It's done. The Esclava group is hers now." The name Elena chose for her salons and the group has always made me smile. Even now.

"How does that make you feel?"

"I haven't really thought about it." My mind is cluttered with other concerns. "I'm just relieved it's over."

Flynn eyes me for a moment, and I think he's going to continue this line of inquiry, but he shifts. "And how are you feeling in general?"

I pause to consider his question, and the truth is, apart from the sabotage of my beloved *Charlie Tango*, and that someone wants me dead, I feel...good. I'm anxious, of course, and I'm pissed Ana won't move in to Escala yet, but I understand that she wants another night with me in her apartment, and that could happen this weekend. The panic rooms are going into the penthouse and we need to be out of there. It's a hotel, *The Grace*, or Ana's.

"I'm good."

"I can see that. I'm surprised." Flynn looks thoughtful.

"Why? What is it?" I ask.

"It's good to see you externalizing your anxiety, rather than turning it in on yourself."

I frown. "I think the threat to my life is external."

He nods. "Yes. It is. But it distracts you from giving yourself a hard time."

"I've not thought of it that way."

"Have you spoken to your father?"

"No."

Flynn remains impassive, his lips tightening slightly.

I sigh. "I'll get around to it."

He glances at the clock. "Time's up."

There's a knock on my office door, and as Andrea enters, I look up from the selection of wedding stationery that Ana has sent me. "Yes?" I ask, surprised by her intrusion.

"Your father is here."

What? "In the office?"

"He's on his way up."

Shit!

"I'm sorry, Mr. Grey," Andrea continues. "I didn't want to leave him in the lobby." She shrugs apologetically. "He's your father."

For heaven's sake. I check the time. It's 5:15 and I'm due to leave at 5:30 for the long weekend.

"Ask him to wait."

"Yes, sir." She leaves and closes the door behind her.

What the hell.

I do not want another conversation with good old Dad. The last one went so well. But thanks to my PA, I have no choice.

Damn.

He never turns up unannounced...unlike my mother. Taking a deep breath, I stand and stretch. I roll down my shirt sleeves and don the cuff links that have been lying on my desk. Grabbing my jacket from the back of the chair, I slip it on and fasten one button. I tug at my shirt cuffs, then straighten my tie and run my hands through my hair.

Showtime, Grey.

Carrick is standing outside my door, holding his battered briefcase. "Dad." I keep my voice neutral.

His lips curl into a warm open smile that reveals twenty-four years of love and paternal pride.

Whoa. It floors me.

"Son," he says.

"Come in. Can I get you anything?" I ask, trying to keep a handle on my suddenly warring emotions.

Does he want a fight? Make peace? What?

"Andrea's already offered me something. I'm fine," he says. "I won't be long." He enters my office and takes a quick look around as I close the door. "It's a while since I've been here."

"Yes," I mutter.

"What a lovely portrait of Ana."

On the wall facing my desk, a monochrome Ana looks captivating as she stares at us, her smile sweet and shy, hinting at her amusement and belying her strength. I like to think she's laughing at me in that way she does; in that way that makes me laugh at myself. "My newly acquired portrait. Her friend from WSU, José Rodriguez, took it. He had an exhibition in Portland. You've met him at my place. The night *Charlie Tango* went down. There's a series. Seven in total. I had this one installed earlier this week. She has such a beautiful smile." I'm babbling.

Carrick's look is warm but guarded, and he runs his hand through his hair.

"Christian, I—" He stops, as if he's had a particularly painful thought.

"What?" I ask.

"I came to apologize."

And just like that all the wind is out of my sails, and I'm becalmed and lost at sea.

"What I said was wrong. I was angry. At myself." His gaze sears mine as his fingers grip the handle of the old valise that he's had for years. My throat tightens and burns as I search for something to say, and I remember how his briefcase always sat on a weathered chair in his study.

"Christian, this is the second school that has been forced to expel you for your belligerent behavior." Dad is beside himself. He's in full asshole mode. *"This is totally unacceptable. Your mother and I are at our wits' end."* He paces in front of his desk, his hands behind his back.

I stand before him, my knuckles raw and throbbing. My side aches from the kicking I've endured. But I don't give a fuck. Wilde deserved it. Stupid bullying prick. He likes to pick on kids smaller than he is. Poorer than he is. He's garbage, and the fucker's been expelled, too.

"Son, we are running out of options."

Dad and Mom are connected. I know they can find some other school. Fuck it, I don't need to further my education.

"We've even discussed military school."

He removes his glasses like he's in a movie and glares at me, waiting and wanting a reaction. But fuck him. Fuck military school. If that's what they want to do to get rid of me, fuck them. Bring it. I lower my eyes and stare at the stupid case he carries everywhere, ignoring the fire in my throat.

Why doesn't he take my side?

Ever.

The guy jumped me.

I stood my ground.

Fuck him.

Now the lines around his eyes are deeper and the lenses in his glasses thicker, and he's watching me, waiting for an answer to his apology in his calm and patient way.

Dad.

I nod. "Me, too," I murmur.

"Good." He clears his throat and glances once more at Ana on my wall. "She's a beautiful girl."

"She is. In every way."

His eyes soften. "Well, I won't keep you."

"Okay."

He flashes me a quick smile and before I can take another breath he's gone, the door closing behind him.

I exhale and the knot at the back of my throat tightens and pulls at my heart.

Fuck. An apology. From my dad. This is a first. I can barely believe it. I look at Ana with her secret smile, and it's as if she knew this was

coming. *Christian, he's your dad. He's only looking out for you.* I hear
her voice in my head and I realize I need to hear her in real time. Now.

I return to my desk and grab my phone.

Ana answers in one ring as if she's been expecting my call. "Hi."
Her tone is soft and breathy, a gentle salve to my ragged soul.

"Hi," I whisper. "I've missed you."

I can almost hear her smile. "I've missed you, too, Christian."

"Ready for this evening?"

"Yes."

"Council of war?"

"Yes," she giggles.

Tonight. We sort the wedding. At her place.

ANA OPENS THE DOOR to her apartment and stands silhouetted
in the kitchen light. She's wearing a floaty floral dress I've not seen
before that's sheer against the light. All her lines and planes and
curves are etched like a fine sculpture, outlined just for me. She's
stunning.

"Hi," she says.

"Hi. Nice dress."

"This old thing?" She does a quick twirl, the skirt clinging to her
legs, and I know she's worn it especially for me.

"I look forward to peeling you out of that later." I hold out the
bunch of blush peonies I bought from Pike Place Market.

"Flowers?" Her face glows as she reaches for them and buries her
nose in the bouquet.

"Can't I buy my fiancée flowers?"

"You may and you do. Though I believe this is the first time I've
had a personal delivery."

"I think you're right. May I come in?"

She laughs, opening her arms, and I step into her embrace and
hold her close. I nuzzle her hair, inhaling her intoxicating fragrance.

Home. Is. Ana.

She is my life.

"Are you okay?" She rests her palm on my cheek, her vivid blue
eyes searching mine.

"I am now." I lean down for a quick kiss. Her lips brush mine, and what I mean to be a grateful, I'm-so-pleased-to-see-you kiss… becomes more. Much more. The fingers from her free hand wind around the nape of my neck and she opens up for me like an exotic flower, her mouth warm and welcoming. She sucks in a breath as my hand skirts down the soft fabric that adheres to her body and squeezes her backside. Her tongue greets mine, in every language, until we're both panting, and desire races through my veins looking for an out.

I groan and pull back, staring down into her beautiful dazed face.

"Okay, Taylor, you can go," I say.

"Thank you, sir." From behind me, Taylor steps out of the shadows of the stairwell, deposits my leather overnight bag inside the door, gives us both a nod, and heads back down the stairs.

Ana giggles. "I didn't know he was there."

"I forgot, too." I grin.

To my great disappointment, Ana releases me. "I have to put these gorgeous flowers in water." I watch as she moves over to the concrete kitchen island and I'm reminded of the last time I was here when Ana was facing an armed and deranged Leila. A shiver runs up my spine. That meeting could have gone so tragically wrong. No wonder Ana's been on about the two of us spending another night here. I'm sure she'd love to supersede the last memory she has of us in this place. Thankfully, Leila's recovered, and far across the country at her parents' place in Connecticut.

"Where's Kate?" I ask, remembering that Ana does not live alone.

"She's out with your brother." She fills a vase with water.

"So we have the place to ourselves." I shrug out of my jacket, take off my tie, and undo the top two buttons of my shirt.

"We do." Ana holds up a notebook. "And I have listed everything we need to discuss for the wedding."

"Can we take a rain check?"

"No. I know what your rain check will involve. And we need to do this, Christian. Council of war, remember?" She waves the book at me, raising that Steele chin in determination.

It's a good look on Ana.

I know she's been stressing about the wedding, though I don't know why. Ms. Gutierrez seems competent and is handling all the arrangements in an unflappable and efficient manner; our discussion should not take long.

"Don't pout," she adds, with her familiar amused smile.

I laugh. "Okay. Let's do this."

AN HOUR LATER WE'RE sitting on barstools at the kitchen counter and we've completed the application for a marriage license. Agreed on stationery. Color scheme. Menus. Cake design. And party favors.

Party favors!

"Christian, I don't think we should have a registry."

"Registry?"

"For wedding gifts."

"God, no."

"But if people want to give something, perhaps they could contribute something to your parents' charity, Coping Together?"

I stare at her, amazed and humbled at once. "That's genius."

Ana nods. "I'm glad you like the idea."

I lean forward and kiss her. "This is why I'm marrying you."

"I thought it was for my cooking."

I nod. "That, too."

She laughs, and it's a joyful sound.

"Okay, I've asked Kate to be my maid of honor," Ana says.

"Makes sense." I ignore my sinking feeling; Katherine is the most irritating woman I know. But she's Ana's best friend...so... *Suck it up, Grey.*

"I'm going to ask Mia to be my bridesmaid."

"Mia would love that, I'm sure."

"You'll need to find a best man."

"Best man?"

"Yes."

Well, it can only be Elliot. I'll have to ask him, and he'll give me shit.

"You don't really enjoy this, do you?" Ana fixes her gaze on me.

"I will enjoy being married to you."

She cocks her head to one side, and I know that she's not satisfied with my answer. I sigh. "No. I don't. I have never enjoyed being the center of attention, which is one of the reasons I'm marrying you."

Ana's brow creases and I run a knuckle down her cheek, because I haven't touched her in minutes. "You'll be the center of attention."

Ana rolls her eyes. "We'll see about that. I'm sure you'll look mighty fine in your wedding regalia, Mr. Grey."

"Do you have a dress?"

"Kate's mother is designing one for me." She looks down at her fingers and adds, "I asked my dad to pay for it."

"He's happy with that?"

She nods. "I think he's relieved he's not footing the bill for the wedding, but he's delighted he can contribute."

I grin. "Anastasia Steele, you're brilliant. I knew you'd find a compromise. You are such a good negotiator." I lean over and give her a peck on her lips.

"Hungry?" she asks.

"Yes."

"I'll cook us some steaks."

"SO, THE PANIC ROOMS, how will they work?" Ana asks as she slices into her filet mignon.

"There's one going into Taylor's office, and our bedroom closet will become one, too. Press a button and the doors will close and they'll be impenetrable. There'll be enough time for help to arrive. That's the plan, anyway."

"Oh." Ana blanches.

I clutch her hand. "It's merely a precaution. Here's hoping we never have to use them." I raise my glass of pinot noir and release her.

"I'll drink to that." She clinks my glass with hers.

"Don't look so worried. I will do everything in my power to keep you safe."

"It's not me I'm worried about, Christian. You know that. How... how is the investigation going?"

"Not fast enough, which is frustrating. But don't think about it. My team is on it." I don't want to trouble Ana with our lack of progress. "That steak was delicious." I put down my knife and fork.

"Thank you," she says, and pushes her empty plate aside.

"What shall we do now?" I ask, and I pitch my voice low, hoping my intention is clear. We have the whole apartment to ourselves, something we don't have at home.

Ana peers at me through her lashes. "I have an idea." Her voice is soft and sultry, and arousing. She skims her tongue across her top lip, and places her hand on my knee. The air is almost crackling between us with my desire.

Ana.

She leans in, giving me a wonderful view of her cleavage, and she murmurs in my ear, "It will involve getting wet."

Oh. She runs her thumb up the inside of my thigh.

Fuck.

"Yes." She leans in farther, her breath tickling my ear. "We could…wash the dishes."

What!

Tease!

Well, this is unexpected. And a challenge.

I stifle my smile, and not taking my eyes off hers, I skim my index finger over her cheek to her chin, then down her throat and her sternum to the *v* in her dress. Her lips part as her breathing deepens. I pinch the soft fabric between my thumb and forefinger and tug, pulling her toward me. "I have a better idea."

She gasps.

"A much better idea," I continue.

"What?"

"We could fuck."

"Christian Grey!"

I grin. I love shocking Ana. "Or we could make love," I add.

Smooth, Grey. Smooth.

"I like your ideas better than mine." Her voice is low and husky for real this time.

"Do you, now?"

"Mm-hmm. I'll take option one." Her eyes are smoky.

Ana, you goddess.

"Good choice. Take that dress off, now. Slowly."

She stands up so that she's between my thighs, and I think she's going to do as she's told, but she bends her head and places her hands on my thighs, then caresses the corner of my mouth with her lips. "You do it," she whispers against my skin, and every hair on my body stands to attention as desire heats my blood.

"As you wish, Miss Steele." I reach for the tie that holds her wrap dress together and gently unravel the bow so that her dress falls open.

Ana's not wearing a bra. *Deep joy.*

I run my hands up her back as she cups my face and starts to kiss me. Her lips are insistent and her tongue demanding. I groan and close my eyes as we revel in each other's kiss. Her skin is soft beneath my fingers as I draw her closer, pressing her to my chest. Her hands twist in my hair. And she tugs, forcing my head up.

Fuck.

Ana takes my bottom lip between her teeth and pulls.

Ow.

Ana!

I yank my head back and grab her wrists. "You're a little wild," I whisper, awed. She shimmies between my legs, her nipples brushing against my shirt and hardening as I watch. Her hair falls over her shoulders and shrouds her breasts while my pants grow tighter by the second.

What has gotten into her?

She's exhilarating. Provocative.

"Are you teasing me?" I ask.

"Yes. Take me."

"Oh, I will. Right here. When I'm ready."

She gasps, eyes sultry and full of invitation, and I think she must have consumed more pinot than I thought. Gently I steer her backward and release her hands as I rise off my seat. I peer down at her as she studies me from beneath her long lashes.

"How about here?" I pat the top of the stool.

She blinks a couple of times as her lips part in surprise.

"Bend over," I whisper.

Her teeth dig into her plump lip, leaving little indent marks, and I know she's doing this on purpose.

"I believe you requested option one," I remind her.

"I did."

"I won't ask you again." I unbutton my pants and slowly tug down my zipper, giving my erection some much-needed room.

Ana stares at me, looking licentious and lovely, dressed only in her pretty open frock, a pair of white panties, and her high-heeled sandals. She raises her hands, and I think she's going to take her dress off.

"Leave it on," I insist, and reaching into my pants, I ease out my cock. "Ready?" I ask, and start to move my hand up and down, pleasuring myself. Her dark gaze strays from my hand to my face, and with a knowing smile, she turns and lies right over the stool.

"Grab the legs," I urge, and she does, wrapping her fingers around the iron struts. Her hair brushes the floor and I move her dress so it hangs down her left side, leaving her glorious ass in view. "Let's get rid of these," I murmur, and run a finger across her skin above the elastic of her underwear. I kneel and slowly drag them down her legs and over her shoes. I toss them to the side and take her ass in my hands and squeeze.

"You look mighty fine from this angle, Miss Steele," I whisper and kiss her butt. She squirms appropriately and I can't help myself. I slap her hard so that she yelps and I ease one finger inside her. Her moan is loud and she strains her body, pushing against my hand.

She wants this.

She's wet.

So wet.

Ana. You never disappoint.

I kiss her ass once more and stand up while moving my finger in. Out. In. Out.

"Legs. Wider," I order as I fondle her backside. She moves her feet. "Wider."

She shuffles them to the side until I'm satisfied.

Perfect.

"Hold on, baby." I withdraw my hand and with infinite care slowly slide into her.

She gasps.

Fuck. She's heaven.

I place my hand on her back and with the other I clutch the edge of the kitchen counter. I do not want to topple us both.

"Hold on," I say once more and ease out of her, then slam into her.

"Ah!" she cries.

"Too much?"

"No. Keep going!" she whimpers.

And her wish is my command. I start to fuck her. Hard. Each stroke. Each push. Takes me away from everything, all my strife, all my worries. There's only Ana. My girl. My lover. My light.

She cries out. Once, twice, three times. Begging me for more. And I keep going, taking her with me. Taking her higher. On and on until she calls out a strangled, loud version of my name. And she comes, over and over, with the force of a spring tide.

"Ana!" I cry and join her.

I collapse over her, then drop to the floor, taking her with me and cradling her in my arms. I kiss her eyelids, her nose, her mouth, and she puts her arms around my neck.

"How was option one?" I ask.

"Hmm…" she hums with a dazed smile.

I grin. "Same for me."

"I'd like some more."

"More? Jesus, Ana."

She kisses my chest where my shirt is open, and I realize I'm still fully dressed.

"Let's try the bed this time," I whisper into her hair.

ANA MOANS. "PLEASE!" Her hands are fastened, courtesy of her robe tie, to the spindles of her bedstead. She's naked, her nipples long and hard, and pointing skyward, courtesy of my lips and tongue. I have her feet in one hand, pushed up on the bed near her behind, so her legs are akimbo and she's straining for release. Slowly I ease my index finger in and out of her while my thumb circles her clitoris.

She can't move.

"How's this?" I ask.

"Please!" She's hoarse.

"Do you like me to tease you?"

"Yes," she cries.

"Do you like teasing me?"

"Yes."

"I like it, too." I stop my thumb and still my hand, my finger still inside her.

"Christian! Don't stop!"

"Tit for tat, Anastasia." She's endeavoring to push her hips up on my hand to find her release. "Still," I whisper. "Stay still."

Her mouth is slack, eyes dark and full of lust and need and all a man could want.

"Please," she whispers, and I can tantalize her no more. I release her feet and withdraw my hand. Taking hold of her knee, I run my nose and lips down her thigh to my ultimate goal.

"Ah!" she yells when my tongue swirls over her swollen clitoris. I slide two fingers inside her, pushing once, twice, and she lets out a boisterous cry and her orgasm washes over me. I kiss her belly, her stomach, between her breasts, then I slowly sink into her as her climax dies.

"I love you, Ana," I whisper, and I start to move.

ANA SLUMBERS BESIDE ME while above me, the tie from her robe is still attached to the bed spindles. I contemplate waking her and having my wicked way with her a third time, marveling that I still want more. Will I ever have enough of Anastasia Steele? But she needs to sleep. Tomorrow we go sailing. Just the two of us and *The Grace*. She'll need her energy to help me on board. We'll be away from everyone for three whole days, enjoying our own July Fourth celebration, and my hope is that I can finally relax, at least for a few days.

My mind drifts to my dad and his surprise apology, to menus and party favors, to the crash and the unknown saboteur. I hope Reynolds and Ryan are okay outside.

They're keeping watch.

Ana's safe. We're safe.

S itting at my desk and staring out at the distant Sound, I can't help but notice the heartwarming glow that's emanating either from my skin or from somewhere deep inside my chest. It could be a combination of sea, sun, and wind from being aboard *The Grace* for the long weekend, or it could be because I've spent three uninterrupted days with Anastasia. Despite all the vexing issues I've dealt with over the past few weeks, I've never felt as relaxed as I did with her on board my catamaran. Ana is food for my soul.

Anastasia is fast asleep. The early morning light shimmers through the portholes skimming over her tousled hair so that it gleams, burnished and beautiful. Sitting down on the edge of the bed, I place a cup of tea on the nightstand, as The Grace *bobs gently on the water in Bowman Bay. I lean over and plant a tender kiss on her cheek.*

"Wake up, sleepy head. I'm lonely."

She groans, but her expression softens. I kiss her again and her eyes flutter open, and her face shines with a breathtaking smile. Reaching up, she caresses my cheek.

"Good morning, husband-to-be."

"Good morning, wife-to-be. I've made you tea."

She chuckles, in disbelief, I think. "You dear man," she says. "This belongs on the list of firsts!"

"I believe it does."

"And I can tell you're very pleased with yourself." Her grin mirrors mine.

"Miss Steele. I am. I make an excellent cup of tea."

She sits up, and to my disappointment pulls up the covers to conceal her naked breasts. She can't seem to stop grinning. "I'm so impressed. It's such a complicated process."

"Indeed, it is," I reply. "I had to boil the water and everything."

"And dip the tea bag. Mr. Grey, you are so competent."

I laugh and narrow my eyes. "Are you belittling my tea-making skills?"

She gasps in mock horror and clutches imaginary pearls. "I wouldn't dare," she says and, reaching over, takes the cup.

"Just checking—"

A knock on my office door brings me back to the now. Andrea pops her head around the door. "Mr. Grey, your tailor is here."

"Oh, great. Show him in."

I need a new suit for the wedding.

MARCO HANDLES THE COMPANY portfolio as well as our Mergers and Acquisitions. This morning he's taking the senior team through GEH's latest additions to our shareholdings. "We now own twenty-five percent of Blue Cee Tech, thirty-four percent of FifteenGenFour, and sixty-six percent of Lincoln Timber." I've been listening with half an ear, but my attention is momentarily piqued by that last piece of news. This is a long-term project of mine, and I'm pleased we now own a majority stake in Lincoln Timber through one of our shell companies. Linc must need the money. Interesting.

Revenge is a dish…

Enough, Grey. Concentrate.

Marco moves on to his latest list of potential acquisitions. There are two companies that he is especially keen to pursue. He's running through the pros while my mind strays to the weekend and Ana.

Ana is at the helm of The Grace *as we glide over the sparkling ocean, past Admiralty Head on Whidbey Island. Her hair is flying in the wind and glinting in the sun. Her smile could melt the hardest of hearts.*

It thawed mine.

She looks beautiful. Relaxed. Free.

"Hold her steady," I shout over the rush of the sea.

"Aye-aye, Captain. I mean, Sir." Ana bites her lip, and I know

she's teasing me, as usual. She salutes when I give her a bogus scowl, and I go back to tightening the bowline, unable to hide my smile.

Marco mentions a solar energy company that's struggling to find investment.

An enticing aroma of batter and bacon welcomes me with open arms as I enter the galley. My girl is making pancakes. She's dressed in a T-shirt and far-too-short denim shorts, and her hair is in pigtails.

"Good morning." I wrap my arms around her, pressing her back to my front, and skim my lips down her neck. She smells so good, of soap and warmth and sweet, sweet Ana.

"Good morning, Mr. Grey." She angles her head, giving me better access to her throat.

"This takes me back," I murmur against her skin, and tug one of her pigtails.

She giggles. "That seems a lifetime ago. These, however, are not cherry-popped-by-would-be-Dominant pancakes. These are Independence Day pancakes. Happy Fourth of July."

"There's no other way I'd like to celebrate than with pancakes." I kiss her beneath her earlobe. "Well, I can think of one way." I gently tug her pigtail once more. "You always get an A."

"Christian," Ros says, her tone abrupt. Seven pairs of eyes are all directed at me. *Shit.* I stare blankly back at Ros, ignoring everyone else, and tilt my head to one side.

"What do you think?" She's barely disguising her irritation, and I assume this is not the first time she's asked.

Come clean, Grey. "I'm sorry, I was miles away."

Her lips form a thin line and she glances at Marco, who gives me a warm smile and proceeds to give me an executive summary of what he's just outlined.

"Okay," I respond when he's finished. "Let's go after Geolumara. They could be a worthwhile addition to the energy division. We need to widen our footprint in green energy."

"The others?"

I shake my head. "We should consolidate. Let's concentrate on Geolumara. Send me all the details."

"Will do."

"We need a decision on the Taiwan shipyard. They are eager for a response from us." Ros looks pointedly at me.

"I read the impact assessment."

"And?"

"This is a gamble."

"It is," she acknowledges.

"But everything in life is a gamble, and at least as a joint venture we'll share the risk and it might secure the future of the shipyard here."

Ros and Marco nod.

"Let's move this forward."

"I'll get the team on that," Marco says.

"Good. I think that's it. Thank you, everyone."

They all rise, except for Ros. "Can I have a quick word?" she asks.

"Sure."

She waits until everyone leaves.

"Well?" And I wait for her to chastise me for my daydreaming.

"Woods has withdrawn his legal threats. We're all good."

"That's not what I was expecting you to say."

"I know. Honestly, Christian, it's like you're on your honeymoon already."

"Honeymoon? I haven't even thought about a honeymoon."

Shit. Something else to organize.

Ros scoffs. "You'd better get on it." She shakes her head. "I know I'd whisk Gwen away to Europe."

I'm surprised by Ros's candor—she rarely discusses her home life, although I know she has a domestic partnership with Gwen. Frequent attempts to legalize gay marriage in Washington have been thwarted. I make a mental note to talk to Senator Blandino about this when we next meet; surely she can apply some pressure to the governor and help push this agenda? "I thought Ana and I might stay somewhere near Bellevue overnight. We're both working."

"Grey, you can do better than that." Ros screws up her face in mock disgust as she starts to gather her papers together.

I laugh. "Yes, I can. And what's more, I'll have fun figuring out what to do. Europe, you say."

Ana's always wanted to see Europe. England especially.

Ros's lips twitch into a benevolent smile as she stands. "Good luck with that." Her parting words echo through the empty room, leaving me to contemplate where the hell I'm going to take the future Mrs. Grey for a honeymoon.

I hope she has a passport.

BACK IN MY OFFICE I check my computer, and there's an e-mail from Ana that she sent an hour ago.

From: Anastasia Steele
Subject: Jibbing and Jibing. Bowlines and Halyards.
Date: July 5 2011 9:54
To: Christian Grey

My darling Mr. Grey
What a spectacular weekend! The best July 4th ever. Thank you.
I am also giving you advance notice that I will be staying at my apartment with Kate on Friday. I will be packing so I can move in with you on Saturday. But, I should warn you, this will be a girls-only evening, so your presence will not be required, but much missed.
Maybe you can write your vows?
Just an idea.
Laters, baby.
Axxx

From: Christian Grey
Subject: Abandoning ship.
Date: July 5 2011 11:03
To: Anastasia Steele

My darling fiancée
Thank YOU for the most relaxed July 4th I've ever experienced.
I will miss you on Friday.
But will help you move in on Saturday.
You make my dreams come true.
I will consider my vows and maybe write a few…

I did not mean that to rhyme!

Christian Grey
CEO & poet, Grey Enterprises Holdings, Inc.

PS: Do you possess a passport?

From: Anastasia Steele
Subject: Citizen of the USA
Date: July 5 2011 11:14
To: Christian Grey

Dear Poet
I'd stick to high finance if I were you.
Though I'm glad your dreams doth come true.
I'm thrilled and honored to report.
I do possess a new passport.
Now you have me thinking why?
Are we off someplace to fly?
I'd love to travel the world with you.
Not as one, but as two.

Curious of Seattle xxx
(And not a poet, as you can tell!)

My future wife is a dreadful poet! Grinning at her response, I grab my gym bag and head out of the office, and down to the basement to face Bastille.

FRESH FROM THE GYM, I finish my chicken-salad sandwich at my desk and pick up the phone. It's time to call Elliot. I've been putting this off because I know he'll give me shit.

"Hotshot. What gives?"

"Hello, Elliot. How are you?"

He laughs. "Jesus, man, you sound bored as fuck!"

Why is this so difficult?

"I'm not bored. I'm working. And taking some time out to talk to you."

"Now you sound pissed."

"I am."

"Something I said?" He cackles over the line, and I'm tempted to hang up and try again later.

I take a deep breath. "I need to ask you something."

"About the new house?"

"No."

Game on, Grey. Ask him.

"Spit it out, man," he says when I don't respond. "This is like waiting for concrete to cure."

"Will you be my best man?"

There. It's done. And there's a deafening silence on the other end of the phone, save for his quick gasp. *Shit.* Is he going to say no?

"Elliot?"

"Sure," he says with uncharacteristic brevity. "Um...I'd be honored." He sounds stunned. Why? Surely he knew this was coming?

"Good. Thank you." My relief is clear in my voice.

He laughs, and I know my brother has recovered his dickwad humor. "Of course, this means I get to organize your goddamned bachelor party!" He whoops like a deranged gorilla.

Bachelor party? He's got to be kidding.

"Whatever, Elliot." An idea pops into my head. "Come over Friday. We can shoot some pool. Ana is spending the evening with Kate."

"Yeah, I heard. Sure thing. We can talk strippers, and where we'll leave you handcuffed at the end of a drunken night!"

I laugh, because he has no idea. "*We?*" I ask.

"I know you have no friends, you fucking recluse. I'll drum up a posse who know how to party."

Oh no.

"Let's talk Friday," I respond.

"Can't wait. By the way, have you been in touch with Gia?"

"Yes, I have. Ana and I had a look at her portfolio online. We both liked what we saw. Ms. Matteo was going with the real estate agent to check out the property so that when we meet she knows what we are talking about."

"I need to see this place, too, hotshot."

"I know. Let's do it Friday. After work."

"Rad. Sounds good."

"Okay. Laters, Elliot." An unexpected surge of warmth fills my chest. "And, um…thank you."

"What are brothers for?"

"So, this is your new office, hotshot." Elliot strolls through the door, as laid-back as his tone.

"Do you have to call me that, Lelliot?" I stress his nickname and wave him toward my white leather couch.

"It's what you are. Look at this place." He waves a hand in the direction of my outer office. Wearing jeans, a T-shirt, and his Aztec jacket from San Diego State, he looks like the proverbial fish out of water here.

I sit down opposite him and notice that his knee is bouncing to a crazy beat and he's avoiding eye contact.

What the hell? He's nervous.

I don't think I've ever seen him this way.

"What is it?" I ask.

He shuffles in his seat and presses his hands together. "I want to start my own construction company." He blurts out the words in a rush.

Ah! "You're looking for investment."

His vibrant blue eyes finally meet mine. "Yes," he says with a steeliness that surprises me.

"How much do you need?"

"About 100K."

I smirk at the irony. That's what I started my business with.

"It's yours."

Elliot balks. "You're not going to ask for a business plan? A pitch?"

"No. You may be an utter fucking asshole sometimes, but you work hard. I see that. You're passionate about what you do. This is your dream. And I believe in it, too. We should all be striving for sustainable living. Besides, you're my brother, and what are brothers for?"

When Elliot smiles, he lights up a room.

Feeling uncomfortable at the sudden swell of feelings for my brother, I dial Welch's number for an update on his investigation.

NIGHT SHROUDS MY STUDY at Escala. I've been poring over the documents Marcus sent me regarding Geolumara. Based in Nevada, their solar farms are already producing enough kilowattage to light up two neighboring towns. They have the expertise to bring cheaper renewable energy to other parts of the U.S. I think they have a great deal of potential. I'm excited to acquire the company and see what we can add to their business model. I e-mail Marcus to confirm my enthusiastic interest, then go find Ana.

She's in the library, curled up in her armchair, laptop on her knees and Snow Patrol playing quietly over the sound system. I assume she's working on an upcoming book, and it occurs to me that we should get her a desk and chair in here.

"Hi," I say when she looks up.

"Hi." She smiles.

"Are you reading another manuscript?"

"I'm doing the first draft of my vows."

"I see." I saunter into the room. "How's that going?"

"It's intimidating, Mr. Grey. A little like you."

"Intimidating? Moi?" I press my hand to my chest and feign surprise.

She purses her lips to hide her smile. "It's your specialty."

Settling into the armchair beside Ana's, I lean toward her, my elbows resting on my knees. "Oh. I thought I had other specialties…" Even from this distance I catch a whisper of her fragrance.

Pure Ana. It's intoxicating.

A pretty pink stains her cheeks. "Well, yes. You are blessed with other specialties. This is true." She closes her laptop, tucks her feet beneath her, and raises her chin with the air of a prim, old-fashioned schoolteacher.

I laugh. I know better. Ana has an inner freak. "As long as you promise to love, honor, and obey, I'm sure your vows will be perfect."

Ana laughs. "Christian, I am not promising to obey you."

"What?" *She thinks I'm joking?*

"No way," she says simply.

"What do you mean you're not going to obey?" My stomach feels like it's dropped twenty feet. I meant my comment to be an amusing quip, but I'm thrown by her response. Ana flicks her hair over her shoulder, and it captures the light from the table lamp, highlighting the few red and gold strands; it's beautiful, distracting me. But my attention shifts to her mouth. Her lips flatten into a stubborn line, as she folds her arms and straightens her shoulders in that way she does when she's gearing up for a fight.

Hell. She's going to argue with me?

"You can't be serious! I'll love and honor you always, Christian. But obey? I don't think so."

"Why not?" I'm perfectly serious.

"Because it's the twenty-first century!"

"And?" *How can she oppose me on this?* The conversation is not going the way I expected.

"Well, I'd hope that we could come to some consensus on issues within our marriage through discussion. You know…communicating with each other," she continues.

"I'm hoping for that, too. But if we can't, and we reach an impasse and you go off and put yourself in unnecessary danger—" All manner of horrific scenarios flit through my mind, and unease spawns exponentially in my gut.

Her face softens as she relaxes, her eyes glowing with understanding. "Christian, you always think the worst. You worry too much." She reaches out to stroke my face, her fingers soft and gentle against my skin.

"Ana. I need this," I whisper.

With a heavy sigh, she withdraws her hand and stares at me, as if she's trying to convey a message via telepathy. "Christian, I'm not religious, but our wedding vows will be sacred, and I'm not prepared to make a vow I might break."

Her response is a gut punch, echoing Carrick's words when he lectured me about Elena. *We are talking about the sanctity of marriage. And if you have no respect for that, then you have no business being married.*

I stare at her as my anxiety boils over into frustration. "Anastasia, be reasonable."

She shakes her head. "Christian. *You* be reasonable. You know you have a tendency to overreact. The answer's no."

Me? Overreact?

I glare at her, and for the first time in a long while I don't know what to say.

"You're just tense about the wedding," she says, gently. "We both are."

"I'm a hell of a lot more tense knowing you're not willing to obey. Ana, reconsider. Please." I sweep my hand through my hair and stare into her big blue eyes, but I see nothing except her determination and courage. She's not budging.

Fuck.

This is getting us nowhere, and the grasp on my temper is slipping. It's time to back away before I say something I regret. I get up and try one last attempt. "Think about it. But for now, I have some work to finish." And before she can stop me, I leave the library and head back into my study, trying to think of some way to get her to see sense.

One of us has to be in charge, for fuck's sake.

I stomp over to my desk and slump into my chair, feeling blindsided by her attitude and resentful that I'm only now finding out that she won't obey.

To hell with it.

I'll have to make her see reason.

How?

Shit.

I'm too wound up to think clearly, so I shelve my frustration and open my computer to look through my e-mails. The good news is that my new sailplane will be arriving from Germany next week. It's being shipped to my hangar at the Port of Ephrata. I allow myself a moment of excitement, a glider built for two. I want to run and tell Ana, but right now I'm mad at her.

Damn.

It's depressing. To cheer myself up I reread the specs for the new aircraft, and when I've exhausted all there is to read, I get back to my financial reports.

A tentative knock interrupts me.

"Come in."

Ana pokes her head around the door. "It's nearly midnight," she says with a winsome smile. She eases the door open and stands on the threshold dressed in one of her satin nightgowns. The soft material caresses her body, molding itself to every curve and dip, leaving nothing to my imagination. My mouth dries and my body responds, hot and heavy with longing.

"Are you coming to bed?" she whispers.

I ignore my arousal. "I have a few more things to do."

"Okay." She smiles, and I half smile in return, because I love her. But I'm not going to concede on this. She has to come to her senses. Ana turns to leave but gives me a quick provocative look over her shoulder before closing the door and leaving.

Once more I'm on my own.

Hell.

I want her.

But she won't obey and that's pissed me off. Big-time.

I turn back to the latest figures from Barney's division at GEH. They're not nearly as seductive as the delectable, and disobedient, Miss Steele.

WEDNESDAY, JULY 6, 2011

Ana is fast asleep when I crawl into bed beside her. Ever thoughtful, she's left my bedside light switched on so I won't be lost in the dark. And yet, that's exactly how I feel. *Lost*. And if I'm being honest, discouraged. Why can't she understand? It's not that big a deal, is it? *Is it?*

Watching her lovely, tranquil face and the steady rise and fall of her breasts as she sleeps, an ugly undercurrent looms beneath my ribs; it's envy. I'm lying here, bewildered and miserable, and she's sleeping like she hasn't a care in the world.

But would I want her any other way?

Of course not. I want her happy and I want to protect her. But how can I do that if she's not willing to obey me?

Deal with it, Grey.

Sighing, I lean over and brush her hair with my lips; it's the gentlest of touches, as I don't want to wake her. But I silently implore her to change her mind.

Please, Ana. Grant me this.

Switching off the light, I stare, unflinching, into the dark, and suddenly the silence in the room is deafening and oppressive. My heart rate doubles and I'm dragged down into a swamp of despair. It's overwhelming. Maybe this is a huge mistake. Our marriage is never going to work if she can't do this.

What was I thinking?

Maybe I want—no, *need*—someone more submissive.

I *need* to be in control.

Always.

Without control, there is chaos. And anger. And hurt, and fear… and pain.

Shit. What am I going to do?

This is an impossible hurdle to overcome.

Isn't it?

But living without Ana would be unbearable. I know what it's like to bathe in her light. She is warmth and life and home. She is everything. I want her by my side. I love her.

How can I get her to reconsider?

I rub my face, trying to fend off my bleak thoughts.

Get a grip, Grey. She'll come around.

I close my eyes and try to utilize Dr. Flynn's mindfulness exercises and find my happy place. Maybe a flowery bower in a boathouse…

I'm walking on air, soaring high in the sky above Ephrata. The Washington landscape is a patchwork beneath me. I wing over and marvel at the quilt of browns and blues and greens crisscrossed by roads and irrigation canals. Catching a thermal I rise above a ridge on the Beezley Hills. The sky is unencumbered, a dazzling, shimmering blue, and I'm at peace. The wind my companion. Constant. Rushing. The only sound. I am alone. Alone. Alone. I wing over again. My world turned upside down. And Ana is in front of the cockpit, her hands stretched out to the canopy, squealing with joy. And wonder. My heart is brimming. This is happiness. This is love. This is what it feels like. I bank, and suddenly I'm in a tailspin. Ana's disappeared. I stamp my feet, but the rudder's gone. I fight the control stick, but the ailerons don't respond. I have no control. All I hear is the roar of the wind and someone screaming. We're going down. Fuck. Spinning. Down. Down. Down. *Shit.* I'm going to hit the ground. *No. No!*

I wake with a start.

Fuck.

I'm wrapped around Ana, and she's threading her fingers through my hair. Her scent is soothing and it's filling the desperate emptiness that's deep in my soul. "Good morning," she says, and immediately I'm calmer. Back to earth.

"Good morning," I whisper, confused. I normally wake before Ana.

"You were having a bad dream."

"What time is it?"

"It's just after seven-thirty."

"Shit. I'm late." I give her a brief, chaste kiss and bound out of bed.

"Christian," she calls.

"I can't stop. I'm late," I mutter as I disappear into the bathroom, recalling her defiance from last night.

And I'm still pissed.

AT MY DESK, I eye the model glider that Anastasia gave me when she left. It took me a whole day to make. Unease circles my gut; maybe it's the echo of that dream or a reminder of the desolation I felt when she was gone. I touch the wing tip, holding the cool plastic between my thumb and forefinger; I never want to feel like that again.

Ever.

I shake off the feeling and take a sip of the espresso that Andrea has prepared, followed by a bite of fresh croissant. I glance at my iMac to see an e-mail has arrived from Ana.

From: Anastasia Steele
Subject: Eat!
Date: July 6 2011 9:22
To: Christian Grey

My dearest husband-to-be
It is not like you to skip breakfast. I missed you.
I hope you're not hungry. I know how disagreeable that is for you.
I hope your day is a good one.
Axxx

I'm comforted by the number of small *x*'s at the end of her message, but I glance at her portrait on my office wall, close the e-mail, and summon Andrea into my office to go through my schedule.

I'm still pissed.

AFTER LUNCH, I'M IN the elevator returning from an external meeting with Eamon Kavanagh when I check my BlackBerry. There's another e-mail from Ana.

From: Anastasia Steele
Subject: Are you okay?
Date: July 6 2011 14:27
To: Christian Grey

My dearest husband-to-be
It's not like you not to reply.
The last time you didn't reply—your helicopter went missing.
Let me know you're okay.

Ana
Worried of SIP

Shit. A twinge of guilt flares in my stomach, especially as there is a distinct lack of kisses on her note.

For fuck's sake.

I'm mad at you, Anastasia.

But I don't want her to worry. I type out a brief reply.

From: Christian Grey
Subject: Are you okay?
Date: July 6 2011 14:32
To: Anastasia Steele

I'm fine.
Busy.

Christian Grey
CEO, Grey Enterprises Holdings, Inc.

I press send and hope my response will alleviate her worries. Andrea eyes me warily when I exit the elevator into the outer office.

"Yes?" I snap.

"It's nothing, Mr. Grey. I just wanted to know if you wanted any coffee?"

"Where's Sarah?"

"She's photocopying the reports you requested."

"Good. And no thanks to coffee," I add in a softer tone. *Why am I being an asshole to my staff?* "Get me Welch on the line."

She nods and picks up the phone.

"Thanks," I mumble, and head into my office. I slouch into my chair and stare despondently out of the window. The day is bright, unlike my mood.

My phone buzzes. "Grey."

"I have Anastasia Steele on the line for you."

Shit. Is she okay?

"Put her through."

"Hi." Her voice wavers, soft and breathy. She sounds uncertain and sad, and a chill grips my heart.

"What is it? Are you okay?" I ask.

"I'm fine. It's you I'm worried about."

My relief turns to irritation. My worry is misplaced. "I'm fine, but busy."

"Let's talk when you get home."

"Okay," I reply, knowing that I'm being abrupt.

She doesn't respond, but I hear her breathing on the other end of the line. She sounds, unsettled, and the chill I felt a moment earlier is replaced by a familiar homesickness.

What is it, Ana? What do you want to say? Silence stretches between us, full of recrimination and unspoken truths.

"Christian," she says eventually.

"Anastasia, I have things to do. I have to go."

"Tonight," she whispers.

"Tonight." I hang up and scowl at the phone.

It's not too much to ask, Anastasia.

"HOME?" TAYLOR ASKS AS he takes the wheel of the Audi.

"Sure," I murmur, distracted. Part of me doesn't want to go home. I still don't have a coherent argument to persuade Ana to change her mind. And I have work to do this evening. A reading project— two weighty reports from the Environmental Sciences Department at WSU—results from the test sites in Africa and Professor Gravett's paper on the microbe responsible for nitrogen fixation in soils. Apparently, microbes are essential to soil regeneration and regeneration holds the key to carbon sequestration. Later this week, I'll be reviewing my funding to her department.

Perhaps I should take Ana out, and we can discuss her vows at dinner. Maybe I can sway her over a glass of wine. I'm reminded of our dinner to discuss the D/s contract.

Hell. That didn't go to plan.

Feeling glum, I stare through the privacy glass at the jostling tourists and commuters, and a sense of righteous indignation settles over me. I'm not asking for much, for fuck's sake. It's the only thing that I want. She can have whatever she likes. Knowing that she'll obey me will give me a sense of security. Does she not understand?

On the sidewalk a young man in shades and loud, flowery shorts is arguing with a woman in an equally loud dress. Their fight is attracting disconcerted looks from passersby.

That will be Ana and me tonight. I know it. And the thought depresses me even more.

I'll just have to tell her what it means to me. I need to keep her safe. Yes. She'll see.

The woman turns, and in a dramatic gesture raises her arms and storms off, leaving the man alone and bewildered on the sidewalk. I think he's drunk.

Asshole.

Maybe I could fuck Ana into agreeing. That might work. The thought gives me a modicum of hope, and I settle back into my seat for the rest of the drive to Escala.

"GOOD EVENING, MR. GREY," Mrs. Jones chimes as I enter the living room. From the enticing aroma I know there's a pot of her delicious Bolognese sauce bubbling on the stove. My mouth waters.

"Hello, Gail. Smells good. Where's Ana?"

"I believe she's in the library, sir."

"Thank you."

"Dinner in half an hour?"

"Works for me. Thanks." I'll have time for a quick run on the treadmill, since I missed my workout this morning.

I head to the bedroom to change, avoiding the library.

THE BOSS BLARES IN my ears as I push my body to its limits. I run three miles in twenty minutes, and I'm a panting hot mess when I come off the treadmill. Dragging air into my lungs and using the back of my hand to wipe the sweat that's pouring off my brow, I bend over to catch my breath and stretch my hamstrings.

It feels good.

When I stand, Anastasia is leaning against the frame in the doorway, watching me, eyes wide and wary. She's wearing a pale gray sleeveless shirt and a tight gray skirt. She looks every bit the publishing executive. But young. So young. And miserable.

Shit.

"Hi," she says.

"Hi," I respond between breaths.

"You didn't say hello when you came in. Are you avoiding me?"

Ana does not beat around the bush. And in that moment, I want to banish the look of misery on her face and her wariness. "I needed to exercise," I pant. "I can say hello now." I open my arms and step toward her, knowing full well I'm soaked with sweat.

Ana laughs, grimacing, and raises her palms. "I'll take a rain check."

I bound up to her and pull her into my arms before she can retreat. She shrieks, shrinking from me, but she's laughing, too. And it's like a weight has lifted from my soul.

I love making her laugh.

"Oh, baby. I missed you." I kiss her, not caring that I'm not fit for human consumption, and to my delight, she kisses me back. Her fingers tighten around my shoulders, her fingernails digging deeper into my flesh as our tongues dance the dance they know so well.

We're both winded when we come up for air. I cradle her face and brush my thumb over her swollen lips, staring into her dazed, beautiful eyes. "Ana," I whisper, imploring her. "Change your vows. Obey. Don't argue with me. I hate it when we argue. Please."

My lips hover above hers, waiting for an answer, but she blinks several times as if she's clearing a haze, then shrugs me off and steps out of my embrace. "No. Christian. Please," she says, condensing her frustration into four syllables.

I drop my hands to my sides as her words douse me with a cold splash of reality.

"If this is a deal breaker for you, please tell me," she continues, her voice rising steadily. "Because it is for me, and I can stop trying to organize our wedding and go back to my apartment and get drunk with Kate."

"You'd leave?" My voice is barely audible; her statement has knocked my world off-kilter.

"Right now. Yes. You're behaving like a spoiled teen."

"That's not fair," I retort. "I need this."

"No, you don't. You just think you do. We're supposed to be grown-ups, for heaven's sake. We'll talk things out. Like adults do."

We gaze at each other, over the gulf between us.

She's not budging.

Fuck.

"I need a shower," I mutter, and she steps out of my way to let me pass.

WHEN I ENTER THE living room Ana is seated at the kitchen counter, where there are two places laid for dinner. Gail hovers over the stove.

"I'm not hungry," I announce. "And I have work to do."

Ana frowns, and opens her mouth as if to say something but shuts it again as I walk past her. I don't miss the look that passes between her and Mrs. Jones.

Are they conspiring?

The thought makes my blood boil, so I storm into my study and slam the door.

Shit.

The noise startles me and it's an abrupt wake-up.

I *am* behaving like a spoiled teen.

Ana's right. *Hell.*

And I'm hungry.

I hate being hungry.

A dark, twisted memory of fear and hunger from before I was Christian Grey threatens to resurface, but I dampen it down.

Don't go there, Grey.

The reports are on my desk where Taylor left them. I sit down, pick up the first one, and start to read.

A GENTLE KNOCK PULLS my attention away from the multiple crop rotations we're trying in Ghana, and my heart stutters.

Ana.

"Come in."

Gail opens the door.

My disappointment is real, my momentary excitement now a sad, deflated balloon that's lost its helium. On the plus side, she's carrying a tray with a bowl of steaming pasta.

She says nothing as she places it on my desk.

"Thank you."

"Ana's idea. She knows you love spaghetti Bolognese." Her tone is clipped, and before I can reply, she turns and leaves, taking her disapproval with her. I scowl at her departing figure. Of course it was Ana's idea. And once again I'm in awe of her thoughtfulness. Why isn't that enough? She says she loves me. So why do I want or need her obedience?

Feeling even more morose, I stare at the long shadows and golden pink hues painted across my study walls by the sun as it sinks into the horizon.

Why does she defy me?

I pick up my fork and dig into my meal, twirling the pasta into a big, solid bite of bliss. It's delicious.

ANA HAS LEFT THE lamp on for me again. She's fast asleep, and as I slide into the bed beside her my body comes alive. I hunger for her.

I contemplate my plan to fuck her into agreeing, but deep down I know she's made up her mind. She might say no, and right now I don't think I'd survive the rejection.

I turn onto my side, away from her, and switch off my light. The room is plunged into darkness, reflecting my mood; I'm more miserable now than I was this morning.

Damn. Why did I let this get so out of hand?

I close my eyes.

Mommy! Mommy! Mommy is asleep on the floor. She has been asleep for a long time. I brush her hair because she likes that. She doesn't wake up. I shake her. *Mommy!* My tummy hurts. It's hungry. He isn't here. I am thirsty. In the kitchen, I pull a chair to the sink, and I have a drink. The water splashes over my blue sweater. Mommy is still asleep. *Mommy, wake up!* She lies still. She is cold. I fetch my blankie, and I cover Mommy, and I lie down on the sticky green rug beside her. Mommy is still asleep. I have two toy cars. They race by the floor where Mommy is sleeping. I think Mommy is sick. I search for something to eat. In the icebox I find peas. They are cold. I eat them slowly. They make my tummy hurt. I sleep beside Mommy. The peas are gone. In the freezer is something. It smells funny. I lick it and my tongue is stuck to it. I eat it slowly. It tastes nasty. I drink some water. I play with my cars, and I sleep beside Mommy. Mommy is so cold, and she won't wake up. The door crashes open. I cover Mommy with my blankie. He's here. *Fuck. What the fuck happened here? Oh, the crazy fucked-up bitch. Shit. Get out of my way, you little shit.* He kicks me, and I hit my head on the floor. My head hurts. He calls somebody and he goes. He locks the door. I lay down beside Mommy. My head hurts. The lady policeman is here. No. No. No. Don't touch me. Don't touch me. Don't touch me. I stay by Mommy. No. Stay away from me. The lady policeman has my blankie, and she grabs me. I scream. Mommy! Mommy! I want my mommy. The words are gone. I can't say the words. Mommy can't hear me. I have no words.

"Christian! Christian!" Her voice is urgent, pulling me from the depths of my nightmare, and my despair. "I'm here. I'm here," she cries.

I wake and Ana's leaning over me, grasping my shoulders, shaking me, her face taut with anguish, eyes wide and brimming with tears.

"Ana." My voice is a hoarse whisper, the taste of fear tarnishing my mouth. "You're here."

"Of course I'm here."

"I had a dream."

"I know. I'm here, I'm here."

"Ana." Her name is an incantation on my lips, a talisman against the dark, choking panic coursing through my body.

"Hush, I'm here." She curls around me, her limbs cocooning mine, her warmth seeping into my soul, forcing back the shadows, forcing back the fear. She is sunshine, she is light. She is mine.

"Please, let's not fight." I wrap my arms around her.

"Okay."

"The vows. No obeying. I can do that. We'll find a way." The words rush out of my mouth in a tumble of emotion and confusion and anxiety.

"Yes. We will. We'll always find a way," Ana whispers, and her lips are on mine, silencing me, bringing me back to the now.

D r. Flynn rubs his chin and I don't know if he's playing for time or genuinely intrigued. "She threatened to leave?"

"Yes."

"Seriously?"

"Yes."

"So, you capitulated."

"I didn't have much choice."

"Christian, you always have a choice. Do you think Anastasia was being unreasonable?"

I meet his gaze and want to shout yes, but deep down I know Ana isn't an unreasonable person.

That's you, Grey.

Unreasonable could be your middle name. Ana's words haunt me. She said that, long ago.

Christ, my negativity is a real prick sometimes.

"How are you feeling now?" Flynn asks.

"Wary," I whisper, and my admission is a jab to the solar plexus, almost winding me.

She could leave me.

"Ah. Your feelings of insecurity and abandonment are coming to the fore again."

I remain mute, distracted by the sliver of afternoon light that brightens the cluster of mini orchids on his coffee table. *What can I say?* I don't want to admit this out loud. It makes my fears real. I loathe feeling this weak. This exposed. Ana has the power to wound me and deliver a fatal blow.

"Is it giving you second thoughts about the wedding?" John asks.

No. Maybe.

I'm afraid she'll hurt me.

Like she did before…when she left.

"No," I answer, because I don't want to lose her.

He nods, as if this is what he wants to hear. "You've relinquished a great deal for her."

"I have." I stifle my indulgent smile. "She's a good negotiator."

Flynn rubs his chin again. "Do you resent that?"

"Yes. Partly. I've given so much and she won't give me this."

"You sound like you're mad at her."

"I am."

"Have you thought about telling her that?"

"How mad I am? No."

"Why not?"

"I'm worried I'll say something I'll regret and she'll leave. She left once before."

"But you hurt her then."

"I did." The memory of her tearful face and her bitter rebuke are never far from my mind. *You are one fucked-up son of a bitch.*

I shudder, but I hide it from Flynn. Whenever I think of that time, my shame almost swallows me whole. "I don't want to hurt her again. Ever."

"That's a good goal to work toward," Flynn says. "But you need to find a healthy way to express and channel your anger. You've directed it inwardly for so long. Too long." He pauses. "But you know my views on that. I am not going to rehash that now, Christian. You're incredibly resilient and resourceful. You had the solution to this impasse all along; you capitulated. Problem solved. Life is not always going to go your way. The key is to recognize those moments. Sometimes it's better to concede the battle to win the war. Communicate and compromise—that's what marriage is all about."

I snort, remembering Ana's e-mail from a lifetime ago.

"What's so funny?"

"Nothing." I shake my head.

"Have a little faith in yourself, and in her."

"Marriage is a huge leap of faith," I mumble.

"It is. For everyone. But you're well equipped to cope. Focus on where you want to be. How you want to be. I think you have over the last few weeks. You've seemed happier."

I meet his gaze.

"This is just a small setback," he says.

I hope so.

"I'll see you next week."

IT'S DUSK, AND ELLIOT and I are standing on the terrace of the new house, admiring the view. "I can see why you bought the place." Elliot whistles his appreciation through his teeth. We're both quiet for a moment, absorbing the majesty of twilight over the Sound: the opal sky, the distant orange haze, the dark purple waters. The beauty. The calm.

"Stunning, isn't it?" I murmur.

"Yep. This is a great spot for a beautiful home."

"Which you're going to remodel." I grin and Elliot play-punches my arm.

"Glad I can help. It's gonna take some hard work, and it ain't gonna be cheap to make this place more sustainable. But, hey, you can afford it. I'll talk to Gia next week and see what she has in mind, and if it's possible."

"I'll close on this sometime before the end of July. I think Ana, you, Gia, and I should meet here once that's done."

"Do it before. Doesn't sound like the results of any survey will stop you from buying this place."

"You're right. I'll look at my schedule. When do you think you might have time?"

"For what?"

"The build, dude. The build."

"Ah. Well, if the Spokani Eden project stays on schedule, maybe early fall?" He shrugs.

"It's going well?"

"Yeah." Elliot looks pleased with himself.

He should. It's an ambitious project, and, once complete, it will be a showcase for his sustainable building methods. He shoves his Seahawks cap back on his head and claps his hands. "T.G.I.F., hotshot. Let's get back to your place and get our beer on." Rolling my eyes, I follow my big brother around the side of the house to where my car is parked in the driveway.

"I WONDER WHAT OUR women are doing?" Elliot says on the drive back to Escala.

"Packing up Ana's things, I hope." I glance at Elliot. He's got his fucking foot on my dashboard, and he's watching the passing scenery as if he doesn't give a shit.

Lord, I envy him.

"They're probably eating pizza, drinking too much wine, and talking about us," he quips.

I hope they're not talking about us!

"Or they could be watching the game." He cackles.

"Kate into baseball?"

"Yeah. She likes all sports."

Of course she does. I'm once more confounded by why she and Ana are friends. Ana doesn't seem interested in sports at all. Though we both enjoyed watching the Mariners recently. "So, do you think of Kate as your woman, then?" I ask, curious.

"Yeah. For now."

"It's not serious between you?"

He shrugs. "She's cool. We'll see. She doesn't hassle me. You know?"

"I don't know, thank God," I mutter to myself, and shake my head. This might be the longest "relationship" he's ever experienced.

"Let's stop at a bar," he says.

"No. I'm not drinking and driving."

"Dude, you're driving like Dad."

"Fuck off, asshole." I put my foot down and the R8 screeches up the on-ramp onto I-5 and we speed toward the city.

"Have you found the prick who totaled your chopper?"

I sigh. "Helicopter, Elliot. And no. It's really pissing me off."

"Man, who would want to do that?"

"I don't know. My team has turned up zilch. I'm waiting for the report from the NTSB. They're taking their sweet time. I've had to up our security. I've got two guys watching Ana and Kate's place tonight."

"No kidding! Don't blame you, man. There are some wackos out there."

I give him a look.

"What? I'm just stating the obvious. I'm glad they'll be safe," he says, and I'm beginning to think he might really care for Kavanagh. "What do you want to do for your bachelor party?" he asks as we come off I-5.

"Elliot, I don't want or need a bachelor party."

"Man, you up and marry the first girl who's given you any serious attention. Of course you need a bachelor party."

I laugh. *Dude, you have no idea.*

"I thought you'd knocked her up."

I go cold. "Fuck off, bro. I'm not that careless. Ana's far too young for kids. We have a life to live before we get into all that shit."

Elliot laughs. "You with kids. That'll loosen you up."

I ignore him. "Have you heard from Mia?"

"She's chasing cock."

"What?"

"Kate's brother. I don't think he's interested."

"I dislike the words *cock* and *Mia* in the same sentence."

"She's not a kid anymore, hotshot. You know, she's only slightly younger than Ana and Kate."

I'd rather not think about that.

"Are we playing pool or watching the game?" He wisely changes the subject.

"Whatever you want, bro, whatever you want." We pull into the underground garage at Escala while I'm still trying not to think about Mia and Ethan Kavanagh.

ELLIOT IS SNORING IN front of the TV. He works too damned hard, he plays too damned hard, but he'll sleep off his overconsumption of beer in the spare bedroom. We've had a chill evening: we watched highlights of the Mariners-Angels game (Mariners lost), he thrashed me at *Call of Duty*, but I won at pool, for a change. Tomorrow morning, I'll be at Ana's apartment to help move the rest of her belongings here. It's taken enough time. I glance at my watch, wondering what she might be doing. My phone buzzes, and it's as if she's heard my thoughts.

> ANA
> I'm packed. Missing you.
> Sleep well. No nightmares.
> This is not a request.
> I'm not there to hold you.
> Love you. ♥

Her words warm my heart. Flynn said our recent fight was just a small setback; I hope he's right. I text back.

> Dream of me.
> I hope to dream of you.
> No nightmares.

> ANA
> Promise?

> No promises.
> Just hope. And dreams.
> And love. For you.

> ANA
> You once said you don't do romance.
> I'm so glad that you're wrong. I'm
> swooning here!
> I love you, Christian.
> Good night xxx.

> Good night, Ana.
> I like to make you swoon.
> I love you. Always. x

I read through the press release that I've rewritten for Sam.

For Immediate Release

**GREY ENTERPRISES HOLDINGS INC.
ACQUIRES SEATTLE INDEPENDENT PUBLISHING**

Seattle, WA, July 11, 2011—Grey Enterprises Holdings, Inc., (GEH) announces the acquisition of Seattle Independent Publishing (SIP) of Seattle, WA, for $15 million.

A spokesperson for GEH stated: "GEH is thrilled to add SIP to its portfolio of local companies." CEO Christian Grey said, "I'm eager to branch into publishing and to use GEH's technological expertise to grow SIP and further develop a solid publishing platform that offers a voice to authors based in the Pacific Northwest."

Seattle Independent Publishing was founded thirty-two years ago by Jeremy Roach, who will continue as CEO. SIP has had considerable success championing local authors, including three-time *USA Today* bestseller Bee Edmonston and poet and performance artist Keon Kinger, whose latest collection, *By the Sound,* was shortlisted for the prestigious Arthur Rense Prize in 2010.

SIP will continue to function independently and will retain all thirty-two of its employees. Roach said, "This is a tremendous opportunity for all the staff and the authors at SIP, and we're very excited to see where our partnership with GEH will take us over the next decade and beyond."

All inquiries to Sam Saster
VP, Director of Publicity, Grey Enterprises Holdings, Inc.

Ana's words come back to me. *Of course I'm mad at you. I mean, what kind of responsible business executive makes decisions based on who he is currently fucking?*

I do, Ana.

But only because I'm fucking *you.*

Memories of her tied to her little white bed, slick and sticky with ice cream, me attempting to chop peppers, her calling me an ass, float into my head. I glance at my glider. Maybe that's why she doesn't want to obey, because she thinks I'm an ass.

Grey. Enough.

Doubt is an ugly, futile feeling.

This is my new mantra. Flynn said our dispute was a small set-back. All relationships have them. She's moved in with me, and we're getting married in less than three weeks. What more do I want?

Damn. I wish we were married already. The wait is shredding my nerves. I don't want her to change her mind. She's been quiet this weekend. We were busy moving her stuff into the apartment, and she's been knee-deep in wedding preparations.

She's just tired.

Stop with the negative, Grey.

Focus on the matter in hand.

I pick up the phone and call Sam.

"Christian."

Sometimes it really grates on my nerves when he uses my first name. In an arctic tone I inform him, "I've sent you a revised, less wordy press release. Brevity is everything. Try and remember that."

"As you wish, Mr. Grey."

Good. Point made.

"And, Sam, delete the price and put 'undisclosed sum.'"

"Will do."

I hang up and turn to my computer. I'm hoping some e-mail banter with my fiancée will improve my disposition and hers.

From: Christian Grey
Subject: The Ultimate Consumer. Consuming.
Date: July 11 2011 08:43
To: Anastasia Steele

My darling Anastasia
I was reminiscing about the day you found out I had purchased SIP. I believe you called me an ass, when I was merely exercising my rights as a citizen of our fine country to purchase whatever I please. As the

Ultimate Consumer (again, your epithet) I am informing you that the news of my most recent acquisition is no longer embargoed and a press release will be issued today.

I'm so glad you've moved in.

I slept well last night knowing you were there.

I love you.

Christian Grey
CEO, Entrepreneur, not an ass, Grey Enterprises Holdings, Inc.

From: Anastasia Steele
Subject: Boss or Bossy
Date: July 11 2011 08:56
To: Christian Grey

My dearest husband-to-be

You were an ass (I stand by that appellation) and my boss's boss's boss. I remember that we enjoyed a thoroughly entertaining and sticky evening. Perhaps a helping of ice cream this evening? It is so warm out…

I love you back. Very much.

I'm preparing an agenda for our meeting this evening with Alondra about final preparations!

Any last-minute requests?

Are you still happy for the rehearsal dinner to take place at Escala?

Anastasia Steele
Acting Editor, Fiction, SIP

From: Christian Grey
Subject: How Many Times!
Date: July 11 2011 08:59
To: Anastasia Steele

My darling Anastasia

Let's make it a short service.

I'm impatient for you to be mine.

Yes, to Escala. Fewer prying eyes there.

Oh, and BLACKBERRY!!!

AND BEN & JERRY'S & ANA.

My favorite dessert.

Christian Grey
Bossy CEO, Grey Enterprises Holdings, Inc.

From: Anastasia Steele
Subject: Uber Bossy
Date: July 11 2011 09:02
To: Christian Grey

Oh fiddle-dee-dee Mr. Grey.
It's my favorite dessert too.
Ana x

I smile. Now she's quoting *Gone with the Wind* at me. She seems happy enough. I shake my head and summon Andrea, my disposition much improved.

Thank you, Miss Steele.

MID-MORNING, ANDREA PUTS Darius Jackson from the Port of Ephrata through.

"Good morning, Christian."

"Darius, it's good to hear your voice. Has she arrived?" Suddenly I'm ten years old again, and it's Christmas. I can barely contain my excitement.

"She has, Mr. Grey, and she's a beauty."

"Have you put her together?"

"Working on it now. I'll send you some photographs when she's complete."

"I can't wait to see her."

"I have the registration ready, and I'm wondering if you want me to take her up for a test flight, or if you'd like to do that."

"No. Take her up. Let me know how she handles."

"I'd be delighted to. When can we expect you?"

"I'll try and get up there this weekend. I'll let you know."

"Okay. I'll get back to her. I don't like to leave a lady waiting." He chuckles, hangs up, and I laugh.

Me neither, Darius, unless she's misbehaved…

I sigh. Perhaps Ana and I can go soaring this weekend.

ANA IS SUBDUED DURING dinner, picking at her risotto.

Maybe she's having second thoughts?

"What's wrong?" I ask.

"Nothing. It was just a long day."

My anxiety simmers. There's something she's not telling me. "Sawyer told me there were paparazzi outside your building," I prompt.

"We left via the loading bay. We managed to avoid them."

So, it's not the continual harassment from the fourth estate that's bugging her. *What is it?* I try a different tack. "What did you do today?"

She snorts. "I spent most of the day on the phone with authors, trying to soften the blow of the news."

I almost spit out my food. *What the hell!*

She laughs at my expression, her reaction immediately lifting my spirits.

"Yes, big business exploiting artistic endeavor," she clarifies.

"Ah."

"Roach called the senior editorial team together this morning to give us all the news of your takeover. Of course, I knew already, when everyone else was in the dark. It was strange. It set me apart...you know."

"I see." Surely that's a good thing—knowledge is power.

"Christian." Her eyes are full of misgiving, and her words pour out in a steady torrent. "My fiancé owns the company I work for. Roach stared at me a few times during the meeting and I didn't know what he was thinking. I remember he went a little crazy when he found out we were getting married. The whole meeting was odd. I felt uncomfortable and self-conscious."

Shit!

"You didn't tell me he went a little crazy." *Asshole.*

"That was a while ago, when he found out we were engaged."

"Did *he* make you feel uncomfortable?"

I'll fire him if he did.

She studies me, her face serious, as if considering my question. "A little. Maybe. Maybe not. Or maybe I'm projecting. I don't know. Anyway, he confirmed my position as editor."

"Today?"

"This afternoon."

Hmm. I've not yet removed the moratorium on hiring new staff.
Wily old bastard.

Reaching over, I grasp her hand. "Congratulations. We should celebrate. Were you worried about telling me?"

"I thought you knew and you hadn't said anything." Her voice trails off.

I laugh. "No, I didn't. But it's great news."

She looks relieved. Is this why she's been so quiet? "Don't sweat it, Ana. To hell with what your colleagues think and what Roach thinks. I hope everyone at the company was reassured by the press release. I'm not planning any changes in the immediate future. And I'm sure your authors were delighted to hear from you."

"Some yes. Some no. There are a few who still miss Jack."

"Really? That amazes me."

"He took a gamble on a couple. They're loyal. I suspect they'll move with him when he finds another job."

He's never going to find another job if I have my way.

She tightens her fingers around mine.

"Anyway, thank you," she says.

"What for?"

"Listening." Her brow furrows once again, and I wonder if she wants to say more.

What, Ana? Tell me.

"Are you ready for the wedding planner?" she asks.

"Of course. Better finish up." I look pointedly at her food. And to my relief she scoops up a large bite of risotto and pops it into her mouth. I slowly unwind; she just wanted to tell me about her promotion and expected me to know about it.

For fuck's sake, Grey.

Relax.

"ALL THAT REMAINS IS to decide what you'll do after the wedding reception." Alondra Gutierrez has an easy smile.

"We haven't discussed that yet." Ana turns to me.

"It's in hand," I tell Ms. Gutierrez, and Ana looks surprised.

Oh, baby. I've got this.

"I'll take this up with you separately, Alondra."

"Very good, Mr. Grey. I can't wait to hear!"

"Neither can I," Ana says.

"You'll have to wait until the big day." I smile.

I hope you enjoy what I have planned.

Ana pushes out her bottom lip in the semblance of a pout, but there's humor in her expression and something else…something darker, more sensual, that speaks to my dick.

Fuck.

Alondra gathers her things, letting us know that we can still make last-minute changes as we thank her for all that she's done.

We all rise as Taylor appears at the entrance to the living room and Alondra takes her leave. We both watch her depart, and once she's out of earshot I turn to Ana.

"She's got it all in hand."

"Alondra's good at her job," she says.

"She is," I agree. "Now what do you want to do?" I add in a whisper.

Ana whips her eyes to mine and her lips part as she gazes at me. We're inches from each other. Not touching. But I feel her. All of her. The silence between us gets louder, expanding to fill the space surrounding us as we each drink the other in.

Suddenly, there's no oxygen in the vast room. There's only us, only our desire, crackling invisibly between us. I see it in the summer of her eyes. Her pupils growing wider. Darker. Reflecting my thirst. My love. Our love.

"You've been so distant." Her voice is barely audible. "All weekend."

"No. Not distant. Afraid."

"No!" she says in a quiet rush of tenderness. She closes the gap between us without moving. Reaching up, her fingertips skim over my stubble, her touch echoing through my every bone and sinew.

I close my eyes as my body responds.

Ana.

Her fingers are at my shirt, undoing the buttons. "Don't be afraid," she breathes, and places a kiss on one of my scars above my pulsing heart. I can bear no more: I cup her face and bring her lips to mine, kissing her ferociously. She's a banquet for a starving man. She tastes of love and lust and Ana.

"Let's go. Now. Vegas. Get married," I implore against her fevered lips. "We can tell everyone we couldn't wait." She moans and I kiss her again, taking all she's got to give, drowning in her desire, drowning in her love, aching for her, desperate for her.

When she pulls back we're both dragging air into our lungs, her dazed eyes on me. "If that's what you want," she says, breathless and brimming with compassion.

I crush her to me.

She'd do this for me.

She won't obey…but she'll do this.

Damn.

And I know I have to give her a wedding she deserves. Not some rushed affair in a chapel of love in Vegas. My girl deserves the best.

"Come to bed," I whisper in her ear, and she laces her fingers into my hair as I lift her into my arms.

"I thought you'd never ask," she says, and I carry her into the bedroom.

SATURDAY, JULY 16, 2011

W ake up, sleepy head." Gently I tug Ana's earlobe with my teeth. "Hmm…" She groans and refuses to open her eyes. I tug again. "Ah!" she gripes and her eyes flutter open.

"Good morning, Miss Steele."

"Good morning." She reaches up to stroke my face. I'm fully dressed and lying stretched out beside her.

"Sleep well?" I kiss her palm.

She gives me a sleepy nod.

"I have a surprise."

"Oh?"

"Up." I slide off the bed.

"What surprise?"

"If I told you…"

She slides her head to one side, unimpressed. She needs an answer.

"Floating above the Pacific Northwest?"

She gasps and sits up immediately. "Soaring?" she asks.

"The very same."

"We can chase the"—she glances out of the window—"rain?" She looks crestfallen.

"It's sunnier where we're going."

"Then we can chase the midday sun!"

"We can. If you get up!"

She squeals with delight and scrambles out of bed, all haste and long limbs. She stops to give me a swift chaste kiss before dashing into the bathroom.

"It should be warm," I call after her with a huge grin. I think she's pleased.

AS WE SPEED DOWN I-90 in the R8, fleeing the dreary weather, I allow myself the luxury of being in the moment. My girl is beside me,

The Killers are on the sound system, and we're going soaring, in my new sailplane. All is right in the world.

Flynn would be proud.

Of course, we're being followed by Sawyer and Reynolds, but a guy can't have everything.

"Where are we going?" Ana asks, peering through the drizzle.

"Ephrata."

From the corner of my eye I see she's perplexed. "It's about two and a half hours away. It's where I keep my sailplanes."

"You have more than one?"

"Two. Now."

"The Blaník?" she asks, and when I frown she continues, sounding a little less certain. "You mentioned it to the pilot when we went soaring in Georgia." She looks down at her fingers and starts twisting her engagement ring. "It's why I bought you the model one." Her voice drops so I have to strain to hear her.

"The only Blaník I have is that little glider. It has pride of place on my desk at work." Reaching over, I grasp her knee, briefly recalling the circumstances when she gifted the little model to me.

Don't go there, Grey.

"I trained to fly in a Blaník. Right now, I have a brand-new, state-of-the-art ASH 30. One of the first in the world. It will be my—our maiden flight in her." I flash her a quick grin.

Ana's face erupts into smile and she shakes her head fondly.

"What?" I ask.

"You."

"Me?"

"Yes. You and your toys."

"A man has to chill, Ana." I wink at her and she blushes.

"You're never going to let me live that down, are you?"

"That and the 'are you gay' question."

Ana laughs. "You enjoy expensive pursuits."

"This is not news."

She stifles her smile and shakes her head again, and I don't know if she's laughing at me or with me.

Plus ça change, Anastasia.

WE TURN INTO THE parking lot at Ephrata Municipal Airport just before eleven. The promised sun has materialized, dispersing the rain clouds and ushering in pretty white cumulus, perfect for soaring. I'm itching to see my new plane and get her airborne. "Ready?" I ask.

"Yes!" Ana's eyes shine, her excitement palpable. Like mine.

"It's so bright, we're going to need shades." From the glove box I take my aviators and hand a pair of Wayfarers to Ana, then retrieve the two Mariners caps.

"Thank you. I forgot my sunglasses."

As I climb out of the car, Sawyer arrives in the Q7 and parks beside the R8. I give him a wave and he rolls down the window. "There's a pilot's lounge if you guys want to wait in there," I say. "Follow us in."

"Mr. Grey, please." Sawyer's tone stops me. And I know he wants to check out the offices before Ana and I go inside. I step out of the way to let Reynolds and Sawyer through.

This is getting old.

I take a deep breath. I won't let his vigilance dampen my spirits—after all, it's what I pay him to do. Taking Ana's hand, I follow our security into the office, where Darius Jackson is waiting.

"Christian Grey," he calls out, and pumps my hand with a hearty shake. It's great to see him. He's a big guy, tall, but rounder than when I last saw him. "You're keeping well," he observes.

"As are you, Darius. This is my fiancée, Anastasia Steele."

"Miss Steele." Darius gives her a broad, brilliant smile.

"Ana," she corrects us both, but smiles and takes his hand.

"Darius was my flight instructor," I explain to Ana.

"You were my star pupil, Christian," he says. "He's a natural."

Ana eyes me, and I think it's pride I see etched on her beautiful face.

"Congratulations on your engagement," Darius says.

"Thanks. Is she ready?" I ask, because I find Ana's pride in me difficult to swallow, and of course I can't wait to see my new sailplane.

"Sure is. She's all lined up for you. My son Marlon is going to spot."

"Whoa! Marlon," I exclaim. Marlon, in his mid-teens now, has close-cropped hair and a smile and handshake that matches his father's. "You've gotten so tall!"

"Kids. They grow." Darius's dark eyes are brimming with paternal love.

"Thanks for helping out, Marlon."

"No worries, Mr. Grey."

Out on the tarmac, N88765CG is waiting. She is without doubt the most graceful sailplane on the planet: a Schleicher ASH 30, she's a gleaming white, with an impressive eighty-seven-foot wingspan and a large canopy. Even from this distance it's obvious she's a marvel of modern engineering.

She's yar.

Darius gives me a play-by-play account of her maiden flight, his face animated by the memory, as the three of us stroll around the glider, taking in her beauty and elegance. "She's got it all, Christian. It's like walking on air," he says, and the awe in his voice is worthy of such a sleek and cutting-edge aircraft.

"She looks mighty fine," I agree.

I open the canopy and Darius talks me through each of the controls. "And I've put more ballast in"—he glances at Ana—"as you'll need it."

"I understand."

"I'll fetch your chutes."

"Wow," Ana exclaims as she gazes into the cockpit. "It has more dials and technical doohickeys than the other glider."

I laugh. "She sure does."

"She?"

"She. But more biddable," I add with a smirk.

Ana cocks her head to one side and squints at me while trying unsuccessfully to hide her amusement. "Biddable, eh?"

I peer down my nose at her. "Easy to handle. Does as she's told…"

Darius returns and hands me the chutes before heading back into the office. I squat down on the ground with Ana's, and help her into it, tightening the straps around her thighs. "As you know, Miss Steele, I like my women biddable."

"To a point, Mr. Grey," she says as I stand. "Sometimes you like to be defied."

I grin. "Only by you." I cinch the shoulder buckles up tight.

"You love doing that, don't you?" she whispers.

"More than you could ever know."

"I think I have a clue. Maybe we should do it later."

I stop and tug her closer so that I can breathe in her scent. "Maybe we should," I murmur. "I'd like that very much."

Ana peeks up at me through her lashes. "So would I." Her words are as soft as the summer breeze and she leans up to kiss me. My breath catches in my throat as her lips touch mine and desire flashes though my body like wild fire. But before I can react, she steps back to give me some room to don my own chute.

Tease.

Eyes blazing, she watches me as I strap on my parachute. I take extra care to tighten my own straps.

"That was hot," she whispers.

Chuckling, and before I make a complete fool of myself and her, I do another circuit of my new plane. This time I'm examining her for anything that looks loose or out of place; all part of my preflight checks. Darius, who taught me to glide, would expect no less.

She's in fine, fine shape.

Like my fiancée.

Ana is still watching me as I run a hand over the tip of her wing.

"She's good," I say when I return to Ana's side. She slides on her cap and threads her ponytail through the gap at the back.

"You look mighty fine, too, Miss Steele," I whisper as I slip on my aviators.

Darius and Marlon join us, and together we push the ASH 30 onto the runway.

Once in position, I help Ana into the front seat of the cockpit and have the pleasure of strapping her in once more. "These should keep you in your place," I whisper with a wicked grin, then jump in behind her and close the canopy.

Darius attaches the tow cable and, with a thumbs-up sign, heads to the waiting single-engine Cessna Skyhawk.

"Ready?" I ask Ana.

"You bet!"

"Don't touch anything."

"Wait."

"What?"

"You've not flown this before."

I laugh. "Nope. I hadn't flown the Blaník L23 before, but we survived that."

She remains silent.

"Ana, they're all the same really. And you have your chute. Don't sweat it."

"Okay." She sounds a little uncertain.

"Honestly. It's going to be fine. Trust me."

I do a thorough check of the controls to orient myself: elevator, ailerons, the stick are all full and free. Straps good. Brakes good and now locked. Canopy locked. Flight instruments good—no cracked glass; shouldn't be, she's new.

Darius's voice crackles over the radio and I let him know that we're ready. A quick glance to the starboard side reveals Marlon standing by, holding the wing tip as Darius fires up the Skyhawk.

"Here we go! Let's chase those thermals and the midday sun," I shout above the shrill whine of the Cessna's engine.

Darius eases forward, and suddenly we're racing across the tarmac. Using the pedals at my feet and the stick in front of me, we sail into the air before the Cessna has left the runway.

She's so quick off the ground!

We climb higher and higher. The Ephrata office building is a child's toy as it disappears into the distance. Darius banks his aircraft and we sail toward the Beezley Hills, where we are sure to find some lift.

"That was so smooth," Ana says, an edge of quiet awe in her voice.

"Much smoother than the Blaník," I agree. ASH is awesome. She's so light and responsive.

We reach 3,000 feet and I radio Darius to let him know I'm releasing the cable. He's flown us into a thermal, and as he pulls away, I hold us in a wide circle, keeping the attitude constant as we rise and rise and rise. Washington falls away beneath us in all her checkered glory.

"Wow," Ana breathes.

"On the port side, you can see the Cascades."

"Port?"

"Left."

"Oh, yes."

There is still a sprinkling of snow kissing the top of the mountains, even in July.

"What's the water down there?"

"Banks Lake."

"Christian, this is beautiful."

We're at 7,000 feet, and I know we could go higher. We could go for miles and miles, and land in some field leagues and leagues away. The thought is appealing—Ana and I alone in some wilderness—but I don't think Sawyer or Reynolds or maybe even Ana would appreciate it.

"Look!" Ana calls. Below us, a substantial dust devil swirls into the air.

The lift!

I make a beeline for it and we travel higher. Fast.

"Wow!" Ana cries, with exhilaration. "No acrobatics today?" she asks.

"I'm just getting the feel of her first."

Fuck it. I love making Ana scream. I wing over and she squeals with delight as we hang above the earth, her hands stretched out, her ponytail tumbling down—the Washington plains beneath us.

"Holy shit!" she exclaims, and I pitch us upright again and Ana laughs and laughs. The sound fills my soul and makes me feel a thousand feet tall. ASH is a dream to fly; she has carried us to the top of the world, where the sun reigns above the clouds; it's tranquil, and we're surrounded by a breathtaking view. The love of my life sits before me, happy and free above the earth. And for the first time in a while a sense of peace unfurls within me. We're together, cradled in the sky, and my heart is full to overflowing.

I don't want this feeling to end.

This high. It's intoxicating.

Focus on where you want to be.

How you want to be.

I think you have for the last few weeks. You've seemed happier.

Flynn's words come back to me.

Ana is my happiness. She holds the key.

The thought is too big, too all-encompassing. I know it could swallow me whole if I let it. To distract myself, I ask Ana if she wants a try.

"No. This is your maiden voyage. You enjoy it, Christian. I'm thrilled to come along for the ride."

I smile. "I bought her for you."

"Really?"

"Yes. I have a single-seater glider made by the same German company but it's for solo flights. This sailplane is a dream. She's fantastic."

"She is." Ana looks ahead at the horizon. "We are floating on air," she says, her voice soft and dreamy.

"That we are, baby...that we are."

WE TOUCH DOWN AN hour later, a landing that's as smooth as the takeoff. I'm thrilled with the new plane. She's everything I knew she would be and more. I'd really like to take her up one day to see how far she'll take us. Perhaps later this summer.

Darius rushes toward us as I unlock the canopy.

"How was it?" he gushes when he reaches us.

"Amazing. She's one helluva plane." Adrenaline is still coursing through my body.

"Ana?" Darius turns his attention to her.

"I agree with Christian. She's amazing."

I undo my straps, clamber out, and stretch. Then lean in to unbuckle Ana's straps.

"This has been inspiring," I whisper, and give her a swift kiss as I make short work of the seat belt.

Her lips part in surprise but I turn to Darius who is still with us. "Let's put her in the hangar."

I'M BEHIND ANA AS we walk back to the cars with Sawyer and Reynolds. Her ponytail swings jauntily behind her. She's still wearing the cap, and beneath the short navy baseball jacket her ass is shielded in tight blue jeans. Her hips sway back and forth, a metronome as she walks, and the rhythm is hypnotizing. She looks so damned hot. I stride around to her side of the car and open the door. "You look great. I don't think I told you that this morning."

"I think you did," she answers with a sweet smile.

"Well, I'd like to tell you again."

"Back at you, Christian Grey." She runs her fingers over my white T-shirt, and the feeling echoes through my chest and the rest of my body.

I need to get her home.

But first. Lunch. A late lunch. I close her door and head to the driver's side.

We stop in Ephrata for pizza.

"Do you mind if we get takeout?" I ask as we enter the small restaurant.

"Eat in your car?"

"Yes."

"Your immaculate R8?"

"The very same."

"Sure." Ana looks puzzled.

"I'm anxious to get home."

"Why?"

I stare at her, quirking an eyebrow with only one thought in my mind. *Why do you think, Ana?*

"Oh," she says, and her teeth drill into her lower lip to suppress her smile, her cheeks flushing that shade of pink I love so much. "Okay. Yes. Takeout," she blurts, and I have to laugh.

"THIS IS THE BEST damn pizza," Ana says with her mouth full. I'm glad I doubled down on paper napkins.

"More?" I ask. And she holds the slice up for me to bite. As I open my mouth, she moves it away and takes another bite.

"Hey!"

She giggles. "My pizza!"

I pout. Because I'm driving and there's nothing else I can do.

"Here," she says, and this time lets me take a bite.

"You know I'll get you back."

"Uh-huh?" she·taunts. "Bring it, Grey."

"Oh, I will. I will…" And I start to contemplate various scenarios, which have an immediate impact on my body. I shift in my seat. "More pizza, please."

Ana continues to feed me. And tease me. Much to her and my delight.

We should do this more often.

"All done," Ana says, and pops the pizza box in her footwell.

I feel sated. I'm with my girl, in my favorite car, Radiohead on play, and we're speeding through the majestic landscape beside the Columbia River toward the Vantage bridge. I'm overwhelmed by a sense of belonging.

Before Ana, how did I spend my weekends?

Soaring, Sailing, Fucking…

I laugh. It doesn't sound like much has changed, but that's simply not true—everything has changed, and all because of the young woman sitting next to me. I didn't know I was lonely until I met her. I didn't know I needed her, and here she is beside me. I glance at Ana, who's sucking the tip of her index finger. The sight is stirring, and I recall her earlier remark about harnesses.

"You love doing that, don't you?"

"More than you could ever know."

"I think I have a clue. Maybe we should do it later."

"Maybe we should…"

The thought drives me wild. Putting my foot down, I push the R8 to ninety. I want to get us home.

MY ANTICIPATION IS at DEFCON 1 when we finally arrive at the garage at Escala. "Home again," Ana breathes when I switch off the ignition. Her voice is husky and quiet, drawing my attention. Her eyes meet mine and we stare at each other as the atmosphere within the R8 slowly simmers.

It's here. Between us. Our desire.

It's almost a separate entity, it's so powerful.

Drawing us together.

Consuming me…us.

"Thank you," she says.

"You're most welcome."

She's looking at me through her lashes, her eyes smoky and full of sensual promise. Compelled, I can't look away. I'm under her powerful spell. Beside us, Sawyer and Reynolds pull up, park, and disembark the Q7, locking it up behind them. They head to the service elevator, and I can't tell if they're waiting for us or not. I don't know. I don't care. Ana and I ignore them, our focus only on each other. The silence in the car is heady, ringing with unspoken thoughts.

"The new glider, that was mind-blowing."

"I like blowing your mind."

A slow, seductive smile tugs at her lips. "I like that, too."

"I have a plan."

"You do?"

I nod, holding my breath as myriad images of Ana harnessed in the playroom run through my head.

"Red Room?" she asks tentatively.

I nod.

Her pupils grow wide and dark, and her breasts rise as she inhales. "Bring it."

And I am out of the car.

She's out when I reach the passenger side. "Come." I take her hand and trek briskly to the elevator. Fortunately, it's waiting for us and we dart in. I squeeze her hand as we both stand against the back wall. She sidles closer to me and her intention is clear as she raises her face to mine.

"No. Wait." I release her hand and step to the side as the elevator climbs.

"Christian," she whispers, her look scorching.

I shake my head.

I'm gonna make you wait, baby.

She presses her lips together, her displeasure obvious, but there's a flash of steel in her eyes. My girl does not back down from a challenge.

The game is on.

The doors of the elevator open and I step back, giving Ana a courtly wave. "Ladies first."

She smirks, and with head held high, sashays out of the elevator into the foyer, where she stops.

Sawyer is waiting for us.

Well, this is inconvenient.

"Mr. Grey, is there anything else you require?" He's aware that Taylor has gone to visit his daughter, and I think he's trying to fill Taylor's shoes. He looks expectantly from me to Ana, whose attention is suddenly concentrated on the floor as she tries not to laugh.

Hiding my amusement, I respond. "I'm good, thank you," then, out of devilment, add, "Ana?"

"All good." She shoots me a what-the-fuck look and it takes all my self-control not to burst out laughing in front of Sawyer. She scuttles out of the foyer.

"You and Reynolds can stand down. We're not going out this evening. Anastasia is going out tomorrow. I'll text you in the morning to let you know when." Ana has a fitting for her wedding dress in the morning.

"Very good, sir." He turns and I follow him out into the corridor. A quick glance in the living room reveals Ana is not there. Sawyer heads into Taylor's office while I go in search of Miss Steele. I find her in the bedroom, where she's unlacing her boots.

She looks up. "Mr. Grey, you are truly evil."

"I try my best. Playroom. Ten minutes." I turn on my heel and leave her, mouth open, in my…our bedroom.

THE PLAYROOM IS SOFTLY illuminated, the light glowing off the red walls. It feels, once more, like my haven. It's been a few weeks since we've been in here. *Why is that? Where does the time go?* I chuckle—I sound like my dad. I strip off my jacket, and remove my shoes and socks, enjoying the warmth of the wooden floor on the soles of my feet. From the bottom of the toy chest, I remove a leather suspension harness; it's going to be fun strapping Ana into this. I can barely contain myself. She won't be fully suspended, so I think she'll be within her limits. I lay it out on the bed, then retrieve a few other items. Putting a couple of them in the back pocket of my jeans, I leave the rest on the chest, then head next door to the en suite in the submissive's room.

I pause when I come out of the bathroom. The room is unchanged since Susannah left. Ana never really occupied this space; it has an empty, abandoned feel. The decor is still neutral. White. Cold. Susannah never wanted to decorate.

Grey, stop.

I don't want to go down that rabbit hole right now. Not when my girl should be waiting for me.

When I enter the room, Ana is barefoot by the bed, examining the harness. The sight of her halts me in my tracks. She's changed into some lacy lingerie. She's all long legs, arms, and black lace, and fine see-through panties.

Just for me.

I can see everything.

Everything.

Shrouded in lace.

My mouth dries as she steps toward me, her hair free, falling and curling under her breasts. "Mr. Grey. You're overdressed."

I could play this one of two ways. We are still finding ourselves in here. Today, the Dominant wins. "You want to play?"

"Yes."

"Yes what?"

Ana's lips part in surprise. "Sir."

"In that case, turn around."

She blinks, astonished at my tone, I think, and a furrow forms on her brow.

"Don't frown."

"Suspension?"

"Not fully, no. Your toes will be on the floor. It'll be intense."

Come on, Ana. Don't lose your nerve.

"We don't have to do this," I whisper.

Her mouth twists into that challenging smirk I know so well, and I think she's considering her options. I cock my head to the side as her eyes stray to the harness on the bed. They linger on it—she's intrigued, I can tell. I tip her chin up and brush my lips against hers. "Do you want to wear this harness or not?"

"What will you do to me?" Her words are breathy and barely audible. She's turned on. Just at the sight of it.

"Whatever I want."

She gasps and turns around immediately.

Yes!

From the top of the chest of drawers, I grab a hair tie and gather her hair in my hands and begin braiding it.

It would never do to get her luscious locks caught in any of the straps.

I make quick work of her braid and, once it's fastened, give it a tug. She steps back into my arms. "You look mighty fine, Miss Steele," I murmur into her ear. "Love the lingerie. Remember, you don't have to do anything you don't want to do. Just tell me to stop. Now, go and assume the position by the door." She gives me a most unsubmissive look, which in another lifetime would have earned her a good spanking, but she moves to the door and kneels, resting her palms on her thighs and parting her legs.

That's my girl.

She looks gorgeous. I could come just looking at her.

Steady, Grey. Get a grip.

Ignoring my arousal, I go back to the chest, pull out my iPod, and place it in the dock. I switch on the Bose system, choose a track, and press repeat.

"Sinnerman." Nina Simone. *Perfect.*

Ana is watching me.

"Eyes down," I warn, and she dutifully casts them to the floor.

I close my eyes. Every time she does as she's told it's music to my soul. I can't get her to obey outside this room, but I'm going to take full advantage in here. I amble back to her and stand directly in front of her. "Legs. Wider."

She shuffles and moves her thighs. I groan in approval, strip off my T-shirt, and toss it on the floor. Slowly I unbuckle my belt and pull it through the belt loops. Ana's fingers flex on her thighs.

Is she wondering what I'm going to do with the belt?

Those days are over, Ana.

But, for maximum effect, I drop it and it clatters to the floor. She flinches at the sound.

Shit.

Reaching down, I caress her hair. "Hey, don't sweat it, Ana."

She gazes up at me, every bit a Dom's wet dream, and I know my cock is bursting in anticipation. Taking my sweet time, I unbutton my fly and tug down the zipper while I tighten my hold on her hair. My intention is clear and she regards me with a look that could set me alight from head to foot, and I think that's a good thing, because she opens her mouth, ready for me.

"No, not yet," I whisper, and, still clutching her hair, I ease my hardened cock from my jeans and run my hand up and down the length. Her eyes do not leave mine. With my thumb, I rub the bead of dew that's emerged, into the head, and run my hand along its length once again. I want nothing more than to take her mouth. But I want to make this moment last. "Kiss me," I murmur.

Ana's breasts are rising and falling faster. Her nipples pebbling under my gaze. She's excited. She puckers her lips and presses them against my dick.

"Open up for me."

She parts her lips and I ease myself into her warm, wet, willing mouth.

Fuck.

I ease back, then push my way in once more. This time she's sheathed her teeth, so the effect is immediate as she sucks me in.

Oh, yes.

Groaning my approval, I grip her hair and move. Back. Forth. Fucking her mouth, and like the goddess she is...she takes me.

All of me.

Over and over. More and more. Deeper and deeper.

On and on. I lose myself in her wondrous mouth.

Fuck. I'm going to come. But I don't care. I release her head and put my hand on the wall to keep me upright and I let go.

I cry out as my orgasm rolls through me in a rush and consumes me while Ana moves, gripping my thighs, taking all I have to give.

"*I need you.*" Nina rasps over the sound system, as I pull out of Ana's mouth and lean against the wall to recover my equilibrium.

Ana peers up at me with a look of triumph. She wipes her mouth with the back of her hand and then licks her lips as I adjust myself and zip up my fly.

"A," I whisper, and she smiles. I give her my hand. "Up." I pull her into my arms and kiss her; pushing her against the wall and spilling all my gratitude into our kiss. She tastes of me and sweet Ana; it's a provocative, potent mix.

When I pull back she's winded, and her lips are a little swollen.

"That's better."

"Hmm…" she responds, the sound a deep, sexy noise in her throat.

I grin. "Now we're going to have some real fun." I lead her to the bed, where the harness is laid out. Now that I've come, I'm calmer, and so ready for part two. I look down at Ana, who is gazing at me expectantly. "As much as I love what you're wearing, we need to get you naked."

She hooks her finger into the waistband of my jeans. "And what about you?"

"All in good time, Miss Steele."

She pushes her lower lip out in a moue and I gently take it between my teeth. "No pouting," I whisper, and start unhooking the basque she's wearing, freeing her beautiful breasts. Slowly, I peel her out of it. Once it's off, I place it beside the harness.

"And now these." Kneeling, I slide her panties gently down her legs, ensuring that my fingertips skate across her skin. When I reach her ankles I stop, and give her time to step out of them. I place them on top of her basque. "Hello there," I address her vulva, and plant a kiss just above her clitoris.

She smirks, and I remember a time that a kiss on this part of her anatomy would make her fidget and blush.

Oh, Ana. We've come a long way.

Standing, I grab the harness. "This is like the parachute earlier today."

"Where you got the idea?"

"Yes. Well, you gave me the idea. So, step in, here." I hold the thigh straps open and Ana grabs on to my biceps and steps into one side and then the other. Once in, I hook the shoulder bindings over her shoulders and proceed to buckle all the straps. This includes the one across her chest, at her back, at her waist, and each of those around her upper arms.

I step back to admire my handiwork and my future wife.

Man, she looks hot.

Oh, Sinnerman, Nina sings.

"Feel okay?" I ask

She nods quickly, her eyes dark and full of carnal curiosity.

Oh, Ana. It gets better.

From the top of the drawers I grab the leather cuffs. I fasten them to each of her wrists and then hook their carabiners to the brass loops embedded in each of the upper arm cuffs. Ana's hands are now tethered, level with her shoulders, and effectively immobile.

"Okay?" I ask.

"Yes," she breathes.

Gently, I tug at one of the hooks embedded in the chest strap and lead Ana to the edge of the restraining system in the ceiling of the playroom. From above, I unhook the trapeze and tug it into position above Ana. From each end of the trapeze there are two short cords with carabiners at the end. I clip these to the hooks in her shoulder straps. She watches me intently as I complete the task.

She's now hooked in place. Her feet flat on the floor. For now.

"So, the exciting feature of this device is that I can do this." I step to the side and from the large brass cleat that's attached to the wall, I unwind the cords that are secured to the trapeze via the restraining system. With both hands I tug, and Ana's suddenly hoisted onto the balls of her feet. Ana gasps and totters from side to side and front and back, attempting to find her balance. I rewrap the cords around the cleat, leaving Ana dancing on the tips of her toes.

She's helpless. And completely at my mercy.

It's a thrilling thought and sight.

"What are you going to do?" she asks.

"Like I said, exactly what I want. I'm a man of my word."

"You won't leave me like this?" She looks panicked.

I grasp her chin. "No. Never. Rule number one: never leave someone who's restrained alone. Ever." I kiss her quickly. "You okay?"

She's breathing hard, excited, and I think she's daunted, but she nods. I kiss her again, this time with infinite tenderness, my lips brushing hers. "Right. You've seen enough." From my back pocket, I retrieve a blindfold and slip it over her head and cover her eyes.

"You look so fucking hot, Ana." Taking a few steps back to the drawers, I pull out the item I require and slip it into my back pocket. I circle Ana, admiring my handiwork, until I'm facing her once more. I run my thumb over her lips, then down her chin, down her sternum.

Power, Nina bellows out through the playroom.

"Are you going to obey me in here?" I whisper.

"Do you want me to?" she asks, her voice all breathy and needy.

I skim my hands over her breasts and her nipples lengthen beneath my thumbs. I tug them both. Hard.

"Ah!" she cries. "Yes. Yes," she says quickly.

"Good girl." I continue kneading her nipples between my thumbs and forefingers. She moans, tossing her head back, and teeters on her toes.

"Oh, baby, feel it. Do you want to come this way?"

"Yes. No. I don't know."

"I think not. I have another plan for you."

Her groan fills the room. I place my hands on her waist and dip my head and suck a nipple into my mouth, taunting it with my tongue and my lips. Ana cries out, and I move to its twin and lavish the same attention on it, until Ana is pulling against her restraints.

When I don't think she can take much more, I kneel at her feet and trail kisses across her belly, my tongue circling her navel and then continuing a journey south. Grabbing her thighs, I hoist her legs over my shoulders and slide her vulva toward my mouth. She tips back in the harness and lets out a guttural cry as my lips and tongue find her clitoris, swollen and ready for my attention. I go to town, dedicating myself to the small powerhouse at the apex of her thighs.

Teasing. Testing. Torturing her with my mouth.

"Christian," she gasps, and I know she's close.

I stop and set her back on her toes. I want her to come with her toes bouncing on the floor. It'll be intense. Standing, I steady her, and from my back pocket, I grab the ridged glass dildo and run it over her belly. "Feel this?"

"Yes. Yes. Cold," she breathes.

"Cold. Good. I'm going to put it inside you. And after you've come, I'm going to put me inside you."

She makes a strangled groan.

"Legs apart," I order.

Ana ignores me. "Ana!"

Tentatively she moves her feet and I run the end of the dildo up her thigh and oh-so-slowly slip it inside her.

"Argh!" she groans. "Cold!" Gently to begin with, I pump my hand, knowing that the glass wand is shaped to hit that potent, sweet, sweet spot inside her. This is not going to take long. With my other hand, I circle her waist, holding her close and kissing her throat, inhaling her rousing scent.

Ana, come apart in my arms.

She's so close. So close. My hand continues to move. Harder. Faster. Taking her higher. Her legs are stiffening and suddenly she goes rigid and screams as her climax rips though her. She bucks against her bindings as I thrust the dildo inside her, making her ride out her orgasm. When her head tips back, her mouth slack, I ease it out of her and toss it onto the bed. I unclip first one and then the other carabiner from her shoulder straps, then carry her to the bed.

I lay her out. Still harnessed. Her hands still tied. I remove the blindfold. Her eyes are closed. I unzip my jeans and swiftly remove them and my boxer briefs. Standing over her, I grab her thighs, lift them to either side of my hips, and slam into her. Then still.

She cries out and opens her eyes.

She's wet. Really wet.

And mine.

Our eyes stay on each other. Hers dazed and full of passion. And want. And need.

"Please," she whispers, and I flex my ass and start to move. Grinding into her. My fingers grip her thighs and she crosses her legs behind me. Holding me. I rock into her. Back and forth. Back and forth. And as I get closer, I release her legs, which she tightens around me, and I lean over her, my hands on either side of her shoulders, my fingers crushing the red satin sheets. "Come on, baby. Again," I shout, and my voice is almost unrecognizable to me.

Ana lets go, taking me with her. I come, long and hard, with a cry and it's her name.

Ana.

I collapse beside her. Utterly. Spent.

As my reason returns, I lean up over her and unclip the wrist restraints and then pull her into my arms. "How was that?" I murmur.

I think she says "mind-blowing" before she closes her eyes and nestles into my arms. I grin and hold her close.

Nina is still singing her heart out. I find the remote on the bed and switch her off, letting silence fall over Ana and me and the playroom. "Well done, Ana Steele. I'm in awe of you," I whisper, but she's fast asleep…in the harness. I smile and kiss the top of head.

Ana, I love you and I love your inner freak.

MONDAY, JULY 18, 2011

It's early and Bastille is his usual tyrannical self as we warm up. "Good cross. Again," he shouts, his words a staccato.

I jab and land a punch on his palm pad.

"Again. Jab. Cross."

I comply.

"Change hands. Leg back."

My right leg is back and I'm in fight stance.

"Go."

I throw my weight behind my right glove and the sound of leather slapping on leather echoes around the basement gym at Grey House.

"Good. Again. Keep going. We gotta keep you in shape, Grey. You gotta look good walking down the aisle." He cackles.

Ignoring his tone, I rain blows on his palm pads.

"Cool. Good. Enough."

I stop and catch my breath. I'm wired. Ready. Bouncing on my toes. Adrenaline flowing through my veins. I'm ready to strike. I'm on top of the fucking world.

"I think that's enough warm-up. Let's blow the corporate bullshit out of your brain."

"You're on, dude. You are going down."

He flashes me a broad, bright grin as he slides his gloves over taped hands. "That's fighting talk, Grey. You know, your girl is making fine progress. She'll keep your ass in line. She'll make one worthy opponent."

She's a worthy opponent now.

And she keeps my ass in line.

And I keep hers—

Don't think about that now!

He raises his fists. "Ready, old man?"

What? I'm ten years his junior.
"Old. I'll give you old, Bastille." I lunge at him.

FEELING REFRESHED AND READY for the day, I take my seat at my desk and fire up the iMac. Ana is waiting at the top of my inbox.

From: Anastasia Steele
Subject: Soaring, In and Out of the Red Room.
Date: July 18 2011 09:32
To: Christian Grey

My dearest Mr. Grey
It's hard to know which I prefer: sailing, soaring or the Red Room of
~~Pain~~ Pleasure. Thank you for yet another unforgettable weekend.
I love flying high in every way with you.
I am, as ever, in awe of your talents…all of them. ;)
Your soon-to-be wife xxxx

My grin in response to Ana's e-mail is out of control. But I don't care. I look up when Andrea places a cup of coffee on my desk, and she looks a little disconcerted.

"Thanks, Andrea."

"Shall I ask Ros to come up?" Andrea asks, recovering her composure.

"Please do." I clear my throat, wondering what's bothering my PA. I type a quick response to Ana.

From: Christian Grey
Subject: Physical Pursuits
Date: July 18 2011 09:58
To: Anastasia Steele

My darling Anastasia
I love soaring with you.
I love playing with you.
I love doing you.
I love you.
Always.

Christian Grey
CEO, Grey Enterprises Holdings, Inc.

PS: Which talent in particular? Inquiring minds need to know.

Ros knocks and enters my office. "Good morning, Christian," she chimes as I press send. She's unusually cheerful. Standing, I wave her to the table.

"Good morning."

"Why the frown?" she asks as she sits down.

"I don't think I've ever seen you so upbeat."

Her smile could rival the Great Sphinx at Giza. "God is good."

I raise my eyebrows. This is very un-Ros-like behavior. Taking a seat opposite her, I wait patiently for an explanation. She shuffles her papers and hands me the agenda for our meeting. It's obvious she's not going to elucidate, and I don't wish to pry. I glance down at the first item. "The Taiwan shipyard?"

"They're offering a full disclosure of their P&L, their assets and liabilities. They want to partner with a U.S. company. They'd like to pitch."

"They sound eager."

"They do," Ros confirms.

"I think we should take them up on the offer and conduct our due diligence. Then we can take it from there. Agreed?"

"I think so. We have nothing to lose at this stage."

"Okay. Let's do it."

"I'll put the paperwork in place." Ros scribbles down a note and moves to the next item on the agenda.

THERE'S AN E-MAIL FROM Ana waiting for me when I've concluded my meeting with Ros.

From: Anastasia Steele
Subject: Your Physical Pursuits
Date: July 18 2011 10:01
To: Christian Grey

Why, Mr. Grey...so rude and so modest! I think you can guess—your sexpertise knows no bounds.
I'm very much looking forward to seeing the house again this evening.
I am in a meeting that concludes at 5 p.m. I'll see you then?
Ax

I pick up my phone and dial her direct line.

"Ana Steele," she answers in her crisp, executive voice.

"Ana Steele, Christian Grey."

"Ah, my talented fiancé. How are you?"

"Very well, thank you. Taylor and I will be there at five."

"Great. Now, I need to get back to daydreaming…I mean work. I don't want my boss's boss's boss to catch me shirking my responsibilities."

"What do you think he'd do if he did?"

She gasps and the sound sends a thrill through my body. "Something unspeakable," she whispers.

"That could be arranged."

"Your twitchy palm?"

"As you know, it's perpetually twitchy. And not been used to its full potential of late."

"Stop. You're making me moist."

What!

"Moist." I clear my throat. "Miss Steele. That word should only be reserved for cakes. I like you wet."

"I like that you like me wet." Her voice is almost inaudible.

I shift in my chair. "Five p.m.," I whisper.

"How can you make three syllables sound so alluring?"

"It's a curse."

"It's a gift." Her voice is husky.

Damn, but she has an answer for everything. "See you at five, Ana. Laters, baby." I'm on top of the world. She giggles in that delightful way she does, and it takes all my willpower to hang up.

I bound out of my chair feeling effervescent. Flirting with Ana is always a joy. And so is discussing the latest prototype of the GEH solar tablet with Fred and Barney. I head out of my office, wondering if I should have studied engineering at school.

AS I'M EATING MY lunch, my phone flashes with Elliot's goofy face.

"Bro?"

"Hey, dude, we still on for later today?"

"Yes. Ana and I are looking forward to it."

"Cool." He pauses.

"What is it?" I ask. "Gia? She'll be there, too."

He scoffs. "Like that would ever be a problem. I'm talking bachelor party, hotshot. Saturday."

"Elliot—"

"Don't be an uptight asshole," he interrupts. "It's happening. Even if I have to kidnap you."

"Fuck—"

"No ifs or buts, bro. I've got the construction crew on standby with duct tape and a cargo van. Suck it up."

My sigh is as exaggerated as I can make it.

Elliot laughs. "What's the worst that can happen?"

"I don't know, Elliot. It depends what you have planned."

"It will take your mind off your woes."

Woes? "What fucking woes?"

"I dunno. Someone trying to kill you?"

Oh, yes. That. "You're so crass. Hard to believe we've been raised by the same people."

He laughs. "Laters, dude." And he hangs up.

Asshole.

But he has a point. Welch has made no further progress in uncovering *Charlie Tango*'s saboteur. I've fired the entire team responsible for her care and maintenance, and I'm still waiting for the report from the NTSB. I'm beginning to wonder if the original FAA assessment was hasty in suspecting malicious interference, or if the damage was a random act of vandalism. Both these outcomes are possible, and give me a modicum of hope, but I don't want to drop my guard yet. Ana's safety is all that I care about. I've had security ramped up around the GEH Gulfstream and she's been on two test flights since *Charlie Tango*'s demise. She'll be taking us to Europe for our honeymoon.

I'm still waiting to hear from Burgess about the yacht, but I have my fingers crossed that I'll get the one I want. I imagine Ana stretched out on deck in a bikini.

Wait. Does she own a bikini?

I don't remember including swimwear in the clothes the personal shopper at Neiman Marcus sourced for Ana. That was a lifetime ago. As my wife, Ana is going to need more clothes—for her vacation, functions, her work... I scroll through my contacts, and when Caroline Acton's name appears, I press call.

From: Christian Grey
Subject: Dedicated Follower of Fashion
Date: July 18 2011 15:22
To: Anastasia Steele

My darling Anastasia
I have made an appointment for us to meet Caroline Acton at 10:30 on Saturday morning to furnish you with a new wardrobe for our honeymoon.
No arguments.
Please.

Christian Grey
CEO, Grey Enterprises Holdings, Inc.

From: Anastasia Steele
Subject: Threads?
Date: July 18 2011 15:27
To: Christian Grey

Me? Argue?
Do I need a new wardrobe?
I don't think so. I have plenty of clothes.
See you at 5 p.m.
Ax

I frown. This is not going to be easy.

From: Christian Grey
Subject: New Threads
Date: July 18 2011 15:29
To: Anastasia Steele

Yes. You do.

Christian Grey
CEO, Grey Enterprises Holdings, Inc.

From: Anastasia Steele
Subject: Men with more money than sense...
Date: July 18 2011 15:32
To: Christian Grey

Is brevity the soul of wit?
Ana

From: Christian Grey
Subject: That's Me.
Date: July 18 2011 15:33
To: Anastasia Steele

Yes. ;)

Christian Grey
CEO, Grey Enterprises Holdings, Inc.

From: Anastasia Steele
Subject: Grrr...
Date: July 18 2011 15:34
To: Christian Grey

I am late for my meeting.
Stop being so funny.
Laters. Baby.
Axx

My phone buzzes. "Yes, Sam."

"Christian, *Star* magazine has gotten hold of some shots of Anastasia and want to run a story on her; a rags-to-riches kinda thing."

"What the fuck?"

"I know."

"What kind of shots?"

"Nothing salacious."

Thank fuck.

Wait. There shouldn't be any salacious shots of Ana. Should there?

"Tell them to fuck off. Rope Ros in. Threaten them with legal action."

Sam takes a deep breath. "They'll be published while you're away on your honeymoon. The photos are okay. If you want my advice, let them run and ignore them. It will be more of a story if you don't."

I can almost hear his *I told you so* vibe over the phone. He wanted us to do a photoshoot; maybe I should have conceded.

Hell.

"Send me what you have," I snap.

Fucking paparazzi!

A moment later his e-mail pops up in my inbox, and I read the attachment quickly. Grudgingly, I admit he might be right. It's not that bad, and the photographs of Ana are okay, if grainy. But they also have her yearbook photo. She looks cute. And young. I call him. "Let me think about this."

AT THE NEW HOUSE, we follow Gia Matteo through each room. "I love the staircase," she enthuses. "I'm not surprised you want to retain it." She beams at me as if it were my idea.

Sweetheart. I wanted to knock this house down and build something new. It's Ana who has fallen in love with the old place.

"I love the period features," Ana asserts.

Gia flashes her a smile. "Of course," she says. We follow her into the main living area. Elliot hangs back; he's uncharacteristically quiet, and I wonder if it's because he has a sexual history with Ms. Matteo—I don't know. She's vocal, with some out-of-the-box ideas, and I remember meeting her briefly when she did the renovation to my house in Aspen. She did a fantastic job on that.

"I love this room," Gia says when we enter the main living room. "It has an airy quality that I think we should embrace." She reaches over and pats my arm.

Damn.

I've spent my life subtly maneuvering myself out of anyone's reach. It's a self-defense mechanism that I've cultivated over the years to keep people out of my space and make them back the hell off. A step here, a slide to the side there, angling my shoulders left or right to avoid physical contact, I have it down to a fine art. I *hate* to be touched. No. I fear it. Except by Ana, of course. Kickboxing has helped. I can tolerate the rough and tumble of a match and a firm handshake…or the bite of a cane or lash.

Don't think about that.

But that's it.

In addition, I've developed a fuck-off-don't-touch-me glare that's proven effective.

However, not on Gia Matteo.

She's fucking touchy-feely.

It's irritating.

And not only with me. She reaches out to Elliot as he enters the main living room and gives him what can only be described as a carnal smile as she takes his arm. Elliot gapes at her cleavage, which is on show for all of us. Ana notices, and I see a frown cross her face. I wonder if what my brother says about Ms. Matteo is true. She's a woman who doesn't take no for an answer, one of those overtly sexual, tactile women who disregards all boundaries.

A bit like Elena.

The unpleasant thought pops into my head and makes me a pause. I don't remember Gia being that way when we met a couple of years ago.

Stop overthinking this, Grey.

But as we walk through the house I find myself putting as much distance as I can between her and me.

"A glass wall would be amazing at this end of the room," Gia says. "It will really open out this whole space."

Ana smiles, but keeps her counsel and takes my hand.

TAYLOR WEAVES THROUGH THE evening traffic back to Escala.

"What did you think?" I ask Ana.

"Of Gia?"

I nod.

"The Gia show," she says.

"Yeah. She has a lot of personality. But she had some great ideas, and we've seen her portfolio. It's impressive."

Ana bursts out laughing. "Yes. Her impressive portfolio was on full display."

I laugh. "I don't know what you mean."

Ana arches a brow. And I laugh again and take her hand. "Thank you for being funny," I whisper, and kiss her knuckles. "What do think? Should we find someone else?"

"She did have some good ideas." Ana sounds almost begrudging, but she smiles. "Let's see what she comes back with."

"Agreed. Shall we go out to eat? We've been cooped up enough at Escala."

"Is it safe?"

"I think so." I turn and catch Taylor's eye in the rearview mirror. "Columbia Tower, please, Taylor."

"Yes, sir."

"Mile High Club?" I suggest to Ana.

"Suits me."

I clasp her hand.

"I did like her idea for opening up the view from the back of the house," Ana says.

"Yes. Me, too, but we're in no rush."

She smiles once more. "I love your ivory tower."

"I love having you there."

Her eyes meet mine and her expression is suddenly serious. "I'm glad, because you're about to commit to having me there for a lifetime."

Whoa. I swallow.

This is huge.

A whole lifetime with Anastasia…will it be enough?

"Good point, well made, Miss Steele."

And from nowhere I'm overwhelmed with a depth of feeling that has become all too familiar, but it's still new and shiny and terrifying. I'm happier than I've ever been before—but I'm afraid, too.

It could all end.

Everything could come crashing down.

Life is ephemeral.

I know this. I've lived it.

From nowhere the image of a pale, still, young woman comes to mind. She's lying on a grubby rug in a grubbier room as a small child tries in vain to shake her awake.

Shit.

The crack whore.

No. Don't think about her!

Reaching over, I take Ana's face between my hands, memorizing every detail: the shape of her nose, her full lower lip, her stunning eyes. I want her with me for a lifetime. I close my eyes and kiss her, pouring all my fear into her.

Don't ever leave me.

Don't die.

What do you think Elliot has planned?" Ana is sprawled over me, her index finger making small circles through my chest hair. It's a weird sensation, one that I'm not entirely comfortable with.

Enough.

I grab her hand, threading my fingers through hers, and plant a kiss on the tip of the offending digit.

"Too much?" she whispers.

I slide her finger into my mouth, clamping my teeth gently around her knuckle and teasing the tip with my tongue.

"Ah!" she coos, as a sensuous spark ignites in her eyes, and she tips her pelvis against my thigh.

Baby.

She tugs her hand and I relax my jaw but close my lips as she eases her finger out of my mouth.

She tastes mighty fine.

Tenderly she kisses the spot on my chest that her finger traced, while I stroke her hair and revel in this quiet moment. It's early, and the only items on today's agenda are my "bachelor party," Ana's bachelorette party, and a shopping excursion with Caroline Acton.

Ana raises her head. "Do you think he'll take you to a…a…strip joint?"

A chuckle rumbles in my chest. "Strip joint?"

Ana giggles. "I don't know what they're called."

I sigh and close my eyes, envisioning the hell that Elliot probably has planned. "Knowing Elliot, it's a distinct possibility."

"I'm not sure how I feel about that," Ana replies, tartly.

I grin and, rolling over, press her into the mattress. "Why, Miss Steele, do you disapprove?" I run my nose down hers and she squirms beneath me.

"Deeply."

"Jealous?"

She makes a face.

"I'd rather be here with you," I reassure her.

"You're not really a party animal, are you?" she says.

"No. More the loner."

"I've figured this out." Her teeth graze my chin.

"Could say the same about you," I murmur.

"I'm the wallflower, nose-in-a-book type."

I skim my lips from her ear to her throat. "You're too beautiful to be a wallflower."

She groans and runs her fingernails over my shoulder blades as her body rises to welcome mine. She's still slick and wet from earlier, and I ease into her and we move together, slower and sweeter this time. Her nails dig into my back as she wraps her legs around mine and she raises her hips to meet me. Over and over. Slow and sweet. She's building.

I stop.

"Christian, don't stop. Please," she begs.

I love it when you beg, baby.

I move slowly and grip her hair at her nape with both hands, so she cannot turn her head. I gaze down at her, marveling at the intricate color of her irises. I move again. Slowly. In. Out. And then stop once more.

"Christian, please," she breathes.

"It will only ever be you, Ana. Always."

Don't be jealous.

"I love you." I start once more. She closes her eyes and tips her head back and comes around me, triggering my own orgasm. With a cry, I fall to her side to catch my breath. When I resurface, I turn over and pull her to me, kissing her hair.

I love waking up to Ana.

Closing my eyes, I imagine every Saturday could be like this. Anastasia Steele has given me a meaningful future, something I've not considered with any seriousness before. And next Saturday, I get the piece of paper that proves it.

She'll be mine.

Until death do us part.

Ana lying on the cold, hard floor flashes before my eyes.

No!

I rub my face.

Stop. Grey. Stop.

I kiss her hair, breathing in her life-affirming fragrance, and I'm calmer.

It must be about 9 a.m. I grab my phone from my nightstand to check the time. There's a text from Elliot.

> **ELLIOT**
> Good morning, Asshole. I'm sitting in
> your vast living room waiting for you to
> get your lazy ass out here. Stop what
> you're doing. Now. You dirty dog.

What the hell?

"What is it?" Ana asks, looking tousled and fuckable.

"Elliot's here."

"Outside?" Ana sounds bemused.

I ease her out of my embrace. "No. He's here."

She frowns.

"Yeah, I don't understand it, either." I get up, stalk into my closet, and drag on a pair of jeans.

Elliot is sprawled on my couch, staring at his phone. "Good morning, hotshot, about time!" he hollers. "Glad you dressed for the occasion." He eyes my naked chest and feet with amused disdain.

"What in God's name are you doing here, dude? It's nine a.m."

"Yep. Surprise! Get your ass in gear. I got the day planned."

What? "I'm supposed to take Ana shopping."

He scoffs, disgusted. "She's a grown woman. She can do her own damn shopping."

"But—"

"Dude. I'm saving you. Shopping with women is hell. Go. Put some clothes on, you pervert. And for fuck's sake have a shower. I can smell the sex from here."

"Fuck off," I reply without heat.

He really is a douche sometimes.

"You'll need hiking boots and sneakers," he calls after me.

Both?

"HOW DID YOU GET in?" I ask as we head down to the garage in the elevator.

"Taylor."

"Ah. That's why we have no security following us."

"Yep. I figured you were leaving with me, so you'd be fine. Your man Taylor was reluctant, but I persuaded him."

I nod, pleased. Being continually dogged by our close protection team has been wearing. Ana and I have been holed up at Escala for what feels like forever. Sawyer and Reynolds will keep an eye on her today, though. That's non-negotiable.

"He's been very helpful," Elliot says.

"Who?"

"Taylor." And with that he hides his sly smile and stops talking.

What does he have planned?

ELLIOT IS IN AN ebullient mood. It's catching. We're cruising in his pickup north along I-5. "Where exactly *are* we going?" I ask, over the godawful yacht-rock blasting through the cab.

"Surprise," he shouts. "Relax. It's going to be fine."

It's too late to tell him I'm not a fan of surprises, so I sit back and enjoy the cityscape as we head out of Seattle. We haven't spent any time together since we went mountain biking near Portland. That was a most interesting night...the first night I slept with Ana. The first night I slept with anyone! And Elliot fucked Ana's best friend—but then Elliot has fucked many of the women with whom he's come into contact. It's not surprising, really; he's good company. Easygoing. Good-looking, I suppose. Women flock to him, I'll give him that. He puts them at ease.

He's always been able to charm our mother. He knows how to treat Grace. I used to envy the easy way he'd spin her around the kitchen floor or hug her or give her a passing peck on her cheek.

He makes it look easy.

As yet, he shows no signs of settling down.

And if he does, I hope to God it's not with Kavanagh.

I send a quick text to Ana.

> No idea what Elliot has in mind.
> This is not how I planned to
> spend the day. Enjoy your
> shopping experience with
> Caroline Acton. Missing you. x

ANA
Missing you, too. Love you. Ax

Elliot leaves I-5 for the 532.

"Camano Island?" I ask.

He winks at me, which is annoying. I check my watch, then my phone.

"Dude! What gives? She'll be fine without you, for fuck's sake. Show some dignity. I packed some snacks. I know how disagreeable you get without food."

"Snacks? Where?"

He opens the car caddy, revealing subs, chips, and Coke. Ah, all of life's pleasures…if you're Elliot.

"Nutritious," I mutter dryly.

"It's all good stuff, bro. Quit complaining. This is your bachelor party."

I laugh, because chips and Coke is not my idea of a good time. Subs, on the other hand…I smirk at my little private joke and reach for a can of Coke.

ABOUT FIVE MILES INTO Camano Island, Elliot turns right. We drive through a farm gate into an open pasture, along a track, and up to a barn, where he pulls into a parking lot.

"We're here."

"Where is here?"

"Friend's place. It's not open to the public yet. But it will be soon. We're guinea pigs."

"What?"

"Well, I figured marriage is pretty much a high-wire activity. I thought you should get some practice."

"What are you talking about?"

"We're going zip-lining." He grins and clambers out of the car.

This! This is my bachelor party? It is not what I was expecting. But hey, zip-lining could be fun.

Elliot greets our hosts, and we're directed into the barn, where a series of hooks hold the safety equipment: hard hats, harnesses, straps, and carabiners. It all looks reassuringly familiar.

"Hey, hotshot, these harnesses are damned freaky. We could get up to some kinky shit in these," Elliot blurts as he slips his on. And for once I'm at a complete loss as to what to say.

Does he know?

Are the tips of my ears red?

Shit! Has Ana talked to Kate?

Elliot looks his usual guileless self, so I assume not, because if he knew, he'd have razzed the shit of me. "You're an idiot. This is like a chute," I reply. Distraction is the best policy. "Got a new sailplane last week. You should come out to Ephrata for a day and we can take her up."

"For two?"

"Yep."

"That would be super cool."

WE'RE ON THE FIRST platform surrounded by pine trees. "To infinity and beyond!" Elliot shouts and leaps off, with all the fearlessness that I associate with his devil-may-fucking-care attitude. He whoops like a gorilla in heat as he whizzes down the line, his joy contagious. He lands surprisingly gracefully on the next platform, about one hundred feet away.

Danielle, one of our guides, radios ahead to say I'm set and clips my lifeline to the zip-line trolley. "Ready, Christian?" she asks with an overeager smile.

"As I'll ever be."

"Off you go."

Taking a deep breath, I grab the carabiner beneath the trolley with one hand, my lifeline with the other, and I jump. I fly through the fresh, lush forest, the pulley whistling above me and the summer breeze on my face. I'm on a roller coaster without a car, sailing between the Douglas firs beneath a brilliant blue sky, and it's thrilling and liberating in equal measure. I land safely on the platform beside Elliot and the other guide.

"Whaddya think?" Elliot claps me on the back.

I grin. "This is pretty fucking excellent."

Danielle is last to land on the platform. "That was our first. They get higher and faster."

"Bring it!" I exclaim.

TWO HOURS LATER, STILL buzzing from our high-wire activity, we're back on the road, Elliot behind the wheel. "Bro, as experiences go, that was right up there," I acknowledge.

"Better than sex?" Elliot cackles. "You've only just discovered it— so probably not."

"I'm a little more discerning in my tastes than you are, dude."

"I just like to spread the love around. The Big E wants what the Big E wants."

I shake my head with a snort of derision. I do not want to think about the Big E. "Can we get some real food now?"

Elliot grins. "Nope, sorry, bro. You don't want a full stomach for what we have planned next. Eat the sub."

"Next? Elliot, the zip line was great. There's more?"

"Oh, yes. Suck it up, buttercup."

Gingerly, I pick up one of the subs.

"Those are made by my own fair hand."

"Don't put me off."

"The finest bologna, tomato, and provolone cheese this side of the Rockies have gone into those sandwiches."

"I'll take your word for it."

"You need to broaden your culinary horizons."

"With bologna?"

"Whatever it takes. Unwrap that for me."

I peel off the parchment paper and hand him the dubious-looking creation. He shoves it in his mouth and starts to chow down. It's not a sight for the fainthearted, and I realize I have no choice, it's bologna or starve.

While I eat, I text Ana.

> Zip-lining. That's what Elliot had planned. And bologna sandwiches. I'm living the dream.

ANA
LOL! I'm spending a great deal of your money. Not entirely consensually. Caroline Acton is a force to be reckoned with. She reminds me of you. Stay safe with whatever Elliot throws at you! Love you. And miss you. xxx

> I love it when you spend my money. It will very soon be your money, too. Will report on Elliot's next "surprise." xxx

Elliot drives smoothly off I-5 onto the 2. *Where the fuck are we going?* I thought we were headed back to Seattle.

"Surprise," he responds to my questioning look.

Seems to be his word of the day.

Fifteen minutes later he pulls into the parking lot at Harvey Airfield.

"Hey, there's a steakhouse here—we could have had some real food," I grumble.

"Maybe later—we've got a class to catch."

"Class?"

"Come on, hotshot, you've not guessed it yet?" He drives past the steakhouse.

"No."

"We're taking the plunge, because you're taking the plunge."

What the hell?

Elliot puts me out of my misery. "Skydiving."

"Oh. Okay." *Fuck!*

"It'll be great. I've done a tandem jump before. It's wild."

Of course he has.

"You'll be fine."

"Yeah. Sure."

"Listen, you get married and women don't let you do this shit. Come on." Together we walk through the parking lot toward the sky-diving school, and my heart races. I like to be in control; tandem jumping means someone else is in control…and I'm strapped to them.

And they're touching me. At a great altitude.

Hell.

I've been as high up as 15,000 feet in my sailplane, and 20,000 feet in *Charlie Tango.* But then I was seated and piloting an aircraft that could fly. Leaping out of a plane? Into the sky? At height?

Never.

Shit.

But I cannot, simply cannot, wimp out in front of Elliot. I swallow my apprehension as we enter the building.

My brother has booked us an exclusive jump. After a short informative video, we sit through a briefing with Ben, our instructor, and I'm grateful that it's just Elliot and me in the class. I was coached on how to use a parachute as part of my glider training, but I've never actually done a jump. While Ben is explaining what we need to do and what to expect, it occurs to me that I haven't provided this training for Ana. She needs to do this before she goes up in ASH 30 again.

When Ben, who looks younger than me, has completed our instruction, he hands us each a waiver. Elliot signs it immediately, while I read through. My anxiety begins to climb, settling in my stomach. I am about to jump out of an aircraft from a high altitude.

Deep breath, Grey.

I realize that if something were to happen to me, Ana would be left with nothing.

To hell with that.

Once I've signed the form, on the back I write:

This is my last will and testament. In the event of my death I leave all my worldly goods to my beloved fiancée, Anastasia Steele, to be dispensed with as she sees fit.
Signed: Christian Grey   Date: 07/23/2011

I take a quick photo with my phone and zap it to Ros, before handing the signed waiver back to Ben, who laughs.

"You'll be fine, Christian."

"Just preparing for all eventualities." I give him a quick, forced smile.

He laughs again. "Okay. Let's get you suited up."

We leave the building and head across the tarmac to an open-air hangar where all the safety gear is located: chutes, helmets, and harnesses.

I'm detecting a theme.

Elliot swaggers to the hangar as if he doesn't have a care in the world; it's infuriating, and right now I envy him more than ever. Ben hands us each a jumpsuit.

Literally. A. Jumpsuit.

Whoa!

"Hey, hotshot. More kinky shit!" Elliot crows as he pulls the safety harness over his attire.

I roll my eyes and turn to Ben. "I apologize for Elliot. He only speaks asshole."

"You two related?" Ben asks.

Elliot and I exchange a look. *Yes. But no. But yes.*

"Brothers," Elliot responds, looking at me, and we both break into *that* secret smile that adopted siblings share. Ben knows he's missing something, but says nothing and helps first Elliot, then me, into our harnesses.

It's decided that I will tandem-jump with Ben, and we're joined by Matt, who will tandem-jump with Elliot. Another instructor, Sandra, tags along, complete with a GoPro to film the whole escapade.

"Hi," Matt says as he shakes our hands. "Special occasion?"

"My brother's bachelor party. He's experiencing the last gasp of freedom," Elliot says.

"Congratulations," Matt says.

"Thanks," I mutter dryly. "This is a surprise."

"Good surprise?"

"Jury's out."

Matt laughs. "You'll love it. Let's go, pilot's ready."

The five of us make our way across the runway to the waiting single-engine Cessna.

Last chance to change your mind, Grey.

There are only two seats at the front of the plane, behind the pilot. But Matt and Ben sit down on the floor and motion for us to sit in front of them. We comply and they start the process of buckling us onto their harnesses. As his hands move over the straps, I realize that I'm not unnerved by the physical contact with Ben; he'll have my life in his hands.

"You flown before?" he asks, raising his voice above the sound of the engine.

"I'm a qualified commercial pilot," I respond. "Rotorcraft. And I have a couple of sailplanes."

"This'll be easy for you."

My laugh is hollow.

Yeah. No. I'm a pilot for a reason.

I'm in control.

I take a deep breath as the plane leaves the runway and begins its ascent. Snohomish Valley falls away as we climb higher and higher into the cloudless sky.

Matt and Elliot are talking crap. Ben joins in. I block them out and think of Ana.

What's she doing? Is her wardrobe complete? I think of her in my arms this morning, wrapped around me. I place my hand on my chest where her finger traced small circles.

Calm, Grey. Calm.

As we near 12,000 feet Ben hands me a leather cap complete with chin strap, and some goggles. As I put them on he runs through a quick reminder of all that I need to know. The other instructor opens the rear door; the draft is almost deafening.

Shit. This is happening.

"You got that?" Ben shouts, referring to his quick refresher.

"Yes."

Ben checks the altimeter on his right wrist. "It's time. Excited? Let's go." We shuffle toward the open door, the sound of the single engine and the wind rush even more thunderous. I glance at Elliot, who gives me a thumbs-up sign and a fuck-you grin.

"You asshole!" I yell, and he laughs. I cross my arms and clutch on to my harness like my life depends on it...because my life depends on it. Then I'm hanging, attached to a man I don't know, over fucking Washington and the Snohomish Valley. I squeeze my eyes shut, and for the first time in a billion years offer a prayer to the God that abandoned me years ago. Then I open them again.

Whoa. I can see the Cascades, Possession Sound, the San Juan Islands—and nothing but air beneath me.

"Here we go," Ben shouts, and launches us out of the aircraft.

"Ffffuuuuuuccccckkkkkk!" I bellow.

And I'm flying.

Really flying, above the earth. Either I don't have time to be afraid or the adrenaline streaking through my body has blotted out the fear. It's super-exhilarating. I can see for miles, and because I'm not behind glass or plastic, it's hyper-real. I'm in the sky, cloaked in it. It's holding me up. The rushing sound of air as we dive to the ground is familiar, like an old friend. I free my hands and hold them out to feel the wind racing through my fingers. Ben holds a thumb up in front of my face and I return the compliment.

This is beyond amazing.

Scanning above, I get a glimpse of Elliot and Matt. And Sandra comes whooshing past us, the camera turned toward Ben and me. My grin is goofy.

"This is great!" I call out to Ben as we surf the sky.

I see Ben raise his wrist. We're at 5,000 feet. He tugs at his rip cord and we slow immediately as above us a multicolored canopy unfurls. The nature of the dive changes from terminal velocity to slow motion, and all is quiet as we hang in the air. My anxiety evaporates, replaced by an inner calm that surprises me. I'm on top of the world, quite literally walking on air. Ben's got this; he knows what he's doing. And from somewhere deep in my mind, the thought materializes in my head: I hope that my marriage to Ana is this thrilling and this easy.

The view is breathtaking.

I wish she were here.

Though it would give me a coronary watching her jump out of a plane.

"Want to steer?" Ben asks.

"Sure."

He hands me the risers; I tug on the left and we turn, slowly and gracefully, in a wide circle.

"Dude, you've got this," Ben calls, patting my upper arm.

We do another circle before Ben takes the risers back in order to steer us toward the landing zone. The ground is approaching at speed, and I lift my knees as instructed as Ben gently drops us to the ground. We both land on our asses, and the ground team is there to welcome us.

Ben unclips his harness from mine and I stand, feeling a little unsteady from the adrenaline rush. Behind us, Elliot and Matt land, Elliot whooping like a gorilla again—his favorite form of expressing excitement.

I pause and catch my breath.

"How was it?" Ben asks.

"Man, that was sublime. Thank you."

"Great!" He offers a fist-bump and I return it.

Elliot rushes over to join us.

"Fuck, man!" I exclaim.

"Rad, huh?"

"I was shitting bricks."

"I know! It's good to see you finally losing your fucking cool for once. It's a rare event, bro." Elliot laughs, but his grin reflects mine. "Better than sex?" he asks.

"No…but close."

FIFTEEN MINUTES LATER WE'RE back in his pickup.

"Dude, I could use a drink after that," I say, and I can't shake my shit-eating grin.

"Me, too. Well, we're going to part three of your bachelor party."

"Fuck, there's more?"

Elliot clams up. *Smug asshole.* He's not telling me. I check my phone.

> **ANA**
> Home. We shopped till we dropped.
> I'm going to have a bath. Then get
> ready to meet Kate. I haven't heard
> from you. You know I worry. Axxx

> We were SKYDIVING!! from
> 12,000 feet. You were right to
> worry. But it was amazing!!
> Reminds me. You need parachute
> training. If I don't see you—enjoy
> your night out. But not too much.

> **ANA**
> Skydiving. Wow! Glad you're safe.
> Parachute training? Didn't we do that
> last weekend in the Red Room? ;)

I laugh out loud.

"What?" Elliot asks.

I shake my head. "Nothing."

Elliot drives back to Escala, though this time he lets me play some decent music from his phone. As we ride the elevator up to the penthouse he says, "You need to get changed. Something smarter."

"What have you got planned?"

He winks.

"Asshole."

"That's a given." He grins.

The doors to the elevator open, and I'm hoping to see Ana.

"My gear is in your spare bedroom. I'll see you down here in half an hour. We're leaving then."

"Okay." I'm hoping to catch Ana in the bath.

She's not in the living room, and I worry that she's left already, but I find her in the bedroom. Halting on the threshold, I watch quietly as she adds the final touches to her makeup.

Wow! Ana looks stunning. Her hair is styled in an elegant chignon. She's wearing high heels and an off-the-shoulder black dress that shimmers. She turns, and is startled when she sees me. She takes my breath away. Hanging from her ears are her second-chance earrings. "I didn't mean to spook you," I whisper. "You look lovely."

She smiles her warm, welcoming smile that's full of love; it swells my heart, and she sashays toward me. "Christian. What a lovely surprise. I wasn't expecting to see you." She raises her lips to mine, and I give her a quick kiss, then pull back. She smells of heaven and home.

"If I kiss you properly, I'm going to mess up your makeup, and peel you out of that elegant dress."

"Oh, that would never do." She giggles and does a quick twirl. Her skirt flares up slightly, revealing a little more leg. "You like?" she asks.

I lean against the doorjamb and cross my arms. "It's not too short. I approve. You look great, Ana. Who's going to be there?" I narrow my eyes, feeling at once ridiculously proud that she's mine, but also territorial—she's mine.

"Kate, Mia, some girlfriends from WSU. Should be fun. We're starting with cocktails."

"Mia?"

Ana nods.

"I haven't seen her in a while. Say hi from me. I hope there's food on your itinerary." I arch a brow in warning. "Drinking rule number one."

She laughs. "Oh, stow your twitchy palm, Christian. We're having a meal."

"Good." I don't want her getting drunk.

She glances at her watch. "I'd better go. I don't want to be late. I'm glad you're back in one piece. I'd never forgive Elliot if anything happened to you."

She offers me her lips once more and I get another swift kiss.

"You look gorgeous, Anastasia."

She picks up her evening bag from the bed. "Laters, baby," she says with a coquettish smile, and she struts past me out of the room, looking like a million dollars. I follow her out and watch her join

Sawyer and Reynolds in the foyer. I salute them, and they all file into the elevator.

I head back into my en suite for a quick shower.

TWENTY MINUTES LATER, DRESSED in a dark navy suit and crisp white shirt, I'm in my kitchen, waiting for Elliot. In the fridge, I find some pretzels.

Fuck, I'm hungry.

Elliot appears in the doorway. He's wearing a dark suit, a gray shirt, and a tie.

Shit.

"Do I need a tie?"

Where the hell are we going?

"No."

"Sure?"

"Yep."

"Why are you wearing one?"

"You get to dress like this all the time. I don't. Changes it up for me. Besides, a suit and tie is catnip to women."

What about Kavanagh?

Elliot smirks at my questioning look, and Taylor joins us.

"Ready, sir?" he asks Elliot.

TAYLOR DRIVES US SOUTH on I-5.

"Where the fuck are we going, Elliot?" I ask.

"Relax, Christian. It's all good." He looks out of the window, seemingly at ease, while I drum my fingers on my knee. I hate not being in the know.

Taylor takes the turn off for Boeing Field, and I wonder if there's some seedy strip club based around here. I glance at my watch: 6:20 p.m. He turns into Signature Flight Support and behind the terminal, sitting on the tarmac, is the GEH Gulfstream.

"What?" I exclaim to Elliot.

From his inside jacket pocket Elliot produces a passport. "You're going to need this."

We're leaving the country?

Taylor drops us at the terminal entrance, and I follow Elliot into the building, bewildered.

"Elliot!" Kavanagh's blond, surfer-dude brother strides up to my brother and shakes his hand. He scrubs up well in his pale gray suit. I note he's not wearing a tie, either.

"Ethan, great to see you," Elliot responds, and claps him on the back.

"Christian." Ethan shakes my hand.

"Hi," I respond.

"Mac!" Elliot exclaims, and Liam McConnell—who works at the GEH shipyard, and also looks after my yacht, *The Grace*—strides toward us.

Mac! We shake hands. "It's good to see you," I tell him. "I'd just like you to know that I have no idea what the hell is going on."

He laughs. "Neither do I."

We all laugh and turn to Elliot as Taylor joins us.

"You knew about this?" I ask Taylor.

"Yes, sir." His look is earnest and amused in equal measure.

I laugh and shake my head.

"Shall we go?" Elliot says.

"CANADA?" I GUESS.

"Correct," Elliot responds.

We are installed in the first four seats of my G550, sipping Cristal champagne and eating the canapés that Sara, our flight attendant, distributed as we taxied onto the runway. Taylor is at the back reading a Lee Child novel. Stephan and First Officer Beighley are at the controls.

"I'm guessing Vancouver," I say to Elliot.

"Bingo! I figured you might have less of a chance being recognized behaving badly in British Columbia."

"What the hell have you got planned?"

"Easy, tiger," Elliot responds, and raises his glass.

Once we're airborne, Sara serves beer and fresh, hot pepperoni pizza, from a local pizzeria in Georgetown. I think this is a first, pizza in my private jet—but this is Elliot's idea of heaven. Frankly, I'm so hungry, it's mine, too. Mac, who's sitting opposite, and I both wolf down our food.

"That didn't touch the sides," Mac says in his Irish brogue.

"Elliot has had me zip-lining and tandem skydiving already today."

"Holy shit! No wonder you're starving."

THE JOURNEY TIME IS less than fifty minutes. When we pull up outside the Vancouver Signature Flight Support terminal Taylor is the first off, carrying our passports for the immigration official who has come to meet the plane.

"Ready?" Elliot says, unbuckling his seat belt and standing up to stretch his legs. Taylor is at the wheel of a Suburban on the tarmac. We all pile in, and he sets off for the bright lights of downtown Vancouver. We have a cooler full of beer. My three companions dive in, but I decline.

"Man, you are not staying sober tonight," Elliot splutters in disgust and hands me a beer.

Fuck. I loathe being drunk. With a roll of my eyes, reluctantly I take the bottle. It's early. We'll be drinking more; I'll need to pace myself. I clink bottles with him, and Mac and Ethan, who are seated behind us. "Cheers, gentlemen." I take a sip and let the drink linger in my hand.

Our first stop is the bar at the Rosewood Georgia hotel. I've been before, on business, but never in the evening. Its wood-paneled walls and leather seats give it an old-world charm and tonight it's heaving with the great and the good of Vancouver. Men in suits, women elegantly dressed. It has a lively vibe. Elliot orders a round, and we sit at a reserved table and our conversation turns to Ethan's endeavors to get into Seattle University to do a master's in psychology. Since Ana moved out, he's now living with Kate, in Ana's old room. Maybe living with his sister is challenging, I wouldn't be surprised—perhaps that's why he's outpacing us on drinks. He's finished his beer first and volunteers to buy the next round.

Mac talks to us about *The Grace.* He's one of the craftsmen who built her, but it seems he's turning his hand to boat design and has some ideas to make the catamaran we custom-build even more aerodynamic.

It's weird, I never do this. It's only when Elliot drags me out, usually with his friends—of whom there are many—that I get to enjoy
the company of men my own age. Elliot is a social glue, sticking us
all together and never letting the conversation lag. He's such a people
person. Our conversation moves, inevitably to the Mariners, then the
Seahawks. We're all fans, it would seem, of both teams. By the end of
the second round we've all relaxed into one another's company, and
I'm enjoying myself.

"Okay. Drink up. Next stop," Elliot announces.

Taylor is waiting outside in the SUV.

Ethan is already buzzed. This could get interesting. I'm tempted
to ask him about Mia but part of me doesn't want to know.

The next venue is in Yaletown, a district renowned for redevel-
oped old warehouses that now house hip bars and restaurants. Taylor
drops us at a nightclub where dance music pulses into the street even
though it's still relatively early. Inside the dark industrial interior, the
bar is doing brisk business and we have a table in the VIP area. I stick
with beer, while Ethan and Mac scan the room, I think to check out
the local talent.

"You're not interested?" I ask Elliot.

He laughs. "Not tonight, hotshot." He side-eyes Ethan, and I wonder if he's holding back the "Big E" because Kate's brother is here.

I glance at my watch, curious to know what Ana is doing, and I'm
tempted to call Sawyer. Frankly, there's only so much socializing I
can tolerate, but our conversation turns to the new house.

After another two rounds Elliot has us on the move again.

Taylor is ready with the SUV, and he drives us to the next venue.
A strip club.

Shit.

"Dude, don't get uptight. This stop is in the bachelor-party rule
book." Ethan claps his hands, but his smile doesn't reach his eyes. I
think he's just as uncomfortable as I am.

"Do not under any circumstances buy me a lap dance," I warn
Elliot. And I'm reminded of a time, not too long ago, when I was in
the dark depths of a private club in Seattle.

Where anything goes.

That was a lifetime ago.

Elliot laughs. "What happens in Vancouver stays in Vancouver." He winks at me as we're led to another VIP table. This time my brother has ordered a bottle of vodka, which arrives with ceremony: sparklers and a chorus of women in short red skirts and bikini tops that barely cover their nipples, who are all cheers and enthusiastic applause. I worry for a moment that they're going to sit down with us, but once the shot glasses are lined up, they move on.

There are beautiful women everywhere. I watch one, a lithe blonde with dark eyes. She starts to remove her clothes with athletic grace, while doing various gymnastic moves and poses on the pole. I can't help thinking that if she were a man, this would be an Olympic sport.

Mac is mesmerized, and I wonder if he has a partner.

"No, I'm single. Looking," he says when I ask. His eyes return to the energetic blonde. I nod, but I'm at a loss as to what to say, because I'm in no position to offer any relationship advice. I'm still amazed that Ana has consented to be mine. In fact, she's consented to a great many things.

I smirk as my mind catapults to thoughts of the Red Room last weekend.

Yeah.

The memory has an arousing effect on my body. I take out my phone.

"No," Elliot says. "Put it away."

"My phone?"

We both laugh. And I sink a shot of vodka.

"Let's go somewhere else," I say.

"You don't like it here?"

"No."

"Jesus, you're one uptight motherfucker."

Dude, this is not my scene.

"Okay. We have one more stop. This was the traditional, customary part of your bachelor party. You know, it's the unwritten law."

"I don't think Ana would be very impressed."

Ethan claps me on the back and I freeze. "So don't tell her."

And something in his tone puts my hackles up. "Are you fucking my sister?"

Ethan jerks his head back as if I've hit him. Shocked, he raises both his hands. "No. No. Dude, no offense. She's attractive and all, but she's just a friend."

"Good. Keep it that way."

He laughs, nervously, I think, and downs two shots of vodka.

My work here is done.

"You going to frighten off all her would-be boyfriends?" Elliot asks.

"Maybe."

He rolls his eyes. "Let's get you out of here. This place is doing nothing for your mood."

"Okay."

We ditch the vodka and I leave an obscene cash tip on the table.

Back in the SUV, my humor is restored. Taylor's at the wheel and we're heading out of downtown Vancouver, in the direction of the airport.

But we don't go back to the plane. Taylor pulls up outside a sprawling, nondescript hotel-and-casino complex that flanks the Fraser River.

"Marriage is a gamble," Elliot says with a grin.

"Life is a gamble, dude. But this is more my scene."

"I figured. You always beat me at cards," he responds. "How are you still sober?"

"It's just math, Elliot. I haven't had that much to drink, and right now, I'm grateful."

Elliot and Ethan head for the craps and roulette tables, while Mac favors the blackjack and I the poker table.

THERE'S A RESPECTFUL BUT expectant hush in the room. I am $118,000 up, and this is the last game I'm going to play. It's getting late; behind me, Elliot is watching. I don't know where Ethan and Mac are. The final hand is in play, and both players beside me fold in turn. I have two jacks, and because this is the final game and I'm on a roll, I raise, and toss $16,000 worth of chips into the pot. The

opponent on my left, a woman who must be in her fifties, folds immediately. "I've got nothing," she grumbles.

My remaining opponent—who reminds me of my dad—glances
at me, then back at his cards, and carefully, counting out chips, he
matches my bet.

Game on, Grey.

The dealer collects the folded cards and briskly lays out the flop.

Hallelujah.

A jack and a pair of nines. I have a full house.

I stare impassively at my rival as he fidgets, checks his cards once
more, his lively, dark eyes flitting to me and back to his cards. He
swallows.

He's got jack shit.

"Check," my challenger says.

Showtime, Grey.

Slowly, for full effect, I tap my finger on the green baize, then gather
my chips together and place $50,000 into the pot. "Raise," I state.

The dealer responds, "Fifty-thousand-dollar raise."

My opponent huffs, picks up his cards, and tosses them in disgust
into the center of the table. Inside, I'm dancing. I've made $134K. Not
bad for forty-five minutes of play.

"I'm done," says the lady beside me, and she nods in my direction.

"Thanks for the game. I've got to go, too." I toss a generous chip to
the dealer as a tip, gather the rest of my winnings, and stand.

"Good night."

Elliot steps forward and helps me with my chips.

"You're a lucky son of a bitch," he says.

JUST BEFORE MIDNIGHT, WE board the plane.

"I'll have an Armagnac, Sara, thank you."

"Now you start drinking!" Elliot exclaims.

"We all came out on top," Mac observes. "Must be your luck rubbing off on us, Christian."

"I'll drink to that," says Ethan.

I smile, settling into the plush leather of my seat. Yes. My win is a
good omen. What a great way to end a most enjoyable evening.

As we begin our descent into Boeing Field I reach for my seat belt and chuckle to myself. I've spent most of today buckling and unbuckling.

Elliot, sitting opposite me, looks up. "What's so funny?"

"Nothing. I just wanted to say thank you. For today. It's been amazing."

Elliot glances at his watch. "Technically, it was yesterday."

"I had a blast. You've acquitted yourself well as best man. Your one remaining duty is to make a speech. Doesn't have to be a long one."

Elliot pales. "Dude. Don't remind me."

"Yeah." I make a face. "I've still got to write my vows."

"Shit. That's heavy." He's horrified. "But this time next week it'll all be over. You'll be married."

"Yeah. And on this plane."

"Cool. Where are you taking Ana?"

"Europe. But it's a surprise. She's never left the U.S."

"Wow."

"I know. I never thought that I, I would...I can't..." My voice trails off as a sudden unexpected surge of emotion sweeps over me. Is it fear, exhilaration, anxiety, or *happiness*? I don't know, but it's overwhelming.

Fuck. I'm getting married.

Elliot frowns. "Dude, why? You're a good-looking guy. You're a douche, but, hey, that's because you're a master of the universe with a big swinging dick." He shakes his head. "I never understood why you weren't interested in any of Mia's friends. They were always crushing on you. Man, I thought you were gay." He shrugs.

I smile, knowing my whole family thought I was gay. "I was just waiting for the right woman."

"I think you found her." His expression softens, but there's a wistful look in his vivid blue eyes.

"I think I have."

"Love suits you," Elliot says, and I roll my eyes at him, because it's possibly the sappiest thing he's ever said to me.

"Get a room, boys," Mac exclaims, and we touch down on the tarmac.

"I'm never going to let you forget that you're the only groom in the Pacific Northwest who remained sober at his own bachelor party."

I laugh. "Well, I'm just grateful I'm not handcuffed naked to a lamppost somewhere in Vegas."

"Dude, if I ever get married, that's exactly how I'd like to finish my bachelor party!" Elliot says.

"I'll make a mental note."

Elliot laughs. "Time to wake Ethan."

TAYLOR IS AT THE wheel of the Q7, driving Elliot and me back to Escala. Mac and Ethan, after some backslapping good-byes, have already left in a waiting cab. "Thanks for this evening, Taylor," I say as I stretch out in the back. Elliot looks like he's asleep.

"It's been a pleasure, sir." His eyes meet mine in the rearview mirror, and even in the surrounding darkness I notice the amused crinkles in the corners. I take my phone out of my jacket pocket.

No messages.

"Have you heard from Sawyer or Reynolds?"

"Yes, sir," Taylor responds. "Miss Steele and Miss Kavanagh are still out."

What? I check my watch. It's after one o'clock in the morning.

"Where is she?" I swallow my alarm and glance at a comatose Elliot.

"At a nightclub."

"Which one?"

"Trinity."

"Pioneer Square?"

"Yes, sir."

"Take me there."

Taylor's eyes flick to mine, his expression doubtful.

"You don't think it's a good idea?" I ask.

"No, sir."

Damn.

Count to ten, Grey.

I remember the one and only time I've been in a nightclub with Ana was at that bar in Portland, where she was celebrating her final exams.

She got so drunk she passed out.

In my arms.

Shit.

"Sir, Sawyer and Reynolds are with her."

This is true.

Put yourself in her shoes. Flynn's words nag me.

This is her night. With her friends.

Grey, leave her be.

"Okay, take us back to Escala."

"Yes, sir."

I hope I've made the right decision.

I ROUSE ELLIOT AS we pull into the underground garage at Escala.

"Wake up, we're here."

"I wanna go home. But if you wanna nightcap or something, I'm up for it." He can barely open his eyes.

"Taylor will take you home, Elliot."

"I'd like to see you into the apartment first, Mr. Grey," Taylor says.

"Okay." I sigh, knowing that he's still in mother-hen mode, concerned about my safety. He parks beside the elevator and climbs out of the car.

Elliot opens his eyes. "I'll stay in the car," he mutters. I reach over to shake his hand, but he grabs it, forcibly. "Fuck off with your fucking handshake," he grumbles, and tugs me into an awkward embrace, which is clumsy and male and…welcome.

"Don't crease the suit," I warn, feeling oddly touched by his gesture. He releases me.

"Good night, bro."

I slap his knee. "Thanks again. Do you need the stuff you left here?"

"I'll be back Friday night for the rehearsal dinner."

"Okay. Good night, Lelliot."

He grins and closes his eyes.

TAYLOR ACCOMPANIES ME UP to the penthouse.

"You know you don't have to do this, Taylor."

"It's my job, sir." He looks straight ahead.

"Are you armed?"

Taylor's eyes flick in my direction. "Yes, sir."

I loathe firearms; I wonder if he took the gun to Canada and, if so, how he got it through security, but I don't want to know the gory details.

Plausible deniability.

"Why don't you ask Ryan to take Elliot home? You must be exhausted."

"I'm good, Mr. Grey."

"Thank you again for your part in all the organization of today."

He turns to me with a warm smile. "It was a pleasure."

The doors to the penthouse open and I wander in. Ryan is standing, waiting for me.

"Good evening, Mr. Grey."

"Ryan, hi. All quiet tonight?"

"Yes, sir. Nothing to report. Do you need anything?"

"No. I'm fine. Good night." I leave him in the foyer and amble into the kitchen. From the fridge I pull a bottle of sparkling mineral water, unscrew the top, and start to drink directly from the bottle.

My apartment is quiet. The low hum of the fridge and the distant rumble of traffic are the only sounds I hear. The place feels empty.

Because Ana's not here.

My footsteps echo across the room as I meander to the window. The moon is high, and it shines in a clear night sky with the promise of another halcyon day, like today. Ana is near, under the same moon. She'll be home soon. *Surely.* I lean my forehead against the glass. It's cool, but not cold. As I let out a long sigh, my breath mists the pane.

Shit.

I saw her a few hours ago, and yet I'm missing her.

For fuck's sake, Grey. You've got it bad. Pull yourself together.

I've had the most fulfilling day. Carefree. Adventurous. Sociable.

Flynn would be proud. I remember when we first sailed on *The Grace*, Ana asked me if I had any friends. Well, now I can say yes. *Maybe.*

I don't understand why I'm suddenly feeling despondent; a familiar sense of loneliness is creeping into my psyche. I recognize its key ingredients: the emptiness, the longing, like I'm missing something. I've not felt it since I was a teenager.

Hell.

I haven't felt lonely for years. I've had my family, though I've kept them at a distance. And there was Elena, of course, and I've been content with my own company and the occasional company of my submissives.

But now, without Ana here, I'm lost.

Her absence is an ache—a scar on my soul.

The silence is becoming intolerable.

I would have thought after all the noise of this evening—the bars, the night club, the casino floor—I would welcome some quiet.

But no.

The silence is oppressive, and it's making me melancholy.

Fuck this.

I stalk over to the piano, lift the lid, and settle onto the stool. Taking a moment to gather my thoughts, I place my hands on the keys, enjoying the grounding feel of the ivory beneath my fingertips. I begin to play the first piece that comes to mind; the Bach-Marcello, and I'm soon lost in the morose melody that perfectly reflects my mood. The second time through the composition I'm distracted by a noise.

"Shh…"

I look up, and Ana is standing by the kitchen counter, swaying slightly. She's carrying her strappy high heels in one hand and she's wearing what looks like a plastic tiara that may have perched on the top of her head at one time, but is now looking decidedly lopsided.

A sash with the word *bride* in an elaborate serif hangs over her shimmering black dress. She has her index finger at her lips.

She is without doubt the most beautiful girl in the world.

And I'm delighted she's home.

Behind her, Sawyer and Reynolds are stony-faced. Rising from the stool, I tip my chin at them in thanks. They smile as one and leave us.

Ana turns and stumbles a little to watch them leave. "Bye!" she almost shouts, and waves them away with a wide sweep of her arm.

She's clearly intoxicated.

Turning back to face me, she rewards me with the biggest, warmest, most drunken smile and stumbles toward me. "Mr. Christian Grey!"

I catch her before she falls and fold her into my arms, and she gazes up at me with unfocused joy. Her expression feeds my soul. "Miss Anastasia Steele. How lovely to see you. Did you have fun?"

"The best!"

"Please tell me you had something to eat."

"Yes! Food has been eaten." She drops her shoes and they clatter on the floor, while she winds her arms around my neck.

"Can I fix your crown?" I try to straighten her tiara.

"You fixed my crown long ago," she slurs.

What?

"You have the most beautiful mouth." She runs her index finger shakily over my lips.

"Do I?"

"Hmm…yes. You do things to me with that mouth."

"I like doing things to you with my mouth."

"Shall we do it now?" Her unfocused gaze moves from my mouth to my eyes.

"Tempting though that sounds, I'm not sure that's a good idea right now."

She sways a little and I tighten my hold on her. "Dance with me," she mumbles, grinning up at me. She lets her hands run down my jacket lapels, and tugs me closer so I feel her down the length of my body.

"We should put you to bed."

"I wanna dance…with you," she whispers, and offers me her lips.

"Ana," I warn, tempted to carry her to bed, but I'm enjoying the feel of her in my arms and the way she's imploring me with her big blue eyes. "Okay. What would you like to dance to?" I'm feeling indulgent.

"Muuuusic."

I laugh, a little exasperated, and move us over to the kitchen counter, where I pick up the remote and press play. Moby's "Bodyrock" starts over the sound system. It's one of my favorites from my youth, but a bit frenetic for now. I skip the track and Nina Simone's "My Baby Just Cares for Me" echoes through the room.

"This?" I state in response to Ana's inebriated smile.

"Yes." She throws her head and arms back with such enthusiasm that I almost drop her.

"Shit. Ana!" I'm glad I have my arm around her waist, otherwise she'd be sprawled on the floor. She starts to stagger and I wonder if she's going to pass out, then realize she's attempting to dance.

Whoa.

I clamp my arms around her. I've never danced with someone as inebriated as Ana. She is all arms and legs and unpredictable spins.

It's an education.

I try to take both her hands and lead her around the room, in a semblance of a dance—that's more a jig—so it's not entirely successful. It's unsettling.

Suddenly she stops and clutches her head. "Oh. The room is spinning."

Oh no. "I think we should go to bed."

She looks up at me between her fingers. "Why? What are you going to do?"

Is she flirting or is this a serious question?

"Let you sleep," I reply, deadpan.

She makes a face, which I interpret as disappointment, but, taking her hand, I guide her back to the kitchen counter. From the cupboard I grab a glass and fill it with water. "Drink this." I pass it to her, and she does as she's told. "All of it."

She narrows her eyes and squints—I suspect to get me in focus. "You've done this before."

"Yes. With you. Last time you were inebriated."

She drains the glass and wipes her mouth with the back of her hand. "Are you going to fuck me?"

"No. Not tonight."

She frowns.

"Come." I guide her to our bedroom suite, switch on the bedside lights from the wall, and release her by the bed. "Do you feel sick?"

"No!" she says emphatically.

That's a relief. "Do you need to use the bathroom?"

"No!"

"Turn around," I demand.

She gives me a lopsided smile, and I remove the tiara.

"Turn around—let me unzip your dress." I drag the ridiculous sash over her head.

"You are so good to me." She lays her hand on my chest, splaying out her fingers.

"Enough. Turn around. I won't ask you again."

She grins. "There he is…"

Oh, baby.

I grasp her shoulders and gently turn her around so I can unfasten her dress. It obliges and falls immediately, pooling at her feet. She's wearing a black lacy bra, matching panties, and a white garter. I undo her bra and step forward, bringing her body flush to mine, and I drag the straps down her arms. She rubs her ass against me and moves her hand behind her to fondle my more-than-interested dick.

Ana!

I allow myself a brief moment of pure pleasure and push my hips forward as her hand fumbles the length of my hardening cock.

Yes!

I drop her bra on the floor, move her hair aside, and run my lips down her neck. "Stop," I whisper.

She continues to rub her hand over me. I groan and step back. Kneeling, I slip the garter—which I suspect came with the sash and tiara—and her panties down her legs, and kiss her behind. "Step." She does, and I remove her underwear and gather her clothes together before pulling back the duvet. "Into bed."

Now she turns around. "Join me," she says with a provocative smile. She's naked and lovely and wanton and tempting.

She's also completely drunk.

"Get into bed. I'll be back."

She sways, sits down, then flops back on the bed, and I lift her feet onto the mattress and cover her up.

"Are you going to punish me?" she slurs.

"Punish you?"

"For getting this drunk. A punishment fuck. You can do anything you want to me," she whispers, and holds out her arms.

Oh God.

A million erotic thoughts flit through my mind, and it takes all my willpower to lean over, gently plant a kiss on her forehead, and leave.

In the closet, which is still full of shopping bags from her earlier trip, I place her clothes in the laundry basket and strip out of my suit and shirt.

I drag on my PJs and a T-shirt and head into the bathroom.

While brushing my teeth I contemplate what I could do to a drunken Ana. She wants punishing? My thoughts do little to ease my erection.

"Pervert," I mouth at my reflection.

I switch off the lights and head back into the bedroom. As I suspected, Ana is out cold, her hair spilling in all directions over the pillows. She looks lovely. I climb in beside her and roll onto my side to watch her sleep.

She's going to have one helluva hangover in the morning.

Leaning over, I kiss her hair. "I love you, Anastasia," I whisper, and I lay back and stare at the ceiling. I'm surprised that I'm not furious with her. No, I found her charming, and funny.

Maybe, I'm growing up. *Finally.*

I hope so. This time next week, I'll be a married man.

I hang up from my call with Troy Whelan, my banker. I've set up a joint account for me and Ana that will go live once she's Mrs. Anastasia Grey. I'm not sure what she'll ever need it for—but, if something happens to me… Jeez. If something happens to her…

My phone buzzes, distracting me from a slew of dark thoughts. "Mr. Grey, I have your mother on the line," Andrea says.

I suppress a groan. "Put her through."

"Will do. Here you go, sir."

"Grace."

"Darling. How are you?"

"I'm good. What is it?"

"Always so brusque. I'm checking up on you, that's all. I talk to Ana more than you these days."

"Well, I'm good. Still here. Still getting married. Thank you for all that you've done. Is there anything specific you want?"

She sighs. "No, darling. I'm looking forward to the rehearsal dinner, and having Ana stay with us the night before the wedding. And of course her mother and her step-father, Bob, too. I'm glad we're meeting them before the big day. Are they on good terms with her dad?"

"With Ray? I think so. But I don't know, you'll need to ask Ana."

"I'll do that. I'm glad he's staying with you."

It was not my idea. "Ana is hoping that we'll bond." Frankly, Raymond Steele intimidates me.

Grace pauses. "I'm sure you will. Do you have a marriage license?"

I scoff. "Of course we do. We picked it up last week."

"Honeymoon?"

"It's all arranged."

"And your suit?"

I direct my eye roll at the phone. "It was delivered today. It fits."

"Rings?"

Rings?

Shit.

Rings!

How the hell did we forget about rings? "In hand," I mutter, and laugh, because both Ana and I have overlooked the rings.

"What's so funny?"

"Nothing, Mom. Anything else?"

"You forgot the rings?"

I sigh. *Busted.* "How did you know?"

"I'm your mother…and you called me Mom. You rarely do that." The humor and warmth in her voice is soothing.

"Perceptive, Dr. Grey."

She chuckles. "Oh, Christian, I love you so much. If you don't have rings, you'd better get some. Everything here is on track; the pavilion goes up tomorrow, and the decorators will follow."

"Thanks, Mom. Thanks for everything."

"See you Friday." She hangs up and I stare out at the Seattle skyline, grateful to all that is holy, for Dr. Grace Trevelyan-Grey.

Mom.

I call Ana.

"Anastasia Steele." She sounds distracted.

"We forgot the rings."

"Rings? Oh! Rings!"

I laugh, because her reaction is the same as mine, and I can imagine her eyes widening in shock. "I know! How could we forget?"

"My mom always says the devil is in the details," Ana agrees.

"She's not wrong. What sort of ring would you like?"

"Oh…um…"

"I thought a platinum band to match your engagement ring?"

"Christian, that would be…that…um…that would be more than mighty fine." Her voice is a whisper.

I smile. "I'll get matching ones."

She gasps. "You'll wear one, too?"

"Why wouldn't I?" I'm surprised by her question.

"I don't know. I'm thrilled that you would."

"Ana, I'm yours. I want the world to know."

"I'm very pleased to hear that."

"You should know this by now."

"I do know," she whispers. "It still gives me all the feels when you say it."

"The feels?"

She giggles. "Yes. The feels."

"Sounds painful."

"No. It's the opposite of painful."

My heart soars. Sometimes she takes my breath away. I swallow, trying to contain my elation. "I'd better get right on this."

"You better!"

"Laters, baby."

"Laters, Christian. I love you."

I let her words settle into my heart.

She loves me.

"Are you going to hang up?" she asks.

"No."

She laughs. "I have to go. I have a meeting and my boss's boss's boss...you know."

"Yeah. He can be an asshole."

"He can...but he can also be the best of men."

I'm staring at her portrait on my office wall; her shy, teasing smile is directed at me. My body and my soul stir. This has to be one of the sweetest things she's ever said to me.

"I'll see you tonight," she says, and the line goes dead before I have a chance to respond.

Anastasia Steele, you are the most disarming woman I know. I stare at her photograph, digesting her words, and I know my smile would light up a dark and soulless night.

Feeling inspired, I find the number for Astoria Fine Jewelry and press call. It's not only rings I need, but a wedding present for my future wife, too.

MY MEETING WITH WELCH is inconclusive: there is still no lead on the perpetrator, and I'm beginning to believe the sabotage is a figment of my overactive imagination. Welch's team is drilling down into all ex-employee records of the companies that GEH has acquired to see if he can find something, but we've been over this ground and I think he's grasping at straws. The only potential suspects we had were Hyde and Woods, but Hyde has been discounted, as he's been in Florida since he was fired, and there's no evidence that links Woods to the crash, yet.

"I know how exasperating this is for you, Grey," Welch says, his voice as gruff as ever. "We are keeping an extra-watchful eye on the Gulfstream."

"I'm wondering if we overreacted to the FAA report."

"No. We did not. Not where your safety is concerned. We'll just have to be patient for the NTSB report. I'm expecting it any day."

"As soon as you have it…" I let the sentence finish itself.

"Yes, sir."

"In the meantime, please liaise with Taylor. He's coming with us to oversee our security while we're on our honeymoon."

"Will do. And congratulations once again."

I nod my thanks. "Okay. That's it. Thanks for coming in."

Welch rises and we shake hands.

BACK AT MY DESK, I check my e-mails.

From: Dr. John Flynn
Subject: FW: For Christian Grey
Date: July 26 2011 14:53
To: Christian Grey

Christian
I received the attached from Leila Williams. We can discuss when I see you on Thursday.
JF

From: Leila Williams
Subject: For Christian Grey
Date: July 26 2011 06:32 EST
To: Dr. John Flynn

Dearest John
Thank you for your continued support. I cannot begin to tell

you what it has meant for me. My parents have embraced me back into the fold. I can hardly believe how considerate they've been, given all the trouble I've caused them. My divorce from my husband should be final next month. At last I'll be able to move on with my life.

My only regret is that I haven't been able to thank Mr. Grey in person. Please pass on this note to him. I would really like to deliver my thanks personally. My life could have taken such a bad turn if not for his and your intervention.

Many thanks
Leila

No fucking way. Leila is the last person in the world I want to see. But I'm glad she's in a better place and healing, and divorcing the cockroach she married. I delete the e-mail and resolve to push her from my mind.

I buzz Andrea. I need coffee. Stat.

IT'S LATE. THE SUN has sunk beneath the horizon, and I'm staring at a blank screen in my study.

Vows.

Drafting them is trickier than I thought. Everything I write will be spoken aloud in front of our nearest and dearest, and I'm trying to find the words to express to Ana how I feel about her, how excited I am to share our life together, and how honored I am that she's chosen me.

Damn it. This is hard.

My thoughts stray to earlier this evening, when Ana and I met with Gia Matteo. Gia wanted our feedback on a few ideas for the new house. Her vision is bold: I like the approach, but I'm not sure that Ana is entirely on board. When we eventually see Gia's drawn-up plans we'll be able to judge.

Fortunately, the meeting was brief. And she touched me once, that's all.

Since then, I've been attempting to write my vows while Ana's been on a call with Alondra Gutierrez. They've each been working tirelessly on this wedding.

I just hope it will be everything Ana wants. And, frankly, as long as Ana's happy, I'm happy.

But most of all, I want to keep her safe.

Life without Ana would be unbearable.

A flurry of images flash unwelcome through my brain: Ana at gunpoint in her old apartment; Ana, not Ros, seated beside me as *Charlie Tango* drops to the ground; Ana lying pale and unmoving on a squalid once-green rug—

Grey, stop. Stop.

I need to get a handle on my morbid thoughts.

Concentrate, Grey. Focus on where you want to be.

With Ana.

I want to give her the world.

I turn back to my screen, to my vows, and start to type.

ANA LOOKS UP WHEN I enter the library, and gives me a sweet but tired smile. She's been reading a manuscript.

"Hi."

"Hi," she answers, as I sit down in the armchair beside her and open my arms. She doesn't hesitate; she uncurls her long legs from beneath her and hops over to me, complete with manuscript, and crawls into my lap. Wrapping her in my arms, I kiss the top of her head and breathe in her scent. She is heaven on earth.

Ana lets out a soft, contented sigh.

She's so good to hold.

A balm to my senses.

My Ana.

We sit in a comfortable, companionable silence. I could never have imagined doing this even three months ago. *No. Two months ago.* I'm changed beyond recognition. The residue of doubt and fear I felt earlier melts away. She's safe, in my arms.

And I'm safe…with her.

The senior management meeting has gone well; everybody is up to speed on what each division is doing, and what steps need to be taken next. I'm leaving my company in safe hands—but then, I never doubted that for a moment. However, if I'm honest, it still makes me anxious. This is the first time I've taken a vacation for more than a few days. As everyone leaves the boardroom, they shake my hand and wish me well. "I'll be here tomorrow," I remind Marcus.

"Christian, you deserve a break," he says. "Enjoy your honeymoon."

"Thank you."

Blowing out a breath, I scrape a hand through my hair. Why the hell am I so apprehensive? Ros sidles up to me when everyone else has left. "The house. It's yours."

"It's done?"

"Signed and sealed."

"Great. Thanks for orchestrating. Keys?"

"They are being biked over."

"I'll give them to my brother. He's going to oversee the renovation."

Her eyes widen. "Renovating, too? You have a great deal on your plate, Christian. I think it's about time you took a vacation."

"You know, I'm ready and looking forward to it."

"Where will you go?"

"I took your advice. Europe."

She brightens. "Gwen and I are really looking forward to Saturday."

"I'll be glad when it's over." I give her a tight smile.

"Christian!" She looks taken aback. "You've got to enjoy the day!"

"I want Ana to enjoy the day."

Ros's stance softens immediately. "You *have* got it bad."

I laugh, because she's never made such a personal comment before. "Guilty as charged."

She grins, her eyes warming. It's a good look on her.

"I'll certainly enjoy my honeymoon knowing that you're heading this place up and keeping the GEH wheels turning."

Her grin broadens. "Don't look so anxious. You'll be in Europe, not on Mars. If I need you, I'll call."

"Thanks, Ros."

"Now, excuse me while I get on with today's business." I step aside and she struts past me. And in that moment, I'm so grateful she's on my team.

"CHRISTIAN, YOU'RE LIKE A caged lion. What is it?" Flynn asks. He's sitting in his chair, regarding me with his usual professional detachment, while I pace up and down his office, treading a path into the thick pile of his rug. I come to a halt at his question and glance through the window to see Taylor waiting by the car. He's watching the street from behind mirrored aviators.

"Nerves?" I hazard a guess, and returning to the couch, I slump into it.

"That's a reasonable reaction to the fact that you're getting married in a couple of days."

"Is it?"

"Of course it is. It's perfectly natural to be nervous. You are publicly going to declare how much Anastasia means to you. It's all getting real."

Yes. It is.

"But it's just taken so long to get to this point and at the last minute we forgot the rings." I throw my hands up in frustration. "What does that say about us?"

"That you're both busy people?" he offers, his tone mollifying.

But his observation doesn't appease me. "Everyone keeps telling me to enjoy myself." My brows knit together.

Flynn looks pensive but remains mute, waiting for me to elucidate.

"I just want it done!"

"Do you? Are you sure you want to go through with this?"

What! I glare at him as if he's sprouted an additional head. "The wedding? Of course I do!"

"I thought so."

"Then why ask me if I have doubts?" I snap.

"Christian, I'm trying to unpack the source of your restlessness."

"I just want it over." I fire the words at him, exasperated. But Flynn says nothing and continues to observe me with a calm and measured expression while I wait for him to offer up some insight. When he doesn't, I know he's testing me.

Damn.

"It's taken so long. I'm not a patient man," I mutter.

"It's been a few weeks, it's not that long."

I huff out a breath as I struggle to unscramble my feelings. "I hope Ana doesn't change her mind."

"I think at this stage Ana is very unlikely to change her mind. Why would she? She loves you." He holds my gaze.

I stare at him, silent, unable to articulate what I want to say. It's frustrating.

"You just want to be married?" Flynn prompts.

"Yes! Then she's mine. And I can protect her. Properly."

"Ah." Flynn nods and lets out a soft sigh. "This isn't just nerves, Christian. Tell me."

Showtime, Grey.

I swallow, and from the depths of my soul, I confess my darkest fear. "Life would be unbearable without her." My words are almost inaudible. "I'm having awful, morbid thoughts."

He nods and taps his lip, and I realize this is what he's been waiting for me to say. "Do you want to talk about them?" he asks.

"No." If I do, I'll make them *real.*

"Why not?"

I shake my head feeling exposed—vulnerable—like I'm naked on top of a treeless hill, the wind howling around me.

John rubs his chin. "Christian, your fears are totally understandable. But they come from the place of an abused, neglected child who was abandoned by the death of his mother."

Closing my eyes, I see the crack whore dead on the floor.

Except she's Ana.

Fuck.

"You're an adult now. A pretty successful one at that," John continues. "None of us have any guarantees in life, but it's extremely unlikely that anything's going to happen to Ana, given everything you've put in place."

I open my eyes to meet Flynn's, and he still wants more.

"I fear for her more than I fear for myself," I whisper.

His expression softens. "I understand, Christian. You love her. But what you have to do is to get that fear into perspective and under control. It's irrational. And fundamentally you know this."

I let out a long breath. "I know. I know."

His forehead creases with a brief frown as he glances at his lap. "I just want to sound a word of caution." He looks up to make sure he has my full attention. "I don't want you to sabotage your happiness, Christian."

"What?"

"I know you feel you don't deserve it and it's a relatively new concept for you, but you should nurture and treasure it."

Where the hell is he going with this?

"I do," I try to reassure him. "But it makes me anxious."

"I know. Just be mindful."

I nod.

"You have the tools to overcome your anxiety. Use them. Free your rational mind."

Okay. Okay.

I'm tiring of this lecture that I've heard before. "Let's move on."

His lips thin. "Are you sure?"

"Yes."

He changes the subject. "Now, speaking of sabotage, do you have any news on the saboteur?"

"No!" The word is an expletive. I wish I had an answer. "I'm beginning to wonder if we overreacted."

"It wouldn't be the first time."

My mouth twists into a half smile. "Ana said that."

"She knows you well."

"She does. Better than anyone. Apart from you."

"You flatter me, Christian. I'm sure she knows you better than

I do. We choose what we show to different people. It's part of what makes us human. I think she's seen the worst and the best of you."

That's true. "She brings out the worst and the best in me."

"If you put your mind to it, you can concentrate on the best. Don't dwell on the negative and be mindful. Use all that you've learned here," he asserts.

"I can try."

"Don't try. Do. You're more than capable, Christian." He crosses his legs and continues. "How are you getting on with your parents?"

"Much better." And I fill him in on my latest interaction with Grace.

"That all sounds great. And your dad?"

"Nothing to report since his surprise apology."

"Good." He pauses. "Did you get the e-mail I forwarded from Leila?"

"Yes. I don't want to see her."

"That's probably wise. I'll let her know."

"Thank you."

He smiles. "You know, you may not be looking forward to your wedding, but my wife is beyond excited."

I laugh.

"We're bringing the boys. I hope you've nailed everything down."

"I think Ros, my chief operating officer, is bringing her kids, too."

"Have you discussed children with Ana?"

"Only generally. We've got years to think about that. We're both young. In fact, I forget how young Ana is sometimes."

Yes, and I'm the sulky teen.

"You're both young." He glances at the clock on the wall behind me. "I think we're done, unless there's anything else you want to talk about? I won't see you in a professional capacity for a while."

"I'm good. Thanks for listening."

"It's my job. Remember. Don't dwell on the negative. Focus on the positive."

I nod and stand.

"And a bit of advice, on a personal level," John says. "Happy wife. Happy life. Trust me on this one."

I chuckle and he grins. "It's good to see you laugh, Christian."

ANA AND I STARE at each other. We lie in my bed...our bed, nose-to-nose, each sated, neither of us sleepy. "That was nice," Ana whispers.

I narrow my eyes. "There's that word again."

She grins, and I run my fingers down her cheek. Her smile fades.

"What is it?" I ask, and she shifts her gaze downward, away from me. "Ana?"

Her eyes find mine, and fix me with an intense stare. "We've not been too hasty, have we?" she asks in a rush, her voice breathy and quiet.

All my senses are suddenly on high alert.

Where the fuck is she going with this?

"No! Why do you think so?"

"It's just that I'm so happy right now, I don't know if I could be any happier. I don't want to change anything."

I close my eyes, savoring my relief. She lays her hand on my cheek. "Are you happy?" she asks.

Opening my eyes, I regard her with all the sincerity I can muster from every fiber of my being. "Of course I'm happy. You have no idea how you've changed my life for the better. But I'll be happier once we're married."

"You're anxious. I can see it in your eyes." Her fingers graze my chin.

"I'm anxious to make you mine."

"I am yours," she murmurs, and her words force a smile.

Mine.

I continue, "And we have to endure two days of enforced socializing."

She giggles. "Yes. There's that."

"I can't wait to take you away."

"I can't wait, either. Where are we going?"

"It's a surprise."

"I like surprises."

"I like you."

"I like you, too, Christian." She leans forward and kisses the tip of my nose.

"Are you sleepy?" I ask.

"No."

Good. "Me neither. I'm not finished with you yet."

E lliot takes a swig of Macallan. It's just after midnight, and he's sprawled out on my couch, feet up, taking up about as much space as he can. The man has no sense of decorum.

"Man, this is good scotch."

"Should be." *It's expensive.*

"What did she get you?" he asks. From my pocket I remove the turquoise Tiffany box that contains my wedding gift from Ana. Opening it up for the second time, I study the platinum cuff links, engraved with an elaborate C entwined with an A. She's never bought me anything like this, and I love them. I'll wear them tomorrow when we marry.

I hand them to Elliot and he nods in approval as he examines them. "Nice gift."

"Yes. They're perfect."

"It's late, bro." He yawns. "We should turn in. In case it's slipped your mind, you're getting hitched in the morning."

"We should." My sip of Armagnac warms the back of my mouth before sliding smoothly down my throat. "It'll be weird sleeping on my own."

Now, there's a sentence I never thought I'd utter.

"Tonight was cool," he says, ignoring me. "I dig Ana's parents. Bob doesn't say much. Come to think of it, Ana's dad doesn't, either."

"They're both taciturn." I arch an eyebrow. "Carla has a type."

Elliot laughs. "It's always the quiet ones. Like you, hotshot." He raises his glass and grins at me.

Fuck off, Elliot. I scowl at him. "Like me? I have no idea what you're alluding to, and I don't even want to think about it. They're my in-laws, for fuck's sake."

"I don't know. Ana's mom's hot. I could get into older women."

I'm not going there with Elliot!

"Dude! What about Kavanagh?"

He gives me a sheepish grin, and I think he's kidding. "Bet you're glad all the parentals hit it off." He steers us to safer ground. "And Ray is a Mariners fan, so he can't be all bad, but the jury is out on the Sounders. I'm not a fan of soccer."

I nod. It's a relief: even Raymond Steele loosened up under Grace's warm and tireless attention. And there's no animosity between him and Ana's mother, so that's good news. Ray has retired for the night. It's ironic that he's sleeping in the bedroom I had hoped would be Ana's, if she'd agreed to be my submissive.

Perhaps it's best if I keep that information to myself.

"And your Mrs. Jones did you proud," Elliot continues.

"She did. Gail is a great cook. I think she likes to stretch her culinary legs on occasion."

Elliot downs his drink and smacks his lips together in appreciation.

Uncouth, bro, uncouth.

"That's damn fine whisky, hotshot. I'm going to turn in. You?"

"I have some business to attend to."

Elliot looks at his watch. "Now? It's late."

"I need to deal with an e-mail that came in before dinner. It won't take long." I'm not sure I can sleep, anyway.

"It's your funeral…well, wedding." He grins and bounds off the couch with his usual spontaneous energy. "Good night. Try and sleep, K?" He punches me on the arm and takes his leave.

"Good night," I call after him. "Don't forget the rings!"

He responds with the finger. In spite of myself, he makes me chuckle. Rising, I slip the Tiffany box back in my pocket.

In my study, I open the e-mail that has been preoccupying me since I received it earlier this evening. It's from Welch, and it contains the report from the NTSB on *Charlie Tango*'s accident.

From: Welch, H. C.
Subject: NTSB Report
Date: July 29 2011 18:57
To: Christian Grey
Cc: J B Taylor

Mr. Grey

Attached is the detailed report from the National Transportation Safety Board. They have been more than thorough and confirm sabotage. The fuel lines were cut, allowing aviation kerosene to leak into the engines.

The report has been forwarded to the FBI and will be used to continue the criminal investigation. Fortunately, the NTSB has kept them updated and the FBI dusted for prints last week as part of their investigation. They are in the process of eliminating the engineers and ground staff from their inquiries, but at present they're no nearer to finding a suspect.

Tomorrow I'd like to move the Gulfstream to Sea-Tac, so you'll depart from there and not Boeing Field. I'll arrange for you to be dropped off airside.

I've added four additional security officers to your wedding detail. Résumés are attached. Taylor has approved them. Two of them have been dispatched to the wedding venue to keep watch overnight.

Apologies for this arriving on the eve of your nuptials.

Leave this with us. And try to enjoy your big day.

Welch

Fuck. Our instincts were right.
But who wants to kill me? Who?
I type a quick response to Welch.

From: Christian Grey
Subject: NTSB Report
Date: July 30 2011 12:23
To: Welch, H. C.
Cc: J B Taylor

Agreed. And thanks.

Christian Grey
CEO, Grey Enterprises Holdings, Inc.

I toss back the remains of my Armagnac and decide to read the full report in bed. I'm on my own because Ana left with my parents to stay at their place tonight.

To hell with these stupid traditions.

She should be here. With me. I miss her.

At least Sawyer went with her. He'll watch over her.

As I gather up the pages of the NTSB report from my printer, my mood grows bleaker. I am done with this shit.

The report is extensive and rather dull, but in spite of my drooping eyelids, I manage to finish it. The next steps are to hand *Charlie Tango* over to the FBI, and once they've finished with her, they'll return her to Eurocopter for a full assessment. I'm hopeful she can be repaired and GEH won't have to deal with any insurance adjusters.

I switch off my side light and stare up at the ceiling.

Why is this happening the night before my wedding?

I'm shrouded in darkness, and conscious of an empty feeling creeping into my chest. I'm now able to recognize it as loneliness; my heart is missing a piece, as Ana is not beside me. Though, strictly speaking, I'm not alone. My future father-in-law is probably asleep above me, Elliot is in the spare bedroom next door, and the staff quarters are almost at capacity. But Anastasia Steele is conspicuous by her absence. I wish she were here; I'd wrap her in my arms and lose myself in her. I'm tempted to text her, but it might wake her, and she needs her sleep. *Fuck it.* Without her, I'm lost. And someone out there wants me dead, and we don't know who.

Damn. Push it from your mind, Grey.

I close my eyes.

Breathe, Grey. Breathe.
I start counting sheep.

We are soaring. Ana is in front of the cockpit, her hands
stretched out to the canopy, squealing with joy and wonder.
My heart is full. This is happiness. This is love. This is what
it feels like. We're on top of the world. Our life stretched
in a colorful patchwork of greens and browns beneath us.
I bank, and suddenly I'm in a tailspin. Ana is screaming.
Screaming. We're in *Charlie Tango* and we're losing height. I
smell the fire. I'm fighting the controls to keep my helicopter
upright. I need to find a place to land. All I hear is the roar
of the engines and Ana screaming. We're going down. *Fuck.*
Spinning. Down. Down. Down. *Shit.* I'm going to hit the
ground. No. No! Ana is lying on a sticky green rug. I'm
shaking her. She won't wake up. Ana. Ana. Ana! There's a
crash. And he fills the doorway. *There you are, you little shit!*
No. *No.* Ana. Ana. *Ana!*

I'm jerked awake, a fine film of sweat bathing my chest and stomach in the first blink of dawn.
It's too early.
I rub my face, bringing my breathing and terror under control,
then close my eyes and turn over. Reaching out, I grab Ana's pillow
and tug it toward me. I immerse myself in her scent. *Ah…*

Grandpa Theodore hands me an apple. It's bright red. And
sweet. There's a light breeze on my face. It's cooling in the
sunshine. We stand together in the orchard. He holds my
hand. His palm is rough with calluses. Mom and Dad and
Elliot are coming. They have a picnic basket. Dad lays out
the blanket. And Ana sits down on the blanket. Ana. She's
here. With me. With us. She laughs. And I laugh. Ana
caresses my face. *Here,* she says. And she hands me Baby
Mia. *Mia.* And suddenly I'm six again. *Mee-a,* I whisper.
Mom looks at me. *What did you say? Mee-a. Yes. Yes.*

Darling boy. You have your words. Mia. Her name is Mia.
And Mommy starts to cry happy tears.

I open my eyes, startled by an image from my dream that I can't quite grasp.

What was I dreaming about?

The sun is higher in the sky, announcing that it's a more acceptable time to rise. I shake my head to rouse myself, and then I remember—today, I make Ana mine.

Today, at 12 p.m.

Yes!

And then I get to spend three weeks with her in Europe. I can't wait to show Ana all the sights. As I lie in bed feeling excited about what I have planned, I have an idea.

Hmm… I'm going to pack a few toys from the playroom to add to the fun.

Yes.

I bound out of bed, grab a T-shirt, and head toward the kitchen. From the corridor I hear voices. Ray is sitting at the kitchen counter, tucking into bacon, eggs, hash browns, and sausages. He's chatting with Mrs. Jones. Unlike me, he's dressed, in his wedding shirt and tuxedo pants. "Good morning," I greet him.

"Good morning, Christian. How are you feeling?"

"Good."

"Morning, Mr. Grey," Gail gushes. "Coffee?"

"Please."

"It's a mighty fine place you have here," Ray says, motioning to the ceiling with his knife.

"Thank you."

"Ana tells me you've bought a house."

"Yes. It's up the coast."

Ray nods. "She says you have a place in Aspen and New York, too."

"Um…yes. You know, property. Um. It's about diversifying my portfolio."

He nods, but gives nothing away. "A lot of places for one person to mind."

"Well, after today, there'll be two of us minding them."

His eyebrows rise high into his forehead, and a slow smile that is either admiration or incredulity spreads across his face. I hope it's admiration. "I guess you're right," he says.

I want to move the conversation off this topic. "Did you sleep well?"

"I did. That room is probably one of the fanciest I've ever stayed in. And that is some view."

"I'm glad you were comfortable."

"Here you are, Mr. Grey." Mrs. Jones places a black coffee on the counter in front of me.

"Thank you, Gail."

"What would you like for breakfast?"

"What Ray's having."

She smiles. "Coming right up, sir."

I slide onto the stool beside Ray and ask him if he's been fishing recently. His eyes light up.

EVEN I HAVE TO admit that Elliot looks good in a tux. We're in the back of the Q7, and nearing our parents' place in Bellevue. "How are you feeling?" he asks.

"I wish people would stop asking me that."

"You? Nervous? You're the coolest dude I know. What gives? Is it because you're saddling yourself to the same woman for the rest of your life? I'd be nervous, too."

I roll my eyes. "Your promiscuity knows no bounds, Elliot. One of these days someone is going to turn your world upside down. I didn't know it would happen to me. And yet here we are."

His eyes cloud, and he looks out of the window as we pull up to our parents' house. There are a number of cars queuing for the valet service, and guests in their wedding finery are following the pale pink carpet to the rear of the house. As Taylor steers us into the driveway, two guys in dark suits, with discreet earpieces and regulation aviators, step forward and open our doors. They're the additional security.

"Ready?" asks Elliot with a quick, reassuring glance at me. "If you want to back out, there's still time."

"Fuck off."

He grins and climbs out of the car.

I take a deep breath.

This is it.

Showtime, Grey.

My phone buzzes and I glance at it.

Fuck. My scalp tingles. It's a text from Elena.

> **ELENA**
> You're making a big mistake. I know
> you. But I'll be here for you when
> your life falls apart. And it will. I'll
> be here because in spite of what I
> said I love you. I'll always love you.

What the everlasting fuck is this?

"Christian," Elliot distracts me. "Are you coming?" He's waiting.

"Yes," I snap. I quickly delete the text and climb out of the car.

Fuck her.

"You okay?" Elliot frowns when I join him.

"Yes. Let's do this." I storm ahead, trying to bring my burst of anger under control. How dare Elena try to derail me on my wedding day! I ignore the young woman who's standing on the path, all smiles. She's carrying a clipboard, but I charge past her, leaving Elliot to check in with her, as I head through the front door. Grace is in the hall.

"Darling, you're here."

"Mother."

"You look so handsome, Christian." She puts her arms around me, gives me a swift, restrained hug, and inclines her head toward me, offering a cheek.

"Mom," I whisper, and she steps back, concern flashing in her eyes. "Are you okay?"

I nod, not trusting myself to speak.

"Ana is upstairs—you can't see her until the wedding. She slept in your room last night. Come with me." She takes my hand and leads me down the hallway into the den.

"Is it nerves, darling? I'd hug you properly, but I don't want to get makeup on your suit," Grace says. "The aesthetician put it on with a trowel. It will take months to get it off."

I laugh, and I'm so grateful that it's Grace I got to see first. "I'm okay, Mom."

She clasps both of my hands. "Are you sure?"

"Yes." My anger has evaporated, beaten back by the woman I call Mom, and I resolve that, today of all days, I will not think about Mrs. Lincoln.

"I'm so excited for you, darling," Grace adds, beaming up at me.

"You look good, Mom. Makeup and all."

"Thank you, dear. Oh, the donations to Coping Together have been unprecedented. I can't thank you enough. It's so generous of you."

I chuckle. "That was Ana's idea. Not mine."

"Oh, that's lovely." She's trying to hide her surprise.

"I told you. She's not acquisitive."

"Of course she isn't. It's a wonderful gesture on both your parts. Are you sure you're okay?"

"Yes. I got an aggravating text from an old business associate."

Grace narrows her eyes, and I think I may have said too much, but she chooses to ignore my explanation and checks her watch. "Kickoff is in fifteen minutes. I have your boutonniere here. Now, do you want to wait here, or go out to the pavilion?"

"I think Elliot and I should go take our seats and wait."

Mom pins the white rose to my lapel and steps back to admire her handiwork.

"Oh, darling." She stops, placing her fingers over her lips, and I think she's going to cry.

Shit. Mom.

My throat tightens, but Elliot steps into the room, saving us both. "What am I, chopped liver?" he chastises Grace, with a wicked gleam in his eye.

"Oh, darling. You look so handsome, too." She recovers and cups his face and pinches his cheeks, and I feel a momentary stab of envy that they have such a touchy-feely relationship.

"Mom, you look like a queen." My brother, charming as ever, plants a kiss on her forehead. She laughs, a girlish, sweet laugh, and she pats her hair.

"You boys," she admonishes us. "You'd better get out there. The ushers will show you where to go. But first let me pin on your boutonniere, Elliot."

AS WE HEAD TO the pavilion, Taylor intercepts me.

"Sir, I've picked up Miss Steele's suitcase, and everything else has been sent on to Sea-Tac."

"Excellent. Thanks, Taylor."

His lips twitch into a smile. "Good luck, sir."

I nod my thanks and continue with Elliot toward the barnlike tent.

A STRING QUARTET IS playing "Halo" by Beyoncé while I wait for Miss Anastasia Steele. My folks have gone all-out; the pavilion looks opulent. Elliot and I are seated at the front of several rows of gold chairs, which are filling up fast. I stare at the scene in front of me, noting all the details, hoping it will distract me from my nerves. A pale pink carpet leads to an impressive, arched flowery bower pitched at the water's edge. It's made of white and pink roses, intertwined with ivy and pale pink peonies that remind me of Ana's blushing cheeks. Reverend Michael Walsh, my mother's friend and her hospital's chaplain, will officiate. He's standing in his designated place patiently waiting, like us. His dark eyes twinkle at Elliot and me. Behind the floral arch the sun skips across the shining waters of Meydenbauer Bay. It's a beautiful day to get married. One of the official photographers is stationed near Walsh, and her lens is directed at me. I look away and turn to Elliot. "You've got the rings?" I ask, probably for the tenth time.

"Yes," he hisses.

"Dude! Just checking."

I turn and survey our guests as they arrive, nodding and waving to those I know. Bastille and his wife are here; Flynn arrives with his wife, Rhian, each holding one of their small boys firmly by the hand.

Taylor and Gail are seated together. The photographer José Rodriguez and his father are here. Ros arrives with her partner, Gwen, and they usher their little girls into their seats. Eamon Kavanagh; his wife, Britt; and Ethan are here—Mia will be pleased. Mac salutes me; he's sitting with a young blond woman I've not seen before. Grandma and Grandpa Trevelyan are shown to their seats near us. Grandma waves enthusiastically at both Elliot and me. Alondra Gutierrez is in the background, directing her small team of people. There are a number of guests that I don't recognize—either friends of my folks or of Ana's parents. My mother and father and Carla and Bob make their way to the front of the gathering to take their seats. My dad breaks rank and dashes toward us. He's brimming with pride, and Elliot and I both stand to greet him.

"Dad." I hold my hand out to shake his, but he takes it and pulls me into a bearlike hug.

"Good luck, son," he enthuses. "I'm so proud of you."

"Thanks, Dad." I squeeze the words past the sudden tangled knot of emotion that's lodged in my throat.

"Elliot." Carrick hugs him, too.

The general buzz of the congregation changes to an expectant hush. Dad scuttles back to his seat behind us as the string quartet breaks into "Chasing Cars."

Of course, Snow Patrol. One of Ana's favorite bands.

She loves this song.

Mia is walking down the central aisle, dressed in a pale pink explosion of tulle. Behind her, Kate Kavanagh looks sleek and elegant in a pale pink silk gown.

Ana.

My mouth dries.

She's stunning.

She's in a fitted white lace dress, her shoulders bare but for a gossamer-thin veil. Her hair is pinned in an updo with a few tendrils framing her beautiful face. Her bridal bouquet is intricate—made of pink and white roses woven together. Ray walks by her side, his hand covering hers as she grips his arm, and it's obvious he's holding back his tears.

Oh shit. The knot tightens in my throat.

Ana's eyes meet mine, and beneath her veil her face lights up like a summer's day, her smile electrifying.

Oh, baby.

They walk up beside us and Ana passes her bouquet to Kate, who stands with Mia. Ray raises Ana's veil and kisses her cheek. "I love you, Annie," I hear him say, his voice hoarse, and, turning to me, he gives me Ana's hand. Our eyes meet, his glistening, and I have to look away because his expression may be my undoing.

"Hi," I say to my bride, because that's all I'm capable of right now.

"Hi," she replies, and squeezes my hand.

"You look lovely."

"So do you." She grins, and all my nerves melt away, as does the music, and it's just Ana and me and Reverend Michael. He clears his throat, commanding everybody's attention, and the wedding begins.

"Dearly beloved, we are gathered here today to witness the joining in matrimony of Christian Trevelyan-Grey and Anastasia Rose Steele." The good reverend smiles benevolently down at both of us, and I tighten my hold on Ana's hand.

He asks the congregation if anyone knows of any impediment to our marriage. Elena's text flits through my mind, and I'm annoyed with myself that I let it. Fortunately, Ana distracts me by glancing back at the crowd. When no one says anything, a collective sigh of relief flutters through the gathering, followed by muffled chuckles and titters. Ana peeks up at me, her eyes sparkling in amusement.

"Phew," I mouth.

Ana stifles her smile.

Reverend Michael asks us each in turn to declare that there's no legal reason why we can't be joined in marriage.

As he addresses us about the seriousness of our commitment to each other, the burning sensation returns to my throat. Ana watches him, absorbed, and I notice she's wearing elegant drop pearl earrings I've not seen before. I wonder if they are a present from her folks.

"And now I invite both of you to offer your vows to each other." He looks encouragingly at me. "Christian?"

I take a deep breath, and gazing at the love of my life, I recite my vows from memory, my words ringing out over the throng: "I, Christian Trevelyan-Grey, do take thee, Anastasia Rose Steele, to be my lawfully wedded wife. I solemnly vow that I will safeguard, and hold dear and deep in my heart, our union and you. I promise to love you faithfully, forsaking all others, through the good times and the bad, in sickness and in health, regardless of where life takes us. I will protect you, trust you, and respect you."

Tears glimmer in Ana's eyes and the tip of her nose turns a fetching pink.

"I will share your joys and sorrows, and comfort you in times of need. I promise to cherish you and uphold your hopes and dreams and keep you safe at my side. All that is mine is now yours. I give you my hand, my heart, and my love, from this moment on, for as long as we both shall live."

Ana wipes a tear from her eye, and I take a deep breath, relieved that I've remembered the words.

"Ana?" the good reverend prompts her. From beneath her sleeve she takes a small slip of pink paper and reads:

"I, Anastasia Rose Steele, do take thee, Christian Trevelyan-Grey, to be my lawfully wedded husband. I give you my solemn vow to be your faithful partner, in sickness and in health, to stand by your side in good times and in bad, to share your joy as well as your sorrow." She gazes up at me and continues her vows without reading, and I stop breathing. "I promise to love you unconditionally, to support you in your goals and dreams, to honor and respect you, to laugh with you and cry with you, to share my hopes and dreams with you, and bring you solace in times of need. And to cherish you for as long as we both shall live." She blinks back her tears, and I fight mine.

"You two will now exchange rings as a symbol of your abiding love for each other. A ring is a constant circle. It is unbroken and everlasting, a symbol of perpetual unity. So, too, will be your commitment to each other and to this marriage, from this day forth, until death do you part.

"Christian, place the ring on Anastasia's finger." Elliot hands me Ana's ring and I position it at the tip of Ana's left ring finger.

"Repeat after me," Reverend Michael says. "Anastasia, I give you this ring as a sign of our enduring faith in each other, our unity and our everlasting love."

I repeat the words, loud and clear, and slip the ring fully onto Ana's finger.

"Anastasia, place the ring on Christian's finger," Reverend Michael says. Elliot flashes a grin at Ana and passes her my ring.

"Repeat after me," the reverend continues. "Christian, I give you this ring as a sign of our enduring faith in each other, our unity and our everlasting love."

Ana's words sound out sweetly for the rest of the congregation to hear, and she slips the ring onto my finger.

Reverend Michael clasps both of our hands in his and says in a booming voice to our audience, "Love is the reason we are here. Marriage is founded on love. These two young people have pledged their everlasting love to each other. We honor them and wish them strength, courage, and trust to grow together, to learn from each other and to remain true to each other on the path that life takes them.

"Christian and Anastasia, you two have agreed to be married and to live together in matrimony. You have declared your love for each other and promised to uphold that love with your vows. With the power vested in me by the state of Washington, I now declare you husband and wife." He releases our hands and Ana beams up at me.

Wife.

Mine.

My heart soars.

"You may kiss the bride," Reverend Michael says with a huge grin.

"Finally, you're mine," I whisper, and pull her into my arms, flush against me, and plant a soft kiss on her lips. There are tiny buttons at the back of her dress and I fantasize about slowly undoing them. I ignore the cheers and applause from our guests, as my body comes alive. "You look beautiful, Ana." I caress her face. "Don't let anyone take that dress off but me, understand?" I gaze down at her, trying to convey a sensual promise. She nods, her eyes darkening with desire.

Oh, Ana.

I want to pick her up and carry her to my boyhood room and consummate our marriage. *Now.* But I'm sure I won't get away with that.

Get a grip, Grey.

"Ready to party, Mrs. Grey?" I smile at my wife.

"Ready as I'll ever be."

I bask in the warmth of her smile. Taking her hand, I extend the other to Reverend Michael.

"Thank you, Reverend. That was a lovely ceremony. And it was brief."

"I had my instructions," he says, and shakes our hands in turn. "Congratulations, both of you."

I have to release Ana as Kate drags her into a hug, and Elliot wraps his arms around me. "Man, you did it. Congratulations."

"Christian!" Mia hollers, and barrels into my arms. "I love Ana! I love you!" she gushes, and crushes me.

"Mia. Steady. I need my ribs intact."

So begins an endless round of congratulations, kisses, and hugs. I gird my loins to tolerate all the unnecessary touching I'm about to endure. It helps that I'm elated. When I turn to my mother, she's sobbing. I give her a brief hug, mindful of her makeup, while Carrick slaps me on the back. Carla and Bob are next. Ray Steele shakes my hand, squeezing harder and harder.

"Congratulations, Christian. You should know, if you hurt her, I'll kill you."

"I'd expect no less, Ray."

"I'm glad we understand each other." He grins and releases my now throbbing hand and claps me on the back. I flex my fingers and remind myself that Raymond Steele is ex-army.

SIPPING A COUPE OF vintage Grande Année Rosé, I watch my beautiful wife as she makes her way toward me. We've just completed what feels like a major photoshoot with the wedding photographers, and now I'm standing near our table in the hope of having a bite to eat—getting married has given me an appetite. Ana stops every so often to talk to our guests, welcoming them and graciously receiving their good wishes. Her light shines so bright, her smile bringing everyone she greets to life.

She's an extraordinary person. A stunning woman.

And she's mine.

When she finally reaches me, I take her hand and pull it to my lips. "Hi," I whisper. "I've missed you."

"Hi. I've missed you, too."

"You've dispensed with your veil. It was lovely."

"It was. But people kept treading on it!"

I cringe. "That must have been annoying."

"It was."

My father takes the microphone. "Good afternoon, all," he says. "Welcome to our home here in Bellevue, and to Christian and Ana's wedding. If you don't know me, I am very proud to say I am Christian's dad, Carrick. I'm hoping to speak to all of you at some point during the afternoon or evening. In the meantime, you should all have a glass of the good stuff and I'd like us all to raise our glasses to Christian and his beautiful wife, Ana. Congratulations you two. Welcome to the family, Ana. And both of you, be kind to each other. To Christian and Ana!"

My father gives me a warm, tender smile, which I feel all the way to my toes. I raise my glass to him as everyone raises their glasses and the words "Christian and Ana" hover around us all.

"Please make your way to your table. We'll be starting lunch shortly," Dad continues.

I pull out Ana's chair; she sits and I take the seat beside her. From here we have the best view of the entire pavilion. I'm thankful to be seated at last. I'm ravenous. The table looks lovely covered in white linen and floral arrangements with white and pink roses. Our parents join us, with Elliot and Kate and Mia and Bob.

Ana and my mom have opted for a buffet, but as the bridal party, we're served our appetizers while our guests find their seats. There's fresh sourdough, with some herby-looking butter, and a delicious cheese soufflé with a delicate garden salad. My wife and I tuck in.

ELLIOT IS GOING TO make a speech. He's had several glasses of champagne, so this could go either way. We've finished our entrée of king salmon en croute and I take a gulp of Bollinger and brace myself.

Elliot winks at me and rises from the table. "Good afternoon, everyone. Welcome. I've drawn the short straw—I mean, I'm honored to be Christian's best man, and his brother, and to be asked to make a speech. But forgive me—public speaking is not my thing. Growing up with Christian Grey was not my thing, either. He was a nightmare of a brother. Just ask my folks."

Fuck! Elliot? But this gets a laugh. Ana squeezes my hand.

"This man can beat the shit out of me and did, frequently. And any of you who have ever kickboxed with him will know, don't mess with him. He's badass. He's a solitary guy. When he was younger he'd rather have had his head stuck in a book than be out tearing up the town with the likes of me. You've all heard how he found school challenging, so I'll gloss over that—but somehow, by some fluke, and not because he's smart or anything, he managed to get some sort of education and even talked his way into Harvard.

"But it turned out Harvard wasn't for him, either. He wanted to throw himself into the world of commerce and high finance. So, he did…he's doing kinda okay with that." Elliot shrugs, apparently unimpressed, and again the audience laughs.

"During this whole time, not once did he show any interest in the opposite sex. None. Well, I'll leave you to deduce what we all thought."

Oh, for fuck's sake. I roll my eyes, and Elliot grins. "So, imagine our collective surprise and delight when not too long ago he shows up with this beautiful young woman, Anastasia Steele. It was obvious from the beginning that she'd captured his heart. And for some strange reason, maybe she was dropped on her head as a child"—he shrugs once more—"she fell for him."

Again, with the laughter from our guests!

"Today they tied the knot, and I just want to say, Christian, Ana, congratulations. We are rooting for you. And no, she's not pregnant!"

There's a communal gasp around all the tables.

"To our bride and groom, Ana and Christian!" He raises his glass. I want to kill him, and judging by Ray Steele's expression, so does he.

Ana's cheeks are pink, and she looks a little shocked.

"Thanks, Elliot," she says, laughing.

I throw my napkin at him and turn to Ana. "Shall we cut the cake?"

"Sure."

THE DJ IS PRIMED and ready as Ana and I make our way to the dance floor. I sweep her into my arms as everyone gathers around us, and Ana settles her arms around my neck. The sweet, soulful words of the song ring through the pavilion, and from the corner of my eye I see Carla clutch her throat in recognition. And then I've only got eyes for my wife as Corinne Bailey Rae starts to sing "Like a Star."

Everyone else fades away. And it's just the two of us gliding across the floor. "Like a star across my sky," Ana whispers. She lifts her lips to mine and I'm lost…and found.

"MOM, THANK YOU FOR not insisting on a Catholic wedding."

"Don't be ridiculous, Christian. I couldn't force it on you. I thought Michael did a wonderful service."

"He did." Leaning forward, I kiss my mother on her forehead. She closes her eyes, and when she opens them again they burn with a curious intensity. "You look so happy, darling. I'm so thrilled for both of you."

"Thanks, Mom."

I glance over to where Kate and Ana are in a deep conversation. Elliot is watching them. No. Elliot is watching Kate. He can't take his eyes off her. Perhaps he cares for her more than he's letting on.

The dance floor is full; Ray and Carla are taking a turn. They really do get on. I glance at my watch—it's 5 p.m.—time we thought about leaving. I amble over toward my wife. Kate hugs her, hard, then grins at me, and I feel slightly less antagonistic toward her.

"Hi, baby." I slip my arms around Ana and kiss her temple. "Kate," I acknowledge her.

"Hello again, Christian. I'm off to find your best man, who happens to be my best man, too." With a smile to us both, she heads over to Elliot, who is drinking with Ethan and José.

"Time to go," I whisper.

I'm done with this party. I want to be alone with my wife.

"Already?" Ana says. "This is the first party I've been to where I don't mind being the center of attention." She turns in my arms and smiles up at me.

"You deserve to be. You look stunning, Anastasia."

"So do you."

"This beautiful dress becomes you." I love how it reveals her enticing shoulders.

"This old thing?" She peers up at me, in that way that she does, all shy and bewitching through her lashes. She's irresistible. Leaning down, I kiss her.

"Let's go. I don't want to share you with all these people anymore."

"Can we leave our own wedding?"

"Baby, it's our party, and we can do whatever we want. We've cut the cake. And right now, I'd like to whisk you away and have you all to myself."

She giggles. "You have me for a lifetime, Mr. Grey."

"I'm very glad to hear that, Mrs. Grey."

"Oh, there you two are! Such lovebirds."

Oh shit. Grandma Trevelyan strikes.

"Christian, darling—one more dance with your grandma?"

"Of course, Grandmother." I swallow my sigh.

"And you, beautiful Anastasia, go and make an old man happy— dance with Theo."

"Theo, Mrs. Trevelyan?"

"Grandpa Trevelyan. And I think you can call me Grandma. Now, you two seriously need to get working on my great-grandkids. I won't last too much longer." Her smile borders on the lecherous.

Grandma! Jesus!

"Come, Grandmother," I say, hastily.

We have years before we have to think about kids.

I lead her slowly onto the dance floor, glancing apologetically back at Ana and rolling my eyes. "Laters, baby!"

Ana gives me a little wave.

"Oh, darling boy, you look so handsome in your suit. And your bride! Stunning. You'll make beautiful children together."

"One day, Grandmother. Are you enjoying the wedding?" I need to move her on to another subject.

"Your parents know how to throw a party. Of course, your mother gets that from me. Theo would rather be puttering around on the farm. But then you know that."

"I do." I have a stack of fond memories of helping Grandpa in his orchard. It's one of my favorite places. "I'll have to bring Ana to visit."

"You must. You promise, now."

"I promise."

We shuffle around the dance floor to "Just the Way You Are," a Bruno Mars track, which morphs into "Moves Like Jagger" by Maroon 5. My grandmother is loving it. I think she may have consumed a little too much Bollinger. But when the first few bars of "Sex on Fire" blast over the speakers, I decide it's time to deliver Grandma back to her table.

Ana is not here. I sit down with Grandpa Trevelyan, and he tells me how he's expecting a bumper harvest this fall. "Those apples'll be the sweetest yet!"

"I can't wait to try one," I shout, because he's a little hard of hearing.

"You happy, boy?" he asks.

"Very."

"Yeah. You look it." He pats my knee. "It's good to see. Your bride, she's a beautiful girl. You take good care of her, mind, and she'll take good care of you."

"I'm going to do just that. Right now, I'm going to find her. Good to see you, Grandpa."

"I think she went to the restroom."

I stand and Flynn approaches me, holding one of his boys, asleep on his shoulder. Rhian, his wife, holds the other—also out for the count.

"John!"

"Christian, congratulations. Lovely wedding." He shakes my hand. "You know, I'd hug you, but I'm burdened with a small child, and I think it might breach my doctor-patient ethics."

I laugh. "You're good. Thanks for coming."

"Good day, Christian," Rhian says. "Great wedding. We have to take these two rascals home."

"They were very well behaved."

"That's because we drugged them." She winks.

I gasp.

"That's a joke." John side-eyes his wife. "Tempting though that might be on occasion, we've not resorted to it yet."

She laughs. "They're exhausted from running around the yard. Your folks have so much space, here."

"Enjoy your honeymoon," Flynn says, and takes Rhian's hand.

"Thank you, good-bye."

I watch them stroll across the lawn toward the house, weighed down by their responsibilities.

Better them than me.

I spy Ana standing on the terrace by the French doors to the house and text Taylor that we'd like to leave. I stick my hands in my pants pockets and amble over the lawn toward my wife. She's pensive as she watches the dancing and the luminous dusk over distant Seattle.

I wonder what she's thinking about.

"Hi," I say as I reach her.

"Hi." She smiles.

"Let's go." I'm a little impatient to be alone with my wife.

"I have to change." She reaches for my hand, and I think she means to drag me inside, but I resist. Her brows knit together in confusion. "I thought you wanted to be the one to take this dress off," she states.

"Correct." I squeeze her hand. "But I'm not undressing you here. We wouldn't leave until…I don't know." I wave my hand, hoping that's enough of an explanation.

She blushes and releases me.

As much as I want to peel her out of that dress, we have a jet waiting for us with an allotted takeoff time. "And don't take your hair down, either," I whisper, trying and failing to keep my desire out of my tone.

"But—" She frowns.

"No buts, Anastasia. You look beautiful. And I want to be the one to undress you. Pack your going-away clothes. You'll need them." For when we arrive at our destination. "Taylor has your main suitcase."

"Okay." She gives me a sweet smile, and I leave her and go in search of my mother and Alondra to tell them we're off. It's Alondra I find first.

"Thank you." I shake her hand. "Everything went so well."

"You're so welcome, Mr. Grey. I'll round everyone up right now."

"Great. Thanks again."

A MISTY-EYED CARLA WATCHES her daughter and ex-husband exchanging an awkward hug while Ana clutches her wedding bouquet. Ana's eyes glisten.

"You'll make one hell of a wife, too," Ray murmurs, and once again tears glint in his eyes. Spying me, he shakes his head, and then my hand, warmly. "Look after my girl, Christian."

"I fully intend to, Ray. Carla." I give Ana's mom a kiss on the cheek.

Outside the French doors, our remaining guests have gathered and formed a human arch from the terrace around the side of the house and all the way to the front.

I check Ana's expression. Her smile is back. "Ready?"

"Yes."

Hand in hand, we duck beneath all the outstretched arms and dash through the arch, where we're showered with rice and good wishes and luck and love. At the end, my mom and dad are waiting.

"Thank you, Mom," I whisper as she hugs me, no longer worried about getting makeup on my suit. Dad pulls me into another hug.

"Well done, son. Have a wonderful honeymoon."

They both kiss and hug Ana, and Grace starts crying again.

Mom! Get it together.

Taylor, standing by the driver's door, moves to open the back passenger door. I shake my head, and instead I open it for Ana, who turns suddenly and tosses her wedding bouquet into the waiting crowd. Mia catches it with a loud whoop of joy that can be heard above the whistles and cheers of approval from everyone gathered to say good-bye.

I help Ana into the Audi, scooping her dress up so it doesn't catch in the door. Giving everyone a quick wave, I sprint to the other side of the car, where Taylor is holding open my door.

"Congratulations, sir," he says warmly.

"Thank you, Taylor." I slide in beside my wife.

Thank God! We're finally leaving. I thought we'd never get away.

Taylor eases the Audi down the driveway to the sound of enthusi-astic cheers and rice pelting the car. Reaching for Ana's hand, I draw her knuckles to my lips and kiss each one in turn. "So far so good, Mrs. Grey?"

"So far so wonderful, Mr. Grey. Where are we going?"

"Sea-Tac."

Ana looks puzzled, so I brush my thumb across her lip.

"Trust me?"

"Implicitly," she breathes.

"How was your wedding?"

"Fantastic. Yours?"

"Amazing." And we're grinning at each other like idiots.

WE DRIVE AIRSIDE THROUGH the security gates at Sea-Tac and steer toward the GEH Gulfstream. "Don't tell me you're misusing company property again!" Ana blurts when she spots the plane. Her eyes shine and she grips my hand, radiating excitement.

"Oh, I hope so, Anastasia." I give her my most wicked grin.

Taylor stops the car at the foot of the steps to the plane, climbs out, and opens my door. I exit. "Thanks again, Taylor. We'll see you in London," I murmur, so Ana doesn't hear.

"I'm looking forward to it, sir. Safe travels."

"You, too."

"I'll grab Mrs. Grey's hand luggage," he says, and my heart warms at Ana's new honorific. I walk around to her door and open it wide. Leaning in, I lift her into my arms.

"What are you doing?" she squeals.

"Carrying you over the threshold."

She giggles, wrapping her arms around my neck, and I carry her up the plane steps, where we're met by Captain Stephan.

"Welcome aboard, sir. Mrs. Grey," he greets us, with a bold grin. I set Ana down and shake his hand. "Congratulations to you both," he continues.

"Thank you, Stephan. Anastasia, you know Stephan. He's our captain today, and this is First Officer Beighley."

"Delighted to meet you," Beighley says to Ana.

Ana looks a little shell-shocked, but she responds in kind to them both.

"All preparations complete?" I ask Beighley.

"Yes, sir," she replies with her usual confidence.

"We have the all clear," Stephan informs us. "Weather is good from here to Boston."

"Turbulence?"

"Not before Boston. There's a weather front over Shannon that might give us a rough ride."

"I see. Well, we hope to sleep through it all."

"We'll get underway, sir," Stephan says. "We'll leave you in the capable care of Natalia, your flight attendant."

Natalia?

Where's Sara?

Natalia looks vaguely familiar.

I ignore my misgivings. "Excellent," I say to Stephan, and taking Ana's hand, I guide her to one of the seats. "Sit."

She does as she's told, folding herself into the seat with surprising grace. I remove my jacket, undo the buttons on my vest, and sit down opposite her.

"Welcome aboard, sir, ma'am, and congratulations," Natalia welcomes us, poised with two crystal flutes of pink champagne.

"Thank you." I take both and offer one to Ana, while Natalia disappears into the galley.

"Here's to a happy married life, Anastasia." I raise my glass to Ana's and we clink.

"Bollinger?" she asks.

"The same." We've been drinking it for most of the afternoon.

"The first time I drank this it was out of teacups." Her eyes have a faraway look.

"I remember that day well. Your graduation."

What a day that was... I think spanking was involved. Hmm... and a discussion about soft and hard limits.

I shift in my seat.

"Where are we going?" Ana drags me back to the now.

"Shannon."

"In Ireland?" she squeaks.

"To refuel."

"Then?" Ana's eyes are out on stalks; her excitement is contagious.

I grin at her and say nothing, tantalizing her.

"Christian!"

I put her out of her misery. "London."

She gasps, looking shocked and awed at once. Then her light-up-Seattle smile is back.

"Then Paris. Then the South of France," I continue.

I think Ana is going to combust.

"I know you've always dreamed of going to Europe. I want to make your dreams come true, Anastasia."

"You are my dreams come true, Christian."

"Back at you, Mrs. Grey." Her words warm my soul, and I take another sip of champagne. "Buckle up."

Ana grins. I think she's pleased. And so am I. We're flying through the sunset to chase the dawn on the other side of the Atlantic.

ONCE WE'RE AIRBORNE, NATALIA serves us dinner. Again, I'm starving.

Why?

Getting married really takes it out of a man. Ana and I discuss our highlights of the wedding. Mine was seeing her for the first time in her beautiful dress.

"Mine was seeing you," Ana confesses. "And that you were *there*!"

"There?"

"Part of me had wondered if this was all a dream and that maybe you wouldn't show up."

"Ana, wild horses couldn't have dragged me away."

"Dessert, Mr. Grey?" Natalia asks.

I decline, and turn to study my wife. Running my finger across my bottom lip, I watch Ana, waiting for her response.

"No, thank you," she says to Natalia, gazing intently at me. Natalia leaves us.

Oh, sweet heaven. I'm going to claim my wife.

"Good," I whisper. "I'd rather planned on having you for dessert."

Ana's eyes meet mine and darken while her teeth tease her bottom lip.

Rising from the table, I offer her my hand. "Come." We head to the back of the cabin, away from the galley and the cockpit. I point to a door at the far end. "There's a bathroom here." Passing through a short corridor, we emerge into the aft cabin where the queen-size bed is ready for us.

I pull Ana into my arms. "I thought we'd spend our wedding night at thirty-five thousand feet. It's something I've never done before."

Ana inhales sharply, and the sound echoes in my groin.

"But first I have to get you out of this fabulous dress."

Her breathing deepens. She wants this, too.

"Turn around," I whisper.

She complies instantly, and I study her updo. Each hairpin has a tiny pearl on it—they're exquisite. *Like Ana.* Gently, I start to extract each one, letting every strand of her hair fall free. My fingertips graze her temple, her neck, her earlobe, but it's the lightest of touches. I want to tease and tantalize the hell out of my wife. And it's working. She's surreptitiously shifting her weight from foot to foot. She's restless. Impatient. Her breathing is louder.

She's aroused.

Just by my touch. And for me, her response is equally arousing.

"You have such beautiful hair, Ana." I breathe the words against her temple, enjoying her delicious fragrance, and a soft sigh escapes her lips. When I've removed all the pins, I ease my fingers into her hair and begin to slowly massage her scalp.

She lets free a heartfelt moan of pleasure and leans back against me. My fingers travel over the back of her head to her nape. I take a fistful of her lush hair and tug, giving me access to her throat. "You're mine." I tease her earlobe with my teeth.

She groans.

"Hush now." I sweep her hair over her shoulder and skim my finger along the lace edging of her dress. A tremor runs through her as I press my lips to her skin above the top button.

"So beautiful," I whisper, and undo it. "You have made me the happiest man alive today." Taking my sweet time, I continue unfastening each delicate button. Her dress falls open, revealing her pale pink corset with delicate hooks at the back.

My cock approves. Big-time.

"I love you so much." I skim my lips from her nape to her shoulder. Murmuring between kisses. "I. Want. You. So. Much. I. Want. To. Be. Inside. You. You. Are. Mine."

She angles her head, offering her throat to me.

"Mine," I utter against her skin, and slip her sleeves down her arms so that her bridal gown falls to her feet, in a delicate shock of silk and lace, leaving her in her corset with garters and stockings.

Sweet Jesus. Stockings. All the blood in my body heads south.

"Turn around." My voice is hoarse.

Inhaling sharply, I study my wife. She looks demure and really fucking hot all at once; her breasts forced up and full beneath her corset and her hair a tumbling riot of lush chestnut.

"You like?" she asks, and she turns a fetching pink that matches her sexy underwear.

"More than like, baby. You look sensational. Here." I offer her my hand, and she steps out of her dress.

"Keep still," I warn, locking my eyes on hers. I run a finger over the soft swell of her breasts. They quiver beneath my touch as she inhales and exhales, faster…and shallower.

I love turning my wife on.

Reluctantly, I lift my finger from her skin and spin it in the air.

Turn around for me.

She does. When she's facing the bed, I ask her to stop. Encircling her waist, I pull her back against my chest and kiss her neck. From this angle, I have a glorious top view of her straining breasts and I can't resist them. I embrace each and hold them, letting my thumbs move over their soft swell to her nipples, circling each over and over. Ana moans.

"Mine," I breathe.

"Yours," she whispers.

She pushes her ass against me and I have to fight my urge to press myself into her. As I skim my hands down the soft satin, over her stomach, her belly, to her thighs—my thumbs briefly skating over her vulva—she leans her head against me, eyes closed, and groans. My fingers find her garters and I unhook both of them at the same time. Then I move my hands to her fine ass.

"Mine," I whisper. As I caress her backside, my fingertips brush beneath her panties.

"Ah," she moans.

She's wet.

Fuck. Ana. You siren.

"Hush." I unclip her garters at the back, then lean down and pull the duvet back. "Sit down." She obliges and I kneel at her feet and tug off each of her shoes, placing them by her dress. I'm aware of her burning gaze as I slowly remove her left stocking, my thumbs skimming over her skin as I peel it off. I do the same with its twin. "This is like unwrapping my Christmas presents," I whisper, and peek up at Ana.

"A present you've had already," she says quietly.

What? Her comment takes me by surprise. "Oh, no, baby," I reassure her, if that's what she needs. "This time it's really mine."

"Christian, I've been yours since I said yes." She moves forward and holds my face between her palms. "I'm yours. I will always be yours, husband of mine."

Husband. It's the first time she's said it since the ceremony.

"Now," she says softly against my lips, "I think you're wearing too many clothes." She leans down to kiss me, but the word *husband* is ringing in my heart.

I'm hers. Really hers.

I kneel up and kiss her, grasping her head with both hands, weaving my fingers into her hair.

"Ana," I whisper. "My Ana." And I kiss her again. Properly. Pushing my tongue into her mouth and tasting her. Tasting my wife. She answers my wordless passion with her own, her tongue finding and embracing mine.

"Clothes," she says when we surface for air, and attempts to remove my vest. I release her and shuck it off while she regards me with her beautiful blue eyes that are darkening with want. "Let me, please," she pleads.

I sit back on my heels, and she leans forward and takes my tie.

That tie.

My favorite.

And she slowly undoes it and pulls it free.

I lift my chin and she unfastens my top button. She moves to my cuffs and removes each of my new cuff links in turn. I hold out my hand, and she places them in my palm. Clasping them in my fist, I kiss my hand and then slip them into my pants pocket.

"Mr. Grey, so romantic."

"For you, Mrs. Grey—hearts and flowers. Always."

She reaches for my hand, and peering up at me through her long, dark lashes, she kisses my wedding ring.

Oh God. I close my eyes and groan. "Ana."

She starts to unbutton my shirt. As she unfastens each one, she plants a soft kiss where the button once was and whispers a word. "You. Make. Me. So. Happy. I. Love. You."

It's too much. I want her.

Fuck, do I want her.

I groan and shake my shirt off, then lift her onto the bed and lay her down beneath me. My lips find hers and I hold her head, keeping her still as we share our first horizontal kiss as husband and wife.

Ana.

My pants are getting too tight. I kneel up between her legs and Ana is panting, her lips swollen from our kisses, and she's staring up at me with want.

Fuck.

"You are so beautiful, wife." I run my hands down each of her legs and grab her left foot. "You have such lovely legs. I want to kiss every inch of them. Starting here." I press my lips to her big toe and graze the pad with my teeth.

"Ah!" Ana makes a garbled sound and closes her eyes. I taste her instep and run my tongue to her heel, which I nip, then run my tongue to her ankle. I leave a path of soft wet kisses up the inside of her calf, and Ana squirms.

"Still, Mrs. Grey," I warn, and for a moment I watch her breasts rising and falling against the constraints of her corset.

It's a thing of beauty.

Enough. It needs to go.

I flip her onto her stomach, and continue my journey of kisses up her body: the backs of her legs, her thighs, her backside. And for a moment I contemplate all that I want to do to her ass.

Ana protests. "Please."

"I want you naked," I murmur, and unhook her corset, one hook at a time, at a languid pace. Once it's off, I plant a soft, wet kiss at the base of her spine, then trail my tongue up the length of her backbone.

Ana wriggles. "Christian, please."

I'm leaning over her, my constrained cock resting against her ass, and she wriggles against me. "What do you want, Mrs. Grey?" I utter the words just beneath her ear.

"You."

"And I you, my love, my life." I undo my pants, kneel up beside her, and turn her onto her back. Standing, I dispense with my pants and underwear while Ana regards me, wide-eyed and wanting. I grasp her panties and whisk them off so that she's naked in all her glory beneath me.

"Mine," I mouth.

"Please," Ana implores me.

I can't help my grin. *Oh, baby. I love it when you beg.*

Crawling onto the bed, I lay a new path of wet kisses up her other leg, getting closer and closer to the top of her thighs. My objective. The sacred apex. When I reach my goal, I push her legs wider apart. She's wet and wanting. Just how I like her. "Ah, wife of mine," I whisper, and I run my tongue over her, tasting her and pinpointing her clitoris.

Hmm… Slowly, I begin to torture her with my mouth. Round and round, my tongue teases her oh-so-sensitive bud. Ana grabs my hair and writhes underneath me, her hips moving in a rhythm I know so well. She bucks once. But I hold her still and continue my sweet torment.

"Christian," she calls, and tugs at my hair.

She's close.

"Not yet." I move up her body, dipping my tongue in her navel.

"No!" she cries out in frustration, and I grin against her belly.

All in good time, my love.

I kiss her soft stomach. "So impatient, Mrs. Grey. We have until we touch down on the Emerald Isle."

When I reach her breasts, I worship each with tender kisses, and take a nipple between my lips and tug. I watch her as I lavish my attention on it; her eyes are dark and her mouth slack. "Husband, I want you. Please."

And I want you.

I cover her body with mine, resting my weight on my elbows, and run my nose down hers. Her hands are on me.

My shoulders.

My back.

My backside.

"Mrs. Grey. Wife. We aim to please." I brush my lips over hers. "I love you."

"I love you, too." She's pushing her hips up for me.

"Eyes open. I want to see you."

Her eyes are a startling blue.

"Christian. Ah," she calls out, as I slowly claim her, inch by inch.

"Ana, oh, Ana," I breathe. Her name is a prayer.

She is heaven. My heaven.

I start to move, relishing the feel of her.

Her fingernails dig into my butt and it drives me on.

And on.

And on.

She's mine.

She's really mine.

Finally, she cries out my name and falls apart beneath me, her climax triggering mine, and I come and come inside my love. My life. My wife.

I t's the sound of the sea lapping against the hull of M.Y. *Fair Lady* that wakes me. The crew are on deck; I hear them, no doubt shining the brass and making their preparations for the day. We are moored in the bay outside Monte Carlo harbor. It's a blissful summer's morning in the Mediterranean, and beside me, Mrs. Anastasia Grey is fast asleep. I turn onto my side and study her, as I have done most mornings since we started our honeymoon. She is sun-kissed. Her hair is a little lighter. Her lips are parted, and she sleeps soundly.

As she should.

I smirk at the memory.

It was a late night. And she came and came and came.

She looks so serene; I envy her that.

Though I have to confess, I've relaxed a little.

There's been the occasional call from Ros and from Marco after the drama of last week's Black Monday. Marco and I avoided any substantial losses with some last-minute repositioning into defensive assets. We're both keeping a watchful eye on the markets and liaising on a strategy to survive the downturn.

But generally, no work and all play has been invigorating.

I smile fondly at Ana, and still she sleeps.

I have discovered new facets to my wife.

She adores London.

She loves afternoon tea at Brown's Hotel.

She loves pubs and the fact that Londoners spill out of them and drink pints and smoke on the sidewalks.

She loves Borough Market, especially the Scotch eggs.

She's not keen on shopping, except at Harrods.

She is not a fan of English ale, but then neither am I. It's warm.

Who drinks warm beer?

She's not keen on shaving…but she'll let me shave her.

Now, that's a memory I'll treasure.

She loves Paris.

She loves the Louvre.

She loves the Pont des Arts, and we left a padlock there to prove it.

She loves the Hall of Mirrors in Versailles.

"Mr. Grey. It is no hardship to see you from every angle in here."

She loves me…or so it would seem.

I'm tempted to wake her, but we enjoyed a late night yesterday. We saw *La Songe*, a ballet based on Shakespeare's *A Midsummer Night's Dream*, at L'Opéra de Monte-Carlo, then went to the casino, where Ana won a few hundred euros at the roulette table. She was thrilled.

Her eyes flicker open, as if I've willed her awake. She smiles. "Hi."

"Hi, Mrs. Grey, good morning. Sleep well?"

She stretches. "I had the best sleep and the best dreams."

"You are the best dream." I kiss her forehead. "Sex, or morning swim around the yacht?"

She smiles her oh-so-sexy smile. "Both," she mouths.

ANA IS BUNDLED UP in a robe fresh from her swim, sipping tea and reading one of her SIP manuscripts as we're served breakfast on deck. "I could get used to this," she says, dreamily.

"Yes. She's a fine, fine vessel." I stare at Ana and swallow the last of my espresso. Ana quirks an eyebrow, but before she can respond, our steward Rebecca sets a plate of scrambled eggs and smoked salmon in front of each of us.

"Breakfast," Rebecca says with a warm smile. "Can I get you anything else?"

"This is great." I return her smile.

"I'm good, thank you," Ana says.

"Let's go to the beach today," I suggest.

RARELY DO I GET the opportunity to read so much. But on my honeymoon I've devoured two thrillers, two books on climate change, and now I'm reading Morgenson and Rosner's tome on how greed and corruption led to the 2008 financial crisis, while Ana is dozing beneath a parasol at the Beach Plaza Monte Carlo. Stretched out on a sunbed in the afternoon sun, she's wearing a rather fetching turquoise bikini that leaves very little to the imagination.

I'm not sure I approve.

I've asked Taylor and his two French cohorts, the Ferreux twins, to keep a lookout for any photographers. The paparazzi are parasites who will stop at nothing to invade our privacy. For some bizarre reason, probably since the *Star* ran its gossip piece on Ana, the press are thirsty for pictures of us. Why, I don't know or understand—it's not like we're celebrities, and it makes me mad. I don't want my wife appearing on Page Six wearing practically nothing just because it's a slow news day.

The sun has shifted so Ana is under its full glare, and it's been a while since I applied her sunscreen. I lean over and whisper in her ear, "You'll burn."

She startles awake and grins. "Only for you."

My heart beats a little faster.

How does she do that with just three short words and a smile?

With a swift tug, I drag her bed into the shade. "Out of the Mediterranean sun, Mrs. Grey."

"Thank you for your altruism, Mr. Grey."

"My pleasure, and I'm not being altruistic at all. If you burn, I won't be able to touch you."

Ana curls her lips in a smirk.

I narrow my eyes. "But I suspect you know that, and you're laughing at me."

"Would I?" She bats her lashes, trying, and frankly failing, to look innocent.

"Yes, you would, and you do. Often." I kiss her. "It's one of the many things I love about you." I nibble at her lower lip.

"I was hoping you'd rub me down with more sunscreen."

Deep joy.

"It's a dirty job, but that's an offer I can't refuse. Sit up."

I love this. Touching her. Out here. In public.

She presents her front to me, and I squirt some sunscreen on my fingers, then slowly and thoroughly, so as not to miss a spot, massage it into her skin. Her shoulders, her neck, her arms, the tops of her breasts, her belly. "You really are very lovely. I'm a lucky man."

"Yes, you are, Mr. Grey." Her coy demeanor stirs my blood.

"Modesty becomes you, Mrs. Grey. Turn over. I want to do your back."

She lies down and I undo the strap of her bikini.

"How would you feel if I went topless, like the other women on the beach?" she asks, her voice soft and languid, like the day.

I squirt more sunscreen on my hand and rub it into her skin.

"Displeased. I'm not very happy about you wearing so little right now." I don't want some sleazy fucking pap ogling my wife through a lens while she's relaxing on the beach. They're everywhere. Like vermin.

Ana looks defiant.

I lean down and whisper in her ear. "Don't push your luck."

"Is that a challenge, Mr. Grey?"

"No. It's a statement of fact, Mrs. Grey."

This isn't a game, Ana.

Her back and legs are done. I slap her backside. "You'll do, wench."

My phone buzzes. I glance at the screen. It's Ros with her morning report.

It's early in Seattle. I hope she's okay.

"My eyes only," I warn Ana half-jokingly, and slap her ass once more before I take the call. Ana wriggles her backside provocatively, and closes her eyes while I talk to Ros.

"Hi, Ros, why so early?" I ask.

"I can't sleep, and I can get work done when the house is quiet."

"Anything wrong?"

"No. It's all good. Yesterday after we spoke, I got a call from Bill. We're being pressured by the Detroit Brownfield Redevelopment Authority. You need to make a decision."

My heart sinks.

Detroit. Damn. "Okay. Okay. Of the three sites that Bill sent through, the second was the best."

"The Schaefer Road site?" she asks.

"That's the one."

"Okay. I'll push on that. There's one more thing. Woods."

Hell. He's still on our list of suspects. "What's that asshole doing now?"

Ros ignores my epithet. "He's rattling his ex-employees."

"Poisoning the well?"

"Yes. I think they need a visit," she says.

"You should go."

"Not from me. You."

"Hmm…something to consider when I get back."

"I think so."

"I fancy a trip to New York. Take the wife."

I hear her smile. "How's the Côte d'Azur?"

My gaze lingers on my dozing wife…and her pert backside. "It's beautiful. Especially the view here."

"Great. Enjoy it. I'll get on with this."

"You do that, Ros."

"You know, I think with you gone, I'm all fired up."

I laugh. "Don't get too used to it. I'll be back."

"Believe it or not, I'm missing you."

I open my mouth to respond, but I'm stumped and don't know what to say.

"Afternoon, Christian." She hangs up, and I stare at my phone, wondering if she's okay.

Grey, she's fine. She's one of the most competent people you know.

I go back to my book.

BY MID-AFTERNOON THE TEMPERATURE is scorching. I order some drinks from the hotel waitress, as I'm parched. Ana wakens and turns her attention to me. "Thirsty?"

"Yes," she replies, sleepily.

She's lovely. "I could watch you all day. Tired?"

In the shade of the parasol, her face flushes. "I didn't get much sleep last night."

"Me neither."

I recall a vision from last night: Ana riding me hard.

My body stirs. *Shit.*

I need to cool down. *Now*. Standing, I make quick work of slipping out of my denim shorts. "Come for a swim with me." I hold out my hand, and Ana blinks, a little dazed. "Swim?" I ask again. When she doesn't answer, I scoop her into my arms. "I think you need a wake-up call."

She squeals and giggles at once. "Christian! Put me down!"

"Only in the sea, baby." Laughing, I carry her across the hellish hot sand, grateful to reach the cooler, damper shoreline. Ana wraps her arms around my neck, her eyes alight with amusement as I wade into the Mediterranean.

This has woken her up. She's clinging to me like a limpet. "You wouldn't," she says, a little breathless.

I can't help my grin. "Oh, Ana, baby, have you learned nothing in the short time we've known each other?" Leaning down, I kiss her and she grasps my head, her fingers running through my hair. Greedily, she kisses me back with a passion that catches me unawares and takes my breath away.

Ana.

I'm grateful I'm waist-deep in the water.

"I know your game," I murmur against her lips, and slowly sink into the sea, kissing her once more. The cool water, her hot, wet mouth against mine, it's arousing. She's wrapped around me, warm and wet, cloaking me in her long, lovely limbs.

This is heaven.

I consume her, our passion building while my mind empties.

It's just Ana, my beautiful girl, and me. In the sea.

I want her.

Here. Now.

"I thought you wanted to swim," she whispers, when we stop for air.

"You're very distracting." I tug her lower lip and suck. "And I'm not sure I want the good people of Monte Carlo to see my wife in the throes of passion."

She grazes my jaw with her teeth.

She wants more.

"Ana," I warn, twisting her ponytail around my wrist. I gently tug so I have access to her throat. She tastes of salt water, coconut sunscreen, sweat, and, best of all, Ana. "Shall I take you in the sea?"

"Yes." Her answer is a whisper that stokes my libido.

Fuck. Enough.

This is getting out of hand.

"Mrs. Grey, you're insatiable and so brazen. What sort of monster have I created?"

"A monster fit for you. Would you have me any other way?"

"I'll take you any way I can get you, you know that. But not right now. Not with an audience." I tilt my head to the shore.

Ana glances at the sunbathers taking an intrusive interest in what we are doing.

Enough, Grey.

Grabbing her around her waist, I boost her into the air and she lands with a satisfying splash in the sea. When she surfaces, she's laughing and spluttering with feigned indignation. "Christian!" she cries, and skates her hand across the surface of the water, splashing me.

I splash her right back, grinning because she looks so disappointed.

I'm not exposing her to an audience while we fuck!

"We have all night," I explain, delighted by her reaction. Before I change my mind and get us both arrested—though this is France, so who knows—I prepare to dive. "Laters, baby," I call, and plunge beneath the calm, clean water and swim away. A fast crawl will cool me down and expend some of this excess energy.

LATER, FEELING CALMER AND much refreshed, I stride up the beach, wondering how my wife is faring.

What the actual fuck!

Ana is topless on her sunbed.

I quicken my pace and scan the beach as I go, catching Taylor's eye from where he sits at the bar. He's sipping Perrier with our French security officers, who happen to be twin brothers. Between them, they survey our surroundings. Taylor shakes his head, and I think he's telling me that he's not spotted any photographers.

I don't fucking care. I think I'm going to have a coronary.

"What the hell do you think you're doing?" I yell, seething at Ana when I reach her.

She opens her eyes.

Was she feigning sleep? On. Her. Back?

She looks around, panicked. "I was on my front. I must have turned over in my sleep," she whispers.

I grab her bikini top off my sunbed and toss it toward her, growling, "Put this on!"

Fucking hell. I specifically asked you not to do this.

Not for my fucking health. But for your privacy!

"Christian, no one is looking."

"Trust me. They're looking. I'm sure Taylor and the security crew are enjoying the show!"

She grabs her breasts.

"Yes," I hiss. "And some sleazy fucking paparazzi could get a shot of you, too. Do you want to be all over the cover of *Star* magazine? Naked this time?"

Ana looks horrified and scrambles to put her top on.

Yeah! Why did you think I said no?

"L'addition!" I snap at the waitress. "We're going," I say to Ana.

"Now?"

"Yes. Now."

Don't argue with me, Ana.

I'm so fucking mad I don't even bother to dry myself. I drag on my shorts and T-shirt, and when the waitress returns I sign the check. Ana dresses hurriedly beside me while I signal to Taylor that we're leaving. He picks up his phone, presumably to call the *Fair Lady* and summon the tender. I gather my book and phone and put on my aviators.

What the hell was she thinking?

"Please don't be mad at me," Ana says quietly as she takes my belongings and places them in her backpack.

"Too late for that," I grumble, trying and utterly failing to bring my temper under control. "Come." I clasp her hand and wave at Taylor and the Ferreux brothers, who follow us through the hotel to the entrance.

"Where are we going?" Ana asks.

"Back to the boat."

I'm relieved to see the tender with its Jet Ski at the dock. Ana hands Taylor her backpack, and he gives her a life jacket. Taylor looks hopefully at me, but I shake my head. He blows out a quick breath of frustration, and I know he wants me to wear one, as well, but I'm too fucking angry. Ignoring him, I check that Ana's straps are cinched tightly. "You'll do," I mutter, and clamber onto the Jet Ski, then offer my hand to Ana. Once she's behind me, I kick us away from the dock and attach the kill-cord to the hem of my T-shirt. "Hold on," I growl, and she settles her arms around me, hugging me hard. I tense when she nuzzles my back, because…old memories, and also I'm mad at her. But, truth is, I love being in her arms. "Steady," I mutter, and twist the ignition, starting the engine. The motor roars to life, and slowly I twist the accelerator and we race forward toward the *Fair Lady*.

As we zip over the water my temper improves.

When the tender catches up with us, Ana tightens her hold around me, and I open the accelerator to the max and we speed ahead.

Ha! I love this!

This is fun.

Big-time fun.

Enjoy the moment, Grey.

The Mediterranean is calm and flat, so it's easy to fly over the brine. We tear past the yacht and out toward the open sea. The summer wind in my face, the spray, the speed at which we race across the water, and Ana clinging to me; it's such a thrill. I steer us in an arc toward the boat—but I want more.

"Again?" I shout at Ana. Her huge smile is all the encouragement I need, and I shoot around the *Fair Lady* and out to open sea again, in Ana's tight embrace.

I want to shout my happiness.

But…I'm still a little pissed at her.

ONE OF THE YOUNG stewards, Gerard, helps Ana off the Jet Ski and onto the *Fair Lady*'s small platform. Ana scoots up the wooden stairs and waits for me on deck. "Mr. Grey," Gerard says, and offers his arm.

I wave him away, climb off the machine, and follow Ana. She looks lovely, if a little apprehensive. Her skin glows from the fresh air and the kiss of the sun. "You've caught the sun," I say absentmindedly and undo her life vest. I hand it to Greg, another of the stewards.

"Will that be all, sir?" he asks.

"Would you like a drink?" I ask Ana.

"Do I need one?"

I frown. "Why would you say that?"

"You know why."

Yes, Ana. I'm mad at you.

"Two gin and tonics, please. And some nuts and olives."

Greg acknowledges my request with a nod. As he leaves, I realize what Ana's implying. "You think I'm going to punish you?" I ask.

"Do you want to?"

"Yes," I answer without hesitation, surprising myself.

Her eyes widen. "How?"

Oh, Ana. You sound interested. "I'll think of something. Maybe when you've had your drink." I let my eyes stray to the horizon as various erotic images float through my mind. "You want to be?"

Her eyes darken. "Depends." Her cheeks flush with telltale interest.

Oh, baby.

"On what?"

"If you want to hurt me or not."

For fuck's sake. I thought we were over this.

Her response irks me, but I lean over and kiss her forehead. "Anastasia, you're my wife, not my sub. I don't ever want to hurt you. You should know that by now." I sigh. "Just...just don't take your clothes off in public. I don't want you naked all over the tabloids. You don't want that, and I'm sure your mom and Ray don't want that, either."

Ana pales.

Yes, Ana. You'd be mortified. Ray would be furious. And he'd probably blame me!

Greg arrives with our drinks and places them on the table.

"Sit," I order, and Ana sits down in one of the director's chairs.

Dismissing the steward with a smile, I take a seat beside her, hand her a drink, and pick up my own. "Cheers, Mrs. Grey."

"Cheers, Mr. Grey." She takes a sip, watching me carefully.

What am I going to do with her?

Some kinky fuckery. I think.

It's been a while.

"Who owns this boat?" she asks, distracting me from my salacious plans.

"A British knight. Sir Somebody-or-Other. His great-grandfather started a grocery store. His daughter is married to one of the crown princes of Europe."

"Wow!" Ana mouths. "Super-rich?"

"Yes."

"Like you."

"Yes. And like you." I take an olive.

"It's odd," she says. "Going from nothing to"—she waves at the deck and the fabulous view of Monte Carlo—"to everything."

"You'll get used to it." *I have.*

"I don't think I'll ever get used to it," she answers, her voice low.

Taylor appears at my right. "Sir, you have a call." He hands me my phone.

"Grey," I snap as I rise from my seat and walk to the rail.

It's Ros.

Again?

She's following up on the meeting I had in London with the European GNSS agency about their Galileo Satellite Navigation. I'm hoping we can incorporate their service into Barney's solar tablet. I answer her queries, surprised that she didn't ask me all this earlier.

"Thanks. I'll let Marco know," she says.

"You know, you could have e-mailed me."

"I will next time. Barney's persistent. He's just sent me another e-mail about this. You know." She laughs, a little embarrassed, I think.

I chuckle in response. "He's eager. I know. That's why he works with us, thank goodness. Is that it? Because I'd really like to get back to my wife."

"You do that, Christian. Thank you. I'll try not to bother you again. Good-bye."

I turn my attention to Ana, who's sipping her gin and tonic and staring at the coastline with a faraway look. She's deep in thought.

What is she thinking about? Going topless? Punishment fucks? My wealth? Our wealth!

I hazard a guess. "You will get used to it," I say as I sit down beside her once more.

"Used to it?"

"The money."

She shoots me an unreadable look and pushes the dish of almonds and cashews toward me. "You're nuts, sir." I notice her half smile. She's trying not to laugh. At me. Again.

My plan crystalizes in my mind. "I'm nuts about you."

And that's the truth.

I take a cashew as I recall that night after her bachelorette party: Ana in bed, naked, holding out her hands to me.

"Are you going to punish me?"

"Punish you?"

"For getting this drunk. A punishment fuck. You can do anything you want to me."

The thought stirs my blood. She wants punishing. It would be rude of me not to oblige. "Drink up. We're going to bed."

She gapes at me.

"Drink," I tell her, quietly.

Ana raises her glass to her lips and drains it in one long gulp.

Wow. Without hesitating, my courageous girl has picked up the gauntlet.

She never backs down.

Game on, Grey.

Standing up, I lean over, resting my hands on the arms of her director's chair, and murmur against her ear, "I'm going to make an example of you. Come. Don't pee."

Her gasp is gratifying, and her face is a picture of shock.

I smirk, knowing where her mind has gone.

No, Ana, don't sweat it, that's not my scene.

"It's not what you think." I hold out my hand. "Trust me?"

Her lips lift in a come-hither smile. "Okay." She places her hand in mine, and together we make our way to the master cabin.

Once inside, I release Ana and lock the door. We don't want to be disturbed. Quickly, I strip out of my clothes and remove my flip-flops, which I shouldn't be wearing anyway, but the crew are too polite to tell me.

Ana is watching me, wide-eyed, unconsciously chewing her bottom lip. I grasp her chin, freeing her plump lower lip, and skim my thumb over the little indentations her teeth have left. "That's better."

From inside the armoire I retrieve my bag of toys and produce two pairs of ankle-to-wrist cuffs, the key for them, and an eye mask. Ana hasn't moved. Her eyes are darker than before.

She's turned on, Grey.

Let's blow her mind.

"These can be quite painful." I hold up a pair so that she has a better view of them. "They can bite into the skin if you pull too hard. But I really want to use them on you now. Here." I step toward her and hand her one set. "Do you want to try them first?" I keep my voice gentle, while trying to keep a grip on my libido.

I want this.

Big-time.

Ana examines the cuffs, turning the cold metal over in her hand. The sight of her handling them is erotic enough. "Where are the keys?" she asks, her voice wavering.

I open the palm of my hand, revealing the key. "This does both sets. In fact, all sets." She looks from my palm to my face, her eyes full of questions, full of curiosity...full of yearning. I caress her cheek with my index finger, trailing it down to her mouth and across her lips. Leaning in, as if to kiss her, I breathe, "Do you want to play?"

"Yes," she answers almost inaudibly.

"Good." I take a deep breath, inhaling her unique scent: Ana and a hint of her arousal.

Already!

Closing my eyes, I pour my gratitude into the gentle kiss I plant on her forehead.

Thank you for this, my love.

"We're going to need a safe word."

Ana shoots her eyes to mine.

"*Stop* won't be enough," I continue hastily, "because you will probably say that, but you won't mean it." I run my nose down hers.

Trust me, Ana.

"This is not going to hurt. It will be intense. Very intense, because I am not going to let you move. Okay?"

She inhales sharply, her breathing labored as her excitement builds.

I love turning you on, baby.

Her eyes drift down to my cock.

Yeah, baby. I'm ready and waiting.

"Okay," she whispers.

"Choose a word, Ana."

A soft furrow puckers her brow.

"A safe word," I clarify.

"Popsicle," she blurts, breathy and flustered.

"Popsicle?" I want to laugh.

"Yes."

"Interesting choice. Lift up your arms."

She does as she's told—which turns me on, too—and I raise her dress over her head, discarding it on the floor. Holding out my palm, she surrenders the handcuffs, and I place those and the other cuffs, key, and blindfold on the nightstand. I yank the quilt off the bed and let it fall to the floor.

"Turn around," I order.

She complies immediately, and I undo her bikini top, letting it fall to the floor. "Tomorrow, I will staple this to you," I mutter, and a kernel of an idea sprouts in my mind.

Love-bites.

I free her hair from its ponytail and gather it in my hand, tugging gently so she's forced to step back against me. Angling her head to one side, I glide my lips from her shoulder to her ear. "You were very disobedient."

"Yes," she says, as if she's proud of herself.

"Hmm. What are we going to do about that?" She tastes exquisite.

"Learn to live with it?" she counters, and I grin against the pulse point beneath her ear.

No backing down from my girl.

God, she's hot.

"Ah, Mrs. Grey. You are ever the optimist." I kiss her neck once more, then set to braiding her hair. Once it's done, I use her hair tie to finish up. Tugging her head to the side once more, I whisper in her ear, "I am going to teach you a lesson." Abruptly, I grab her around the waist and sit down on the bed, pulling her over my knee. I smack her beautiful behind. Once. Hard. Then toss her, faceup, onto the bed. Leaning over her, I run my fingertips up her thigh as we drink each other in.

"Do you know how beautiful you are?" I whisper, as she squirms on the bed, panting.

Waiting.

Her eyes dark with longing.

Keeping my gaze on her, I stand and reach for the cuffs. I grasp her left ankle and cuff it with one set of the cuffs. I take the other set and fasten a cuff to her right ankle. "Sit up."

She does.

"Now hug your knees."

With a quizzical look at me, she draws her legs up and wraps her arms around her knees. Reaching down, I lift her chin and brush her lips with a soft, wet kiss before slipping the eye mask over her eyes.

"What's the safe word, Anastasia?"

"Popsicle."

"Good." I snap the left cuff on around her left wrist, and the one attached to her right ankle around her right wrist. She yanks on both and realizes she's unable to straighten her legs.

This is going to be intense.

For you. And for me.

"Now," I whisper. "I'm going to fuck you till you scream."

And I can't wait.

She gasps, and I grab both her heels and tip her feet up so she falls backward onto the bed. I ease her ankles apart, and for a moment I enjoy the sight of her, open and helpless before me. Frankly, I could come over her right now. I'm tempted to. But I kneel down at her altar, and kiss my way up her inner thigh. She moans, pulling on the cuffs.

Careful, Ana. They will bite you.

"You're going to have to absorb all the pleasure, Anastasia. No moving." I shift so I can reach her bikini briefs, and run my lips over her taut belly. The string fastenings on both sides unravel with a simple tug, and her briefs are no more.

I kiss her belly, my tongue dipping into her navel.

"Ah!" Ana groans. Her breasts rise and fall rapidly, as I continue with my trail of wet kisses across her stomach.

"Shh," I murmur. "You're so beautiful, Ana."

She moans, louder this time, and tugs against her metal restraints. "Argh!" she cries as she feels the bite of the cuffs while I continue my conquest of her body, kissing and grazing my teeth against her fragrant skin.

"You drive me crazy," I whisper. "So I'm going to drive you crazy." I kiss her breasts, my tongue, my lips, and my teeth provoking Ana's passionate cries, her heavy breathing, her head thrashing from side to side. I roll each of her nipples between a thumb and forefinger and feel them harden and lengthen under my not-so-tender ministration. I suck hard around each nipple, leaving a telltale little mark each time.

She's breathless now.

Trying to move.

She can't.

She's mine.

And I don't stop.

"Christian," she pleads, and I know I'm driving her crazy.

"Shall I make you come this way?" I blow on her nipple. "You know I can." I take it in my mouth, sucking. Hard.

She cries out, a guttural cry of pleasure.

And I'm fully aroused.

Straining to be inside her.

"Yes," she whimpers.

"Oh, baby, that would be too easy."

"Oh, please."

"Hush." My teeth graze her chin, then I capture her mouth with mine, thrusting my tongue between her lips to meet hers. She tastes of Ana and fresh gin and tonic with a hint of lemon.

Delicious.

But she's greedy. Kissing me back. Wanting more. And more.

Fuck. She tastes so good. She gives as good as she takes. Her head lifting off the sheets.

Oh, baby.

I release her lips and grasp her chin. "Still, baby. I want you still," I whisper.

"I want to see you," she breathes, desperate and needy.

"Oh, no, Ana. You'll feel more this way." I ease my hips forward, knowing we're lined up, and ease my way inside her, just a little.

She can't move.

And I ease back, teasing her.

"Ah! Christian, please!"

"Again?" I ask, and I don't recognize my own voice.

"Christian!"

I push myself into her again, a little farther this time, but pull back and let my fingers tease her right nipple.

"No!" she wails in disappointment. She does not want me to withdraw.

"Do you want me, Anastasia?"

"Yes!" she cries.

"Tell me." My voice is hoarse. I need to hear her say it, and I tease her with my cock once more. In. Out.

"I want you," she whimpers. "Please."

I love it when she begs.

"And have me you will, Anastasia." I slam into her and she screams, pulling against the cuffs.

I know she's helpless.

And I take full advantage. Stilling. Feeling her around me, then circling my hips. She groans.

"Why do you defy me, Ana?"

"Christian, stop."

It's not the safe word. I circle my hips once more, deep, deep inside her. Then pull out and slam into her once more.

Don't come! I will myself. "Tell me. Why?" *I need to know.*

She cries out, and her pleasure is my pleasure.

"Tell me," I plead.

"Christian!"

"Ana, I need to know." I thrust into her once more.

Tell me. Please.

"I don't know!" she wails. "Because I can! Because I love you! Please, Christian."

I groan loudly, and finally let myself love her, cocooning her head beneath my hands as I claim her. Pleasure her. And pleasure myself. She's fighting against the cuffs. Gasping. Keening. Building beneath me.

She's close. I feel it.

She cries out.

"That's it," I grind out between gritted teeth. "Feel it, baby!"

Ana screams as she comes. And comes. And comes. Shattering beneath me. Her head back. Her mouth open. Her face screwed up. I kneel up, taking her with me, pulling her into my lap. Riding out her climax. Holding her tightly, burying my head against her neck as I let go.

FUCK!

My orgasm is relentless.

When I'm finally spent, I rip off her blindfold and kiss my wife. Her eyelids. Her nose. Her cheeks.

Thank you, Ana.

She's crying. I kiss the tracks of her tears while I cup her face. "I love you, Mrs. Grey," I whisper. "Even though you make me so mad—I feel so alive with you."

She's exhausted—listless in my arms—so I lay her down on the bed and ease out of her. "No," she mumbles, feeling the loss of contact, I think.

Oh, baby.

You're so done.

From the nightstand I grab the key and release her from each of the cuffs, rubbing her wrists and ankles as I do. I lay down beside her as she stretches out her legs, and wrap her in my arms. She sighs, a small, satisfied smile on her lips, and her breathing slows. She's gone to sleep. I kiss her hair and cover us both.

Boy, that was intense for me, too.

Ana. What you do to me.

I WAKE FIFTEEN MINUTES later from my doze. Ana is still in my arms, sleeping soundly. I kiss her forehead, untangle myself from her limbs, and get up to use the bathroom. She's still out for the count when I return from my shower. I dress quickly, unlock the cabin door, and head up on deck to find the captain to discuss staying on board this evening.

She's still asleep when I return. I put away the cuffs and grab my laptop to check through my e-mails, and also check on the brown-field sites in Detroit, just to make sure that I made the correct call with Ros earlier.

On deck and around the boat, the crew ready the *Fair Lady*. I hear the loud clanking of the anchor as it's winched on board and the distant rumble of the engines as they're fired up. We're setting sail.

DUSK HAS BEEN AND gone and it's dark outside when Ana stirs.

"Hi," I murmur, eager to see her. *I've missed you while you were sleeping.*

"Hi." Her voice is hesitant, and she pulls the cover up to her chin.

Has she gone all shy on me?

"How long have I been asleep?" she asks.

"Just an hour or so."

"We're moving?"

"I figured since we ate out last night, and went to the ballet and the casino, that we'd dine on board tonight. A quiet night à deux."

She grins—relieved, I think, to be spending the evening on board. "Where are we going?"

"Cannes."

"Okay." She stretches out beside me, then gets up, grabs her robe, and slips it on.

Shit.

She has a few love-bites. It's what I planned, but now, seeing the purple blotches on her skin, I'm not so sure it was a good idea.

This could go either way.

She ambles into the en suite bathroom and closes the door.

Hours. Minutes. Seconds. I don't know how long she's in there, but it takes forever. Eventually, she appears, but deliberately—it seems—she avoids eye contact with me as she darts into the closet.

This does not look good.

Maybe she's just tired.

I wait. Again.

She's in there for too long.

I can't bear it. "Anastasia, are you okay?"

No answer.

Damn.

Suddenly, she bursts out of the closet, a blur of arms and hair, and hurls a hairbrush at me. *Shit.* I raise my arm in time to protect my head, and the hairbrush smacks me below my wrist. Ana storms out of the room and slams the cabin door.

Fuck.

She's not impressed.

I don't think I've ever seen her this mad. Not even over the vows, when she threatened to cancel the wedding.

Grey, what have you done?

My good humor evaporates, replaced by an anxiety I've not felt since before we got married. Warily, I get up, dump my laptop on the nightstand, and go in search of my furious wife.

She's leaning on the rail at the bow, staring at the distant shore. It's a beautiful evening and the *Fair Lady*, like the Queen of the Seas that she is, coasts effortlessly over the Mediterranean.

Ana looks desolate. It's chastening.

"You're mad at me," I whisper.

"No shit, Sherlock!" she hisses, but she doesn't turn to look at me.

"How mad?"

"Scale of one to ten, I think I'm at fifty. Apt, huh?"

Wow. "That mad."

"Yes. Pushed-to-violence mad," she seethes. Finally, she looks at me, her expression raw and angry…and I know she sees me. Sees me for who I am. *You are one fucked-up son of a bitch.* Her recrimination from months ago echoes in my head.

Hell. It's been weeks since I've felt as shitty as this.

Flynn's words float back to me: *communicate and compromise.*

Ana takes a deep breath and stands taller, squaring her shoulders. "Christian, you have to stop unilaterally trying to bring me to heel. You made your point on the beach. Very effectively, as I recall."

"Well, you won't take your top off again," I grunt, and even to my own ears I sound like a petulant teen.

She glares at me. "I don't like you leaving marks on me. Well, not this many, anyway. It's a hard limit!" She spits at me like a cornered kitten.

"I don't like you taking your clothes off in public. That's a hard limit for me," I counter.

I warned you, Ana.

"I think we've established that," she continues in the same vein. "Look at me!" She tugs down her top, exposing the love-bites I've left on her. I count six. I didn't know my plan would be quite so effective.

But I don't want to fight.

I raise my hands, palms up in surrender. "Okay, I get it."

Maybe I overreacted.

"Good!" she snaps.

I run my hand through my hair, feeling helpless.

I'm lost. What more can I do? "I'm sorry. Please don't be mad at me." *I don't want to fight. Ana. Please.*

"You are such an adolescent sometimes." Ana shakes her head, but she sounds more resigned than forthright. I take a step forward and tuck a loose tendril behind her ear.

"I know, I have a lot to learn."

"We both do." She sighs and slowly raises her hand and places it over my heart.

Ana.

I place my hand over hers and give her an apologetic smile. "I've just learned that you've got a good arm and a good aim, Mrs. Grey. I would never have figured that, but then I constantly underestimate you. You always surprise me."

Her lips form a half smile and she arches a brow. "Target practice with Ray. I can throw and shoot straight, Mr. Grey, and you'd do well to remember that."

"I will endeavor to do that or ensure that all potential projectile objects are nailed down and that you don't have access to a gun."

She narrows her eyes. "I'm resourceful."

Oh, Ana. I don't doubt it. "That you are," I whisper, and releasing her hand, I fold her into my arms. Her hands move over my back and she returns my embrace. I plant my nose in her hair, inhaling her soothing scent. "Am I forgiven?" I ask, quietly.

"Am I?"

"Yes," I respond.

"Ditto."

We stand at the bow, the French Riviera passing us by, and we just…*are*.

For a moment, it's the best feeling in the world.

"Hungry?" I ask.

"Yes. Famished. All the, um, activity has given me an appetite. But I'm not dressed for dinner."

"You look good to me, Anastasia. Besides, it's our boat for the week. We can dress how we like. Think of it as dress-down Tuesday on the Côte d'Azur. Anyway, I thought we'd eat on deck."

"Yes, I'd like that."

I reach under her chin and raise her lips to mine and kiss her. Slowly. Gently.

Forgive me, Ana.

She smiles and together we walk hand in hand back to where our dinner awaits.

"WHY DO YOU ALWAYS braid my hair?" Ana asks as I'm about to tuck into my crème brûlée.

I frown, because the answer's obvious. "I don't want your hair catching in anything." *I've always done it. Hair and toys don't mix.* "Habit, I think, I add. And from nowhere a vision of a young woman singing an eighties pop song as she brushes out her long dark hair comes to mind. She turns and smiles at me, the dust motes circling in the air around her.

Hey, Maggot. Do you want to brush my hair?

And I'm back in a godforsaken slum in Detroit, a lifetime ago. Ana caresses my chin and runs a finger across my lips, bringing me back to the *Fair Lady.*

Why is the crack whore haunting me now?

"It doesn't matter," Ana whispers. "I don't need to know. I was just curious." She smiles and leans forward to kiss the corner of my lips. "I love you," she whispers. "I'll always love you, Christian."

"And I you." I'm thankful that she's here to drag me back from the dark abyss of my early childhood.

"In spite of my disobedience?" She smirks, immediately lightening the mood.

I chuckle, feeling better. "Because of your disobedience, Anastasia."

She bashes the caramelized sugar of her dessert with her spoon and scoops up a mouthful, and all thoughts of the crack whore fade.

ONCE REBECCA HAS CLEARED our plates, I offer Ana more rosé. She looks past me to check we're alone, then leans toward me with a conspiratorial air. "What's with the no-going-to-the-bathroom thing?" she asks.

Always curious. "You really want to know?"

"Do I?"

I smile. "The fuller your bladder, the more intense your orgasm, Ana."

"Oh. I see." A sweet blush colors her cheeks, and I know she's embarrassed.

Don't be, baby.

"Yes. Well…" She takes a swift gulp of wine.

"What do you want to do for the rest of the evening?" I ask, to move us on to a more comfortable topic. She raises her right shoulder in a shrug, a suggestive shrug, I think.

Again, Ana?

And I know I could make up for my transgression in bed. But I want more. "I know what I want to do." I pick up my glass of wine and stand, holding out my hand to her. "Come."

We move to the main salon and I guide her to the dresser, where my iPod is plugged into an impressive speaker. I select a song, something sweet and romantic for my girl. "Dance with me," I ask, and sweep her into my arms.

"If you insist."

"I insist, Mrs. Grey."

Michael Bublé is singing the Lou Rawls classic "You'll Never Find Another Love Like Mine."

We start to move, Ana following my lead. I dip her low and she giggles. I right her, then spin her around beneath my arm. She laughs. "You dance so well." Her voice is a little husky. "It's like I can dance."

I love dancing with you, baby.

Elena flits, unwelcome, into my mind, and while I'm grateful to her for teaching me to dance, I'm not happy that she's in my head.

Don't go there, Grey.

She's history.

Let's just enjoy this.

I dip Ana again, then kiss her when she's upright once more.

"I'd miss your love," she whispers, echoing the lyrics.

"I'd more than miss your love," I respond, and sing the next few lines softly in her ear. The song fades and we stop moving, and just gaze at each other.

I watch as her pupils grow larger and darker.

It's magic. Our special alchemy bubbling between us.

"Come to bed with me," I beg her.

Her coy smile brightens her face, and she places her hand on my heart. Beneath my chest, it starts hammering with my love for her—my wife—a beautiful woman who knows how to forgive me.

Mommy is pretty today. She laughs as she sits on her bed.
It is sunny and lots of little dots float in the air around her
like she's a princess. *Hey, Maggot, brush my hair.* I pull the
brush through her long hair. It is hard for me because of
tangles. But Mommy likes it. She sings. *What's love got to
do, got to do with it.* She smiles her special smile. It is her
smile for me. Only me. She shakes her hair so it is silky
down her back. I stroke it. It smells of clean. She splits it into
three snakes. And then she ties them together to make one
bumpy snake. *There, it's out of the way, Maggot.* She picks
up her hairbrush. And she brushes my hair. No! Mommy. It
hurts. Too many tangles. *Don't fight, Maggot.* No! Mommy.
I try to make her stop. There is a loud noise. A crash. He's
back. No! *Where the fuck are you, bitch? Got a friend here. A
friend with dough.* Mommy stands and takes my hand and
pushes me into her closet. I sit on her shoes. I am quiet. Like
a mouse. I cover my ears and close my eyes. If I am small he
won't see me. The clothes smell of Mommy. I like the smell.
I like being here. Away from him. He is shouting. *Where is
the little fucking runt?* He has my hair and he pulls me out
of the closet. He waves the hairbrush at Mommy. *Don't want
this little prick spoiling the party.* He slaps Mommy hard on
her face with her hairbrush. *Put your fucking hooker heels on
and make it good for my friend, then you get your fix, bitch.*
Mommy looks at me and she has tears. Don't cry, Mommy.
Another man comes into the room. A big man with dirty
coveralls. Blue coveralls. The big man smiles at Mommy. I
am pulled into the other room. He pushes me onto the floor
and I hurt my knees. He waves the hairbrush at me. *Now,*

what am I going to do with you, you piece of shit? He smells
bad. He smells of beer and he is smoking a cigarette.

I wake suddenly, fear clawing at my throat.

Where am I?

Gasping, I suck precious air into my lungs and try to steady my
racing heart. It takes me a moment to orient myself.

I'm on the *Fair Lady*. With my fair lady. I look frantically to my
right, and Ana is fast asleep in the shadows beside me.

Thank heavens.

I'm immediately calmed, just by the sight of her.

I take a deep, cleansing breath.

Why am I having nightmares?

Arguing with Ana?

I hate fighting with her.

Judging by the light that's seeping through the curtains over the
portholes, it's early dawn. I should sleep some more. I cuddle up to
Ana, and put my arm around her, breathing in her unique calming
fragrance…and I drift.

IT'S MUCH LIGHTER IN the cabin when I wake later, with Ana still
slumbering beside me. I watch her for a few moments, enjoying this
quiet time.

Will she ever really know what she means to me?

I kiss her hair, get up, and slip on a pair of swim trunks. I'm going
for a swim around the boat. Maybe I can shake the unease that
lingers.

AS I SHAVE, I'M still rattled by my nightmare.

Why? I don't get it.

I've had these dreams before.

Why am I so hung up on this one, now?

The bathroom door opens and Ana stands before me, a ray of
light, and I mute my dark thoughts. "Good morning, Mrs. Grey." I
welcome her with a cheery smile.

"Good morning yourself." She grins and leans against the wall, raising her chin, imitating me as I shave under my jaw. From the corner of my eye, I watch her as she mimics my actions.

"Enjoying the show?" I ask.

"One of my all-time favorites."

She's forgiven me.

I lean over and kiss her, grateful that she's with me, and leave a small smudge of shaving foam on her face. "Shall I do this to you again?" I whisper, brandishing my razor, recalling the moment when I shaved her in our suite at Brown's Hotel.

Ana purses her lips. "No. I'll wax next time."

"But that was fun."

You beguiled me, Ana.

"For you maybe." She pouts, but there's a spark of amusement and perhaps carnal appreciation in her eyes.

I see you, Ana.

"I seem to recall the aftermath was very satisfying." I continue shaving, but Ana's gone very quiet. "Hey, I'm just teasing. Isn't that what husbands who are hopelessly in love with their wives do?" I tip her chin up and scrutinize her expression. Perhaps she's still mad at me.

She squares her shoulders.

Uh-oh.

"Sit," she orders.

What?

She splays her hands on my naked chest and pushes me gently toward a stool in the bathroom.

Okay, I'll play. I sit down and she takes my razor.

"Ana," I warn. But she ignores me and leans down and kisses me.

"Head back," she says against my lips.

When I hesitate, she cocks her head to one side. "Tit for tat, Mr. Grey." And I know she's provoking me. How can I walk away from a challenge when my wife never does?

"You know what you're doing?" I ask.

She shakes her head.

Well, what's she going to do, Grey?

Slit my throat?

Taking a deep breath, I close my eyes and raise my chin, offering myself to her. She slides her fingers into my hair and grips hard while I scrunch my eyes tighter. She's standing so close to me. I can smell her. Sea. Sunshine. Sex. Sweetness. Ana.

It's heady.

With the utmost tenderness she glides my razor from my neck to my chin, shaving me. I release the breath I was holding.

"Did you think I was going to hurt you?" I hear the tremor in her voice.

"I never know what you're going to do, Ana, but no—not intentionally."

Sliding the razor across my skin again, she says quietly, "I would never intentionally hurt you, Christian." She sounds so sincere. Opening my eyes, I curl my arms around her as she shaves my cheek.

"I know," I whisper.

She hurt me when she left, that one time.

And I deserved it. I hurt her.

You are one fucked-up son of a bitch!

Grey, don't go there.

I angle my cheek, making it easier for her to finish the job, and two strokes of the razor later, she's completed her work. "All done, and not a drop of blood spilled." She beams at me.

I run my hands up her leg and ease her onto my lap until she's sitting astride me. "Can I take you somewhere today?"

"No sunbathing?" Ana's tone is disingenuous, but I ignore it.

"No. No sunbathing today. I thought you might prefer something else."

"Well, since you've covered me in hickeys and effectively put the kibosh on that, sure, why not?"

Hickeys? We're not in high school!

"You never really had an adolescence—emotionally speaking. I think you're experiencing it now."

Hell.

Ignoring Flynn's words and Ana's reference to my bad behavior, I continue, "It's a drive, but it's worth a visit, from what I've read. My dad recommended we visit. It's a hilltop village called

Saint-Paul-de-Vence. There are some galleries there. I thought we could pick out some paintings or sculptures for the new house, if we find anything we like."

She presses her lips together and leans back to study me.

"What?" I ask, alarmed at her expression.

"I know nothing about art, Christian."

I shrug. "We'll buy only what we like. This isn't about investment."

She looks a little less alarmed, but preoccupied nevertheless.

"What?" I ask again. "Look, I know we only got the architect's drawings the other day—but there's no harm in looking, and the town is an ancient, medieval place."

Her expression remains the same.

"What now?" I ask. *Fuck, Ana. Are you still angry about yesterday?* She shakes her head.

"Tell me," I beg, but she gives nothing away. "You're not still mad about what I did yesterday?" I can't look her in the eye; instead, I bow my head and nuzzle between her breasts.

"No. I'm hungry," she says.

"Why didn't you say?" I ease her off my lap.

ANA AND I FALL under Saint-Paul-de-Vence's spell. We wander the narrow, cobbled streets, breathing in the Gallic wonder of it all, followed from a discreet distance by Taylor and Philippe Ferreux. Ana is tucked under my arm, where she fits perfectly. "How did you know about this place?" she asks.

"Dad e-mailed me when we were in London. He and Mom came here back in the day."

"It's beautiful." Ana waves her hand in homage to our spectacular surroundings.

We stop at a small gallery with some striking abstract art in the window and decide to venture in. I'm taken by some erotic photographs that are on display inside. They're beautifully composed. "Not quite what I had in mind," Ana says, her tone wry.

I grin down at her. "Me neither." My hand finds hers as we study some still-life paintings, all vegetables and fruit. They're good.

"I like those." Ana points to some peppers. "They remind me

of you chopping vegetables in my apartment." She giggles, her eyes alive with mischief and memories—of our reconciliation—maybe?

"I thought I managed that quite competently. I was just a bit slow, and anyway"—I embrace her and nuzzle her ear—"you were distracting me. Where would you put them?"

Ana gasps, distracted by my teasing lips. "What?"

"The paintings—where would you put them?" I graze her earlobe with my teeth.

"Kitchen," she breathes.

"Hmm. Nice idea, Mrs. Grey."

"They're really expensive!"

"So?" I kiss the spot behind her ear. "Get used to it, Ana." I release her and approach the sales assistant to purchase all three of the paintings and give her my credit card and our address in Escala for shipping.

"Merci, monsieur," she simpers, with a flirtatious smile.

Sweetheart, I'm married.

I raise my left hand to stroke my chin, making my ring obvious, then return to Ana, who is looking at the nudes.

"Changed your mind?" I ask.

She laughs. "No. They're good, though. And the photographer's female."

I cast my eye over them again. One catches my attention: a woman kneels up on a chair, her back to the camera. She's naked, except for hooker heels, her long, dark hair loose. A memory I don't want stirs in the back of my mind and I'm reminded of the bleak black-and-white photo on my bulletin board.

The crack whore.

Fuck.

I look away and take Ana's hand. "Let's go. Are you hungry?"

"Sure," she says with an uncertain look as I open the door and step out into the fresh air. I'm grateful to get back outside where I can breathe again.

What the hell is wrong with me?

PROTECTED FROM THE FIERCE Mediterranean sun, we sit beneath bright red parasols on an archaic stone terrace at a hotel restaurant. We're surrounded by geraniums and ancient ivied walls. It really is stunning. The food is off the charts, too. Damn, but the French can cook. I hope Mia's learned some of these skills. I'll have to persuade her to make dinner for us someday.

When I pay the check, I give the waiter a hefty tip.

Ana is sipping coffee, admiring the view. She's been quiet, and I wonder once more what she's thinking about.

Yesterday?

I shift in my seat.

I'm still trying to shake off my nightmare. Fragments keep haunting me and it's unsettling. I'm reminded of Ana's question yesterday evening about braids. Did it stir something from my subconscious?

Communicate and compromise. Flynn's words circle my brain.

Maybe I should talk to Ana. Tell her the truth. Perhaps that's why I'm getting these vivid flashbacks. I take a deep breath. "You asked me why I braid your hair."

Ana looks up, expectant. "Yes."

"The crack whore used to let me play with her hair, I think. I don't know if it's a memory or a dream."

Ana blinks, in that way she does when she's processing information, but her eyes are wide and clear, and all I see in them is her compassion. "I like it when you play with my hair," she says, but her voice wavers, and I think she's just trying to reassure me.

"Do you?"

"Yes!" The vehemence in her tone surprises me. She clasps my hand. "I think you loved your birth mother, Christian."

Time stills, and it's like she's knocked all the air out of my lungs. I'm in free-fall.

Why does she say shit like this?

She says she doesn't want to hurt me.

And yet…

My eyes stay glued to hers, because in spite of what she's just said, Ana's my life raft, and I'm drowning in a wave of uncertainty that I don't understand or know how to process.

I can't do this.

I don't want to think about the past.

It's been. It's done.

It's too painful.

My gaze drifts to her hand in mine and to the red mark around her wrist. It's a stark reminder of what I did to her yesterday.

I hurt her.

"Say something," she whispers.

I need to get out of here. "Let's go."

In the street, feeling adrift and unsure of myself, I reach for her hand once more. "Where do you want to go?" I ask, but it's more to distract myself from what's hovering at the edge of my memory. Whatever it is, it's dredging up these unwanted and unsettling... feelings.

She smiles. "I'm just glad you're still speaking to me."

Only just! You mentioned "love" and the crack whore in the same sentence.

"You know I don't like talking about all that shit. It's done. Finished."

I'm expecting her to sulk or berate me, but as I watch a kaleidoscope of emotions cross her face, what settles in her gaze is love.

Her love.

For me.

I think.

All the wrongs right themselves, and my world spins on its proper axis once more. I fold my arm around her and she slips her hand into my back pocket, her palm against my ass. It's a possessive gesture, and I live for it.

We walk down one of the cobbled streets, stalked by our security, when a fine jeweler's store catches my eye. We pause outside, and I have a sudden urge to buy Ana a piece. Grasping her free hand, I rub my thumb along the red wheal left by the handcuff yesterday. "It's not sore," Ana says, correctly interpreting my look of concern. I shift so Ana has no choice but to take her other hand out of my pocket. Around *that* wrist, she's wearing my wedding gift to her, which I purchased in the crazy rush to buy our rings from Astoria Fine Jewelry. It's a white gold Omega De Ville with diamonds; I had it inscribed.

Anastasia
You Are My More
My Love, My Life
Christian

And that was never truer than now.

Yet beneath the strap lies a red mark.

That I gave her.

And all those hickeys, too.

Because I was pissed at her.

Damn. Releasing her, I gently grasp her chin and raise her eyes to mine. She stares back at me, as guileless as ever, and with the same look of love.

"They don't hurt," she whispers, and I take her hand again, and plant a soft kiss on her wrist.

I'm sorry, Ana.

"Come." We head into the shop because there's a Chanel bracelet that's caught my eye in the window. Once inside, I waste no time and purchase it. I know if I ask Ana, she'll politely refuse. It's pretty—white gold with small diamonds—and it'll look lovely on her.

"Here." I fasten it around her wrist. It covers the red line. "There, that's better," I mutter.

"Better?" Her brow creases a little.

"You know why."

"I don't need this." She rotates her wrist and the diamonds on the bracelet sparkle in the sunlight, throwing little rainbows around the store.

"*I* do," I whisper.

It's an apology. I just don't know how to do this, Ana.

"No, Christian, you don't. You've given me so much already. A magical honeymoon, London, Paris, the Côte d'Azur, and you. I'm a very lucky girl."

"No, Anastasia, I'm a very lucky man."

"Thank you." She stretches up and puts her arms around my neck and kisses me, properly. In front of everyone.

Oh, baby.

I love you.

"Come. We should head back," I murmur against her lips. She slips her hand into my back pocket again, and together we make our way back to the car.

THE MERCEDES CRUISES BACK to Cannes. Taylor is in the passenger seat up front and Ferreux is driving, but we're hampered by the traffic. I stare out of the window, trying to figure out why I'm so agitated.

It can't have just been my dream.

My argument with Ana, yesterday?

The fact that I've marked her?

I don't understand why this feels so weird. I've marked women before. Not permanently. *Fuck, no. Never!* That's not my scene. Two of my submissives hated it, so that was fine, and I didn't do it. And, of course, I never marked Elena. That was impossible. She was married. And then there was Susannah. She loved that shit. Whenever she was marked, she liked me to photograph her.

Ana grips my hand, distracting me from my thoughts. She's wearing a short skirt that exposes her legs. I look across at her and caress her knee. She has such lovely legs.

Her ankles!

They're probably marked, too.

Shit.

Reaching down, I grasp her ankle and gently ease her foot onto my lap. She swivels in her seat and faces me. "I want the other one, too." I need to see for myself. She looks toward Taylor and Ferreux.

She's shy?

What does she think I'm going to do?

I press the privacy screen button and it slowly rises out of the panel in front of us until we're partitioned off from them. "I want to look at your ankles."

She frowns and places her other foot in my lap. I skim my thumb up her instep and she squirms.

She's ticklish. I don't know why I haven't registered this before.

I undo the strap on her sandal. And there it is. Another mark. Darker than those on her wrists. "Doesn't hurt," she says.

I'm an inconsiderate asshole.

I massage the line in the hope that it will disappear, and look back out of the window at the passing countryside. She wriggles her foot, and her sandal falls into the footwell. But I ignore it.

"Hey. What did you expect?" she asks.

She's gazing at me as if I've beamed down from Mars.

I shrug. "I didn't expect to feel like I do looking at these marks."

"How do you feel?"

Shitty.

"Uncomfortable," I mutter.

And I don't really know why.

Suddenly she unbuckles her seat belt and scoots closer to me and grabs both of my hands. "It's the hickeys I don't like," she hisses. "Everything else...what you did"—her voice drops lower—"with the handcuffs, I enjoyed that. Well, more than enjoyed. It was mind-blowing. You can do that to me again anytime."

Oh.

"Mind-blowing?" Her words are a small boost to my mood and my libido.

"Yes." She grins and curls her toes around my more-than-interested dick.

"You should really be wearing your seat belt, Mrs. Grey."

She teases me with her toes once more.

I glance at the glass. Could we...? But my lascivious thoughts are interrupted by my phone vibrating. *Shit.* I remove it from my shirt pocket.

It's work. I check my watch. It's early in Seattle.

"Barney," I answer, while Ana tries to withdraw her feet from the close proximity of my dick. I tighten my hold on her feet.

"Mr. Grey. There's been a fire in the server room."

What? "In the server room?" *How the hell did that happen?*

"Yes, sir."

The servers? Fuck! "Did it activate the fire-suppression system?"

Ana removes her feet from my lap, and this time I let her.

"Yes, sir. It did."

I hit the button to lower the privacy glass so Taylor can hear me. "Anyone injured?"

"No, sir," Barney responds.

"Damage?"

"Very little, from what I've been told."

"I see."

"Security were quick to call."

"When?" I glance at my watch again.

"Just now. The fire's out, but they want to know if we should call the fire department."

"No, not the fire department or the police. Not yet anyway."

I need to think.

"Welch has just called me on the other line," Barney says.

"Has he?"

"He's probably trying to get ahold of you. I'll text him."

"Good."

"I'm heading to Grey House now."

"Okay. I want a detailed damage report. And a complete rundown of everyone who had access over the last five days, including the cleaning staff."

"Yes, sir."

"Get ahold of Andrea and get her to call me."

"Will do. It was a good move to change from the outdated suppression system," Barney says as he blows out a breath.

"Yeah, sounds like the argon is just as effective, worth its weight in gold."

"Yes, sir."

"I realize it's early."

"I was awake. There'll be no traffic now," Barney continues. "I'll be there in no time. And I'll see what's up."

"E-mail me in two hours."

"I hope you don't mind that I called."

"No, I need to know. Thank you for calling me." I hang up and call Welch, who is heading to Grey House as we speak. During a brief exchange, we agree to increase security at the off-site data center as a precaution, and that we'll talk in an hour. When I end my call with him, I direct Philippe to get us back on board as soon as possible.

"Monsieur." Ferreux speeds up.

I wonder what could have gone wrong in the server room? An electrical fault? Something overheated? Arson?

Ana looks wary. "Anyone hurt?" she asks.

I shake my head. "Very little damage." Though I haven't had a damage report, I want to reassure her. Reaching over, I take her hand and give it a comforting squeeze. "Don't worry about this. My team is on it."

"Where was the fire?"

"Server room."

"Grey House?"

"Yes."

"Why so little damage?"

"The server room is fitted with a state-of-the-art fire-suppression system. Ana, please, don't worry."

"I'm not worried," she whispers, but I'm not convinced.

"We don't know for sure that it was arson." And that's my biggest fear.

I'M IN THE SMALL study aboard *Fair Lady.* Welch and Barney are at GEH and Andrea is making her way into the office early. Now that Welch has inspected the damage, he's advised that we get the fire department in so an expert can establish what started the fire. He doesn't want a stream of people in the server room contaminating any evidence. We run through a list of protocols, and as I feared, he's not ruling out arson. He's compiling lists of everyone who has had access to the server room in advance of the fire department's report.

Andrea calls when she arrives at the office and I pace the floor as I talk her through what's happened. I'm leaning against the desk when there's a knock on the door. It's my wife. "Andrea, hold please."

Ana's expression is one of determination—it's a look I know well, the one she wears when we're going to fight. My shoulders tense in preparation for a showdown. "I'm going shopping. I'll take security with me," she says with a too-bright smile.

Is that it? "Sure, take one of the twins and Taylor, too," I reply. She doesn't leave. "Anything else?"

"Can I get you anything?"

"No, baby, I'm good. The crew will look after me."

"Okay." She hesitates, then strides toward me, places her hands on my chest, and gives me a quick peck on my lips.

"Andrea, I'll call you back."

"Yes, Mr. Grey," Andrea says, and I'm sure she's smiling on the other end of the phone. Hanging up, I place my phone on the desk, pull Ana into my arms, and kiss her. Properly. Her mouth is sweet and wet and warm, and a welcome diversion. She's breathless when I stop. "You're distracting me," I whisper, staring down into dazed eyes. "I need to sort this out, so I can get back to my honeymoon." I run my finger down her cheek and clasp her chin.

"Okay. I'm sorry."

"Please don't apologize, Mrs. Grey. I love your distractions." I kiss the corner of her mouth. "Go spend some money." I step back, letting her go.

"Will do." With a girlish smile, she sashays to the door and is gone, though there's something about her demeanor that makes me pause.

What isn't she telling me?

Dismissing the thought, I call Andrea back.

"Mr. Grey, while I have you on the phone, Ros mentioned that you might go to New York next week. If so, I wanted to remind you that the Telecommunications Alliance Organization fundraiser is on Thursday in Manhattan. They really want you there."

"That trip's not definite. But let them know that I'm considering their invitation, and if I accept it, it will be for two. We might want to think about any other meetings I could do in New York while I'm there."

"Yes, sir."

"I think that's all for now. Can you put me through to Ros?"

"Will do."

I update Ros and ask her to liaise with Barney and Welch.

From somewhere close to the yacht, the sound of a Jet Ski start-ing up sidetracks me. It stalls. It starts and stalls again. I peer through the windows on the starboard side and Ana is on one of the Jet Skis. Fully clothed.

I thought she was going shopping.

"Ros. I'll call you back!" I hang up and scramble out of the study to the starboard walkway, but she's gone. I dash around to the port side, and Ana's tearing across the water on the Jet Ski with the tender in hot pursuit. She waves at me.

No. Ana! Don't let go. My heart leaps into my mouth.

Hesitantly, I raise my hand and wave back.

This was her plan?

I watch as she races toward the marina with the tender in her wake. I pull out my phone and call Taylor.

"Sir."

"What the hell are you and Anastasia playing at!" I shout.

"Mr. Grey, Mrs. Grey wanted to try the Jet Ski."

"But she could fall. Drown—fuck!" Words fail me.

"She's quite competent on it, sir."

"For fuck's sake, don't let her come back on it!"

I hear Taylor's sigh. But I don't give a fuck. "Yes, sir."

"Thank you!" I press end call.

In the salon, I find the binoculars and watch as Ana pulls up beside the tender. Taylor helps her in, then onto the dock.

I call her number and watch as she fumbles in her purse for her phone.

"Hi," she answers, a little breathlessly.

"Hi."

"I'll come back on the boat. Don't be mad."

Oh. I'm expecting a fight. "Um."

"It was fun, though," she whispers, sounding exhilarated. And I see her once more in my head, flying past the boat, the wind in her hair and a huge smile on her face.

I sigh. "Well, far be it for me to curtail your fun, Mrs. Grey. Just be careful. Please."

"I will. Anything you want from town?"

"Just you, back in one piece."

"I'll do my best to comply, Mr. Grey."

"I'm glad to hear it, Mrs. Grey."

"We aim to please." She giggles, and the sweet sound makes me smile. My phone beeps.

"I have another call. Laters, baby."

"Laters, Christian."

I hang up and Grace is on the line. "Hello, darling, how are you?"

"I'm good, Mom."

"I'm just calling to check that you're all okay."

"Why wouldn't I be okay?" *Shit. Maybe she knows.* "Are you calling about the fire?"

"What fire?" she asks, suddenly terse.

"It's nothing, Mother."

"What. Fire. Christian." Her tone is intimidating.

Sighing, I quickly fill her in on what's happened at Grey House, sparing no details. "Mom, it's no big deal. No damage." The last thing I want to do is worry Grace.

"Will you come home?"

"I don't see any reason to cut my honeymoon short. The fire was contained and hasn't done any damage."

She's quiet for a moment.

"Grace. It's okay."

She sighs. "If you say so, darling. How is your honeymoon going?"

"Well, up until this incident—it's been wonderful. Ana loves London and Paris and the yacht, she's yar."

"Sounds heavenly. Did you go to Saint-Paul-de-Vence?"

"We did. Today. It was magical."

"I fell in love with the place. I won't keep you, I know you'll have a lot to think about and do. The reason I called was to invite you and Ana to lunch on Sunday, when you're home."

"Sure. That sounds great."

"Lovely. See you then. And, Christian, remember, we love you."

"Yes, Mom. Thanks for the call."

WHEN I HANG UP there's an e-mail from Ana.

From: Anastasia Grey
Subject: Thank You
Date: August 17 2011 16:55
To: Christian Grey

For not being too grouchy.
Your loving wife
xxx

I type back.

From: Christian Grey
Subject: Trying to Stay Calm
Date: August 17 2011 16:59
To: Anastasia Grey

You're welcome.
Come back in one piece.
This is not a request.
x

Christian Grey
CEO & Overprotective Husband, Grey Enterprises Holdings, Inc.

A COUPLE OF HOURS later, I'm sitting at the small desk in the study and I get the call I've been dreading. "It's arson," Welch says.

"Fuck." My heart sinks.

Who the hell is doing this to me? What do they want?

"Exactly. A small incendiary device was placed beside one of the server cabinets. Interestingly, it was designed to set off smoke, but that's it. I think it's a warning."

A *warning?*

"Any idea when it was placed?" I ask.

"We don't have that information, yet. We've already doubled security. I'll post a guard 24/7 outside the server room. I know it's the lifeblood of the company."

"Good idea."

"Will you come back early?"

"Do I need to?" I don't want to end our honeymoon.

"No. I don't think so. I think the biggest question for me right now is if this is linked to your EC135."

"Let's assume it is. That's the worst-case scenario."

"Yes. I think that's prudent," Welch responds.

"There's nothing I can achieve there that I can't do here. Besides, I think we're safer on the boat."

"There's that," he agrees, then pauses. "I know all our leads for a potential suspect have led to nothing. But we'll double-check all the footage in and around Grey House. We will find this person."

"Do. Nail the prick."

"The police forensics team are in the server room right now, dusting for prints."

"I bet Barney's thrilled about that."

Welch's laugh is wry. "He's not."

"Goddamn it, this is frustrating," I mutter into the phone.

"I know, Christian. The EC135 was dusted for prints by the FBI a few weeks ago. We're still waiting to see if that yields a suspect. Eurocopter have the helicopter now. They're assessing the damage to see if it can be repaired."

"Okay."

"I'll call if there's an update."

"Thank you." I hang up and stare at the coastline, where the city lights of Cannes are beginning to wake and welcome the dusk.

What the hell am I going to do?

What have I done to deserve this?

Grey, don't go there.

The tender is being craned onto the bridge deck, which means Ana must have returned.

Ana. My girl.

She might get caught in this crossfire. I put my head in my hands in an attempt to drive the image of Ana lying unmoving on the floor from my psyche.

If anything happened to her…

The thought is torture. I need to see that she's back in one piece. Now.

Quelling my morbid thoughts, I go in search of her. Stopping out-side the master cabin door, I take a deep breath to calm my anxiety, and step inside. Ana is sitting on the bed with a parcel beside her.

"You were gone some time."

Startled, she looks up and eyes me warily. "Everything in control at your office?"

"More or less." I don't tell her more; I don't want to worry her.

"I did a little shopping," she says with a sweet smile.

"What did you buy?"

"This." She places her foot on the bed, and around her ankle there's a silver ankle chain.

"Very nice." I run my fingers over the little bells that hang from the chain. They have a sweet, delicate chime, but the chain doesn't hide the faint red line from the cuff yesterday.

The mark I left on her.

Hell.

"And this." She holds out a wrapped gift box, a little too eagerly—to distract me, I think. Of course, she's bought me something, and my mood switches to curious delight.

"For me?" The package is surprisingly heavy. Sitting down beside her, I give it a quick shake. Grinning, I clasp her chin and kiss her. "Thank you."

"You haven't opened it yet."

"I'll love it, whatever it is. I don't get many presents."

"It's hard to buy you things. You have everything."

"I have you."

"You do." She smiles.

I unwrap the paper to find a digital SLR camera. "A Nikon?"

"I know you have your compact digital camera, but this is for… portraits and the like. It comes with two lenses."

Portraits?

Where is she going with this?

My anxiety returns in full force, prickling my scalp.

"Today in the gallery you liked the Florence D'elle photographs. And I remember what you said in the Louvre. And, of course, there were those other photographs." Her voice drops.

Oh good God. I don't want to talk about them!

"I thought you might, um, like to take pictures of me."

"Pictures? Of you?"

She nods, blinking, her uncertainty obvious, and I examine the box, playing for time. It's a state-of-the-art camera, a thoughtful gift from my thoughtful wife, but it makes me uncomfortable. Really uncomfortable

Why does she think I want to photograph her naked?

That isn't my life anymore.

I look up at her. "Why do you think I want this?" I whisper.

A frisson of alarm crosses her face. "Don't you?" she asks.

No, Ana. You've got this all wrong.

Suddenly, I see it clearly: my old life and my new one careening together like a car crash and inflicting untold damage. Those photographs were fundamentally to protect me—to protect my position and my family. I have to make her understand that I don't need this from her...but I don't want to hurt her feelings.

Try the truth, Grey. Communicate.

"For me, photos like those have usually been an insurance policy, Ana."

And for your pleasure, Grey. Yes. It felt intimate, but deep down I knew I was safe viewing my subject through a lens. I was always at a remove; the camera put a wall between me and my sub, even though it was a thrill to capture them in the most intimate poses.

Fuck. Shame washes over me, and I'm in the confessional spilling my darkest secrets. "I know I've objectified women for so long."

Ana tucks her hair behind her ear, and looks as confounded as I feel. "And you think taking pictures of me is objectifying me?" she whispers.

I close my eyes. *What is happening here?*

Why wouldn't I do this with her?

"I'm so confused," I murmur.

"Why do you say that?" she asks gently.

Opening my eyes, I look down at her wrist, which still bears the marks that I left on her. I'm trying to protect her from my old life. And this is what I do?

How can I keep her safe, when I can't even keep her safe from me?

"Christian, these don't matter." She holds up her hand so the welt is on show. "You gave me a safe word. Shit—yesterday was fun. I enjoyed it. Stop brooding about it. I like rough sex, I've told you that before." She sounds panicked. "Is this about the fire? Do you think it's connected somehow to *Charlie Tango*? Is this why you're worried? Talk to me, Christian, please."

Don't frighten her further, Grey.

She frowns. "Don't overthink this, Christian." She reaches for the box, opens it, and removes the camera. Switching it on, she takes the lens cap off, and raises the Nikon to her face, pointing it at me.

I loathe having my photograph taken. The last time I did it willingly was at the wedding, and before that it was for her, not so long ago, at The Heathman. That was before my life changed irrevocably. Before I knew her. She presses the button and holds it, taking a burst of photographs.

"I'll objectify you, then," she mutters. And once more I know she's laughing at me, and not putting up with my bullshit. She edges closer, still looking at me through the lens. One, two, three, she takes several photos. She pokes her tongue between her teeth as she snaps each one, but I know she's unaware that she's doing it and I'm beguiled. She smiles and captures my answering smile.

Only you, Ana.

Only you can drag me back into the light.

I pose for her, pursing my lips in an exaggerated fashion.

Her grin broadens and she giggles, and it's such a wonderful sound.

"I thought it was *my* present," I grumble.

"Well, it was supposed to be fun, but apparently, it's a symbol of women's oppression." She takes more photographs.

She's laughing at me!

Game on, Ana.

"You want to be oppressed?" A delightful vision of her kneeling in front of me, hands tied while she services my cock, forms in my mind.

"Not oppressed. No," she whispers, continuing to take photographs.

"I could oppress you big-time, Mrs. Grey."

"I know you can, Mr. Grey. And you do, frequently."

Oh. Fuck. She's serious!

She lowers the camera and stares at me. "What's wrong, Christian?"

I just want to keep you safe.

She frowns and lifts the camera to her eye once more. "Tell me," she insists.

Get a grip, Grey.

I damp down my feelings. I can't deal with them right now. "Nothing," I answer, and drop out of her line of sight, remove the camera box from the bed, and grab Ana, dragging her down onto the comforter and sitting astride her.

"Hey!" she protests, and takes more photographs of me smiling down at her until I take the camera from her and frame her beautiful face in the viewfinder. I press the shutter and capture her loveliness for posterity.

"So, you want me to take pictures of you, Mrs. Grey?" She looks so earnest, through the lens. "Well, for a start, I think you should be laughing." Reaching down, I start to tickle her with my free hand. She squeals and struggles beneath me and I take picture after picture.

This is fun.

She laughs and laughs. "No! Stop!"

"Are you kidding?" I've never tickled anyone, and hers is a particularly gratifying reaction. I put the camera down and use both hands.

"Christian!" she squeals, and thrashes around beneath me. "Christian, stop!" she pleads, and I take pity on her. Grabbing both her hands, I hold them down on either side of her head. She's winded, flushed, her eyes dark, her hair a mess. She's stunning. She takes my breath away.

"You. Are. So. Beautiful," I whisper.

I don't deserve her.

Leaning down, I close my eyes and kiss her. Her lips are soft. Her mouth welcoming. I cradle her head in my hands, my fingers weaving into her hair, and I deepen our kiss, wanting more, wanting to lose myself in her. She responds, her body rising, her hands traveling up my arms and grasping my biceps.

Her response is a torch to my arousal.

No, it's more than that.

I want her, yes, but I *need* her more.

My body stands at attention, hungering for her. She's my life raft, while I'm adrift, trying to make sense of what's happening to me. When I'm with her, in her, all is right with the world. "Oh, what you do to me." I groan, yearning for her. I shift quickly so I'm lying on top of her, feeling her body along the length of mine. My hand skates down to her breast, her waist, her hip, and her behind, squeezing as I go. I kiss her again, pushing my knee between her legs, running my hand down her thigh and hitching her leg over my hip. I grind against her, wanting her. Her fingers are in my hair and she tugs and holds me to her mouth, while I take all I want.

I think I'm going to combust, I want her so badly.

Fuck.

Abruptly, I stop. *I need her. Now.*

Standing, I pull her off the bed and undo her shorts. Kneeling down, I drag them and her panties off, then we're back on the bed with her beneath me. My fingers make light work of my fly and free my impatient dick.

With one move, I'm inside her. Hard. Deep.

"Yes!" I hiss as she cries out.

I still and examine her face. Her eyes are closed, her head tipped back and her mouth open. I swivel my hips and drive myself deeper.

She groans and wraps her arms around me.

"I need you," I growl, and graze my teeth along her jaw, and then I'm kissing her again, taking her mouth and all she has to give while she binds herself to me, wrapping her legs and arms around me. I'm unleashed. My need for her greater than I ever imagined. I want to crawl inside her skin so she can keep me in one piece; keep me whole. She meets me stroke for stroke. Encouraging me with her soft cries of need. Her passion, loud and hot in my ear.

I feel her. She's close. So close. Reaching. With me. As I drive her higher. As she drives me higher.

"Come with me," I rasp, and rear up over her. "Open your eyes. I need to see you." She peers up at me, eyes dazed with longing, and she lets go, tipping her head back and screaming her orgasm for all to hear.

It pushes me over the edge and I climax, driving myself into her and calling out her name. I collapse to the side, bringing her with me, and turn us both so that she's sprawled on top of me. I drag precious air into my lungs while still inside her, holding her tightly.

My beacon. My dream catcher. My love. My life.

Someone wants to kill us. Damn them.

She kisses my chest, soft, sweet kisses. "Tell me, Christian, what's wrong?"

I tighten my hold on her and close my eyes.

I don't want to lose you.

"I give you my solemn vow," she whispers, "to be your faithful partner in sickness and in health, to stand by your side in good times and in bad, to share your joy as well as your sorrow."

I still. She's reciting her vows. I open my eyes. Her face is a picture of sincerity and her love-light shines so bright from her beautiful face. "I promise to love you unconditionally, to support you in your goals and dreams, to honor and respect you, to laugh with you and cry with you, to share my hopes and dreams with you, and bring you solace in times of need. And to cherish you for as long as we both shall live." She sighs, gazing at me and willing me to speak.

"Oh, Ana," I murmur, and move, easing out of her, so that we're lying side by side, lost in each other's eyes. I stroke her face with my knuckles and thumb. From memory, I recite my vows, my voice hoarse as I try to contain my emotion. "I solemnly vow that I will safeguard and hold dear and deep in my heart our union and you. I promise to love you faithfully, forsaking all others, through the good times and the bad, in sickness and in health, regardless of where life takes us. I will protect you, trust you, and respect you. I will share your joys and sorrows and comfort you in times of need. I promise to cherish you and uphold your hopes and dreams and keep you safe at my side. All that is mine is now yours. I give you my hand, my heart, and my love from this moment on for as long as we both shall live."

Tears well in her eyes.

"Don't cry," I whisper, brushing away a stray tear with my thumb.

"Why won't you talk to me? Please, Christian."

I close my eyes.

Talking about it makes it real, Ana.

"I vowed I would bring you solace in times of need. Please don't make me break my vows," she pleads.

I have no defenses against her.

I love her.

Before Ana, I didn't feel *anything*. And now, I feel *everything*. Every emotion is so heightened. It's hard to process. Hard to understand.

Her expression hasn't changed. She's begging me.

I sigh, defeated. "It's arson," I whisper, as if this is a huge failing on my part. "And my biggest worry is that they are after me. And if they are after me—" The next thought is unbearable.

"They might get me," Ana finishes the sentence in a whisper and caresses my face as her eyes soften. "Thank you."

"What for?"

"For telling me."

I shake my head. "You can be very persuasive, Mrs. Grey."

"And you can brood and internalize all your feelings and worry yourself to death. You'll probably die of a heart attack before you're forty, and I want you around far longer than that."

"You'll be the death of me. The sight of you on the Jet Ski—I nearly did have a coronary." I flop back on the bed and cover my eyes with the back of my hand to blot out the memory. But it doesn't work. In my mind, she's lying on the cold, hard floor. I shudder.

"Christian, it's a Jet Ski. Even kids ride Jet Skis. Can you imagine what you'll be like when we visit your place in Aspen and I go skiing for the first time?"

I gasp and turn to look at her, alarmed. *Skiing. No!*

"Our place," I remind her.

She's wearing that smile—the one I stare at every day in my office. Is she laughing at me? No. I don't think so. It's her compassion. "I'm a grown-up, Christian, and much tougher than I look. When are you going to learn this?"

I shrug. She doesn't look tough to me—not when I see her out cold on a sticky green rug.

"So, the fire. Do the police know about the arson?"

"Yes," I respond.

"Good."

"Security is going to get tighter," I tell her.

"I understand." Her eyes sweep down over my body, and suddenly her lips quirk up.

"What?"

"You."

"Me?"

"Yes. You. Still dressed."

"Oh." I glance down. I'm still dressed. I grin when I look back at Ana and let her know how hard it is for me to keep my hands off of her, especially when she's giggling.

Her eyes brighten immediately and she moves quickly, straddling me.

Shit. I grab her wrists, somehow knowing what she's going to do.

"No," I whisper, as the darkness makes an unwelcome return to my chest, ready to claw its way out. I take a deep breath. "Please don't," I plead. "I couldn't bear it. I was never tickled as a child." Ana puts her hands down and I continue, "I used to watch Carrick with Elliot and Mia, tickling them, and it looked like such fun, but I, I—"

She puts her finger on my lips. "Hush, I know." She removes her finger and plants a sweet kiss in its place. Scooting down, she rests her cheek to my chest, and I hold her, pressing my nose into her hair. Her scent is soothing, mixed with the pungent fragrance of sex. We lie for several minutes in our calm after the storm, before she interrupts our quiet, comfortable silence. "What is the longest you've gone without seeing Dr. Flynn?"

"Two weeks. Why? Do you have an incorrigible urge to tickle me?"

"No." She laughs. "I think he helps you."

I snort. "He should. I pay him enough." I stroke her hair and she turns her face to me. "Are you concerned for my well-being, Mrs. Grey?"

"Every good wife is concerned for her beloved husband's well-being, Mr. Grey."

"Beloved?" I whisper, wanting to say the word out loud, to hear it ring between us with all its significance.

"Very much beloved." She leans up to kiss me.

It's a relief that she knows the truth and yet she still loves me. My anxiety has evaporated, replaced by hunger. I smile down at her. "Do you want to go ashore to eat?"

"I want to eat wherever you're happiest."

"Good. Aboard is where I can keep you safe. Thank you for my present." I reach for it and, turning it around, hold it at arm's length and snap a picture of the two of us wrapped around each other.

WE TAKE COFFEE POST-DINNER inside the impressive dining room on the *Fair Lady*. "What are you thinking about?" I ask, as Ana looks wistfully out the window.

"Versailles."

"Ostentatious, wasn't it?"

Ana looks at our surroundings.

"This is hardly ostentatious," I observe.

"I know. It's lovely. The best honeymoon a girl could want."

"Really?" I smile. Pleased.

"Of course it is."

"We only have two more days. Is there anything you'd like to see or do?"

"Just be with you," she says.

I rise and come around the table and drop a kiss on her forehead

"Well, can you do without me for about an hour? I need to check my e-mails, find out what's happening at home."

"Sure," she says.

"Thank you for the camera."

As I head into the study, I notice that for some reason, I'm feeling far more settled. Could it be the delicious dinner, the sex, or telling Ana about the arson? It could be a combination of all those. I pull my phone out of my pocket and notice a missed call from my dad.

"Son," he says when he answers his phone.

"Hi, Dad."

"How's the South of France?"

"It's great."

"And Ana?"

"She's great, too." I can't help my smile.

"You sound happy."

"Yes. The only fly in the ointment is the fire."

"Your mother told me about that. But not much damage, I hear."

"No."

"What's the matter, Christian?" He adopts a serious tone, probably in response to my monosyllabic reply.

"It was arson."

"Shit. Police involved?"

"Yes."

"Good. This and your helicopter. It's a lot to deal with."

"Welch is on it. But we don't have a clue who it might be. Have you noticed anything unusual?"

"No, I can't say that I have. But I'll keep a watchful eye."

"Do," I insist.

"Is the jet safe?" he asks.

"The Gulfstream? Yes. I think so."

"Perhaps you should fly back commercial."

Why?

"It's just a thought. I don't want to worry you. I'll let you go."

"Thanks for checking in, Dad."

"Christian. I'm here for you. Always. Enjoy the rest of your evening." He hangs up, and I wonder what he's going to do with the information I've just given him. I don't dwell on it, but call Ros for an update.

I'M STILL ON THE phone when Ana pops her head around the door later. She blows a kiss at me and leaves me to my conversation with Andrea, who is sorting our flights back to Seattle.

Ana is curled up asleep when I return to our cabin. I slip into bed beside her and pull her into my arms without waking her. I kiss her hair and close my eyes.

I have to keep her safe. I have to keep her safe…

Through the lens, I watch my wife sleep soundly at last. Earlier, Ana was talking, begging someone in her dreams not to go. I wonder who? Me? Where would I go without her? She's been plagued by nightmares since the arson at Grey House was confirmed. She's even taken to sucking her thumb on the odd occasion while she sleeps. I wonder if it might have been better for us to fly home earlier. But I was reluctant to leave the tranquility of *Fair Lady*, and so was Ana. And at least I've been able to comfort her after her night terrors—hold her. Soothe her. Like she holds me, when I have mine.

We have to catch this asshole.

How dare he, or she, frighten my wife.

I've taken my father's advice and we're flying commercial. It's been a while for me, but Ana has never flown international first class, so it will be a new experience for her. We're leaving out of London, and I've grounded the jet in Nice until it's had a thorough inspection. I'm not taking any chances, not with my crew and not with my wife.

Apart from the nightmares, the remaining days of our honeymoon have been blissful. Reading. Eating. Swimming. Sunbathing on board. Making love. These have been magical days. There's just one more activity I want to do, before we go.

I push the shutter and hope that the sound won't wake her. The camera's been a welcome gift, and I've rediscovered my passion for photography. We're in such a splendid, photogenic setting after all; the *Fair Lady* is yar.

Ana stirs and stretches her hand out, to my side of the bed, looking for me. The gesture warms my heart.

I'm not far away, baby.

She opens her eyes, startled, I think, so I put the camera on the floor and quickly lie down beside her. "Hey, don't panic. Everything's fine," I whisper. I hate her wary look. I push her hair off her face. "You've been so jumpy these last couple of days."

"I'm okay, Christian," she lies. Her forced smile is for my sake. "Were you watching me sleep?"

"Yes. You were talking."

"Oh?" Her eyes widen.

"You're worried." I kiss the soft spot above her nose to try to reassure her. "When you frown, a little *v* forms just here. It's soft to kiss. Don't worry, baby, I'll look after you."

"It's not me I'm worried about, it's you," she grumbles. "Who's looking after you?"

"I'm big enough and ugly enough to look after myself. Come. Get up. There's one thing I'd like to do before we head home."

Something fun.

I slap her ass, and I'm rewarded with a gratifying squeal.

I bound off the bed, and she follows.

"Shower later. Put your swimsuit on."

"Okay."

THE CREW HAVE LOWERED the Jet Ski into the water. My life vest is on, and I'm helping Ana into hers. I strap the ignition key and kill cord to her wrist.

"You want me to drive?" she asks, incredulous.

"Yes." I grin. "That's not too tight?"

"It's fine. Is that why you're wearing a life jacket?" She arches a brow, unimpressed.

"Yes."

"Such confidence in my driving capabilities, Mr. Grey."

"As ever, Mrs. Grey."

"Well, don't lecture me," she warns, and I know she's talking from bitter experience.

I hold up my palms in surrender. "Would I dare?"

"Yes, you would, and yes, you do, and we can't pull over and argue on the sidewalk here."

"Fair point well made, Mrs. Grey. Are we going to stand on this platform all day debating your driving skills, or are we going to have some fun?"

"Fair point well made, Mr. Grey." She climbs onto the craft, and I slide on behind her and look up to find we've attracted a small audience on deck: the crew, our French security, and Taylor. I kick us away from the small pontoon and wrap my arms and clamp my thighs around Ana. She inserts the ignition key, presses the start button, and the engine powers into life with a gutsy roar. "Ready?" she shouts.

"As I'll ever be."

Slowly, she opens up the accelerator and the Jet Ski glides away from the ship.

Steady, Ana.

I tighten my hold on her as Ana increases our speed and we shoot across the water. "Whoa!" I shout, but it doesn't stop her. She leans forward, taking me with her, and speeds toward the open sea, then veers toward the shore, where the runway at Nice airport juts out into the Mediterranean.

"Next time we do this we'll have two Jet Skis," I shout.

That would be fun. Racing together.

Ana soars across the waves. We bounce a little, as it's choppier on the water today with the brisk summer breeze. As she nears the shore, a plane flies overheard. The noise is deafening.

Shit.

Ana swerves suddenly. I shout, but I'm too late, and we're both bucked off the craft and into the Mediterranean. The water closes over my head, into my eyes and my mouth, but I kick up and surface immediately, shaking my head and looking for Ana. The Jet Ski bobs, lifeless and harmless, not far from us, and Ana is wiping the water from her eyes. I swim toward her, relieved she's surfaced. "You okay?" I ask when I get close.

"Yes," she croaks. And she's grinning from ear to ear.

Why is she smiling? She just catapulted us into the cold sea.

I pull her into my wet embrace and hold her face between my palms, checking to see that she wasn't hit by the Jet Ski.

"See, that wasn't so bad!" she gushes, and I know she's okay.

"No, I guess it wasn't. Except I'm wet."

"I'm wet, too."

"I like you wet." I leer at her.

"Christian!" She admonishes me for my lewd look, and I can't help myself. I kiss her.

No.

I consume her. We're both winded when I pull away.

"Come. Let's head back. We have to shower. I'll drive." I swim over to the Jet Ski, vault onto it, and pull her up behind me.

"Was that fun, Mrs. Grey?"

"It was. Thank you."

"No, thank *you*. Shall we go home now?"

"Yes. Please."

ANASTASIA IS SIPPING CHAMPAGNE and reading off her iPad as we sit in the Concorde lounge at Heathrow and wait for our connecting flight to Seattle. This is one of the things I loathe about traveling on a scheduled flight: the waiting. But Ana seems happy enough. Occasionally, from the corner of my eye, I notice her surreptitious glances in my direction.

Inside, I'm dancing. I love that she's watching me.

I'm reading the *Financial Times*. It makes for sober reading. The global markets are still skittish in the wake of the recent budget deficit issues and Black Monday. The dollar is sinking. Also there's an article on whether the rich should pay more tax; Warren Buffett seems to think we should, and maybe he's right.

Ana takes a photograph, with the flash on, surprising me. I blink the blur of the bright lights out of my eyes and watch as she switches the flash off.

"How are you, Mrs. Grey?" I ask.

"Sad to be going home." She pouts. "I like having you to myself."

I take her hand and kiss her knuckles in turn. "Me, too," I whisper.

"But?" she asks.

Damn. She heard my unspoken doubt. Her eyes narrow, shrewd and interrogative. She's not going to let this go until I tell her. I sigh. "I want this arsonist caught and out of our lives."

"Oh."

Exactly.

"I'll have Welch's balls on a platter if he lets anything like that happen again." My tone sounds cold and sinister, even to me.

But this has gone on too long. We need to catch the fucker.

Ana gapes at me, then raises the camera and takes a quick shot. "Gotcha."

I smile, relieved that she's lightened the mood. "I think it's time to board our flight. Come."

"SAWYER, CAN WE GO through the front?" I ask, and he pulls the Audi up to the curb outside Escala. Taylor climbs out and opens my door. Ana is fast asleep.

"Thanks, Taylor," I say as I stretch my legs. "It's good to be back."

"It is, sir."

"I'll wake Ana." Opening her door, I lean over her. "Hey, sleepyhead, we're home." I unbuckle her seat belt.

"Hmm," she hums, and I lift her into my arms. "Hey, I can walk," she grumbles sleepily.

Oh, no, baby. "I need to carry you over the threshold."

She puts her arms around my neck. "Up all thirty floors?"

"Mrs. Grey, I am very pleased to announce that you've put on some weight."

"What?"

"So, if you don't mind, we'll use the elevator."

Taylor opens the doors to the Escala lobby and smiles. "Welcome home, Mr. Grey, Mrs. Grey."

"Thanks, Taylor," I answer.

We head into the lobby. "What do you mean I've put on weight?" Ana glares at me.

She's pissed.

"Not much." I grin to reassure her. Tightening my hold on her as I walk to the elevator, I recall how she looked when I picked her up from SIP, after we split up. How thin and sad she was. The memory is sobering.

"What is it?" she asks.

"You've put on some of the weight you lost when you left me." My answer is quiet. *That was me. I was responsible for her sadness.*

I never want to see her like that again.

I press the call button.

"Hey." Ana caresses my face and her fingers entwine in my hair. "If I hadn't gone, would you be standing here, like this, now?"

And just like that, she pours oil on my troubled waters.

"No." I smile. Because it's true. I step into the elevator, holding my wife, and lightly brush my lips over hers. "No, Mrs. Grey, I wouldn't. But I would know I could keep you safe, because you wouldn't defy me."

"I like defying you," she says with her coquettish smile.

I chuckle. "I know. And it's made me so happy."

"Even though I'm fat?" She pouts.

I laugh. "Even though you're fat." My lips capture hers once more, and she tightens her hold on my hair as we lose ourselves in each other.

The elevator pings, and we are back at Escala for the first time as husband and wife. "Very happy," I whisper, my body stirring. I carry her into the foyer and I want to bypass everything and everyone and take her to bed. "Welcome home, Mrs. Grey." I kiss her once more.

"Welcome home, Mr. Grey." Her face is alight with joy.

I carry her into the main living room and set her down on the kitchen island. From the cupboard, I take down two champagne flutes, and from the fridge I retrieve a chilled bottle of Grand Année Bollinger, our favorite rosé. Opening the bottle with a quick twist of the cork, I pour the pale pink sparkling liquid into each glass. I hand one to Ana, who's still sitting on the counter, and stand between her legs. "Here's to us, Mrs. Grey."

"To us, Mr. Grey," she answers with a shy smile.

We clink glasses and each take a sip.

"I know you're tired." I run my nose against hers. "But I'd really like to go to bed, and not to sleep." I kiss the corner of her sweet mouth. "It's our first night back here, and you're really mine."

She moans, closes her eyes, and raises her head, giving me access to her throat.

Ana. You goddess.

My love.

My life.

My wife.

I'm expecting the smooth roll of the *Fair Lady* as she floats on the Mediterranean, and the sounds of the crew readying her for the day. But when I open my eyes, I'm at home. Outside, the golden dawn heralds a beautiful morning, and beneath my arm Ana tenses. She's staring at the ceiling, trying to stay still.

"What's wrong?" I whisper.

Her eyes meet mine, and for a moment she looks lost. "Nothing." Her face softens as she smiles. "Go back to sleep." My dick responds enthusiastically to her smile, far more roused than me. Blinking, I rub my face and stretch my limbs in an effort to wake my mind and the rest of my body.

"Jet lag?" I ask.

"Is that what this is? I can't sleep."

"I have the universal panacea right here, just for you, baby." Grinning, I nudge her hip with my erection. She giggles, rolling her eyes, and her teeth tease my earlobe as her hand skates down my body to my waiting cock.

WHEN I STIR AN hour or so later, it's early morning. I've slept well, and Ana is still asleep beside me. I let her rest and get up quietly; a quick run in my gym is what I need. While I'm on the treadmill with Four Tet blaring in my ears, I check the markets and watch the news. It's going to be quite the adjustment to return to my routine. Ana and I have been in a blissful bubble for the last few weeks, but now I'm ready to go back to work. I'm excited. My wife and I are going to forge this new life together, and as of yet I have no idea what that will entail. Maybe we could travel; I could take Ana to see the Great Wall of China, the Pyramids—hell, all the Wonders of the World. I could ease up at the office—Ros has done a great job since I've been away—and Ana could stop working. After all, she won't need the money.

But she loves her job, and she's good at it.

Maybe she has great ambitions in publishing.

I shake my head; she would be safer if she stayed at home.

Damn. Don't dwell on the negative, Grey.

ANA IS IN THE shower when I enter the bathroom, and I cannot resist. I step in behind her. "Good morning. Let me scrub your back, Mrs. Grey." She hands me the sponge and body wash with a distracted smile. Lathering up the sponge, I start soaping her neck. "Don't forget we're going to my parents' for lunch. I hope you don't mind. Kate will be there." I kiss her ear.

"Hmm," she murmurs, eyes closed.

"You okay?" I ask. "You're quiet."

"I'm good, Christian. Getting pruny." She wiggles her fingers.

"I'll let you go."

She smiles, exits the shower cubicle, and grabs her robe on the way out. She seems happy enough, but I think my girl is preoccupied. Something's up.

Ana is in the kitchen making breakfast when I enter. She looks lovely wearing a black strappy top and the skirt she wore on our walk around Saint-Paul-de-Vence.

"Coffee?" she asks.

"Please."

"Sourdough toast?"

"Please."

"Preserves?"

"Apricot. Thanks." I kiss her cheek. "I've got some things to do before we leave for lunch."

"Okay, I'll bring breakfast to you."

IN MY STUDY, I find Gia Matteo's latest plans for the house on my desk where Gail must have left them. Setting them aside to review later, I fire up my iMac and get to work. Welch and Barney are combing through all of the past week's footage from the CCTV cameras at

Grey House, but there's no news on the arsonist yet. Welch has been rolling out additional security at each of the GEH sites. I read through the schedule for our personal protection, to find it includes an additional operative. Her name is Belinda Prescott. But today, it's Ryan and Sawyer who will accompany us to my parents' place—Taylor, quite rightly, has gone to visit his daughter after so many weeks away.

Ana pushes the door open using her back, and places coffee and toast on my desk.

"Thank you, wife."

"You're welcome, husband." Her smile is thin. "I'm going to unpack."

"You don't have to, Gail can do it."

"It's okay. I want to be busy."

"Hey." I get up and catch her hand before she leaves, scrutinizing her face. "What's wrong?"

"Nothing." She leans up to kiss my cheek. "I'll be ready to leave midday."

I frown and release her. "Okay."

Something's up.

But I have no idea what it could be.

It's unsettling.

Perhaps Ana needs time to readjust to this time zone. She leaves, and I turn my attention to work, setting aside my disquiet for now. I have an e-mail from Gia Matteo, who wants to see us tomorrow to discuss her latest plans. I let her know that's fine and suggest a meeting for early evening.

There's good news from Eurocopter: they can replace both of *Charlie Tango*'s engines, so she should be back, fully functioning, within a couple of weeks; however, there's still no progress in the FBI investigation into her sabotage. It's irritating.

Why is it taking so long?

I move on and review the latest e-mails from Ros; the sooner I get through these, the sooner I can get back to my wife.

THE DRIVE TO MY parents' home is a joy. I haven't driven my R8 for weeks, and with my wife by my side, I'm enjoying the lush greenery of urban Seattle. After the old-world charm of the South of France, the landscape is pleasingly familiar. It's good to be home. I've missed driving, especially in this car. I check the rearview mirror and, sure enough, Sawyer and Ryan are on our tail.

Ana is quiet beside me, gazing at the scenery that's dappled with summer sun as we speed, top down, along I-5. "Would you let me drive this?" she asks out of the blue.

Is that what she's been thinking about?

"Of course. What's mine is yours. If you dent it, though, I will take you into the Red Room of Pain." I give her a wolfish grin, knowing that I'm using her spurious name for the playroom, not mine.

Her mouth drops open. "You're kidding. You'd punish me for denting your car? You love your car more than you love me?" She sounds incredulous.

"It's close," I tease, reaching over to squeeze her knee. "But she doesn't keep me warm at night."

"I'm sure it could be arranged. You could sleep in her," Ana retorts.

I laugh, loving her banter. "We haven't been home one day and you're kicking me out already?"

"Why are you so pleased?"

I flash her a quick grin, while keeping my eyes on the road. "Because this conversation is so…normal."

Isn't this what marriage is all about? The to and fro between us?

"Normal!" she scoffs. "Not after three weeks of marriage! Surely."

What? My smile withers. *She was serious? She's gonna kick me out?*

"I'm kidding, Christian."

Hell. So was I!

She presses her lips together, looking sullen, then mutters, "Don't worry, I'll stick to the Saab." She turns to stare at the scenery once more.

So much for marital banter. "Hey. What's wrong?" I ask.

"Nothing."

"You're so frustrating sometimes, Ana. Tell me."

She turns her head to me, a smirk twisting her lips. "Back at you, Grey."

I'm the problem? Me?

Shit.

"I'm trying," I respond.

"I know. Me, too." She smiles, and I think she's okay. But I'm not sure. Maybe her heart is still in the Côte d'Azur.

Or perhaps she's upset over the arson?

Maybe the increased security?

Hell, I wish I knew.

"BRO!" IT'S ELLIOT WHO answers the front door at my parents' home. "How's it hanging?" He grabs my hand and pulls me into a bear hug.

"Perpendicular," I mutter. "How are you, Elliot?"

"It's great to see you, hotshot. You're looking good. You got a little sun." Then he turns his attention to Ana. "Sister!" he bellows, and he sweeps my wife off her feet.

"Hello, Elliot." She giggles, and it's a relief to hear her laugh. He sets her down.

"Looking beautiful, Ana. He treating you well?"

"Mostly."

"Come in." Elliot steps aside. "Dad's in charge of the BBQ."

MY PARENTS ARE EXPERT hosts and love entertaining. We're on the terrace in the backyard, sitting around the table. Across the lawn, there's the familiar view of the bay and Seattle's skyline in the distance. It's still stunning. Grace has gone all out, as usual, so there's plenty of food. Carrick holds us captive with family camping stories and his BBQ skills, and we're seated with Elliot, Kate, Mia, and Ethan. It's weird, I've always felt removed from my family, not that they excluded me—it's more that I siloed myself, to protect myself. Sitting here now, watching them laugh and tease one another—and me—and take such a keen interest in my wife and our honeymoon—I kind of regret having been so guarded. To think of all those years I missed locked in an ivory tower of my own making—an accusation that Ana frequently levels at me.

Perhaps she's right.

Our hands are entwined, and I fondle the rings on her finger, reluctant to release her. She seems to have brightened up, the way she's laughing with Kate, whatever was bothering her forgotten, I hope.

Elliot is talking about the new house. "So if you can get the plans finalized with Gia, I have a window September through to mid-November and can get the whole crew on it." Elliot puts his arm around Kate and clasps her shoulder. His thumb lightly brushes her skin. I think he really likes her. This has to be a first.

"Gia is due to come over to discuss the plans tomorrow evening," I reply. "I hope we can finalize everything then." I look at Ana.

"Sure." She smiles, but some of the light in her eyes fades.

What is it?

She's driving me crazy.

"To the happy couple." Dad raises a glass, and a smile, and everyone seconds the sentiment.

"And congratulations to Ethan for getting into the psych program at Seattle," Mia interjects, pride ringing in her voice. She's obviously smitten, and I wonder if she's gotten into his pants yet. It's difficult to tell from the smirk he gives her.

My family is thirsty for information about our honeymoon, so I give them an executive summary of the last three weeks.

Ana remains quiet.

Is she regretting all this?

No, I can't let myself go there.

Grey, get a grip.

Elliot makes some crude joke and stretches his arms, sending his glass flying onto the flagstones, where it smashes rather dramatically. My mother leaps up, as do Mia and Kate, while Elliot sits there like the dope he is.

Seizing the opportunity this distraction presents, I lean over and whisper to Ana, "I am going to take you to the boathouse and finally spank you in there if you don't snap out of this mood."

She gasps and checks that no one is listening. "You wouldn't dare!" she challenges, her voice husky.

I raise a brow.

Bring it, Ana.

"You'd have to catch me first—and I'm wearing flats," she hisses for my ears only.

"I'd have fun trying."

Ana turns a delightful and familiar shade of pink and stifles her smile.

There she is, my girl.

Mom serves us strawberries and whipped cream, which reminds me of London; this and Eton mess were the staple summer desserts there. As we finish up, we're caught short by a sudden shower. "Ah! Everyone inside," Grace cries as she gathers the serving dish.

We all grab plates, cutlery, and glasses and bolt back into the kitchen.

Ana looks happier, her hair a little wet, while she giggles with Mia. It warms my heart to see her with my family—they have fallen in love with her, like I have. Perhaps Mia will tell her what's happening with Ethan. I smile; inquiring minds need to know.

We head into the den to shelter from the rain and I take a seat at the upright piano. It's an old, worn, but much-loved Steinway, with a warm, rich tone. I press the middle C key and the sound rings through the room perfectly in tune. I smile, thinking of Grace. I suspect she keeps it tuned, as she plays on the odd occasion, though I haven't heard her play for years. And I haven't played here for so long—I can't even remember the last time. As a child, music was my refuge. It was somewhere I could escape and lose myself, at first in the tedious repetition of scales and arpeggios, and then in each piece I learned.

Music and literature got me through puberty.

There's sheet music on the rest, and I wonder who it belongs to, maybe Grace, maybe her housekeeper—she plays, I think. It's a song I know, "Wherever You Will Go" by The Calling. My family gathers, continuing their conversations, while I read the music. My fingers flex, instinctively following the song.

I could play this.

And before I know it, I've started to play. The words are on the sheet music and I sing along. A few bars later I'm lost in the melody and the poignant lyrics—it's just me and the piano and the music.

It's a beautiful song. About loss…and love.

"I'll go wherever you go…"

Slowly, the silence in the room intrudes into my consciousness.

The chatting has ceased. I stop playing, and turn around on the stool to find out what has caught everyone's attention. All eyes are on me.

What the hell!

"Go on," Grace prompts, her voice wavering with emotion. "I've never heard you sing, Christian. Ever." She's almost inaudible, but I can hear her because of the oppressive silence in the room. Her face glows with pride and wonder and love.

It's a gut punch.

Mom.

A well of feeling pours from my heart into my chest, filling me up and threatening to drown me.

I can't breathe.

No. I cannot do this.

I shrug and surreptitiously take a deep breath and look at my wife, my anchor. She seems puzzled, possibly by the weird reaction of my family. In an effort to blot them out for a moment, I turn and stare through the French windows.

This is why I distance myself.

This.

To escape these...*feelings.*

There's a sudden and almost spontaneous burst of chatter, and I get up and stand at the window. From the corner of my eye, I see Grace embrace my wife with an unbridled enthusiasm that surprises Ana. My mother whispers in her ear, and my throat burns with the same choking emotion from a moment ago. With a beseeching look, Grace kisses Ana's cheek, then announces in a throaty voice, "I am going to make some tea."

Ana takes pity on me and comes to my rescue. "Hi," she says.

"Hi." I slip my arm around her and tug her to my side, finding comfort in her warmth. She slides her hand in the back pocket of my jeans. Together, we watch the rain through the French window, the sun still in the distance. Somewhere there must be a rainbow.

"Feeling better?" I ask her.

She nods.

"Good."

"You certainly know how to silence a room," she says.

"I do it all the time." I grin down at her.

"At work, yes, but not here."

"True, not here."

"No one's ever heard you sing? Ever?"

"It appears not." My tone is wry.

She stares up at me as if she's trying to solve a puzzle.

It's just me, Ana. "Shall we go?"

"You going to spank me?" she whispers.

What?

Ana is, as ever, unexpected. Her words twist and turn through me, awakening my desire. "I don't want to hurt you, but I'm more than happy to play."

Ana nervously scans the room.

Baby, no one can hear us. I tilt my head and whisper in her ear, "Only if you misbehave, Mrs. Grey."

She squirms in my arms, and her face breaks into an impish grin. "I'll see what I can do."

Does she know how adrift I felt a moment ago?

Does she say this stuff to bring me back?

I don't know, but right now, my heart swells with my love for her.

My answering grin is just as broad. "Let's go."

"IT'S SO GOOD TO see you so happy, darling," Grace says, her gaze unwavering as she presses her palm against my cheek.

"Thanks for lunch." I give her a quick peck.

"You are welcome, always, Christian. This is your home, too."

"Thank you, Mom." I pull her into an impulsive hug. She beams up at me, then turns her attention to Ana, hugging her hard. When I manage to pry Ana from my mother's clutches, we wave our good-byes to everyone else and head to the car. As we do, it occurs to me that her decrepit Beetle must have been a stick shift too.

Let's do this, Grey.

"Here." I toss the R8 key at Anastasia. She catches it with one hand. "Don't bend it or I will be fucking pissed."

"Are you sure?" Her voice is full of excitement.

"Yes, before I change my mind."

What's mine is yours, baby. Even this...I think.

She lights up like Christmas, and rolling my eyes at her elation, I open the driver's door to let her in. She starts the engine before I'm even in the car.

"Eager, Mrs. Grey?" I ask as I fasten my seat belt.

"Very." She flashes me a wild-eyed smile and I wonder if I've made a huge mistake. She doesn't take the top down—my girl is not wasting any time. Slowly, she reverses so that she can turn the car around in the driveway. I glance behind us, and Sawyer and Ryan are scrambling into the SUV.

Where were they?

Ana reaches the end of the driveway and glances nervously at me. Her early bravado has slipped a little. "You're sure about this?"

"Yes," I lie.

She inches out into the road and I brace myself. As soon as she's on the pavement, she puts the pedal to the metal and we shoot down the street.

Fuck. "Whoa! Ana! Slow down! You'll kill us both!"

She eases off the accelerator. "Sorry," she says, but I know from her tone she's anything but, and I'm reminded of our time, only yesterday, on the Jet Ski.

I smirk at her. "Well, that counts as misbehaving."

Ana slows down a little more.

Good. That's got her attention.

She drives steadily along Lake Washington Boulevard and through the Tenth Street intersection. My phone buzzes. "Shit." I struggle to retrieve it from my jeans. It's Sawyer. "What?" I snap.

"Sorry to disturb you, Mr. Grey. Are you aware of the Black Dodge following you?"

"No." Turning around, I survey the street behind us through the cramped rear window of the R8, but as we're on a bend, I don't see any cars.

"Mrs. Grey is driving?"

"Yes. She is." Ana turns onto Eighty-Fourth Avenue.

"The Dodge set off after you left. The driver was waiting in the car. We ran the plates. They're fake. We don't want to take any chances. Could be nothing. Or it could be something."

"I see." Myriad thoughts dart through my mind. Maybe this is just a coincidence. No. After everything that's happened recently, this can't be a coincidence. And whoever is following us could be armed. My scalp prickles with alarm. How could this have happened? Sawyer and Ryan were out there the whole time. Weren't they? They didn't think it odd that someone was sitting in a car? Did it follow us to my parents' place?

"Do you want to try to lose them?" Sawyer asks.

"Yes."

"Will Mrs. Grey be okay?"

"I don't know."

When has she ever let me down?

Ana is concentrating on the road ahead, but her earlier spirit has vanished and her grip on the steering wheel has tightened; she's figured out something's wrong. "We're fine. Keep going," I tell her in the most soothing tone I can muster.

Her eyes widen, and I know I've failed to reassure her.

Shit. I pick up the phone again. Sawyer is talking. "We haven't been able to get a close look at the driver. The 520 is probably the best place to try. Mrs. Grey could try to lose them there, too. The Dodge is no match for the R8."

"Okay, on the 520. As soon as we hit it." I say.

Damn, I wish I was driving.

"We'll be right behind the Dodge. We'll try to come alongside it. Are you okay with this?

"Yes."

"Do you want to put us on speaker, so Mrs. Grey can hear us?"

"I will."

I slot the phone onto the speaker cradle.

"What's wrong, Christian?"

"Just look where you're going, baby," I murmur gently. "I don't want you to panic, but as soon as we're on the 520 proper, I want you to step on the gas. We're being followed."

Ana blinks several times as she absorbs this news, and the color drains from her cheeks

Shit.

She sits up straighter and squints into the rearview mirror, no doubt trying to identify our pursuer.

"Keep your eyes on the road, baby." I speak softly. Calmly. I don't want to spook Ana any more than she's spooked already. We just need to get back to Escala as quickly as possible and lose this asshole.

"How do we know we're being followed?" Her voice is high-pitched and breathless.

"The Dodge behind us has false license plates."

She drives carefully across the Twenty-Eighth Street intersection, around the roundabout and up the 520 on-ramp. Traffic is light, so that's something. Ana's eyes flick to the rearview mirror, then she takes a deep breath and abruptly seems to slow down.

Ana, what are you doing?

She's studying the flow of traffic; suddenly she drops a gear and floors the gas so we shoot forward through a break in the traffic onto the highway. The Dodge has to slow right down to a crawl to wait for a gap to follow us.

Whoa. Ana. Clever girl!

But we're going too fast!

"Steady, baby." I keep my voice even, though inside my stomach is in knots. She drops her speed and starts to weave between the two lanes. Knotting my hands together, I hold them in my lap so I don't distract her. "Good girl." I glance behind us. "I can't see the Dodge."

"We're right behind the unsub, Mr. Grey," Sawyer's voice says over the speaker. "He's trying to catch up with you, sir. We're going to try to come alongside. Put ourselves between your car and the Dodge."

"Good. Mrs. Grey is doing well. At this rate, provided the traffic remains light, and from what I can see it is, we'll be off the bridge in a few minutes."

"Sir."

We speed past the bridge control tower. We're halfway. Ana is traveling fast, but smoothly and confidently. She's got this. "You're doing really well, Ana."

"Where am I headed?"

"Mrs. Grey, head for I-5 and then south. We want to see if the Dodge follows you all the way."

The lights on the bridge are green, thank goodness, and Ana continues at speed. "Shit." There are cars backed up coming off the bridge. Ana slows, and I see her glance in the rearview mirror, looking for the Dodge.

"Ten or so cars back?" she says.

Staring behind us, I spot it. "Yeah, I see it. I wonder who the fuck it is?"

"Me, too. Do we know if it's a man driving?" Ana directs her comment to my phone.

"No, Mrs. Grey. Could be a man or woman. The tint is too dark."

"A woman?" I ask.

Ana shrugs. "Your Mrs. Robinson?"

What? No!

I've not heard from Elena since—well, since the wedding, when she sent that fucking text. I reach for my phone and pull it out of the cradle to mute it.

"She's not my Mrs. Robinson," I grumble. "I haven't spoken to her since my birthday."

That's not right, Grey. I called her when I gifted her the business, but now is not the time to mention that. "Elena wouldn't do this. It's not her style."

"Leila?"

"She's in Connecticut with her parents. I told you."

"Are you sure?"

"No. But if she'd absconded, I'm sure her folks would have let Flynn know. Let's discuss this when we're home. Concentrate on what you're doing."

"But it might just be some random car."

"I'm not taking any risks. Not where you're concerned." I sound brusque, but I don't care. Ana, as ever, is challenging. Unmuting my BlackBerry, I place it back in the speaker cradle.

The traffic starts to ease, and Ana's able to increase her speed along the intersection.

"What if we get stopped by the cops?" she asks.

"That would be a good thing."

"Not for my license."

"Don't worry about that." The arson attempt and *Charlie Tango*'s sabotage are all part of a police investigation. I'm sure any police officer would be more interested in our stalker.

"He's cleared the traffic and picked up speed." Sawyer's disembodied voice is calm and informative. "He's doing ninety."

Ana accelerates and my beautiful car responds like the finely honed machine she is, climbing to ninety-five with ease.

"Keep it up, Ana," I assure her.

Ana coasts onto I-5 and immediately crosses several lanes to get into the fast lane.

Smooth, baby. Smooth.

"He's hit one hundred miles per hour, sir."

Fuck. "Stay with him, Luke," I bark at Sawyer.

A semi lurches into our lane and Ana hits the brakes, so we're thrown forward. "Fucking idiot!" I shout.

Christ. He could have killed us!

"Go around him, baby," I grit between clenched teeth. Ana maneuvers across three lanes, past several cars and the fucking semi, then back into the passing lane, leaving the asshole behind us. "Nice move, Mrs. Grey. Where are the cops when you need them?"

"I don't want a ticket, Christian," she says without heat. "Have you had a speeding ticket driving this?"

"No." But nearly.

"Have you been stopped?"

"Yes."

"Oh."

"Charm. It all comes down to charm."

Yes, Mrs. Grey. Believe it or not, I can be charming.

"Now concentrate. Where's the Dodge, Sawyer?" I ask.

"He's just hit one hundred and ten, sir," Sawyer says.

Ana gasps and she puts her foot down so the Audi picks up speed. There's a Ford Mustang in our way.

Fucking hell.

"Flash the headlights," I yell.

"But that would make me an asshole."

"So be an asshole!" I hiss, trying to keep my anger at the Mustang and my spiraling anxiety in check.

"Um, where are the headlights?" Ana asks.

"The indicator. Pull it toward you."

The prick gets the message and moves over, giving us the finger. "He's the asshole," I mutter. "Get off on Stewart," I tell Ana. "We're taking the Stewart Street exit," I inform Sawyer.

"Head straight to Escala, sir."

Ana glances in the mirror, her brow furrowed. She signals and moves across four lanes of the highway, straight down the off-ramp, slowing down and then turning smoothly onto Stewart Street.

She's amazing.

"We've been damned lucky with the traffic. But that means the Dodge has, too. Don't slow down, Ana. Get us home."

"I can't remember the way," she squeaks.

"Head south on Stewart. Keep going until I tell you when."

She cruises down the street.

Shit, the lights at Yale are on yellow.

"Run them, Ana," I urge.

Ana overreacts and we're thrown back as we speed through the intersection. The light on red.

"He's taking Stewart," Sawyer says.

"Stay with him, Luke."

"Luke?"

"That's his name." Didn't you know?

She glances at me.

"Eyes on the road!" I yell.

"Luke Sawyer?"

"Yes!" *Why are we talking about this now?*

"Ah."

"That's me, ma'am," Sawyer says. "The unsub is heading down Stewart, sir. He's really picking up speed."

"Go, Ana. Less of the fucking chitchat."

"We're stopped at the first light on Stewart," Sawyer informs us.

"Ana—quick—in here." I point to the parking lot on the south side of Boren Avenue. She turns sharply, gripping the steering wheel, and the expensive tires on my magnificent R8 squeal in disapproval, but Ana holds it, and swerves into the crowded lot.

Shit. That must have been a quarter-inch off the tread.

"Drive around. Quick."

Ana takes us to the back of the parking lot. "In there." I point to an empty space. Ana gives me a quick, panicked look. "Just fucking do it," I growl. And she does. Perfectly. As if she'd spent her whole life driving my car.

Well done, Ana.

"We're hidden in the parking lot between Stewart and Boren," I tell Sawyer.

"Okay, sir. Stay where you are; we'll follow the unsub." He sounds a little irritated.

Tough.

I turn to Ana. "You okay?"

"Sure." Her voice is deathly quiet, and I know she's really shaken.

I try for humor to calm us both. "Whoever's driving that Dodge can't hear us, you know."

Ana laughs. Loudly. Too loudly. She's masking her fear.

"We're passing Stewart and Boren now. I see the lot. He's gone straight past you, sir."

Thank Christ. The relief is instant, for Ana, too. I blow out a breath. "Well done, Mrs. Grey. Good driving." Reaching up, I startle her when I stroke my fingertips down her face. She takes a huge gulp of air.

"Does this mean you'll stop complaining about my driving?" she asks.

I laugh, and it's cathartic. "I wouldn't go so far as to say that."

"Thank you for letting me drive your car. Under such exciting circumstances, too." She's trying to stay bright, but she sounds brittle as if she's about to break.

I switch off the ignition, as she's made no attempt to do so. "Maybe I should drive," I offer.

"To be honest, I don't think I can climb out right now, to let you sit here. My legs feel like Jell-O." Her hands are shaking.

"It's the adrenaline, baby. You did amazingly well, as usual. You blow me away, Ana. You never let me down." I stroke her cheek again with the back of my hand because I need to touch her, to reassure her and me that we're safe. Tears well in her eyes, and her choked sob surprises us both as tears start coursing down her face. "No, baby, no. Please don't cry." I can't bear to see her cry. Reaching over, I unbuckle her seat belt, grasp her waist, and pull her over the center console into my lap; her feet remain on the driver's seat. Smoothing her hair off her face, I kiss her eyelids, and her cheeks, then bury my nose in her hair as she curls her arms around my neck and sobs into my throat. Cradling her close, I let her cry it out.

Ana. Ana. Ana. You did so well.

Sawyer's voice startles us. "The unsub has slowed outside Escala. He's casing the joint."

"Follow him," I order.

Ana wipes her nose with the back of her hand, sniffles, and takes a deep breath.

"Use my shirt," I offer, and kiss her temple.

"Sorry," she says.

"What for? Don't be."

She wipes her nose again, and I hold her chin, tipping it up and kissing her tenderly. "Your lips are so soft when you cry, my beautiful, brave girl." I keep my voice low, conscious of our security at the other end of the phone.

"Kiss me again," she whispers, and all I hear is the need in her voice. It lights a fire in my soul. "Kiss me." Her voice is husky and insistent. Retrieving my BlackBerry from its cradle, I hang up and toss it on the seat, next to her feet. I weave my fingers through her hair, holding her in place while my lips find hers and my tongue finds hers. She welcomes it, her tongue caressing mine and kissing me back with an intensity that steals my breath away. She clutches my face, her fingers skimming over stubble as she takes all I have to offer.

I groan. And my body responds. All the adrenaline heading south.

Fuck. I want her.

I move my hand down her body, feeling her, brushing her breast, her waist, and landing on her backside. She moves, sliding on top of my trapped dick. "Ah!" I pull away, panting.

"What?" she says against my lips.

"Ana, we're in a car lot in Seattle."

"So?"

"Well, right now I want to fuck you, and you're shifting around on me; it's uncomfortable."

"Fuck me, then." She kisses the corner of my mouth, as her words take me by surprise. I stare into her dark, dark eyes that are nearly all pupil. All lust. All need.

"Here?" I breathe, shocked.

"Yes. I want you. Now."

I can't believe she's said that. "Mrs. Grey, how very brazen." I scan our environs. We're well hidden. There's no one here. We won't be seen. We can do this. My hunger for her goes into overdrive. I tighten my grip on her hair, holding her where I want her, and kiss her again. Harder. Deeper. Taking. Taking. More and more.

My other hand skims again down her body to her thigh.

She grips my hair.

"I'm so glad you're wearing a skirt." My hand travels up her thigh. She wriggles on top of me.

Ah!

"Keep still," I grunt, tightening my grasp on her hair at the nape.

She's going to unman me.

I cup her through her lace panties; they're damp already.

Oh, baby.

With my thumb, I circle her clitoris, once, twice, and she groans, her body quivering at my touch. "Still," I whisper, and capture her lips with mine while my thumb teases the swollen bud beneath the dewy lace. I move the material aside and sink two fingers inside her.

She groans and tips her hips toward my hand in greeting.

Oh, my greedy girl.

"Please," she whispers.

"Oh. You're so ready," I murmur in appreciation, and slowly slide my fingers in. And out. And in. And out. And in. "Do car chases turn you on?"

"You turn me on."

Her words feed my hunger, and I withdraw my hand and slide my arm beneath her knees and lift her so she's fully on my lap, facing the windshield.

She gasps. But she starts grinding down on me.

I groan. "Place your legs either side of mine," I order, and run my hands down her outer thighs, then back up, yanking her skirt out of the way. "Hands on my knees, baby. Lean forward, lift that glorious ass in the air. Mind your head." She raises her beautiful behind and I unzip my jeans, freeing my heavy cock. Putting one arm around her waist, with my other hand I tug her panties sideways and, lifting my hips, force her down and thrust balls-deep inside her in one swift move.

My breath whistles through my lips. *Yes!*

"Ah," Ana cries out for anyone to hear, and she grinds down on me.

I groan, teeth clenched. She feels out of this world. I grasp her jaw and lean her back against me and angle her head so I can kiss her throat. Grabbing her hip with my other hand to keep her steady, I move into her, and I'm in deep. She pushes up and starts to ride me. Hard. Fast. Frantic.

Ah… I bite down on her earlobe.

She moans and moves and together we set a heady, desperate pace.

Her rising and falling. Me, bucking into her.

I move my fingers to her clitoris and start to tease her through her panties.

Ana makes a garbled cry, and the sound does nothing for my restraint.

Shit. I'm going to come. "Be. Quick," I rasp in her ear. "We need to do this quick, Ana."

Sweat beads on my brow, and I increase the pressure on her clitoris, circling around and around with my fingers.

"Oh," Ana cries.

"Come on, baby. I want to hear you."

We move. And move. And then I feel her. Building. Ready.

Oh, thank God. I slam into her once more and she tips her head back on my shoulder so she's facing the roof of the car.

"Yes!" I grind out between my teeth and she comes. Loudly.

"Oh, Ana." I wrap her in my arms and climax deep inside her.

When I return to reality, my head is bent against hers, and she's limp on top of me. I run my nose along her jaw and kiss her throat, her cheek, and her temple. "Tension relieved, Mrs. Grey?" I tug her earlobe. She whimpers, in a good way, and I smile. That's a great sound. "Certainly helped with mine," I murmur, and shift her forward, withdrawing from her. "Lost your voice?"

"Yes," she breathes.

"Well, aren't you the wanton creature? I had no idea you were such an exhibitionist."

She sits up immediately, watchful and wary. Her fatigue, a memory. "No one's watching, are they?" She scours the parking lot.

"Do you think I'd let anyone watch my wife come?" I stroke my hand down her back and she calms, turning around to give me a sweet playful smile.

"Car sex!" she exclaims, and her eyes flare with a sense of achievement, I think.

I grin. *Yes. It's a first for me, too, Ana.* I tuck a wayward strand of hair behind her ear. "Let's head back. I'll drive." Leaning forward, I open the car door, and Ana clambers off my lap so I can do up my fly.

When I'm back in the driver's seat I call our security detail.

"Mr. Grey, it's Ryan."

"Where's Sawyer?" I snap.

"At Escala."

"And the Dodge?"

"I'm following the Dodge south on I-5."

"How come Sawyer's not with you?"

"He thought it better to wait at Escala once we saw her—"

"Her?" I gasp.

"Yes. The driver is a woman," says Ryan. "I was going to follow her to see if we can ID her."

"Stick with her."

"Will do."

I hang up and look at Ana.

"The driver of the Dodge is female?" She sounds shocked.

"So it would appear." I have no idea who it might be. It can't be

Elena, and surely not Leila. Not after all the work that Flynn has put in with her. "Let's get you home."

The R8 growls to life, and I reverse out of the space and head home.

"Where's the, um, unsub? What does that mean, by the way? Sounds very BDSM."

"It stands for *unknown subject.* Ryan is ex-FBI."

"Ex-FBI?"

"Don't ask." That's a long story about doing the right thing, protecting an innocent, and getting fired for it. I'll tell her over dinner. He's probably why we know the plates on the Dodge were false. He has extensive connections.

"Well, where is this female unsub?" Ana continues.

"On I-5, heading south." Whoever it is drove past our place, scouted it out, and left. Who the hell is it?

Ana reaches over and runs her fingers down my inner thigh.

Whoa.

We're stopped at a red. I scoop her hand into mine to stop its progress to my dick. "No. We've made it this far. You don't want me to have an accident three blocks from home." I kiss her index finger and release her, and concentrate on getting us back in one piece. I need a thorough debrief from Sawyer. I'm pissed that there was someone waiting for us outside my parents' house. Surely they should have seen the Dodge.

What the hell am I paying them for?

Ana is quiet until we approach the garage at Escala. "Female?" she says out of nowhere. She sounds incredulous.

"Apparently so." I sigh and punch in the code to raise the gate to the garage.

Yeah. I wish I knew who. Welch has investigated all my exsubmissives, even those from the private club I used to frequent. They're all in the clear, as I knew they would be. I'll check on Leila via Flynn, but last I heard she was happy back in the bosom of her family.

I ease the R8 into her designated space.

"I really like this car," Ana says, giving me a welcome break from my dark thoughts.

"Me too. And I like how you handled it—and how you managed not to break it."

She smirks. "You can buy me one for my birthday."

Anastasia Ste...Grey! I gape at her, shocked. I don't think she's ever asked me for anything, but she steps out of the car before I can respond. I'm so astonished I don't know what to say. Once out, before she closes the door, she bends down and flashes me a sassy grin. "A white one, I think."

I laugh. White. Apt choice. She is the light to my darkness. "Anastasia Grey, you never cease to amaze me."

She shuts the door and I get out after her. She's waiting by the trunk, looking every bit the just-fucked goddess who wants a two-hundred-thousand-dollar car.

She's never asked me for anything.

Why is that so hot?

Leaning down, I whisper, "You like the car. I like the car. I've fucked you in it. Perhaps I should fuck you on it."

She gasps and her cheeks pink in that delightful way I love. The sound of a car pulling into the garage distracts me. It's a silver 3 Series BMW.

Cockblocker.

"But it looks like we have company. Come." Taking her hand, I guide her to the elevator. Sadly, we have to wait and we're joined by Mr. BMW Cockblocker. He looks my age. Maybe younger.

"Hi," he says, with an appreciative smile aimed at my wife.

I put my arm around Ana.

Back off, bud.

"I've just moved in. Apartment sixteen," he gushes at her.

"Hello," Ana says, her tone nothing but friendly.

We're saved by the elevator. Once inside, I keep Ana close. I glance down at her, willing her not to engage with this stranger.

"You're Christian Grey," he says.

Yep. That's me.

"Noah Logan." He holds out his hand. Reluctantly, I extend mine and he gives me a damp, overenthusiastic handshake. "Which floor?" he asks.

"I have to input a code."

"Oh."

"Penthouse."

"Oh. Of course." He presses the button for his floor and the doors close. "Mrs. Grey, I presume." He simpers like a nervous eighth-grader with an epic crush.

"Yes." She gives him a sweet smile, and they shake hands and the fucker blushes.

Blushes!

"When did you move in?" Ana asks, and I tighten my hold on her. *Don't encourage him.*

"Last weekend. I love the place."

She smiles. *Again!*

Mercifully, the elevator stops at his floor. "Great to meet you both," he says, sounding relieved, and steps out. The doors close behind him, and I enter the code for the penthouse into the keypad.

"He seemed nice," Ana says. "I've never met any of the neighbors before."

I grimace. "I prefer it that way."

"That's because you're a hermit. I thought he was pleasant enough."

"A hermit?"

"Hermit. Stuck in your ivory tower," Ana says, deadpan.

I try, really try, to suppress my smile. "*Our* ivory tower," I correct her. "And I think you have another name to add to the list of your admirers, Mrs. Grey."

She rolls her eyes heavenward. "Christian, you think everyone is an admirer."

Oh. Sweet. Joy.

"Did you just roll your eyes at me?"

She looks up at me from beneath her lashes. "I sure did," she whispers.

Oh, Mrs. Grey.

I cock my head to one side. The day has just improved one thousand percent. "What shall we do about that?"

"Something rough."

Fuck. Her words are arousing.

"Rough?" I swallow.

"Please."

"You want more?"

She nods, not taking her eyes off me. It's so fucking hot.

The doors of the elevator open, but neither of us step out. We just stare at each other, our attraction, our yearning, sparking between us like static. Ana's eyes darken, like mine, I'm sure.

"How rough?" I ask.

Ana's teeth sink into her full lower lip, but she says nothing.

Oh. Dear. God.

I close my eyes to savor this sensual moment, then grab her hand and march out of the elevator and through the double doors of the foyer. Sawyer is waiting.

Hell.

"Sawyer, I'd like to be debriefed in an hour," I state, wanting him gone.

"Yes, sir." He heads back into Taylor's office.

Good. I look down at my wife. "Rough?"

She nods, her expression serious.

"Well, Mrs. Grey, you're in luck. I'm taking requests today." My mind races with possibilities. "Do you have anything in mind?"

She raises her left shoulder in a coquettish shrug.

What does that mean? "Kinky fuckery?" I ask, to be clear.

She nods an emphatic yes, but her face flushes.

"Carte blanche?" I ask.

Her eyes flick to mine, and they're brimming with curiosity and sensuality. "Yes." Her husky affirmation feeds the flames of my desire.

"Come." We head upstairs to the playroom. "After you, Mrs. Grey." I unlock the door and step aside, and Ana strolls into my favorite room. I follow her in, switching on the lights. Ana turns, watching me as I lock the door.

Take a breath, Grey.

I love this moment.

Building anticipation.

It's exhilarating.

She stands there, waiting. Wanting. *Mine.*

Last time we were in here, I put her in the harness.

A memory of that flits through my mind. That was fun.

What shall I do with her today?

"What do you want, Anastasia?"

"You."

"You've got me. You've had me since you fell into my office."

"Surprise me, then, Mr. Grey."

She's so bold. "As you wish, Mrs. Grey." Folding my arms, I tap my index finger against my lip.

I know what I'd like to do.

I've wanted to do it for a long, long time.

But first things first.

"I think we'll start by ridding you of your clothes." Stepping forward, I grasp her short denim jacket, ease it off her shoulders, and drop it to the floor; her camisole is next. "Lift your arms." She does as she's told and I peel it off her lovely body. I offer her a soft, sweet kiss, then discard her top so it lands on her jacket. She's wearing a lacy black bra, her nipples visible and pressing through the fabric.

My wife is hot.

"Here," she says and, to my surprise, offers me a hair tie.

My dark confession in Saint-Paul-de-Vence has done nothing to discourage her, or to keep her away from me.

Don't overthink this, Grey.

I take it from her. "Turn around."

She does, with a small, private smile, and I wonder what she's thinking about.

Don't go there, either, Grey.

Quickly, I braid her hair and fasten it. With a tug, I pull her head back. "Good thinking, Mrs. Grey," I murmur, my lips brushing her ear, then I nip her earlobe. "Now turn around and take your skirt off. Let it fall to the floor."

She steps forward, turns on her heel, and with her eyes on mine, she unfastens her skirt and slides the zipper down, slowly. Her skirt flares out like a parasol and drifts to her feet.

She is Aphrodite.

"Step out from your skirt."

She complies and I kneel at her feet and grasp her ankle, unbuckling each of her sandals in turn. Once they're off, I sit back on my heels and gaze up at my wife. In black lacy underwear, she's spectacular. "You're a fine sight, Mrs. Grey." Kneeling up, I grab her hips and yank her forward, burying my nose at the blessed junction of her thighs.

She gasps as I inhale. "And you smell of you and me and sex. It's intoxicating." I kiss the top of her sweet cleft through the lace, then release her and gather her clothes and shoes before standing. With my hands full, I point with my chin. "Go and stand beside the table." I make my way to the chest of drawers. When I glance back at Ana, she's watching me like a hawk.

This will never do.

"Face the wall. That way you won't know what I'm planning. We aim to please, Mrs. Grey, and you wanted a surprise."

Ana obeys, and I drop her shoes beside the door and place her clothes on the chest. I strip off my shirt, remove my own shoes, and glance at her. She's still facing the wall. *Good.* From the butt drawer, I extract what I need, and leave the items on the chest while I find some music on the iPod: Pink Floyd, "The Great Gig in the Sky."

Okay. Let's see if she goes for this.

Moving back to Ana, I place my haul on the table, out of her sight line.

"Rough, you say, Mrs. Grey?" I whisper into her ear.

"Hmm."

"You must tell me to stop if it's too much. If you say stop, I will stop immediately. Do you understand?"

"Yes."

"I need your promise."

"I promise," she whispers, her tone husky with want.

"Good girl." I kiss her shoulder and then hook my finger beneath the bra strap across her back and gently run my finger under it, skimming over her flesh. "Take it off," I order.

I want her naked.

Hastily, she unhooks the back and lets it fall. Coasting my hands down her back to her hips, I hook my thumbs into her panties and slip them down her lovely legs. When I reach her ankles, I ask her to step out of them, and she obliges.

At eye level with her beautiful behind, I kiss one cheek, knowing that we're about to get better acquainted, and I stand. A thrill runs through me; I've been waiting for this moment.

"I'm going to blindfold you so that everything will be more intense," I murmur, and slip an airline eye mask over her eyes. Around us, the music swells and the singer lets loose, as if she's mid-climax.

Apt.

"Bend down and lie flat on the table. Now."

Ana's shoulders rise and fall quickly as her breathing escalates, but she does as she's told and lays down over the table.

"Stretch your arms up and hold on to the edge."

She reaches up and clutches the far edge. The table is wide, so her arms are fully extended.

"If you let go, I will spank you. Do you understand?"

"Yes."

"Do you want me to spank you, Anastasia?"

Her lips part as she takes in a breath. "Yes," she whispers, her voice hoarse.

"Why?" I ask.

She doesn't answer, though I think she's trying to shrug.

"Tell me," I prompt.

"Um."

I smack her hard across her ass, the sound echoing over the music and through the playroom. "Ah!" she cries out. For me, both sounds are deeply, deeply satisfying.

"Hush now." I gently rub her backside. Standing right behind her, I bend over her body, my cock straining against my jeans, and my fly digging into the soft swell of her behind as I plant a kiss between her shoulder blades. Slowly, I leave a trail of wet kisses across her back. When I stand, my saliva glistens in little patches on her skin.

"Open your legs."

She shuffles her feet apart.

"Wider."

She moans and does as she's told.

"Good girl," I whisper, and run my index finger down her spine, down to her coccyx, and over her anus. It shrinks and puckers beneath my touch. "We're going to have some fun with this," I whisper.

She tenses. But she doesn't stop me, so I skim my finger over her perineum and slowly ease it into her vagina.

Sweet. Heaven.

"I see you're very wet, Anastasia. From earlier or from now?"

She groans as I slip my finger in and out and she pushes back against my hand, wanting more. "Oh, Ana, I think it's both." My fingers move back and forth. "I think you love being here. Like this. Mine."

She moans, closing her eyes, and I withdraw my finger and smack her fine ass once more.

"Ah."

"Tell me." My voice is hoarse with my passion.

"Yes, I do," she whispers. I spank her again and she cries out, then I slide two fingers inside her and twist them once around to lubricate them. When I withdraw, I spread her essence up, and over and around her anus.

She tenses a little, once more. "What are you going to do?"

"It's not what you think," I reassure her. "I told you, one step at a time with this, baby." I reach for the lube and squirt a generous amount on my fingers, then massage it around her small, puckered hole. She squirms, her back rising and falling more rapidly with her accelerated breathing. Her lips part. She's excited. I smack her hard, aiming slightly lower, so my fingertips strike her labia that's soaked from her passion.

She moans and wiggles her ass, begging for more.

"Keep still," I order. "And don't let go." I squirt more lube on my fingers.

"Ah."

"This is lube." I spread some more over and around her anus. "I have wanted to do this to you for some time now, Ana." I grab the small, metal butt plug.

She groans and I drag the plug slowly down her spine. "I have a small present for you here," I whisper, and slide it down between her buttocks. "I am going to push this inside you, very slowly."

She inhales, breathless. "Will it hurt?"

"No, baby. It's small. Once it's inside you, I'm going to fuck you real hard."

Her lips part and she quivers. Leaning over her, I kiss her once again between her shoulder blades.

"Ready?"

Because I am.

My cock is almost bursting.

"Yes," she breathes.

With the plug in my left hand, I quickly coat it in lube, then skim my right thumb down between her buttocks, over her anus, and sink it into her vagina, circling inside her. My fingers brush against her clitoris, slowly, methodically taunting her eager bud while I move my thumb. She groans loudly with pleasure. And that's my cue. Very slowly, I push the plug into her ass.

"Ah!" she moans.

I'm met with a little resistance, so I circle my thumb inside her vagina, teasing the sweet spot inside her with the tip of my thumb, and push harder on the plug. Joy of joys, it slips inside her. Easily.

"Oh, baby." I swirl my thumb inside her again and feel the weight of the plug inside her butt. Slowly, I twist the plug, and Ana mewls, a strange sound of pure pleasure.

Whoa.

"Christian," she whimpers, lewd and needy, and I withdraw my thumb.

She's breathless.

"Good girl," I murmur. Leaving the plug in its place, I trace my fingers down her side until I reach her hip. Undoing my fly and freeing my dick, I grasp her hips with both hands, and pull her ass toward me. With my foot, I force her to widen her stance. "Don't let go of the table, Ana."

"No," she pants.

"Something rough? Tell me if I'm too rough. Understand?"

"Yes," she whispers. And in one swift move, I yank her toward me and slam inside her, to the hilt.

"Fuck!" she cries.

And I still, relishing the feel of my girl around me.

She's doing good, her breathing as harsh as mine. I reach between us and gently tug on the plug.

She lets out a breathtaking moan of pleasure.

It almost tips me over the edge.

"Again?" I whisper.

"Yes," she says, and she sounds desperate, begging for more.

"Stay flat," I insist, and ease out of her, then slam into her again.

"Yes," she hisses with loud, sibilant fervor. I pick up the pace, slamming inside her with a wild abandon that's exhilarating.

It's never felt like this.

Taking Ana to a darker side.

I fucking love it.

"Oh, Ana," I pant, and twist the plug around again.

She cries out as I keep rocking into her. Taking her. Consuming her. Owning her.

"Oh, fuck," she cries.

And I know she's close.

"Yes, baby," I whisper.

"Please," she begs.

"That's right."

You goddess, Ana.

I slap her hard and she lets go, screaming out loud and proud as she's gripped by her orgasm. I tug the plug out and toss it in the bowl.

"Fuck!" she screams, and I tighten my hold on her hips and let go, holding her to me and losing myself in my release.

I sag over her, spent but elated. Pulling her into my arms, I sink to the floor, curling her into my embrace as I catch my breath. She's gulping in air, her head resting on my chest.

"Welcome back," I say, removing the blindfold. She blinks, a little dazed, as her eyes adjust to the muted light. She looks okay. I tip her head back and press my lips to hers, anxiously trying to gauge how she's feeling.

Reaching up, she strokes my face.

I smile with relief. "Well, did I fulfill the brief?" I ask.

Her brow creases. "Brief?"

"You wanted rough." My tone is cautious.

Her face brightens. "Yes. I think you did."

Her words wrap around my soul. "I'm very glad to hear it. You look thoroughly well fucked and beautiful at this moment." I caress her cheek.

"I feel it," she hums. Holding her face, I kiss her with all the tenderness that she deserves. Because I love her.

"You never disappoint." *Ever.* "How do you feel?" I breathe.

"Good," she whispers and a telltale flush crosses her face. "Thoroughly well fucked." Her smile is shy and sweet and telling. And totally at odds with her profanity.

"Why, Mrs. Grey, you have a dirty, dirty mouth."

"That's because I'm married to a dirty, dirty boy, Mr. Grey."

I can't argue with that.

And I'm buoyant, grinning back at her. I must resemble the Cheshire Cat. "I'm glad you're married to him." My fingers grasp her braid, and I lift the end to my lips and kiss it. *I love you, Ana. Never leave me.*

She reaches for my left hand and, raising it to her lips, kisses my wedding ring. "Mine," she whispers.

"Yours," I answer, and I tighten my hold on her and drive my nose in her hair. "Shall I run you a bath?"

"Hmm. Only if you join me in it."

"Okay." I help Ana to her feet and stand up.

She points to the jeans I'm still wearing. "Will you wear your, er, other jeans?"

"Other jeans?"

"The ones you used to wear in here."

"Those jeans?" *My Dom jeans. The DJs.*

"You look very hot in them."

"Do I?"

"Yeah. I mean, really hot."

How could I refuse? I want to look hot for my wife.

"Well, for you, Mrs. Grey, maybe I will." I kiss her and grab the small bowl that contains our afternoon's entertainment, and I walk over to the chest of drawers to switch off the music.

"Who cleans these toys?" Ana asks.

Oh. Ah. "Me. Mrs. Jones."

"What?" Ana gasps in shock.

Yep. Gail knows everything, all my dirty little secrets, and she still works for me.

Ana is still gaping at me as if she expects more information. I switch off the iPod. "Well. Um—"

"Your subs used to do it?" Ana says, finally figuring it out.

All I have is an apologetic shrug. "Here." I offer her my shirt and she dons it quickly, and says no more about toy-cleaning. I leave our stuff on the chest and, taking Ana's hand, unlock the playroom door, and we head downstairs to our bathroom. She pauses on the threshold, yawns and stretches, a secret smile etched on her face.

"What is it?" I ask, turning on the faucets.

Ana shakes her head, avoiding eye contact.

Is she feeling shy all of a sudden?

"Tell me," I coax, as I pour bath oil into the running water.

Her cheeks develop a rosy flush. "I just feel better."

"Yes, you've been in a strange mood today, Mrs. Grey." I embrace her. "I know you're worrying about these recent events. I'm sorry you're caught up in them. I don't know if it's a vendetta, an ex-employee, or a business rival. If anything were to happen to you because of me—" The horrific image, of her lying in place of the crack whore, haunts me.

Stop, Grey. Stop.

She hugs me. "What if something happens to you, Christian?" She sounds bleak.

"We'll figure this out. Now let's get you out of this shirt and into this bath."

"Shouldn't you talk to Sawyer?"

"He can wait." My tone is clipped; I have a few choice words for him.

I slip my shirt off Ana.

Shit. The marks I left on her body are still there. Faded. But still present, reminding me that I'm an asshole.

"I wonder if Ryan has caught up with the Dodge?" Ana says, and I know she's ignoring my reaction.

"We'll see, after this bath. Get in." I offer her my hand, and she steps into the foam-filled tub. Gingerly, she sits down.

"Ow." She winces as her ass hits the hot water.

"Easy, baby," I whisper, but she smiles when she settles, submerged in the water. I strip out of my jeans and join her, sinking down behind her and gathering her to my chest.

Slowly I let myself relax.

Be in the moment, Grey.

That was really something.

Ana did so well. I nuzzle her hair and marvel at how easy it is to just *be* in her company. I don't have to talk; she doesn't have to talk. We can just lie and unwind in a bath together.

I close my eyes and reflect on the day.

What a crazy end to our honeymoon.

A car chase, which Ana handled brilliantly, like a pro.

I run the end of her braid through my fingers, absently.

And she let me have fun in the playroom, doing something I've wanted to do forever, and she's never done before.

My girl. My beautiful girl.

A few moments later, I remember that Gia Matteo will be joining us tomorrow evening. I break the comfortable silence between us. "We need to go over the plans for the new house. Later this evening?"

"Sure," Ana responds, and she sounds resigned. "I must get my things ready for work," she adds.

Her braid slips through my fingers. "You know you don't have to go back to work."

Ana's shoulders tense against me. "Christian, we've been through this. Please don't resurrect that argument."

Okay. I gently tug her braid, slanting her face toward me. "Just saying." I brush my lips over hers.

LEAVING ANA TO SOAK a little longer in the bath, I get dressed and wander through to my study for Sawyer's debrief. Mrs. Jones is in the kitchen.

"Evening, Gail."

"Mr. Grey. Welcome home, and congratulations once again."

"Thank you. Your sister okay?"

"All good, sir. Would you like anything?"

"No, thanks. I have some work to do."

"Mrs. Grey?"

I grin. "She's in the bath."

Gail smiles and nods. "I'll ask her when she's out, sir."

At my desk, I check my e-mails. Then buzz Sawyer. A moment later there's a brisk knock at my door.

"Come in."

Sawyer enters and stands before me, looking cool, calm, and professional in his suit and tie. His demeanor makes me so mad. Slowly, I get up from my desk and, placing both hands on it, lean toward him. "Where the fuck were you?" I shout.

He takes a small step back, surprised by my outburst.

"What the hell were you doing that you weren't ready to leave when we were?" I fold my arms, keeping a rein on my temper.

"Mr. Grey." He holds up his hands. "We were patrolling the grounds, like you asked us to do. And we didn't know you were leaving."

Oh.

"Also," he adds, getting into his stride, "I'd noticed the unsub. It arrived while we were out patrolling and I was going to investigate, when you came out of the house."

Ah.

I sigh, somewhat mollified. "I see. Okay." I should have told them we were leaving. And I know if Taylor had been with us, he would have left his colleague in the car.

"And Mrs. Grey set off at one hell of a pace." He raises a disapproving eyebrow.

I want to laugh at his response. I feel his pain, but I remain impassive. "She did," I admit. "Though you should have caught up. You're both trained in defensive driving."

"Yes, sir."

"Don't let it happen again."

"Yes, Mr. Grey." He looks a little contrite. "Sir," he says. "The unsub didn't follow us. He or she arrived shortly before you were leaving. I logged the exact time I noticed the car. It was 14:53 and they did not exit the vehicle. They knew where you were."

I pale. "What does that mean?"

"That someone could be watching your parents' house, sir. Or watching us here. Though I think we would have noticed if we were followed to Bellevue."

"Shit."

"Precisely. I've written a report for you and forwarded it to Taylor and Mr. Welch."

"I'll read it. Where's Ryan?"

"He's still on the road to Portland."

"Still?"

"Yes. Let's hope the unsub runs out of gas," Sawyer says.

"Why do you think the driver's a woman?" I ask.

"From the brief glimpse I got, I thought their hair was tied back."

"That's not definitive."

"No, sir."

"Keep me updated."

"Will do."

"Thank you, Luke. You can go."

He turns without a word and leaves my study while I sit back down at my desk, relieved that I don't have to fire him or Ryan, though I'll be glad when Taylor's back with us tomorrow evening. I contemplate Sawyer's theory; perhaps someone is watching my parents' place. But why? I should call my father, but I don't want to worry him, or my mother.

Shit. What to do?

My iMac has been nagging me about the latest update to its operating system, so I decide to install it, and open my laptop to check my e-mails and Sawyer's report.

I'm reading when my phone buzzes.

"Barney," I answer, surprised that he's contacting me on a Sunday.

"Welcome home, Mr. Grey."

"Thank you. What is it?"

"I've been going through the CCTV footage in the server room and I've uncovered something."

"You have?"

"Yes, sir. I couldn't wait until tomorrow to share it with you. I hope you don't mind. But I figured you'd want to know. I'll e-mail you a link and you can take a look yourself."

"You figured right. E-mail it to me now."

"Doing it."

"Will you stay on the line?"

"Yes, sir. I'm anxious for you to see it."

I smile. Barney is protective of his server room. I bet he's as pissed as I am by the unwelcome breach. His e-mail pops into my inbox; I open it and click on the link and I'm taken to a site I've not seen before. There are four different boxes that look like they might be monochrome views of my server room at Grey House. "Barney, you there?"

"Yes, Mr. Grey."

"What am I looking at?"

"This is the GEH security hub. If you click the play button in the menu on the left-hand side of the screen at the top, the footage from all the cameras within the server room will play." I do as I'm asked, and the footage plays four different views of the room. At the bottom center of each feed there's a date with a timer. It reads 08/10/11 07:03:10:05 and the milliseconds on the clock fly by. Via these four views, I watch a tall, slim man enter the room. He has scruffy dark hair and he's in pale, possibly white, coveralls. He walks to one of the servers, bends to the floor, and places a small black item that's hard to identify between two of the server cabinets. He stands and glances down at his handiwork, then, keeping his face fixed on the door, leaves.

"This is him?"

"I believe so, sir. It's not anyone we can identify. And that's where the incendiary device was found."

"That's over a week ago. How the fuck did he get in there?"

"The pass that correlates to that time of entry to the server room was issued to the cleaning crew."

"What?" How the hell did he get ahold of that?

"Exactly. We'll have to check that out tomorrow." The footage freezes.

"Did you just stop the feeds?" I ask.

"Yes, sir."

"Can you put these in a sequence?"

"Yes, sir."

"Quickly?"

"I can do it now."

"Has Welch seen this?"

"His team notified me of it. They've been combing the footage."

"Good."

A moment or so later my screen changes so I'm only looking at one feed. I press play again, and this time the sequence is longer, cutting between views. Each time one view finishes, I press play for the next.

"I can try and enhance the image," Barney says, his enthusiasm bubbling over in his tone. He wants to nail this son of a bitch, too.

"Do."

The image on my screen changes. It's sharper.

Suddenly, my study door opens. I look up, surprised, about to rebuke the intruder. It's Ana.

"So, you can't enhance it further?" I ask Barney.

"Let me try something." He's silent as Ana walks toward me with a look of quiet determination, and before I can do or say anything she crawls into my lap.

"I think that's as good as it's going to get," Barney says.

Ana puts her arms around my neck and snuggles beneath my chin, and I tighten my hold on her.

Is something wrong?

"Um, yes, Barney. Could you hold one moment?"

"Yes, sir."

I lift one shoulder to trap and hold my phone.

"Ana, what's wrong?"

She shakes her head, refusing to answer me. I grasp her chin and study her face, but her expression is unreadable. She frees her chin from my fingers and cuddles into me. I have no idea what's wrong, and frankly, I'm too engrossed in what Barney has found. I drop a kiss on her head. "Okay, Barney, what were you saying?"

"I can enhance the picture a little more."

I press play. The grainy black-and-white image of the arsonist appears on-screen. I press play once more, the arsonist moves closer to the camera, and I freeze the frame. "Okay, Barney, one more time."

"Let me see what I can do."

A dashed box appears around the head of the arsonist and suddenly zooms in.

Ana sits up and stares at the image. "Is Barney doing this?" she asks.

"Yes." And I know I sound as awed as she looks by Barney's technical prowess. "Can you sharpen the picture at all?" I ask him. The picture blurs, then refocuses moderately sharper on the asshole. He's looking down at the floor. Ana tenses and squints at the screen.

"Christian," she whispers. "That's Jack Hyde."

What!

"You think?" I squint at the image.

"It's the line of his jaw." Ana points at the screen following the monochromatic line of his chin. "And the earrings and the shape of his shoulders. He's the right build, too. He must be wearing a wig, or he's cut and dyed his hair."

I feel the blood drain from my face. *Hyde. Jack fucking Hyde!*

"Barney, are you getting this?" I put the phone down and switch to hands-free, then whisper to Ana, "You seem to have studied your ex-boss in some detail, Mrs. Grey."

Ana grimaces and shudders while anger surges like sulfuric acid through me.

"Yes, sir. I heard Mrs. Grey. I'm running facial-recognition software on all the digitized CCTV footage right now. See where else this asshole—I'm sorry, ma'am—this man has been within the organization."

"Why would he do this?" Ana asks.

I shrug, trying to mask my rage.

Fucking Hyde.

I put a stop to his creepy shit. Fired him. Punched him and broke his nose.

"Revenge, perhaps," I offer, darkly. "I don't know. You can't fathom why some people behave the way they do. I'm just angry that you ever worked so closely with him."

We have to get this information to the police, the FBI, and Welch, though he has some explaining to do. Hyde is obviously not in Florida. Why the hell did Welch think he was? I need to talk to him. And maybe, given all this time, Hyde may have skulked back to his apartment, here in Seattle. Welch needs to find him sooner rather than later, and if he does, I hope I get to punch that fucker's lights out again. One thing's for sure, I need to keep him away from my wife, keep her safe. I curl my arm around her waist.

"We have the contents of his hard drive, too, sir," Barney adds.

I interrupt Barney with the first thought that comes into my head. "Yes, I remember. Do you have an address for Mr. Hyde?" I don't want to alarm Ana with the details of what was on Hyde's old computer.

"Yes, sir, I do," Barney says.

"Alert Welch." Welch needs to make sure Hyde's not back home.

"Sure will. I'm also going to scan the city CCTV and see if I can track his movements."

"Check what vehicle he owns."

"Sir."

"Barney can do all this?" Ana whispers, clearly impressed.

I nod, feeling a little smug that he works for me.

"What was on his hard drive?" she asks.

I shake my head. "Nothing much."

"Tell me."

"No."

"Was it about you, or me?"

She is not going to drop this.

"Me." I sigh.

"What sort of things? About your lifestyle?"

No. I shake my head and place my index finger on her lips.

We are not alone, Ana.

She scowls at me but keeps quiet.

"It's a 2006 Camaro," Barney pipes up, excited. "I'll send the license details to Welch, too."

I'm sure he has them, but it doesn't hurt to be sure. "Good. Let me know where else that fucker has been in my building. And check this image against the one from his SIP personnel file. I want to be sure we have a match."

"Already done, sir, and Mrs. Grey is correct. This is Jack Hyde."

Ana grins, practically preening, she's so pleased with herself.

As she should be.

I run my hand down her back, proud of her. "Well done, Mrs. Grey." To Barney, I add, "Let me know when you've tracked all his movements at HQ. Also check out any other GEH property he may have had access to, and let the security teams know so they can make another sweep of all those buildings."

"Sir."

"Thanks, Barney." I hang up the phone. "Well, Mrs. Grey, it seems that you are not only decorative, but useful, too," I tease.

"Decorative?"

"Very." I press a soft kiss to her lips.

"You're much more decorative than I am, Mr. Grey."

I wind her braid around my wrist and hold her, pouring my gratitude into a deep and tender kiss. She's done so much today. And identified our perpetrator!

She pulls away.

"Hungry?" I ask.

"No."

"I am," I confess.

"What for?" She eyes me warily.

"Well—food, actually."

She giggles. "I'll make you something."

"I love that sound."

"Of me offering you food?"

"Your giggling." I kiss her head, and she eases herself off my lap.

"So, what would you like to eat, Sir?" she asks with faux sweetness.

She's making fun of me. Again.

I narrow my eyes. "Are you being cute, Mrs. Grey?"

"Always, Mr. Grey, Sir."

I see how it is.

"I can still put you over my knee," I whisper. Frankly, not much would give me greater pleasure.

"I know." Ana grins and places her hands on the arms of my office chair. She bends down and kisses me. "That's one of the things I love about you. But stow your twitching palm, you're hungry."

"Oh, Mrs. Grey, what am I going to do with you?"

"You're going to answer my question. What would you like to eat?"

"Something light. Surprise me."

"I'll see what I can do." She turns and struts out of my office, like she owns the place, which, of course, as my wife, she does.

I call Welch to interrogate him about what Barney and Ana have uncovered.

"Hyde?" While usually gruff, his voice is high-pitched with incredulity.

"Yes. In my fucking server room."

"We tracked his cell phone to Orlando. It's been there ever since. We assumed he'd been staying with his mother, as the phone was tracked to her condominium in Orlando. There are no records of him traveling elsewhere."

"Well. He's here." I take a deep breath, trying to keep a lid on my frustration.

He sighs, obviously annoyed. "So it would seem. I'll put the team straight on this. I don't know how he slipped through our fingers. I'll make inquiries and find out how and where we messed up."

"You do that. I want to know."

"It's a damned shame there are no prints from the server room," he says.

"None?

"No."

"Hell. He was probably wearing gloves, though it's difficult to tell from the footage," I speculate. "Perhaps Hyde's prints are on file somewhere."

"Interesting thought. In fact, the FBI recovered a partial print but has no match."

"From *Charlie Tango*?" I ask.

"Yes."

"Why didn't you let me know?"

"They didn't have a match, and it's only a partial print," Welch explains.

"Could Hyde be behind the sabotage of my EC135?"

"In the absence of any other suspects, I think it's a possibility," Welch's gravelly voice echoes over the phone.

"We had him on our list of suspects and he was right there this whole time."

I can't believe it.

"We dismissed him for three reasons," Welch clarifies. "First, we thought he was in Florida. He'd not been in his apartment in Seattle for some time, but we'll check on that now. Second, he's not withdrawn any cash from an ATM in the Seattle area. And third, his misdeeds seemed limited to harassing female colleagues."

"You should let the FBI know about all this," I say.

"I'll brief them," he says, and then changes tack. "Sawyer's informed me about the chase."

"He thinks my parents' house was being watched."

"It's a possibility. We'll need to track this Dodge down to be sure."

"The driver could have been Hyde."

"Yes. In light of what you've uncovered, could be."

"Given that he still poses a threat, I think we should provide security for all my family."

"That's a good idea. There were extensive details about all of them on Hyde's computer. You should consider letting your parents know."

I sigh. I don't want to alarm my family.

"We'll concentrate our efforts on locating Hyde."

"Find him."

"We'll redouble our efforts."

"You'd better," I warn. "Barney will be in touch and you can submit the server room footage as evidence to the police. I'll talk to my dad and get back to you."

"Yes, sir. We'll get on it." He hangs up.

I call my parents' landline, but it diverts to the answering machine. I try my dad's cell, but that goes straight to voice mail, too. They must be at evening Mass. I leave a message asking Dad to call me in the morning.

I gather Gia Matteo's plans and go in search of my wife and food.

Placing the plans on the kitchen island, I stroll over to Ana, who I have to say looks fetching even in sweatpants and her camisole. She's preparing some food; the mashed avocado looks good. I fold my arms around her and kiss her neck. "Barefoot and in the kitchen," I whisper into her fragrant skin.

"Shouldn't that be barefoot and pregnant in the kitchen?"

Pregnant! I tense. Shit. No. Kids. Hell no. "Not yet," I state, as I try to calm my suddenly spiked heart rate.

"No. Not yet!" Ana sounds as panicked as me.

I take a deep breath. "On that we can agree, Mrs. Grey."

She stops mashing the avocado. "You do want kids, though, don't you?"

"Sure, yes. Eventually. But I'm not ready to share you yet." I kiss her neck.

One day. Sure.

"What are you making? Looks good." I nuzzle her ear. She quivers and gives me a wicked grin.

"Subs." She smirks.

God, I love this woman's sense of humor.

I nip her earlobe. "My favorite," I whisper in her ear, and am rewarded with a poke in my side from her elbow. "Mrs. Grey, you wound me." I clutch my damaged side in a performance worthy of an Oscar winner.

"Wimp," Ana teases.

"Wimp?" Playfully, I slap her behind. "Hurry up with my food, wench. And later I'll show you how wimpy I can be." I spank her again and head to the fridge. "Would you like a glass of wine?" I ask.

Ana flashes me a quick smile. "Please."

ANA DOES GOOD SUB. What can I say?

Taking both our plates, I leave them in the sink for Gail. I top off both our wineglasses, then spread out Gia's plans over the breakfast bar. We pore over her drawings; she's worked hard and produced thorough and detailed elevations. Her designs are impressive. But what does my wife think?

Ana looks up at me. "I love her proposal to make the entire downstairs back wall glass, but…"

"But?" I prompt.

She sighs. "I don't want to take all the character out of the house."

"Character?"

"Yes. What Gia is proposing is quite radical, but, well, I fell in love with the house as it is, warts and all."

Oh. I think this house is in need of a serious update.

"I kind of like it the way it is," she says quietly, her expression serious.

In that moment, everything becomes clear to me. "I want this house to be the way you want. Whatever you want. It's yours."

She frowns. "I want you to like it, too. To be happy in it, too."

"I'll be happy wherever you are. It's that simple, Ana." *I mean it. You* are what will make the house a home, and I want you happy. *Always.*

"Well—" Her breath catches in her throat. "I like the glass wall. Maybe we could ask her to incorporate it into the house a little more sympathetically."

"Sure. Whatever you want. What about the plans for upstairs and the basement?"

"I'm cool with those."

"Good."

She bites her lip. "Do you want to put in a playroom?" she blurts, and her question completely takes me by surprise. She flushes.

Ana, Ana, Ana, even after today, you're still shy about what we do?

I hide my smile. "Do you?" I ask.

She raises one narrow shoulder, trying to look nonchalant. "Um, if you want."

I think she does.

"Let's leave our options open for the moment. After all, this will be a family home. Besides, we can improvise."

"I like improvising," she whispers.

Me, too, baby.

"There's something I want to discuss." I don't want separate bathrooms. I like showering with Ana too much.

Fortunately, she agrees.

"Are you going back to work?" Ana asks as I roll up the plans.

"Not if you don't want me to. What would you like to do?"

"We could watch TV."

"Okay." I deposit the plans on the dining table and we both head into the TV room.

On the couch, I pick up the remote and switch on the TV and start flicking through the channels, while Ana curls up beside me and rests her head on my shoulder.

This is nice.

"Any specific drivel you want to see?" I ask her.

"You don't like TV much, do you?" Ana says.

I shake my head. "Waste of time. But I'll watch something with you."

"I thought we could make out."

"Make out?" I stop flicking and stare at her.

"Yes." Ana frowns.

"We could go to bed and make out."

"We do that all the time. When was the last time you made out in front of the TV?" she asks with a shy smile.

Um... Never?

I shrug and shake my head, embarrassed to answer. I didn't do the make-out thing. I would have liked to. I remember Elliot bringing home girl after girl and making out with them

I used to burn with envy.

But I couldn't bear to be touched.

How can you kiss and cuddle someone when you can't tolerate their hands on you?

Fuck. Those were tough years.

I flick through the channels, and an old episode of *The X-Files* pops up.

Ha! Scully, my first adolescent crush.

"Christian?" Ana asks, bringing me back from my fucked-up past.

"I've never done that," I answer, quickly. *Can we move on?*

"Never?"

"No."

"Not even with Mrs. Robinson?"

I laugh. "Baby, I did a lot of things with Mrs. Robinson. Making out was not one of them." Ana looks horrified, and I want to kick myself for allowing Elena into our conversation. And then it occurs to me—maybe Ana has made out with countless boys. I narrow my eyes. "Have you?"

"Of course." She's scandalized that I would think otherwise.

"What! Who with?"

Ana clams up.

What the fuck? Does she have some first great love? I know nothing about her love life. I assumed, stupidly, that she didn't have one, because she was a virgin. "Tell me," I press her.

She gazes down at her hands, knotted in her lap. I place my hand over hers, and she glances up at me.

I'm just curious, Ana. "I want to know. So, I can beat whoever it was to a pulp."

She giggles. "Well, the first time—"

"The first time! There's more than one fucker?"

"Why so surprised, Mr. Grey?"

I run a hand through my hair. The thought of anyone touching Ana is…annoying. "I just am. I mean—given your lack of experience."

"I've certainly made up for that since I met you."

"You have." I grin. "Tell me. I want to know."

"You really want me to tell you?"

I'm interested in everything about you, Ana.

She takes a deep breath. "I was briefly in Texas with Mom and Husband Number Three. I was in tenth grade. His name was Bradley, and he was my lab partner in physics."

"How old were you?"

"Fifteen."

"And what's he doing now?"

"I don't know."

"What base did he get to?"

"Christian!" she chastises me, and we stare at each other.

Fuck this Bradley. What kind of a name is that, anyway?

I grab her knees, then her ankles, and tip her up so she falls back on the couch, and I lay down on top of her.

"Ah," she cries out.

I grab both her hands and raise them above her head. "So, this Bradley. Did he get to first base?" I whisper and run my nose down hers and leave soft kisses at the corner of her mouth.

"Yes," she breathes. I release one of her hands and clasp her chin and kiss her, properly, my tongue caressing hers, and her body rises to meet mine, her tongue twisting with mine.

"Like this?" I whisper.

"No. Nothing like that." Ana is breathless.

Releasing her chin, I skim my fingers down her body, then back to her breast. "Did he do this? Touch you like this?" Through the soft material of her top, my thumb skates repeatedly over her nipple, and it perks up at my touch.

"No." She writhes beneath me.

"Did he get to second base?" I blow the words gently in her ear as my hand travels down to her hip. My lips suck gently on her earlobe before my teeth tug it into my mouth.

"No." The word is a husky whisper.

I mute the TV. *The X-Files* can wait. I gaze down at Ana; she's tousled and dazed and looking up at me with big blue eyes that I could drown in. "What about Joe Schmo number two? Did he make it past second base?"

I move to her side and slip my hand into her sweatpants, keeping her pinned with my gaze.

"No."

"Good." I hold her in the palm of my hand, the gateway to heaven. "No underwear, Mrs. Grey. I approve." I kiss her again, and my thumb strokes her clitoris in a steady rhythm and I ease my index finger inside her.

"We're supposed to be making out," she murmurs with a moan.

I stop. "I thought we were?"

"No. No sex."

"What?" *Why?*

"No sex."

"No sex, huh?" I gently ease my finger out of her and remove my hand from her pants. "Here." I circle her mouth with my finger, then push it between her lips and onto her tongue. Once. Twice. Again.

Taste good, Ana?

I shift so I'm lying on top of her, between her legs, and I rock against her, giving my cock some relief.

She groans.

Oh, wow.

I grind against her. "This what you want?" And I repeat the action, hitting her sweet spot with my erection.

It feels good.

"Yes."

I tease her nipple with my fingers, tugging gently, feeling it lengthen beneath my touch. My teeth graze her jaw. She smells of Ana and jasmine and her arousal. "Do you know how hot you are, Ana?"

Her mouth opens, slack and wanting, as I tantalize her further, pushing at the junction of her thighs. She lets out an inarticulate moan and I seize the moment, tugging at her bottom lip, then invading her mouth with my tongue, tasting her arousal on mine.

It's so fucking hot.

I release her remaining hand and her fingers feel their way over my biceps and over my shoulders and into my hair. She tugs and I groan, staring down at her.

"Do you like me touching you?" she asks.

Why would she ask me that now?

I stop rubbing against her. "Of course I do." I'm breathless. "I love you touching me, Ana. I'm like a starving man at a banquet when it comes to your touch." Kneeling up between her legs, I maneuver her to a sitting position and remove her top in one swift move. I do the same with my shirt, yanking it over my head and throwing our clothes on the floor. While still kneeling, I seat her on my lap and rest my hands on her behind. "Touch me," I whisper.

She takes full advantage, brushing the tips of her fingers over my sternum and over my scars. I inhale sharply as her touch radiates through my body with the promise of fulfilment. My eyes stay on hers as she skims her fingers over my skin to my nipple, then to its twin; each react to her touch, hardening, erect, mirroring another part of my anatomy. She leans forward and presses her lips in a soft, sweet line across my chest. Her hands hold my shoulders, and she squeezes, and I feel her nails pinching my skin.

It's heady.

And to think a few months ago I would have said this was impossible.

Yet, here she is. Touching me. Loving me.

And I welcome it. All of it.

"I want you," I whisper, and her hands move to my head, her fingers in my hair. She yanks my head back and takes my mouth with hers. Claiming my tongue with hers.

Fuck. I groan loudly and push Ana back down on the couch, divesting her of her sweatpants in one hasty move, and freeing my erection at the same time. I move on her. "Home run," I murmur, and fill her in one rapid move.

She lets out a deep, guttural cry and I still, holding her face between my hands. "I love you, Mrs. Grey." And very slowly, I make sweet love to my wife until she cries out and falls apart in my arms, taking me with her and cocooning me with her limbs and keeping me safe.

ANA IS SPRAWLED ON my chest. I think it's the end of *The X-Files*.

"You know, we completely bypassed third base." Her fingers trace a pattern on my chest.

I chuckle. "Next time." I nuzzle her hair, inhaling her magical scent, and kiss her head. The end credits roll for *The X-Files* and, using the remote, I switch the sound back on.

"You liked that show?" Ana asks.

"When I was a kid."

Ana goes quiet.

"You?" I ask.

"Before my time."

"You're so young." I hug her tightly. "I like making out with you, Mrs. Grey."

"Likewise, Mr. Grey." She kisses my chest and the commercials start on the TV.

Why are we watching these?

Because I like being here, with her lying on me.

This is married life.

I could get used to this…

"It's been a heavenly three weeks," she says airily. "Car chases and fires and psycho ex-bosses notwithstanding. Like being in our own private bubble."

"Hmm." I tighten my arms around her. "I'm not sure I'm ready to share you with the rest of the world yet."

"Back to reality tomorrow." She sounds a little sad.

"Security will be tight—"

Ana silences me with her index finger. "I know. I'll be good. I promise." She leans up on her elbows, scrutinizing me. "Why were you shouting at Sawyer?"

"Because we were followed."

"That wasn't Sawyer's fault."

"They should never have let you get so far in front. They know that."

"That wasn't—"

"Enough." Sawyer fucked up and he knows it. "This is not up for discussion, Anastasia. It's a fact, and they won't let it happen again."

"Okay," she says. "Did Ryan catch up with the woman in the Dodge?"

"No. And I'm not convinced it was a woman."

"Oh?"

"Sawyer saw someone with their hair tied back, but it was a brief look. He assumed it was a woman. Now, given that you've identified that fucker, maybe it was him. He wore his hair like that."

That piece of shit is dead if I ever get ahold of him.

I run my hand down Ana's back, my fingers stroking her skin. Grounding me. Calming me. "If anything happened to you." The thought is unbearable.

"I know. I feel the same about you." She shivers.

"Come. You're getting cold." I sit up, taking her with me. "Let's go to bed. We can cover third base there."

To our relief, there are no photographers outside SIP when we pull up in the Q7. I'm hoping that the intense press scrutiny and intrusion into our lives will now ease off. Ana gathers up her briefcase when Ryan stops the car, and I can't resist one more try. "You know you don't have to do this."

"I know," she answers quietly, so Ryan and Sawyer can't hear. "But I want to. You know this." Her sweet kiss does little to mollify me. We both have to go back to reality. Don't we?

"What's wrong?" she asks, and I realize I'm frowning.

I'm not going to see her until this evening. We've spent the last three weeks or so in each other's company, and it's been the best time of my life. Sawyer climbs out of the car to open her door, and I seize my opportunity. "I'll miss having you to myself."

She places her palm on my cheek. "Me, too." Her lips brush mine. "It was a wonderful honeymoon. Thank you."

It was for me as well, Ana.

"Go to work, Mrs. Grey."

"You, too, Mr. Grey."

Sawyer opens her door, she squeezes my hand, and I watch both of them head into the building.

"Take me to Grey House," I instruct Ryan, and stare out of the window. It's a cooler, cloudy day—a precise match for my mood. I'm strangely out of sorts. Perhaps this is what Ana was feeling yesterday, though she never managed to articulate it to me.

If this was what you were experiencing, Ana, I get it. It's a case of the post-honeymoon blues.

AS RYAN AND I walk up to the entrance at Grey House I notice Barry and an additional security guard who I don't recognize on the other side of the glass doors. Barry typically stands by the elevator, and is usually the only security operative in reception.

"Good morning, Mr. Grey. Welcome back," he says as he holds open the door.

"Thank you, Barry. Good morning."

They are checking that all GEH staff are wearing their passes. I'm not wearing mine, but then I'm the exception to the rule. Welch was not lying when he said he was doubling down on all our security measures.

Greeting both of the receptionists with a salute, I head to the elevators. They both wave back, and I notice they're wearing their passes, too. It's reassuring.

Andrea and Sarah look up as the elevator doors open; each have ID lanyards. "Welcome back, Mr. Grey," Andrea says.

"Good morning. How are you? Oh, these are for you and Sarah." I place a bag that contains a large box of chocolates—from Ladurée, near the Jardin des Tuileries in Paris—that Ana insisted I buy for them on the desk. Andrea blushes, speechless.

Yes. I don't blame her. Apart from her wedding present, this is a first.

"Thank you," Sarah blurts, eyeing the bag with keen interest.

"You're welcome. I would have bought some of their world-famous macarons, too, but was advised that the chocolates have a longer shelf life."

"Thank you, Mr. Grey," Andrea says, recovering her composure. "Coffee?"

"Please. Black."

"Coming up."

I head into my office, leaving Sarah's giggles and Andrea's quiet hushing behind me. Rolling my eyes, I shut the door and cut off their chatter.

At my desk, I call Welch for an update on Jack Hyde.

Once that call is over, I e-mail Ana, wondering how she is adapting to life back at SIP.

From: Christian Grey
Subject: Bubble
Date: August 22 2011 09:32
To: Anastasia Grey

Mrs. Grey
Love covering all the bases with you.
Have a great first day back.
Miss our bubble already.
x

Christian Grey
Back in the Real World CEO, Grey Enterprises Holdings, Inc.

My phone buzzes. "Mr. Grey, I have your father on the line," Andrea says.

"Put him through."

"Christian, you called?"

"Dad." I tell him everything that has happened with Jack Hyde since I fired him in mid-June. "His vendetta against me is out of hand. We're submitting the server room footage to the FBI and the police. They can press charges. They just have to locate him first. But given what we found on his hard drive, I think I should extend our security protocols to you, Mom, Mia, and Elliot."

"That seems excessive."

"Dad, he's a bright guy. I wouldn't put anything past him."

Carrick blows out a breath. "Well, if you think it's necessary."

"I do. We were followed from your house yesterday. He knows where you live."

"Fuck!"

Dad!

My father sighs. "Get on it. I'll talk to Mom and Mia."

"I'll tell Elliot."

"Thanks, Christian. I'm sorry it's come to this."

"Me, too."

With my father's reluctant agreement secured, I phone Welch back to implement enhanced security measures for my family.

I just have to tell Elliot. I don't know how he'll take the news.

When I look at my e-mails I notice the one I sent to Ana has bounced. Maybe she hasn't had a chance to change her e-mail address at work.

Let's have some fun with this.

I forward the e-mail I sent her.

From: Christian Grey
Subject: Errant Wives
Date: August 22 2011 09:56
To: Anastasia Steele

Wife
I sent the e-mail below and it bounced.
And it's because you haven't changed your name.
Something you want to tell me?

Christian Grey
CEO, Grey Enterprises Holdings, Inc.

Andrea knocks on the door with another coffee.

"Thanks, Andrea. Shall we go through the schedule?"

She takes the chair opposite my desk and we discuss my appointments for the week and the coming month.

"...You have the Seattle Assistance Union Gala for Hope on Wednesday evening, I have two tickets. Your mother is involved with that charity," she says.

"Okay."

"And the Telecommunications Alliance Organization fundraiser is on Thursday evening in New York," Andrea continues. "I have tickets for two. The Gulfstream will be back. Everything has checked out. Stephan is flying in from Maine tomorrow."

"My plans aren't set yet. I'll talk to Ros to see if a visit to GEH Fiber Optics is still required."

"Okay. Stephan will be on standby should you decide to go. And I'll have your Tribeca apartment serviced, too, unless you'd like me to make a reservation at The Lowell."

My mind whirrs. "If I do go to New York, then I could come back via DC. There are two meetings we could set up for Friday, one with the Securities and Exchange Commission, the other with Senator Blandino."

"Do you want me to arrange those?"

"I'll talk to Vanessa about the Securities and Exchange Commission. But provisionally yes for Blandino."

"Sir."

"Okay. I should see Ros, and can you get Flynn on the line for me? Oh, and find time for Bastille tomorrow. Please."

"Will do." She gets up and leaves, and I turn my attention to my computer. An e-mail from Ana arrived a short while ago.

From: Anastasia Steele
Subject: Don't Burst the Bubble
Date: August 22 2011 09:58
To: Christian Grey

Husband
I am all for a baseball metaphor with you, Mr. Grey.
I want to keep my name here.
I'll explain this evening.
I am going into a meeting now.
Miss our bubble, too…
PS: Thought I had to use my BlackBerry?

Anastasia Steele
Editor, SIP

I stare at her e-mail.

She's not going to take my name.

She's. Not. Going. To. Take. My. Name.

Why?

She doesn't want my name.

Not now, Maggot.

It's a gut punch.

I gape at the screen, shocked and momentarily paralyzed.

Don't fight, Maggot!

Why didn't she tell me? This is how I find out?

Damn it. To hell with this.

I'm going to get her to change her mind.

Like you did about her obeying you, Grey?

My phone buzzes. It's Andrea. "Ros is on the way up."

"Thanks. Send her in when she gets here."

I don't know what to say to Ana, so I push her e-mail from my thoughts and await my meeting with my chief operating officer.

Ros is in sparkling form. She sails through a concise agenda and brings me up to speed on everything within an hour.

"You've done a great job," I tell her.

"Christian, I've loved it. But in all honesty, I missed you."

I smile, because I don't know how I should react. I'm not used to compliments from my staff. "In all honesty, I can't say the same," I reply.

She grins. "That's as it should be. I'm sure you had a wonderful time."

"I did, thank you."

Except my wife doesn't want my name.

She gives me a brief speculative look, but I force a smile. "I'll get on to the Detroit people," she says, "and I'll give Hassan a call about whether you need to visit the New York operation this week."

"Thursday would be good if they need me to go."

"I'll let you know."

After she's gone, I reread Ana's e-mail. It's as discouraging as it was the first time I read it. While I'm contemplating how to respond, Andrea puts Flynn through.

"Christian. Welcome back. How was your honeymoon?" He sounds hale and hearty, and very British. He must have been back to the UK recently.

"Good. Thanks."

He hesitates, and I know he senses something's wrong.

"Can I come and see you?" I ask.

"I'm sorry, but my schedule is full today."

When I don't respond, he sighs. "Janet, my secretary, will kill me, but I can squeeze you in at lunchtime, though you'll have to watch me eating my cheese-and-pickle sandwiches."

"Okay. What time is that?"

"Twelve thirty."

"I'll see you then." I hang up and call Elliot to give him the full story on Hyde and brief him about security.

"What a fucker!" Elliot sneers.

"Yes. That's him in a nutshell. Don't tell Kate about this. I know what a newshound she is."

"Dude—" Elliot protests, but I cut him off.

"Elliot, I don't want to argue. She's tenacious. I met my wife because of Kate's constant badgering, and I don't want her fucking up the police investigation by becoming involved."

Elliot is silent.

"No disrespect meant," I add.

He sighs. "Okay, man. Hope the police catch the bastard."

"Me, too."

"I've got to be on-site, but let me know how your meeting with Gia goes this evening. I can't wait to see the plans and we can start ordering the materials we'll need."

"Will do."

"I HAVE HALF AN hour, Christian," Flynn says when I march into his office.

"She won't take my name."

"What?"

"Anastasia."

"She won't take your name?" He looks momentarily confused. "Anastasia Grey?"

"Yes. She sent me an e-mail this morning, telling me so."

"Sit," he says, and points to the couch, and rather than take his usual chair, he sits down on the couch opposite. There is a plate of sandwiches, their crusts removed, and what looks like cola in a glass in front of him on the coffee table. "Lunch," he says.

"Please, go ahead. Don't mind me."

"So, Christian, let's just back up a bit. I last saw you on your wedding day. It was a joyous occasion. How was the honeymoon?" He takes a large bite out of a sandwich while my mind casts back to a few days ago. I relax, a little, remembering the calm waters of the deep blue Med; the scent of the bougainvillea, how accommodating and efficient the crew of *Fair Lady* were...how much I loved being in Anastasia's company.

"It was sublime."

John smiles. "Good. Any issues?"

"None that I want to discuss." I'm not prepared to tell him about the hickey incident yet.

He gives me a direct, level look. "Because you are encroaching on my lunchtime, I'm going to tell you that's not very helpful."

I sigh. "Nothing serious. We had one fight."

"Was that about your name?"

I flush. "Um. No."

"Okay, when and if you want to discuss that, we can. So, what's happened since then?"

I tell him at length about Hyde, about firing him, about the incendiary device, and the fact that he had information about me, my family, and Ana on his SIP hard drive. I tell him about the car chase.

"Crikey!" Flynn exclaims when I finish.

"He's now the chief suspect in my helicopter's sabotage."

"Holy crap," he mouths, and takes a bite of his sandwich.

"But that's not the reason I'm here. This morning I got an e-mail from Ana saying she doesn't want to take my name. I would have expected a discussion at least. Not just an e-mail."

"I see." His expression is thoughtful. "Finding out your wife's ex-boss is trying to burn down your building, and may be responsible for a near-fatal accident in your helicopter is a big deal, Christian. Plus, a car chase. Have you considered that you may be channeling your stress from all these incidents into your reaction to the e-mail that you received from your wife?"

I frown. "I don't think so."

He strokes his chin. "Knowing how anxious you are about Ana's safety, all of these events had to have had an effect on you. As I've learned over the last few months, she is your primary concern. Always."

"True."

"You do a great deal for her," he says gently.

I do.

"You've given up a great deal for her."

I say nothing. *Where is he going with this?*

"Then you might be interpreting her e-mail as a rejection, especially after all that you've done for her, and that wounds you."

I take a deep breath.

Yes. It does. "I just can't believe she didn't talk to me about it. It's like she's dismissing me and all that I have worked to become. I wasn't born a Grey."

Flynn frowns. "There's a lot to unpack in that sentence, Christian. And, sadly, I don't have the time to do that right now. I hate to break it to you, but Anastasia keeping her name might be more about how she feels about herself, and may have nothing to do with you."

How could this not be about me? It's my name. It's the only one I have…the only one I acknowledge.

There you are, Maggot.

I gaze at him, remaining impassive.

"The best thing to do is to talk to her. Tell her how you feel," Flynn adds. "We spoke about this before. Ana is not an unreasonable person."

She's not. Except about the obey vow.

"This obviously means a great deal to you. Talk to her. I think we have an appointment on Wednesday. We can discuss this in more detail then. And maybe, in the meantime, you'll have worked out some kind of compromise."

"Compromise?"

She either takes my name or she doesn't. Where's the compromise in that?

"Ask her why, Christian," he says gently. "Communicate and compromise."

"Yeah, yeah. 'It's better to concede the battle to win the war.'" I parrot his words from one of our earlier sessions.

"Precisely."

I get up. "Thanks for seeing me at such short notice."

"Well, I hope I've been helpful."

"I think so." *I'm going to talk to Ana right now.*

"I'll see you Wednesday."

"One more thing. Leila Williams—is she in Connecticut?" I ask.

"I think so. She starts college today in Hamden. I had an e-mail from her last night. She's excited to begin her studies." He angles his head to one side in an unspoken "why?"

"It's nothing. See you Wednesday."

"RYAN, TAKE ME TO SIP."

"Yes, sir."

On the short journey to Ana's workplace, I contemplate what I'm going to say to her. We had three weeks to discuss the issue of her name while we were on our honeymoon. Why didn't she bring it up then? I've done nothing but call her Mrs. Grey. She didn't object. Maybe I've made a stupid assumption about her name, but she knows I have…issues. I've told her to manage my expectations.

I want people to know she's *my* wife, even where she works.

My name does that. It represents all that is good in my life.

My parents. *My father.*

It represents everything he's done for me. For Elliot and for Mia, too.

Even though he's an asshole sometimes.

I still want to emulate him.

And every time I stood in front of his desk while he gave me a dressing-down, I knew I'd failed and disappointed him.

He has pushed me to be a better person, a better man.

I admire him.

I love him.

Fuck.

Maybe I should wait until this evening.

No. It can't wait. I will burst a blood vessel.

This is too important to me.

As I stare out of the car window, looking at everyone going about their business, my resentment simmers. Why the hell didn't she tell me?

By the time I stalk into SIP, I'm hanging on to my temper by a silken thread. The first person I meet is Jerry Roach, who's standing in the reception area and talking to a willowy woman with long, out-of-control dark hair.

"Christian Grey," he says in disbelief.

"Jerry. How are you?"

"Um. Good. This is Elizabeth Morgan, our head of HR."

"Hi," I mutter tightly, as we shake hands.

"Mr. Grey. I've heard a great deal about you." Her smile doesn't reach her eyes, and I doubt Ana's confided in her about me—so where she's heard about me, I don't know, but I've got no time to speculate on this now.

"What can we do for you?" Roach asks, pleasantly.

"I need a quick word with Ms. Steele."

"Ana? Of course. I'll take you to her. Follow me." His fawning small talk leaves a lot to be desired, and I listen with half an ear as we head through the double doors behind reception and through to Ana's office. I recall her saying that he went a little crazy when he found out that we were engaged. This does not endear him to me. Idly, I wonder how he would feel if he worked for Ana. That would surely make him crazy.

There's a thought.

That would teach him.

Ana is in Hyde's old office. I nod in greeting to Sawyer, who's standing outside, while Roach raps on the door. Ana calls, "Come in." The office is as small and shabby as I remember—still in need of updating and a lick of paint—though there are flowers on Ana's desk, and the shelves are ordered and tidy. She's eating her lunch with a young woman who I assume is her assistant. Both of them gape at me. I turn to her PA. "Hello, you must be Hannah. I'm Christian Grey."

Hannah leaps to her feet and offers me her hand. "Mr. Grey. H-how nice to m-meet you," she says as we shake hands. "Can I fetch you a coffee?"

"Please." I give her a polite smile and she rushes out of the room. I turn to Roach. "If you'll excuse me, Roach, I'd like a word with *Ms.* Steele."

"Of course, Mr. Grey. Ana." Roach leaves, closing the door behind him. I turn my attention to my wife, who looks guilty—like I've caught her doing something illicit—though she's as lovely as ever.

A little pale, perhaps.

A little hostile, perhaps.

Shit. My anger recedes, leaving anxiety in its wake, as she squares her shoulders.

"Mr. Grey, how nice to see you." Her smile is saccharine, and I know our honeymoon is over, and I have a fight on my hands. My spirit nosedives once more.

"Ms. Steele, may I sit down?" I nod toward the worn leather chair facing Ana's desk that's been vacated by Hannah.

"It's your company." Ana offers me the chair with a dismissive wave of her hand.

"Yes, it is." I grin back with an equally saccharine look.

Yes, baby. Mine.

We are circling each other—boxers in a ring—sizing each other up. Dampening down my bitterness, I steel myself for the battle ahead. This issue is important to me. "Your office is very small," I note as I take the seat.

"It suits me." Her tone is clipped and irritated; she's mad at me. "So, what can I do for you, Christian?"

"I'm just looking over my assets."

"Your assets?" she scoffs. "All of them?"

"All of them. Some of them need rebranding."

"Rebranding?" Her eyebrows shoot up. "In what way?"

"I think you know."

She sighs. "Please don't tell me you have interrupted your day, after three weeks away, to come over here and fight with me about my name."

That's exactly what I've done.

I cross my legs and remove a speck of lint from my pants, playing for time.

Steady, Grey. "Not exactly fight. No."

She narrows her eyes. Pissed. "Christian, I'm working."

"Looked like you were gossiping with your assistant to me."

"We were going through our schedules," she hisses, as her cheeks color. "And you haven't answered my question."

There's a knock on the door. "Come in!" Ana yells, surprising us both. Hannah enters, bearing a small tray with coffee, which she places on Ana's desk.

"Thank you, Hannah," Ana mutters, subdued.

"Do you need anything else, Mr. Grey?" Hannah asks.

"No, thank you. That's all." Deliberately, I give her my most excellent smile. It has the desired effect, and she scuttles out. "Now, *Ms. Steele,* where were we?"

"You were rudely interrupting my workday to fight with me about my name." Ana spits the words at me, her fervor taking me by surprise.

She is really mad.

So. Am. I.

She should have told me.

"I like to make the odd impromptu visit. It keeps management on their toes, wives in their place. You know."

"I had no idea you could spare the time," she retorts.

Enough. Cut to the chase, Grey.

Striving to keep my tone respectful, I ask, quietly, "Why don't you want to change your name here?"

"Christian, do we have to discuss this now?"

"I'm here. I don't see why not." *This is important to me, Ana.*

"I have a ton of work to do, having been away for the last three weeks."

"Are you ashamed of me?" I inquire, surprising myself, and inadvertently revealing the darkness that resides in my soul.

I hadn't intended to go here.

I hold my breath.

Don't fight, Maggot.

"No! Christian, of course not." She grimaces, appalled. "This is about me, not you."

"How is this not about me?" I cock my head, willing her to explain. Of course this is about me; it's my name.

Her expression softens. "Christian, when I took this job, I'd only just met you." It's like she's talking to a child. "I didn't know you were going to buy the company—" She closes her eyes, as if this is a particularly painful memory, and puts her head in her hands. "Why is it so important to you?" she asks and looks up, beseeching me.

"I want everyone to know that you're mine."

"I am yours—look." She holds up her hand, which bears her wedding and engagement rings.

"It's not enough," I whisper.

"Not enough that I married you?" Her voice is almost inaudible, and her eyes widen.

"That's not what I mean." *Ana, don't distort what I'm trying to say to you.*

"What do you mean?" she demands.

"I want your world to begin and end with me."

Her eyes are impossibly blue. "It does," she says, and I don't know if I've ever heard two words filled with such quiet passion before; they suck the air out of the room and take my breath away. "I'm just trying to establish a career," she continues, warming to her subject, "and I don't want to trade on your name. I have to do something, Christian."

I swallow down my rising emotion, listening hard, as she speaks.

"I can't stay imprisoned at Escala or the new house with nothing to do. I'll go crazy. I'll suffocate. I've always worked, and I enjoy this. This is my dream job; it's all I've ever wanted. But doing this doesn't mean I love you less. You are the world to me." Her voice is hoarse and her eyes dewy with unshed tears.

We hold each other's gaze, testing the silence between us.

You are my world, Ana.

But I want you bound to me in every way.

I need that.

I need you…maybe too much.

"I suffocate you?" I whisper.

"No. Yes. No." She sounds exasperated; she closes her eyes and rubs her forehead. "Look, we were talking about my name. I want to keep my name here because I want to put some distance between you and me, but only here, that's all. You know everyone thinks I got the job because of you, when the reality is—" She stops and sits back, staring at my expression in shock.

Shit. How does she read me so well?

Fess up, Grey.

"Do you want to know why you got the job, Anastasia?"

"What? What do you mean?"

"The management here gave you Hyde's job to babysit. They didn't want the expense of hiring a senior executive when the company was mid-sale. They had no idea what the new owner would do with it once it passed into his ownership, and, wisely, they didn't want an expensive redundancy. So they gave you Hyde's job to caretake until the new owner—namely, me—took over."

That's the truth.

"What are you saying?" She looks offended and horrified.

Baby. Don't sweat this. "Relax. You've more than risen to the challenge. You've done very well."

You're very good at what you do, Anastasia Steele.

"Oh," she says, and she looks lost.

And it all becomes crystal clear.

This is what she wants.

This is her dream, and I can make it come true.

I vowed I would uphold her dreams during our wedding.

I don't want to stifle her; I want to help her reach her full potential. I want her to fly…but just not too far away from me.

"I don't want to suffocate you, Ana. I don't want to put you in a gilded cage. Well… Well, the rational part of me doesn't."

It's a gamble, but I play my most ambitious hand yet, voicing the idea that I've had on the spur of this moment. "So, one of the reasons I'm here—apart from dealing with my errant wife—is to discuss what I am going to do with this company."

Ana scowls. "So, what are your plans?" Her sarcasm is threaded through each word and she cocks her head to one side, like I do… copying me, laughing at me, I suspect.

God, I love her; she's recovered her backbone.

"I'm changing the name of the company—to Grey Publishing."

Ana blinks.

"And in a year's time, it will be yours."

Her mouth drops open.

"This is my wedding present to you."

She shuts her mouth, opens it again, then shuts it again, looking shell-shocked.

"So, do I need to change the name to Steele Publishing?"

"Christian, you gave me a watch. I can't run a business."

"I ran my own business from the age of twenty-one."

"But you're, *you*. Control freak and whiz-kid extraordinaire. Jeez, Christian, you majored in economics at Harvard before you dropped out. At least you have some idea. I sold paint and cable ties for three years on a part-time basis, for heaven's sake. I've seen so little of the world, and I know next to nothing!"

Well, that's not true.

"You're also the most well-read person I know." I have to pitch this to her. "You love a good book. You couldn't leave your job while we were on our honeymoon. You read how many manuscripts? Four?"

"Five," she whispers.

"And you wrote full reports on all of them. You're a very bright woman, Anastasia. I'm sure you'll manage."

"Are you crazy?"

"Crazy for you." *Always.*

She snorts, trying not to laugh. "You'll be a laughingstock. Buying a company for the little woman, who has only had a full-time job for a few months of her adult life."

I dismiss her concerns with a wave of my hand. "Do you think I give a fuck what people think? Besides, you won't be on your own."

"Christian, I—" She stalls, lost for words, and I cherish the moment—it doesn't happen often. She lays her head in her hands again. When she looks up, she's trying not to laugh.

"Something amusing you, *Ms.* Steele?"

"Yes. You."

Her amusement is contagious, and I find myself smiling. This is what she does. Disarms me.

Every time.

"Laughing at your husband? That will never do." Her teeth sink into her lovely lower lip. "And you're biting your lip," I mutter darkly; it's a stirring sight.

She sits back. "Don't even think about it," she warns.

"Think about what, Anastasia?"

Fucking you in your office? Lust streaks through my bloodstream like lightning.

"I know that look. We're at work," she whispers.

Can't you feel this, Ana? The sorcery between us is potent. Raw.

I lean forward to get closer to her, to catch her scent, to touch her. "We're in a small, reasonably soundproofed office with a lockable door," I whisper.

I want to seduce my wife.

"Gross. Moral. Turpitude." Each word is a bullet forming a shield around her.

"Not with your husband."

"With my boss's boss's boss," she hisses.

"You're my wife."

"Christian, no. I mean it. You can fuck me seven shades of Sunday this evening. But not now. Not here!"

Hell. I take a deep breath as I come to my senses and the temperature in the room drops back to normal. I laugh, releasing my tension. "Seven shades of Sunday?" I arch a brow, intrigued. "I may hold you to that, *Ms.* Steele."

"Oh, stop with the Ms. Steele!" she snaps and hammers her hand on her desk, making us both jump. "For heaven's sake, Christian. If it means so much to you, I'll change my name!"

What?

She's agreeing?

I feel a sudden rush of relief.

My face erupts in a huge grin. I've succeeded in a negotiation with my wife. I think this might be a first.

Thank you, Ana.

"Good." I clap my hands and stand. "Mission accomplished. Now, I have work to do. If you'll excuse me, Mrs. Grey."

She gawks at me. "But—"

"But what, Mrs. Grey?"

She shakes her head and closes her eyes, looking thoroughly exasperated. "Just go."

"I intend to. I'll see you this evening. I'm looking forward to seven shades of Sunday." I ignore her scowl. "Oh, and I have a stack of business-related social engagements coming up, and I'd like you to accompany me."

She frowns.

"I'll have Andrea call Hannah to put the dates in your calendar.

There are some people you need to meet. You should get Hannah to handle your schedule from now on."

"Okay," she mumbles, sounding bewildered.

I lean over the desk, staring straight into her dazed baby blues. "Love doing business with you, Mrs. Grey." She doesn't move, and I plant a soft kiss on her lips. "Laters, baby," I whisper, then turn and leave.

Outside SIP, I sink into the plush leather in the back of the waiting Audi and ask Ryan to take me back to Grey House.

Thank heavens.

My relief is proportionate to the anxiety I felt before I went into the building. It appears my wife can be reasonable. I reach for my phone to send her an e-mail, and find that she's beaten me to it.

From: Anastasia Steele
Subject: NOT AN ASSET!
Date: August 22 2011 14:23
To: Christian Grey

Mr. Grey
Next time you come and see me, make an appointment, so I can at least have some prior warning of your adolescent overbearing megalomania.
Yours

Anastasia Grey ⟵ please note name.
Editor, SIP

Overbearing megalomaniac, eh?
My wife has a way with words.

From: Christian Grey
Subject: Seven Shades of Sunday
Date: August 22 2011 14:34
To: Anastasia Steele

My Dear Mrs. Grey (emphasis on My)
What can I say in my defense? I was in the neighborhood.
And no, you are not an asset, you are my beloved wife.
As ever, you make my day.

Christian Grey
CEO & Overbearing Megalomaniac, Grey Enterprises Holdings, Inc.

In a calmer frame of mind, I head back to my office. I need lunch.

THROUGHOUT THE AFTERNOON, I check my e-mails to see if she's responded. She hasn't, and I presume that's the end of it, I hope.

LATER, I'M SITTING IN the car waiting for Ana outside SIP. Ryan is tapping his index fingers on the steering wheel, and it's driving me crazy.

For fuck's sake.

Taylor will be back this evening, so I'm endeavoring to keep my cool. I keep glancing toward the door to see if Ana is on her way. According to my watch, it's 5:35, precisely. She's five minutes late. We have a meeting with Gia later; I hope Ana hasn't forgotten.

Where is she?

Sawyer appears, holding the office door open for Ana. Ryan gets out and strolls around the car to the rear passenger door.

What's he playing at?

Head down, Ana walks briskly toward us, followed by Sawyer, who heads to the driver's seat while Ana climbs into the car. Ryan takes the passenger seat.

"Hi," she says, avoiding eye contact.

"Hi."

"Disrupt anyone else's work today?" Her tone is frostier than an arctic night.

"Only Flynn's."

Her eyes flick to me in surprise, but she looks ahead. "Next time you go to see him, I'll give you a list of topics I want covered." She's bristling like a feral kitten beside me.

She's still mad.

I clear my throat. "You seem out of sorts, Mrs. Grey."

She doesn't answer. She just stares ahead, ignoring me. I shuffle a little closer and reach for her hand. "Hey," I whisper. But she snatches her hand out of mine. "You're mad at me?"

"Yes," she spits, and folds her arms, turning away from me and staring through the window.

Damn.

Seattle streams past my window, and I stare out, unseeing, feeling miserable and out of my depth. I thought we'd resolved this.

Sawyer stops outside Escala, and Ana grabs her briefcase and is out of the car before any of us are ready.

"Ana!" I call.

"I've got this," Ryan says, and scoots out in pursuit.

Not waiting for Sawyer to open my door, I scramble out after them, in time to watch Ana stomp into the building with Ryan at her heels.

I'm right behind them when he dashes ahead to reach the elevator before her, to press the call button.

"What?" she snaps at him.

He flushes, shocked, I think, by her tone. "Apologies, ma'am," he says. He steps back when I join them.

"So, it's not just me you're mad at?" I observe, wryly.

"Are you laughing at me?" she seethes, her eyes narrowing.

"I wouldn't dare." I hold my hands up in surrender. I am no match for my wife's bad mood.

"You need a haircut." She scowls as she steps into the elevator.

"Do I?" Taking my life in my hands and brushing my hair off my forehead, I follow her in.

"Yes." She stabs the code for our floor into the keypad.

"So, you're talking to me now?"

"Just."

"What exactly are you mad about? I need an indication." *So I'm sure.*

She stares at me, horrified. "Do you really have no idea? Surely, for someone so bright, you must have an inkling? I can't believe you're that obtuse."

Wow.

I take a step back. "You really are mad. I thought we had sorted all this in your office."

"Christian, I just capitulated to your petulant demands. That's all."

I have no answer to that.

The elevator doors open and Ana storms out. "Hi, Taylor," I hear her say.

I follow her into the foyer. "Mrs. Grey," Taylor says, and glances at me with raised eyebrows. She dumps her briefcase in the hallway.

"Good to see you," I quietly address Taylor.

"Sir," he says, and I follow my wife into the living room.

"Hi, Mrs. Jones," Ana says, and stomps straight to the fridge.

I nod at Gail, who's at the stove, preparing dinner.

Ana pulls out a bottle of wine and a glass from the cupboard while I remove my jacket, wondering what to say to her. "Do you want a drink?" she asks in a syrupy tone.

"No thanks." I watch her as I take off my tie and undo my shirt collar. She pours herself a large glass of wine while Mrs. Jones, with a swift, unreadable look at me, exits the kitchen.

So, Ana's frightened off all the staff.

I am the last man standing.

I run my hand through my hair, feeling helpless, while she takes a sip of wine, closing her eyes and enjoying the taste, or so it would seem.

Enough.

"Stop this," I whisper, stepping toward her. Tucking her hair behind her ear, I then gently tug on her earlobe, because I want to touch her. She takes a breath, then shakes me off. "Talk to me," I whisper.

"What's the point? You don't listen to me."

"Yes, I do. You're one of the few people I listen to."

Her eyes don't leave mine as she takes another swig of wine.

"Is this about your name?" I ask.

"Yes and no. It's about how you dealt with the fact that I disagreed with you." She sounds surly.

"Ana, you know I have…issues. It's hard for me to let go where you're concerned. You know that."

"But I'm not a child, and I'm not an asset."

"I know." I sigh.

"Then stop treating me as though I am," she beseeches me with quiet fortitude.

I can't bear not touching her. Brushing my fingers down her cheek, I run the tip of my thumb across her bottom lip. "Don't be mad. You're so precious to me. Like a priceless asset. Like a child."

"I'm neither of those things, Christian. I'm your wife. If you were hurt that I wasn't going to take your name, you should have said."

"Hurt?" I frown. *Hurt? Yes. I am. Was…shit.*

This is confusing. This is what Flynn said. I glance at my watch. "The architect will be here in just under an hour. We should eat."

Ana looks dismayed, the *v* between her brows deeper than usual. "This discussion isn't finished."

"What else is there to discuss?"

"You could sell the company."

"Sell it?" I scoff.

"Yes."

Why would I do that? "You think I'd find a buyer in today's market?"

"How much did it cost you?"

"It was relatively cheap."

"So, if it folds?"

"We'll survive. But I won't let it fold, Anastasia. Not while you're there."

"And if I leave?"

"And do what?"

"I don't know. Something else."

"You've already said this is your dream job. And forgive me if I'm wrong, but I promised before God, Reverend Walsh, and a congregation of our nearest and dearest to 'cherish you, uphold your hopes and dreams, and keep you safe at my side.'"

"Quoting your wedding vows to me is not playing fair."

"I've never promised to play fair where you're concerned. Besides, you've wielded your vows at me like a weapon before."

She scowls.

"Anastasia, if you're still angry with me, take it out on me in bed later." Her mouth pops open, and I know how I'd like to fill it.

Right now.

Here.

Then I remember. "Seven shades of Sunday," I whisper. "Looking forward to it."

She closes, then opens her mouth again.

Oh, baby. What I'd like to do to that mouth.

Stop, Grey.

"Gail!" I call, and a few moments later she comes back into the kitchen.

"Mr. Grey?" she says.

"We'd like to eat now, please."

"Very good, sir."

I watch Ana, who has gone worryingly quiet, as she takes another sip of wine.

"I think I'll join you in a glass," I mutter, and run a hand through my hair. She's right, it's too long, but I don't think she'd approve if I went to Esclava to have it cut.

Ana is monosyllabic as we eat. Well, I'm eating, Ana is pushing her food around her plate, but given how mad she is at me, I decide not to chide her about it.

It's frustrating.

Hell. I can't stay quiet. "You're not going to finish?"

"No."

I wonder if she's doing this on purpose. But before I can ask her, she stands and takes my empty plate and hers from the dining table.

"Gia will be with us shortly," she says.

"I'll take those, Mrs. Grey," Mrs. Jones says.

"Thank you."

"You didn't like it?" Gail asks, concerned.

"It was fine. I'm just not hungry."

Mrs. Jones gives Ana a pitying smile, and I suppress my eye roll. "I'm going to make a couple of calls," I mumble, to escape them both.

The spectacular sunset over the distant Sound does little to improve my temper. I wish for a moment that Ana and I were on *The Grace* or back on the *Fair Lady.* We didn't argue then. Well, apart from after the hickey incident.

I dwell on Flynn's words. *Marriage is a serious business.*

It sure is.

Sometimes too serious, especially if your wife doesn't agree with you.

Communicate and compromise.

This should be my new mantra.

Why is this so hard?

"I don't want you to sabotage your happiness, Christian."

Flynn is still in my head.

Shit, is that what I'm doing?

Sullenly, I pick up the phone and call my dad to let him know that all the arrangements are in place for additional security. It's a short conversation, and when I'm done, I gather up Gia Matteo's designs and head back into the living room.

There's no sign of Ana, or Mrs. Jones, who has cleaned up the kitchen and dining area. I spread the plans out on the dining table, then, using the remote, I scroll through the list of music. I chance upon Fauré's Requiem.

This should soothe my soul.

And maybe Ana's, too.

I press play and wait. The notes from a church organ echo through the living room, and they're joined by the celestial voice of the choir, their voices rising and falling to the lament.

It's stunning.

Calming.

Elevating.

Perfect.

Ana appears on the threshold, where she stops and inclines her head, listening to the music. She looks different; she's shrouded in silver-gray, her hair backlit and shining from the hall lights. She looks like an angel.

"Mrs. Grey."

"What's this?" she asks.

"Fauré's Requiem. You look different."

"Oh. I've not heard it before."

"It's very calming, relaxing. Have you done something to your hair?"

"Brushed it," she says, and there's too much distance between us. Transported by my stunning wife and the music, I make my way over to her. "Dance with me?" I whisper.

"To this? It's a requiem," she squeaks, shocked.

"Yes." *And?*

I tug her into my arms and hold her, my nose in her hair, inhaling her sweet but stirring fragrance. She wraps her arms around me and nuzzles my chest, and together we start to sway. Slowly. Side to side.

Ana. This is what I've missed. You. In my arms.

"I hate fighting with you," I whisper.

"Well, stop being such an arse."

I chuckle and draw her closer. "Arse?"

"Ass."

"I prefer arse."

"You should. It suits you."

I laugh and kiss the top of her head, remembering that she was very taken with the word when she overheard it in Harrods.

London. Happy times.

"A requiem?" There's a trace of censure in her murmur.

I shrug. "It's just a lovely piece of music, Ana." *And I get to hold you.*

Taylor coughs, and grudgingly I release her. "Miss Matteo is here," he announces.

"Show her in." I clasp Ana's hand as Gia enters.

"Christian. Ana." She beams at us, and we each shake her hand.

"Gia," I respond, politely.

"You both look so well after your honeymoon," she purrs.

I pull Ana close. "We had a wonderful time, thank you." I plant a soft kiss on my wife's temple and she slips her hand into my back pocket, and, to my delight, squeezes my butt.

Gia's smile falters a little. "Have you managed to look over the plans?" she asks brightly.

"We have," Ana says with a quick glance at me. I can't help my grin. Ana's gone all territorial and is laying claim to me. I like it.

"Please, the plans are here." I wave in the direction of our dining table. Reluctantly, I pull away from Ana, but hold her hand.

"Would you like something to drink?" Ana asks Gia. "A glass of wine?"

"That would be lovely. Dry white if you have it," she responds.

I switch off the music as Gia joins me by the table.

"Would you like some more wine, Christian?" Ana calls.

"Please, baby." I watch as she retrieves the wineglasses.

Gia stands beside me. "This is good work, Gia," I say, as she moves a little too close. "This especially." I point at the rear elevation of her CAD drawing. "I think Ana has some opinions on the glass wall, but generally we're both pleased with the ideas you've come up with."

"Oh, I'm glad," Gia coos, and she pats my arm.

Keep your fucking distance. She's wearing a cloying, rich perfume that's almost suffocating.

I step out of her reach and call to Ana. "Thirsty here."

"Coming right up," Ana responds.

A beat later, she's back with glasses of wine for each of us, and she inserts herself between Gia and me—deliberately, I think. Has she noticed how Gia is incapable of keeping her hands to herself?

"Cheers." I offer up my glass in thanks to Ana and take a sip of wine.

"Ana, you have some issues with the glass wall?" Gia prompts.

"Yes. I love it—don't get me wrong. But I was hoping that we could incorporate it more organically into the house. After all, I fell in love with the house as it was, and I don't want to make any radical changes."

"I see." Gia's eyes flick to mine, and I look at Ana.

She continues, "I just want the design to be sympathetic, you know, more in keeping with the original house." Ana glances at me.

"No major renovations?" I say.

"No."

"You like it as it is?"

"Mostly, yes. I always knew it just needed some TLC."

Ana's eyes are glowing, reflecting mine, I'm sure.

Are we talking about the house, or me?

"Okay." Gia gives us a quick glance before pitching a revised plan. "I think I get where you're coming from, Ana. How about if we retain the glass wall, but have it open out onto a larger deck that's in keeping with the Mediterranean style. We have the stone terrace there already. We can put in pillars in matching stone, widely spaced so you'll still have the view. Add a glass roof, or tile it as per the rest of the house. It'll also make a sheltered alfresco dining and seating area."

Ana looks impressed.

Gia continues, "Or instead of the deck, we could incorporate a wood color of your choice into the glass doors—that might help to keep the Mediterranean spirit."

"Like the bright blue shutters in the South of France," Ana says, looking at me.

I'm not keen on the idea, but I'm not going to shoot her down in front of Ms. Matteo. Besides, if that's what Ana wants, she can have it. I'll learn to live with it. I ignore Gia, preening beside me.

"Ana, what do you want to do?" I ask.

"I like the deck idea."

"Me, too."

Ana turns her attention to Gia. "I think I'd like to see revised drawings, showing the bigger deck and pillars that are in keeping with the house."

"Sure," Gia says to Ana. "Any other issues?"

"Christian wants to remodel the master suite," Ana says.

Another discreet cough interrupts us.

"Taylor?" He's standing on the threshold.

"I need to confer with you on an urgent matter, Mr. Grey."

I squeeze Ana's shoulders and address Gia. "Mrs. Grey is in charge of this project. She has absolute carte blanche. Whatever she wants, it's hers. I completely trust her instincts. She's very shrewd." Ana reaches up and pats my hand.

"If you'll excuse me." I leave them, and follow Taylor into his office. Prescott is there, seated at the CCTV monitor bank. Over her shoulder, all the feeds from around the apartment and also from the perimeter of Escala and the garage are on display.

"Mr. Grey," Prescott greets me.

"Evening. What gives?"

Taylor grabs a chair from his small conference table and places it beside Prescott. He gestures to me to sit down. I comply and look at them expectantly.

"Prescott has been going through all the tapes from over the weekend from downstairs and outside. She found this." Taylor nods at her, and using her mouse, Prescott clicks start on one of the screens.

A grainy image begins to play. It shows a man in coveralls walking toward the front entrance of the building, and inspecting the camera itself. She freezes it as the man looks directly at the camera.

Fuck. "It's Jack Hyde," I murmur, and he has his hair tied back. "When was this?"

"It's Saturday, August 20, at around nine forty-five in the morning."

His hair is lighter here; he must have been wearing a wig in the server room at Grey House.

"Sir, I've isolated all the footage I can find of him at around this time," Prescott says.

"Interesting. What else do you have?"

She runs through several clips of Hyde: at the front door, at the opening to the garage, at the fire escapes. He's carrying a broom, which he uses occasionally so he looks like a street cleaner.

Cunning bastard.

It's weirdly fascinating to watch him.

"Have you sent this to Welch?"

"Not yet," Taylor says. "I thought you'd better see it first."

"Send it to him. Perhaps he can track where he goes from here."

"Will do. This might be just the clue they need. Though, I learned today they haven't found him yet. He's still not been to his apartment, sir."

"Oh, that's news."

"I spoke with Welch for a full update about an hour ago," Taylor clarifies.

"No doubt he'll fill me in tomorrow. This is good work. Well done, Prescott." I give her a quick smile.

"Thank you, sir."

"We'll have to be extra careful, knowing that he's prowling around the building."

"Indeed," Taylor agrees.

"I'd better head back. Thank you. Both of you."

It looks like Ana and Gia are finishing up when I enter the living room. "All done?" I ask, as I put my arm around Ana.

"Yes, Mr. Grey." Gia smiles brightly, though her smile looks forced. "I'll have the revised plans to you in a couple of days."

Oh. I'm Mr. Grey now.

Interesting.

"Excellent. You're happy?" I ask Ana, and I want to know what she's said to Gia. Ana nods, looking rather pleased with herself.

"I'd better be going," Gia says, again too brightly. She offers her hand to Ana first, then to me.

"Until next time, Gia," Ana says with a charming smile.

"Yes, Mrs. Grey. Mr. Grey."

Taylor appears at the entrance of the great room.

"Taylor will see you out," Ana says, and arm in arm, we watch her join Taylor in the hallway.

When she's out of earshot, I look down at my wife. "She was noticeably cooler."

"Was she? I didn't notice." Ana shrugs, trying and failing miserably to look nonchalant. My wife is an appalling liar. "What did Taylor want?" She's changing the subject.

Releasing her, I turn and start rolling up the plans. "It was about Hyde."

"What about Hyde?" She pales.

Shit. I don't want to add to her nightmares.

"It's nothing to worry about, Ana." Abandoning the plans, I draw her into my arms. "It turns out he hasn't been in his apartment for weeks, that's all." I kiss her hair and go back to rolling up Gia's designs. "So, what did you decide on?"

"Only what you and I discussed. I think she likes you," Ana says quietly.

I think so, too! "Did you say something to her?"

She stares down at her hands. She's knotting her fingers.

"We were Christian and Ana when she arrived, and Mr. and Mrs. Grey when she left," I prompt.

"I may have said something," she admits.

Oh, baby, you're going into battle for me?

I've met Gia's type before. Always in a business context. "She's only reacting to this face."

Ana looks alarmed.

"What? You're not jealous, are you?" I'm shocked that she could even think this. Her cheeks color, and she doesn't answer me, but looks down at her hands again, and I know I have my answer. I remember Elliot alluding to Gia's nature and it reminded me of Elena—a woman who doesn't take no for an answer. A woman who gets what she wants. "Ana, she's a sexual predator. Not my type at all. How can you be jealous of her? Of anyone? Nothing about her interests me." I run a hand through my hair, at a loss. "It's only you, Ana. It will only ever be you."

Abandoning the drawings again, I move quickly toward her and grasp her chin. "How can you think otherwise? Have I ever given you any indication that I could be remotely interested in anyone else?"

"No," she whispers. "I'm being silly. It's just today. You—" She stops.

"What about me?"

"Oh, Christian." Tears well in her eyes. "I'm trying to adapt to this new life, that I had never imagined for myself. Everything is being handed to me on a plate—the job, you, my beautiful husband, who I never...I never knew I'd love this way, this hard, this fast, this... indelibly."

I stare at her, paralyzed, as she takes a deep breath. "But you're like a freight train, and I don't want to get railroaded because the girl you fell in love with will be crushed. And what'll be left? All that would be left is a vacuous social X-ray, flitting from charity function to charity function."

Whoa! Ana!

"And now you want me to be a company CEO, which has never even been on my radar. I'm bouncing between all these ideas, struggling. You want me at home. You want me to run a company. It's so confusing." She fights down a sob. "You've got to let me make my own decisions, take my own risks, and make my own mistakes, and let me learn from them. I need to walk before I can run, Christian, don't you see? I want some independence. That's what my name means to me."

This is about her!

Shit.

"You feel railroaded?" I whisper.

She nods.

I close my eyes. "I just want to give you the world, Ana, everything and anything you want. And save you from it, too. Keep you safe. But I also want everyone to know you're mine. I panicked today when I got your e-mail. Why didn't you tell me about your name?"

She flushes. "I only thought about it while we were on our honeymoon, and, well, I didn't want to burst the bubble, and I forgot about it. I only remembered yesterday evening. And then Jack—you know—it was distracting. I'm sorry, I should have told you or discussed it with you, but I could never seem to find the right time."

I study her, measuring her words. Yes. It would have resulted in an argument on our honeymoon.

"Why did you panic?" she asks.

I want to be worthy of you and your e-mail derailed me.

Stop, Grey. "I just don't want you to slip through my fingers."

"For heaven's sake, I'm not going anywhere. When are you going to get that through your incredibly thick skull? I. Love. You." She waves her hand in the air looking for inspiration—like I do. "More than 'eyesight, space, or liberty.'"

Shakespeare? "A daughter's love?" *I hope not!*

"No." She laughs. "It's the only quote that came to mind."

"Mad King Lear?"

"Dear, dear mad King Lear." She reaches up and strokes my cheek and I lean in to her hand, closing my eyes and reveling in her touch. "Would you change your name to Christian Steele, so everyone would know that you belong to me?"

Opening my eyes, I stare at her. "Belong to you?"

"Mine," she says.

"Yours," I repeat. "Yes, I would. If it meant that much to you." I remember surrendering myself to her here, before we were married, when I thought she was leaving.

"Does it mean that much to you?" she asks.

"Yes."

"Okay," she says.

"I thought you'd already agreed to this."

"Yes, I have, but now that we've discussed it further, I'm happier with my decision."

"Oh."

Flynn was right. This was about her and how she feels.

But I'm glad she's come around. It's a relief—our feud is over. I beam at her and she smiles back, so I swoop down, grab her by her waist, and swing her high.

Thank you, Anastasia.

She giggles, and I set her on her feet. "Mrs. Grey, do you know what this means to me?"

"I do now."

I kiss her, threading my fingers through the softness of her hair, and whisper against her lips, "It means seven shades of Sunday." I run my nose down hers.

"You think?" She leans back, her eyes narrowed, but she's trying to hide her smile.

"Certain promises were made. An offer extended, a deal brokered," I whisper.

And I want you.

After this fight, I need to know we're okay.

"Um…" Ana regards me as if I've lost mind.

Hell, she's backing out. "You reneging on me?" A plan pops, fully formed, into my mind. "I have an idea. A really important matter to attend to."

Ana's expression intensifies; she thinks I'm crazy.

"Yes, Mrs. Grey. A matter of the gravest importance." I'm sure there's a wicked gleam in my eye. This is a means to an end.

She narrows hers, once more. "What?" she asks.

"I need you to cut my hair. Apparently, it's overlong, and my wife doesn't like it."

"I can't cut your hair!" she exclaims, in amused disbelief.

"Yes, you can." I shake my head and my hair falls into my eyes.

How have I not noticed this?

"Well, if Mrs. Jones has a pudding bowl." Ana giggles.

I laugh. "Okay, good point well made. I'll get Franco to do it."

Her laugh turns to a grimace, and after a moment's hesitation she grabs my hand with surprising strength. "Come." She drags me all the way to our bathroom and releases me there.

Looks like she's going to cut my hair.

I stand watching her as she drags the bathroom chair in front of her sink. Her high heels emphasize her legs and the tight pencil skirt sculpts her beautiful behind. This is a show worth watching.

She turns and points to the chair. "Sit."

"Are you going to wash my hair?"

She nods.

Whoa. I can't remember anyone washing my hair. Ever.

"Okay." Without taking my eyes off hers, I slowly unbutton my shirt, and when it's undone I present her with my right wrist. The cuff is held together with one of my cuff links.

Undo this, baby.

With a darkening look, she undoes the right, then the left cuff, her fingertips tantalizing my skin with a soft sweep or two over each pulse. Her blouse is undone, one button too far, and I glimpse the soft swell of her breasts encased in fine lace.

It's a most inspiring sight. She steps closer, and I catch a hint of her lovely fragrance as she pushes my shirt off my shoulders and lets it drop to the floor.

"Ready?" she whispers, and that one word holds so much promise. It's arousing. Deeply arousing.

"For whatever you want, Ana."

Her eyes stray to my lips and she leans in for a kiss.

"No," I breathe, and in a monumental act of self-sacrifice, I grasp her shoulders. "Don't. If you do that, I'll never get my hair cut."

Her mouth forms a perfect o.

"I want this," I whisper, surprising myself.

"Why?"

Because no one's washed my hair... Ever. "Because it'll make me feel cherished."

She gasps at my softly spoken confession, and before I can do so much as blink, she embraces me, holding me close. She kisses my chest with soft, gentle kisses, where only two months ago I couldn't bear to be touched.

"Ana. My Ana." Closing my eyes, I gather her in my arms while my heart overflows.

I think I'm forgiven for railroading her.

I think we're okay.

We stand in our embrace in the middle of our bathroom for an age, her warmth and her love soaking into me.

Eventually, Ana leans back, the love-light shining in her eyes. "You really want me to do this?"

I nod, and her smile matches mine. She steps out of my arms and points to the chair again. "Then sit." I do as she asks while she kicks off her shoes and retrieves my shampoo from the shower. "Would Sir like this?" She holds it up as if she's on a cheesy shopping channel, selling it to me. "Hand-delivered from the South of France. I like the smell of this." She pops the top. "It smells of you."

"Please."

She places the shampoo on the vanity unit, then reaches for a small towel. "Lean forward," she orders, and drapes the towel over my shoulders and turns the taps on behind me.

"Lean back."

She's bossy.

I like it.

I try to lean back, but it doesn't work because I'm too tall. I shuffle the chair forward and then tip it so it rests against the sink.

Success. I tilt my head backward over the sink and watch Ana.

Slowly, using a glass to scoop up the warm water, she anoints my head, leaning over me. "You smell so good, Mrs. Grey." I close my eyes, enjoying her hands on me as she continues to wet my hair.

Abruptly, she pours water over my forehead and it flows into my eyes.

"Sorry!" she squeals.

I laugh and wipe the excess off with the corner of my towel. "Hey, I know I'm an arse, but don't drown me."

She giggles and plants a tender kiss on my forehead. "Don't tempt me," she whispers. Reaching up, I place my hand on her neck and guide her lips to mine. Her breath is sweet; she tastes of Ana, and sauvignon blanc. An enticing combination.

"Mm," I murmur, savoring the taste. Releasing her, I lean back, ready for her to continue. She smiles down at me, and I hear the sound of liquid squirting from the tube as she squeezes it into her hand. Gently, she starts to massage the shampoo into my scalp—from my temples, she works her way over my head—and I close my eyes, relishing her touch.

Sweet Jesus.

Who knew heaven resided in my wife's fingertips?

When Franco's cut my hair, he's always used a spray. I've never had my hair washed.

Why not, Grey? This is so relaxing.

Or perhaps it's just Ana—I'm so acutely aware of her. Her leg grazing mine, her arm skimming my cheek, her touch, her scent…"That feels good," I murmur.

"Yes, it does." Her lips graze my forehead.

"I like it when you scratch my scalp with your fingernails."

"Head up," she says, and I lift my head so she soaps the back using her fingernails on my scalp.

Bliss.

"Back."

I do as I'm told, and she pours water over my head again, rinsing out the suds.

"Once more?" she asks.

"Please." When I open my eyes, she's smiling down at me.

"Coming right up, Mr. Grey." She releases me and fills my sink. "For rinsing," she explains.

Closing my eyes, I surrender myself to her ministrations. She washes my hair again, anointing me with more water, massaging more shampoo into my scalp, and using her fingernails.

I have found nirvana.

This is pure paradise.

Her fingers caress my cheek and I open heavy eyelids to watch her. She kisses me, and her kiss is soft, sweet, chaste.

I sigh, my contentment complete.

She moves over me and her breasts brush my face.

Fuck.

Hello!

Behind me, the water gurgles down the drain, but with my eyes closed, I reach up and grab her hips, then slide my fingers over her magnificent behind.

"No fondling the help," she warns.

"Don't forget I'm deaf." Slowly I start to hitch up her skirt, but she swats my arm. I grin, feeling like I've been caught with my hand in the cookie jar. I stop misbehaving, but I keep my hands on her fine backside while she rinses my hair. I imagine I'm playing the Moonlight Sonata on her ass, my fingers flexing through the notes. She wiggles deliciously against my fingers and I growl in appreciation.

"There, all rinsed," she announces.

"Good." My fingers tighten around her hips and I sit up, dripping water everywhere and pulling Ana sidesaddle onto my lap. I curl my fingers around her nape, and with my other hand I hold her jaw. She gasps and I take full advantage, pressing my lips to hers and kissing her. My tongue seeking more.

Hot. Hungry. Ready.

I don't care that I'm spraying water all over the bathroom and soaking my wife. Ana's fingers tighten in my wet hair as she returns my kiss with a ferocity of her own.

Desire courses through my veins.

Demanding release.

I'm tempted to rip off her blouse, but I tug the top button. "Enough of this primping. I want to fuck you seven shades of Sunday, and we can do it in here or in the bedroom. You decide."

Ana's expression is dazed.

"What's it to be, Anastasia?"

"You're wet," she whispers.

Holding her hips, I tip my head forward and rub my wet hair all over the front of her blouse. She squeals once more and squirms, but I tighten my hold. "Oh, no you don't, baby."

When I look up, her blouse is sticking to her like a second skin, her lacy bra obvious, her nipples pert beneath the lace. She's gorgeous, but she's also outraged, amused, and aroused at once. "Love the view," I whisper, and lean down to run my nose around her wet, waiting nipple. She groans and wriggles on me. "Answer me, Ana. Here or the bedroom?"

"Here," she whispers.

"Good choice, Mrs. Grey," I murmur against the corner of her mouth, and move my hand from her jaw to her leg. Skimming my fingers over her pantyhose toward her thigh, I raise her skirt higher and higher while placing tender kisses along her jaw. "Oh, what shall I do to you?" I murmur.

Oh. My fingers reach the firm flesh of her thighs.

She's wearing stockings!

Deep joy.

"I like these." I run a finger under the stocking top and across the soft skin of her upper thigh. Ana squirms in delight. I groan. "If I'm going to fuck you seven shades of Sunday, I want you to keep still."

"Make me," she demands, and the challenge in her eyes goes straight to my cock.

"Oh, Mrs. Grey. You have only to ask." I slide my hand up to her panties, glad that she's wearing them over her garter belt. "Let's divest you of these." I tug gently, and she shifts on top of my erection.

Fuck. My breath hisses through my teeth. "Keep still," I grumble.

"I'm helping." She pouts in protest, and I suck her bottom lip between my teeth.

"Still," I warn, then release her lip and tug her panties down her legs, crushing them into my hand; I have a plan for them. I raise Ana's skirt so it's bunched up around her hips and take a brief moment to appreciate how beautiful her legs are in stockings with lacy tops. I lift her. "Sit. Astride me."

Keeping her darkening eyes on mine, she obeys, but tilts her chin up wearing her *Bring it* expression.

Oh, Ana.

"Mrs. Grey, are you goading me?"

We could have some fun with this.

My pants feel two sizes too small.

"Yes. What are you going to do about it?"

God, I love a challenge.

"Clasp your hands together behind your back."

She does, and I bind her wrists with her panties and pull them tight. Now she's helpless. "My panties? Mr. Grey, you have no shame," she chides me, breathless.

"Not where you're concerned, Mrs. Grey, but you know that."

I love the provocation in her smoky blue eyes. It's such a turn-on. I push her backward on my lap so I have more room to work. She chews her lip, her eyes on mine, and gently I skim my hands down to her knees, pushing her legs wider apart. Then I widen my legs, to give my dick some more room and to make her more available to me.

Also, it will be more intense for her this way.

My fingers move to the buttons on her wet blouse. "I don't think we need this." Slowly, I undo each button, revealing her breasts, still slick from their earlier soaking. They rise and fall rapidly as she inhales sharply, and I leave her blouse gaping open.

Desire shines in her eyes and they stay glued to mine.

I caress her face and brush my thumb across her bottom lip, then abruptly push it into her mouth. "Suck." She closes her mouth around me and does exactly what she's been told to do.

Hard.

My girl does not back down.

This I know.

She scrapes her teeth gently over my skin and bites the pad.

I moan, then ease my thumb from her mouth and paint her chin, her throat, and her sternum with her saliva. I hook my thumb into her bra cup and tug it down, freeing her breast, then tuck the cup beneath, pushing her breast up so it's poised and ready for me. We stare at each other, her mouth opens and closes, her eyes filled with yearning. I love watching her reaction to everything I do. She bites down on her lip as I free her other breast, so it, too, is helpless and waiting for me. They are too tempting. I hold both of them and slowly graze my thumbs over her nipples in a tight circle, torturing each one so that they stand proud beneath my touch. Ana starts panting and arching her back, thrusting her breasts into my palms. I don't stop, but continue to tease her so that she throws her head back and lets out a long, low moan of pleasure.

"Shh," I whisper, not letting up on the slow, sweet rhythm I've set for my thumbs. Ana's hips shift. "Still, baby, still." Reaching behind her head, I gather her hair in one hand and hold her neck.

I want her still.

Leaning down, I tease her right nipple with my lips, then suck hard as my fingers move to continue taunting its twin, gently tugging and twisting.

"Ah! Christian!" she groans, and rocks her hips forward on my lap.

Oh, no, baby.

I don't let up. My lips tasting and teasing, my fingers tweaking and tugging.

"Christian, please," she mewls.

"Hmm. I want you to come like this," I whisper against my captive peak, and I return to it, but this time I tug tenderly and carefully with my teeth.

"Ah!" Ana calls, and writhes on my lap, but I hold her still and I don't stop.

"Please." She's breathless and begging, and I watch her, her mouth slack, her head back, as she has no choice but to absorb all the pleasure.

I know she's close. "You have such beautiful breasts, Ana. One day I'll fuck them."

She arches her back fully, surrendering to me, her breathing rapid. Her thighs straining against mine.

She's close.

So close.

"Let go," I whisper, and she does, her eyes scrunched closed as she cries out and her body quivers through her orgasm. I tighten my hold on her as she sails down from her high.

Her eyes flicker open, dazed, and beautiful.

"God, I love to watch you come, Ana."

"That was…" She stops, overwhelmed, I think.

"I know." I kiss her, angling her head so I can claim her, and tell her with my tongue that she is everything to me.

She blinks up at me when I pull away.

"Now I'm going to fuck you, hard." I grab her around the waist and move her farther back on my lap once more. With one hand on her thigh, I reach for my pants zipper and free my impatient cock. Ana's eyes darken, her pupils dilating. "You like?" I whisper.

"Hm." She makes a delicious rumbling noise of approval in throat.

I wrap my fingers around my erection and move them up and down as she watches.

"You're biting your lip, Mrs. Grey."

"That's because I'm hungry."

"Hungry?"

Anastasia Grey, my day's just improved a thousandfold.

She makes that noise again, the sexy one deep in her throat, and licks her lips while I continue to pleasure myself.

"I see. You should have eaten your dinner." I'm almost tempted to spank her, but I'm not sure that would be welcome. "But maybe I can oblige." I put my hands around her waist so that she keeps her balance. "Stand," I order.

She does, indecently quickly. She's keen.

"Kneel," I murmur, watching her. Her eyes flick to mine shining with sensuous delight and she does, surprisingly gracefully, considering her hands are tied. I slide forward on the chair, holding my erection. "Kiss me," I order, offering her my cock. She glances from my dick to my face, and I run my tongue over my teeth.

Come on, baby.

She leans forward and plants a soft kiss on the tip. Her eyes on mine. It's so fucking hot. I could come over her right now.

I lay my hand against her cheek and she runs her tongue around the head of my erection. I gasp, and suddenly she pounces, pulling my dick into her mouth and sucking, really hard.

"Ah!" Ana's mouth is heaven.

I flex my hips forward, diving deeper into her throat, and she takes me, all of me.

Fuck.

She moves her head, up and down, consuming me.

Ah. She's so good at this.

But I don't want to come in her mouth. I hold her head with both hands to slow her down and control her pace.

Easy, baby.

Panting hard, I guide her mouth. Down. Up. On. Me. Her tongue works its magic. "Jesus, Ana," I whisper, and screw my eyes up, and lose myself in her rhythm.

She draws her lips back, so I feel her teeth.

Fuck. I stop and grab her, moving her onto my lap. "Enough!" I growl. I tug her panties off her wrists and she looks so fucking pleased with herself. As she should. She's a goddess, her expression sultry beneath her long lashes. She licks her lips and wraps her fingers around my dick and scoots forward and lowers herself oh-so-fucking-slowly onto me.

Oh, the feel of her.

Groaning, in tribute to her, I tug her blouse off so it falls to the floor. I steady her hips with my hands to stall her. "Still," I order. "Please, let me savor this. Savor you."

She stops moving, and her dark, dark eyes glow with her love and innate sensuality; her lips are parted and moist where she's been biting her bottom lip.

She is my life.

I flex my butt, driving deeper into her, and she moans and closes her eyes. "This is my favorite place," I murmur. "Inside you. Inside my wife."

Ana's fingers fist in my wet hair, her lips find mine, and her tongue finds mine as she starts to move, rising up and down, riding me.

Riding me, fast. Her pace frantic.

I moan, weaving my hands in her hair, and my tongue welcomes hers, as they dance a dance they know so well.

She's greedy.

Like me.

Too fast, baby.

My hands move to her ass, and I guide her once more, to a quick but even tempo.

"Ah!" she cries out.

"Yes. Yes, Ana," I hiss through my teeth, as I try to prolong this exquisite pleasure. "Baby," I murmur as my passion builds, and I take her mouth once more.

Ana. Ana. Will it always be like this?

This. Hot.

This. Elemental.

This. Extreme.

"Oh, Christian, I love you. I will always love you."

Her words are my undoing. I can't hold on, after all the tension between us today. I clasp her to me and let go, crying out as I come hard and fast, triggering her release. She cries out and surrenders herself to me, shuddering around me, until we're both still.

Together, we resurface.

She's crying. "Hey." I tip her chin back. "Why are you crying? Did I hurt you?"

"No," she says in a breathless rush of denial. I push her hair off her face and wipe the tear that's slipped down her cheek with my thumb, and kiss her. I shift, pulling out of her, and she winces as I do.

"What's wrong, Ana? Tell me."

Watery eyes stare into mine. "It's just, it's just sometimes I'm over-whelmed by how much I love you," she whispers.

My heart melts and mends into one glorious whole. "You have the same effect on me." I touch my lips to hers in the softest of kisses. "Do I?"

Ana. "You know you do."

"Sometimes I know. Not all the time."

"Back at you, Mrs. Grey."

What a pair we make, Anastasia.

Her smile lights a path for my dark soul and she leaves a trail of soft, sweet kisses over my chest and cuddles up to me, her cheek against my heart. I stroke her hair and run my fingers down her back. She's still wearing her bra. It can't be very comfortable; I undo it, tug down each of the straps so it falls to the floor, joining her blouse.

"Hmm. Skin on skin." I fold her into my arms and graze my lips over her shoulder and up to her ear. "You smell like heaven, Mrs. Grey."

"So do you, Mr. Grey." She kisses my chest again and relaxes into me, letting out what I think is a sigh of contentment.

I don't know how long we sit, wrapped around each other, but it's a balm to my soul. We are one. The tension between us gone. I kiss her hair, inhale my wife's scent, and all is right in my world once more.

"IT'S LATE." I'M STROKING her back and I don't want to move.

"Your hair still needs cutting."

I laugh. "That it does, Mrs. Grey. Do you have the energy to finish the job you started?"

"For you, Mr. Grey, anything." She drops another kiss on my chest and stands up.

"Don't go." I capture her hips and turn her around. Quickly, I unzip her skirt so it falls to the floor and I offer Ana my hand so she steps free of it. I take a moment to appreciate my wife wearing nothing but her stockings and garter belt. "You are a mighty fine sight, Mrs. Grey." Sitting back in the chair, I cross my arms and gawk.

She opens her arms and twirls for me.

"God, I'm a lucky son of a bitch," I whisper in awe.

"Yes, you are."

"Put my shirt on and you can cut my hair. Like this, you'll distract me, and we'll never get to bed."

Her wicked smile is sexy. What is she planning? I zip up my pants as she waltzes over to where my shirt lies on the floor, her hips swaying in a sensual rhythm. She bends from her waist, in a pose worthy of *Penthouse* magazine, leaving nothing to my imagination, collects my shirt, smells it, then, with a coy glance at me, shrugs it on.

Down, boy.

"That's quite a floor show, Mrs. Grey."

"Do we have any scissors?" she asks, wearing my shirt and a cheeky smile.

"My study." My voice is hoarse.

"I'll go search." She prances out of the bathroom, leaving me with a semi-hard-on.

Mrs. Mrs. Mrs. Grey.

While Ana is finding scissors, I collect her clothes, fold them, and place them on the vanity. I glance at myself in the mirror, hardly recognizing the man staring back at me.

Giving up a little control in matters sexual with Ana, is extremely satisfying.

I like frantic Ana.

And greedy Ana.

I love that she loves my dick.

Yes. Especially that.

And she's agreed to be Mrs. Grey in name, too.

I'd call that a good result.

We just have to get better at communicating with each other.

Communicate and compromise.

Ana dashes into the bathroom, catching her breath.

"What's wrong?" I ask.

"I just ran into Taylor."

"Oh." I frown. "Dressed like that?"

Ana's eyes widen in alarm at my expression. "That's not Taylor's fault," she says quickly.

"No. But still." I don't want anyone eyeing my nearly naked wife.

"I'm dressed."

"Barely."

"I don't know who was more embarrassed, me or him."

I bet. Poor Taylor. Or lucky Taylor. I'm not sure how I feel about that. I remember the bikini-top incident and push that quickly from my mind.

"Did you know he and Gail are, well, together?" she says, sounding a little shocked.

I laugh. "Yes, of course I knew."

"And you never told me?"

"I thought you knew, too."

"No."

"Ana, they're adults. They live under the same roof. Both unattached. Both attractive."

She blushes. Why, I don't know. I'm glad they have each other.

"Well, if you put it like that," she mutters. "I just thought Gail was older than Taylor."

"She is, but not by much. Some men like older women—"

Shit.

"I know that," Ana snaps, scowling.

Shit. Why did I say that? Will Elena always loom over and between us?

"That reminds me," I change the subject.

"What?" Ana sounds sulky. She takes the chair and turns it so it faces the sinks. "Sit," she orders.

My bossy wife.

I do as I'm told, trying to hide my amusement.

See. I can behave.

"I was thinking we could convert the rooms over the garages for them at the new place," I say. "Make it a home. Then maybe Taylor's daughter could stay with him more often." I watch Ana's reaction in the mirror as she combs my hair.

She frowns. "Why doesn't she stay here?"

"Taylor's never asked me."

"Perhaps you should offer. But we'd have to behave ourselves."

"I hadn't thought of that." *Kids. They ruin all the fun.*

"Perhaps that's why Taylor hasn't asked. Have you met her?"

"Yes. She's a sweet thing. Shy. Very pretty. I pay for her schooling."

Ana stops combing my hair, and our eyes meet in the mirror. "I had no idea."

I shrug it off. "Seemed the least I could do. Also, it means he won't quit."

"I'm sure he likes working for you."

"I don't know."

"I think he's very fond of you, Christian." She runs the comb through my hair again. It feels nice.

"You think?" I ask. It's never crossed my mind.

"Yes. I do."

Well, how about that? I have enormous respect for Taylor. I'd like him to stay working for me—for us, indefinitely. I trust him. "Good. Will you talk to Gia about the rooms over the garage?"

"Yes, of course." Her lips curl in a secret smile, and I wonder what she's thinking about. She glances at me in the mirror. "You sure about this? Your last chance to bail."

"Do your worst, Mrs. Grey. I don't have to look at me, you do."

Her smile illuminates the room. "Christian, I could look at you all day."

I shake my head. "It's just a pretty face, baby."

"And behind it is a very pretty man." She kisses my temple. "My man."

Her man.

I like that.

I sit still and let her work. Her tongue escapes between her teeth while she concentrates. It's cute and arousing, so I close my eyes, and think back to our honeymoon, enjoying the many memories we made. Occasionally, I crack open an eyelid to take a quick peek at her.

"Finished," she announces. I open my eyes and check her handiwork.

It's a haircut. And it looks fine.

"Great job, Mrs. Grey." I pull her to me and nuzzle her belly. "Thank you."

"My pleasure." She gives me a quick kiss.

"It's late. Bed." I smack her behind, because she's waving it in front of me and it's too tempting.

"Ah! I should clean up in here," she exclaims.

There are small clumps of my hair all over the floor. "Okay, I'll get the broom," I mutter, and stand up. "I don't want you embarrassing the staff with your lack of appropriate attire."

"Do you know where the broom is?"

I stare at Ana. "Um, no."

She laughs. "I'll go." And with a quick grin, she sashays out of the bathroom.

How do I not know where the broom is?

I turn to the sink and check my hair again. Ana's done a good job. It looks fine. Smiling, impressed by her handiwork, I reach for my toothbrush.

ANA IS LAUGHING TO herself when I join her in bed.

"What?" I ask.

"Nothing. Just an idea."

"What idea?" I turn on my side and watch her.

"Christian, I don't think I want to run a company."

I shift onto my elbow. "Why do you say that?"

"Because it's not something that has ever appealed to me."

"You're more than capable, Anastasia."

"I like to read books, Christian. Running a company will take me away from that."

"You could be the creative head."

She looks pensive, and I don't know if she hates the idea or is considering it. I persist. "You see, running a successful company is all about embracing the talent of the individuals you have at your disposal. If that's where your talents and your interests lie, then you structure the company to enable that. Don't dismiss it out of hand, Anastasia. You're a very capable woman. I think you could do anything you wanted if you put your mind to it."

She's not convinced. "I'm also worried it will take up too much of my time."

I hadn't considered that.

"Time I could devote to you," she murmurs.

I see your game, Mrs. Grey. "I know what you're doing."

"What?"

"You're trying to distract me from the issue at hand. You always do that. Just don't dismiss the idea, Ana. Think about it. That's all I ask." I plant a swift kiss on her lips and run my thumb down her cheek.

You are so lovely.

You are more than capable.

"Can I ask you something?" Ana says.

"Of course."

"Earlier today you said if I was angry with you, I should take it out on you in bed. What did you mean?"

"What did you think I meant?" I ask.

"That you wanted me to tie you up."

What? "Um...no. That's not what I meant at all." I just want some...resistance in bed.

"Oh." Ana looks disappointed.

"You want to tie me up?" I ask.

I'm not sure I could do that...not yet, anyway.

Ana blushes. "Well."

"Ana, I—" That would mean complete loss of control, and total surrender. I offered that to her once before, and she didn't want it. I'm not sure I could deal with that kind of rejection from her again. Besides, I've only just learned to tolerate—no, revel—in her touch. I don't want to derail that.

"Christian," she whispers, and scrambles up so she's facing me. She places her palm on my cheek. "Christian, stop. It doesn't matter. I thought that's what you meant."

Taking her hand, I place it on my chest, where beneath my skin and bone my heart is hammering with my anxiety. "Ana, I don't know how I'd feel about you touching me if I were restrained."

Her eyes grow wider.

"This is still too new." I'm confessing my darkest fears to her again.

Ana leans toward me, and I don't know what she's going to do, but she kisses the corner of my mouth. "Christian, I got the wrong idea. Please don't worry about it. Please don't think about it." She kisses me again, and I close my eyes and kiss her back, hungrily. I grab the back of her head, holding her in place, and press her into the mattress, banishing my demons as I do.

Scarlet nails rake across my chest. I can't move. I can't see. I can only feel. *You don't like this, do you?* I can't speak. Silenced by the ball gag. Frantically I shake my head as the darkness slithers inside me, trying to crawl its way out, while her talons wreak their havoc on the outside. *Hush, now. You'll get your reward.* The flogger strikes my chest, the small beads pinching my skin in a stinging rebuke that silences the darkness with pain. Sweat beads on my brow. *Such beautiful skin.* She hits me again. Lower. And I pull against the restraints as the flogger sings its song across my belly. *Fuck.* She's going lower. The pain will be hard to take. I steel myself. Waiting. Ana stands over me. She's caressing my face while wearing my fur glove. Her hand moves down my throat, across my chest, the fur sliding over my skin. Soothing. Quieting the darkness. Ana watches me, her hair mussed, her eyes shining with her love. *Ana.* Her hand moves lower to my belly and sweeps over my stomach with the softest caress. Then her fingers are in my hair.

Opening my eyes, I find I'm wrapped around Ana like swaddling, my head on her chest. My gray eyes meet sparkling summer blue. "Hi," I murmur, delighted to see her.

"Hi." My joy is mirrored in her face.

Her satin nightgown is perfectly designed, revealing that special valley between her breasts. I kiss her there as the rest of my body wakes…fully. My hand skims over her hip. "What a tempting morsel you are," I mutter. "But, tempting though you are"—the radio alarm reads 7:30—"I have to get up." Reluctantly, I disentangle myself from my wife and climb out of bed. She puts her hands behind her head and watches me as I strip, teasing her top lip with her tongue.

"Admiring the view, Mrs. Grey?"

"It's a mighty fine view, Mr. Grey." Her mouth twists into a smug grin, so I throw my pajama pants at her.

She catches them, giggling.

To hell with work.

I hoist the duvet off of her, kneel on the bed, and grab Ana's ankles, drawing her toward me so that her nightgown rides up over her thighs, and up, and up, revealing my favorite place.

She squeals. It's a stimulating sound, and I lean down and start a path of kisses from her knee, to her thigh, to my favorite place.

Good morning, Ana.

Ah! She groans.

MRS. JONES IS BUSYING herself in the kitchen when I stroll in. "Good morning, Mr. Grey. Coffee?"

"Good morning, Gail. Please."

"And what would you like for breakfast?"

I'm famished after this morning's, and yesterday evening's, activities. "Omelet. Please."

"Ham, cheese, and mushrooms?"

"Great."

"Mrs. Grey did an excellent job on your hair, sir." Mrs. Jones smiles, and there's a teasing glint in her eye.

I grin back. "That she did." I perch on one of the barstools at the kitchen counter, where she's laid two place settings. "Ana will be with us shortly."

"Very good, sir." She hands me a coffee, and while my omelet is cooking she lays out granola, yogurt, and blueberries for Ana. I check the markets on my phone.

"Good morning, Mrs. Grey." Gail hands Ana a cup of tea as she greets her.

My wife is wearing a pretty blue shift dress that complements her eyes. She looks ever the cool publishing executive, and not the sex siren that I know, intimately, and often. She sits down beside me. "How are you, Mrs. Grey?" I ask, knowing that she was well pleasured, and loud about it, this morning.

"I think you know, Mr. Grey." She gazes up at me through her lashes, giving me that look that goads my libido.

I smirk. "Eat. You didn't eat yesterday."

"That's because you were being an arse."

Mrs. Jones drops a plate that she's washing beneath a tap into the sink; the sound startles Ana.

"Arse or not—eat."

Don't fuck with me on this, Ana.

Ana rolls her eyes. "Okay! Picking up spoon, eating granola." She sounds exasperated, but proceeds to serve herself yogurt and blueberries and makes a start on her breakfast.

I relax and remember what I wanted to talk to her about. "I may have to go to New York later in the week."

"Oh."

"It'll mean an overnight. I want you to come with me."

"Christian, I won't get the time off."

I peer down at her. *Oh, I think we can work that out.*

She sighs. "I know you own the company, but I've been away for three weeks. Please. How can you expect me to run the business if I'm never there? I'll be fine here. I'm assuming you'll take Taylor with you, but Sawyer and Ryan will be here—" She stops.

As ever, my wife makes a good point.

"What?" she asks.

"Nothing. Just you." *And your negotiation skills.*

She gives me a sideways look, but the amusement in her expression abruptly vanishes.

"How are you getting to New York?"

"The company jet, why?"

"I just wanted to check if you were taking *Charlie Tango.*" Her face loses color as she shudders.

"I wouldn't fly to New York in *Charlie Tango.* She doesn't have that kind of range. Besides, she won't be back from the engineers for another two weeks."

She looks relieved. "Well, I'm glad she's nearly fixed, but—" She stops and looks down at her granola.

"What?" I ask.

She shrugs.

I hate it when she does this. "Ana?" *Tell me.*

"I just…you know. Last time you flew in her…I thought, we th-thought, you'd—" She stutters and then stops.

Oh.

Ana.

"Hey." I brush my fingers down her face. "That was sabotage."

And we suspect your ex-boss.

"I couldn't bear to lose you," she says.

"Five people have been fired because of that, Ana. It won't happen again."

"Five?"

I nod.

She frowns. "That reminds me. There's a gun in your desk."

How the hell does she know that?

The scissors.

Shit.

"It's Leila's."

"It's fully loaded."

"How do you know?" I ask.

"I checked it yesterday."

What! "I don't want you messing with guns. I hope you put the safety back on."

She looks at me as if I've grown an additional head. "Christian, there's no safety on that revolver. Don't you know anything about guns?"

"Um, no."

Taylor clears his throat. He's waiting for us at the entrance. I check my watch; it's later than I thought.

That's because you made love to your wife this morning, Grey.

"We have to go." Standing up, I don my jacket, and Ana follows me out to the hallway, where we both greet Taylor.

"I am just going to brush my teeth," Ana says, and Taylor and I watch her retreat toward the bathroom.

I turn to Taylor. "That reminds me. It's Ana's birthday in September. She wants an R8. A white one."

Taylor raises his eyebrows.

I laugh. "Yeah. Surprised me, too. Can you order one?"

Taylor grins. "With great pleasure, sir. A Spyder like yours?"

"Yes. I think so. Same spec."

Taylor rubs his hands in ill-disguised glee. "I'll get onto it."

"We need it by the latest September 9."

"I'm sure I can source one in time."

Ana returns and we head into the elevator. "You should ask Taylor to teach you how to shoot," she says.

"Should I, now?" My tone is wry.

"Yes."

"Anastasia, I despise guns. My mom has patched up too many victims of gun crime, and my dad is vehemently antigun. I grew up with their ethos. I support at least two gun-control initiatives here in Washington."

"Oh. Does Taylor carry a gun?"

I glance at Taylor and hope that the utter disdain I feel for firearms doesn't show on my face. "Sometimes."

"You don't approve?" Ana asks, as I usher her out of the elevator.

"No. Let's just say that Taylor and I hold very different views with regard to gun control."

In the car, Ana reaches over and grasps my hand. "Please," she says.

"Please what?"

"Learn how to shoot."

I roll my eyes. "No. End of discussion, Anastasia."

She opens her mouth, but closes it again, and folds her arms and gazes out of the window. I suppose being an ex-soldier's daughter will give you a different perspective on guns. Being a doctor's son formed mine.

"Where is Leila?" Ana pipes up.

Why is she thinking about my ex-sub?

"I told you. She's in Connecticut with her folks."

"Did you check? After all, she does have long hair. It could have been her driving the Dodge."

"Yes, I checked. She's enrolled in an art school in Hamden. She started this week."

"You've spoken to her?" Ana pales, her voice quietly ringing with shock.

"No. Flynn has."

"I see," she mutters.

"What?"

"Nothing."

I sigh. This is the second time this morning she's done this. "Ana. What is it?"

Communicate and compromise.

She shrugs, and I have no idea what she's thinking. About Leila? Maybe Ana needs reassuring. "I'm keeping tabs on her," I say, "checking that she stays on her side of the continent. She's better, Ana. Flynn has referred her to a shrink in New Haven, and all the reports are very positive. She's always been interested in art, so..." I stop, trying to find a clue in Ana's face as to what she's thinking. "Don't sweat this, Anastasia." I squeeze her hand, and I'm heartened when she returns the gesture.

"NICE HAIRCUT, MR. GREY." Barry is effusive as he opens the glass door to Grey House.

"Er, thank you, Barry."

Well, that's a first.

"How's your boy?" I ask.

"He's great, sir. Doing well at school." Barry glows with paternal pride.

I can't help my smile. "Good to hear it."

Ros and Sam are in the elevator.

"Haircut?" Ros asks.

"Yes. Thanks."

"Looks good."

"Yes," says Sam.

"Thanks."

What the hell has gotten into my staff?

AFTER MY UPDATE WITH Barney on the tablet prototype, I send an e-mail to Ana. I take a gamble that she's managed to have her e-mail name changed.

From: Christian Grey
Subject: Flattery
Date: August 23 2011 09:54
To: Anastasia Grey

Mrs. Grey
I have received three compliments on my new haircut. Compliments
from my staff are new. It must be the ridiculous smile I'm wearing
whenever I think about last night. You are indeed a wonderful,
talented, beautiful woman.
And all mine.

Christian Grey
CEO, Grey Enterprises Holdings, Inc.

I'm delighted when it doesn't bounce, though I don't get an
immediate answer.

I'm between meetings when her response arrives.

From: Anastasia Grey
Subject: Trying to Concentrate Here
Date: August 23 2011 10:48
To: Christian Grey

Mr. Grey
I am trying to work and don't want to be distracted by delicious
memories.
Is now the time to confess that I used to cut Ray's hair regularly? I
had no idea it would be such useful training.
And yes, I am yours and you, my dear, overbearing husband who
refuses to exercise his constitutional right under the Second
Amendment to bear arms, are mine. But don't worry because I shall
protect you. Always.

Anastasia Grey
Editor, SIP

She used to cut Ray's hair. Well, damn it, that's why she did such
a good job. And she's going to protect me.

Of course, she is. I turn to my computer and Google "gun phobia."

From: Christian Grey
Subject: Annie Oakley
Date: August 23 2011 10:53
To: Anastasia Grey

Mrs. Grey
I am delighted to see you have spoken to the IT dept and changed your name. :D
I shall sleep safe in my bed knowing that my gun-toting wife sleeps beside me.

Christian Grey
CEO & Hoplophobe, Grey Enterprises Holdings, Inc.

From: Anastasia Grey
Subject: Long Words
Date: August 23 2011 10:58
To: Christian Grey

Mr. Grey
Once more you dazzle me with your linguistic prowess.
In fact, your prowess in general, and I think you know what I'm referring to.

Anastasia Grey
Editor, SIP

Her reply makes me grin.

From: Christian Grey
Subject: Gasp!
Date: August 23 2011 11:01
To: Anastasia Grey

Mrs. Grey
Are you flirting with me?

Christian Grey
Shocked CEO, Grey Enterprises Holdings, Inc.

From: Anastasia Grey
Subject: Would you rather…
Date: August 23 2011 11:04
To: Christian Grey

I flirted with someone else?

Anastasia Grey
Brave Editor, SIP

From: Christian Grey
Subject: Grrrrr
Date: August 23 2011 11:09
To: Anastasia Grey

NO!

Christian Grey
Possessive CEO, Grey Enterprises Holdings, Inc.

From: Anastasia Grey
Subject: Wow…
Date: August 23 2011 11:14
To: Christian Grey

Are you growling at me? 'Cause that's kinda hot.

Anastasia Grey
Squirming (in a good way) Editor, SIP

I love making her squirm via e-mail.

From: Christian Grey
Subject: Beware
Date: August 23 2011 11:16
To: Anastasia Grey

Flirting and toying with me, Mrs. Grey?
I may pay you a visit this afternoon.

Christian Grey
Priapic CEO, Grey Enterprises Holdings, Inc.

From: Anastasia Grey
Subject: Oh No!
Date: August 23 2011 11:20
To: Christian Grey

I'll behave. I wouldn't want my boss's boss's boss getting on top of me at work. ;)
Now let me get on with my job. My boss's boss's boss may fire my ass.

Anastasia Grey
Editor, SIP

From: Christian Grey
Subject: &*%$&*&*
Date: August 23 2011 11:23
To: Anastasia Grey

Believe me when I say there are a great many things he'd like to do to your ass right now. Firing you is not one of them.

Christian Grey
CEO & Ass man, Grey Enterprises Holdings, Inc.

From: Anastasia Grey
Subject: Go Away!
Date: August 23 2011 11:26
To: Christian Grey

Don't you have an empire to run?
Stop bothering me.
My next appointment is here.
I thought you were a breast man...
Think about my ass, and I'll think about yours...
ILY x

Anastasia Grey
Now Moist Editor, SIP

Moist? There's that word again. I shake my head. I like her wet. Moist doesn't do it for me, at all. But sadly, I must cease, as my meeting with Marco and his team starts in four minutes.

It's a great meeting. Marco has gone aggressively after Geolumara and our bid has been successful. This acquisition will take us into a new area of green energy, via a cheaper and easier-to-manufacture solar panel.

It's also looking likely that either I'll have to go to Taiwan or the shipyard owners will come to us. But first they want a phone conference. Ros is arranging a time.

When we finish up, she asks for a word. We wait for the others to leave.

"Hassan would like you to go to New York," she says. "Morale is low because of how Woods left. He wasn't well liked, and because he kicked up a fuss in the press, the tech team is skittish. We don't want to lose any of them. They're all good people."

"Hassan can't reassure them?"

"He can only do so much, Christian. Your visit would signal real support. You're good at rallying the troops."

"Okay."

"I'll let him know you'll be there Thursday."

"Thanks."

"Oh, and Gwen is pregnant."

"Wow. Congratulations!"

I wonder how all that works, but I don't want to pry.

"Yes. She's at twelve weeks, so we're telling people."

"Three kids! Wow!"

"Yes. We'll probably stop there."

I grin. "Well, congratulations once more."

When I get back to my desk, I call Welch for an update. He's viewed the footage from outside Escala. "Mr. Grey, I'd like to talk to Hyde's former assistants again. See if they'll talk this time."

"Couldn't do any harm."

"My thoughts exactly."

"Let me know how you get on."

"Will do."

I hang up and let Ana know I'm off to New York.

From: Christian Grey
Subject: The Big Apple
Date: August 23 2011 12:59
To: Anastasia Grey

Dearest Wife
My empire requires that I go to NYC on Thursday.
I'll be back on Friday evening.
Are you sure I can't persuade you to come with me?
Your boss's boss's boss needs you.

Christian Grey
CEO, Breast & Ass man, Grey Enterprises Holdings, Inc.

From: Anastasia Grey
Subject: NYC NoNo
Date: August 23 2011 13:02
To: Christian Grey

I think my boss's boss's boss can manage a night without me
and my breasts and ass!
As they say, absence makes the...heart grow fonder.
I'll behave. I promise.

Anastasia Grey
Editor, SIP

Thursday, August 25, 2011

I t's pre-dawn, and my wife is curled up beneath the covers. Beside her on the floor is the remains of a cable tie. I pick it up, smirking, remembering last night, and slip it into my pants pocket.

Fun times.

Leaning over her, I catch a hint of her scent. Ana and sex; the most seductive perfume in the world. I plant a gentle kiss on her forehead.

"Too early," she grumbles.

Damn. I've woken her, and I know from experience that Ana is not a fan of the early morning. "I'll see you tomorrow night," I whisper.

"Don't go," she says sleepily, and she's so tempting.

"I have to." I stroke her cheek. "Miss me."

"I will." She gives me a sleepy smile and puckers her lips.

I grin. An early morning good-bye kiss from my girl. "Bye," I whisper against her lips, and reluctantly, I leave her to sleep.

FROM THE BACK OF the car I send Ana an e-mail while Ryan drives Taylor and me to Boeing Field.

From: Christian Grey
Subject: Miss You Already
Date: August 25 2011 04:32
To: Anastasia Grey

Mrs. Grey
You were adorable this morning.
Behave while I'm away.
I love you.

Christian Grey
CEO, Grey Enterprises Holdings, Inc.

·

Captain Stephan and First Officer Beighley are on hand, and we're soon airborne for NYC. I strip down in the small bedroom, hoping to catch an hour or so of sleep. As I lay down, I recall our evening. Ana and I went to the Seattle Assistance Union Gala; she looked elegant in her pale pink dress and second-chance earrings. She looked even more elegant when I undressed her last night.

She should be with me now. I close my eyes and my mind drifts to our honeymoon night, on board this Gulfstream.

Hmm…I hope to dream of my wife.

I WAKE WHEN WE'RE about an hour out of New York and, feeling refreshed, dress quickly. Taylor is in the main cabin, eating what looks like a ham-and-cheese croissant.

"Good morning, sir."

"Hi. Breakfast. Great. Did you get some sleep?"

Taylor nods, looking his usual, immaculate self. "I did, thank you."

I take my seat as the captain joins us.

"Sleep well, sir?" Stephan asks.

"Yes. Thanks. Everything okay?" I ask.

"We're being rerouted to JFK. There's been an incident at Teterboro."

"An incident?"

"As far as I know, it's nothing major, it's just hit our landing time."

"This will give me less time at GEH Fiber Optics," I say to Taylor.

"I've been in touch with the ground crew at Sheltair, and we're rerouting your car from Teterboro," Stephan says.

"Good. Will you get the Gulfstream to Teterboro after we land? It's more convenient to leave from there."

"I'll see what we can do." Stephan smiles and heads back into the cockpit.

FORTY MINUTES LATER WE land at JFK. As we taxi to the terminal, I check my e-mails. There's one from Ana.

From: Anastasia Grey
Subject: Behave Yourself!
Date: August 25 2011 09:03
To: Christian Grey

Let me know when you land—I'll worry until you do.
And I shall behave. I mean, how much trouble can I get into with
Kate?

Anastasia Grey
Editor, SIP

Kate? I imagine she could get into a lot of trouble with Kate. The
second time I met Miss Kavanagh, Ana was inebriated. That's how
we spent our first night together. *Shit!* I press call.

"Ana St—Grey."

It's such a pleasure to hear her voice. "Hi."

"Hi! How was your flight?"

"Long. What are you doing with Kate?"

"We're just going out for a quiet drink."

Out? With Hyde at large? Fuck!

"Sawyer and the new woman—Prescott—are coming to watch
over us," she says sweetly.

Then I remember. "I thought Kate was coming to the apartment."

"She is, after a quick drink."

I sigh. "Why didn't you tell me?" I'm not in Seattle. If something
happens to them…to her, and I'm not there, I'll never forgive myself.

"Christian, we'll be fine. I have Ryan, Sawyer, and Prescott here.
It's a quick drink. I've seen her only a few times since you and I met.
Please. She's my best friend."

"Ana, I don't want to keep you from your friends. But I thought
she was coming back to the apartment."

She sighs. "Okay. We'll stay in."

"Only while this lunatic is out there. Please."

"I've said okay," she mutters, and I know by the tone of her voice
she's exasperated.

I chuckle, relieved that she's reverting to type. "I always know
when you're rolling your eyes at me."

"Look, I'm sorry. I didn't mean to worry you. I'll tell Kate."

"Good." I blow out a breath. I can go about the rest of my day and not worry about her.

"Where are you?"

"On the tarmac at JFK."

"Oh, so you just landed?"

"Yes. You asked me to call the moment I landed."

"Well, Mr. Grey, I'm glad one of us is punctilious."

"Mrs. Grey, your gift for hyperbole knows no bounds. What am I going to do with you?"

"I am sure you'll think of something imaginative. You usually do," she whispers.

"Are you flirting with me?"

"Yes." She sounds breathless and even from this far away, and over the phone her voice is arousing.

I grin. "I'd better go. Ana, do as you're told, please. The security team knows what they're doing."

"Yes, Christian, I will." I sense more eye rolling.

"I'll see you tomorrow evening. I'll call you later."

"To check up on me?"

"Yes."

"Oh, Christian!" she chides me.

"Au revoir, Mrs. Grey."

"Au revoir, Christian. I love you."

Hearing her say those three words will never get old. "And I you, Ana."

Neither of us hangs up.

"Hang up, Christian," she murmurs.

"You're a bossy little thing, aren't you?"

"Your bossy little thing."

"Mine," I whisper. "Do as you're told. Hang up."

"Yes, Sir," she purrs, and hangs up.

And the disappointment is real.

Ana.

I type a quick e-mail.

From: Christian Grey
Subject: Twitching Palms
Date: August 25 2011 13:42 EDT
To: Anastasia Grey

Mrs. Grey
You are as entertaining as ever on the phone.
I mean it. Do as you're told.
I need to know you're safe.
I love you.

Christian Grey
CEO, Grey Enterprises Holdings, Inc.

The plane pulls to a stop outside the terminal. Our car is waiting for us on the tarmac. It's time to head to the Flatiron district and rally the troops.

I loathe the tedious drive from JFK to Manhattan. The traffic is always gridlocked, and even when it's moving, it's slow. That's why I prefer to travel from Teterboro. I occupy myself with e-mails until I glance out of the car window. We're driving through Queens on the expressway, heading to the Midtown Tunnel, and there she is— Manhattan. There is something magical about her skyline. I've not been to New York for a few months; well, since before I met Ana. And I know I must bring her here soon, as she's never been before, if only to see this iconic view.

We head straight to the GEH Fiber Optics division, which is based in an old building on East Twenty-Second Street. We pull up outside, and I can feel the bustling energy of the city. It's invigorating. As I step out of the car into the Manhattan throng, I'm hyped for my first meeting of the day.

The engineering team blows me away. Young. Creative. Energetic. I feel at home here. Over a long lunch of sandwiches and beer, I tell them how their technology is going to revolutionize Kavanagh Media's operation and how the work they're doing now is vital in future-proofing Kavanagh's expansion plans. His will be the first major media outlet to use their technology, and when I show them how we intend to deploy their expertise in other fields, they're all buzzing with excitement.

Ros was right—I needed to do this. Hassan, who is now the senior vice president of the company, is smart, young, and driven; he reminds me of myself. He's far superior to Woods, an inspiring and worthy successor with vision and drive. One only has to see the premises that Woods has inflicted on his team to know he had a short-term, narrow perspective. What was he thinking? While the reception area is remarkably upscale and frankly pretentious, the offices are cramped, shabby, and in need of substantial refurbishment. We need to relocate. I've instructed Rachel Morris, their logistics chief, to get on that. She's keen to do so, which is great, but it's no wonder morale is low; the place is grim. I e-mail Ros and ask her to go through the lease to see if we can get out before the end of the term, which has another two years to run.

When I leave it's after 6 p.m., and we're behind schedule. I have just enough time to get to my apartment in Tribeca, change into my tux, then head out again to the Telecommunications Alliance Organization fundraiser near Union Square.

In the car I try to call Ana, but I can't get a signal.

Hell.

The irony is not lost on me. I'll try again later.

The event, as I expected, is convivial enough, and it gives me a chance to network with fellow senior executives and entrepreneurs in my field. But yesterday I attended a charity gala in Seattle with Ana, and it was more enjoyable for that reason alone.

While the gathered guests enjoy canapés and cocktails, I call her once more, but her phone goes to voice mail. I'm about to leave a message when I'm interrupted by the host, Dr. Alan Michaels, who is delighted to see me.

At 9:30 p.m., during the entrée, Taylor sidles up to me.

"Sir. Mrs. Grey is having a drink with Kate Kavanagh at the Zig Zag Café."

"Really?" Ana said she would go back to the apartment. I check my watch. It's 6:30 p.m. in Seattle. "Who's with her?"

"Sawyer and Prescott."

"Okay." *Maybe it's just one drink.* "Let me know when she leaves."

She said she would stay at home.

Why would she do this?

She knows I'm concerned about her welfare.

Hyde is at large. He's obviously crazy and unpredictable.

My mood sours, and I find it difficult to concentrate on the conversation that floats around me. I'm sitting at a table occupied by some of the titans of our industry and their wives—and a husband, in one case. We are here to raise money to provide technology for schools in less privileged and underserved communities across the country. But there are only nine of us at our table and one empty seat; my wife is conspicuous by her absence.

She's also absent from our home.

"Where's your wife this evening?" Callista Michaels asks me. Seated on my left, she's the organizer of the event and Dr. Michaels's wife. She's older, maybe in her late fifties, and dripping in diamonds.

"She's in Seattle."

At a fucking bar.

"Shame she couldn't come tonight," she says.

"She works. And she enjoys her job."

"Oh. How quaint. What does she do?"

I grit my teeth. "She's in publishing."

And I wish she were here.

Or I were back in Seattle.

My mood grows bleaker. My sirloin with béarnaise sauce doesn't taste quite as good as it did. It's weird. I've always attended these events without a date; now I don't know what possessed me to accept the invitation without Ana.

Well, I thought Ana would come with me.

Though, now that I think about it, she was a little bored at the benefit we attended yesterday.

And tonight, she's out drinking. With Kate.

Having fun.

Shit.

Every time I've known them to go out together, Ana has had too much to drink. The first night we slept together in Portland she was so drunk she passed out in my arms. She was totally inebriated when she got home after her bachelorette party. An image of her naked in bed, her arms beckoning me, her sweet, seductive tone, calls to me. *"You can do anything you want to me."*

Fuck!

It's always when she's out with Kavanagh.

Keep it together, Grey. The security team is with her.

What harm can she come to?

Hyde. He's out there, somewhere. And he wants revenge? I don't know.

He's a maniac.

I look up at Taylor, who is standing on the other side of the room. He shakes his head.

She's still out. She's still drinking. With Kavanagh.

I'm dragged back into the now, and a conversation about conflict minerals and reliable sources of ethically mined materials.

After the delicious and frankly comforting dark chocolate torte, I look up at Taylor again.

He shakes his head.

Hell.

That's time for how many drinks?

I hope she's had something to eat.

"Excuse me, I have to make a call." I leave the table and call Ana from the lobby. She doesn't pick up. I try her again. No answer. I try once more. Still no answer.

Fuck.

I text her.

WHERE THE HELL ARE YOU!

She should be home. Or here.

And I know I'm being petulant, but she won't even pick up my calls.

I storm back into the ballroom, where a charity auction is about to begin. I listen to the first two lots. Both involve golf.

Fuck this.

I write a check for one hundred thousand dollars and hand it to Mrs. Michaels. "I am sorry, Callista, but I have to go. Thank you for hosting a lovely evening. I'll pledge the same again for next year. It's a worthy cause."

"Christian, that's so generous. Thank you." I get up to leave, as does she, and she kisses me on both cheeks, which I'm not expecting.

"Good night," I say to Callista, and I shake her husband's hand.

I eye Taylor at the edge of the room, and I think he's already calling the car.

Even with its high ceilings and great views over the city, the place suddenly feels claustrophobic, and I'm grateful when we get outside into the balmy evening heat of New York.

"Sir, the car will be a couple of minutes."

"Okay. She's still there? At the Zig Zag?"

"Yes, sir."

"Let's go home."

Taylor tilts his head. "Tribeca?"

"No, Seattle."

He stares at me, his face giving nothing away, but I know he thinks I'm crazy.

I sigh. "Yes. I'm sure. I want to go home." I answer his unspoken question.

"I'll call Stephan," he says.

He wanders over to the side of the main entrance and makes the call. I try Ana again, and her phone goes to voice mail. I don't trust myself to leave a message. I realize I could call Sawyer, but I have only a flimsy hold on my temper.

Taylor could call him. But what would that achieve? It's not like Sawyer can physically remove Ana from the bar.

Could he?

Grey! Behave.

Taylor finishes his call and walks back to me, his expression grim.

What the hell?

"Sir, the Gulfstream is at Teterboro. It can be ready to fly in an hour."

"Good. Let's go."

"Do you want to go back to the apartment?" he asks.

"No, I don't need anything there. Do you need to go back there?"

"No, sir."

"We'll go straight to the airport."

In the car I brood. I have a nagging suspicion that I'm behaving badly, but not as badly as my wife. Why can't she do what she says? Or let me know?

Hyde is out for revenge, and I'm scared.

For her.

And for me, if I lose her.

Once we're on board, I remove my bow tie, fold it, and stuff it into the outside breast pocket of my tux. Taylor hangs my jacket with his in the small closet, and I grab a blanket for each of us, then take a seat in the main cabin.

I gaze out into the New Jersey darkness, tension leaching from my muscles into my bones. While we were in the terminal waiting for the Gulfstream, I managed to restrain myself from calling Ana again. But I can bear it no longer, and as Stephan and Beighley do their final checks, I call Sawyer.

"Mr. Grey," he says, above the background hum of the bar. People are out, enjoying themselves. Like Ana.

"Sawyer, good evening. Is Mrs. Grey still with you?"

"She is, sir."

I'm tempted to ask him to hand his phone to her, but I know I will lose my shit and she's probably having a good time. I'm reassured that she's under Sawyer's watchful eye.

"Do you want to talk to her?" he asks.

"No. Stick close to her. Keep her safe."

Hyde could be anywhere.

"Yes, sir. Prescott and I have her covered," Sawyer replies. I hang up and glance at Taylor, who is sitting diagonally opposite me, watching me impassively.

I look back down at my phone and I'm so mad at my wife, I didn't even tell Sawyer that we were on our way home. Taylor must think I'm crazy.

I am crazy—crazy for my fucking wife, who cannot be trusted to do as she says. Taylor's seen me sitting on the floor of my foyer, staring at the elevator, after she left me. And he had glue for the little glider.

"Sir, she'll be fine," he says gently.

I look up at him again and bite my tongue.

This is none of his goddamn business.

This is between me and my wife.

Deep down I think she's going to be fine.

But I have to be sure.

Why the hell couldn't she do what I needed her to do?

Just once.

Just now.

My temper simmers and I fire off a quick e-mail to her.

From: Christian Grey
Subject: Angry. You've Not Seen Angry
Date: August 26 2011 00:42 EST
To: Anastasia Grey

Anastasia
Sawyer tells me that you are drinking cocktails in a bar when you said you wouldn't.
Do you have any idea how mad I am at the moment?
I'll see you tomorrow.

Christian Grey
CEO, Grey Enterprises Holdings, Inc.

Beighley announces that we will be taking off shortly. I buckle up as Taylor does the same. "You can take the bed, if you'd like to sleep," I offer. "I think it will elude me."

"I'm good, sir."

Okay. I lay back and close my eyes, grateful that Beighley likes a nap and has slept all afternoon. She's going to fly us home.

I SLEEP FITFULLY, MY dreams a tangled mess of dominance and submission—standing over Ana with a cane in my hand. Elena standing with a cane over me.

It's confusing and unsettling.

I try not to sleep.

To stay awake, I pace. Feeling like a caged animal, though that sense is exacerbated because the Gulfstream is not exactly designed for pacing.

Hell. I want to howl at the moon.

I want to be home.

I want to curl up with Ana.

THE PLANE LANDING AT Boeing Field wakes me from my restless sleep. Opening my eyes, which are gritty from lack of sleep and dry from the air-conditioning, I pick up my phone.

Taylor is awake. I wonder if he's slept at all. "What's the time?" I ask as Beighley brings the plane to a stop at the end of the runway.

"It's ten after four."

"That's early. Will we be met?"

"I did e-mail Ryan. Let's hope he got the message." We both switch on our phones at the same time.

Shit. I have several messages. And judging by the irritating notifications coming from his phone, so does Taylor. There's a text and missed call from Ana. I read her text first.

> ANA
> I'M STILL IN ONE PIECE. I HAD A
> NICE TIME. MISSING YOU—PLEASE
> DON'T BE MAD.

Too late, Ana.

At least she missed me.

She's left a voice mail, which I listen to next. Her voice is breathy and anxious. "Hi. It's me. Please don't be mad. We've had an incident at the apartment. But it's under control, so don't worry. No one is hurt. Call me."

What the fuck?

And my first thought is Leila has broken in again. Maybe it *was* her driving the Dodge. When I glance at Taylor, his face is ashen. "Hyde was caught in the apartment. Ryan took him down. He's in police custody," he says.

My world grinds to a screeching halt.

"Ana?" I whisper, as all the breath evaporates from my body.

"She's fine."

"Gail?"

"She's fine, too."

"What the hell?"

"Exactly." Taylor looks as shaken as I feel. The plane taxies to a stop, and I call Ana immediately, but her phone goes straight to voice mail.

Shit.

Hyde. In the apartment? How? Why? What?

I'm trying to wrap my head around this, but exhaustion is clouding my thinking. Ana's not answering; she must be asleep. I hope so. I'm relieved she's okay, but I need to see her to make sure. Stephan has opened the aircraft door, and the early morning chill seeps into the main cabin and my bones. Shivering, I get up, and take my jacket from Taylor, who is first off the plane.

"Thanks, Beighley. Stephan," I say, as I don my tux jacket to ward off the cool pre-dawn air.

"You're welcome, sir," she says.

"No. I mean it. Thank you. For the last-minute scramble of it all."

"It's not a problem."

"Get some rest." I shake both their hands and follow Taylor out to where Sawyer is waiting with the Audi.

Sawyer gives us a debrief during the drive back to Escala. While Ana and Kate were carousing at the Zig Zag Café, Hyde, dressed in coveralls, arrived at Escala and buzzed the apartment service entrance. Ryan recognized him. Let him in. And took him down. This all happened just before Ana, Sawyer, and Prescott returned home. The police and paramedics came. Took Hyde away. They questioned everyone.

What the actual fuck!

"Was he armed?" Taylor asks.

"Yes," Sawyer responds.

"Is Ryan okay?" I ask.

"Yes. But there was an altercation. One of the doors needs repair."

"Altercation?" *I don't believe it!*

"They fought."

Fuck. "But Ryan's okay?"

"Yes, sir."

"And Gail. She was there?" Taylor presses.

"In the panic room."

Thank you, Ros Bailey! I glance at Taylor, who rubs his forehead, his eyes screwed shut.

Hell. Both of our women threatened by that evil motherfucker Hyde.

"Who called the police?" Taylor asks.

"I did. Mrs. Grey insisted."

"She did the right thing," I mutter. "What the hell was he hoping to achieve?"

"I don't know, sir," Sawyer replies. "One more thing. The press were outside last night."

Damn. And after they'd lost interest in us. This day just keeps getting better and better, and it's only—I glance at my watch—4:40 a.m.

"Ryan didn't get your e-mail until he turned in," Sawyer says. "It was too late to let everyone know you were on your way back."

"So Ana and Gail don't know," I ask.

"No, sir."

"Okay."

We're quiet for the rest of the short journey. Each of us with our own haunting thoughts. If Ana had been home, she'd have been in the panic room with Gail, and Ryan would have had backup and wouldn't have had to face Hyde alone.

Why can't she do as she's told?

Sawyer parks the Audi in the garage, and both Taylor and I fly out of the car and into the elevator.

"Glad we came home when we did," I say to Taylor.

"Yes, sir." He nods in agreement.

"What a fucking mess."

"Indeed." He remains tight-lipped.

"We should have a full debrief when everyone has had some sleep."

"Agreed."

The elevator doors open and we spill out into the foyer, each of us with one goal: to check on our woman. I head straight for our bedroom, and I know that's exactly what Taylor is doing. I barrel down the hallway and into the room, grateful that the thick carpet absorbs the sound of my footsteps.

Ana is fast asleep on my side of the bed. She's curled up in a small ball, wearing one of my T-shirts.

She's here.

She's fine.

My relief almost brings me to my knees, but I stand and watch her. I can't risk touching her, as I know I'll wake her if I do.

Wake her and bury myself in her.

I wonder how drunk she was last night.

Ana. Ana. Ana.

What a shock to come back here to Hyde.

I steel myself and brush my forefinger over her cheek. She mumbles something in her sleep, and I freeze. I don't want to wake her. When she settles, I slink out and head back to the living room. I need a drink.

As I pass the foyer door I notice that it's hanging off its hinges. There are scuff marks over the walls. But no blood, that I can see.

Thank God. An altercation? It looks like it was a full-on fight.

And Hyde had a gun. He could have murdered Ryan right here in my home.

The thought is sickening.

In the living room I head over to the bar cart and pour myself a Laphroaig. I toss the contents of the glass down in one swallow, appreciating the burn as it sears my throat, the warmth spreading downward and joining the maelstrom in my gut. I take a deep breath and pour another, larger glass and head back into the bedroom.

I should really get some sleep, but I'm too wired.

And too mad.

No. Not mad. I'm raging.

The sanctity of my home invaded by that cocksucking, mother-fucking asshole.

Quietly, I drag the bedroom chair from its position by the window to my side of the bed. Sitting down, I watch Ana sleep as I slowly sip my scotch and pinch the bridge of my nose, trying to quiet the ferocious storm inside me.

It doesn't work.

He wanted to harm my wife.

That's the only conclusion I can come to.

Kidnap her? Kill her?

To get back at me.

And Ana…she wasn't here.

Where I asked her to be.

Told her to be.

My anger simmers, curdling into bitter rage.

And I have no outlet.

Only this drink, and the fire it leaves in its wake with each sip.

I re-cross my legs and tap my finger against my lip as I think of all the ways I'd like to end Hyde.

Strangulation. Suffocation. Beat him to death. Shoot him. I have Leila's gun.

And punish Ana for not doing as she's told.

Paddle. Flogger. Cane… Belt.

But I can't. She won't let me.

Fuck.

As dawn breaks, it gradually lights the room.

Ana stirs, and her eyes flutter open. Her lips part as she gasps in surprise when she realizes I'm sitting and watching her. "Hi," she whispers. I finish my drink and place the glass on the bedside table while I contemplate what I'm going to say to her. "Hello," I murmur, and it feels like someone else is talking. Someone robotic. Someone without feeling.

"You're back."

"It would appear so."

She sits up, eyes bright, and blue, and lovely. "How long have you been sitting there watching me sleep?"

"Long enough."

"You're still mad," she whispers.

Oh, I wish I was just *mad.* Robotic me says the word out loud, testing it. But it's not enough. "No, Ana. I am way, way beyond mad."

"Way beyond mad. That doesn't sound good."

No. It's not. We gaze at each other and I wish I could stand up and yell and scream and tell her how I feel. How disappointed and relieved I am.

How frightened I am.

How fucking furious I am.

I don't think I've ever experienced the depth of these conflicting feelings that plague me right now. But robotic me doesn't know what to do; all systems are offline, trying to contain my rage.

She reaches over, grabs her glass, and takes a sip of water. "Ryan caught Jack," she says, placing the glass back down.

"I know."

Her brow creases. "Are you going to be monosyllabic for long?"

Is she trying to be funny? "Yes," I respond, because it's all I can manage.

Her frown deepens. "I'm sorry I stayed out."

"Are you?"

"No."

"Why say it, then?"

"Because I don't want you to be mad at me."

It's too late for that, Ana. I sigh and run a hand through my hair.

"I think Detective Clark wants to talk to you," she says.

"I'm sure he does."

"Christian, please…"

"Please what?"

"Don't be so cold."

Cold? "Anastasia, cold is not what I'm feeling at the moment. I'm burning. Burning with rage. I don't know how to deal with these"—I wave my hand seeking inspiration—"feelings."

Her eyes widen farther, and before I can stop her, she clambers out of bed and onto my lap. It's so unexpected—a welcome, disarming diversion from my rage. Slowly and carefully, so I don't break her, I wrap my arms around her and bury my nose in her hair, inhaling her unique Ana scent.

She's here.

She's okay.

My throat burns with my unshed tears of gratitude.

Thank heavens she's safe.

She embraces me and kisses my neck.

"Oh, Mrs. Grey. What am I going to do with you?" My voice is hoarse, and I kiss the top of her head.

"How much have you had to drink?"

"Why?"

"You don't normally drink hard liquor."

"This is my second glass. I've had a trying night, Anastasia. Give a man a break."

I sense her smile. "If you insist, Mr. Grey." She nuzzles my throat, once more. "You smell heavenly. I slept on your side of the bed because your pillow smells of you."

Oh, Ana.

I kiss her hair. "Did you, now? I wondered why you were on this side. I'm still mad at you."

"I know," she whispers. My hand moves rhythmically down her back; touching her brings me solace and starts to ground me in the now. "And I'm mad at you," she says.

I stop caressing her back. "And what, pray, have I done to deserve your ire?"

"I'll tell you later when you're no longer burning with rage." She kisses my neck and I close my eyes and hold her.

Tight.

I never want to let her go.

I could have lost her. She could have been killed by that asshole. "When I think of what might have happened…" I squeeze the words past the knot of fury that's still lodged in my throat.

"I'm okay."

"Oh, Ana," I choke out, and I want to cry.

"I'm okay. We're all okay. A bit shaken. But Gail is fine. Ryan is fine. And Jack is gone."

"No thanks to you," I mutter.

She leans back and glares at me. "What do you mean?"

"I don't want to argue about it right now, Ana."

I think she's weighing my words, and for whatever reason, she cuddles into me once more. She wouldn't if she knew the truth.

She knows the truth.

She knows me.

The bad seed.

She's seen the monster. "I want to punish you." I whisper, like it's a deep, dark confession, "really beat the shit out of you."

She stills. "I know," she whispers.

That's not what I expect her to say. "Maybe I will."

"I hope not," she says, her voice quiet but unwavering.

I sigh. It's never going to happen. This I know and I reconciled myself to that when she came back after leaving me.

But I want to.

Really fucking want to.

But she left the last time I did.

Now she's my wife and here we are.

I hug her tighter. "Ana, Ana, Ana. You'd try the patience of a saint."

"I could accuse you of many things, Mr. Grey, but being a saint isn't one of them."

And there she is.

My girl.

I chuckle, and though it sounds hollow, even to my ears, it's cathartic. "Fair point well made as ever, Mrs. Grey." I kiss her forehead. "Back to bed. You had a late night, too." I pick her up and deposit her back on the bed.

"Lie down with me?" she says, her eyes imploring me to stay.

"No. I have things to do." I reach for my empty glass. "Go back to sleep. I'll wake you in a couple of hours."

"Are you still mad at me?"

"Yes."

"I'll go back to sleep, then."

"Good." I tuck her in and kiss her forehead. "Sleep."

I stride out of the room before I change my mind.

And I know that I'm running from her, because she has the power to wound me like no other. If Hyde had gotten to her...*shit*. Her absence from this world would hurt me more than anything I've experienced so far.

I wander into the kitchen, deposit the glass by the sink, and head into my study. I need an action plan. I scribble down everything that I need to do, then send Andrea an e-mail to cancel my meetings in Washington, DC. I tell her I've had to return to Seattle, but can still have the meetings via WebEx or phone. I press send, knowing that once the news cycle picks up on Hyde's arrest, it will be self-explanatory.

I pull out Hyde's file to have another look through the information Welch has provided, to see if there are any clues to Hyde's insanity.

I keep coming back to one detail that's been nagging at me since I read it the first time. I wonder if it's a coincidence or material to this mess.

Jackson "Jack" Daniel Hyde.

DOB: Feb 26, 1979, Brightmoor, Detroit, MI

Hell. I'm so tired my brain is fried, but I know I won't sleep. I need some fresh air to clear the fear and anxiety from my system.

Quietly, I sneak into the closet and change into my running gear, but before I go out, I check on Ana. She's fast asleep. With my iPod strapped to my arm, I head down to the lobby in the elevator.

As the doors open, I note the two photographers outside. I slip through the rear doors to the utility area, then through a series of corridors and out into the passage behind the building. I hit the early morning streets of Seattle, The Verve's "Bitter Sweet Symphony" playing loud and proud through my earbuds.

I run and run and run, down Fifth Avenue to Vine. I run past Ana's old apartment, where Kate Kavanagh should be sleeping off her hangover. I run along Western, veering off to go through Pike Place Market. It's grueling. But I don't stop until I'm back outside Escala. And then I do it all over again.

I return a sweaty mess with my Mariners cap pulled low over my face. I make my way unrecognized through the press gathered outside the building and safely into the elevator.

Mrs. Jones is in the kitchen.

"Gail! How are you?" I ask as soon as I see her.

"Good, Mr. Grey. Glad you and Taylor are back."

"Tell me what happened."

As I fill and drink a glass of water, she gives me a quick run-through of last night's events. How Ryan ushered her into the panic room. And afterward, once Hyde was caught, what happened with the police and paramedics. "I never thought we'd have to use that room."

"I'm glad I had it installed."

"Yes, sir. I'm grateful, too. Do you want a coffee?"

"Not yet. I'll have some orange juice for Ana."

She smiles. "Coming right up."

"Is Taylor awake?"

"No, sir."

"Good. Let him rest."

She hands me the juice, and I leave her to go wake Ana.

She's still asleep.

"There's some orange juice for you here." I place it on her bedside table and she stirs, her eyes are on me, her teeth toying with her bottom lip. "I'm going to take a shower," I mutter and leave.

I strip quickly, leaving my clothes on the bathroom floor. My run has done little to improve my temper. I start washing my hair vigorously, and mentally run through a checklist of what I have to do this morning. I sense Ana before I hear her. She closes the shower door, then steps up behind me and places her arms around me. I stiffen at her touch.

Everywhere.

Don't touch me.

Ignoring my reaction, she pulls me closer, so that I feel her warm, naked body against me. She presses her cheek to my back.

We're skin on skin.

And it's unbearable.

I'm too mad at you right now.

I'm too mad at myself.

I shift so we're both under the water and continue rinsing the suds out of my hair. She presses her lips against me in small, soft kisses.

No. "Ana," I caution her.

"Hmm."

Stop.

I burn for her.

But my thoughts are too dark.

I'm too angry.

Her hand skims down over my belly, and I know what she has in mind. But I want none of it.

I want all of it.

All of her.

No!

I place both of mine on hers and shake my head. "Don't," I whisper.

She steps back, immediately, as if I've slapped her, so I turn around and her eyes flit to my erection.

It's just biology, baby.

I clasp her chin. "I'm still fucking mad at you," I whisper, and rest my forehead against hers, closing my eyes.

And I'm fucking mad at myself.

I should have stayed in Seattle.

She reaches up and strokes my cheek, and I desperately want to give in to her tender touch.

"Don't be mad at me, please. I think you're overreacting," she says.

What!

I straighten, so her hand falls to her side, and glare at her. "Overreacting?" I rant. "Some fucking lunatic gets into my apartment to kidnap my wife, and you think I'm overreacting!"

She gazes up at me, but she doesn't back away. "No, um, that's not what I was referring to. I thought this was about me staying out."

Oh. I close my eyes. I left her for one night, and she could have been kidnapped or worse. Murdered by that asshole.

"Christian, I wasn't here," she whispers in the gentlest of tones.

"I know." I open my eyes, feeling hopeless and worthless at once. "And all because you can't follow a simple fucking request. I don't want to discuss this now, in the shower. I am still fucking mad at you, Anastasia. You're making me question my judgment."

I leave her and grab a towel as I stalk out of the bathroom. I want to hang on to my anger. It protects me and keeps her away from me.

It keeps me safe.

Safe from more complex and difficult feelings.

I towel myself dry. I'm still damp as I dress, but I don't give a damn. I storm out of the closet and along the corridor to the kitchen.

"Coffee?" Gail calls after me, as I head toward my study.

"Please."

At my desk I look once more through Hyde's background check.

There's something here. I can feel it. Gail appears and leaves a black coffee on my desk.

"Thanks."

I take a sip; it's hot and dark. Damn, it tastes good.

I call Welch.

"Good morning, Grey. I hear you're back in Seattle," Welch says.

"I am. Who told you?"

"I just got an update from Taylor."

"So you've heard about Hyde."

"Yes. I've put a call in to my contact at King County PD. Find out what's going on."

"Thanks."

"And I've heard from the FBI."

There's a knock at my door, and Ana stands in the doorway, wearing the purple dress that reveals every womanly curve she possesses. Her hair is in a bun, and there are diamonds in her ears. She looks prim and proper, hiding her inner freak, and it's arousing as hell. I shake my head, dismissing her, noting the downturn of her mouth as she turns away.

"Sorry, Welch—what did you say?"

"The FBI. There's a match. The partial print in the EC135."

"It's Hyde?"

"Yes, sir. The FBI uncovered his convictions as a minor in Detroit."

Detroit again.

"They match," he says, "though those documents are supposed to be sealed, which is why it's taken a few days."

"What does that mean?"

"They may be inadmissible."

"Shit, really? Well, there's also the footage we have of Hyde outside Escala that Prescott found earlier this week. It's obvious he was checking the place out. And, of course, the CCTV from GEH's server room."

"The police have been wanting to question him about the incident at GEH, but they hadn't been able to locate him."

"They have him now."

"Indeed," Welch growls. "And the two investigations are going to compare Hyde's prints for a match."

"About time. Did you get anything out of his former assistants?"

"No. They're reluctant to talk. They all say he was an excellent boss."

"I find that hard to believe."

"Agreed, given the hushed-up harassment claims," Welch mutters. "We've only spoken to four. I'll keep pushing."

"Okay."

"What do you want to do about the heightened security around your family?"

"Let's keep it for now and see where this goes with Hyde. We have no idea if he's working alone or with someone."

"Okay. I'll report back when I've heard from my contact."

"Great. Thanks."

I check my e-mails. There's one from Sam letting me know that he's been inundated with press inquiries about last night. I respond, telling him to send all inquiries to the King County PD press office.

Taylor enters. "Good morning, sir."

"Did you get some sleep?"

He blows out a breath. "A few hours. Enough."

"Good. We have a great deal to cover."

He pulls up a chair and we run through my to-do list.

"…and, finally, get a carpenter to fix the door."

"Will do. Briefing at ten with the entire team. I'll let them know," Taylor says.

"Please."

"Sawyer and Ryan are in their racks. I'm assuming they're still asleep. Prescott is sifting through the CCTV from last night to find out how Hyde got into the building."

"Good."

"Sir," he says, in a way that gets my immediate attention.

"Yes?"

"I'm grateful we came home last night. Maybe you have a sixth sense or something."

I'm taken aback. "Taylor, I was just mad at my wife."

His sudden smile is wry and world weary. "Happens to us all, sir."

I nod, but his words are not reassuring; he's divorced.

Don't go there, Grey.

"Thank God Ana and Gail are safe," I add, as I get up. I'm hungry for my breakfast.

"Yes, sir." He follows me out of the study.

"I've made you an omelet," Gail says to me, and she gives us both a huge smile.

Maybe Taylor and Gail will tie the knot.

Who knows?

Ignoring them, I take a seat at the kitchen counter, and once Taylor has left the room I ask Gail if Ana ate. "She did, Mr. Grey. An omelet, too."

"Good."

As if I've conjured her by mentioning her name, Ana appears in the doorway wearing her jacket.

"You're going?" I ask in disbelief.

"To work? Yes, of course." She moves closer. "Christian, we've hardly been back a week. I have to go to work."

"But—" I rake my hand through my hair, feeling anxious.

What about yesterday? Hyde! The kidnapping!

Out of the corner of my eye, I notice Gail leave the kitchen. "I know we have a great deal to talk about," Ana continues. "Perhaps if you've calmed down, we can do it this evening."

"Calmed down?" I whisper and I'm immediately incandescent again. This woman is pressing every single button I have this morning.

She flushes, embarrassed. "You know what I mean."

"No, Anastasia, I don't know what you mean."

"I don't want to fight. I was coming to ask you if I could take my car."

"No. You can't," I snap.

"Okay," she says, quietly.

And just like that all the wind is out of my sails, and I'm no longer mad, just tired. I was expecting a battle. "Prescott will accompany you." My tone is softer.

"Okay," she says, and she steps toward me again.

Ana. What are you doing? She leans up and kisses me, sweetly, at the corner of my mouth. As her lips press against my skin, I close my eyes, savoring her touch. I don't deserve this.

I don't deserve her.

"Don't hate me," she whispers.

I grab her hand. "I don't hate you." *Ana, I could never hate you.*

"You haven't kissed me," she whispers.

"I know." *But I want to.*

Damn, Grey. Carpe diem.

Standing abruptly, I grasp her face between my hands and raise her mouth to mine. Her lips part in surprise and I pounce, pushing my tongue into her mouth, tasting and testing her.

She tastes of heaven, and better times and minty toothpaste.

Ana. I love you.

You. Just. Drive. Me. Crazy.

I release her before she can properly respond. I know she'll never get to work if I don't back away. I'm breathing harder. "Taylor will take you and Prescott to SIP." I fight to recover my composure and dampen my desire.

Ana blinks at me, her breathing labored, too.

"Taylor!" I call.

"Sir." Taylor is standing in the doorway.

"Tell Prescott Mrs. Grey is going to work. Can you drive them, please?"

"Certainly." Taylor turns on his heel and disappears.

Feeling more myself, I look back at Ana. "If you could try to stay out of trouble today, I would appreciate it," I mutter.

"I'll see what I can do." Her eyes shine with amusement, and it's impossible not to respond.

"I'll see you later, then," I reply.

"Laters," she whispers, and leaves with Taylor and Prescott in tow.

After breakfast I head back into my study and call Andrea. I tell her I'll be working from home, as I wasn't planning to be in the office anyway. She puts me through to Sam and we have a tedious discussion about "owning the message" with regard to Hyde's break-in.

"No, we don't, Sam, not in this instance."

"But—" he protests.

"No buts. This is a police matter. All press inquiries about this incident to them. End of discussion."

He sighs. Sam is such a publicity whore. "Very well, Mr. Grey." He sounds sullen, but I don't care. I hang up and call my dad to tell him about Hyde. We agree to keep up the security for the next week just in case.

"Will you tell Mom?"

"Yes, son. You take care."

"Will do."

I hang up and my phone buzzes with a text from Elliot.

> ELLIOT
> Yo Bro! You ok? Hyde! Fuck!

He's brief and to the point, as ever. He must have seen the news, or Ana's told Kate. I call to fill him in on events, and we agree to meet up over the weekend. He wants to talk about something, but not over the phone.

"Whatever, dude," I say. "And by the way, your girlfriend has been leading my wife astray. She should have been here in the panic room—instead, she was out getting drunk with Katherine."

"Katherine, eh?"

"Kate." I roll my eyes. "Whatever."

"And you're telling me this why?"

"I don't know, dude, just sharing my thoughts."

Elliot sighs. "You'll have to take it up with her."

Oh. Have they split up? What does that mean?

He continues before I can ask any questions. "This guy who follows me around. Do I still need him?"

"Let's see what happens with Hyde over the next few days."

"Okay, hotshot. It's your money."

"Laters, Elliot."

RYAN AND SAWYER GIVE Taylor and me a full debrief. I can't decide if Ryan is a hero or an idiot for letting Hyde into the apartment. His face is pretty battered, and he has a cut over one eye after their "altercation." Judging from his bruised face, he must have had quite the skirmish with our intruder. He says he only let Hyde in because Ana wasn't here. I glance at Taylor, whose mouth is set in a grim line. Ryan put Gail at risk, panic room or not.

The good news is that Prescott, before she left this morning, located the CCTV footage of Hyde arriving in the basement garage. His van is still down there.

I ask Sawyer to let Detective Clark know.

"Yes, sir."

"Is that all?" Taylor asks Ryan and Sawyer.

"Yes, sir," they say in unison.

"Thank you. For everything," I tell them. "I'm grateful you caught the bastard, Ryan."

"I felt an enormous sense of satisfaction knowing I brought the guy down."

"Let's hope the police charge him," I add.

Ryan and Sawyer leave.

"I have a carpenter arriving in about half an hour to repair the broken door," Taylor informs me.

"Good. I'm going to scour what was on Hyde's computer to see if I can find any further clues as to what could be behind all this."

"Sir, we have a potential problem," Taylor says.

"What?"

"Technically, Ryan did grant Hyde access to the apartment."

I pale. "Only under unique circumstances. And Hyde was armed."

"True. But it's something to bear in mind when speaking with the cops."

"Yes. Agreed. Talk to Ryan."

"Will do."

"Taylor, take the night off. Gail, too. In fact, all of you."

"Mr. Grey—"

"You had a very late night and little sleep, as did Sawyer and Prescott, watching my wife last night."

Taylor looks grim. "I'd like to leave Ryan on lookout. He's in no fit state to go out."

"Okay."

"Thank you, sir." Taylor nods and exits while I turn my attention to my computer. Specifically, the files that Barney recovered from Hyde's hard drive.

At 10:45 I stop combing through his creepy, obsessive collection of all things Grey, and log on to WebEx. Vanessa is online, too, and we start our conference with the Securities and Exchange Commission. It's a brief and convivial chat, and GEH is co-opted onto a task force that will examine the issue of conflict minerals in tech.

When we hang up with the SEC, Vanessa informs me that she's located Sebastian Miller, the truck driver who rescued Ros and me when *Charlie Tango* went down. She's introduced him to our logistics team and he'll shortly become an affiliate with the haulage contractor that GEH uses.

"That's great news."

"Mr. Grey, he was stunned to get the call."

"I bet. Thanks for tracking him down."

When that's over I call Senator Blandino.

Our conversation is short and we resolve to have lunch next time she's in Seattle.

Taylor is standing in the doorway when I finish the call.

"Yes?"

"Detective Clark is here, sir."

"Show him in."

Detective Clark has a firm handshake and a curmudgeonly, hangdog appearance. "Mr. Grey, thank you for seeing me."

"Please sit." I direct him to the chair in front of my desk.

"Thank you. I was hoping to get a brief history of your dealings with Jackson Hyde."

"Of course." I explain that I own SIP, and that Ana used to work for him, until he was fired, and all the circumstances around that, including my run-in with him at SIP.

"You assaulted him?" Clark's eyebrows are raised.

"I taught him some manners. He attacked my wife."

"I see."

"If you check his employment history, he has a track record of being fired for assaulting his female colleagues."

"Hmm… You think he's behind the GEH arson attempt?"

"I do. We have the CCTV from Grey House."

"Yes. I've seen it. And thank you for the CCTV from the garage. The forensic team have been examining the van."

"Did they find anything?"

"This." He pulls out a plastic evidence bag. In it is a note. He shows it to me so I can read the note through the bag. It's scrawled in black Sharpie:

> Grey, Do you know who I am?
> Because I know who you are, Baby Bird.

I look at the words blankly.

What a weird note.

"Do you know what this means?" Clark asks.

I shake my head. "No idea."

He slides it back into the inside breast pocket of his jacket.

"I have some more questions for Mrs. Grey. How is she?"

"She's good. She's remarkably tough."

"Hmm… Is she here?"

"She's at work. You could phone her."

"I see. I prefer a more hands-on approach. I'd like to talk to her again, face-to-face," Clark grunts.

"I'm sure I can make that happen. Given the intense press interest in my wife and me, I would request that you go to her office."

"I can do that." He nods and sits quietly while I send a quick e-mail to Hannah to see when Ana might be free.

"Hyde had a gun. Does he have a license for it?"

"We're checking."

"Have you spoken with the FBI team investigating the sabotage of my helicopter?"

"We've been in touch."

"Good. I suspect he might be behind that, too."

"Hmm… He does seem a little obsessed."

"A little." I tell him about Hyde's computer hard drive, and all the information he had accumulated about my family.

Clark frowns. "Interesting. Can we have access to that?"

"By all means. I'll ask my IT people to send it to you."

My computer pings, announcing a response from Hannah.

"My wife is free at three this afternoon at her office."

"Excellent. Well, I won't keep you, Mr. Grey."

He stands, as do I. "I'm relieved you have him. And hopefully he'll stay behind bars for a long time."

Clark's smile is menacing, and I suspect he's thinking the same. "Great view you have from up here," he says.

"Thank you."

Taylor shows him out and I compose an e-mail.

From: Christian Grey
Subject: Statement
Date: August 26 2011 13:04
To: Anastasia Grey

Anastasia
Detective Clark will be visiting your office today at 3 p.m. to take your statement.
I have insisted that he should come to you, as I don't want you going to the police station.

Christian Grey
CEO, Grey Enterprises Holdings, Inc.

I go back to searching through the contents of Hyde's computer. An e-mail arrives from Ana.

From: Anastasia Grey
Subject: Statement
Date: August 26 2011 13:12
To: Christian Grey

Okay.
A x

Anastasia Grey
Editor, SIP

At least I get a kiss.

I open up Hyde's files once more. He has a great deal about Carrick in one of the files. *Why is he so interested in my dad? I don't get it.*

Notification of an e-mail from Ana pops up on my screen.

From: Anastasia Grey
Subject: Your Flight
Date: August 26 2011 13:24
To: Christian Grey

What time did you decide to come back to Seattle yesterday?

Anastasia Grey
Editor, SIP

The kiss is missing. I respond.

From: Christian Grey
Subject: Your Flight
Date: August 26 2011 13:26
To: Anastasia Grey

Why?

Christian Grey
CEO, Grey Enterprises Holdings, Inc.

From: Anastasia Grey
Subject: Your Flight
Date: August 26 2011 13:29
To: Christian Grey

Call it curiosity.

Anastasia Grey
Editor, SIP

What is she trying to find out? I send a glib answer.

From: Christian Grey
Subject: Your Flight
Date: August 26 2011 13:32
To: Anastasia Grey

Curiosity killed the cat.

Christian Grey
CEO, Grey Enterprises Holdings, Inc.

From: Anastasia Grey
Subject: Huh?
Date: August 26 2011 13:35
To: Christian Grey

What is that oblique reference to? Another threat?
You know where I am going with this, don't you?
Did you decide to return because I went out for a drink with my friend
after you asked me not to, or did you return because a madman was
in your apartment?

Anastasia Grey
Editor, SIP

Hell. I stare at the screen, uncertain what to say. It wasn't a threat.
Jesus.

She knows I came back before I knew about Hyde. If she doesn't,
she hasn't done the time-zone math.

What can I say?

I'm staring blankly out of the window when Mrs. Jones knocks on
my office door.

"Would you like some lunch?"

"Yeah. Sure. Thank you, Gail."

"Very good, Mr. Grey." With a polite smile she leaves me with
my thoughts. I'm still trying to think of something to respond to Ana,
when I hear the ping of a new message arriving from my iMac.

From: Anastasia Grey
Subject: Here's the Thing…
Date: August 26 2011 13:56
To: Christian Grey

I will take your silence as an admission that you did indeed return
to Seattle because I CHANGED MY MIND. I am an adult female and
went for a drink with my friend. I did not understand the security
ramifications of CHANGING MY MIND because YOU NEVER TELL
ME ANYTHING. I found out from Kate that security has, in fact,
been stepped up for all the Greys, not just us. I think you generally
overreact where my safety is concerned, and I understand why, but
you're like the boy crying wolf.

I never have a clue about what is a real concern or merely something
that is perceived as a concern by you. I had two of the security detail
with me. I thought both Kate and I would be safe. Fact is, we were
safer in that bar than at the apartment. Had I been FULLY INFORMED
of the situation, I would have taken a different course of action.

I understand your concerns are something to do with material that
was on Jack's computer here—or so Kate believes. Do you know how
annoying it is to find out my best friend knows more about what's
going on with you than I do? And I am your WIFE. So are you going to
tell me? Or will you continue to treat me like a child, guaranteeing that
I continue to behave like one?

You are not the only one who is fucking pissed. Okay?
Ana

Anastasia Grey
Editor, SIP

Cursing and shouty capitals, too. Two can play at that game.

From: Christian Grey
Subject: Here's the Thing…
Date: August 26 2011 13:59
To: Anastasia Grey

As ever, Mrs. Grey, you are forthright and challenging in e-mail.
Perhaps we can discuss this when you get home to **OUR** apartment.
You should watch your language. I am still fucking pissed, too.

Christian Grey
CEO, Grey Enterprises Holdings, Inc.

Fuck it. I don't want an e-mail fight with Ana. I storm out of my office and into the living area. My temper eases at the sight of the cold chicken salad that Mrs. Jones has prepared for my lunch.

Maybe I'm so mad because I'm hungry.

"Thanks," I mumble.

"I'm going to the Greek deli that Mrs. Grey likes, to pick up her favorite foods from there for this evening. She'll just have to pop them in the oven or microwave to heat them up."

"Great," I say, distracted. *Why are Ana and I always fighting these days?*

"Mr. Grey—" Mrs. Jones is trying to get my attention.

"Yes."

"Thank you for this evening. But I must say you look tired. Have you thought about taking a quick nap?"

I frown. A nap? I'm not a child. "No."

"It's just an idea."

"I'll take it under advisement," I mutter, and bring my salad into my office.

Welch calls while I'm eating.

"Welch."

"Interesting development in the Hyde case," he rasps in his gruff voice. "Turns out Hyde's van in the garage was kitted out with a mattress and enough ketamine to fell a Texas rodeo."

"Ketamine. Shit." *I was right!*

"Yes, sir. And syringes."

I grimace. I loathe syringes.

Welch continues, "Looks like our boy will be charged with attempted kidnapping, first degree. They'll probably throw in criminal trespass, robbery, and illegal possession of a firearm, too. Also, there was a note."

"Clark showed me the note."

"Mean anything to you?"

"No. And Hyde left it in the van. Maybe he changed his mind about that, because it's nonsensical."

"Maybe. He was delivering lights to one of the new tenants in the building," Welch growls.

"Delivering lights? What do you mean?"

"Yes. He was working for a courier company. The client lives at apartment sixteen."

"Oh, yes. I've met him. Young guy. That's how Hyde got access; he's a wily bastard."

"That he is, sir," Welch agrees. "One more thing. I've heard from King County PD and the FBI. The prints match."

"We have him!"

"It looks like it."

"There must be a Detroit connection, but I'm damned if I know what it is," I mutter.

"I'll keep digging," Welch responds. "That's it for now."

"Thanks for the update."

He hangs up, and I look at the remains of my lunch. My appetite has evaporated. What the hell did that evil motherfucker have planned for my wife? Kidnap. Rape. Murder. And he had syringes. Perhaps he was going to inject her with a filthy, dirty syringe. Bile rises in my throat, but I swallow it down.

Fuck.

I have to get out of here and get some fresh air. Abandoning my lunch, I walk out through the living room and, ignoring Gail's anxious look, take the elevator down to the main lobby. The photographers have gone, so I slip out the front entrance and walk. And walk. And walk.

Life in the Emerald City goes on. People are going about their business; the streets are crowded, but I manage to weave my way through the throng.

My poor wife.

He could have killed her.

If I ever get my hands on that evil, twisted asshole. I will end him. Once more I imagine all the ways I could do that.

Shit.

Grey, get a grip.

I'm outside Nordstrom. Maybe I should buy something for Ana. Anything. I check that my wallet's in my back pocket and head in. I'm in the scarf section. A silk scarf… Yeah. That works.

I'M CALMER WHEN I get back to the apartment.

"You didn't like your lunch? Would you like something else?" Gail offers.

"No, thanks. I think I'll take your advice. I'm going to lie down. I'm exhausted."

Gail's smile is sympathetic.

Once in our bedroom, I take off my shoes, lie down, and close my eyes.

Ana is laid out before me, naked. She holds out her arms. *You can do anything you want to me. A punishment fuck.* She's in the harness. In the playroom. *What will you do to me?* I stand behind her, a cane in my hand. *Whatever I want.* She's on the table. Facedown. She cannot move. She's tied. I slap a paddle against my hand. Her buttocks clench in anticipation. She's on her knees, her forehead pressed to the floor. Her hands tied behind her back. *I want your mouth. Your cunt. Your ass. Your body. Your soul.* She kneels before me. *I'm yours. I will always be yours, husband of mine. Mine. Yours.*

I wake. Disoriented.

I'm at home. It's late afternoon, by the look of the light. I check the time; it's 5:30. Ana won't be home yet. I rub my face and walk into the bathroom, a plan hatching in my mind. I'm anticipating one hell of a fight. Ana says she's pissed at me. In the closet I remove my shirt, replace it with a T-shirt, and change into my playroom jeans in readiness for her return. I tuck the new scarf into my pocket.

Maybe we can both get what we want.

In my office, I print out her e-mail and notice that she hasn't sent me any messages since our last exchange. My wife does not back down from a challenge. This evening will be interesting.

Gail is absent. As is Taylor. Idly, I wonder what they are doing.

Ryan is in Taylor's office; he stands when I enter. "Good evening, Mr. Grey."

"You can hang out upstairs. I'd like to give everyone the night off. We'll call you if we need you."

He hesitates before agreeing. "Okay, sir."

And with that I wander back into the living room and over to the piano to await my wife's return.

Behind me, the late-afternoon sun is drifting toward the horizon, and I'm in my corner of the ring, waiting for the match to start. Gloves on. Mouth guard in.

How many rounds will I go with Mrs. Grey?

The soft ping of the elevator rings through the foyer.

She's here.

Showtime, Grey.

The thud of Ana's briefcase hitting the floor in the hall is followed by her footsteps into the living room. She stops when she sees me.

"Good evening, Mrs. Grey." Barefoot, I swagger toward her, like a gunfighter in an old black-and-white movie, my eyes fixed on her. "Good to have you home. I've been waiting for you."

"Have you, now?" she whispers. She's as beautiful as she looked this morning, though her eyes are wide and wary; her guard is up.

Game on, Ana.

"I have," I answer.

"I like your jeans," she murmurs, eyeing me from head to toe.

I wore them for you. I give her a wolfish grin and halt in front of her. She licks her lips, and swallows, but she doesn't look away.

"I understand you have issues, Mrs. Grey." From my back pocket I pull out her shouty-capped e-mail and unfold it in front of her, trying to intimidate her with a look.

I fail.

"Yes, I have issues," she responds, gazing at me, her manner forthright but her voice betraying her, all breathy and sexy.

Leaning down, I run my nose along hers, relishing the contact. Her eyes close and she utters the softest of sighs.

"So do I," I murmur against her fragrant skin.

Her eyes flutter open and I straighten up.

"I think I'm familiar with your issues, Christian." She raises a brow, and humor hovers behind her eyes.

I narrow mine.

Don't make me laugh, Ana.

I remember her saying that to me, not so long ago.

She takes a step back. "Why did you fly back from New York?" she asks, her voice kitten-soft, belying the lioness I know.

"You know why."

"Because I went out with Kate?"

"Because you went back on your word, and you defied me, putting yourself at unnecessary risk."

"Went back on my word? Is that how you see it?"

"Yes."

She looks heavenward, then stops when she notices my scowl, but I'm not sure a spanking would be a good idea right now. "Christian," she says in the same soft voice, "I changed my mind. I'm a woman. We're renowned for it. That's what we do." When I don't respond, she continues, "If I had thought for one minute that you would cancel your business trip…" She stops, seemingly at a loss.

"You changed your mind?"

"Yes."

"And you didn't think to call me?"

How could you be so inconsiderate?

"What's more, you left the security detail short here and put Ryan at risk."

Her cheeks pink. "I should have called, but I didn't want to worry you. If I had, I'm sure you would have forbidden me to go, and I've missed Kate. I wanted to see her. Besides, it kept me out of the way when Jack was here. Ryan shouldn't have let him in."

But he did.

And had you been here…

Fuck. Enough, Grey.

I reach for her, pulling her into my arms. "Oh, Ana," I whisper, and hold her as close as I can. "If something were to happen to you—"

He had a gun.

He had a syringe.

"It didn't," she whispers.

"But it could have. I've died a thousand deaths today, thinking about what might have happened. I was so mad, Ana. Mad at you. Mad at myself. Mad at everyone. I can't remember being this angry…except—"

"Except?" she asks.

"Once in your old apartment. When Leila was there."

Someone else with a fucking gun.

"You were so cold this morning." Her voice breaks into a sob on the last word.

No. Ana. Don't cry. I loosen my grip and tip her head up. "I don't know how to deal with this anger," I whisper.

I used to have a way. But that's lost to me now.

Shit. Don't go there, Grey.

I gaze down into troubled blue eyes that draw the truth from me. "I don't *think* I want to hurt you." That's why I was cold. I was raging. "This morning, I wanted to punish you, badly, and—"

How do I explain that?

I want to rage at the world, and you are my world.

"You were worried you'd hurt me?" she asks.

"I didn't trust myself."

"Christian, I know you'd never hurt me. Not physically, anyway." She clasps my face.

"Do you?"

"Yes. I knew what you said was an empty, idle threat. I know you're not going to beat the shit out of me."

"I wanted to."

"No, you didn't. You just thought you did."

"I don't know if that's true."

"Think about it," she says, embracing me and nuzzling my chest. "About how you felt when I left. You've told me often enough what that did to you. How it altered your view of the world, of me. I know what you've given up for me. Think about how you felt about the cuff marks on our honeymoon."

She has a point. Thinking back, I felt like an asshole, and I don't want her to leave me again. She tightens her arms around me and gently rubs my back, and slowly, oh-so-slowly, my tension eases. She presses her cheek to my chest, and I can resist her no more. Leaning down, I kiss her hair, and she turns her face up, offering her mouth to me. I kiss her, my lips begging her to do as she's told, begging her not to go, begging her to stay. She kisses me back.

"You have such faith in me," I murmur.

"I do."

I stroke her face, staring into her beautiful eyes, seeing her compassion, her love, and her desire.

What did I do to deserve her?

She smiles. "Besides," she whispers, an impish look on her face, "you don't have the paperwork."

I laugh and clutch her to my chest. "You're right. I don't." We hold each other, and a quiet peace settles between us; it's the first time I've felt any tranquility since my trip to New York. Is this the end of hostilities?

"Come to bed," I whisper.

"Christian, we need to talk."

"Later."

"Christian, please. Talk to me."

Damn. I sigh as my spirits sink. Perhaps we're just in the eye of the storm. "About what?" Even to my own ears, I sound petulant.

"You know. You keep me in the dark."

"I want to protect you."

"I'm not a child."

"I am fully aware of that, Mrs. Grey." I skim my hands over her body and fondle her backside, pressing my interested cock against her.

"Christian!" she scolds. "Talk to me."

Ana is as persistent as ever. "What do you want to know?" Releasing her, I pick up her e-mail that's fallen to the floor and take her hand.

"Lots of things," she says, as I lead her to the couch.

"Sit." She obeys, and I take a seat beside her. Putting my head in my hands, I steel myself for her onslaught of questions. Then I turn to face her. "Ask me."

"Why the additional security for your family?"

"Hyde was a threat to them."

"How do you know?"

"From his computer. It held personal details about me and the rest of my family. Especially Carrick."

"Carrick? Why him?"

"I don't know yet." This feels like the Inquisition. I change tack. "Let's go to bed."

"Christian, tell me!"

"Tell you what?"

"You are so exasperating," she says, holding up her hands.

"So are you."

She sighs. "You didn't ramp up the security when you first found out there was information about your family on the computer. So what happened? Why now?"

"I didn't know he was going to attempt to burn down my building, or—" I stop. I don't want to tell her about *Charlie Tango*. She'll worry. I change tack again. "We thought it was an unwelcome obsession, but you know"—I shrug—"when you're in the public eye, people are interested. It was random stuff: news reports on me from when I was at Harvard—my rowing, my career. Reports on Carrick—following his career, following my mom's career—and, to some extent, Elliot and Mia."

She frowns. "You said 'or.'"

"Or what?"

"You said 'attempt to burn down my building, or…' Like you were going to say something else."

She misses nothing.

"Are you hungry?" I try distraction and, on cue, her stomach rumbles. "Did you eat today?" She flushes, and I have my answer. "As I thought. You know how I feel about you not eating. Come." Standing, I hold out my hand, and my mood softens. "Let me feed you."

"Feed me?"

I guide Ana over to the kitchen, and I grab a barstool and drag it around to the other side of the island. "Sit."

"Where's Mrs. Jones?" Ana perches on the stool.

"I've given her and Taylor the night off."

"Why?" She looks incredulous.

They deserve an evening off after last night. "Because I can." Simple.

"So you're going to cook?" Now she sounds incredulous.

"Oh, ye of little faith, Mrs. Grey. Close your eyes."

She looks at me askance, still unsure.

"Close them!"

With a withering look, she complies.

"Hmm. Not good enough." From my back pocket I pull out the scarf I bought earlier, and I'm pleased to see it's a good match for her dress. She raises a brow. "Close. No peeking."

"You're going to blindfold me?" Her voice is soft and high-pitched.
"Yes."

"Christian—" She's about to object, but I gently press a finger to her lips.

"We'll talk later. I want you to eat now. You said you were hungry." I skim my lips over hers, then place the scarf over her eyes, tying it behind her head. "Can you see?"

"No," she grumbles, lifting her head in that way she does when she rolls her eyes. It makes me chuckle. She's so predictable sometimes.

"I can tell when you're rolling your eyes, and you know how that makes me feel."

She huffs and purses her lips. "Can we just get this over and done with?"

"Such impatience, Mrs. Grey. So eager to talk."
"Yes!"

"I must feed you first." I place a soft kiss on her temple. She has no idea how hot she looks perched primly on the stool, blindfolded and with her hair restrained in its bun. I'm almost tempted to grab my camera.

But I must feed her.

From the fridge I extract a bottle of Sancerre and the various serving dishes into which Gail has transferred the Greek deli food; the lamb is in a Pyrex bowl.

Shit. How long do I cook this for?

I pop it in the microwave and set it to heat for five minutes on full power. That should be enough. I place two pitas in the toaster.

"Yes. I am eager to talk," Ana says, and the way she's tilting her head, it's obvious she's listening to what I'm doing. I grab the bottle of wine and a corkscrew as Ana shifts in her chair.

"Be still, Anastasia—I want you to behave," I murmur, close to her ear. "And don't bite your lip." I tug her bottom lip free from her teeth and she smiles.

Finally!

A smile.

I open the bottle, easing out the cork, and fill a glass.

Now for some musical accompaniment. I switch on the surround speakers and select Chris Isaak's "Wicked Game" from the iPod. The pluck of a guitar string resonates through the room.

Yes. This song works.

I turn it down and pick up the glass of wine. "A drink first, I think," I say, almost to myself. "Head back." She lifts her chin. "Farther." Ana obliges and I take a swig of cool, crisp wine and kiss her, pouring the wine into her mouth.

"Mm." She swallows.

"You like the wine?"

"Yes," she breathes.

"More?"

"I always want more, with you."

I grin. *More.* Our word. She grins, too.

"Mrs. Grey, are you flirting with me?"

"Yes."

Good. I love it when she flirts with me.

I take another large sip of wine, then, holding the knot of the scarf, gently tug her head back. I kiss her, drizzling the wine into her mouth. She drinks, greedily. "Hungry?" I ask her against her lips.

"I think we've already established that, Mr. Grey." Her voice is dripping with sarcasm.

Ah, there she is again…my girl.

The microwave pings, announcing that the lamb is ready. Its appetizing aroma has filled the kitchen. I pick up a cloth, open the microwave door, and grab the dish. "Shit! Christ!" It's scalding hot where my finger touches it without the cloth. I drop it and it clatters on the counter.

"You okay?" Ana asks.

"Yes!"

No.

Ow!

I abandon the dish, wanting some TLC. "I just burned myself. Here." I ease my poor finger into her mouth. "Maybe you could suck it better."

Ana grabs my hand and slowly draws my finger out of her mouth.

"There, there," she whispers, and pouts prettily and blows gently on my smarting skin.

Oh.

She might as well be blowing on my dick.

She kisses my knuckle, twice, then slowly reinserts my digit into her mouth, her tongue cradling and sucking me.

She might as well be sucking my dick.

Lust surges like a tidal wave, south.

Ana.

As she fellates my finger her forehead creases.

"What are you thinking?" I whisper, as I draw my finger out of her mouth and attempt to bring my body under control.

"How mercurial you are."

This is not news. "Fifty Shades, baby." I plant a kiss at the corner of her mouth.

"My Fifty Shades." She grabs my T-shirt and tugs me closer.

"Oh, no you don't, Mrs. Grey. No touching. Not yet." I pry her hand from my shirt and kiss each of her fingers. "Sit up." Ana pouts. "I will spank you if you pout."

I stick a fork into the lamb dish, then into the accompanying sauce of yogurt and mint. "Now open wide." She opens her mouth and I slide a forkful between her lips.

"Hmm," she hums in appreciation.

"You like?"

"Yes."

I try some, too, and it's a party of delicious flavors in my mouth. I realize how hungry I am. "More?" I ask Ana. She nods, and I feed her another forkful. While she's chewing, I tear some of the pita bread and dip it into the hummus. "Open." Ana indulges me and eats this latest morsel with enthusiasm.

I join her.

This really is the best hummus in Seattle.

"More?" I ask.

She nods. "More of everything. Please. I'm starving."

Her words are music to my soul. I feed her and myself, alternating between the bread and hummus and the lamb. Ana is lapping it up, thoroughly enjoying the feast, and it's a pleasure to watch her savor the food and to feed her. Occasionally I offer her more wine, using my tried-and-trusted mouth-to-mouth technique.

When the lamb is finished, I turn to the stuffed grape leaves. "Open wide, then bite."

She does. "I love these," she mumbles with a full mouth.

"I agree. They're delicious."

When I finish feeding her, she licks my fingers clean. One by one. "More?" My voice is husky.

She shakes her head.

"Good," I murmur against her ear, "because it's time for my favorite course. You." I pick her up suddenly and she squeaks with surprise.

"Can I take the blindfold off?"

"No. Playroom." Ana stills in my arms while I cradle her to my chest. "You up for the challenge?" I ask.

"Bring it on," she says, as I knew she would. She feels a little lighter in my arms as I carry her upstairs. "I think you've lost weight," I mutter. She smiles, pleased, I think. Outside the playroom, I slide her down my body and onto her feet, keeping my arm around her waist while I unlock the door. I usher her inside, turning on the lights as we enter.

In the middle of the room, I release her, undo the scarf, and slowly draw the hairpins from her bun, freeing her braid. Grasping it as it swings between her shoulder blades, I tug gently so she steps back against me. "I have a plan," I whisper in her ear.

"I thought you might," she answers, as I kiss that spot beneath her ear where her pulse beats.

"Oh, Mrs. Grey, I do." Still holding her braid, I tilt Ana's head, exposing her neck, and skim my lips down her throat. "First we have to get you naked." When I turn her around, her eyes flit down to the unfastened top button on my jeans. Before I can stop her, she inserts her finger into the waistband, teasing the hair at the base of my belly.

Ah!

She glances up at me from behind long lashes. "You should keep these on," she says.

"I fully intend to, Anastasia." I fold her in my arms, one hand at her neck, the other splayed on her backside, and I kiss her, my tongue testing and tasting her. While we kiss, I walk her backward until she's against the playroom cross, where I press my body into hers. Her lips are greedy, her tongue as eager as mine. I pull back. "Let's get rid of this dress." I grasp the hem and slowly divest her of her dress, revealing her body an inch at a time as I peel it off. "Lean forward," I say, and she complies. The dress ends up on the floor as my wife stands before me in her seductive lingerie and her sandals. Threading my fingers through hers, I raise her hands over her head and incline mine in a question.

Restraints, Ana?

Her gaze is intense, missing nothing. I bathe in it, feeling it in my groin. She swallows and then nods.

My sweet girl. She never lets me down.

I clip her wrists in the leather cuffs above her head and take the scarf from my back pocket once more. "Think you've seen enough," I whisper, and blindfold her again. I run my nose down hers and deliver a promise: "I'm going to drive you wild."

Grasping her hips, I run my hands down her body, removing her panties as I go. "Lift your feet, one at a time." She obliges and I remove her panties, then each of her sandals in turn. Sliding my fingers around her ankle, I tug her right leg to the right. "Step," I order. She does, and I cuff her right ankle to the cross. I repeat the process with her left ankle, buckling her up tight. When she's secure I stand and step close to her, bathing in her warmth and her growing excitement. Holding her chin, I plant a soft, chaste kiss on her lips. "Some music and toys, I think. You look beautiful like this, Mrs. Grey. I may take a moment to admire the view." Stepping back, I do exactly that, knowing that the longer I look at her and do nothing, the wetter she'll get…and the harder I'll get.

She is a mighty fine sight.

But right now, I want to teach her about orgasm denial.

I pad over to the drawers and pull out a wand and the iPod. There's a small tin of Tiger Balm beside the wand, and I contemplate spreading a little on her clitoris.

That would heat her up.

No. Not right now. That's too next-level.

I switch on the music system and choose something unsettling, to suit my mood.

Yes. Bach. Aria from Goldberg Variations. Perfect.

I press play, and the crisp, bright, cool notes sing out through my playroom.

Our playroom.

I put the wand in my back pocket, pull off my T-shirt, and return to my wife, who is biting her lip. Taking her chin between my fingers, I startle her, then tug so that she releases her bottom lip. Her smile is shy and sweet, and I know she was unaware of what she was doing.

Oh, Ana. What I have in store for you.

Maybe I'll let you come.

Maybe I won't.

I run the backs of my fingers over the soft skin of her throat to her sternum, then, using my thumb, I tug her bra cup down, freeing her breast. She has such beautiful breasts. While I kiss her throat, I release her other breast from its bra cup and toy with her nipple. My lips and my fingers tug and tease each of them, until they're both erect and begging for more.

Ana squirms against her restraints. "Ah," she groans. But I don't stop; my mouth and fingers continue their slow, sensual torment. I know how easy it is to arouse her to orgasm this way.

She's breathing hard. "Christian," she begs.

"I know." My voice is husky with want. "This is what you make me feel."

She gasps.

And I continue.

Her hips press forward and her legs start to tremble. "Please," she pleads.

Oh, baby. Feel it.

My cock is pressing against soft denim, wanting release. *All in good time, Grey.*

I stop and stand up, looking down at her face. Her mouth is hanging open as she drags air in to her lungs, and she writhes against the leather cuffs. I run my hands down the side of her body, leaving one to linger at her hip while I skirt the fingers of my other hand down her belly. Again, she pushes her hips forward, offering herself to me. "Let's see how you're doing," I murmur. I brush my fingers over her sex, and she soaks my fingers.

My jeans get tighter.

I skate my thumb over the excited little nub at the junction of her thighs and she cries out, pushing herself into my hands.

Oh, Ana. So keen. So wet for me.

And you're so far from coming.

If—and it's a big if—I let you come at all.

Slowly, I insert my middle, then index finger inside her. She groans and continues to strain against my hand, searching for release. "Oh, Anastasia, you're so ready." I circle my fingers inside her, stroking her, tantalizing her, while my thumb continues to rouse her clitoris. Her legs start to tremble again as she strains toward me. It's the only part of her body I'm touching. Her head is thrown back as she absorbs the pleasure. She's close.

With my other hand, I pull out the wand from my back pocket and switch it on.

"What?" she murmurs at the sound.

"Hush." My lips swoop down on hers, and she kisses me greedily. I pull back while my fingers still work away inside her. "This is a wand, baby. It vibrates." I hold it against her sternum and let it float over her so it oscillates against her skin. My thumb and fingers still tease her sex, and I drag the vibrating wand down between her breasts, then across each nipple in turn.

"Ah!" she moans out loud, and her legs stiffen as she throws her head back once more and groans loudly. I stop moving my fingers and lift the wand from her skin.

"No! Christian," she cries, and pushes her hips fruitlessly toward me.

So close. And yet so far.

"Still, baby," I whisper, and kiss her. "Frustrating, isn't it?"

She gasps. "Christian, please."

"Hush." I kiss her and slowly start to move my fingers inside her, grazing the wand across her skin between the two peaks of her breasts. I move so I'm leaning into her, my cock hard and ready against her.

She starts to climb again and I bring her close.

So close.

Then stop once more.

"No," she whimpers, and I plant kisses on her shoulder as I withdraw my fingers from inside her and stop teasing her clitoris with my thumb. Instead, I increase the speed of the wand and let it travel down her stomach, over her belly and over the tiny swollen bud between her thighs.

"Ah!" she cries out, and pulls on her shackles.

And I stop once more, removing the wand from her skin.

"Christian!" she calls.

"Frustrating, yes?" I whisper against her throat. "Just like you. Promising one thing and then…"

"Christian, please!"

I let the wand touch her again.

And stop.

And start.

And stop.

She's panting hard.

"Each time I stop, it feels more intense when I start again. Right?"

"Please," she begs, and I switch the wand off and place it on the small shelf beside the cross and kiss her. Her lips are eager—no, *desperate*—for my touch. I run my nose down hers and whisper, "You are the most frustrating woman I have ever met."

She shakes her head. "Christian, I never promised to obey you. Please, please—" I grab her behind and push my still clothed cock against her; rubbing myself over her. She groans, and I peel off the blindfold and grasp her chin; wild blue eyes meet mine.

"You drive me crazy." My voice is hoarse as I flex my hips against her, once, twice, thrice, and she tips her head back, ready to come— and I stop. She closes her eyes and takes a deep breath.

"Please," she whispers, and looks up at me.

Oh, baby, you can take more. I know you can.

My fingers skim her breast as they travel down her body, and she stiffens beneath my touch, and turns her face away from me. "Red," she whimpers. "Red. Red." As tears spill down her face.

I freeze.

Fuck.

No. No.

"No!" I breathe. "Jesus Christ, no." I unclip her hands, and, holding her, I bend down and unclip her ankles. She puts her head in her hands and starts to weep.

"No, no, no. Ana, please. No." I've gone too far. I pick her up and sit down on the bed, cradling her in my lap while she sobs. Reaching for the satin sheet behind me, I pull it off the bed and wrap it around her, and I hug her close, rocking her gently, backward and forward. "I'm sorry. I'm sorry," I whisper, feeling like an asshole, and shower her hair with kisses. "Ana, forgive me, please."

She says nothing. She continues to weep; each sob a twist of the knife in my dark, dark soul.

What was I thinking?

Ana. I'm sorry.

I'm a fucking asshole.

She buries her face in my neck, and her tears scorch my skin. "Please switch the music off."

"Yes, of course." I move with her on my lap, easing the remote out of my back pocket, and switch off the music. All I hear is her quiet keening interspersed with her shuddering breaths.

It's hell.

"Better?" I ask.

She nods, and gently I wipe away her tears with my thumb. "Not a fan of Bach's Goldberg Variations?" I make a desperate attempt at humor.

"Not that piece." She looks up at me, her eyes dulled by her inner pain, and shame washes over me in a torrent.

"I'm sorry," I whisper.

"W-why did you d-do that?" she stutters between shudders.

I shake my head and close my eyes. "I got lost in the moment."

Her brows knit together.

I sigh. I have to explain. "Ana, orgasm denial is a standard tool in— You never—"

What's the use?

I stop and she shifts; her weight slams against my semi-erect dick and I wince.

"Sorry," she mumbles, as her pale cheeks pink. Even now, she's apologizing to me. This woman puts me to shame. Disgusted with myself, I lie back and take her with me so that we're both lying on the bed, my arms around her.

She squirms and starts to readjust her bra.

"Need a hand?" I ask.

She shakes her head vehemently, and I know she doesn't want me to touch her.

Fuck.

Ana. I'm. Sorry.

I can't bear it. I move so that we're facing each other. I raise my hand and wait a beat to see if she withdraws, but she doesn't, and I stroke the backs of my fingers gently down her tearstained face. Tears well in her eyes again.

"Please don't cry," I mutter, as we gaze at each other.

She looks so damned hurt. It's heartrending.

"I never what?" she asks, and it takes me a split second to realize what she's referring to—my unfinished sentence.

"Do as you're told. You changed your mind; you didn't tell me where you were. Ana, I was in New York, powerless and livid. If I'd been in Seattle, I'd have brought you home."

"So you are punishing me?"

Yes. No. Yes. I close my eyes, unable to face her.

"You have to stop doing this," she says.

I frown.

"For a start, you only end up feeling shittier about yourself."

I snort. "That's true. I don't like to see you like this."

"And I don't like feeling like this. You said on the *Fair Lady* that you hadn't married a submissive."

"I know. I know."

"Well, stop treating me like one. I'm sorry I didn't call you. I won't be so selfish again. I know you worry about me."

We stare at each other while I weigh her words. "Okay. Good." I lean over to kiss her. But I stop before my lips touch hers, asking for permission and begging for forgiveness. She raises her lips to mine and I kiss her with tenderness.

"Your lips are always so soft when you've been crying."

"I never promised to obey you, Christian."

"I know."

"Deal with it, please. For both our sakes. And I will try to be more considerate of your controlling tendencies."

I have no answer to that, except "I'll try."

She sighs. "Please do. Besides, if I *had* been here…" Her eyes grow wide.

"I know," I whisper, feeling like all the blood is draining from my face. I lie back and fling my arm across my eyes, imagining for the thousandth time what could have happened.

He could have killed her.

She curls around me and lays her head on my chest while I hold her. My fingers twirl her braid, then untie it and slowly untangle her hair. It's soothing, feeling her soft hair spill through my fingers.

Ana, I'm so sorry.

We lie for several moments, until Ana interrupts my thoughts. "What did you mean earlier, when you said 'or'?"

"Or?" I ask.

"Something about Jack."

I peer at her. "You don't give up, do you?"

She rests her chin on my sternum. "Give up? Never. Tell me. I don't like being kept in the dark. You seem to have some overblown idea that I need protecting. You don't even know how to shoot—I do." She's on a roll. "Do you think I can't handle whatever it is you won't tell me, Christian? I've had your stalker ex-sub pull a gun on me, your pedophile ex-lover harass me—"

Ana!

"And don't look at me like that. Your mother feels the same way about her."

What? "You talked to my mother about Elena?" I don't believe it.

"Yes, Grace and I talked about her."

I gape at her, and Ana continues, "She's very upset about it. Blames herself."

"I can't believe you spoke to my mother. Shit!" I put my arm over my face again, as yet more shame washes through me.

"I didn't go into any specifics."

"I should hope not. Grace doesn't need all the gory details. Christ, Ana. My dad, too?"

"No!" she says, shocked, I think. "Anyway, you're trying to distract me—again. Jack. What about him?"

I lift my arm to check on her and she's sporting her expectant talk-to-me-now, I'm-taking-none-of-your-bullshit look. Sighing, I put my arm back over my eyes, and I let the words spill out in a rush. "Hyde is implicated in *Charlie Tango*'s sabotage. The investigators found a partial print—just partial, so they couldn't make a match. But then you recognized Hyde in the server room. He has convictions as a minor in Detroit, and the prints matched his. This morning, a cargo van was found in the garage here. Hyde was the driver. Yesterday, he delivered some shit to that new guy who's moved in. The guy we met in the elevator."

"I don't remember his name," Ana mutters.

"Me neither. But that's how Hyde managed to get into the building legitimately. He was working for a delivery company—"

"And? What's so important about the van?"

Damn.

"Christian, tell me," Ana insists.

"The cops found things in the van." I stop. I don't want to give her nightmares. I tighten my hold around her.

"What things?" she presses.

I stay silent. But then I know she'll keep pushing me. "A mattress, enough horse tranquilizer to take down a dozen horses, and a note." I try to hide my horror, and I don't tell her about the syringes.

"Note?"

"Addressed to me."

"What did it say?"

I shake my head. *It was gibberish.*

"Hyde came here last night with the intention of kidnapping you." She shudders. "Shit."

"Quite."

"I don't understand why," she says. "It doesn't make sense to me."

"I know. The police are digging further, and so is Welch. But we think Detroit is the connection."

"Detroit?" Ana sounds confused.

"Yeah. There's something there."

"I still don't understand."

I raise my arm and gaze at her, realizing that she doesn't know. "Ana, I was born in Detroit."

"I thought you were born here in Seattle."

No. Reaching behind me, I grab one of the pillows and place it under my head. With my other hand, I continue to run my fingers through her hair. "No. Elliot and I were both adopted in Detroit. We moved here shortly after my adoption. Grace wanted to be on the West Coast, away from the urban sprawl, and she got a job at Northwest Hospital. I have very little memory of that time. Mia was adopted here."

"So, Jack is from Detroit?"

"Yes."

"How do you know?"

"I ran a background check when you went to work for him."

She gives me a sideways look. "Do you have a manila file on him, too?" She smirks.

I hide my smile. "I think it's pale blue."

"What does it say in his file?"

I stroke her cheek. "You really want to know?"

"Is it that bad?"

I shrug. "I've known worse." My sad and sorry start in life springs to mind.

Ana cuddles into me, pulling the red satin sheet over the two of us before laying her cheek on my chest. She looks thoughtful.

"What?" I ask. Something's on her mind.

"Nothing," she murmurs.

"No, no. This works both ways, Ana. What is it?"

She glances at me, her eyebrows drawn together. She rests her cheek on my chest once more. "Sometimes I picture you as a child before you came to live with the Greys."

I tense beneath her. I do not want to talk about this. "I wasn't talking about me. I don't want your pity, Anastasia. That part of my life is done. Gone."

"It's not pity. It's sympathy and sorrow, sorrow that anyone could do that to a child." She stops and swallows, then continues, her voice soft and low. "That part of your life is not done, Christian. How can you say that? You live every day with your past. You told me yourself—fifty shades, remember?"

I sigh and run my hand through my hair. *Drop it, Ana.*

"I know it's why you feel the need to control me. Keep me safe."

"And yet you choose to defy me." I'm bewildered. This is what I find most confusing about her. She knows that I have issues, yet she still challenges me.

"Dr. Flynn said I should give you the benefit of the doubt. I think I do, I'm not sure. Perhaps it's my way of bringing you into the here and now—away from your past," she mutters. "I don't know. I just can't seem to get a handle on how far you'll overreact."

"Fucking Flynn," I mumble.

"He said I should continue to behave the way I've always behaved with you."

"Did he, now?" I observe wryly.

I have him to blame.

She takes a deep breath. "Christian, I know you loved your mom, and you couldn't save her. It wasn't your job to do that. But I'm not her."

Fuck. What? Stop. Now.

I lay paralyzed beneath her. "Don't," I whisper.

I don't want to discuss the fucking crack whore.

I'm floating above a deep well of harrowing, painful feelings that I don't want to acknowledge, and I certainly don't want to *feel*.

"No, listen. Please." Ana lifts her head, her bright blue eyes penetrating my shield, and I realize I'm holding my breath. "I'm not her," Ana says. "I'm much stronger than she was. I have you, and you're so much stronger now, and I know you love me. I love you, too."

"Do you still love me?" I whisper.

"Of course I do. Christian, I will always love you. No matter what you do to me."

Ana, you're crazy.

I close my eyes and place my arm over my eyes again, holding her closer to me.

"Don't hide from me," she says, and she pries my arm off my face. "You've spent your life hiding. Please don't, not from me."

Me?

I stare at her, bewildered. "Hiding?"

"Yes."

I roll onto my side, smooth her hair off her face, and tuck it behind her ear. "You asked me earlier today if I hated you. I didn't understand why, and now—"

"You still think I hate you?" she asks.

"No." I shake my head. "Not now. But I need to know, why did you safe-word, Ana?"

She swallows, and I watch the play of emotions that cross her face. "Because…because you were so angry and distant and cold. I didn't know how far you'd go."

I realize that she asked me and asked me and asked me to let her come. And I didn't.

I betrayed her trust.

Thank heaven for safe words.

"Were you going to let me come?" Her gaze is unwavering, in spite of her blush.

Yes. No. I don't know.

"No," I answer. But the truth is, I don't know.

"That's harsh."

I caress her cheek with my knuckle, the one with the burn. "But effective," I whisper.

And you stopped me.

We will always have safe words. If I go too far.

Even when I said we didn't need them.

"I'm glad you did," I mutter.

"Really?" She doesn't believe me.

I try to smile at her. "Yes. I don't want to hurt you. I got carried away." I kiss her. "Lost in the moment." I kiss her again. "Happens a lot with you."

Her face brightens with a grin.

It's catching. "I don't know why you're grinning, Mrs. Grey."

"Me neither."

I embrace her, holding her close, and place my head on her chest. She strokes my naked back with one hand and runs her fingers through my hair with the other. And I crave her touch.

"It means I can trust you, to stop me. I never want to hurt you," I confess. "I need—"

Tell her, Grey.

"You need what?"

"I need control, Ana. Like I need you. It's the only way I can function. I can't let go of it. I can't. I've tried. And yet, with you..." I shake my head in exasperation.

"I need you, too," she says, hugging me tighter. "I'll try, Christian. I'll try to be more considerate."

"I want you to need me."

"I do!" she says emphatically.

"I want to look after you."

"You do. All the time. I missed you so much while you were away."

"You did?"

"Yes, of course. I hate you going away."

I smile. "You could have come with me."

"Christian, please. Let's not rehash that argument. I want to work."

I sigh as she runs her fingers through my hair, chasing away my tension, helping me relax. "I love you, Ana."

"I love you, too, Christian. I will always love you."

We lie entwined in red satin, almost naked, me wearing jeans, Ana in her bra.

What a pair we are...

Her breathing evens out, she's sleeping. I close my eyes.

Mommy is sitting on the couch. She is quiet. She looks at the wall and blinks sometimes. I stand in front of her with my cars, but she doesn't see me. I wave and she sees me, but she waves me away. *No, Maggot, not now.* He comes here.

He hurts Mommy. *Get up, you stupid Bitch.* He hurts me.
I hate him. He makes me so mad. I run to my kitchen and
hide under the table. *Get up, you stupid Bitch.* He shouts.
He is loud. Mommy screams. *No.* I put my hands over my
ears. *Mommy.* He comes into the kitchen with his boots and
smell. *Where are you, little shit? There you are. Stay here,
you little prick. I'm going to fuck your bitch of a mother. I
don't want to see your fuck-ugly face for the rest of the evening.
Understand?* When I don't reply, he slaps my face. Hard. My
cheek stings. *Or you get the burn, you little prick.* No. No. I
don't like that. I don't like the burn. It hurts. He smokes his
cigarette and waves it in front of me. *Do you want the burn,
you little shit? Do you?* He laughs. He has some teeth gone.
He laughs. And laughs. *I'm going to cook something for that
bitch. Gonna need a spoon. Then it's going into this.* He holds
an in-jec-shun up for me to see. *She loves this. She loves this
more than she loves you or me, you little shit.* He turns away.
He changes. He's Jack Hyde and Ana lies on the floor beside
him and he's plunging the syringe into her thigh.

"No!" I bellow to the world.

"Christian, please. Wake up!"

I open my eyes. She is here. Shaking me. "Christian, you're having a nightmare. You're home. You're safe." I look around. We're on
the bed in the playroom.

"Ana!" She's here. She's safe. I grab her face and pull her lips to
mine, seeking the comfort and solace of her mouth. She is everything
wholesome in my life. My love. My light.

Ana.

Desire rockets through my body like lightning; I'm aroused. I roll
us over, pressing her into the mattress.

I want her. I need her.

Holding her chin, I place my hand on her head to keep her still
while I part her legs with my knee, resting my bursting dick, still clad
in denim, against her sex. "Ana," I breathe, and gaze down into her
startled blue eyes. Her pupils grow bigger and darker.

She feels it, too.

She wants it, too.

My lips capture her mouth again, tasting her, taking her. And I rock my dick against her. I kiss her face, her eyelids, her cheeks, along her jawline. I want her.

Now.

"I'm here," she whispers, and wraps her arms around my shoulders and grinds against me.

"Oh, Ana. I need you." I'm breathless, yearning for her.

"Me, too," she rasps, clutching at my back.

I rip open my button fly, freeing my dick, and I shift, ready to take her.

Yes? No? Ana? I gaze into her dark, dark eyes and see a reflection of my need and want.

"Yes. Please," she says.

I bury myself in her in one thrust.

"Ah!" she cries, and I groan, cherishing the feel of her.

Ana. I honor her mouth once more, my tongue insistent as I drive into her, chasing away my fear and my nightmare. Losing myself in her love and lust. She is frantic, too. Needy. Greedy. Joining me, thrust for thrust, on and on.

"Ana!" I growl and let go, coming inside her over and over, losing all sense of self and falling under her powerful spell. She makes me whole.

She heals me. She is my light.

She holds me, hard and tight, while I drag air into my lungs.

I ease out of her and tighten my arms around her while the earth rights itself on its axis.

Wow.

That was…

Quick!

I shake my head and lean up on my elbows, staring down into her beautiful face. "Oh, Ana. Sweet Jesus." I kiss her.

"You okay?" She places her palm on my cheek.

I nod as I finally settle back on earth. "You?" I ask.

"Um…" She wriggles beneath me, pressing herself against my

sated cock. I give her a wicked, carnal smile. I know what she's trying to tell me. This is a language I understand.

"Mrs. Grey, you have needs," I whisper. I drop a quick kiss on her lips, and before she can say anything, I get up. Kneeling at the end of the bed, I grab Ana's legs and tug her toward me so that her ass hangs on the edge of the bed. "Sit up," I tell her, and she does as she's told. Her hair tumbles down to her breasts, and with my eyes on hers, I gently push her legs apart. She leans back on her hands, her breasts rising and falling as her breathing quickens. Her lips are parted. I don't think she can quite believe what I'm going to do.

"You are so fucking beautiful, Ana," I murmur, and press soft kisses up her inner thigh. I glance at her through my lashes, like she does to me.

"Watch," I breathe, as my tongue laps at her clitoris.

"Ah!" she cries out. She tastes of Ana and sex and me and I don't let up. After what I did to her earlier, she must be wound up tighter than an old-fashioned watch. I keep her legs apart, holding her in place while my mouth works its magic, lavishing her with unyielding attention.

Her body starts to tremble.

"No...ah!" she says, and it's my cue to slowly slide a finger inside her. She groans and collapses onto the bed while I stoke the fire inside her, taunting her sweet spot over and over, my tongue continuing to bathe her clitoris.

She's so close. Her legs stiffen.

Ana. Let it go.

She cries out my name, her back arching off the bed as she comes and comes and comes. I ease my finger out of her and strip out of my jeans. Leaning up, I nuzzle her belly as she runs her fingers through my hair. "I'm not finished with you yet," I whisper, and kneeling back, I tug her off the bed, onto my lap and my waiting erection.

She gasps as I fill her. "Oh, baby," I breathe, as I wrap my arms around her while cradling her head and raining soft kisses on her face. I flex my hips, and she clutches my upper arms, with a wild-eyed look at me. I grab her ass and lift her, flexing my butt once more and driving into her.

"Ah," she groans, and we kiss while I slowly ease in and out of her. She tightens her thighs around me as we ride each other.

Slowly. Sweetly.

She raises her face to the ceiling, her mouth open wide in a silent cry of joy.

"Ana," I murmur against her throat as I kiss her.

We move.

Together.

In bliss.

"I love you, Ana."

She folds her hands around my neck. "I love you, too, Christian." She opens her eyes and we watch each other.

Building.

Climbing.

Higher.

She's there.

"Come for me, baby," I whisper, and she screws her eyes shut and she hollers out as she submits to her release.

Ah!

I lean my forehead against hers, and whisper her name as her body pulls mine into a sweet, slow orgasm.

When I've come down from my high, I lift her onto the bed and we lie in each other's arms. "Better now?" I ask, as I nuzzle her neck.

"Hmm."

"Shall we go to bed, or do you want to sleep here?"

"Hmm."

I grin. "Mrs. Grey, talk to me."

"Hmm."

"Is that the best you can do?"

"Hmm."

"Come. Let me put you to bed. I don't like sleeping here."

She moves. "Wait," she murmurs.

What now?

"Are you okay?" she asks.

I can't help my smug smile. "I am now."

"Oh, Christian," she admonishes me, and reaches up to stroke my face. "I was talking about your nightmare."

Nightmare?

Shit.

Fleeting visions of the horror I witnessed in my sleep flicker through my mind. I hold her close, and hide from them by burying my face in her neck. "Don't," I mutter.

Ana. Don't remind me.

She gasps. "I'm sorry." She holds me, running her hands through my hair and down my back. "It's okay. It's okay," she whispers.

"Let's go to bed," I say. Getting up, I pick my jeans up off the floor and slip them on. She follows me, keeping the sheet wrapped around herself to preserve her modesty. "Leave those," I say, as she bends to gather her clothes. I scoop her into my arms, cradling her against my chest. "I don't want you to trip over this sheet and break your neck." I carry her downstairs to the bedroom and set her down. She slips on her nightdress while I take off my jeans and drag on my pajama bottoms, and together we climb into bed. "Let's sleep," I mutter. She gives me a sleepy smile and nestles into my arms.

I lie staring at the ceiling, trying to rid my mind of my morbid thoughts. We have Hyde, now. I should be asleep, like Ana is beside me. It never takes her long. I envy her that.

I close my eyes, grateful that she's still here, in one piece, in our bed.

Ana's on her knees. Bowed. Naked. In front of me. Her forehead pressed to the playroom floor. Her hair a burnished coronet against the wooden boards. Her hand stretched out. Splayed. She's begging. I stand with a crop in hand. I want more. I always want more. But she can't take it. *Red. Red. Red.* No! There's a crash. The door flies open. His frame fills the doorway. He roars and the bloodcurdling sound fills the room. *Fuck. No. No. No.* He's here. He knows. *Ana screams. Red. Red. Red.* He hits me. A right hook to my chin. I fall. And fall. My head spins. I'm faint. No. Stop the screaming. *Red. Red. Red.* Stop. It goes on. And on. Then it stops. I open my eyes and Hyde looms over her body. Syringe in hand. He leers. Ana is still. Pale. Cold. I shake her. She doesn't move. *Ana!* She lies unresponsive in my arms. I shake her once more. *Wake up.* She's gone. Gone! *Gone!* No. Kneeling on a sticky green rug, I clutch her to me and tip my head back and howl. Ana. Ana. *Ana!*

I'm startled awake, dragging air into my lungs.

Ana!

A quick twist of my head confirms that she's peacefully asleep beside me.

Thank Christ.

Clasping my head in my hands, I stare up at the ceiling.

What the hell?

Why am I letting that asshole into my psyche?

He's in custody. We've got him.

I take a long, calming breath as my thoughts wander.

Baby Bird? What the hell does that mean? From the depths of my brain something stirs but vanishes instantly. My mind spins, trying to chase it through the shadows, but without success. I suspect it's from a part of my psyche that stores all the memories I try to forget. I shudder.

Don't go there.

I know I'm not going back to sleep anytime soon. With a sigh, I get up, grab my phone, and pad into the kitchen for a glass of water. Standing by the sink, I run my hand through my hair.

Get it together, Grey.

Tomorrow we could do something special. Take our minds off Hyde.

Sailing? Soaring?

New York? No, it's too far and given that I've just been there—and all the shenanigans that have ensued since I returned—I don't think it's a good idea.

Aspen.

I could take her to Aspen. She's never seen the house. The press won't find us there. What's more, I could ask Elliot and Mia to join us. She said she wanted to see more of Kate.

Yes.

From my study, I send e-mails to Stephan, to Taylor, and to Mr. and Mrs. Bentley, the caretakers of our Aspen property, about a possible trip in the morning. Then I e-mail Mia and Elliot.

From: Christian Grey
Subject: Aspen TODAY!
Date: August 27 2011 02:48
To: Elliot Grey; Mia G. Chef Extraordinaire

Mia, Elliot
As a surprise for Ana, I'm taking the jet to Aspen just for the night, Sat 27.
Come with us. Kate and Ethan are welcome to join us. We'll be back Sunday evening.
Let me know if you're up for it.

Christian Grey
CEO, Grey Enterprises Holdings, Inc.

I press send and a few seconds later my phone buzzes.

ELLIOT
Sounds great, hotshot.

He's awake.

Why the hell is he up at this time? He normally sleeps like the dead.

Can't sleep?

ELLIOT
No. You?

I roll my eyes.

Obviously!

ELLIOT
All the Hyde shit?

Yeah.

My phone vibrates. Elliot is calling me.

What the hell?

"Dude, it's late," I answer.

"I can't believe I'm doing this," he mutters.

"Doing what?"

"Taking advice from someone who married the first girl they dated. But how did you know?"

"How did I know what?"

"That Ana was the one," he says.

What? Why's he asking me this?

How did I know?

"It was instant," I respond.

"What do you mean?"

I conjure an image of Ana falling into my office during *that* interview.

It's a lifetime ago.

"When I met her, she looked at me with her big blues eyes, and I knew. She saw past all the bullshit. She saw *me*. It was terrifying."

"Yeah. I get that."

"Why are you asking me?" *Please don't tell me it's about Kavanagh!*

"It's Kate, man."

Shit.

He continues, "I remember when I first saw her. I mean, she's hot—no arguments there. And then we were dancing in that bar in Portland, and I thought…You don't have to try so hard. You've got me, and what's more, it's only been her since then."

I blow out a breath. This is not Elliot's usual M.O.—he's the most promiscuous person I know. "So, what's the problem?" I ask.

"I dunno. Is she the one? I dunno."

We've never had this kind of conversation before; there have been so many women in Elliot's life. I don't know what to say. "Well, as you know, she kept Ana out late last night, and whenever she's with Ana, Ana comes back drunk," I grumble. And she's a major pain in the ass, but I can't say that to him.

"Kate's a good-time girl. Maybe that's it. I just don't know how she feels."

"Dude, I am not the person to ask for advice. Believe me. You'll have to figure this out for yourself."

"I guess," he says.

"Aspen might be the place."

"Yes. I'll text her."

"She's not with you?"

"No. But I want her to be. I'm just playing it cool."

"Whatever, dude. I'll send details of where to go in the morning."

"It is the morning, bro."

"True. This trip is a surprise for Ana. Tell Kate. I don't want her blowing it."

"Copy."

"Good night, Elliot."

"Dude." He hangs up.

I stand staring at my phone, not quite believing the conversation we've just had. Elliot's never asked me for advice on his love life. Ever. And as I suspected, he's really fallen for Kavanagh. I don't get it. She's the most irritating woman on the planet.

It's late, and I should head back to bed. But I'm drawn to the piano; some music will quiet my mind. I lift the lid, sit down, and focus. The keys are cool and familiar beneath my fingers, and I start to play Chopin. Melancholic music wraps around me like a soothing blanket, smothering my thoughts, the plaintive, somber notes a perfect match for my frame of mind. I play it once, twice, three times, losing myself in the melody and forgetting everything; it's just me and the music. While I'm playing the piece for a fourth time, Ana appears at the edge of my vision dressed in her robe. I don't stop, but I shift to make room for her on the stool. She sits down beside me and lays her head on my shoulder. Kissing her hair, I continue to play.

When I finish, I ask if I woke her.

"Only because you were gone. What's that piece called?"

"It's Chopin. It's one of his preludes in E minor. It's called 'Suffocation.'" I almost smile at the irony: it's what she accuses me of doing to her.

She takes my hand. "You're really shaken by all this, aren't you?"

"A deranged asshole gets into my apartment to kidnap my wife. She won't do as she's told. She drives me crazy. She safe-words on me." I close my eyes. "Yeah, I'm pretty shaken up."

She squeezes my hand. "I'm sorry."

I press my forehead to hers, and I'm in the confessional, whispering my darkest fear. "I dreamed you were dead. Lying on the floor—so cold—and you wouldn't wake up." I swallow down the image that lingers from my nightmare.

"Hey." Ana's voice is soothing. "It was just a bad dream." She holds my head, her hands on my cheeks. "I'm here, and I'm cold without you in bed. Come back to bed, please." She stands, taking my hand, and after a heartbeat, I follow her.

She slips out of her robe, and we both climb into bed. I hold her close. "Sleep," she whispers, and kisses my hair, and I shut my eyes.

IT'S THE WARMTH I become aware of first, the warmth of her body and the scent of her hair. When I open my eyes, I am wrapped around my wife. I lift my head off her chest.

"Good morning, Mr. Grey," she says with a soft smile.

"Good morning, Mrs. Grey. Did you sleep well?" I stretch out beside her, feeling remarkably fresh after such a disturbed night.

"Once my husband stopped making that terrible racket on the piano, yes, I did."

"Terrible racket? I'll be sure to e-mail Miss Kathie and let her know." I grin back at her.

"Miss Kathie?"

"My piano teacher."

She giggles.

"That's a lovely sound. Shall we have a better day today?"

"Okay," she agrees. "What do you want to do?"

"After I have made love to my wife, and she's cooked me breakfast, I'd like to take her to Aspen."

Ana looks dumbfounded. "Aspen?"

"Yes."

"Aspen, Colorado?"

"The very same. Unless they've moved it. After all, you did pay twenty-four thousand dollars for the experience."

She gives me her most superior smile. "That was your money."

"Our money," I correct her.

"It was your money when I made the bid." She rolls her eyes.

"Oh, Mrs. Grey, you and your eye rolling." I run my hand up her thigh.

"Won't it take hours to get to Colorado?" she asks.

"Not by jet," I mutter, as my hand cradles my favorite place.

MY PLAN HAS COME together, with surprising ease. I have a full crew and our guests are on board, waiting for us; I'm excited to see Ana's reaction. As we pull up to the Gulfstream, I squeeze her hand. "I have a surprise for you." I kiss her knuckles.

"Good surprise?"

"I hope so."

She tilts her head, amused but curious, as Sawyer and Taylor simultaneously climb out of the car to open our doors.

With Ana behind me, I greet Stephan at the top of the plane

steps. "Thanks for doing this on such short notice." I grin back at him. "Our guests here?"

"Yes, sir."

Ana looks around to see Kate, Elliot, Mia, and Ethan all seated in the main cabin. She gapes at me.

"Surprise!"

"How? When? Who?" she says in a breathless rush.

"You said you didn't see enough of your friends." I shrug.

So, here we are, with your friends.

"Oh, Christian, thank you." She throws her arms around me, planting her lips firmly on my mine. *Whoa.* I'm stunned by her unexpected ardor, but soon lost in her passion, taking all that she has to give. My hands find her hips, pulling her to me. "Keep this up and I'll drag you into the bedroom," I whisper.

"You wouldn't dare." Her breath is soft and sweet against my lips.

"Oh, Anastasia."

Gauntlet. Thrown.

When will she learn that neither of us will back down from a challenge? Grinning, I stoop quickly, grab her thighs, and carefully hoist her over my shoulder. "Christian, put me down!" She smacks my behind as I wave a welcome to our guests and walk through the cabin.

"If you'll excuse me, I need to have a word with my wife in private." I think Mia, Kate, and Ethan are shocked. Elliot is cheering like the Mariners are about to score a home run. *Ha! Maybe I will.*

"Christian!" Ana shouts. "Put me down!"

"All in good time, baby."

Carrying her into the rear cabin, I close the door and slide her down my body to set her on her feet. She looks less than impressed. "That was quite a show, Mr. Grey." She crosses her arms, and I think she's pretending to be pissed.

"That was fun, Mrs. Grey."

"Are you going to follow through?" There's a dare in her tone, but I'm not sure if she's serious. She glances at the bed and blushes. Perhaps she's remembering our wedding night. Her gaze returns to mine, and a slow smile spreads across her face until we're grinning at each other like idiots. I think that's exactly what she's remembering.

"I think it might be rude to keep our guests waiting," I murmur.

Tempting though you are.

I step toward her and run my nose down hers. "Good surprise?" I ask, because I need to know.

She looks delighted. "Oh, Christian, fantastic surprise." She kisses me once more. "When did you organize this?" Her fingers linger in my hair.

"Last night, when I couldn't sleep. I e-mailed Elliot and Mia, and here they are."

"It's very thoughtful. Thank you. I'm sure we'll have a great time."

"I hope so. I thought it would be easier to avoid the press in Aspen than at home. Come. We'd better take our seats—Stephan will be taking off shortly." I offer her my hand and together we go back into the main cabin.

Elliot cheers when we enter. "That sure was speedy in-flight service!"

Dude! Calm the hell down.

I ignore him and nod greetings at Mia and Ethan, as Stephan announces our imminent takeoff. Taylor has taken a seat at the rear.

"Good morning, Mr. Grey, Mrs. Grey," says Natalia, our flight attendant. Returning her welcoming smile, I sit down opposite Elliot. Ana hugs Kate before sitting down beside me. I ask if she's packed her hiking boots.

"We're not going skiing?"

"That would be a challenge, in August."

She rolls her eyes, and I wonder if she was being sarcastic.

"Do you ski, Ana?" Elliot asks her.

"No."

The thought of Ana on skis as a beginner is troubling. I grasp her hand.

"I'm sure my little brother can teach you." Elliot winks at her. "He's pretty fast on the slopes, too." I ignore him and watch Natalia run through the safety procedures as our plane taxis to the runway.

"You okay?" I overhear Kate ask Ana. "I mean, following the Hyde business?"

Ana nods.

"So why did he go postal?" she asks.

"I fired his ass," I intervene, hoping that will shut her up.

"Oh? Why?" Kate looks intently at both of us.

Damn. More questions.

"He made a pass at me," Ana says tightly.

"When?" Kate's eyes are on stalks. She's shocked.

"Ages ago."

"You never told me he made a pass at you!"

Ana shrugs.

"It can't just be a grudge about that, surely," Kate says. "I mean, his reaction is way too extreme." She turns her attention to me. "Is he mentally unstable? What about all the information he has on you Greys?"

She really doesn't let up. I sigh. "We think there's a connection with Detroit."

"Hyde is from Detroit, too?"

I nod. *How the hell does she know all this stuff?*

Ana grips my hand as the plane accelerates. My fearless girl is not a fan of takeoffs and landings. I brush my thumb across her knuckles.

We're okay, baby.

"What *do* you know about him?" Elliot is serious for once, and I have no choice but to reveal what I know. I shoot Kate a warning look.

"This is off the record," I tell her, and rattle off what I remember from his background check. "We know a little about him. His dad died in a brawl in a bar. His mother drank herself into oblivion. He was in and out of foster homes as a kid. In and out of trouble, too. Mainly boosting cars. Spent time in juvie. His mom got back on track through some outreach program, and Hyde turned himself around. Won a scholarship to Princeton."

"Princeton?" Kate squeaks, surprised.

"Yep. He's a bright boy." I shrug.

"Not that bright. He got caught," Elliot observes wryly.

"But surely he can't have pulled this stunt alone?" Kate asks.

Christ, she's irritating. This is none of her damned business. "We don't know yet," I growl, trying to keep a rein on my temper. Ana looks up at me in alarm. I squeeze her hand to reassure her as we sail into the air. She leans in to me.

"How old is he?" she whispers, so neither Kate or Elliot hear us.

"Thirty-two. Why?"

"Curious, that's all."

"Don't be curious about Hyde. I'm just glad the fucker's locked up."

"Do you think he's working with someone?" She sounds anxious.

"I don't know."

"Maybe someone who has a grudge against you? Like Elena?"

For fuck's sake, Ana. I check that Kate and Elliot aren't listening, but they're deep in their own conversation. "You do like to demonize her, don't you?" I mutter. "She may hold a grudge, but she wouldn't do this kind of thing. Let's not discuss her. I know she's not your favorite topic of conversation."

"Have you confronted her?"

"Ana, I haven't spoken to her since my birthday party." *Well, I haven't spoken to her in person.* "Please, drop it. I don't want to talk about her." I kiss her knuckles.

"Get a room," Elliot interrupts my thoughts. "Oh, right—you already have, but you didn't need it for long."

"Fuck off, Elliot."

"Dude, just telling you how it is." Elliot looks so pleased with himself.

"Like you'd know," I retort.

"You married your first girlfriend." Elliot gestures to Ana.

"Can you blame me?" I kiss Ana's hand again, and give her a smile.

"No." Elliot laughs and shakes his head.

Kate slaps Elliot's thigh. "Stop being an ass."

"Listen to your girlfriend." Maybe Kavanagh can keep him in line. She scowls at Elliot while Stephan announces our altitude and flight time, and tells us we're free to move around the cabin.

Natalia appears from the galley. "May I offer anyone coffee?"

WHEN THE GULFSTREAM PULLS to a stop at Aspen Pitkin airport, Taylor is off the plane first.

"Good landing." I shake Stephan's hand as the rest of our guests prepare to disembark.

"It's all about the density altitude, sir. Beighley here is good at math."

"You nailed it, Beighley. Smooth landing."

"Thank you, sir." Her grin is rightly smug.

"Enjoy your weekend, Mr. Grey, Mrs. Grey. We'll see you tomorrow." Stephan steps aside to let us deplane, and we descend the aircraft steps to where Taylor is waiting with our ride.

"Minivan?" I raise a brow. With an apologetic smile, he slides open the door. "Last minute, I know," I offer. I turn to Ana. "Want to make out in the back of the van?"

She giggles.

"Come on, you two. Get in," Mia nags from behind us. We climb on board, scrambling to the backseat, where we sit down. I put my arm around Ana as she cuddles into me.

"Comfortable?"

"Yes." Ana smiles and I kiss her forehead, delighted that we're here together. I've been on trips like this before, with my parents, to their place in Montana, and with Mia and Elliot when they've included their friends. But I've always gone solo.

This is another first.

As a teenager I didn't have friends, and as an adult I've been too busy and too solitary to enjoy this kind of outing.

And I still don't have many friends.

Once Elliot and Taylor have loaded the luggage, we set off toward town. As I enjoy the scenery, my thoughts drift to our house on Red Mountain. I wonder if Ana will like it.

I hope so. I love it here.

Aspen in late summer is as green as Seattle, more so at this time of year. It's what I love about the place. The grass in the pastures is lush and tall and the mountains are smothered in forests in full leaf. Today, the sun is high in the sky, though there are dark clouds on the horizon toward the west. I hope that's not an omen.

Ethan turns in his seat to face us. "Have you been to Aspen before, Ana?"

"No, first time. You?"

"Kate and I used to come here a lot when we were teens. Dad's a keen skier. Mom less so."

"I'm hoping my husband will teach me how to ski." She peers at me.

"Don't bet on it," I mutter.

"I won't be that bad!"

"You might break your neck." A shiver runs down my spine.

"How long have you had this place?" she asks.

"Nearly two years. It's yours now, too, Mrs. Grey."

"I know," she whispers, and kisses my jaw before settling in to my side once more.

Ethan asks me which are my favorite slopes, and I run through them. I'm not as fearless as Elliot, though. He could ski downhill, backward, with his eyes closed, anywhere.

"I can ski, too," Mia pipes up, glaring at Ethan. He smiles indulgently at her and I wonder how her campaign to capture his heart—*or his dick*—is going. He says she's not his type, but the way she's making eyes at him, he's definitely hers.

"Why did you choose Aspen?" Ana asks me as we cruise down Main Street.

"What?"

"To buy a place."

"Mom and Dad used to bring us here when we were kids. I learned to ski here, and I like the place. I hope you do, too—otherwise, we'll sell the house and choose somewhere else." I tuck a loose strand of her hair behind her ear. "You look lovely today." She blushes prettily and I cannot resist kissing her.

The traffic is fairly light, and Taylor reaches the center of town in good time. He turns north on Mill Street and we cross the Roaring Fork River and head up on Red Mountain. Taylor steers around the bend at the ridge and I inhale sharply.

"What's wrong?" Ana asks.

"I hope you like it," I answer. "We're here." Taylor parks in the driveway and Ana turns to look at the house, while our guests pile out of the van. When she turns back to me, her eyes are luminous with excitement. "Home," I mouth.

"Looks good."

"Come. See." I grab her hand, anxious to show her around.

Mia has dashed ahead, into the arms of Carmella Bentley.

"Who's that?" Ana asks of the slight figure in the doorway who's welcoming our guests.

"Mrs. Bentley. She lives here with her husband. They look after the place."

Mia introduces Ethan and Kate to Mrs. Bentley, while Elliot gives her a hug.

"Welcome back, Mr. Grey." Carmella smiles.

"Carmella, this is my wife, Anastasia."

"Mrs. Grey."

Ana beams at her as they shake hands.

"I hope you've had a pleasant flight. The weather is supposed to be fine all weekend, though I'm not sure." She eyes the darkening gray clouds behind us. "Lunch is ready whenever you want," she says with a warm welcome.

I think she approves of my wife.

"Here." I grab Ana and swing her into my arms.

"What are you doing?" she squeals.

"Carrying you over yet another threshold."

Everyone stands aside as I carry my wife into the wide hallway where I give her a swift kiss and set her onto the hardwood floor.

Behind us, Mia grabs Ethan's hand and drags him toward the stairs.

Where the hell is she going?

Kate whistles loudly. "Nice place."

"Tour?" I ask Ana.

"Sure." She offers me a brief smile.

I take her hand, excited to show her around and guide her through a whistle-stop tour of her vacation home: kitchen, sitting room, dining area, nook, downstairs den complete with bar and billiard table. Ana blushes at the sight of it. "Fancy a game?" I ask with a husky timbre to my voice.

I thoroughly enjoyed the last game we played.

She shakes her head.

"Through there is a home office, and Mr. and Mrs. Bentley's rooms."

She nods, distracted.

Maybe she doesn't like the place.

I find the thought depressing.

Feeling a little deflated, I take her up to the second floor, where there are four guest bedrooms and the master suite. The view from the picture window in the master bedroom is stunning and the reason I bought the house. Ana wanders in and stares out at the scenery. "That's Ajax Mountain, or Aspen Mountain, if you like," I inform her from the doorway.

She nods.

"You're very quiet." My voice is tentative.

"It's lovely, Christian." Her gaze is wide-eyed and wary. Striding over to her, I tug her chin, freeing her lip from her teeth.

"What is it?" I ask, searching her eyes for a clue.

"You're very rich."

Is that all?

I temper my relief. "Yes." I'm reminded of how quiet she was when I first took her to Escala; that's where I've seen her like this before.

"Sometimes it just takes me by surprise how wealthy you are."

"We are," I remind her, yet again.

"We are," she breathes, her eyes widening further.

"Don't stress about this, Ana, please. It's just a house."

"And what did Gia do here, exactly?"

"Gia?"

"Yes. She remodeled this place?" Ana asks.

"She did. She designed the den downstairs. Elliot did the build." I rake my hand through my hair, wondering where she is going with this. "Why are we talking about Gia?"

"Did you know she had a fling with Elliot?"

I pause for a second, wondering what I should tell her. She knows nothing of Elliot's dissolute habits. I sigh. "Elliot's fucked most of Seattle, Ana."

She gasps.

"Mainly women, I understand." I shrug and hide my amusement at her shocked expression.

"No!"

"It's none of my business." I hold up my palms; I don't really want to discuss this.

"I don't think Kate knows," Ana squeaks, appalled.

"I'm not sure he broadcasts that information. Kate seems to be holding her own." He's discreet, so that's a plus. Her eyes are on mine, and I'm trying to work out what she's thinking. "This can't just be about Gia's or Elliot's promiscuity," I whisper.

"I know. I'm sorry. After all that's happened this week, it's just…" She lifts her shoulder as tears well in her eyes.

No. Ana. Don't cry. I fold her into my embrace. "I know," I murmur into her hair. "I'm sorry, too. Let's relax and enjoy ourselves, okay? You can stay here and read, watch godawful TV, shop, go hiking—fishing, even. Whatever you want to do. And forget what I said about Elliot. That was indiscreet of me."

"Goes some way to explain why he's always teasing you," she says, her cheek against my chest.

"He really has no idea about my past. I told you, my family assumed I was gay. Celibate, but gay."

She giggles. "I thought you were celibate. How wrong I was." She draws me closer, and I sense her smile.

"Mrs. Grey, are you smirking at me?"

"Maybe a little. You know what I don't understand is why you have this place."

"What do you mean?" I kiss her hair.

"You have the boat, which I get, you have the place in New York for business—but why here? It's not like you shared it with anyone."

"I was waiting for you."

"That's…that's such a lovely thing to say," she whispers; bright blue eyes meet mine.

"It's true. I didn't know it at the time."

"I'm glad you waited."

"You are worth waiting for, Mrs. Grey." I run my finger beneath her jaw, tip her lips toward mine, and kiss her.

"So are you." She smiles. "Though I feel like I cheated. I didn't have to wait long for you at all."

I grin in disbelief. "Am I that much of a prize?"

"Christian, you are the state lottery, the cure for cancer, and the three wishes from Aladdin's lamp all rolled into one."

What? Even after yesterday?

I still, trying to wrap my head around her compliment.

"When will you realize this?" She semi-scowls at me. "You were a very eligible bachelor. And I don't mean all this." She waves an arm at the view. "I mean in here." She rests her hand on my heart while I flounder for something to say. "Believe me, Christian, please." Holding my face, she brings my lips to hers, and we're soon lost in a healing, searing kiss, her tongue sparring with mine.

I want to christen the bed.

But we can't. Not yet.

I pull away, my eyes burning into hers, knowing how strong she is and how much she could wound me if she chose to…by leaving.

Don't go there, Grey.

"When are you going to get it through your exceptionally thick skull that I love you?"

I swallow. "One day."

Her smile is heartwarming—lighting me up on the inside. "Come." I'm uncomfortable with our conversation. "Let's have some lunch—the others will be wondering where we are. We can discuss what we all want to do."

DURING THE IMPRESSIVE MEAL that Mrs. Bentley has laid out for us, we decide on an afternoon walk. But as we finish up, the room darkens. "Oh no!" Kate says suddenly. "Look." Outside, the threatened rain has arrived.

"There goes our hike," Elliot says, but he sounds relieved.

"We could go into town," Mia says.

"Perfect weather for fishing," I suggest.

"I'll go fish," Ethan says.

"Let's split up." Mia claps her hands. "Girls, shopping—boys, outdoor boring stuff."

"Ana, what do you want to do?" I ask.

"I don't mind," she says. "But I'm more than happy to go shopping." She smiles at Kate and Mia.

She hates shopping.

"I can stay here with you, if you'd like," I offer, thinking again about how we could christen the bed.

"No, you go fish," she says, but she gives me a scorching look, her eyes smoky, making me think she'd prefer to stay home.

With me. I feel ten feet tall.

"Sounds like a plan." Kate rises from the table.

"Taylor will accompany you," I announce. He'll keep Ana safe.

"We don't need babysitting," Kate huffs, her irritation obvious.

Ana puts her hand on her arm. "Kate, Taylor should come."

Listen to my wife. This is not up for discussion. That woman makes my hackles rise; I don't know what my brother sees in her.

Elliot frowns. "I need to pick up a battery for my watch in town."

Today? Can't he do that at home?

"Take the Audi, Elliot. When you come back we can go fishing."

"Yeah." His voice wavers. "Good plan."

What's up with him?

TAYLOR MANEUVERS THE MINIVAN carrying Ana and Co. out of the driveway and sets off toward town. I hand Mrs. Bentley's Audi keys to Elliot. He's told me and Ethan to go ahead without him. "We'll be on the Roaring Fork. Usual place, I think," I say.

As he takes the keys, his expression is odd, like he's about to face a firing squad. "Thanks, bro," he mutters.

I frown. "You okay?"

He swallows. "I'm going to do it."

"What?"

"A ring."

"Ring?"

"I'm going to buy a ring. I think it's time."

Shit. "You're going to ask Kate to marry you?"

He nods.

"Are you sure?"

"Yeah. She's the one."

I think my mouth drops open. *Kavanagh?*

"Hey, hotshot, marital bliss seems to be working for you." He grins, recovering his usual devil-may-care demeanor in an instant. "You're gonna catch flies with that mouth open, dude. Go catch some fish instead." He laughs as I shut my mouth, and dumbfounded, I watch him climb into the A4 wagon.

Hot damn. He's going to marry Kavanagh. That woman will be a thorn in my side forever. Maybe she'll say no. But as I watch him reverse out of the driveway, something tells me she won't. With a brisk wave, he's gone. I shake my head. *Elliot Grey, I hope to God you know what you're doing.*

Ethan is in the mudroom, checking out the line of fishing rods. "Float or fly?" I ask him.

"Let's wade. We'll be wet anyway, with this rain," Ethan replies with a grin.

"The gear's there." I point to one of the cupboards. "I'm going to get changed. You can wear what you like from whatever's in there."

"Cool." Ethan opens the cupboard and pulls out a pair of waders.

WE LOAD OUR BACKPACKS and our fishing gear into my pickup and I reverse out of the garage and head down the mountain; even in the rain, the scenery is inspiring. Our first stop is the local angling store, where I purchase our fishing licenses. From there we drive to one of my favorite spots on the Roaring Fork River.

"You fished around here before?" I ask Ethan as we make our way to the bank.

"Here, no. But around the Yakima. My dad's a big fan."

"He is?" *Now, there's another reason to like Eamon Kavanagh.*

"Yeah. Dad told me you're working with him," Ethan says.

"GEH is updating his fiber-optic network."

"He's pleased."

I grin. "I enjoy working with him. He's got a good head on his shoulders."

Ethan nods. "He says the same about you."

"I'm glad to hear that." From my backpack, I remove a box of flies. Inside is an impressive collection. "Carmella's husband makes these. They're great for trout."

"Cool." He selects one and examines it closely.

"Yeah." I choose one. "The mayflies are hatching around now."

"These should do it. Let's hook some lips. I'll give you some room," he says, and we both move over the rock-strewn bank in opposite directions.

My reel is attached, but I quickly assemble the rest of the rod and run the fly-line through the guides and attach my fly to the tippet. I'm ready. A glance at Ethan, who must be twenty-five feet away, tells me he's ready, too. He makes his first cast. It's smooth and graceful, and the fly lands in what looks like a sweet spot in the water. He knows what he's doing.

The Roaring Fork gurgles westward at my feet, flanked by rocks and silver birches. It's a perfect, peaceful setting. The mere sight of this wilderness is enough to make me exhale. I gaze intently at the water as it rushes past me, and slowly wade into the shallows.

Dad is standing with me in the water.

We're in waders. He scans the river.

Here, son, you've got to learn to read the water like you do a book.

Look for those telltale signs of Mr. Trout.

He could be hiding under rocks in the river.

He could be in the seam.

You see the seam, where the slow water hits the fast water.

And look for the bubbles. He could be feeding there.

He loves to eat mayflies, especially this time of year.

This guy, he holds up a fly. We'll fool him with this.

Take your fly and fasten to the tippet. Here. Like this. Dad knots the fly.

Now you do it. After a few goes, I do. It's a good knot because Dad's shown me how.

Good going, Christian. Remember to cast like you're flicking paint off a brush. It's all in your wrist.

The mayfly lands and I let her drift on top of the water like Dad said. I get a bite. A trout.

Good going, Christian!

Together we reel it in.

My dad was a good teacher. I make a couple of casts upstream to the far bank and let the fly drift toward me, and soon I'm lost in concentration. Everything slips from my mind as I set about conquering the river.

A heron lands upstream.

The drizzle eases.

It's so quiet. In spite of the weather, it's great out here.

I get a bite.

It's a trout.

A big one.

Hell yes.

The trout backflips and snaps the line.

Shit. Lost him. And the fly.

ETHAN HAS BETTER LUCK than me. I suspect he hooks the same fish I lost.

"The one that got away," I complain.

Ethan grins. "This one had my name on it."

I check the time; we should go.

"He's big enough to eat. Can we take him?" Ethan says.

"We shouldn't."

He grimaces. "Just this once?"

I smile. "Let's load up. And head back."

"Elliot never showed," Ethan says, as we climb into the truck.

"His business in town must have taken longer than he thought."

Ethan nods, pensive. "He's a good guy. I think my sister is pretty stuck on him."

"I think he's pretty stuck on her, too. Speaking of sisters, how are things with Mia?" I hope I sound casual.

"Your sister is a real force of nature." He shakes his head, amused by something. "But we're still just friends."

"I think she'd like to be more than friends."

"Yeah. I think so, too." He blows out a breath.

We pull into the driveway and I activate the garage door. We both climb out of the truck to start unloading, as the garage door slowly rises to reveal Ana and Kate standing beside Elliot astride one of my

KTM dirt bikes. They're all staring at us. "Garage band?" I ask, as I saunter toward Ana. She's a little flushed, as if she's been drinking. She grins as her eyes travel down my body; she's amused at my attire.

Fishing gear, baby. Or maybe she recognizes the coveralls she sold me at Clayton's. "Hi," I say, wondering what the hell they're all doing in the garage.

"Hi. Nice coveralls," coos Ana.

"Lots of pockets. Very handy for fishing." I remember how attractive but awkward she was when I was at the hardware store. Her cheeks grow rosier.

Oh, baby, we've come a long way since then.

From the corner of my eye, I see Kate roll her eyes, but I ignore her.

"You're wet," Ana breathes.

"It was raining. What are you guys doing in the garage?"

"Ana came to fetch some wood." Elliot smirks.

Dude!

"I tried to tempt her to take a ride." He pats the bike.

Fuck. No. In this weather? And enough of the smut talk, bro!

"She said no. That you wouldn't like it," Elliot says quickly.

I slide my eyes to Ana. "Did she, now?"

Her cheeks grow rosier still.

"Listen, I'm all for standing around discussing what Ana did next, but shall we go back inside?" Kate snaps. She picks up two logs and marches out of the garage. Elliot sighs and swings his leg off the bike and follows her.

I turn back to Ana. "You can ride a motorcycle?"

"Not very well. Ethan taught me."

Did he, now? My sister and my wife…

"You made the right decision. The ground's very hard at the moment, and the rain's made it treacherous and slippery."

"Where do you want the fishing gear?" Ethan asks.

"Leave it, Ethan—Taylor will take care of it."

"What about the fish?" Ethan continues, his voice vaguely taunting.

"You caught a fish?" Ana asks.

No. "Not me. Kavanagh did." I pout.

Ana starts laughing.

"Mrs. Bentley will deal with that," I call. With a smug grin, Ethan takes it into the house. "Am I amusing you, Mrs. Grey?"

"Very much so. You're wet. Let me run you a bath."

"As long as you join me." I plant a kiss on her lips. "I'll see you up in the bedroom. I've just got to get out of my coveralls."

Ana cocks her head to the side.

"Do you want to watch?" I grin at her.

"Always. But right now, I'll go run your bath, Sir."

I smirk and watch her leave, then head into the mudroom.

"Man, that was great," Ethan says, as he strips out of his waders.

"Yeah. It's a good spot."

"I'm happy to sort the gear." He sounds sincere.

"Okay. I'll help you."

"No, man. Your wife is waiting for you. I'll bring it in." He waves me away as he goes back out to the truck. I don't argue; instead, I strip out of my gear and leave the coveralls on a peg in the mudroom.

On my way to join Ana, I run into Mia at the bottom of the stairs.

"Hey, big brother." She hugs me, taking me by surprise.

"Mia." I think she's a little tipsy.

"Where's Ethan?"

"He's outside. Unloading the truck."

She puts her hands on her hips. "Christian Grey, did you make him unload it on his own?"

"He offered."

"You know, I don't hear from you at all since you got married. It's like I don't exist." She sounds sullen.

"Hey." I kiss her forehead. "You exist. How about I take you for lunch next week?"

She claps her hands in delight.

"What have you been drinking?" I call after her.

"Strawberry daiquiris." She dashes out to find Ethan and I shake my head.

Taking the stairs two at a time, I go in search of my wife.

Ana is hanging a silvery-looking garment in the closet. She must have bought it in town. "Did you have a good time?" I ask, as I enter and close the door.

"Yes," she says, staring at me.

"What is it?"

"I was thinking how much I've missed you."

My heart skips a beat at the warmth in her voice. "You sound like you have it bad, Mrs. Grey."

"I have, Mr. Grey," she whispers.

I stroll over and stand before her, feeling the heat emanating from her body. "What did you buy?" I whisper, basking in her warmth.

"A dress, some shoes, a necklace. I spent a great deal of your money." She peers up at me as if she's guilty of some terrible crime.

Oh, this will never do.

"Good," I stress quietly while my fingers ease a stray lock of her hair behind her ear. "And for the billionth time, *our* money." The scent of jasmine and the sound of the bath filling with water drift from the en suite. With a gentle tug, I release her bottom lip from her teeth. I run my index finger down the front of her T-shirt, between her breasts, over her stomach and belly, to the hem. "You won't be needing this in the bath." I grip her T-shirt with both hands and slowly pull it up. "Lift your arms." Ana cooperates, her luminous eyes on mine, and I tug off her top, dropping it on the floor.

"I thought we were just having a bath." Her voice is breathy with desire.

"I want to make you good and dirty first. I've missed you, too." I lean down and kiss her. Her hands creep into my hair as she welcomes the touch of my lips, and we're soon lost in each other.

ANA'S HEAD IS OFF the side of the bed, tipped back as she cries out her orgasm. Her response triggers mine, and I come fast and hard inside her. Panting, I pull her onto my chest and we lie dazed and replete while I stare up at the ceiling.

"Shit, the water!" Ana cries, and tries to sit up. I keep hold of her. *Don't go.*

"Christian, the bath!" She stares down at me in horror.

I laugh. "Relax—it's a wet room." I roll onto her, pressing her into the mattress once more and kiss her, quickly. "I'll switch off the faucet." Feeling far more relaxed than I have for days, I get up, saunter into the bathroom, and turn off the water. Sure enough, the bath is overflowing, which will make for a fun time with my wife. She follows me in and gapes at the floor.

"See?" I point to where the water is circling the drain. She grins, and together we climb in, laughing as the water splashes out around us. She's piled her hair into an impossible topknot perched precariously on her head, tendrils falling around her face.

She looks lovely.

And she's all mine.

We sit at opposite ends of the overflowing tub. "Foot," I command, and she places her left foot in my hand. I start massaging her sole with my thumbs. She closes her eyes and, as earlier, tips her head back and groans. "You like?" I whisper.

"Yes," she breathes. Tugging each of her toes, I watch her lips pucker as she absorbs the pleasure. I kiss each toe in turn and graze my teeth along her little toe.

"Aaah!" she groans once more, and her eyes pop open.

"Like that?"

"Hmm." I start massaging again, and she closes her eyes. "I saw Gia in town," she says airily.

"Really? I think she has a place here."

"She was with Elliot."

My hands still, and Ana opens her eyes.

"What do you mean 'with Elliot'?"

"We were in a boutique opposite a jeweler. I saw him go in alone, and I thought he must be buying the watch battery. He came out with Gia Matteo. She laughed at something he said, then he kissed her cheek and left."

Maybe Gia helped him select a ring?

"Ana, they're just friends. I think Elliot is pretty stuck on Kate." Unfortunately. "In fact, I know he's pretty stuck on her." Though why, I have no idea.

"Kate is gorgeous." Ana bridles, and I wonder once more if she can read my mind.

"Still glad it was you who fell into my office." I kiss her big toe, pick up her right foot, and begin the process over again. Ana lays back once more as I lavish attention on her sole and we stop talking about Elliot and Gia and Kate.

I wonder when he's going to propose?

I LEAVE ANA TO get ready for dinner while I head down to my study to check my e-mails. I sit down at my desk and open my laptop. As I go through my inbox, there are a couple of irritating work issues that I need to deal with, but I shelve them for the moment. It's the e-mail from Leila that stops me in my tracks. My scalp tingles with apprehension. What the hell does she want?

From: Leila Williams
Subject: Thank you
Date: August 27 2011 14:00 EST
To: Christian Grey

Sir, or should I just call you Mr. Grey?
I don't know anymore.
I wanted to say thank you.
For everything.
In person.
Please.
Leila

I scowl at the screen, and at Leila's audacity. I've asked her, via Flynn, not to contact me directly, and yet she's sent me this e-mail. I send it on to Flynn and ask him to remind her of my precondition to paying for her treatment and her tuition fees. Hopefully she won't contact me again.

To add to my annoyance, there's an e-mail from Ros telling me that the Taiwanese would like to talk tomorrow at 2:30 p.m. their time. On a Sunday? What time is that here?

I google it—shit. That's half-past midnight, tonight.

What the hell?

I call Ros.

"Christian, hi. How are you?" She sounds upbeat, which only adds to my annoyance.

"Pissed. Can you change the time of this call?"

"I know. It's ridiculous. But no. One of their execs is only avail-able then."

"On a Sunday?"

"It's something to do with them having to be off-site when they make this call."

I sigh. "Okay."

"I'll be on the call, too," she says, in an attempt to mollify me, I suspect. "And we'll have an interpreter."

"Okay, I'll speak to you then." I hang up, irritated.

To hell with this.

I head into the den, where Elliot and Ethan are playing pool and drinking beer. I join them for a drink. Taylor has booked a table at a local restaurant for the six of us, but they have time for a game.

"So, what's the deal with you and Mia?" Elliot asks Ethan.

Ethan chuckles. "You're as bad as your brother." He eyes me. "Like I said to Christian, we're just friends."

Elliot raises an eyebrow and directs a look at me.

I take a long swig of cool, clean-tasting beer.

"Did you get what you needed from town?" I ask Elliot as we watch Ethan slam in a couple of solids.

"Yeah." He grins.

"Did you get some help?"

Elliot cocks his head to one side. "Why do you ask?"

"Little bird told me."

Elliot scowls and Ethan fouls the white ball, so he goes to take his shot.

My phone buzzes in my back pocket. I have an e-mail from my wife.

From: Anastasia Grey
Subject: Does My Butt Look Big in This?
Date: August 27 2011 18:53 MST
To: Christian Grey

Mr. Grey
I need your sartorial advice.
Yours
Mrs. G x

Now, this I have to see. I type a quick response.

From: Christian Grey
Subject: Peachy
Date: August 27 2011 18:55 MST
To: Anastasia Grey

Mrs. Grey
I seriously doubt it.
But I will come and give your butt a thorough examination just to
make sure.
Yours in anticipation
Mr. G x

Christian Grey
CEO, Grey Enterprises Holdings and Butt Inspectorate, Inc.

I abandon my beer, bound up two sets of stairs, and open our
bedroom door.

Wow.

Anastasia Grey. Wow.

Paralyzed, I stand on the threshold. Ana's in front of the full-
length mirror. She's dressed—in a sense—in a tiny silver dress, and
towering stilettos. Her hair is a glossy veil edging her beautiful face.
Kohl frames her eyes, and dark red lipstick paints her mouth.

She looks sensational; my body comes alive in response.

She flicks her hair to the side. "Well?" she whispers.

"Ana, you look… Wow."

"You like it?"

"Yes, I guess so." My voice is husky, betraying my desire. I want to
mess up her hair and smudge her lipstick. I want her to be my Ana,
not this version of her. This powerful, seductive woman is, frankly, a
little intimidating.

And hot.

Ball-tighteningly hot.

I enter the room, bewitched by my wife, and close the door behind
me, glad that I put my jacket back on. She has endless, shapely legs.
A vision of her feet in those shoes, hooked over my shoulders, comes
to the forefront of my mind.

Fuck.

Placing my hands on her naked shoulders, I turn her around so we're both facing the mirror.

Christ!

This *dress* hardly has a back.

At least it covers her backside. Just.

Our eyes meet in the glass, smoky blue to darkening gray.

She looks every inch the goddess I know. And tall. Really tall!

I glance down at her naked back, and I cannot resist her. I glide a knuckle down her spine and she slowly arches her back into my touch.

Oh, Ana.

I stop where the dress starts at the small of her back. "This is very revealing," I whisper. My hand skates lower, over her pert behind, which is provocatively accentuated in the tight clinging material, to the hem. My fingers hover over her skin at her thigh. Gently, I caress her, teasing her flesh as my fingers move around her thigh, her eyes following their path. She inhales sharply, her mouth forming a perfectly fuckable o.

"It's not far from here." I run my fingers around the hem, then higher up her thigh. "To here." I touch her panties and stroke her through the thin material. She gasps as I ease my fingers against her, feeling the fabric dampen beneath my touch.

Oh, baby.

"And your point is?" Her voice is hoarse.

"My point is…it's not far from here"—I glide my fingers over her panties to the edge and slip my index finger around the fabric so we're skin on skin—"to here. And then…to here." As we gaze at each other, I slide my finger inside her.

She's warm and wet around me, and she closes her eyes as she groans.

"This is mine." I drip the words into her ear and, closing my eyes, slowly move my finger in and out of her. "I don't want anyone else to see this."

She starts to pant, and I open my eyes to watch as I pleasure her. "So be a good girl and don't bend down, and you should be fine."

"You approve?" she breathes.

"No, but I'm not going to stop you from wearing it. You look stunning, Anastasia."

Enough.

I want to fuck her. But we don't have time. And as much as I want to smudge her makeup, I'm sure she won't appreciate it. Slowly, I withdraw my hand, and move so I'm in front of her. Gently I trace her bottom lip with the slick tip of my index finger. She puckers her scarlet lips to kiss it.

The contact echoes in my groin.

I grin. A wicked grin.

This is what I love about my girl.

She does not back down from a challenge.

I slip my finger in my mouth.

She tastes mighty fine. I lick my lips and Ana flushes.

Yes. There she is. My girl.

Grinning, I take her hand. "Come."

Hand in hand, we head downstairs to join our guests, and I'm not immune to the admiring looks they all give my wife.

"Ana! You look like a million dollars," Mia gushes, giving her a hug.

I release Ana and open the closet door. "Whose coat is this?" I ask, holding up a trench coat.

"Mine," Mia says.

"Were you going to wear it?"

"Not tonight."

"Good. Can I borrow it?"

"It'll be a bit small for you," Mia quips.

Ignoring her, I hold up the coat for Ana. She rolls her eyes, but acquiesces and lets me slip it on her.

Good.

She might be cold later.

And no one will see her ass.

THE FOOD AT MONTAGNA is excellent, as is—to my surprise— the conversation. It must be the company. I've discovered that I love watching my wife interact with people; she's charming, funny, and smart. Well, I knew that before I married her, but today her shyness is in check and she's making it look easy. I wonder if it's the amount of alcohol she's consumed that's making her more gregarious, but right now I don't care. I could watch her all day. She is bewitching and she offers me hope for our future together. We could do this more often: bring friends here, entertain them, enjoy time with them. I never thought that would be my thing, but maybe it is.

I'm warming more and more to Ethan. He's passionate about his academic field and excited to be joining the postgraduate psychology program at Seattle U. "Man, you know a lot about this shit," he says as we await dessert.

I chuckle. "I should. I've seen enough shrinks."

He frowns as if he doesn't quite believe me. "Really?"

You have no idea.

Elliot stands suddenly, his chair scraping across the floor, the noise ringing over the general level of chatter. We all turn to look at him. He's gazing down at Kate, and she's gazing up at him as if he's grown an extra head. Elliot drops to one knee.

Oh, fuck.

Dude.

Here?

He takes her hand, and I think he has the attention of the entire restaurant. "My beautiful Kate, I love you. Your grace, your beauty, and your fiery spirit have no equal, and you have captured my heart. Spend your life with me. Marry me."

There's a collective intake of breath. Ana grabs my hand, and all eyes turn to Kavanagh, who just gapes at Elliot in shock. A tear trickles down her cheek and she splays her hand on her chest, as if she's trying to contain her emotion. Finally, she smiles. "Yes," she whispers.

The patrons in the place erupt with cheers, applause, catcalls. This is so Elliot—in a crowded restaurant, in front of everyone. The guy is fearless. My admiration for him grows exponentially. From his pocket he produces a ring box and opens it, showing her the ring inside. Kate throws her arms around him and they kiss.

I laugh as their audience goes wild. Elliot stands, takes a

well-deserved bow, and sits down beside his fiancée with a ridiculous grin plastered on his face.

Ana is crying and squeezing my hand.

Shit.

I remember when I first asked her to marry me. She cried then, too. We were on the floor of the living room in Escala, and I had confessed my worst. I wonder what Ethan Kavanagh would make of that if he knew.

Don't go there, Grey.

Elliot is sliding the ring onto Kate's finger—which reminds me that I have lost the feeling in mine. I squeeze Ana's hand, and she lets go, letting the blood rush back into my fingertips. Ana has the grace to look embarrassed. "Ow." I mouth the word.

"Sorry. Did you know about this?" she whispers.

I give her my best sphinxlike smile and summon the waiter. "Two bottles of the Cristal, please. The 2002, if you have it." He gives me a wide grin and rushes off.

Ana smirks.

"What?" I ask.

"Because the 2002 is so much better than the 2003," she teases me.

I laugh. She's right. But I don't have to tell her that. "To the discerning palate, Anastasia."

"You have a very discerning palate, Mr. Grey, and singular tastes."

"That I do, Mrs. Grey." I lean closer, catching a trace of her scent. "You taste best." I kiss the pulse point beneath her ear.

Mia is up and hugging Kate and Elliot. Ana follows.

"Kate, I am so happy for you. Congratulations," Ana says while she clutches Kate.

I hold out my hand to Elliot, he grins, and he looks so relieved and happy that I pull him into a hug, surprising us both. "Way to go, Lelliot."

Elliot stills for a nanosecond, no doubt shocked by my sudden display of affection, then he embraces me. "Thanks, Christian," he says, his voice cracking on my name.

I hug Kate, quickly. "I hope you are as happy in your marriage as I am in mine."

"Thank you, Christian. I hope so, too," she says sweetly.

She can be sweet!

Maybe she's not as annoying as I thought she was.

The waiter opens the champagne and pours it into our flutes. Taking mine, I hold it up to the happy couple in a toast. "To Kate and my dear brother, Elliot—congratulations."

"Kate and Elliot," we all murmur.

Ana is smiling.

"What are you thinking about?" I ask.

"The first time I drank this champagne."

I frown, filing through the myriad memories I have of Ana.

"We were at your club," she says.

The elevator. I grin. Ana with no panties. "Oh, yes. I remember." I wink at her.

"Elliot, have you set a date?" Mia pipes up.

Elliot shakes his head, his exasperation obvious. "I've only just asked Kate, so we'll get back to you on that, 'kay?"

"Oh, make it a Christmas wedding. That would be so romantic, and you'd have no trouble remembering your anniversary." Mia claps her hands.

"I'll take that under advisement." Elliot smirks at her.

"After the champagne, can we please go clubbing?" Mia turns and gives me her most pleading look.

"I think we should ask Elliot and Kate what they'd like to do."

Elliot shrugs and Kate blushes. I think she wants to return home to the seclusion of their room.

I WALK TO THE front of the line with our guests and we're ushered into Zax, the nightclub that Mia has set her heart on attending. The music is already thumping through the small lobby. I don't know how long I'm going to last here.

"Mr. Grey, welcome back," the receptionist says. "Max will take your coat." Her words are directed at Ana. A young man dressed in black appears at her side. I think he approves of my wife's appearance—a little too much, for my liking.

"Nice coat," he says, admiring Ana's...physique.

I glare at the little prick. *Back off, bud.*

He hastily hands me a coat-check ticket.

"Let me show you to your table." The hostess bats her eyelashes at me, and Ana tightens her grip on my arm. I glance down at her, but her eyes are on the hostess, and we follow her into the club to a VIP seating area near the dance floor. "There'll be someone along to take your order shortly." The hostess waltzes off while we sit down.

"Champagne?" I ask, as Ethan and Mia both head to the dance floor, holding hands. Ethan gives me a thumbs-up.

"Show me your ring," Ana asks Kate, while I turn my attention to my sister and Ethan on the dance floor. She's making her usual crazy moves, but Ethan seems unconcerned and is following her lead.

The waitress arrives for our drink order.

Ignoring Elliot's protest about paying, I reel off, "Bottle of Cristal, three Peronis, and a bottle of iced mineral water, six glasses."

"Thank you, sir. Coming right up."

Ana is shaking her head.

"What?" I ask her.

"She didn't flutter her eyelashes at you."

I must be losing my touch. I try hard not to grin. "Oh. Was she supposed to?"

"Women usually do."

I smile. "Mrs. Grey, are you jealous?" And tipsy?

"Not in the slightest." Though she pouts. I take her hand and bring it to my lips, kissing each knuckle.

"You have nothing to be jealous of, Mrs. Grey."

"I know."

"Good."

The waitress returns with our drinks and opens the bottle of champagne with little fuss. She pours it, and Ana takes a sip.

"Here." I hand her a glass of water. "Drink this."

Ana frowns and I sigh. "Three glasses of white wine at dinner and two of champagne, after a strawberry daiquiri and two glasses of Frascati at lunchtime. Drink. Now, Ana."

She scowls at me, probably because I'm keeping score. But she does as she's told. I'm hoping she'll avoid a hangover tomorrow. She wipes her hand over her mouth in a less-than-decorous way. I'm assuming it's her version of a protest at my high-handedness. "Good girl. You've vomited on me once already. I don't wish to experience that again in a hurry."

"I don't know what you're complaining about. You got to sleep with me."

This is true. "Yeah, I did."

"Ethan's had enough, for now," Mia exclaims when they return from the dance floor. "Come on, girls. Let's hit the floor. Strike a pose, throw some shapes, work off the calories from the chocolate mousse."

Kate stands up. "Coming?" she asks Elliot.

"Let me watch you," he says.

"I'm going to burn some calories," Ana says, then leans down so I get a glimpse of some fine cleavage, and she whispers, "You can watch me."

"Don't bend over," I warn.

"Okay." She stands upright quickly and grabs my shoulder.

Shit. I reach up to support her as she sways, but I don't think she notices. She's dizzy or drunk or both. "Perhaps you should have some more water," I offer.

Perhaps I should take her home.

"I'm fine. These seats are low and my heels are high." She smiles, and Kate takes her hand as they head onto the dance floor.

I'm not sure how I feel about this.

Kate hugs Ana.

And then they both start to move.

Mia is…well, Mia. I'm used to watching her lost in her own world, dancing around the room. She rarely keeps still.

Kavanagh can dance.

And so can my wife. She sets the dance floor alight, in that scrap of material she calls a dress. Legs, back, ass, hair: she's letting loose in a most provocative way.

She closes her eyes and surrenders herself to the thumping beat.

Fuck. My mouth dries as I watch her move.

In my previous life, I enjoyed watching dancing like this, but it was always in the privacy of my apartment, and always at my command. I run my thumb over my bottom lip and shift in my chair as my body responds to my wife. Maybe I could persuade Ana to do this at home. For my eyes only. The lyrics of the song are apt.

Damn, you's a sexy bitch.

As the music pulses through the club, more and more people crowd onto the dance floor. I glance at Elliot, who grins back at me, and we both laugh. "This is a good game," I mutter.

"Sure is." His grin is wicked, and I know exactly what he's thinking.

Dirty dog.

"You did it," I say over the thumping music.

"What?"

"Proposed. In public."

"Yeah. It was a now-or-never moment."

"Happy?"

He nods, beaming. "Very."

I glance back at Ana just in time to see a haystack of a man looming over her, and Ana smacking him across his face.

What the fuck?

Adrenaline courses through my veins, followed closely by a rage that's baying for blood. Springing up from my seat, I knock over my beer, but I don't give a shit.

Did he put his hands on my wife?

I'm going to fucking kill him.

At lightning speed I weave through the throng as Ana looks around frantically. *I'm here, baby.* Slipping my arm around her waist, I move her to my side. The motherfucker in front of her is half a head taller than me, and too broad, like he's overdone the steroids. He's young. And stupid. "Keep your fucking hands off my wife."

"She can take care of herself," he shouts.

I hit him. Hard. An uppercut to his chin.

And he drops to the floor.

Stay down, asshole.

I'm wound so tight, every sinew and muscle on high alert.

I'm ready. Bring it.

"Christian, no!" Ana moves in front of me and I'm vaguely aware of the panic in her voice. "I already hit him," she shouts, her hands pushing at my chest. But I don't take my eyes off the cocksucker on the floor. He scrambles hastily to his feet, and I feel another hand tighten around my arm. I tense, ready to hit that person, too.

It's Elliot.

The haystack holds up his palms in defeat. "Take it easy, okay? Didn't mean any harm." He moves away, tail between his legs, and I have to quell the urge to follow him and teach him some fucking manners. My heart is pounding to the same beat that's shaking the room. I hear it, the blood thumping against my eardrums.

Or is it the music? I don't know.

Elliot eases his hold on me and finally lets go.

I'm frozen. In place. Battling to stay afloat and not descend into the abyss.

I take a deep breath, and finally look down at Ana. Her arms are around my neck, her eyes wide and fearful.

Shit. "Are you okay?" I ask.

"Yes." She slides her hands from my neck to my chest, her eyes searing my soul. She's scared.

For me?

For her?

For the haystack?

"Do you want to sit down?" I ask.

Ana shakes her head. "No. Dance with me."

She wants to dance? Now?

I remain impassive as I fight to bring my fury under control, my mind replaying the last fifteen seconds in a loop.

"Dance with me," she says again, pleading. "Dance. Christian, please." She takes my hands while I watch the asshole make his way to the exit. Ana starts to move against me. Her warmth, her heat, brushing up against me and seeping into my veins.

It's...distracting.

"You hit him?" I want to check that I didn't imagine that.

"Of course I did." My hands fist, because I want to smack him again. She continues, "I thought it was you, but his hands were hairier. Please dance with me." Her fingers curl around my balled fists and she moves closer so I catch a trace of her scent.

Ana. Grabbing her wrists, I haul her against my body and pin her hands beneath mine. "You wanna dance? Let's dance," I growl in her ear, and roll my hips against her, enjoying the feel of her against my groin. I don't let go, but when she smiles, I release her and she moves her hands up my arms to my shoulders.

We move.

Together.

Forehead against forehead.

Eye to eye.

Body to body

Soul to soul.

I keep her close.

As she relaxes, she throws her head back.

God, she's sexy. I am one lucky man.

I spin her across the floor to watch her hair fly out around her.

Then pull her back to me as the throbbing rhythm infects us both.

I've never done this.

In a club.

We danced at our wedding…but not like this.

It's liberating.

When the song changes, she's breathless, her eyes shining.

And my equilibrium has returned. I must download this song onto my iPod. I think it's called "Touch Me."

Apt. I've not heard it before.

"Can we sit?" she gasps.

"Sure." We head back toward our table.

"You've made me rather hot and sweaty," she whispers.

I wrap my arms around her. "I like you hot and sweaty. Though I prefer to make you hot and sweaty in private." Exhilarated, we sit down. I'm relieved to see that my spilled beer has been cleaned up and replenished. As has our water.

The others are still on the dance floor. Ana takes a sip of her champagne.

"Here." I place a glass of sparkling mineral water in front of her, and I'm relieved to watch her down the entire glass. I grab myself a beer from the ice bucket and take a long swig.

What a night.

"What if there had been press here?" Ana asks.

I shrug. "I have expensive lawyers."

She frowns. "But you're not above the law, Christian. I did have the situation under control."

Really? "No one touches what's mine." I insert the right amount of venom into that statement. Ana takes another sip of champagne and closes her eyes. Suddenly she looks weary. I grasp her hand. "Come, let's go. I want to get you home."

"You going?" asks Kate, as she and Elliot arrive back at the table.

"Yes."

"Good, we'll come with you."

ANA FALLS ASLEEP IN the minivan on the way back, her head on my shoulder. She's fried. I shake her gently when Taylor pulls up outside the house. "Wake up, Ana."

She staggers out into the cool air, where Taylor is waiting patiently.

"Do I need to carry you?" I ask her.

She shakes her head.

"I'll go fetch Miss Grey and Mr. Kavanagh," Taylor says.

Ana clings to me as she tiptoes up the stone steps to the oak front door. Taking pity on her, I bend down, unstrap and remove each of her shoes. "Better?"

She nods and gives me a bleary smile. She's tipsy.

"I had delightful visions of these around my ears," I whisper, looking wistfully down at her fuck-me heels, but she's too tired for that. I open the door and we head upstairs to our bedroom. She stands, swaying, beside our bed, eyes closed, hands loose at her sides. "You're wrecked, aren't you?" I stare down into her sleepy face.

She nods and I start to unbuckle her coat.

"I'll do it," she mumbles, and tries to brush me off.

"Let me."

She sighs and resigns herself to her fate.

"It's the altitude. You're not used to it. And the drinking, of course." I smirk down at her and ease her out of her coat, tossing it aside onto a chair. Taking her hand, I lead her into the bathroom.

She frowns.

"Sit," I order.

She slumps onto the chair and closes her eyes. She might fall asleep if I'm not quick enough. In the vanity I find the Advil, cotton balls, and moisturizer that Mrs. Bentley has supplied, and fill a small glass with water. I turn back to Ana and gently tip her head back. She opens eyes that are smudged with makeup. "Eyes closed," I order.

She obliges, and gently I clean the makeup off until, finally, she's smudge-free. "Ah. There's the woman I married."

"You don't like makeup?"

"I like it well enough, but I prefer what's beneath it." I kiss her forehead. "Here. Take these." I place the tablets on her palm and hand her the water.

She gazes up at me, pouting.

What?

"Take them." *You'll feel worse tomorrow if you don't.*

She rolls her eyes but does as she's told.

"Good. Do you need a private moment?"

She scoffs. "So coy, Mr. Grey. Yes, I need to pee."

I laugh. "You expect me to leave?"

She giggles. "You want to stay?"

I cock my head to one side. It's tempting.

"You are one kinky son of a bitch. Out. I don't want you to watch me pee. That's a step too far." She stands up and waves me out of the bathroom.

I suppress my laughter and leave her to it. In the bedroom, I strip out of my clothes, change into my pajama bottoms, and hang my jacket in the closet. When I turn around, Ana is watching me. Grabbing a T-shirt, I stroll up to her, appreciating her frankly lascivious appraisal of my body. "Enjoying the view?"

"Al-ways," she slurs.

"I think you're slightly drunk, Mrs. Grey."

"I think, for once, I have to agree with you, Mr. Grey."

"Let me help you out of what little there is of this dress. It really should come with a health warning." I turn her around, sweep her hair to the side, and undo the single button at the halter neck.

"You were so mad," she says.

"Yes. I was."

"At me?"

"No. Not at you." I kiss her shoulder. "For once."

"Makes a nice change."

"Yes. It does." I kiss her other shoulder, then tug her dress over her behind. Hooking my thumbs into her panties, I bend down and remove them together. I take her hand. "Step." She does, tightening her fingers around mine as she wobbles. I toss her clothes on top of the coat. "Arms up." I slip the T-shirt over her head and pull her into my arms and kiss her. She tastes of champagne and toothpaste and my favorite flavor, Ana. "As much as I'd love to bury myself in you, Mrs. Grey—you've had too much to drink, you're at nearly eight thousand feet, and you didn't sleep well last night. Come. Get into bed." I pull back the duvet and let her climb in. She snuggles down as I cover her up and kiss her forehead.

"Close your eyes. When I come back to bed, I'll expect you to be asleep."

"Don't go."

"I have some calls to make, Ana."

"It's Saturday. It's late. Please." She looks up at me with her soul-searching eyes.

I run my hand through my hair. "Ana, if I come to bed with you now, you won't get any rest. Sleep." She pouts once more, but without any real passion. She's too tired. I brush my lips against her forehead again. "Good night, baby." I turn and leave her. I have to get Taipei on the line.

Sunday, August 28, 2011

Ana is comatose when I return to bed. Slipping beneath the covers, I lean over and kiss her hair. She mumbles something unintelligible, but remains fast asleep. I close my eyes. My conversation with the owners of the Taiwanese shipyard was a success: a brother and sister in business together—it's a first for me—and they're keen to discuss terms in person. We just have to settle on a date. It's the icing on the cake of a good day. Well, apart from losing it at the club and punching that asshole's lights out. I grin into the darkness. No, that felt pretty good, too. With a self-satisfied smile on my face, I drift.

ANA SQUIRMS AGAINST ME and I wake, fully. As usual, my limbs are entwined with hers. "What's wrong?" I ask.

"Nothing." She's luminous in the early morning sunshine. "Good morning." She runs her fingers through my hair.

"Mrs. Grey, you look lovely this morning." I press my lips to her cheek.

Her eyes search mine. "Thank you for taking care of me last night."

"I like taking care of you. It's what I want to do." *Always.*

"You make me feel cherished." Her smile warms my heart.

"That's because you are." More than you'll ever know. I grasp her hand and she winces. I release her immediately. *Shit!* "The punch?" I ask.

I knew I should have hit that prick again.

"I slapped him. I didn't punch him."

"That fucker! I can't bear that he touched you." My temper flares.

"He didn't hurt me—he was just inappropriate, Christian. I'm okay. My hand's a little red, that's all. Surely you know what that's like?" She smirks, laughing at me as usual, and my brief burst of anger dissolves.

"Why, Mrs. Grey, I am very familiar with that. I could reacquaint myself with that feeling this minute, should you so wish."

"Oh, stow your twitching palm, Mr. Grey." She runs her fingertips over my cheek and then tugs the little hairs of my sideburn. I'm not sure I like the feeling. I take her hand and kiss her palm.

"Why didn't you tell me this hurt last night?"

"Um, I didn't really feel it last night. It's okay now."

Ah, yes. Alcohol deadened the pain. "How are you feeling?"

"Better than I deserve."

"That's quite a right arm you have there, Mrs. Grey."

"You'd do well to remember that, Mr. Grey." And there's a challenge in her tone.

"Oh, really?" I roll onto her and grab her wrists, holding them above her head. "I'd fight you any day. In fact, subduing you in bed is a fantasy of mine." I kiss her throat, wondering what that would be like. The idea is arousing.

"I thought you subdued me all the time."

"Hmm, but I'd like some resistance," I murmur, running my nose along her jaw, wondering if she'd ever agree to that. She stills beneath me and I know I have her attention, and possibly her interest. Releasing her hands, I lean up on my elbows.

"You want me to fight you? Here?" she whispers, trying to contain her surprise.

I nod. *Why not?* I've always wanted to do this but couldn't— because I couldn't bear to have anyone touch me.

"Now?" she asks.

I shrug. Part of me can't believe she's even entertaining the idea, but I'm thrilled that she might. I nod again, as my dick grows rigid against her soft flesh. Ana toys with her bottom lip as she gazes at me, and I know she's considering the notion.

"Is this what you meant about coming to bed angry?"

Yes. Exactly. I nod. "Don't bite your lip."

She narrows her eyes, but there's a flash of amusement, and possibly desire, in their depths as her pupils enlarge. "I think you have me at a disadvantage, Mr. Grey." She wriggles beneath me and flutters her lashes, and I want her all the more.

"Disadvantage?"

"Surely you've already got me where you want me?" Her smile is coy as I press my eager cock against her.

"Good point well made, Mrs. Grey." I kiss her quickly and roll over, taking her with me so she's astride my belly. She grabs my hands, pinning them to the bed on each side of my head. Her eyes sparkle with carnal mischief, and her hair tumbles down over my face. She shakes her head to torture me, the ends of her hair tickling my face.

"So, you want to play rough?" she asks while she teases me, her groin skimming over mine.

I inhale suddenly. "Yes."

She sits up and releases my hands. "Wait." Reaching for the glass of sparkling water I left for her on the nightstand, she takes a long draft, while I skate my fingers in circles up her thighs to her ass. I give it a good squeeze. She leans down and kisses me, pouring cool water into my mouth.

"Very tasty, Mrs. Grey," I murmur, trying to contain my excitement at our new game. Placing the glass back on the nightstand, she grabs my hands from her behind and pins them on either side of my head once more.

"So I'm supposed to be unwilling?" She sounds amused.

"Yes."

"I'm not much of an actress."

I grin. "Try."

Leaning down, she kisses me once more. "Okay, I'll play," she murmurs, and I close my eyes, inwardly rejoicing as she skims her teeth along my jaw. I groan deep in my throat and move, quickly, pinning her beneath me. Ana cries out in surprise and I make a play to grab her hands, but she's too quick. She pushes against my chest as I try to part her legs with my knee, but her thighs are firmly clamped together. I capture her wrist, but she grabs my hair with her other hand and yanks it. Hard.

Fuck. This. Is. Hot.

"Ah!" I twist my head free and stare down at her.

Her eyes are wide and wild, her breathing erratic.

She's turned on, too.

It's a torch to my libido. "Savage," I whisper, my lust laced through each syllable. Ana is unleashed—she tries to wrest her hand from mine as she attempts to buck me off. I grab her free hand with my left, so I have both of her wrists pinned above her head, leaving my right hand to linger over her body. My fingers travel down, my aim to lift the hem of her T-shirt, but I love the feel of her flesh beneath the soft material. Her nipple is hard, ready for me, and I greet it with a tweak.

Ana yelps and tries in vain to buck me off once more.

I lean down to kiss her and she turns her face away from me.

No.

I clasp her chin and hold her in place while my teeth graze her jaw, as she did to me earlier. "Oh, baby, fight me." My voice is husky with need.

She twists and writhes one more, trying to free herself, but I keep my hold on her and it's such a kick—a heady, euphoric feeling of dominance. Teasing her lower lip with my teeth, I try to invade her mouth, but suddenly she softens beneath me, granting my tongue access and kissing me back, her passion taking me by surprise. I release her wrists, and her hands are in my hair while she wraps her legs around me, her heels at my ass, pushing down my pajamas. She tips her pelvis up to me as we kiss. "Ana," I whisper, her name a talisman as she bewitches me. We're no longer fighting. We're surrendering to each other. I cannot get enough of her. She's on me, I'm on her. We're lips and tongues, and mouths and hands.

Fuck. I want her.

"Skin," I mumble, panting. I haul her up and remove her T-shirt in one fast move, throwing it on the floor.

"You," she whispers, and she yanks down my pajamas and grabs my cock, squeezing me hard as she tightens her hand around me.

"Fuck!"

I grab her thighs, lifting them so she falls back on the bed, but she doesn't let go of me. Her fingers move over me, hot and fevered, her thumb teasing me, while my hands caress her body: her hips, her stomach, her breasts.

She slips her thumb in her mouth.

"Taste good?" I ask, as she stares at me, her eyes burning with desire.

"Yes. Here." She shoves her thumb into my mouth as I hover over her. Tasting and biting the pad, I suck her thumb and marvel at her audacity. She groans, her fingers tugging on my hair, bringing my mouth to hers. She folds around me, pushing my pajamas off with her feet. My teeth skim her jaw, nipping gently.

"You're so beautiful." My lips continue their journey down her throat. "Such beautiful skin." Across her chest and onward to her breasts.

Ana writhes beneath me. "Christian," she begs, tightening her hands in my hair.

"Hush." My tongue circles her nipple, honoring it, before my lips close around it and I tug.

"Ah!" she moans, tilting her hips so that we're slick against each other. I grin against her skin. I'm going to make her wait. Gliding my lips to her other breast, I greet its erect and eager nipple with my mouth.

"Impatient, Mrs. Grey?" I suck hard on her, and Ana yanks hard on my hair, eliciting a long groan from me. I narrow my eyes in warning. "I'll restrain you."

"Take me," she beseeches.

"All in good time." My lips and tongue pay homage to her breast and nipple, while Ana continues to squirm beneath me. She moans, loudly, her pelvis thrusting against my ready dick.

Suddenly she twists and bucks, trying to throw me off her again. "What the—" I grab her hands and pin her down into the mattress.

Ana is panting underneath me. "You wanted resistance," she rasps.

I take some of my weight on my elbows and gaze down at her, trying to understand her sudden change of heart…again. Her heels dig into my ass.

She wants me.

Now.

"You don't want to play nice?" My cock is straining.

"I just want you to make love to me, Christian," she says through gritted teeth. "Please." Her heels press into my ass again, with more force this time.

Fuck. What's going on here?

Releasing her hands, I sit back on my haunches, pulling her into my lap. "Okay, Mrs. Grey, we'll do this your way." Lifting her, I lower her onto my waiting erection.

"Ah," she groans, closing her eyes and tipping back her head.

God, she feels so good.

She curls her arms around my neck, her fingers clamped over my head, and she starts to move. Fast. Frantic. My lips find hers, and I surrender to her pace, and her supercharged rhythm, until we both shout out as we come, and collapse back on the bed.

Wow.

That was...different.

We both lie there, catching our breath. She runs her fingertips through my chest hair and I thrum my fingers down her back, enjoying the contact.

"You're quiet," Ana says eventually, and kisses my shoulder. I turn to look at her, trying to understand what just happened. "That was fun," she says, but as her eyes search mine, she looks uncertain.

"You confound me, Ana."

"Confound you?"

I turn so we're face-to-face. "Yes. You. Calling the shots. It's different."

The small *v* forms between her brows as she frowns. "Good different or bad different?" She traces her finger over my lips, and I pucker them to kiss her fingertip as I contemplate her question.

"Good different." *Frantic, though.* I would have liked that to last longer.

"You've never indulged this little fantasy before?"

"No, Anastasia. You can touch me." *And it was fucking hot. I'd like to do it again.*

"Mrs. Robinson could touch you."

My eyes find hers while I wonder why she would bring up Elena at this time. "That was different," I whisper.

Ana's eyes widen, seeing through me, as ever. "Good different or bad different?" she asks.

The searing pain of Elena's touch flares in my imagination.

Her hands on me. Her nails scraping my skin while the darkness flailed and clawed at me from within, trying to throw her off.

It was unbearable.

I swallow, trying to dispel the memory. "Bad, I think." The words are less than a whisper.

"I thought you liked it."

"I did. At the time."

"Not now?"

Ana's eyes are a guileless blue, impossible to escape. Slowly, I shake my head.

"Oh, Christian." She launches herself at me, an unstoppable force of good, kissing my face, my chest, each of my scars. I groan and answer her kiss with my own passion and my love. And we're soon lost, making love at my pace. Slowly, tenderly, so I can show her how much I love her.

ANA IS BRUSHING HER teeth as I finish dressing. "I'll go and check on our guests."

Her eyes meet mine in the bathroom mirror. "I have a question."

I lean against the doorjamb. "Pray, what do you wish to know, Mrs. Grey?"

She turns to face me, dressed only in a towel. "Does Mrs. Bentley know about your…um…your—"

"Predilections?" I offer.

Ana flushes and I laugh, because Ana can still blush at anything to do with sex, and because Mr. and Mrs. Bentley have no idea.

"No. No playroom here. We'll have to bring some toys." I wink at her and turn to go, leaving her mouth open.

Kate and Mrs. Bentley are chatting in the kitchen. They're the only ones up, it seems, on such a beautiful morning. I greet them both.

"Good morning, Mr. Grey," Carmella says.

Kate smiles, and frankly it's unnerving. I'm more used to her snarling at me.

"We could go for a hike and a picnic before heading home," I suggest to Kate.

"Sounds great."

"Waffles okay today?" Mrs. Bentley asks.

"Great. Picnic for later, would that be possible?"

"Of course," she says, with a look that tells me I shouldn't dare doubt her culinary abilities. "Oh, and Martin would like a word with you," she continues. "He's somewhere in the yard."

"I'll go find him."

Martin Bentley is weeding what Mrs. Bentley calls the kitchen garden. We exchange pleasantries and he takes me on a tour of the grounds. He's a thoughtful, introspective man with some ideas on how to improve the yard. Not only does he maintain my property, but also a couple of the other properties in the near vicinity, and he's a volunteer for the fire department.

While we walk, we discuss putting in a hot tub, and maybe a pool. I notice a bamboo cane that's been discarded, and I pick it up as we continue to talk. It's been a while since I held a cane. It's a little heavy, and not very flexible. Absentmindedly, I swipe it through the air.

"It'll be expensive," Martin says, referring to the notional pool, "and, to be honest, how often would you use it?"

"Good point. Perhaps we could go for a tennis court instead."

"Or you could leave it all be and let the meadow flowers bloom." His grin is infectious.

I survey the yard: pool, or tennis court, or meadow flowers? I wonder which Ana would prefer. I swipe the cane through the air once more as Mr. Bentley opens the door into the basement. I don't know what it is that makes me glance up, but I do, to discover Ana is watching me from the kitchen window. She waves, but looks guilty for some reason—why? I don't know. She turns away, and I hand the cane to Martin and head back into the house. I'm hungry for waffles.

THE FLIGHT HOME IS smooth. Ana slumbers beside me while I go through the draft deal terms for the acquisition of Geolumara. I think everyone is tired after the forced-march hike up the Red Mountain Road trail that Elliot led us on. But it was worth it for the view. The late night, the altitude, and the alcohol are catching up with all of us: Elliot and Ana are sleeping, Kate and Ethan are dozing, Mia is reading. She and Ethan appear to have had an argument. I suspect Ethan's "we're just friends" has finally registered in Mia's stubborn mind.

Stephan announces that we're beginning our descent into Seattle. "Hey, sleepyhead." I wake Ana. "We're about to land. Buckle up."

She stirs and fumbles for her belt, but I fasten it for her and kiss her forehead. She snuggles against me and I drop a kiss in her hair.

This trip has been a success, I think. But for me, it's also been disturbing. I'm sensing a growing feeling of…contentment. It's a strange and frightening sentiment. One that could disappear in a heartbeat. I glance down at Ana, trying to dismiss the worrisome feeling. It's too new. And too fragile. Turning my attention back to the paperwork in front of me, I continue to read, making notes in the margins with my queries.

Don't dwell on your happiness, Grey.

It will only lead to pain.

Flynn's recent advice echoes in my mind. *Nurture and treasure it.*

Shit. How?

Hell.

Elliot wakes and teases Ana while First Officer Beighley announces our final approach. I take Ana's hand.

"Christian, Ana. Thank you for a fantastic weekend," Kate says, threading her fingers through Elliot's.

"You're welcome," I answer. And there it is again, that *contentment.*

"HOW WAS YOUR WEEKEND, Mrs. Grey?" I ask once we're en route to Escala.

Ryan is driving, with Taylor in the passenger seat. Even he looks relaxed.

"Good, thank you."

"We can go anytime. Take anyone you wish to take."

"We should take Ray. He'd like the fishing."

"That's a good idea."

"How was it for you?" she asks.

I glance at her.

Fantastic. Scarily so…

"Good," I say, eventually. "Real good."

"You seemed to relax."

"I knew you were safe."

She frowns. "Christian, I'm safe most of the time. I've told you before, you'll keel over at forty if you keep up this level of anxiety. And I want to grow old and gray with you." Ana reaches out taking my hand. I raise it to my lips and kiss her fingers.

I will always worry about you, baby.

You are my life.

"How's your hand?" I ask, to change the subject.

"It's better, thank you."

"Very good, Mrs. Grey. You ready to face Gia again?"

Ana rolls her eyes. "I might want to keep you out of the way, keep you safe."

"Protecting me?" Well, how the tables have turned. I want to laugh.

"As ever, Mr. Grey. From all sexual predators," she teases, keeping her voice low, so Ryan and Taylor don't overhear her.

I BRUSH MY TEETH, glad that we've approved Gia's plans. Elliot's team will start on the build Monday. I tick through a mental checklist. I have much to do over the coming week, but chiefly I want to make sure we nail Hyde's ass to the wall and keep him incarcerated. Welch will need to keep digging to see if the asshole's been working with anyone.

I hope not.

I hope this is over.

"Everything okay?" Ana asks, when I join her in the bedroom. She's wearing one of her satin nightdresses and looks every inch a goddess.

I nod as I climb into bed beside her, putting aside my thoughts about next week.

"I'm not looking forward to going back to reality," she says.

"No?"

She shakes her head and caresses my face. "I had a wonderful weekend. Thank you."

"You're my reality, Ana." I kiss her.

"Do you miss it?"

"Miss what?"

"You know. The caning, and stuff," she whispers.

Why is she asking me this? I rack my brain. The bamboo cane. This morning?

"No, Anastasia, I don't." I stroke her cheek with the back of my knuckles. "Dr. Flynn said something to me when you left, something that's stayed with me. He said I couldn't be that way if you weren't so inclined. It was a revelation." John encouraged me to try our relationship her way.

And look where we are…

"I didn't know any other way, Ana. Now I do. It's been educational."

"Me, educate you?" she scoffs.

I smile. "Do you miss it?"

"I don't want you to hurt me, but I like to play, Christian. You know that. If you wanted to do something…" She lifts her left shoulder in a coy shrug.

"Something?"

"You know, with a flogger or your crop—" She stops as her face colors.

Crops and floggers, eh?

"Well, we'll see. Right now, I'd like some good old-fashioned vanilla." My thumb skims her bottom lip, and I kiss her once more.

THURSDAY, SEPTEMBER 1, 2011

Bastille is kicking my ass. "Marriage is making you soft, Grey," he taunts, flicking his dreads to the side as I struggle to my feet once more. That is the third time he has knocked me on my butt. "Maybe this is what happiness looks like." His face brightens with a benign grin and he comes at me again with a roundhouse kick. But I block him and feint right, then bring him down with my left leg.

"Yeah," I respond, adrenaline flying through my veins. "Maybe it does." I bounce on my feet, fists raised, ready to take him down once more, as he leaps to his feet.

"That's more like it, man."

AS I SIP MY coffee at my desk, I contemplate the last few days and Bastille's words. *Maybe this is what happiness looks like.*

Happiness.

It's a strange and unsettling emotion, one that I've felt often enough since I met Ana. But I've always thought of those as fleeting moments, sometimes euphoric, sometimes just pure joy. It's never been my constant companion. It's crept up on me, and now it's with me, always—but it's an uneasy feeling, a tightness in my chest. And I know it's because it could be snatched from me at any moment, and I'd be left devastated.

"*I don't want you to sabotage your happiness, Christian. I know you feel you don't deserve it.*" Flynn's words echo once more through my thoughts.

Sabotage my happiness?

How and why would I do that?

It's like love. That was a frightening prospect, too, yet I let that in.

Shit. Why can't I just accept this feeling and enjoy it? I could bathe in its fire and rise reborn like a phoenix...or will I perish in its flames, with what's left of my heart destroyed?

Flowery, Grey. I snort. *Get a grip.*

Maybe Bastille has a point. These last few days have been idyllic. Work is going well. I've not had any further arguments with my wife, just fun and frolics.

She's been…*Ana. My Ana.*

I recall the Shipbuilding Association dinner, a few nights back, where—at my request—Ana wore Kegel balls throughout the long meal. How she held it together I'll never know. She didn't when we got home. I shift in my seat, remembering her need.

My phone buzzes, interrupting my erotic reminiscence.

"Yes?"

"I have Welch for you."

"Thanks, Andrea."

"Mr. Grey." His gravelly voice kills any residual lust that's lingering in my body. "Hyde's bail hearing is this afternoon. I'll report back when the judge has given her verdict."

"Let's hope she makes the right decision."

He clears his throat, "He's a flight risk. I think she will."

"Great. Let me know."

As I put the phone down, my BlackBerry buzzes with a text.

> **LEILA**
> I wanted to thank you personally for
> everything you've done for me. I am
> trying to understand why you won't see
> me. It's hard. I owe you so much. Leila.

What the hell?

I switch my phone off and return to my coffee. I am not in the mood to deal with Leila Williams. She shouldn't be texting me at all. I had hoped that Flynn had talked to her, but I'll discuss Leila's persistence with him later today when I see him.

MIA IS MORE ANIMATED than usual when we meet for an early lunch at my favorite sushi restaurant. She hurls herself at me, fizzing with excitement, kissing my cheek. "It's so good to see you," she gushes.

"You saw me last weekend." I return her hug, my tone wry.

"But I get you to myself—and I have news! I have a job." She raises her hands and does a celebratory twirl before she takes her seat.

"What! Finally?" Her joy is contagious, and I'm eager to hear the details.

"It's taken forever. But I'm thrilled. I'm working for Crissy Scales."

"The caterer?"

"Yes. Weddings. Events. All those gigs. I want to start my own business one day, but she's going to show me the ropes. I'm super-excited."

"Great. When do you start?"

"Next Friday."

"Tell me everything."

No one can enthuse like my little sister, and I can't remember the last time we spent a long lunch together, just the two of us. Over our sashimi and maki rolls she regales me with her hopes for her new career, and with her latest attempts to win Ethan Kavanagh's heart.

"Mia, I'm not sure I can deal with you having a love life."

"Oh, Christian, of course I have a love life. I had so much fun in Paris."

"What?"

"Yes. There was Victor, Alexandre—"

"There's a list? Christ. Stop."

"Don't be such a prude, Christian," she scolds.

"Moi?" I place my hands on my chest in feigned outrage.

She laughs.

"So, you think you have a chance with Ethan?" I ask.

"Yes." She's definitive, and that's one of the many things I love about her, her determination and resilience.

"Okay. Good luck with that." I signal for the check.

"Can we do this again? I miss you."

"Of course. But right now I have to get back to work for a meeting."

I'M SITTING WITH BARNEY and Fred in the lab, examining the latest prototype of the solar tablet—the lighter, simpler, cheaper version for struggling economies in the developing world. This is the part of my job that I love most. Barney is in full flow. "Took eight hours to charge and it's giving us three days of use."

"Can we get more?"

"I think we're at our limit with the battery technology at the moment." Fred glides his glasses up his nose. "It's the black-and-white E-ink screen that saves us on power. And it's more robust."

"And for the home market?"

"Color touchscreen." Barney hands me the other prototype.

I weigh it in my hands. "It's quite a bit heavier."

"Color screens are."

"Feels expensive." I grin.

"We're only getting four hours from it so far, with eight hours in the sun."

"Makes sense. But it can be charged conventionally?"

"Yes. Here." Barney points out the charging port on the bottom of the device. "It's standard, nonproprietary USB. Saves on landfill."

"That's a good marketing angle." My phone buzzes, and Welch's name pops up on the screen.

"Guys, I've got to get this." I step away from the workbench and answer. "What gives?"

"He didn't make bail. No trial set yet."

"He doesn't deserve bail. Thanks for letting me know." I hang up and send a quick e-mail to Ana.

From: Christian Grey
Subject: Hyde
Date: September 1 2011 15:24
To: Anastasia Grey

Anastasia
For your information, Hyde has been refused bail and remanded in custody. He's charged with attempted kidnapping and arson. As yet no date has been set for the trial.

Christian Grey
CEO, Grey Enterprises Holdings, Inc.

I turn back to Fred and Barney to continue our discussion of the tablet and next steps.

BACK IN MY OFFICE, I notice Ana's reply to my earlier message.

From: Anastasia Grey
Subject: Hyde
Date: September 1 2011 15:53
To: Christian Grey

That's good news.
Does this mean you'll lighten up on security?
I really don't see eye to eye with Prescott.
Ana x

Anastasia Grey
Editor, SIP

From: Christian Grey
Subject: Hyde
Date: September 1 2011 15:59
To: Anastasia Grey

No. Security will remain in place. No arguments.
What's wrong with Prescott? If you don't like her, we'll replace her.

Christian Grey
CEO, Grey Enterprises Holdings, Inc.

There's a knock on the door. I'm expecting Ros for our four o'clock, but it's Andrea who pops her head around the door. "Mr. Grey, Ros is running late. She'll be with you in ten minutes. Can I get you anything?"

"I'm good, Andrea, thanks." She closes the door and I open the revised deal terms for Geolumara. I need to read it through and check that all my suggestions have been incorporated. When I look up, I have a response from Ana.

From: Anastasia Grey
Subject: Keep Your Hair On!
Date: September 1 2011 16:03
To: Christian Grey

I was just asking (rolls eyes). And I'll think about Prescott.

Stow that twitchy palm!
Ana x

Anastasia Grey
Editor, SIP

From: Christian Grey
Subject: Don't Tempt Me
Date: September 1 2011 16:11
To: Anastasia Grey

I can assure you, Mrs. Grey, that my hair is very firmly attached—has
this not been demonstrated often enough by your good self?
My palm, however, is twitching.
I might do something about that tonight.
x

Christian Grey
Not Bald Yet CEO, Grey Enterprises Holdings, Inc.

I send a quick e-mail to Ros to bring signature copies for the
Geolumara deal with her, and there's another e-mail from my wife.

From: Anastasia Grey
Subject: Squirm
Date: September 1 2011 16:20
To: Christian Grey

Promises, promises...
Now stop pestering me. I am trying to work. I have an impromptu
meeting with an author. Will try not to be distracted by thoughts of
you during the meeting.
A x

Anastasia Grey
Editor, SIP

There's a knock on the door, and this time it's Ros, twenty minutes late.

"YOU LOOK WELL." FLYNN motions me into his office.

"I am, thank you." I take my usual seat and wait patiently for him
to take his. When he's ready, he gives me his expectant look.

"So, what's occurring?" he asks.

I fill him in on the week's events, starting with my rushed flight back from New York. Hiding my amusement, I watch his eyebrows ascend farther up his forehead as my tale unfolds.

"That's it?" he asks, when I finish.

"More or less."

"So, let me get this straight. You canceled two important meetings to fly home to check on Anastasia, because you were angry with her that she hadn't followed your instructions, only to find this Hyde character had broken into your apartment to kidnap your wife."

"In a nutshell. Yes."

"She safe-words on you, and that's never happened before—I don't want to know the details, unless you really feel a need to tell me—but you resolve your differences, and following that, you have a nightmare that she dies."

I nod, trying to dampen my sudden anxiety as I remember fragments of my dream.

"Anything else?"

"I took her to Aspen with some friends. I punched a guy's lights out because he touched her. And this afternoon Hyde was refused bail. And I got a text from Leila."

He closes his eyes, and I don't know if it's because he can't believe what he's just heard, or because he's collecting his thoughts, or because he's pissed at Leila.

"Christian, that's a hell of a lot to take on board. I'm surprised you're not more stressed."

"Yes. You'd think. But my stress has been tempered by something altogether unfamiliar and frankly alarming."

"Oh?"

"Yes. Something you alluded to in our last couple of meetings."

"Go on," Flynn prompts.

"I have a general and creeping sense of happiness. It's quite unsettling."

"Ah. I see."

"You do?"

"It's obvious. To me anyway." His expression, frustratingly, gives nothing away.

"Please. Enlighten me."

"Well, I would hazard a guess that Jack Hyde's kidnap attempt and his subsequent incarceration have justified your feelings about Ana's security, but the threat he posed has now been eliminated. So, you've been able to let down your guard. Ana's safe."

Ah! Makes sense.

"But I would also say this is not a new phenomenon. You've experienced a great deal of happiness over the last few months. Your engagement. The wedding. The honeymoon. We've talked about this before. You have a tendency to focus on the end result and not the journey to get there. You were focused on getting married and anxious that wouldn't happen. Yet it did." He pauses, I imagine for emphasis. "Christian, you are the master of your own happiness. I imagine that in your subconscious you don't think you deserve to be happy. But let me set you right on that. You do. You are *allowed* to be happy. After all, it's an unalienable right written into your constitution."

"I think you'll find it's the *pursuit* of happiness that's enshrined in the Constitution."

"Hmm...semantics. But what I'm reading into this situation is that you hold the key to your happiness. You're in control. You just need to let it in. And not deliberately put obstacles in its way."

I glance down at the mini orchids on his coffee table. "Can I?" The words are out before I realize I've said them out loud.

"Can you what?"

"Let it in."

"That's entirely up to you."

"But what if she leaves?"

He sighs. "There are no certainties in life except death and taxes. Everyone runs the risk of being hurt; you know this. You've had more than your fair share of that as a child. But you're not a child anymore. Give yourself permission to enjoy your life and your wife."

Is it as simple as that?

"Now. Leila," he says, and I know we've moved on.

Taylor pulls away from the curb as I watch Ana and Prescott disappear into SIP. My uneasy sense of bliss lingers. We've had an amazing weekend…more fun and frolics with Mrs. Grey. This is what I've been missing from my life.

"Sir." Taylor distracts me from my happy place.

"Yes?"

"The R8 Spyder for Mrs. Grey will be ready at the end of the week."

"Excellent. Thanks."

His gaze does not leave mine in the rearview mirror.

"What?"

"Gail has a suggestion for you, with regard to Mrs. Grey's birthday."

"Oh?" I wait for him to tell me more, but he continues to drive. "Are you going to tell me?"

His eyes flick back to mine in the rearview mirror, and in them I see a silent plea. He doesn't want to rain on her parade.

"I'll talk to her."

"Thank you, sir."

My phone buzzes.

> ELLIOT
> It begins!

He's attached a photograph of his team taking down one of the rear walls of our house on the coast. It's a dramatic shot: blue skies, a gaping hole in a wall, clouds of brick dust, and five hulking men in yellow hard hats wielding sledgehammers.

Whoa! Leave some of it standing!

ELLIOT
Don't get your panties in a wad. We're
following the plans.

I'd expect no less. Good luck.

IN THE ELEVATOR AT Grey House, I check my e-mails.

From: Anastasia Grey
Subject: Sailing & Soaring & Spanking
Date: September 5 2011 09:18
To: Christian Grey

Husband
You sure know how to show a girl a good time.
I shall of course be expecting this kind of treatment every weekend.
You are spoiling me. I love it.
Your wife
xox

Anastasia Grey
Editor, SIP

At my desk, I respond.

From: Christian Grey
Subject: My Life's Mission…
Date: September 5 2011 09:25
To: Anastasia Grey

Is to spoil you, Mrs. Grey.
And keep you safe because I love you.

Christian Grey
Smitten CEO, Grey Enterprises Holdings, Inc.

Smitten doesn't cover it. I want to do something special for her birthday, and I wonder what Mrs. Jones has in mind. I'll talk to her this evening. In the meantime, I'd like to get Ana something other than the car…a gift that requires a little more creative thought.

As I sip my coffee, an idea slowly forms in my mind.

Something to celebrate all our *firsts*.
When I finish my coffee, her response is in my inbox.

From: Anastasia Grey
Subject: My Life's Mission...
Date: September 5 2011 09:33
To: Christian Grey

Is to let you—because I love you, too.
Now stop being so sappy.
You are making me cry.

Anastasia Grey
Equally Smitten Editor, SIP

I grin. We're both smitten.

Astoria Fine Jewelry has outdone itself. My lunchtime quest was a success, and I'm delighted with the gift I've bought for Ana. I hope she likes it, too. Glancing at her beautiful face on my office wall, I admire her secret smile as she peers down at me, but as ever, she gives nothing away.

Lord, she is lovely.

I find myself grinning at her portrait like the lovesick fool I am.

A man in love with his wife.

Get a grip, Grey.

My plans for Ana's birthday are falling into place. Mrs. Jones has volunteered to cook a surprise dinner party for Ana, and I'm waiting to hear if all our guests can make it. I've offered to send the jet to collect Carla and Bob, Ray is on, and my siblings have both said yes, but I've yet to hear from my folks. Ana knows nothing of this, and the event will be the first surprise party I've ever organized. I remember, when I bought my apartment pre-construction, how the real estate agent had waxed lyrical about the expansive entertainment space within. I never thought I'd actually get to use it. That wasn't my life. And now, two years later, I'm hosting a party.

For my wife. Who knew.

It should be fun.

Perhaps we could take everyone to see the new house on Sunday after lunch and check out how Elliot and his team are doing. Or perhaps we could go before, just Ana and me. Maybe on Friday. I check my schedule, but I'm interrupted by a text from Taylor, and a nanosecond later, an e-mail from Ana. I open the e-mail first.

From: Anastasia Grey
Subject: Visitors
Date: September 6 2011 15:27
To: Christian Grey

Christian
Leila is here to see me. I will see her with Prescott.
I'll use my newly acquired slapping skills with my now-healed hand,
should I need to.
Try, and I mean try, not to worry.
I am a big girl.
Will call once we've spoken.
A x

Anastasia Grey
Editor, SIP

What!
Leila?
Fuck!
I dial Ana's number immediately.
No fucking way is she meeting with Leila.
The phone rings and rings, ignored by Ana, and my blood pressure climbs with each unanswered chime until it reaches a dizzying height. Eventually her voice mail kicks in, asking me to leave a message. I hang up, not trusting myself to speak.
Hell.
I check Taylor's text.

> TAYLOR
> Mrs. Grey is meeting with Leila
> Williams. Prescott is attending the
> meeting. I'm heading to the car.

Prescott must have told him. "Andrea!" My bellow practically shakes the window behind me. I text Taylor back.

> You going to SIP?

Andrea doesn't bother to knock and comes barreling into my office.

"Mr. Grey?"

"Get me Ana's assistant on the line. Now."

"Yes, sir."

What the hell is Leila playing at? She knows this is forbidden. And as for Prescott—Leila is on the watch list, she knows this is prohibited.

My office phone buzzes and Andrea puts Hannah through.

"Mr. Grey, good afternoon." Hannah sounds irritatingly cheery.

"I need to speak to my wife. Now." I am not in the mood for pleasantries.

"Oh. Um. I'm afraid she's in a meeting."

I'm going to have a coronary. "I'm fully aware of that. Get her out of the meeting."

"Um. I'm not—"

"Do it, now, or you're fired," I seethe through gritted teeth.

"Yes, sir," she squeaks, and the phone clatters to her desk, the noise an assault on my eardrum.

Shit.

I'm left hanging. Waiting once more for Anastasia Stee—Grey.

My fingers drum a frantic tattoo on my desk.

Perhaps I should just get up and go.

That's absurd.

Did John speak to Leila?

My BlackBerry buzzes.

> TAYLOR
> I'm in the car. Outside.

>> Wait for me.

> TAYLOR
> Copy.

I don't understand what Prescott is playing at. How did she let this happen?

The phone scrapes along the desk and is dropped back onto the hard surface, the noise deafening again.

Fucking hell. Hannah is clumsy!

"Um. M-Mr. Grey?"

"Yes." The word hisses out at her in frustration.

Get on with it!

"Ana says she's sorry, but she's b-busy and she'll c-call you b-back shortly."

Jesus Christ. She's a tongue-tied mess.

"Fine," I snap, and hang up.

Shit. What to do?

Prescott! Of course.

Ana said Prescott would be in the meeting with her. She has a phone, though I don't think I have her number. "Andrea!" I shout once more, and a moment later she's in the doorway, her demeanor tentative. "Get me Prescott on her mobile."

Andrea looks momentarily baffled, and I think I'm going to explode.

"Belinda Prescott, Ana's security," I snap. "Now!"

"Ah, yes." Andrea disappears.

Don't be an asshole, Grey.

Taking a deep breath in an effort to calm myself, I get up and pace behind my desk, knowing it will be a moment before Andrea has Prescott's number. I'm suffocated by my anxiety. Loosening my tie, I undo my top button to ameliorate the situation. But an image of Leila—bedraggled and destitute, holding a gun at Ana—remains at the forefront of my mind.

It's torture.

My anger and apprehension rise several notches on the Richter scale.

When my phone rings, I grab it. "Mrs. Grey's security for you," Andrea says.

"Mr. Grey," Prescott says.

"Prescott, I cannot begin to articulate how disappointed I am in you right now. Let me talk my wife."

"Yes, sir," she answers.

There's a beat of muffled chatter. "Christian," Ana snaps, and from her tone I know she's on her high-fucking-horse, condescending to talk to me.

"What the fuck are you playing at?" I bark down the phone.

"Don't shout at me." Her retort only fuels my temper.

"What do you mean, don't shout at you?" My voice bellows around the room and into the phone. "I gave specific instructions, which you have completely disregarded—again. Hell, Ana, I am fucking furious."

"When you are calmer, we will talk about this."

Oh, no! "Don't you hang up on me!"

"Good-bye, Christian."

"Ana! Ana!" The line is dead, and I think I'm going to erupt like Mount St. Helens. Incandescent with fury, I grab my jacket and my phone, and storm out of my office. "Cancel the rest of my meetings today," I growl at Andrea. "And let Taylor know I'm on my way down."

"Yes, sir."

The elevator takes an eternal sixteen seconds to arrive. I know because I count each and every one in an effort to rein in my temper. After I step in and jab the button for the lobby, I clench my fists so tightly that my fingernails dig into my palms, and I know I have lost the fight. Andrea glances up, consternation writ large on her face, but I remain impassive, ignoring her as the doors close.

I am ready to do battle.

With my wife.

Again.

And with Leila. *What the fuck is she thinking?*

Taylor is standing by the car, holding the door open. I'm grateful that at least he's on the case. We drive in silence to SIP as my anger simmers, ready to boil over at the slightest provocation. From the back of the car I call Flynn's office, but I get his secretary Janet's voice mail. I hang up, frustrated that I can't even vent my anger on Flynn.

Was this Leila's plan all along?

She knew that if she accosted my wife, then I would come running.

I'm playing into her hands, but I don't give a fuck.

After an agonizing journey, Taylor pulls up outside SIP and I'm out of the car as soon as he stops at the curb. I don't bother with reception, but head straight through the double doors toward Ana's office. At her desk, Hannah looks up. I ignore her, too.

"Mr. G-Grey—"

I burst into Ana's office, so forcefully that a few papers fall to the floor, amplifying the room's emptiness.

Shit.

Feeling like a complete idiot, I turn around and glare at Hannah. "Where is she?" I snap, trying not to lose it. She pales and points toward the opposite end of the open-plan floor.

"In the meeting room. I-I'll take you."

"I'll manage, thank you." Scowling at her, my tone glacial and clipped, I blaze back in the direction I've come from, a storm cloud about to burst. I have to remind myself that it's not her fault. Ignoring the curious glances from the staff at their desks, I pass by the double doors to reception. They open, and Taylor stalks through to join me, but beyond him I catch a glimpse of Susannah Shaw sitting on one of the Chesterfields in the waiting area.

What the hell?

Are all my ex-submissives here?

She's reading a magazine, so she doesn't see me.

I haven't got time for this.

I spot Leila through the glass wall of the conference room. Without knocking, I barge in and am met by three surprised pairs of eyes. Ana stares at me in shock, then fury. Leila's eyes widen, but she drops her gaze to the table, as she should. Prescott stares ahead. My first response is relief that Ana is unharmed, but it's swiftly swept aside by my anger.

"You," I address Prescott. "You're fired. Get out now." Prescott nods—resigned, I think—and makes her way around the table to leave.

Ana gapes at me. "Christian—" She pushes her chair back, and I know she's going to stand up and berate me. I hold a finger up in warning.

"Don't." I keep my voice low while I struggle to contain my fury. Prescott, her face expressionless, walks past me out of the room. Shutting the door behind her, I turn to confront Leila.

She looks as I remember when she was with me: healthy and well adjusted. It's a relief to see her looking like her old self, and I'd tell her that, if I wasn't so fucking angry with her right now. Splaying my fingers onto the cool surface of the polished wood, I lean forward, tension tightening every muscle in my body, and snarl, "What the fuck are you doing here?"

"Christian!" Ana exclaims, shocked, I think, but I ignore her and concentrate my attention on Miss Leila Williams.

"Well?" I demand.

Leila's eyes dart to mine, her face slowly draining of color. "I wanted to see you, and you wouldn't let me," she whispers.

"So you came here to harass my wife?"

Leila examines the tabletop again.

Well, I'm here now. You got what you wanted.

I'm mad that I've been played, but more livid that she's here with Ana.

"Leila, if you come anywhere near my wife again, I will cut off all support. Doctors, art school, medical insurance—all of it—gone. Do you understand?"

"Christian!" Ana tries to interject. She looks distraught, but right now I don't give a shit, and I silence her with a look.

"Yes," Leila says, her voice almost inaudible.

"What's Susannah doing in reception?"

"She came with me."

I stand upright and run a hand through my hair.

What am I going to do with her?

"Christian, please," Ana interjects again. "Leila just wants to say thank you. That's all."

Ignoring Ana, I direct a question at Leila. "Did you stay with Susannah while you were sick?"

"Yes."

"Did she know what you were doing while you were staying with her?"

"No. She was away on vacation."

I can't imagine that Susannah would have stood by and let Leila lose her mind. She always struck me as a caring and considerate person.

I sigh. "Why do you need to see me? You know you should send any requests through Flynn. Do you need something?"

Leila traces her finger along the edge of the table and the silence fills the room. Abruptly, she looks up. "I had to know," she declares, looking directly at me.

"Had to know what?"

"That you're okay."

What the fuck? "That I'm okay?" I don't believe her.

"Yes." She's not backing down.

"I'm fine. There, question answered. Now Taylor will run you to Sea-Tac so you can go back to the East Coast. And if you take one step west of the Mississippi, it's all gone. Understand?"

"Yes. I understand," Leila says quietly, her expression finally contrite. It goes a long way to calming me.

"Good," I mutter.

"It might not be convenient for Leila to go back now. She has plans," Ana intervenes again.

"Anastasia." My tone is arctic. "This does not concern you." The stubborn scowl that I know so well forms on her face.

"Leila came to see me, not you," she snaps.

Leila turns to look at Ana. "I had my instructions, Mrs. Grey. I disobeyed them." She glances at me, then back to my wife. "This is the Christian Grey I know," she says, and her tone is almost wistful.

What?

That's not fair.

We role-played a relationship, for fuck's sake. And the last time she was in a room with my wife, she had her at gunpoint! I will go to the ends of the earth to keep Anastasia safe. Leila rises, and I want to leap to my own defense, but if that's how she'd like to rewrite history, then so be it. I don't give a flying fuck.

"I'd like to stay until tomorrow. My flight is at noon," she states.

"I'll have someone collect you at ten to take you to the airport."

"Thank you."

"You're at Susannah's?"

"Yes."

"Okay."

Leila turns to Ana. "Good-bye, Mrs. Grey. Thank you for seeing me."

Ana rises and holds out her hand, and they shake. "Um, good-bye. Good luck," she says.

Leila nods with a faint, sincere smile and turns to me. "Good-bye, Christian."

"Good-bye, Leila. Dr. Flynn, remember."

"Yes, Sir."

I open the door for her to leave, but she pauses in front of me. "I'm glad you're happy. You deserve to be," she says, and then she's out the door. I watch her leave, baffled by our exchange.

What the hell was that all about?

I close the door and, taking a deep breath, turn to face my wife.

"Don't even think about being angry with me," she snarls. "Call Claude Bastille and kick the shit out of him, or go see Flynn." Her cheeks pink with her rising anger.

Wow. Attack as the first form of defense.

But that's not what this is about.

"You promised you wouldn't do this."

"Do what?" she spits at me.

"Defy me."

"No, I didn't. I said I'd be more considerate. I told you she was here. I had Prescott search her, and your other little friend, too. Prescott was with me the entire time. Now you've fired the poor woman, when she was only doing what I asked." Ana is on a roll. "I told you not to worry, yet here you are. I don't remember receiving your papal bull decreeing that I couldn't see Leila. I didn't know that my visitors were subject to a proscribed list." She's mad, really mad, her voice rising and her eyes flashing with righteous indignation.

Impressive, Mrs. Grey.

I marvel at how she always stands up to me and remains as disarming as ever. And she's funny, sucking the venom of the room with her choice of words. "Papal bull?" I ask, because it's the most amusing and disrespectful thing I've heard in a while, and I hope to raise a smile.

Ana remains stony-faced.

Shit. "What?" I ask, exasperated. I had hoped that we could move on, now that she's got everything off her chest.

"You. Why were you so callous toward her?"

What? I wasn't callous, I was mad. She shouldn't be here.

Hell.

Sighing, I lean against the table. "Anastasia, you don't understand. Leila, Susannah—all of them—they were a pleasant, diverting pastime. But that's all. You are the center of my universe. And the last time you two were in a room together, she had you at gunpoint. I don't want her anywhere near you."

"But, Christian, she was ill."

"I know that, and I know she's better now, but I'm not giving her the benefit of the doubt anymore. What she did was unforgivable."

"But you've just played right into her hands. She wanted to see you again, and she knew you'd come running if she came to see me."

I shrug. "I don't want you tainted with my old life."

Ana frowns. "Christian, you are who you are because of your old life, your new life, whatever. What touches you touches me. I accepted that when I agreed to marry you, because I love you."

Where is she going with this?

Her expression is raw, full of compassion.

But this time it's not for me, but for Leila.

Who knew Leila would find an advocate in my wife?

"She didn't hurt me. She loves you, too."

"I don't give a fuck."

And no, she doesn't love me. How could she?

Leila knows only too well what I'm capable of…

Ana stares at me as if she's seeing me for the first time.

Oh, baby. I told you a long time ago. Fifty Shades.

"Why are you championing her cause all of a sudden?" I ask, baffled.

"Look, Christian, I don't think Leila and I will be swapping recipes and knitting patterns anytime soon. But I didn't think you'd be so heartless to her."

"I told you once, I don't have a heart," I mutter, and even to my own ears I sound petulant.

She rolls her eyes. "That's just not true, Christian. You're being ridiculous. You do care about her. You wouldn't be paying for art classes and the rest of that stuff if you didn't."

I remember Leila, broken and filthy as I bathed her in Ana's old apartment and how I felt seeing her like that.

Hell. I've had enough of this shit.

"This discussion is over. Let's go home."

Ana glances at her watch. "It's too early."

"Home!" I insist.

Please. Ana.

"Christian, I'm tired of having the same argument with you." She sounds weary.

What argument?

"You know," she continues, correctly interpreting my frown, "I do something you don't like, and you think of some way to get back at me. Usually involving some of your kinky fuckery, which is either mind-blowing or cruel." She shrugs.

Cruel? Shit.

Yeah, she safe-worded on you, Grey.

Fuck.

"Mind-blowing?" I ask, because I don't want to dwell on *cruel.*

"Usually, yes."

"What was mind-blowing?"

Ana looks exasperated. "You know."

"I can guess." Various erotic memories cloud my imagination. Ana in a spreader bar, shackled to the bed, the cross...in my childhood bedroom...

"Christian, I—" She sounds breathless; distracting her has worked.

"I like to please you." I brush my thumb over her bottom lip.

"You do." Her voice is petal-soft, caressing me. *Everywhere.*

"I know." I whisper in her ear, "It's the one thing I *do* know." When I stand, Ana's eyes are closed. She opens them abruptly and purses her lips, probably in response to my wicked smile.

I want her.

I don't want to argue.

"What was mind-blowing, Anastasia?" I coax her.

"You want the list?"

"There's a list?"

"Well, the handcuffs," she mumbles, and for a moment she looks lost in the memory of our honeymoon tryst.

No. I grab her hand and skim my thumb around her wrist. "I don't want to mark you." My eyes meet hers, imploring her. "Come home."

"I have work to do."

"Home."

Please, Ana. I don't want to fight.

We gaze at each other, our battlefield the space between us as I try desperately to understand what she might be thinking. I know I've angered her, and at the back of my mind I'm concerned that I might be doing exactly what Flynn has warned me against—sabotaging our relationship and killing my own happiness.

I need to know we're okay.

Her pupils widen, growing larger and darkening her eyes. I can't resist her. Raising my hand, I caress her cheek with the back of my fingers. "We could stay here." My voice is hoarse, betraying my desire and my need to reconnect with my wife.

Ana blinks and shakes her head, stepping back. "Christian, I don't want to have sex here. Your mistress has just been in this room."

"She was never my mistress."

Only Elena fits that title.

Don't go there, Grey.

"That's just semantics, Christian." She sounds weary, once more.

"Don't overthink this, Ana. She's history." And I don't know if I'm referring to Leila or Elena, but the same applies to both of them.

They're history.

Ana sighs, and she regards me as if I'm a complex riddle to solve, her eyes beseeching me, but for what I don't know. Suddenly, her expression changes to one of alarm, and she gasps, and I think she says no.

But she *is* history. "Yes," I implore her, and press my lips to hers, to drive away her doubt.

"Oh, Christian," she whispers, "you scare me sometimes." She grasps my head in her hands and pulls my lips to hers, kissing me.

I'm lost. *Scare her?*

I fold her in my arms and whisper against her lips, "Why?"

"You could turn away from her so easily."

This time I know she's referring to my attitude to Leila. "And you think I might turn away from you, Ana? Why the hell would you think that? What's brought this on?"

"Nothing. Kiss me. Take me home." Her lips find mine once more, but this time there's a desperate edge to her kiss.

What's wrong, Ana?

The thought is fleeting as I surrender to her tongue.

ANA WRITHES BENEATH ME. "Oh, please," she begs.

"All in good time." I have her exactly where I want her, on our bed in Escala, trussed up and available. She groans and pulls on the leather restraints that bind each elbow to each knee. She's completely open to me, and helpless, as I focus my attention and the tip of my tongue on her clitoris. She groans as I tease the potent powerhouse buried in her flesh, feeling it harden under my relentless ministration.

God, I love this.

Her fingers find my hair, tugging it hard.

But I don't stop.

She's trying to straighten her legs. She's close. "Don't come." My words float over her wet flesh. "I will spank you if you come."

She groans and tugs harder.

"Control, Ana. It's all about control." And I double down on my efforts, my tongue continuing to provoke her, bringing her closer and closer. I know this is a losing battle for her, she's so near.

"Ah!" she cries, and her climax spirals through her body. She raises her face to the ceiling and arches her back as she comes.

Yes!

I don't stop until she screams. "Oh, Ana," I chide her, nipping her thigh. "You came." Flipping her onto her front, I smack her hard on her behind, so she cries out.

"Control," I repeat, and grabbing her hips, I drive into her.

She cries out again.

And I still.

Reveling in her.

This is where I want to be.

My happy place.

Leaning forward, I unclip each cuff in turn so she's free, and pull her fully onto my lap, driving deeper inside her.

Ana. I wrap my arm around her and caress her jaw, enjoying the feel of her back against my front.

"Move." I whisper my demand in her ear.

She moans and rises on my lap, then back down.

Too slow.

"Faster," I order.

And she moves. Fast. Faster. Faster still. Taking me with her.

Ah, baby.

This is heaven.

The feel of her.

I ease her head back, kissing her throat as my other hand skims down her body, caressing her skin. From her hip I trail my fingers down to cup her vulva. She whimpers as I brush my fingers against her already-sensitized clitoris. "Yes. Ana. You are mine. Only you."

"Yes," she cries out, and I can't believe she's so close. Her readiness fuels my desire. She tips her head back.

And the first shocks are there. "Come for me," I whisper.

She lets go, and I hold her still while I ride out her orgasm.

"Christian!" she calls, my name tipping me over the edge.

"Oh, Ana, I love you." I groan, and I come, all the tension from earlier spiraling out of my body as I find my release.

WE LIE SPRAWLED TOGETHER, and we're a tangle of limbs and cuffs. I kiss her shoulder and stroke her hair from her face before propping myself up on my elbow. While I knead her backside where I smacked her, I ask, "Does that make the list, Mrs. Grey?"

"Hmm."

"Is that a yes?"

"Hmm." Her lips lift in a glorious smile.

I grin. She's incoherent.

Job done, Grey.

I kiss her shoulder again and she rolls over to face me. "Well?" I ask.

"Yes. It makes the list." Her eyes sparkle with mischief. "But it's a long list."

She makes me feel ten feet tall.

My earlier anger is forgotten.

Thank you, Ana. I kiss her. "Good. Shall we have dinner?"

She nods and her fingers dance over my chest. "I want you to tell me something." Sincere, curious blue eyes meet mine.

"What?"

"Don't get mad."

"What is it, Ana?"

"You *do* care." She says the words with such compassionate sincerity that all the air is sucked from my lungs. "I want you to admit that you care. Because the Christian I know and love would care."

Why does she do this?

From nowhere images of Leila, and Susannah, and the rest of my subs cloud my brain. All that we did. All that they did. For me. All that I did, and do for them.

Leila broken and filthy.

Hell.

That was torture. I wouldn't want her or any of them to experience that. *Ever.*

"Yes. Yes, I care. Happy?"

Ana's eyes soften. "Yes. Very."

I frown. "I can't believe I'm talking to you now, here in our bed, about—"

She places a finger on my lips. "We're not. Let's eat. I'm hungry."

I sigh and shake my head.

This woman confounds me. In every way.

Why is this so important to her?

My sweet, compassionate wife. "You beguile and bewilder me, Mrs. Grey."

"Good." She kisses me, her tongue finding mine, and soon we're lost in each other again.

G ood morning, Mr. Grey." Andrea is bright and chirpy.
A little like me. Married life agrees with her, too, it would seem.
"Good morning, Andrea." I give her a quick, sincere smile.

"Coffee?"

"Please. Where's Sarah?"

"On an errand for the meeting this morning. Black?"

"Yes. And let's go through the preparations for today and the weekend."

Sitting down at my desk, I review the documents laid out in front of me. Today we meet the Hwangs from Taiwan to discuss our joint venture with their shipyard. I have their stats, their management structure, details of their suppliers and subcontractors, and a list of their clients. It's impressive, but part of me is still wondering why they would want to partner with a company in the U.S. In fact, this is what has been nagging me throughout our discussions with them. They told us during our recent call that they want to expand throughout the Pacific rim to be less reliant on the domestic and East Asian market. But GEH could be entering a political minefield.

Well, today we get to ask all the difficult questions.

Andrea joins me. She makes a mighty fine cup of coffee. "This is great." I raise my cup to her, and am rewarded with a smile. "Where are you with the travel arrangements for Ana's surprise party?"

"Your family arrives tomorrow. Raymond Steele will be driving in from his fishing trip in Oregon tomorrow. The Gulfstream is due to take off this afternoon for Savannah to collect Mr. and Mrs. Adams. They'll fly into Seattle tomorrow afternoon. I wanted to check that you didn't need hotel reservations for them."

"No, thanks. They'll be staying with us."

"I think that's all with regard to the weekend. I've been liaising with Mrs. Jones."

"Great. Now, the Taiwanese delegation." I check my watch. "They should be here by eleven."

"Everything's in place." Andrea is exuding her usual efficiency. "They're coming from the Fairmont Olympic. In addition to the owners, Mr. and Miss Hwang, and their chief operating officer, Mr. Chen, they're bringing their interpreter; I'm sorry that I don't have his or her name yet. Marco will meet them in reception and escort them to the conference room."

"Odd that they are bringing an interpreter. They all speak fluent English."

Andrea shrugs. "Lunch is booked in your name, at the Four Seasons at one thirty p.m."

"Thanks, Andrea, sounds like everything is in hand."

"Will that be all?"

"For now."

Once she's gone, I turn to my iMac and check my e-mail. The title of Ana's jumps out at me.

From: Anastasia Grey
Subject: The List
Date: September 9 2011 09:33
To: Christian Grey

That's definitely at the top.
:D
A x

Anastasia Grey
Editor, SIP

I laugh out loud and shift in my seat as I remember the spreader bar and how exceptionally accommodating my wife was last night. Then again, she has been every night since Leila intruded on our lives. Thankfully, that drama is over—Leila is home and Flynn has reassured me that she's happily settled back into her life in Connecticut.

Ana is as insatiable as ever.

I am a lucky, lucky man.

From: Christian Grey
Subject: Tell Me Something New
Date: September 9 2011 09:42
To: Anastasia Grey

You've said that for the last three days.
Make your mind up.
Or...we could try something else.
;)

Christian Grey
CEO, Enjoying This Game, Grey Enterprises Holdings, Inc.

Our only source of conflict has been Ana's campaign to rehire Prescott, in spite of the fact that Ana herself said she wasn't certain about her. I've reassured Ana that I'll give Prescott a good reference, but that's it, and for me the matter is closed. I return to the documents in front of me for a reread; I need to be on my game.

That done, I check for any further e-mails from Ana, but there are none. I'm restless for the meeting to start, but with forty-five minutes to go, I need to stretch my legs. Leaping up, I grab my phone and head out of my office.

"Andrea, I'm just going to see Ros. I've got my phone." I wave it in front of her, and notice it needs charging.

Damn. "Can you charge this for me?"

"Yes, Mr. Grey."

With a need to burn off some of my excess energy prior to the meeting, I vault down the stairs to Ros's office.

ROS HAS A REAM of final questions for the Hwangs, and we're discussing tactics when there's a knock on the door. It's Andrea. "Mrs. Grey called you. She wanted to talk to you urgently. I thought you would want to know." She hands me my phone.

"Thank you." Frowning, I step out of Ros's office and dial Ana's number.

"Christian," Ana gasps, breathless and choked.

A frisson runs up my spine. "Christ, Ana. What's wrong?"

"It's Ray—he's been in an accident."

"Shit!"

"I'm on my way to Portland."

"Portland? Please tell me Sawyer is with you."

"Yes, he's driving."

"Where's Ray?"

"At OHSU."

Ros steps out of her office, distracting me. "Christian, they'll be here shortly." My eyes dart to the clock on the wall. It's 10:48.

"Yes, Ros, I know!" The meeting will take at least two hours. *Hell.* I was going to take them to lunch.

Ros and Marco can do it.

"Sorry, baby—I can be there in about three hours. I have business I need to finish here. I'll fly down." Thank God *Charlie Tango* is back in operation. "I have a meeting with some guys over from Taiwan. I can't blow them off. It's a deal we've been hammering out for months. I'll leave as soon as I can."

"Okay," she whispers, her voice small and scared.

A fist tightens around my heart. This is not Ana's usual demeanor. "Oh, baby," I murmur, overwhelmed with the need to drop everything and join her.

She needs me.

But I can't. I have responsibilities here.

Sawyer is with her.

"I'll be okay, Christian. Take your time. Don't rush. I don't want to worry about you, too. Fly safely."

"I will."

"Love you."

"I love you, too, baby. I'll be with you as soon as I can. Keep Luke close."

"Yes, I will."

"I'll see you later."

"Bye." She hangs up.

"Everything okay?" Ros asks.

I shake my head. "No. Ana's dad has had an accident."

"Oh no…"

"He's in OHSU hospital in Portland. She's heading there now. I have to make a quick call." I speed-dial my mother, and by some miracle Grace answers her cell.

"Christian, darling. How lovely to hear from you."

"Mom, Ana's dad has been in an accident."

"Oh no, poor Ray. Is he okay? Where is he?"

"OHSU."

"Is it serious?"

"I don't know. Ana's on her way down there. Unfortunately, I have a meeting here that I need to take before I can join her."

"I see. A friend from Yale works there. I'll make some calls."

"Thanks, Mom. I've got to go."

I call Andrea, hoping that she's back at her desk.

"Mr. Grey."

"Ana's dad has been in an accident. I'll need Stephan to fly with me to Portland in *Charlie Tango* after my meeting. Can you ask Beighley to fly the Gulfstream to Savannah? We'll need to find a second pilot to go with her. And liaise with Taylor—I need him to come with me."

"Yes, sir. I'll get right on it." I hang up. Ros is gathering her papers from her desk. "You'll have to entertain the Hwangs after this meeting. Take them to lunch. I have a table booked at the Four Seasons. I'll have to join Ana."

"Of course. I'll ask Marco to join me."

"We'd better head up."

RYAN DRIVES TAYLOR AND me to the helipad in downtown Seattle. It was Andrea's idea that we leave from here, rather than Boeing Field, to save time. The meeting with the Hwangs has been a huge success. I've acquired a shipyard, and the settlement we've reached appears to be satisfactory to all parties, but I've left Ros and Marco to iron out the details. Ros and I have an invitation to visit the shipyard next week, but right now I need to support my wife and find out about my father-in-law's condition.

As Ryan parks the Audi outside the building, I'm reminded of the last time I used this helipad—to take Ana to José's exhibition in Portland. All part of my campaign to win her back.

I allow myself a brief moment of triumph.

I succeeded.

She's now my wife.

Who would have thought, Grey?

Taylor and I make our way to the elevator, which whisks us up to the rooftop helipad. The doors slide open and there she is: *Charlie Tango.*

My pride and joy restored to her former glory.

I left her burnt out and abandoned in a clearing in a wild and desolate corner of Gifford National Forest. Now she has two new engines, and after a thorough cleanup at Eurocopter, she stands tall and proud, gleaming like new in the early afternoon sun. It's a joy to see her. Stephan climbs out of the cockpit, beaming, as we walk toward him. "She's handling just like she used to, and she's looking good, too," he says by way of a greeting.

"I can't wait to take her up." In spite of my anxiety about Ana, I can barely contain my excitement to be at *Charlie Tango*'s controls again.

"Thought you'd say that." With a grin, he holds the pilot's door open, then takes the seat beside me while Taylor hops into the back. Once I've buckled up, I don my headphones and run through my preflight checks.

"Have I forgotten anything?" I ask Stephan.

"No, sir. Well remembered."

I check the rotor rpm then radio the tower.

"Okay, guys. You ready?"

"Copy," Taylor says over his headset, and Stephan gives me a thumbs-up. Gently, I ease back the collective, and *Charlie Tango* rises like a phoenix into the Seattle sunshine. It's a rush and a relief, knowing I'll be with my wife in just over an hour.

The flight to Oregon is a welcome diversion from my worries about Ana and her dad. *Charlie Tango* is as responsive, smooth, and elegant as she's always been. She lands with her usual grace on the Portland helipad.

"You'll keep her warm?" I ask Stephan.

"With pleasure, sir." He's agreed to stand by for further instructions, as I don't know when, or if, we'll be heading home today.

Outside the building, there's a Suburban waiting for us. The rental agent hands the keys to Taylor, and we set off for the hospital. While he drives, I fish out my phone to contact Ana, but there's a missed call and voice mail from my mother. I call Grace, rather than listen to her message, but she doesn't pick up. *Hell.* I hang up and listen to her voice mail. Her tone is crisp and concise, her doctor's voice. "Christian, I don't have much information on your father-in-law. I know he's in the OR and has been there for some time. He's in serious condition. We'll find out more when they're finished with him. I don't have a time yet. If you're at the hospital, call me."

I scowl at my phone. My mother's message is disturbing; *serious* does not sound good. "Taylor, we may have to stay overnight. Can you pick up some essentials for Ana and me?"

"Toiletries?"

"Yes. And a change of clothes or two. For both of us. Casual attire. Please."

"Yes, sir."

I call Andrea and she picks up on the first ring. "Mr. Grey."

"Andrea, we may need to stay in Portland tonight. Check that The Heathman has a suite."

"Will do. Shall I courier your laptop to you?"

"I have it. Taylor picked it up."

Shit. It's Ana's birthday tomorrow.

"Call Mrs. Jones. I'm not sure we'll be able to make dinner tomorrow. I'll update her later."

"Shall I turn the Gulfstream around?"

"No. Let them land in Savannah. Ana may want her mother here. I'll come back to you when I know more." I hang up.

What to do?

Taylor catches my eye.

"What is it?" I ask.

"Sir, I could drop you at the hospital. Shop for your essentials. Leave the shopping bags at your hotel, then fly back to Seattle with

Stephan and bring the R8 down for Mrs. Grey so it's here tomorrow morning."

"That's an idea. Let's see how her father is before we do anything. But yes, that's a good plan. You could also collect a few items for me, too."

"Yes, sir."

Perhaps we'll have to reschedule Ana's birthday celebrations to later in the month. While I chew on that, I remember that Mia starts her new job today. I send her a quick good-luck text as Taylor pulls up outside the main OHSU building.

I gird my loins. In spite of my mother's chosen profession, I loathe hospitals.

IN THE ELEVATOR, on my way to the OR floor, my phone buzzes with a text from Andrea. She's reserved my usual suite at The Heathman. A nurse at the reception desk on the third floor directs me to the waiting room. Taking a deep breath, I open the door. Inside the stark, utilitarian room I find Ana seated on a plastic chair. Pale, scared, and swamped in a man's leather jacket, she's clutching José Rodriguez's hand. His father sits in a wheelchair beside him.

"Christian," she cries. The relief and hope on her face as she leaps up to greet me extinguish the brief flash of jealousy that flared in my gut. When she's in my arms, I close my eyes and hold her close. She smells of apples and orchards and Ana, and the unmistakable aroma of cheap cologne and sweaty nights out.

José's jacket?

I wrinkle my nose and hope no one notices. José stands, but José Rodriguez senior remains in the wheelchair, looking pretty banged up.

Shit. He must have been in the accident, too.

"Any news?" I direct my question at Ana.

She shakes her head.

"José." I nod a greeting while keeping hold of my wife. Sawyer is seated in the corner. He acknowledges me with a quick nod; I'm grateful that he's been here with Ana.

"Christian, this is my father, José Senior," José says.

"Mr. Rodriguez—we met at the wedding. You were in the accident, too?" Gently, I shake his free hand.

"We all were," José replies. "We were driving to Astoria for a day's fishing." His face hardens, and his fresh-faced boyishness disappears, revealing the menacing man beneath. "But we were hit by a drunk driver on the way. He totaled my dad's car. Miraculously, I was unharmed. My dad got beat up, but Ray—" He stops and swallows to collect himself, then, with a swift, anxious glance at Ana, continues, "He was bad. He was airlifted from Astoria community hospital to here."

I tighten my arm around Ana.

"After they patched my father up, we followed," he finishes, and I raise my brows in surprise. Mr. Rodriguez Senior has a leg and an arm in casts, and one side of his face is bruised. He doesn't look fit to travel.

"Yeah." José shakes his head in exasperation, as if he can read my mind. "My dad insisted."

"Are you both well enough to be here?" I ask.

"We don't want to be anywhere else." Mr. Rodriguez's face contorts; he looks and sounds like he's in pain.

Maybe they should go home.

But I don't press them; they're here for Ray. Taking Ana's hand, I guide her back to one of the seats and sit down beside her. "Have you eaten?"

She shakes her head.

"Are you hungry?"

She shakes her head.

"But you're cold?" I ask, catching another whiff of José's jacket. She nods and wraps the offending garment more snugly around her. The door opens and a man in scrubs enters—dark-haired, tall, and with a weary air of battle fatigue; his expression is grave.

Shit.

Ana stumbles to her feet, and I stand quickly to steady her. All eyes in the room are on the young doctor.

"Ray Steele," Ana says with quiet trepidation.

"You're his next of kin?" the doctor asks.

"I'm his daughter, Ana."

"Miss Steele—"

"Mrs. Grey," I mutter, correcting him.

"My apologies," the doctor stammers. "I'm Dr. Crowe. Your father is stable, but in critical condition."

Ana crumples in my arms as the doctor delivers each blow about Ray's condition. "He suffered severe internal injuries, principally to his diaphragm, but we've managed to repair them, and we were able to save his spleen. Unfortunately, he suffered a cardiac arrest during the operation because of blood loss. We managed to get his heart going again, but this remains a concern."

Jesus!

"However," Dr. Crowe continues, "our gravest concern is that he suffered severe contusions to the head, and the MRI shows that he has swelling in his brain. We've induced a coma to keep him quiet and still while we monitor the brain swelling."

Ana gasps, sagging against me some more.

"It's standard procedure in these cases. For now, we just have to wait and see."

"And what's the prognosis?" I ask, trying to mask the distress in my voice.

"Mr. Grey, it's difficult to say at the moment. It's possible he could make a complete recovery, but that's in God's hands now."

"How long will you keep him in a coma?"

"That depends on how his brain responds. Usually seventy-two to ninety-six hours."

"Can I see him?" Ana's breathless with anxiety.

"Yes, you should be able to see him in about half an hour. He's been taken to the ICU on the sixth floor."

"Thank you, Doctor."

Dr. Crowe nods a good-bye and leaves us.

"Well, he's alive," Ana whispers, trying to sound hopeful, but tears pool in her eyes and spill down her ashen face.

No. Ana, baby. "Sit down," I tell her, easing her back to the seat.

"Papa," José says to his father, "I think we should go. You need to rest. We won't know anything for a while. We can come back this evening, after you've rested. That's okay, isn't it, Ana?" José turns to Ana.

"Of course," she responds.

"Are you staying in Portland?" I ask, and José nods. "Do you need a ride home?"

José frowns. "I was going to order a cab."

"Luke can take you."

Sawyer stands, while José looks confused.

"Luke Sawyer," Ana says.

"Oh. Sure. Yeah, we'd appreciate it. Thanks, Christian."

Ana offers Mr. Rodriguez a careful hug, and a less careful one to José. He whispers in her ear, but I'm close enough to hear. "Stay strong, Ana. He's a fit and healthy man. The odds are in his favor."

"I hope so," she replies, her voice distressingly small. Her words slice through me like a scythe, because there's nothing I can do to help. She shrugs off José's pungent jacket and hands it back to him.

Thank God.

"Keep it, if you're still cold," he offers.

"No, I'm okay. Thanks," she says, and I take her hand. "If there's any change, I'll let you know right away."

José gives her a faint smile and wheels his father toward the door that Sawyer props open. Mr. Rodriguez raises his hand, and José stops. "He'll be in my prayers, Ana." The older man's voice cracks. "It's been so good to reconnect with him after all these years. He's become a good friend."

"I know," Ana says, her voice strained with emotion.

The three of them exit, and we're finally alone. I caress her cheek. "You're pale. Come here." Taking a seat, I gather her onto my lap, folding my arms around her. She burrows into my chest, and I kiss her hair.

We sit.

Together.

Each of us with our own thoughts.

What do I say to comfort her?

I have no idea. I'm helpless and I hate it.

Taking her hand, I offer her what I hope is a reassuring squeeze.

Ray is a strong man. He'll pull through; he's got to.

"How was *Charlie Tango*?" she asks eventually, and I marvel that even in this situation she's thinking of me. I think my spontaneous grin is answer enough.

My EC135 is back. And what a joy she was to fly. "Oh, she was yar."

She smiles. "Yar?"

"It's a line from *The Philadelphia Story*. Grace's favorite film."

"I don't know it."

"I think I have it on Blu-Ray at home. We can watch it and make out." Brushing my lips against her hair, I inhale her fragrance, sweeter now that José's jacket has left with him. "Can I persuade you to eat something?"

"Not now. I want to see Ray first."

I don't push her.

"How were the Taiwanese?" she asks, and I think she's steering the conversation to stop me from brooding about food.

"Amenable."

"Amenable how?"

"They let me buy their shipyard for less than the price I was willing to pay."

"That's good?"

"Yes. That's good."

"But I thought you had a shipyard over here."

"I do. We're going to use that to do the fitting-out. Build the hulls in the Far East. It's cheaper."

"What about the workforce at the shipyard here?"

Good question, Mrs. Grey.

"We'll redeploy. We should be able to keep redundancies to a minimum."

I hope.

I kiss her once more. "Shall we check on Ray?"

RAYMOND STEELE IS IN the last bed in the ICU ward. It's a shock to see him out cold and hooked up to a range of high-tech medical equipment. This man intimidates me more than anyone I know, but right now, he looks vulnerable and sick. *Real sick.* He's in an induced coma and on a ventilator; his leg is in plaster and his chest is wrapped in a surgical dressing. His modesty's protected by a thin blanket.

Jesus. Ana is stunned when she sees him and blinks back tears of shock.

Her anguish is hard to witness.

What do I do? What do I say?

I can't make this better for her.

A nurse is checking his various monitors. Her badge identifies her as KELLIE RN.

"Can I touch him?" Ana asks, and she reaches for Ray's hand without waiting for a response.

"Yes," Kellie says kindly. Standing at the end of the bed, I watch as Ana carefully covers Ray's hand with hers. Abruptly, she sinks into the chair beside the bed, lays her head on his arm, and starts sobbing.

Oh no.

I move quickly to comfort her.

"Oh, Daddy. Please get better," she pleads quietly. "Please."

Feeling utterly fucking powerless, I place my hand on her shoulder and clasp it tightly, trying to offer her some reassurance. "All Mr. Steele's vitals are good," Kellie says quietly.

"Thank you," I mutter, because I don't know what else to say.

"Can he hear me?" Ana asks.

"He's in a deep sleep. But who knows?"

"Can I sit for a while?"

"Sure thing." Kellie gives Ana a warm smile.

Ana is where she needs to be right now, and I should make arrangements for us to stay in Portland. There's no way we're going home tonight. I squeeze her shoulder once more and she raises her eyes to mine. "I need to make a call." I drop a kiss on her head. "I'll be outside. I'll give you some alone time with your dad."

FROM THE SIXTH FLOOR waiting room I call my mother. This time she answers, and I update her on Raymond Steele's condition.

She takes a deep breath. "It sounds critical. I want to come and see him—"

"Mom. You don't—"

"No. Christian. I want to. Ana is family. I have to come down and check on him myself. Carrick and I will drive down."

"I can fly you down."

"What?"

"My helicopter is here, but Taylor is taking it back to Seattle. Stephan can fly you down here."

"That sounds good. Let's do that."

"Okay. I'll let Taylor know, and you can liaise with him."

"I'll do that. Christian, Ray is in good hands."

"Thanks, Mom."

I call Taylor and let him know about my mother.

Then I call Andrea. "Mr. Grey. How's Mr. Steele?"

"He's in serious condition. We'll be here for at least two nights. I'm going to have to do something for Ana's birthday here, if we do anything at all. Maybe a private dinner, if she's up to it. I'd like her family and our friends to attend, too. But we should see how Ray does during the night."

"I can talk to The Heathman and see if they'll accommodate a private dinner."

"Good. Ana needs her mom, so let's bring her and her husband out as planned. Book rooms for them, for my folks and the rest of our guests, and make provisional arrangements to get them here. My mother will be joining us this evening. Please book her into The Heathman tonight."

"Will do."

"Find out José Rodriguez's cell number. I'd like to invite him, too."

"I'll text you."

"Thanks, Andrea." I hang up and call Mrs. Jones to confirm that tomorrow's surprise dinner party at Escala is canceled.

"I hope Mr. Steele makes a swift recovery," Gail says.

"Yes. I do, too. I'm sorry about tomorrow."

"It's no trouble, Mr. Grey. There'll be another time."

"There will. Thanks, Gail." I hang up and return to the ICU. At the nurses' station I give Kellie my cell number and Ana's, with instructions to call us if there's a change in Ray's condition. It's time I took my wife for something to eat.

When I return to Ray's bedside, Ana is talking to him and her tears have ceased. She's composed and her face shines with her love for the man out cold and prostrate beside her.

It's an affecting sight.

And I feel I'm intruding.

But I don't want to go.

Quietly, I take a seat and listen to her soft, sweet voice. She's asking him to come to Aspen, where I'll take him fishing. Her words tug at my heart. Ana is my family now, like my mother said, and by extension, so is Ray. I see us side by side, casting flies in the Roaring Fork River or up on Snowmass Lake. Ray taciturn. Me relaxed and equally taciturn.

The two of us sharing a beer later.

"Mr. Rodriguez and José will be welcome, too. It's such a beautiful house. There's room for all of you. Please be here to do that, Daddy. Please."

Okay. Ray, José Senior, José, and me fishing together.

Yes. I could do that.

She turns and notices me.

"Hi," I murmur.

"Hi."

"So, I'm going fishing with your dad, Mr. Rodriguez, and José?"

She nods.

"Okay." I smile in agreement. "Let's go eat. Let him sleep." Ana frowns, and I know she doesn't want to leave her father. "Ana, he's in a coma. I've given our cell numbers to the nurses here. If there's any change, they'll call us. We'll eat, check in to a hotel, rest up, then come back this evening."

She looks longingly at Ray, then back at me. "Okay," she capitulates.

ANA STANDS IN THE doorway of our suite at The Heathman, surveying the familiar room. She looks shell-shocked.

Or perhaps she's remembering the first time I brought her here, though that's doubtful, as she was blind drunk at the time. I place her briefcase beside one of the sofas. "Home away from home," I murmur.

It was certainly home to me while I was pursuing Miss Steele to be my submissive.

And now here we are.

Husband and wife.

Finally she enters, and stands in the middle of the room, looking lost and forlorn.

Oh, Ana. What can I do? "Do you want a shower? A bath? What do you need, Ana?" I'm desperate to help her in any way I can.

"A bath. I'd like a bath," she mutters.

"Bath. Good. Yes." I stride into the en suite, relieved to have a purpose, and turn on the faucets. The water pours in, and I add some sweet-smelling bath oil, which instantly begins to foam. I slip out of my jacket and take off my tie as my phone buzzes. It's a text from Andrea with José's mobile number. I'll deal with that later.

Ana's in the bedroom, staring at the Nordstrom bags, when I reenter. "I sent Taylor to get some things. Nightwear. You know." She nods but says nothing, her desolation obvious in her blank look. My heart yearns to take her pain away. "Oh, Ana, I've not seen you like this. You're normally so brave and strong."

She returns my gaze, mute and helpless.

Slowly, she crosses her arms, hugging herself as if caught in an icy draft, and I can bear it no more. I fold her into my embrace, offering her the warmth of my body. "Baby, he's alive. His vital signs are good. We just have to be patient." She shudders, and I don't know if she's cold, or if it's the shock of seeing Ray brought so low. "Come." Taking her hand, I lead her into the bathroom, slowly undress her, and help her into the bath. She fastens her hair in a gravity-defying bun, slips beneath the foam, and closes her eyes. I take it as my cue to undress and join her. Climbing in behind her, I settle into the hot water and pull her against my front so we're both lying in the warm, soothing waters, her feet on mine.

As time moves on, Ana relaxes against me.

I let out a sigh of relief and allow myself a moment of respite from the dread that lingers in the pit of my stomach.

I hope to God that Ray will be okay.

Ana will fall apart if he's not.

And I'm powerless to help.

Idly I kiss her hair, grateful that she can take a moment to unwind as she pops the bubbles in the foam.

"You didn't get into the bath with Leila, did you? That time you bathed her?" she asks out of the blue.

"Um, no!"

"I thought so. Good."

Where is this coming from?

Tugging her haphazard topknot of hair, I angle her head so I can see her face. I'm curious. "Why do you ask?"

She shrugs. "Morbid curiosity. I don't know…seeing her this week." *Hopefully you'll never see her again.* "I see. Less of the morbid."

"How long are you going to support her?"

"Until she's on her feet. I don't know. Why?"

"Are there others?"

"Others?" I ask.

"Exes who you support."

"There was one, yes. No longer, though."

"Oh?"

"She was studying to be a doctor. She's qualified now and has someone else."

"Another Dominant?"

"Yes."

"Leila says you have two of her paintings," Ana mutters.

"I used to. I didn't really care for them. They had technical merit, but they were too colorful for me. I think Elliot has them. As we know, he has no taste."

Ana giggles, and it's such a wonderful sound that I wrap both arms around her, with a little too much enthusiasm, and the bath water slops over the sides and onto the floor with a satisfying splash.

"That's better." I kiss her temple.

"He's marrying my best friend."

"Then I'd better shut my mouth." I smile down at her and am rewarded with her answering smile. "We should eat."

Ana's face falls, but I'm not going to take no for an answer. I sit her up and clamber out of the bath, grabbing a robe as I do.

"You soak. I'm going to order some room service."

Once I've ordered some food, I rummage through the shopping bags and change into fresh clothes. Taylor has done well. I like the black jeans and a grey cashmere sweater that he's chosen. In the living room, I unpack my laptop and fire it up to check e-mails. While I'm scrolling through them, I have an idea.

From: Christian Grey
Subject: Drunk Driver. Astoria PD.
Date: September 9 2011 17:34
To: Grey, Carrick

Hi, Dad
Mom has probably told you that Raymond Steele was in an accident. His car was hit by a drunk driver this morning in Astoria. Ray is now in the ICU. Can you use your police department contacts to find out any information about the guy who hit him?
Thanks.

Christian Grey
CEO, Grey Enterprises Holdings, Inc.

I saunter back toward the bedroom and lean against the door frame, watching Ana search through the Nordstrom bags.

"Apart from harassing me at Clayton's, have you ever actually gone into a store and just bought stuff?" she asks.

"Harassing you?" I amble over to her, trying to hide my amusement. She half smiles. "Yes. Harassing me."

"You were flustered, if I recall. And that young boy was all over you. What was his name?"

"Paul."

"One of your many admirers."

She rolls her eyes, and I cannot help my smile. I plant a quick kiss on her lips. "There's my girl." I knew she couldn't be far away. "Get dressed. I don't want you getting cold again."

ANA IS NOT SEDUCED by the food I ordered. She eats two fries and half a crab cake, but that's all. Sighing in disappointment, I watch her leave the table and head back into the bedroom. I know I can't force her to eat, but it worries me when she doesn't. While I debate what to do, I text José to invite him and his father to Ana's surprise birthday dinner if—and it's a big if—it goes ahead tomorrow and if José Senior is up for it, too.

At my laptop I check e-mails. There's one from Carrick.

From: Grey, Carrick
Subject: Drunk Driver. Astoria PD.
Date: September 9 2011 17:42
To: Christian Grey.

Will do. Your mother should be in Portland now.
Dad.

Carrick Grey, Partner
Grey, Krueger, Davis, and Holt LLP

This is good news. My mom should be with Ray by the time we're back at the hospital.

When Ana returns to the living room, she's wearing a light blue hooded sweatshirt, chucks, and jeans. "Ready," she murmurs. Maybe it's because she's sad and anxious, and her face is pale, but she looks younger.

But then, she's still only twenty-one.

"You look so young—and to think you'll be a whole year older tomorrow," I murmur.

Her sad smile tears me in two. "I don't feel much like celebrating. Can we go see Ray now?"

"Sure. I wish you'd eat something. You barely touched your food."

"Christian, please. I'm just not hungry. Maybe after we've seen Ray. I want to wish him good night."

JOSÉ IS LEAVING THE ICU as we arrive. "Ana, Christian, hi."

"Where's your dad?" Ana asks.

"He was too tired to come back. He was in a car accident this morning."

I think that's José's idea of a joke as he forces a grin.

"And his painkillers have kicked in," he continues. "He was out for the count. I had to fight to get in to see Ray, since I'm not next of kin."

"And?" Ana's voice cracks with anxiety.

"He's good, Ana. Same, but all good."

She nods, relieved, I think.

"See you tomorrow, birthday girl."

Hell. Don't blow the surprise!

"Sure. We'll be here," Ana responds.

José glances at me, then pulls her into a brief hug, closing his eyes as he holds her. "Mañana," he whispers.

Dude. Are you still holding a torch for my wife?

He releases her, and we wish him good night, watching him walk down the corridor toward the elevators.

I sigh. "He's still nuts about you."

"No, he's not. And even if he is…" She shrugs. She doesn't care. "Well done," she says.

What?

"For not frothing at the mouth," she clarifies, her eyes sparkling with amusement.

Even now, she's making fun of me. "I've never frothed!" I try to sound offended, but her lips twitch in a slight smile, which was my intention. "Let's see your dad. I have a surprise for you."

"Surprise?"

"Come." I take her hand.

My mother is standing at the end of Ray's bed, her head bowed, as she listens to Dr. Crowe and a woman dressed in scrubs. Grace perks up when she sees us.

"Christian." She kisses my cheek, then hugs my wife. "Ana. How are you holding up?"

"I'm fine. It's my father I'm worried about."

"He's in good hands. Dr. Sluder is an expert in her field. We trained together at Yale."

"Mrs. Grey." Dr. Sluder shakes Ana's hand. She has a soft southern accent, her words sounding like a lullaby. "As the lead physician for your father, I'm pleased to tell you that all is on track. His vital signs are stable and strong. We have every faith that he'll make a complete recovery. The brain swelling has stopped and shows signs of decreasing. This is very encouraging after such a short time."

"That's good news," Ana says, a little color returning to her cheeks.

"It is, Mrs. Grey. We're taking real good care of him. Great to see you again, Grace."

"Likewise, Lorraina."

"Dr. Crowe, let's leave these good people to visit with Mr. Steele." Crowe follows Dr. Sluder out of the ward.

Ana looks down at Ray, who is still sleeping peacefully. Grace takes her hand. "Ana, sweetheart, sit with him. Talk to him. It's all good. I'll visit with Christian in the waiting room."

"HOW'S SHE DOING?" GRACE asks.

"It's hard to tell. She's bearing up, but I know she's extremely anxious. She's normally so strong."

"It must be a shock to her, darling. Thank heavens you're here with her."

"Thank you for coming, Mom. What you said was really reassuring, and I'm sure it made a huge difference to Ana."

Grace smiles at me. "You love her so."

"I do."

"What will you do for her birthday tomorrow?"

"I'm undecided, but I thought we might go ahead and have a low-key celebration here."

"I think that's a good idea. I'll stay in Portland tonight. It's not often I get some time to myself."

"Andrea has booked a room for you and dad at The Heathman."

She smiles. "Christian, you're so capable. You think of everything."

Her words spread like warm summer sunshine through my body.

I STRIP OUT OF my white T-shirt, and Ana grabs it and slips it over her head before climbing into bed.

"You seem brighter." I don my pajamas, pleased that Ana wants to wear my T-shirt.

"Yes. I think talking to Dr. Sluder and your mom made a big difference. Did you ask Grace to come here?"

Sliding into bed, I pull her into my arms, her back to my front; it's the best position to spoon with my girl. "No. She wanted to come and check on your dad herself."

"How did she know?"

"I called her this morning."

Ana sighs.

"Baby, you're exhausted. You should sleep."

"Hmm," she mumbles, then turns her head to look at me, frowning.

What?

She turns over and curls herself around me, her warmth permeating my skin as I stroke her hair. Whatever she was thinking about, it seems to have gone.

"Promise me something," I ask.

"Hmm?"

"Promise me you'll eat something tomorrow. I can just about tolerate you wearing another man's jacket without frothing at the mouth, but, Ana, you must eat. Please."

"Hmm," she grunts in agreement and I kiss her hair. "Thank you for being here," she mumbles, and kisses my chest.

"Where else would I be? I want to be wherever you are, Ana."

Always.

You are my wife. My family now.

And family comes first.

I stare up at the ceiling, remembering the first time we slept together in this room.

So long ago. And yet, not so long ago.

It was a revelation.

Sleeping with someone.

Sleeping with her.

"Being here makes me think of how far we've come. And the night I first slept with you." I whisper, "What a night that was. I watched you for hours. You were just…yar."

I sense Ana's tired smile against my chest.

Oh, baby.

"Sleep," I murmur, and it's not a request.

Grandpa Theodore hands me an apple. It's bright red. And tastes sweet; of home and long rich summers when the days went on forever. There's a light breeze on my face. It's cooling in the sunshine. We stand eye to eye in the orchard. His face sun-worn and weather-beaten, the etched lines in his skin telling a thousand stories. He reaches up, and a tremor runs through his hand. He's not as steady as he once was…*Grandpa!* He grasps my shoulder, his eyes hooded but still shining with wisdom and love… For me. I see it now. *Remember how we made the sweet apples when you were a boy?* I grin. They're still sweet. The trees are still giving. He smiles, his skin crinkling around his eyes. *Boy, you were an odd one. Wouldn't talk. Awful shy. Now look at you. Master of your own universe. I'm proud of you, son. You done good.* The warmth of his words matches the warmth of the sun. Behind him, Mom, Dad, Elliot, Mia, and Ana are walking through the long, lush grass to join us with a blanket and a picnic basket. Ana laughs at something Mia says. She tips her head back, her hair free and catching the golden light. My mom joins in. Laughing, too. *It's all about family, boy. Always. Family first.* Ana turns and beams at me. The sunshine of her smile lighting me from within. My light. My love. My family. *Ana.*

I wake, but before I open my eyes, I savor my contentment. All is right in the world, everything is as it should be, and I know I'm enjoying the remnants of a now-forgotten dream.

I open my eyes.
Where am I?
The Heathman.

Shit—Ray.

Grim reality intrudes, but I turn my head and am comforted to see Ana curled up beside me, still slumbering. From the light filtering through the curtains I know it's early. I lie still for a moment, making a mental list of all that I need to do today.

It's her birthday.

And Ray is lying injured in the hospital.

It will be a delicate balancing act, to celebrate and commiserate all at once with her.

I slip out of bed carefully.

Don't wake the wife!

When I'm showered and dressed, I move quietly into the living room and let Ana sleep. I have to make a decision on whether to proceed with Ana's birthday dinner, so my first task of the day is to call the ICU. I speak to one of Ray's nurses, who reports that he's spent a comfortable night and that his vitals are good. She then hands me over to the attending physician, who explains that all is as it should be and we should remain optimistic. At this encouraging news, and Dr. Sluder's report yesterday, I decide to go ahead with the dinner.

In the meantime, I need her gifts—both of which are in Taylor's hands. I check my watch—7:35 a.m.—and text Taylor, who's staying somewhere in the hotel.

> Good morning.
> Do you have Ana's present?

> TAYLOR
> Yes, sir.
> Shall I bring the box up?

> Please. She's still asleep!

A few moments later there's a gentle tap on the door, and Taylor is his usual smart-suited self on the other side. "Hello," I whisper, mindful of sleeping beauty. I prop the door open with my foot and join Taylor in the corridor.

"Good morning," he says, whispering, too. "Here." He places a beautifully wrapped package, all pale pink paper and satin ribbons, in my palm.

"Nice wrapping. Your handiwork?" I raise a brow, and Taylor flushes.

"For Mrs. Grey," he mutters, and I know this is reason enough. "Here's the card that came with the box."

"Thanks. I'm taking a gamble and going ahead with the small dinner party for Ana. We'll need to coordinate the arrival of our guests today."

"Andrea has been keeping me up-to-date, and Sawyer is here. Between the two of us I think we've got this," he says.

"And we'll have the new car, so Ana and I won't need ferrying around."

"I took the liberty of bringing both keys." He holds up the R8 key. "The spare is with the valet."

"Smart thinking." I slip the key into my pocket. "I think we'll be at least an hour. I'll text you when we're ready to leave so you can bring the Audi around to the front."

"I may not get a signal in the garage. I'll liaise with the concierge and he can call me at the valet station."

"Okay. I'll give him a sign when we're in the foyer. How was she?"

"The R8?"

I nod, and his broad grin tells me all I need to know.

"Great." I grin back. "I'll see you later."

He turns on his heel and I smile at his departing figure. Have I ever had a whispered conversation in a hotel corridor before? With Taylor? Ex-Marine? I shake my head at the ridiculousness of the two of us, and step back inside the suite.

When I check on Ana, she's still out for the count. I'm not surprised; she must be shattered from yesterday. I have time to e-mail Andrea.

From: Christian Grey
Subject: Ana's Birthday Dinner
Date: September 10 2011 07:45
To: Andrea Parker

Good morning, Andrea.
I want to go ahead with the surprise dinner for Ana.

Please confirm with the hotel and organize a cake (chocolate!).
Keep me informed about the travel arrangements for everyone.
Sawyer and Taylor are here so will be able to do airport pickups.
Coordinate with them.
Thanks.

Christian Grey
CEO, Grey Enterprises Holdings, Inc.

What else do I need to do?

Sitting down at the desk with Ana's gift in my hand, I stare at the blank card. Fortunately, I know exactly what I want to say.

For all our firsts on your first birthday
as my beloved wife.
I love you.
C x

I slide the card into its envelope and turn to my laptop. Ana will want something a little dressier for dinner, and bearing in mind what she said yesterday, I'd rather pick a dress for her myself than send Taylor. I check out the Nordstrom website and discover that the local store has a "buy and pick up" service. And it's two blocks from The Heathman.

Perfect.

I start browsing.

Twenty minutes later I've purchased everything Ana will need; I hope she likes my choices. I text Taylor to let him know, and he texts me back that he'll send Luke to Nordstrom when we're out visiting Ray.

Time to wake Ana.

She stirs as I sit down on the edge of the bed, and opens her eyes, blinking in the morning light. For a moment she looks relaxed and well rested, but abruptly her expression changes. "Shit! Daddy!" she exclaims in alarm.

"Hey." I stroke her cheek, so that she looks directly up at me. "I called the ICU this morning. Ray had a good night. It's all good." She thanks me as she sits up, looking relieved. Leaning in, I kiss her forehead and, closing my eyes, inhale her scent.

Sleep and Ana.

Delectable.

"Good morning, Ana." I kiss her temple.

"Hi."

"Hi. I want to wish you happy birthday. Is that okay?"

Her smile is uncertain, but she caresses my cheek, her eyes bright with sincerity. "Yes, of course. Thank you. For everything."

"Everything?"

"Everything," she says with conviction.

Why is she thanking me? It's bewildering. But I'm anxious to give her my gift, so I ignore the feeling. "Here."

Ana's eyes dart to mine, shining with excitement as she takes the package and opens the card. Her expression softens as she reads it. "I love you, too."

I grin. "Open it."

Returning my smile, she unravels the ribbon and gently removes the wrapping paper, revealing the Cartier leather box. Her eyes widen when she opens it to find a white-gold bracelet with charms that represent our firsts we've experienced together: a helicopter, a catamaran, a glider, a London black cab, the Eiffel Tower, a bed. Her forehead creases as she examines the sugar cone, and she glances up at me with a bemused expression.

"Vanilla?" I offer with a sheepish shrug.

She laughs. "Christian, this is beautiful. Thank you. It's yar." Her fingers fondle the small heart on the bracelet. It's a locket: I thought it appropriate, as I've never given anyone my heart before. Ana's been the one to unlock it, walk right in, and make herself at home there.

Sappy, Grey. "You can put a picture or whatever in that."

"A picture of you." She peers at me through her lashes. "Always in my heart."

She makes me feel ten feet tall.

Her fingertips brush over the C and A letter charms that signify the two of us, then over the white-gold key. She looks up again, a question burning in her bright blue eyes.

"To my heart and soul," I whisper. She lets out a strangled cry and launches herself at me, taking me by surprise as she throws her arms around my neck. I cradle her in my lap.

"It's such a thoughtful present. I love it. Thank you." Her voice breaks on the last word.

Oh, baby. I tighten my arms around her.

"I don't know what I'd do without you," she says through her tears.

I swallow, trying to digest her words and ignore the pang deep in my chest. "Please don't cry." My voice is husky with emotion. I love that she needs me.

She sniffs. "I'm sorry. I'm just so happy and sad and anxious at the same time. It's bittersweet."

"Hey." I tip her head back and press my lips to hers. "I understand."

"I know," she says with a sad smile.

"I wish we were in happier circumstances, and at home. But we're here." I give her an apologetic hug. Neither of us could have foreseen this situation. "Come, up you go. After breakfast, we'll check on Ray."

"Okay." Her smile is a little cheerier when I leave her so she can dress.

In the living room I order granola, yogurt, and berries for Ana, an omelet for me.

IT'S GRATIFYING TO SEE that Ana's appetite has returned. She wolfs down her breakfast, a woman on a mission, but I don't comment. It's her birthday and I want her happy.

Actually, I want her happy pretty much all the time.

"Thank you for ordering my favorite breakfast."

"It's your birthday. And you have to stop thanking me."

"I just want you to know that I appreciate it."

"Anastasia, it's what I do."

I want to take care of you. I've told you more than once.

She smiles. "Yes, it is."

Once she's finished her breakfast, I ask as nonchalantly as possible if we should go. I'm excited to give her the car.

"I'll just brush my teeth."

I smirk. "Okay."

The little *v* forms between her brows as she frowns—I think she suspects something's afoot—but she says nothing and heads to the bathroom. I text Taylor to let him know that we're leaving imminently.

As we walk to the elevators, I notice that Ana is wearing her new charm bracelet. Grasping her hand, I kiss her knuckles. My thumb grazes the helicopter charm. "You like?"

"More than like. I love it. Very much. Like you."

I kiss her fingers once more while we wait for the elevator.

The elevator.

Where it all started. Where I lost control.

Ceded control, Grey.

Yes. She's had you on a tight leash since you met her.

Ana's eyes flit to mine as we enter.

Is she thinking what I'm thinking? "Don't," I whisper, as I push the button for the lobby and the doors slide shut.

"Don't what?" She peeks at me through her lashes, coy and provocative at once.

"Look at me like that."

"Fuck the paperwork," she says, with a wide grin.

I laugh and tug her into my arms and tilt her face to mine. "Someday, I'll rent this elevator for a whole afternoon."

"Just the afternoon?" She raises an eyebrow, and it's a challenge.

"Mrs. Grey, you're greedy."

"When it comes to you, I am."

"I'm very glad to hear it." I plant a tender kiss on her lips, but as I pull away, Ana's fingers curl around the nape of my neck, pulling my mouth to hers. Her tongue is insistent, demanding access, and she pushes me against the wall, pressing her body against mine. I kiss her back as desire flares like a comet inside me.

What I thought would be a courtly, respectful expression of affection becomes darker, needier, hotter.

More.

So much more.

Her tongue is relentless, mating with mine.

Fuck.

I want her. Here. In this elevator.

Again.

We kiss. Tongues. Lips. Hands. All playing a role.

My fingers tightening in her hair while her hands caress my face. "Ana," I breathe, fighting my desire.

"I love you, Christian Grey." She's breathy and restless, her eyes full of promise. "Don't forget that." The elevator stops, the doors open, and she puts some space between us.

Hell.

My blood is running fast and thick through my body.

"Let's go see your father before I decide to rent this today." I kiss her quickly and, taking her hand, head out into the lobby. I'm grateful that I'm wearing my jacket.

The concierge sees us, and I give him a nod. Ana notices our exchange, but I give my girl my patented I-so-own-you-and-I've-got-a-surprise-for-you smile, and she frowns. "Where's Taylor?" she asks.

"We'll see him shortly."

"Sawyer?"

"Running errands."

We head outside and stop on the wide sidewalk. It's a beautiful late-summer day; the trees on Broadway are in full leaf, but there's a hint of the coming fall in the air. There's no sign of Taylor. Ana looks up and down the street, following my lead. "What is it?" she asks. I lift my shoulders, trying for nonchalance, not wanting to give the game away.

Then I hear it: the growl of the R8's throaty engine. Taylor steers the white, pristine vehicle that is Ana's brand-new Audi to a stop in front of us.

Ana takes a step back, and in stunned disbelief looks from the car to me.

Okay, last time I tried to give her a car, it didn't go so well.

This could go either way.

You said it, Ana. *You can buy me one for my birthday. A white one.*

"Happy birthday," I murmur, and from my pocket I produce the key.

Her mouth drops open. "You are completely over the top." Each word is a quiet staccato, then she turns to admire the marvel of engineering parked at the curb. Her consternation is short-lived; her face lights up and she jumps up and down on the spot. She turns and barrels into my waiting arms, and I swing her around, delighted at her reaction.

"You have more money than sense!" she cries. "I love it! Thank you."

I dip her low, surprising her, so she gasps and grips my biceps. "Anything for you, Mrs. Grey." I kiss her. "Come. Let's go see your dad."

"Yes!" she exclaims. "And I get to drive?"

Smiling down at her, and against my better judgment, I acquiesce. "Of course. It's yours." I pull her to her feet, and she dances to the driver's door, which Taylor is holding open for her.

"Happy birthday, Mrs. Grey." He beams.

"Thank you, Taylor." She hugs him while I roll my eyes and climb into the passenger seat. Ana clambers in beside me and slides her hands around the steering wheel, grinning with glee, as Taylor closes her door.

"Drive safe, Mrs. Grey," he says, his affection obvious despite the gruff tone. For some unfathomable reason it makes me smile.

"Will do," Ana replies, buzzing with excitement. She puts the key in the ignition, and I tense beside her.

I hate being driven.

Except by Taylor.

But she knows this.

"Take it easy," I caution. "Nobody chasing us now." She turns the key, and the R8 roars to life. Ana quickly adjusts the side and rearview mirrors, puts the car in drive, and pulls out into the street at a harrowing speed.

"Whoa!" I cry out, clutching my seat.

"What?"

"I don't want you in the ICU beside your father. Slow down," I yell, wondering if the R8 was a good idea. She slows immediately.

"Better?" She gives me a dazzling smile.

"Much," I mutter, grateful that we're both still alive. "Take it easy, Ana."

SEVEN MINUTES LATER WE'RE in the hospital parking lot, and
I've aged at least ten years with each minute of the journey. My pulse
must be at 180 bpm; being driven by my wife is not for the faint of
heart. "Ana, you have to slow down. Don't make me regret buying
you this." I glare at her as she turns off the ignition. "Your dad is
upstairs because he was involved in a car accident."

"You're right," she whispers, reaching over and clasping my hand.
"I'll behave."

I want to say more, but I don't. It's her birthday and her dad's in
the ICU.

And you bought her the car, Grey.

"Okay. Good. Let's go."

WHILE ANA IS VISITING with Ray, I hole up in the waiting room
and make some calls. First, Andrea.

"Mr. Grey. Good morning."

"Good morning. What news?"

"Everyone is lined up to come to Portland. I'm liaising with
Stephan later this morning. I'm still waiting to hear from The
Heathman, and if they can't source a cake, I've found a bakery in
Portland that can do it today."

"Good work."

"Mr. and Mrs. Adams will take off at ten thirty this morning
Pacific time. They should be in Portland by four thirty."

"Do they know why we've moved the surprise party to Portland?"

"I haven't elaborated."

Good. I don't want Carla to spend the flight worrying about Ray.

Andrea continues, "Mrs. Adams said she's deliberately not contacting Mrs. Grey, to add to the surprise."

"Okay. Let me know when they've left Savannah."

"Will do."

"Thanks for organizing all this."

"It's a pleasure, sir. I hope Mr. Steele continues to improve."

"We'll talk later." I hang up and open the e-mail that has caught
my attention.

From: Grey, Carrick
Subject: Drunk Driver. Astoria PD.
Date: September 10 2011 09:37
To: Christian Grey

Your mother says that Raymond Steele is in good hands.
I'll be joining her later for Ana's birthday celebrations.
With regard to the driver, I have some information which I'd rather talk
you through, either in person or over the phone.
See you this evening, son.
Dad.

Carrick Grey, Partner
Grey, Krueger, Davis, and Holt LLP

I call Carrick but get his voice mail. I leave a message, then sit down and peruse the notes Ros has sent me regarding our meeting yesterday with the Hwangs.

Half an hour later my dad calls.

"Christian."

"Dad. Hello. You have news?" I stare out at the Portland skyline.

"I spoke with one of my contacts at the Astoria PD. The perpetrator's name is Jeffrey Lance. He's well known to the police, not only in Astoria but also in southeast Portland, where he's from. He lives in a trailer park there."

"He was a long way from home."

"His blood alcohol level was 0.28 percent."

"What does that mean?"

I turn around; unbeknownst to me, Ana has crept into the waiting room and is watching me warily.

"It means he was three and a half times over the legal limit," Dad says, pulling me back into the conversation.

"*How* far above the limit?" I don't believe it. *Fucking drunks. I loathe them.* From deep in that part of my brain that holds my most painful memories, the smell of stale Camel cigarette smoke, bourbon, and body odor seeps into my consciousness.

"*There you are, you little prick.*"

Fuck. The crack whore's pimp.

"Three and half times," Dad mutters, disgusted.

"I see."

"And it isn't his first offense. His driver's license was suspended. He has no insurance. The police are assessing all the charges and his lawyer is trying to get a plea bargain, but—"

"All charges, everything," I interrupt. My blood's boiling. *What an asshole.* "Ana's father is in the ICU. I want you to throw the fucking book at him, Dad."

"Son—I can't get involved, because of the family connection. But one of the women I work with specializes in this kind of law. With your permission, she can act on behalf of your father-in-law, and she'll press for the heaviest penalties."

I blow out a breath, trying to calm down. "Good," I mutter.

"I have to go, son. There's another call on the line. See you later."

"Keep me informed."

"Will do."

"The other driver?" Ana asks, when I've hung up.

"Some drunken asshole from southeast Portland."

Her eyes widen, probably at my tone, but Jeffrey Lance deserves it. Taking a deep breath to calm myself, I amble over to her. "Finished with Ray? Do you want to go?"

"Um, no." She looks anxious.

"What's wrong?"

"Nothing. Ray's being taken to radiology for a CT scan to check the swelling in his brain. I'd like to wait for the results."

"Okay. We'll wait." Sitting down, I hold out my arms and she climbs into my lap. I stroke her back and inhale the scent of her hair. It's soothing. "This is not how I envisaged spending today," I murmur against her temple.

"Me neither, but I'm feeling more positive now. Your mom was very reassuring. It was kind of her to come last night."

"My mom is an amazing woman." I continue caressing her back and rest my chin on her head.

"She is. You're very lucky to have her."

I couldn't agree more, Ana.

"I should call my mom. Tell her about Ray," she says.

Uh-oh. At this moment her mom should be en route to Portland.

"I'm surprised she hasn't called me." She frowns, and I feel a little guilty about my subterfuge.

"Maybe she did," I offer.

Ana fishes her phone out of her pocket but finds no missed calls. She looks through her texts, and from what I can see she's received birthday wishes from her friends, but as I suspected, nothing from her mother. She shakes her head.

"Call her now," I say, knowing she won't get a reply. Ana does, but she soon hangs up.

"She's not there. I'll call later when I know the results of the brain scan."

Drawing her closer, I kiss her hair. I long to tell her, but that would blow the surprise. My own phone buzzes. Without letting go of Ana, I tug it out of my pocket.

"Andrea."

"Mr. Grey. Just to let you know that Mr. and Mrs. Adams took off from Savannah fifteen minutes ago."

"Good."

"Taylor is primed to pick them up from the airport."

"ETA is what time?" I don't want Ana and me to run into them at the hotel.

"At present, four thirty-five."

"And the other, um"—I glance down at Ana, not wanting to give the game away—"packages?"

"They're all set. Your father is driving down. Your brother, sister, Kate, and Ethan Kavanagh will be flying down with Stephan. They can't leave until five thirty because of your sister's new job, but they should be with you by six thirty."

"Does The Heathman have all the details?"

"Rooms have been booked for all of them. Dinner is booked for twelve people at seven thirty. They are offering the full menu and a cake—chocolate, as requested."

"Good."

"Ros wanted to know if you got her notes on the shipyard deal. If you're happy with them, she can send the Heads of Agreement for signing."

"Yes. It can hold until Monday morning, but e-mail it just in case—I'll print, sign, and scan it back to you."

"Samir and Helena have an HR issue they want to discuss, and Marco needs two minutes."

"They can wait. Go home, Andrea."

I think I hear her smile on the end of the phone. "Is there anything else you need? I'm on my cell if you do."

"No, we're good, thank you." I hang up.

"Everything okay?" Ana asks.

"Yes."

"Is this your Taiwan thing?"

"Yes."

"Am I too heavy?"

As if! "No, baby."

She asks me if I'm worried about the Taiwan deal and I assure her I'm not.

"I thought it was important."

"It is. The shipyard here depends on it. There are lots of jobs at stake. We just have to sell it to the unions. That's Sam and Ros's job. But the way the economy's heading, none of us have a lot of choice."

Ana yawns.

"Am I boring you, Mrs. Grey?" Amused, I kiss her hair once more.

"No! Never. I'm just very comfortable on your lap," she murmurs. "I like hearing about your business."

"You do?"

"Of course. I like hearing any bit of information you deign to share with me." She smirks, and I know she's teasing me.

"Always hungry for more information, Mrs. Grey."

"Tell me." She rests her head against my chest again.

"Tell you what?"

"Why you do it."

"Do what?"

"Work the way you do."

I snort, amused, because it's obvious, isn't it? "A guy's got to earn a living."

"Christian, you earn more than a living," she says, her eyes as guileless as ever, demanding the truth.

"I don't want to be poor. I've done that. I'm not going back there again."

The hunger.

The insecurity.

The vulnerability.

…The fear.

Grey, lighten up. It's her birthday.

"Besides, it's a game. It's about winning. A game I've always found very easy."

"Unlike life," she mutters, almost to herself.

"Yes, I suppose." I've never thought of it that way. I smile at her. *Perceptive, Mrs. Grey.* "Though it's easier with you."

She hugs me. "It can't all be a game. You're very philanthropic."

I shrug. "About some things, maybe." *Ana, don't lionize me. I can afford to be generous.*

"I love philanthropic Christian," she whispers.

"Just him?"

"Oh, I love megalomaniac Christian, too, and control-freak Christian, sexpertise Christian, kinky Christian, romantic Christian, shy Christian—the list is endless."

"That's a whole lot of Christians."

"I'd say at least fifty."

I laugh. "Fifty Shades," I whisper into her hair.

"My Fifty Shades."

I sit back, tip her head up, and kiss her. "Well, Mrs. Shades, let's see how your dad is doing."

"Okay."

Dr. Sluder has good news. The swelling in Ray's brain has subsided, so she's decided to wake him from his coma tomorrow morning.

"I'm pleased with his progress. He's come a long way in a short period of time. His recovery is proceeding well. It's all good, Mrs. Grey."

"Thank you, Doctor," Ana gushes, her eyes shining with gratitude.

I take Ana's hand. "Let's go get some lunch."

"CAN WE GO FOR a drive?" she asks as she starts the ignition.

"Sure. It's your birthday—we can do anything you want." For a moment I'm transported to a parking lot in Seattle, where an insatiable Ana took matters into her own hands.

She stares at me, her eyes darkening. "Anything?" Her voice is husky.

"Anything," I offer.

"Well." Her tone is seductive. "I want to drive."

"Then drive, baby." We grin at each other like the fools we are, and I resist the urge to pounce on her.

Behave, Grey.

Ana steers us out of the lot, and at a sedate speed that keeps my blood pressure normal she takes us to I-5. Once there, she puts her foot down, throwing us back into our seats. *Damn!* She was lulling me into a false sense of security. "Ana! Steady, baby," I warn, and she slows down. We cruise over the bridge; luckily, the traffic is light. I stare down at the Willamette River and remember all the times I went running along its banks when I stayed in Portland during my pursuit of Miss Anastasia Steele.

And now here we are and she's Mrs. Anastasia Grey.

"Have you planned lunch?" she asks.

"No. You're hungry?" I hear the hope in my voice.

"Yes."

"Where do you want to go? It's your day, Ana."

"I know just the place."

She diverts off I-5, back across the river, and into downtown Portland. Eventually she pulls up outside the restaurant where we ate after José Rodriguez's photography exhibition. *The day I won her back.*

"For one minute I thought you were going to take me to that dreadful bar you drunk-dialed me from," I tease her.

"Why would I do that?"

"To check the azaleas are still alive." I give her a sideways look, and she blushes.

Oh, yes, baby. You vomited at my feet.

"Don't remind me! Besides, you still took me to your hotel room." Smirking, she lifts her chin in that stubborn, triumphant way that she has.

"Best decision I ever made."

"Yes. It was." She leans over and kisses me.

"Do you think that supercilious fucker is still waiting tables?" I ask.

"Supercilious? I thought he was fine."

"He was trying to impress you."

"Well, he succeeded."

Ana, you're too easily impressed.

"Shall we go see?" she says, amused.

"Lead on, Mrs. Grey."

I PINCH THE BRIDGE of my nose. For the last couple of hours I've been working in the confines of the ICU waiting room. Ana has been at Ray's bedside since we returned from lunch; last time I checked, she was reading to him. She's a kind and considerate daughter—he must have been a wonderful father to inspire such devotion.

I've read through the Shipyard Heads of Agreement, and I have a list of questions, which I've e-mailed to Ros. I'm not signing anything until we've spoken, but all that can wait until Monday at the earliest.

My phone buzzes. It's Taylor, calling to say he's delivered Ana's mother and her husband to The Heathman. I check the time, noting it's just after 5 p.m. Carla needs to know about Ray—I can't put that off any longer. Reluctantly, I call the hotel and ask to be put through to the Adamses' room.

I'm not looking forward to this.

"Hello," Carla answers.

I take a deep breath. "Carla, it's Christian."

"Christian," she gushes. "We had such a wonderful flight over here. Thank you so much."

"I'm glad you had a pleasant journey. I have some bad news, though."

"Oh no! Is Ana okay?"

"Ana's fine. It's Ray. He was involved in a car accident and he's in the ICU here in Portland. That's why we're in Portland and not Seattle. His condition is improving. Though he's in an induced coma at the moment, but he'll be coming out of it tomorrow."

"Oh no," she breathes. "How's Ana?"

"She's holding up. And because all the news from the ICU is good, I thought we'd go ahead and celebrate her birthday."

"Yes. Yes, of course."

"I thought you should know before this evening. But I'd still like to keep your arrival a surprise."

"Yes. Yes," she says. "I've deliberately not called or texted Ana to keep the surprise."

"I appreciate that, and I'm sorry to be the bearer of this news. It must be upsetting."

"No. Christian. Thank you for telling me. I'm very fond of Ray."

"I'll see you later this evening."

"Yes. You will. Bye for now." She hangs up.

That was not as bad as I anticipated.

It's time to go back to the hotel. I pack up my laptop, then stand and stretch. These are not the most comfortable seats.

Ana is still reading off her phone to Ray. I watch from the end of the bed as she caresses his hand and glances at him occasionally, her lovelight burning bright.

She notices me as Nurse Kellie approaches.

"It's time to go, Ana," I say gently.

She tightens her hold on Ray's hand, making it clear she doesn't want to leave him.

"I want to feed you. Come. It's late," I insist.

"I'm about to give Mr. Steele a sponge bath," Nurse Kellie says.

"Okay," Ana acquiesces. "We'll be back tomorrow morning." Leaning over, she kisses Ray's cheek.

SHE'S QUIET AND THOUGHTFUL as we walk across the parking lot.

"Do you want me to drive?" I ask.

Her face whips to mine. "No. I'm good," she says, and opens the driver's door.

There's my girl.

I grin and climb in beside her.

IN THE ELEVATOR SHE'S quiet again. Her mind is with Ray, I'm sure of it. Wrapping her in my arms, I offer her the only comfort I can.

Me. And the warmth of my body.

I hold her close as we travel up to our floor.

"I thought we'd dine downstairs. In a private room." I open the door to our suite and usher her in.

"Really? Finish what you started a few months ago?" Ana raises a brow.

"If you're very lucky, Mrs. Grey."

She laughs. "Christian, I don't have anything dressy to wear."

Oh, ye of little faith, Ana.

In the bedroom, I open the closet door. There, hanging where Sawyer said it would be, is a dress bag.

"Taylor?" Ana's surprised.

"Christian," I state, feeling a little aggrieved that she would doubt me.

She laughs, in that indulgent way she has sometimes, unzips the bag, and takes out the dress. She draws a sharp breath as she holds it up. "It's lovely," she says. "Thank you. I hope it fits."

"It will." *I hope.* "And here." From the depths of the closet I retrieve the box. "Shoes to match."

High-heeled fuck-me pumps. My favorite.

"You think of everything. Thank you." She kisses me, a sweet, chaste peck, and I flash her a quick grin, pleased.

"I do." I hand her a second, smaller Nordstrom bag that weighs nothing and seems to be all tissue. Ana ferrets around inside and discovers the black lace lingerie to complement the dress. Tilting her chin up, I plant a soft kiss on her lips. "I look forward to taking this off you later."

"So do I," she whispers, and her words inspire my cock.

Not now, Grey.

"Shall I run you a bath?" I ask.

"Please."

WHILE ANA IS SOAKING in the tub, I check with the hotel that all of Andrea's arrangements are in place. It seems she's thought of everything, right down to the decorations.

Give the woman a raise, Grey.

I have to wait for Ana, so I open my laptop, pull up Geolumara's P&L, and spend several minutes running through it.

Hmm…their sales could be better—but their cash deposits are healthy, given it's a fairly new company. However, with their considerable expenses their profit margins aren't as high as I would expect. We can get them there. I make a few notes of what we could do, until the sound of a hair dryer coming to life next door pulls me from the spreadsheet.

I've lost track of time.

Ambling into the bedroom I find a squeaky clean Ana sitting on the edge of the bed wrapped in a towel, drying her hair. "Here, let me," I offer, and point to the chair by the dressing table.

"Dry my hair?" Her disbelief is obvious.

Ana, this is not my first rodeo.

But I'm not sure she'd like to hear that I used to do this for my submissives as a reward for good behavior.

"Come," I coax her. She seats herself in the chair, throwing me a quizzical look in the mirror. But as I brush her hair she surrenders herself to my ministrations. It's an absorbing task, and I soon find myself lost in it…detangling strands of her hair, then drying them. It takes me back, much further back than I want to go.

To a small, shabby room in a slum in Detroit.

I halt those thoughts immediately.

"You're no stranger to this." Ana interrupts my reverie, and I smile at her in the mirror, but say nothing.

You don't want to know, Ana.

When I'm finished, her hair is soft and lush, capturing the light from a lamp on the dressing table.

Beautiful.

"Thank you," she says, shaking her head and letting her hair tumble down her back. I drop a kiss on her naked shoulder and tell her that I'll have a quick shower. She smiles, though I see her sadness and it makes me wonder if I've made the right decision to host this party.

Hell.

These thoughts weigh heavily on me as I step under the cascade of hot water.

So much so that I offer a silent prayer to God.

Make Ray better.

Please, Lord.

WHEN I COME OUT of the bathroom, Ana's waiting for me. She looks stunning. The dress fits perfectly, accentuating her beautiful body, and the bracelet sparkles on her wrist. She does a quick twirl, then stops so I can zip her up. "You look gorgeous, as you should on your birthday," I whisper.

She turns and places her hands on my naked chest. "So do you." She peeks up at me, through long lashes, in that way that heats my blood.

Ana.

"I'd better get dressed, before I change my mind about dinner and unzip that dress."

"You chose well, Mr. Grey."

"You wear it well, Mrs. Grey."

MIA HAS TEXTED TO let me know everyone has gathered in the room. Squeezing Ana's hand as we step out of the elevator onto the mezzanine level, I hope she likes surprises. I steer us toward the private dining rooms, my stunning wife seemingly oblivious to the admiring glances she's attracting. At the end of the corridor, I pause for the briefest moment before I open the door, then in we go—to a rousing chorus of "Surprise!"

Mom, Dad, Kate, Elliot, both Josés, Mia, Ethan, Bob, and Carla all raise their glasses, cheering, as we stand together before our family and friends. Ana turns and gawks at me. I grin, squeezing her hand, delighted that this has all come together, and Carla steps forward, sweeping Ana into her arms.

"Darling, you look beautiful. Happy birthday."

"Mom!" Ana sobs. It's a bittersweet sound and I step away to give them some privacy, and to greet the rest of our guests.

I'm actually pleased to see everyone—even José. He and his father are looking well rested, and less battered than yesterday. Elliot and Ethan rave about *Charlie Tango*, Mia and Kate about The Heathman.

"And I got to fly in your helicopter! Thank you so much!" Mia throws her arms around me. I ask her how her job's going. "So far so good." She grins. "Oh, my turn for Ana!" She darts off to pester my wife.

"Thanks for all this, Christian," Kate says. "I'm sure Ana appreciates it."

"I hope so."

When I return to her, Elliot has Ana in a tight embrace. Taking her hand, I ease her to my side. "Enough fondling my wife. Go fondle your fiancée," I say without rancor. Elliot winks at Kate.

A waiter presents Ana and me with flutes of rosé champagne—our usual, Grande Année, of course. I clear my throat; the general hum in the room dies down as everyone gives me their attention. "This would be a perfect day if Ray were here with us, but he's not far away. He's doing well, and I know he'd like you to enjoy yourself, Ana. To all of you—thank you for coming to share my beautiful wife's birthday, the first of many to come. Happy birthday, my love." I raise my glass to my girl, amid a chorus of "happy birthdays," and tears shine in her eyes.

Oh, baby.

I kiss her temple, longing to take her hurt away. "Good surprise?" I ask, suddenly nervous.

"Very good surprise. Thank you, you darling man." She raises her lips to mine, and I give her a quick, chaste peck, suitable for family viewing.

Ana is not her usual self during dinner—she's subdued, but I understand; she's worried about her father. She follows the conversations, laughs in the right places, and I *think* she's buoyed by the merriment of our family and friends. But deep down my girl is aching: she's pale, she's chewing her lip, and occasionally, she's distracted—probably lost in her dark thoughts.

I see her pain and I'm powerless to help.

It's frustrating.

She picks at her food, but I don't nag her. I'm just grateful she ate a hearty lunch.

Elliot and José are in top form. I had no idea the photographer had such a sharp sense of humor. Kate, too, has noticed Ana's state; she's solicitous, and during a hushed conversation I watch them laughing. Ana shows off her new bracelet and Kate makes the right appreciative noises. My feelings toward Kavanagh thaw a little more.

Make my wife laugh. She needs the distraction right now.

Finally, a magnificent chocolate cake with twenty-two candles ablaze is delivered by two waitstaff. Elliot starts a spirited rendition of "Happy Birthday," and we all join in. Ana's smile is wistful.

"Make a wish," I whisper to her, and she screws her eyes shut like a child might, then blows out every candle in one breath. She looks up at me, anxiously, and I know she's thinking of Ray. "He'll be fine, Ana. Just give him time."

BIDDING GOOD NIGHT TO all our guests, we wander up to our hotel room. I think the night has been a success. Ana seems more content, and I'm surprised, given the circumstances, how much I enjoyed everyone's company. I close the door to our suite and lean against it as Ana turns to face me. "Alone at last," I mutter.

She must be exhausted.

She steps toward me and runs her fingers over my lapels. "Thank you for a wonderful birthday. You really are the most thoughtful, considerate, generous husband."

"My pleasure."

"Yes, your pleasure. Let's do something about that," she whispers, and raises her lips to mine.

A na is curled up on the sofa in our suite, reading a manuscript that she's had printed out at the hotel. She's calm and focused, that little *v* forming between her brows as she scribbles her blue-penciled hieroglyphics in the margins. Occasionally she chews her plump lower lip, and I don't know if it's a judgment on what she's reading or if she's immersed in the narrative, but it has the usual effect on my body.

I want to bite that lip.

Smiling to myself, I remember my surprise wake-up call this morning. Ana is becoming more and more proactive when it comes to sex, but as the beneficiary of her passion, I'm not complaining. I think seeing her nearest and dearest at this difficult time has been therapeutic.

Having said that, it's been an emotional morning. After a convivial breakfast with our family and friends, we said good-bye to everyone, except Carla and Bob. My parents have driven back to Seattle; Stephan has flown Elliot, Mia, Kate, and Ethan back home in *Charlie Tango*. Ryan, who's still in Seattle, will pick them up at Boeing Field.

After everyone left, Carla, Ana, and I visited Ray. Well, Carla and Ana did; I gave them some privacy and worked in the waiting room until it was time to take Carla and Bob to the airport. We delivered them into the safe hands of First Officer Beighley and her copilot, who were standing by with the Gulfstream. Ana said a tearful farewell to her mother, and now we're back in our suite, cooling our heels after a light lunch. I think Ana is reading to distract herself from thinking about Ray.

I'd just like to go home.

But I guess that depends on Ray's recovery.

I hope he wakes shortly, and we can make plans to move him to

Seattle and return to Escala. I don't mention this to Ana, though—I don't want to add to her worries.

I've had my fill of reading, so to pass the time, I've started assembling a collage of photographs of my wife to use as a screensaver on my laptop and phone. I have so many photographs of her from our honeymoon—and in all of them, Ana is stunning. I'm delighted to have captured her in so many different moods: laughing, pensive, pouting, amused, relaxed, happy, and in some, she's scowling at me. Those are the photos that make me grin.

I'm reminded of the shock at seeing her image, large and lovely, at José Rodriguez's exhibition, and our conversation afterward.

I want you that relaxed with me.

I glance over at her again. Here she is. Relaxed. Absorbed in her work.

Mission accomplished, Grey.

We'll hang the other photographs in our new house, and maybe I'll put one of them in the study at Escala.

She looks up. "What?"

I tap my index finger against my lips and shake my head. "Nothing. How's the book?"

"It's a political thriller. Set in a dystopian surreal future."

"Sounds riveting."

"It is. It's a take on Dante's *Inferno* by a new writer who's based in Seattle. Boyce Fox." Ana's eyes shine, animated with the thrill of a good book.

"I can't wait to read it."

She smiles and returns to her manuscript.

Smiling, I return to my collage.

A LITTLE LATER SHE gets up and wanders over to me, her expression hopeful. "Can we go back?"

"Of course." I close my laptop, pleased with my photomontage of Mrs. Anastasia Grey.

"Will you drive?" she asks.

"Sure." Taylor is visiting his daughter, and I've given Sawyer the day off.

"I want to grab a copy of *The Oregonian* on the way, so I can read Dad the sports page."

"Good idea. I'm sure they'll have one at reception. Let's go." I grab my jacket and my laptop, and we head out.

RAY LIES PEACEFULLY ASLEEP in his hospital bed, and it takes a few seconds for Ana and me to realize that he's no longer on a ventilator. The repetitive, measured blast of air that had been his constant companion is no more; he's breathing on his own. Ana's face glows in relief. With infinite tenderness she strokes his stubbled chin and wipes his spittle with a tissue.

I look away.

I'm intruding. This wordless expression of love from a daughter to her father is too intimate for me to witness. I know Ray would be mortified if he knew I was standing here watching him at his most vulnerable. I stalk off to find one of his doctors for an update. Nurse Kellie and her colleague Liz are at the nurses' station. "Dr. Sluder is in surgery." Kellie picks up the phone. "She's due out any minute. Do you want me to page her?"

"No. That's fine. Thanks." I leave both nurses and head back to the all-too-familiar waiting room. Again, I'm here alone; slumping into one of the chairs I open my laptop and pull up the latest iteration of my Ana collage. I've decided I want to add a few photographs from our wedding.

I'm completely absorbed in the task when Ana bursts into the room, dragging me from the screen. Her eyes are red-rimmed from fresh tears, but she's brimming with elation. "He's awake," she exclaims.

Thank God. At last.

Setting aside my laptop, I stand up to embrace her. "How is he?"

She snuggles against my chest, her eyes closed, as she wraps her arms around me. "Talking, thirsty, bewildered. He doesn't remember the accident at all."

"That's understandable. Now that he's awake, I want to get him moved to Seattle. Then we can go home, and my mom can keep an eye on him."

"I'm not sure he's well enough to be moved."

"I'll talk to Dr. Sluder. Get her opinion."

"You miss home?" Ana looks up at me.

"Yes." *Very much.*

"Okay." She smiles, and together we return to the ward, where we find Ray is sitting up in bed. He looks a little shell-shocked, and frankly embarrassed that I'm there.

"Ray. It's good to see you back with us."

"Thanks, Christian," he grumbles. "Awful lot of trouble for you kids to be here."

"Dad, it's no trouble. We don't want to be anywhere else." Ana tries to reassure him.

Dr. Sluder joins us, bristling with efficiency. "Mr. Steele. Welcome back," she says.

"YOU HAVEN'T STOPPED SMILING." I tuck a strand of Ana's hair behind her ear as she pulls up outside The Heathman in the R8.

"I'm very relieved. And happy." She flashes me a smile.

"Good." We climb out and Ana hands her keys to the valet. It's getting darker and cooler and Ana shivers, so I drape my arm around her shoulders, and we wander into the hotel. From the foyer, I eye the Marble Bar. "Shall we celebrate?"

"Celebrate?" Ana frowns.

"Your dad."

She chuckles. "Oh, him."

"I've missed that sound." I kiss her hair.

"Can we just eat in our room? You know, have a quiet night in?"

"Sure. Come." Taking her hand, we walk to the elevators.

ANA DEVOURS HER DINNER. "That was delicious." She pushes her plate away. "They sure know how to make a fine tarte tatin here."

That they do, Ana. "That's the most I've seen you eat the entire time we've been here."

"I was hungry." She sits back, replete, and it's most gratifying to witness. She's fresh and clean from our bath earlier and wearing nothing but my T-shirt and her panties. She's all eyes and smiles and ponytail and legs…especially legs.

Lifting my glass of wine, I take a sip. "What would you like to do now?" I keep my tone gentle, and hopefully a little seductive. My iPod is playing some serene tunes in the background. I know what I want to do, but she's had an emotional day.

"What do *you* want to do?"

Is this a trick question?

I raise a brow, amused. "What I always want to do."

"And that is?"

"Mrs. Grey, don't be coy."

She purses her lips with her secret smile and, reaching across the table, grasps my hand and turns it over. With great care, she skates her index finger over my palm, which tingles in response. It's an odd feeling that takes my breath away.

"I'd like you to touch me with this." Her voice is low and provocative as her fingertip continues brushing over my index finger.

Her touch echoes. *Everywhere.*

Fuck.

I shift in my chair. "Just that?"

"Maybe this." She traces a line along my middle finger and back to my palm. "And this." She weaves a path up to my wedding ring. "Definitely this." She stops, her finger pressed against my platinum ring. "This is very sexy."

"Is it, now?"

"It sure is. It says 'this man is mine.'"

Hell. I'm hard.

Yes. Ana. Yours.

Using her fingernail, she outlines the small callus that's formed where my palm rubs against my ring, her eyes on mine. Her pupils dilate—the dark overcoming the bright blue.

She beguiles me.

Leaning forward, I capture her chin in my hand. "Mrs. Grey, are you seducing me?"

"I hope so."

"Anastasia, I'm a given." *Always.* "Come here." I pull her into my lap and hold her. "I like having unfettered access to you." To prove it, I run my hand up her naked thigh to her behind, then clasping the nape of her neck with my other hand, I angle her head and kiss her. Thoroughly. Exploring her mouth and savoring the feel of her tongue against mine, as her fingers find my hair.

She tastes of apple pie and Ana.

With a hint of fine Chablis.

It's a stimulating combination in every sense. We're both breathing hard when I pull away. "Let's go to bed," I whisper against her lips.

"Bed?" she scoffs.

Oh!

I lean back and tug her hair so I'm looking directly into her eyes. "Where would you prefer, Mrs. Grey?"

She shrugs, nonchalant. Challenging. "Surprise me."

"You're feisty this evening." I run my nose down hers while a list of possibilities forms in my mind.

"Maybe I need to be restrained."

"Maybe you do. You're getting mighty bossy in your old age."

"What are you going to do about it?" She squares her shoulders, in that way she does, ready for battle.

Oh, Ana. "I know what I'd like to do about it. Depends if you're up to it."

"Oh, Mr. Grey, you've been very gentle with me these last couple of days. I'm not made of glass, you know."

"You don't like gentle?"

"With you, of course. But you know…variety is the spice of life." She flutters her eyelashes.

"You're after something less gentle?"

"Something life-affirming."

Wow. "Life-affirming?" Astonished, I gaze at her, as all manner of sexual scenarios pop most welcome into my mind. She nods, gazing into my eyes and teasing her lower lip with her teeth.

On purpose.

She's goading me.

She wants life-affirming, I can oblige. "Don't bite your lip." I tighten my grip on her and rise, holding her close. She gasps in surprise and grabs my arms while I carry her across the room and settle her on the farthest sofa.

I have a plan. I want to see how far her newfound sexual confidence extends.

And I want to watch.

"Wait here. Don't move." She turns her head, her eyes tracking me as I head to the bedroom. I scan the room and remember one of the presents she opened this morning at breakfast—some fancy toiletries from Kate. In the smart presentation box, I discover a small bottle of scented moisturizing oil, dark amber and sandalwood.

Perfect. I slip it into the rear pocket of my jeans. From the bathroom I retrieve both belts from our hotel bathrobes and grab one of the largest bath towels.

Back in the living room, I'm pleased to find Ana has stayed on the couch.

Obedience! At last!

She can't see me as I approach her from behind, or hear me, as I'm barefoot. She gasps when I lean over and grab the hem of her T-shirt. "I think we'll dispense with this." I drag it over her head and toss it on the floor, admiring how her nipples peak in response to the brush of the material and the cooler temperature in the room. I grab her ponytail, tipping her head back and claiming her mouth with a brief kiss.

"Stand up," I murmur against her skin. She obliges, naked except for her panties. I lay the towel over the sofa, not wishing to get oil, or anything else, on the fabric.

"Take your panties off." I look directly at Ana. She swallows, but with her eyes fixed on mine she obeys, without hesitating.

I like this version of Ana.

"Sit."

She does as she's told, and I grasp her ponytail once more, twirling her soft hair between my fingers. I tug it, pulling back her head, and stand over her. "You'll tell me to stop if this gets too much, yes?"

She nods.

Damn it, Ana. "Say it."

"Yes," she answers, her voice a little shrill and breathy, betraying her excitement.

I smirk and pitch my voice low. "Good. So, Mrs. Grey—by

popular demand, I'm going to restrain you." I've chosen this, the only sofa that has finials, for a reason. "Bring your knees up. And sit right back." Once more she complies, without hesitation. Taking her left leg, I wrap a belt from one of the robes around her lower thigh and tie a slip knot above her knee.

"Bathrobes?" Ana asks.

"I'm improvising." I tie the other end to the finial at the back left-hand corner of the sofa and tug, parting her thighs. "Don't move." I do the same with her right leg, tying the other belt to the back-right finial.

Ana is splayed out, her legs spread wide, revealing all she has to offer, her hands by her sides.

"Okay?" I ask, drinking in the view from above.

She nods and looks up at me, soft, sweet, vulnerable. *Mine.*

Bending down, I kiss her. "You have no idea how hot you look right now." I rub my nose against hers, fighting my anticipation of what's to come. "Change of music, I think." I wander over to my iPod.

I scroll through artists. Select a track. Press repeat and play.

"Sweet About Me." Perfect.

As Gabriella Cilmi's sugared, sultry voice fills the room, I turn and lock eyes with my trussed-up, naked wife and saunter back to her. Her gaze doesn't leave mine, as I sink down onto my knees in front of her, to worship at her altar.

Her mouth parts as she inhales.

Oh, Ana. Let's see how far your confidence has grown.

I know what she's feeling. "Exposed? Vulnerable?" I ask.

She licks her lips and nods.

"Good," I whisper.

Baby, you've got this. "Hold out your hands." From my back pocket I withdraw the small bottle of oil. Ana holds up her cupped palms and I pour a little oil into her hands. The scent is heavy but not unpleasant. "Rub your hands."

She wriggles on the couch.

Oh, this will never do. "Keep still," I warn.

Ana stops squirming.

"Now, Anastasia, I want you to touch yourself."

She blinks—surprised, I think.

"Start at your throat and work down."

Her teeth dig into that bottom lip.

"Don't be shy, Ana. Come. Do it."

Come on, Ana.

She places her hands on either side of her neck, then glides them down to the tops of her breasts, leaving a slick shine over her skin in their wake.

"Lower," I whisper.

After a beat, her hands embrace her breasts.

"Tease yourself."

Tentatively, her darkening eyes on mine, she takes each of her nipples between thumb and forefinger and gently tugs on both.

"Harder," I urge her, feeling like the serpent in the garden. "Like I would," I add, gripping my own thighs to keep myself from touching her. She groans in response and squeezes and tugs harder. I watch each pucker and lengthen under her touch.

Damn, she's hot.

"Yes. Like that. Again."

She closes her eyes and moans, and rolls and twists them between her fingers and thumbs.

"Open your eyes." My voice is hoarse.

She blinks them open.

"Again," I order. "I want to see you. See you enjoy your touch."

She continues, her eyes clouded with dark longing—her breathing increasing as desire consumes her—while my yearning matches hers.

This must be making her so wet...

My pants are getting tighter by the second. *Enough.* "Hands. Lower."

She squirms.

"Keep still, Ana. Absorb the pleasure. Lower."

"You do it," she whispers.

"Oh, I will. Soon. You. Lower. Now." She has no idea how fucking hot she looks right now. She glides her hands beneath her breasts, over her stomach, toward her belly, as she writhes, pulling on the robe restraints.

No. No. I shake my head. "Still." Placing my hands on each of her knees, I hold her in place. "Come on, Ana—lower." Her hands slide down to her belly.

"Lower," I mouth.

"Christian, please," she begs. I skim my hands from her knees, along her thighs, toward the exposed junction at the top of her legs.

My end goal.

Her goal.

"Come on, Ana. Touch yourself."

Her left hand grazes her vulva, then she starts to rub her fingers in a slow circle over her clitoris. "Ah!" she breathes, her mouth forming a badly drawn *o*.

"Again." The word is a whisper and a command.

She groans, gasping for air, and closes her eyes, tipping her head back against the sofa as her hand moves.

"Again."

She groans again, and I don't want her to come without me. Grabbing her hands, I hold them firmly, and bend down between her thighs, running my nose and tongue over her clitoris. Back and forth. Again. Taking her higher.

She's so wet. Dripping with her lust.

"Ah!" she cries and tries to move her hands. I tighten my fingers around her wrists while I continue my sensual onslaught.

"I'll restrain these, too. Keep still," I breathe, against her most intimate place.

Ana groans, and I release her, then slowly ease two fingers inside her.

So wet.

So ready.

So greedy.

The heel of my hand pushes up against her clitoris.

"I'm going to make you come quickly, Ana. Ready?"

"Yes," she breathes, nodding frantically.

I move my hand. Hard. Fast. Stimulating her both inside and out. She mewls above me. Her head twisting to and fro, her toes curling, and her fingers clawing at the towel beneath her. I know she wants to straighten her legs to lessen the intense feeling. But she can't; she's close.

So close.

But I don't stop.

And I feel it.

The beginning.

Of the end.

Her orgasm. Coming.

"Surrender," I whisper, and she cries out. Loud and proud, and I press the heel of my hand against her clitoris, and ride out her orgasm, which goes on and on.

Wow. Ana.

With my other hand I untie the robe belts, one at a time.

As she descends back to earth, I murmur, "My turn." Withdrawing my fingers from inside her, I ease back and I flip her over so she's facedown on the sofa, her knees on the floor. I yank open my jeans, spread her legs with my knee, and slap her hard across her beautiful backside.

"Ah!" she cries, and I drive into her, as deep as I can. She cries out again.

"Oh, Ana," I breathe, and gripping her hips, I start to move. Hard. Fast.

Again. Taking my pleasure. She wanted it rough.

We. Aim. To. Please.

I drive into her. Losing myself. In her. *So in her.*

Her cries taking me higher.

Fuck.

She's building again.

I feel it.

"Come on, Ana!" I shout, and she comes once more, taking me over the edge with her.

I EASE HER OFF the sofa and we lie down on the floor, where she sprawls on top of me, facing the ceiling. We're quiet, catching our collective breath.

"Life-affirming enough for you?" I ask eventually, as I kiss her hair.

"Oh, yes." Her hands settle on my thighs, and she tugs at the material of my jeans. "I think we should go again. No clothes for you this time."

Again! "Christ, Ana. Give a man a chance."

She giggles, and I can't help laughing with her. "I'm glad Ray's conscious. Seems all your appetites are back."

She turns over, still on top of me, and scowls. "Are you forgetting about last night and this morning?" she pouts and rests her chin on her hands, on my chest.

"Nothing forgettable about either of those." I grin and grab her bountiful behind with both hands. "You have a fantastic ass, Mrs. Grey."

"So do you." She arches a brow. "Though yours is still under cover."

"And what are you going to do about that, Mrs. Grey?"

"Why, I'm going to undress you, Mr. Grey. All of you."

Her enthusiasm is infectious.

"And I think there's a lot that's sweet about you," she whispers, repeating the song lyric, her eyes radiating her warmth and love.

Shit.

"You are," she stresses, and kisses the corner of my mouth. Closing my eyes, I tighten my arms around her.

Why are you talking about this?

"Christian, you are. You made this weekend so special—in spite of what happened to Ray. Thank you."

Large, luminous eyes meet mine.

"Because I love you," I murmur.

"I know," she says. "I love you, too." She runs her fingertips down my cheek. "And you're precious to me, too. You do know that, don't you?"

Precious. *Me?*

Suddenly, I'm helpless and panicked. And completely disarmed.

What do I say?

Not now, Maggot.

Fuck. I close my eyes. I don't want that in my head.

"Believe me," she whispers, and I open them once more, gray eyes to blue.

"It's not easy." My words are almost inaudible.

I don't want to talk about this.

It's too raw. Right now. For some reason I don't understand.

She holds such power over me. That's why.

"Try. Try hard, because it's true." She caresses my face, and I know she means what she says. If only I could hear it without panicking inside.

"You'll get cold. Come." I move her to one side and stand, pulling her to her feet, too.

Leaving the detritus of our lovemaking, Ana slips her arm around me. I switch off the iPod and we stroll back into the bedroom, while I wonder about my reaction.

Why is it still so hard to hear her declarations of love sometimes?

I shake my head.

"Shall we watch TV?" Ana asks, and I know she's trying to recapture our former levity.

"I was hoping for round two."

She eyes me speculatively. "Well, in that case, I think I'll be in charge."

Oh!

She pushes me suddenly with such force that I fall onto the bed. Before I know it, she's straddled me and is pinning my arms down on either side of my head.

"Well, Mrs. Grey, now that you've got me, what are you going to do with me?"

Leaning down, her breath tickling my ear, she whispers, "I am going to fuck you with my mouth."

Oh boy.

I close my eyes as she runs her teeth along my jaw, and I surrender to her. I surrender to the love of my life.

Ana is still asleep when I step out of the en suite. Frankly, I'm not surprised; she was persistent last night.

Sex-mad and insatiable indeed.

I'm not complaining.

That delectable memory fresh in my mind, I gather my clothes together and step into the living room to get dressed. The remnants from last night's tryst are still all over the sofa. I untie the bathrobe belts and grab the towel, wondering what housekeeping would have made of this scenario if they'd come in early to clean. Folding the items, I place them on the console beside the bedroom door.

I order breakfast—it will take half an hour and I'm hungry. To distract myself, I sit down at the desk and open my laptop. Today, I want to arrange moving Ray to Northwest Hospital, where my mother can watch over him. I fire up my e-mails, and to my surprise there's one from Detective Clark. He has questions for Ana about that asshole Hyde.

What the hell?

I send a brief reply to let him know we're in Portland and he'll have to wait until we return to Seattle. I call my mom and leave a message about moving Ray, then breeze through my other e-mails. There's one from Ros: the Hwangs are inviting us to visit later this week.

That will depend on Ray.

I guess.

I e-mail Ros to say that it's likely that I'll be able to go, but I can't confirm yet, as we're not sure what's happening with my father-in-law.

I don't want to leave Ana to deal with this on her own.

As I press send, I receive a reply from Clark.

He's coming to Portland.

Shit.

What can be that important?

"Good morning." Ana's sweet tone interrupts my thoughts. When I turn around she's standing in the bedroom doorway, wearing nothing but a sheet and a shy smile. Her hair is a tousled mess that falls to her breasts, her bright eyes intent on me.

She looks like a Greek goddess.

"Mrs. Grey. You're up early." I hold out my arms, and in spite of the sheet, she bolts across the room, offering me a welcome flash of legs, and lands in my lap.

"As are you," she says.

I cradle her against me and kiss her hair. "I was just working."

"What?" she asks, leaning back to scrutinize me. She knows something is off.

I blow out a breath. "I got an e-mail from Detective Clark. He wants to talk to you about that fucker Hyde."

"Really?"

"Yes. I told him you're in Portland for the time being, so he'll have to wait. But he says he'd like to interview you here."

"He's coming here?"

"Apparently so."

She frowns. "What's so important that it can't wait?"

"Exactly."

"When's he coming?"

"Today. I'll e-mail him back."

"I have nothing to hide. I wonder what he wants to know?"

"We'll find out when he gets here. I'm intrigued, too." I move in my chair. "Breakfast will be here shortly. Let's eat, then we can go see your dad."

"You can stay here if you want. I can see you're busy."

"No, I want to come with you."

"Okay." She grins, pleased, I think, that I want to accompany her. She kisses me, then waltzes back toward the bedroom and, with a suggestive glance at me, lets the sheet drop as she crosses the doorway.

Damn. Goddess indeed.

That's my cue. E-mails and breakfast can wait.

I follow her into the bedroom to make good on her invitation.

RAY IS AWAKE, BUT it would appear that he's not in the best of tempers. After saying good morning, I leave Ana to deal with him and head to the waiting room—my new office, or so it seems. I've already received tentative approval from Dr. Sluder to move Ray to Seattle, and I'm waiting for my mother to confirm that there's a bed for him at Northwest before I organize the helicopter transfer. Dr. Sluder thinks we can relocate him as early as tomorrow, but she'll confirm that later today, once she's run more tests.

I call Andrea.

"Good morning, Mr. Grey."

"Andrea, hello. I'm hoping we can move Raymond Steele tomorrow. Can you find an air ambulance service, please? Portland OHSU to Northwest Hospital. My mother should know a reliable company. I'll ask Ray's doctor if there's any specific medical equipment that should be on board. Either she or I will send that through."

"I'll call Dr. Grey."

"Do. I'm waiting to hear from her if there's a room available."

"Okay, I'll take care of it."

"Taiwan. Ros and I may fly out on Thursday evening. We'll need the jet."

"You're at WSU on Thursday morning."

"I know. But get Stephan and the crew prepped. It's still tentative."

"Yes, sir. Actually, Ros wants a word."

"Okay. Thanks. Put me through."

Ros and I have a quick catch-up and decide that signatures on the Heads of Agreement for the Taiwan shipyard can wait until tomorrow, when I'm hopefully back in Seattle. As soon as I hang up, my phone buzzes. It's Clark.

"Mr. Grey. Thank you for seeing me today. Is four o'clock a good time?"

"Sure. We're at The Heathman."

"I'll see you then."

Ana wanders into the waiting room. She looks serious.

Is there a problem?

"Okay," I respond to Clark, and hang up. "Clark will be here at four this afternoon."

She frowns. "Okay. Ray wants coffee and doughnuts."

I laugh, not expecting that response. "I think I would, too, if I'd been in an accident. Ask Taylor to go."

"No, I'll go."

"Take Taylor with you."

Ana rolls her eyes. "Okay." She sounds like an exasperated teen.

I smirk and cock my head to one side. "There's no one here."

Her eyes widen a fraction as she catches my drift; her interest is clearly piqued. She sets her shoulders as if she's going to challenge me and raises that stubborn Steele chin.

A young couple enters the room behind her and the man has his arms around his weeping companion. The woman is visibly distraught. *Shit, something is seriously wrong.*

Ana's eyes widen with compassion, then she turns to me and lifts a shoulder in regret.

Oh. Maybe she was game for a spanking. The thought is appealing. *Very appealing.*

Picking up my laptop, I take her hand, and we head out of the room. "They need the privacy more than we do," I mutter. "We'll have our fun later."

Taylor is outside, waiting in the car. "Let's all go get coffee and doughnuts," I say. We could use a treat.

Ana returns my smile. "Voodoo Doughnut in Portland. Best doughnuts in the world," she says, and climbs into the back of the SUV.

DETECTIVE CLARK IS PUNCTUAL. Taylor shows him into our suite and he wanders in, looking as rumpled and curmudgeonly as ever. "Mr. Grey, Mrs. Grey, thank you for seeing me."

"Detective Clark." I shake his hand and direct him to sit down, then step over to join Ana on the sofa that I tied her to last night.

"It's Mrs. Grey I wish to see," Clark says, his tone a little abrasive, and I know he's addressing Taylor and me.

Oh. Now I definitely want to hear what he has to say.

I nod to Taylor, who acknowledges my cue and leaves, closing the door behind him.

"Anything you wish to say to my wife you can say in front of me." If this is about Hyde, I'm not leaving my wife's side.

"Are you sure you'd like your husband to be present?" Clark asks Ana.

She looks puzzled. "Of course. I have nothing to hide. You are just interviewing me?"

"Yes, ma'am."

"I'd like my husband to stay."

There. Told you so. I glare at him, pleased that Ana has taken my side. I sit down beside her, trying to mask my simmering irritation.

"All right," murmurs Clark. He coughs to clear his throat, and I wonder if he's nervous. "Mrs. Grey, Mr. Hyde maintains that you sexually harassed him and made several lewd advances toward him."

What the fuck!

Ana looks both shocked and amused at once. She places her hand on my thigh, but it doesn't stop me. "That's preposterous," I exclaim. Her fingernails dig into my leg—I suspect in an attempt to shut me up.

"That's not true." Ana looks him squarely in the eye, the embodiment of serenity as she addresses Clark. "In fact, it was the other way around. He propositioned me in a very aggressive manner, and he was fired."

Clark's mouth flattens, as if he'd been expecting this response. "Hyde alleges that you fabricated a tale about sexual harassment in order to get him fired. He says that you did this because he refused your advances and because you wanted his job."

Ana's face twists in disgust. "That's not true."

This is fucking absurd.

"Detective, please don't tell me you have driven all this way to harass my wife with these ridiculous accusations."

Clark graces me with a resigned look. "I need to hear this from Mrs. Grey, sir." Ana grasps my thigh again, and I know she wants me to shut up.

"You don't have to listen to this shit, Ana."

"I think I should let Detective Clark know what happened." She pins me with bright blue eyes, imploring me to shut the fuck up.

Okay, baby. Have it your way.

Waving at her to continue, I endeavor to stay quiet and keep my temper in check. She folds her hands in her lap and continues, "What Hyde says is simply not true." Her voice rings calm and clear through the room. "Mr. Hyde accosted me in the office kitchen one evening. He told me that it was thanks to him that I'd been hired, and that he expected sexual favors in return. He tried to blackmail me, using e-mails that I'd sent to Christian, who wasn't my husband then. I didn't know Hyde had been monitoring my e-mails. He's delusional. He even accused me of being a spy sent by Christian, presumably to help him take over the company. He didn't know that Christian had already bought SIP." She shakes her head and knits her hands together. "In the end, I–I took him down."

"Took him down?" Clark interjects, puzzled.

"My father is ex-army. Hyde, um, touched me, and I know how to defend myself." Her eyes flick to mine, and I can't hide my pride and awe for my girl.

Don't mess with my girl.

She's a warrior.

"I see." Clark huffs out a breath and sits back on the sofa.

"Have you spoken to any of Hyde's former personal assistants?" I ask. I'm curious to know if the cops have made more progress than Welch.

"Yes, we have. But the truth is, we can't get any of his assistants to talk to us. They all say he was an exemplary boss, even though none of them lasted more than three months."

Damn. "We've had that problem, too. My security chief, he's interviewed Hyde's past five PAs."

This news piques Clark's interest. He frowns, his eyes boring into me. "And why's that?"

"Because my wife worked for him, and I run security checks on anyone my wife works with."

Clark's face reddens. "I see." His bushy brows draw together. "I think there's more to this than meets the eye, Mr. Grey. We are conducting a more thorough search of his apartment tomorrow, so maybe something will present itself then. Though by all accounts he hasn't lived there for some time."

"You've searched already?"

"Yes. We're doing it again. A fingertip search this time."

"You've still not charged him with the attempted murder of Ros Bailey and myself?"

Maybe that's the FBI's prerogative?

"We're hoping to find more evidence in regard to the sabotage of your aircraft, Mr. Grey. We need more than a partial print, and while he's in custody, we can build a case."

"Is this all you came down here for?"

Clark stiffens. "Yes, Mr. Grey, it is, unless you've had any further thoughts about the note?"

Again, Ana's eyes scrutinize mine, but this time she's frowning.

"No. I told you. It means nothing to me." *My wife does not need to know about that!* "And I don't see why we couldn't have done this over the phone."

"I think I told you, I prefer a hands-on approach. And," he adds, slightly sheepishly, "I'm visiting my great-aunt, who lives in Portland. Two birds—one stone."

"Well, if we're all done, I have work to attend to." I stand, hoping that Clark will take the hint.

He does. "Thank you for your time, Mrs. Grey."

Ana nods.

"Mr. Grey."

I open the door and he shuffles out.

Thank fuck.

Ana leans back into the sofa.

"Can you believe that asshole?" I run my hands through my hair.

"Clark?" Ana says.

"No. That fucker, Hyde."

"No, I can't." She looks bemused.

"What's his fucking game?"

"I don't know. Do you think Clark believed me?"

"Of course he did. He knows Hyde is a fucked-up asshole—"

"You're very sweary," Ana chastises me.

"Sweary? Is that even a word?"

"It is now."

And just like that, her humor smothers my anger, and it's gone.

Marveling at the spell she casts, I sit down beside her and pull her into my arms. "Don't think about that fucker. Let's go see your dad and try to talk about the move tomorrow."

"He was adamant that he wanted to stay in Portland and not be a bother," Ana says.

"I'll talk to him."

She fingers the buttons on my shirt. "I want to travel with him."

That should be possible. "Okay. I'll come, too. Sawyer and Taylor can take the cars. I'll let Sawyer drive your R8 tonight."

She offers me a sweet smile of thanks, and I feel ten feet tall.

RAY HAS CAPITULATED; HE'S in far better spirits than he was this morning. The doughnuts must have worked their magic, and I think he's secretly pleased that he'll get to ride in a helicopter tomorrow. He doesn't remember anything of his flight here from Astoria. I make a mental note to take him up in *Charlie Tango* at some point.

While Ana sits with him, I head to the waiting room to finalize Ray's move.

Andrea has everything organized. She is, without doubt, the best PA I've ever had.

"Thanks, Andrea."

"You're welcome, Mr. Grey. Anything else?"

"No, it's all good. Go home."

"Will do, sir."

I fire off a quick e-mail to Samir to review Andrea's salary and recommend a generous raise.

Before I head back to the ward, I reflect on Clark's visit and what he did and didn't say. He's obviously liaising with the FBI with regard to *Charlie Tango*'s sabotage, but mentioned that he's searching Hyde's apartment again. Why? Does he have another lead? Or is it something else that he's not telling us? And where *was* Hyde while he was planning his kidnap attempt? It's obvious he was still in Seattle; I have the CCTV footage to prove it. This is worth exploring.

I e-mail Welch and Barney and ask them if they tracked the movements of the white van that Hyde used before he arrived at Escala.

Perhaps they'll come up with something.

I hang up from my phone conversation with my mother and catch Ana's monochrome eye. She's gazing down at me from my office wall with her disarming smile, her eyes bright and brimming with intelligence. It's been only three hours since I saw her, but I miss her already. I wonder what she's doing right now? She's probably at work and if all has gone to plan, Ray should be settled in his room at Northwest Hospital where my mother will keep an eye on him. I hope he's comfortable, or as comfortable as he can be. He seemed to enjoy the flight from OHSU to Boeing Field, but he's not a man who likes to be the center of attention—quite the opposite, in fact. A little like his daughter.

And here I am, missing her.

Last time I saw her, she was heading to the hospital in an ambulance with her father.

I glance at my watch.

She'll definitely be at work.

I type a quick e-mail.

From: Christian Grey
Subject: Missing You
Date: September 13 2011 13:58
To: Anastasia Grey

Mrs. Grey
I've been back in the office for only three hours, and I'm missing you already.
Hope Ray has settled into his new room okay. Mom is going to see him this afternoon and check up on him.
I'll collect you around six this evening, and we can go see him before heading home.
Sound good?

Your loving husband

Christian Grey
CEO, Grey Enterprises Holdings, Inc.

I press send, then open the report on my desk and start to read. But almost immediately the ping of a new e-mail distracts me. Ana? No. It's from Barney.

From: Barney Sullivan
Subject: Jack Hyde
Date: September 13 2011 14:09
To: Christian Grey

CCTV around Seattle tracks the white van from South Irving Street. Before that I can find no trace, so Hyde must have been based in that area.

As Welch has told you, the unsub car was rented with a false license by an unknown female, though nothing that ties it to the South Irving Street area.

Details of known GEH and SIP employees who live in the area are in the attached file, which I have forwarded to Welch, too.

There was nothing on Hyde's SIP computer about his former PAs.

As a reminder, here is a list of what was retrieved from Hyde's SIP computer.

Greys' Home Addresses:
Five properties in Seattle
Two properties in Detroit

Detailed Résumés for:
Carrick Grey
Elliot Grey
Christian Grey
Dr. Grace Trevelyan
Anastasia Steele
Mia Grey

Newspaper and online articles relating to:
Dr. Grace Trevelyan
Carrick Grey
Christian Grey
Elliot Grey

Photographs:
Carrick Grey
Dr. Grace Trevelyan
Christian Grey
Elliot Grey
Mia Grey

I'll continue my investigation, see what else I can find.

B Sullivan
Head of IT, GEH

I gaze at the contents of his e-mail and wonder when Hyde started scouring the internet for information on my family. Was it before Ana started working with him? Or was it after he'd met me? I'm about to pen a response to Barney when Ana's reply to my earlier e-mail pops into my inbox.

From: Anastasia Grey
Subject: Missing You
Date: September 13 2011 14:10
To: Christian Grey

Sure.
x

Anastasia Grey
Editor, SIP

Oh. Feeling a tad deflated, I glance at the enigmatic, smiling goddess on the wall. I thought we might indulge in some e-mail banter.
She's normally so good at that.
This is not like her.

From: Christian Grey
Subject: Missing You
Date: September 13 2011 14:14
To: Anastasia Grey

Are you okay?

Christian Grey
CEO, Grey Enterprises Holdings, Inc.

While I wait for her reply, I sift through the address file that Barney has attached to his e-mail. A couple of GEH employee names, and one from SIP, jump out at me: the highest-profile name is Elizabeth Morgan, the HR director at SIP. Her name stirs something in the back of my brain, but whatever it is, it remains elusive. I'll ask Welch to follow up on her when we next speak, but it's hard to conceive that any of these people could be involved with Hyde.

I dismiss that train of thought and wonder what's up with Ana. I'm tempted to pick up the phone and call her, but as I reach for it, another e-mail arrives from her.

From: Anastasia Grey
Subject: Missing You
Date: September 13 2011 14:17
To: Christian Grey

Fine. Just busy.
See you at six.
x

Anastasia Grey
Editor, SIP

Of course she's busy. She's missed a few days of work, and my girl is nothing but conscientious.

Grey, keep it together.

I go back to Barney's e-mail and read through his list one more time. It doesn't yield any further insights, but maybe he can answer a question for me.

From: Christian Grey
Subject: Jack Hyde
Date: September 13 2011 14:23
To: Barney Sullivan

Barney
Thanks for the e-mail. Can you track when Hyde began these internet searches?

Christian Grey
CEO, Grey Enterprises Holdings, Inc.

I check the time; I have a catch-up with Ros.

TAYLOR AND I WAIT for Ana outside SIP. I glance anxiously toward the entrance, hoping that she'll be out at any moment. An e-mail alert appears on my phone.

From: Barney Sullivan
Subject: Jack Hyde
Date: September 13 2011 17:35
To: Christian Grey

Internet searches on the topics in Hyde's e-mail happened between 19:32 Monday, June 13, 2011, and 17:14 Wednesday, June 15, 2011.

B Sullivan
Head of IT, GEH

Hmm… Interesting. I remember I'd met him the Friday before, at the bar when I'd arranged to meet Ana. He was a loudmouthed asshole then. I wonder if he was looking for anything specific on my family, and if he found it. I glance out of the window, and finally Ana appears. She dashes toward the car, dodging the rain, Sawyer at her heels. I smile as I watch her, but my heart sinks when she glances into the car.

Her face is a stark alabaster in the gray rain.

Shit!

Sawyer opens her door, and she slides in beside me.

"Hi." The inflection in my voice is tentative. *What is it, Ana?*

"Hi." Her eyes flick to my face, briefly—too briefly, and all I see is her turmoil flashing back at me.

"What's wrong?"

She shakes her head as Taylor pulls into traffic. "Nothing."

I don't think that's true. "Is work all right?"

"Yes. Fine. Thanks." Her tone is clipped.

Tell me! "Ana, what's wrong?" My words are harsher than I intend, as they're loaded with my anxiety.

"I've just missed you, that's all. And I've been worried about Ray."

Oh, of course. Thank God. I brighten immediately. "Ray's good." I try to reassure her. "I spoke to Mom this afternoon, and she's impressed with his progress." I reach for her hand. It's freezing. "Boy, your hand is cold. Have you eaten today?"

She flushes.

"Ana." *Why does she do this?*

"I'll eat this evening. I haven't really had time."

I rub her hand in an attempt to warm it. "Do you want me to add 'feed my wife' to the security detail's list of duties?" I catch Taylor's eye in the rearview mirror.

"I'm sorry. I'll eat. It's just been a weird day. You know, moving Dad and all."

I guess. She turns away and stares out the window, leaving me to flounder.

Something's not right.

It *has* been a weird day.

Take her at her word, Grey.

I give her my news to test the water. "I may have to go to Taiwan."

"Oh. When?" This gets her attention.

"Later this week. Maybe next week."

"Okay."

"I want you to come with me."

Her lips thin. "Christian, please. I have my job. Let's not rehash this argument again."

I blow out a breath, unable to conceal my disappointment. "Thought I'd ask."

"How long will you go for?" Ana's voice is soft, but distracted.

This is not my girl. She's too quiet and hesitant.

"Not more than a couple of days. I wish you'd tell me what's bothering you."

"Well, now that my beloved husband is going away…" Her voice fades as I raise her hand to my lips and kiss her knuckles.

"I won't be away for long."

"Good." She gives me a thin smile, but I know she's preoccupied.

I gaze out the window and go through several scenarios that might be bothering Ana. Only one rings true: her father has just been in a major accident and his recovery will take some time.

Yes.

That's it.

Grey, get a grip.

RAYMOND STEELE IS HAPPY to see us. "Can't thank you enough for organizing all this." He waves at the airy room, his dark eyes full of quiet sincerity.

"Ray, you're most welcome." Uncomfortable with his gratitude, I change the subject. "I see you have a stack of sports magazines."

"From Annie. I've been reading about the Mariners, and the season they've been having." Ray launches into a diatribe about how disappointed he is with the M's this year. I have to say, I'm with him; it's not been a stellar season. Our conversation moves on to fishing. He's sorry to miss out on his angling trip in Astoria, and I mention my recent fishing expedition in Aspen.

"Roaring Fork—I know it," he says.

"You should come and stay. Maybe for a weekend, once you're up and about."

"I'd appreciate that, Christian."

Throughout our discussion Ana is quiet.

Too quiet. She's tuning out and going elsewhere.

It's frustrating. *Ana. What's wrong?*

Ray yawns. Ana glances at me, and I know it's time to go. "Daddy, we'll leave you to sleep."

"Thanks, Ana honey. I like that you drop by. Saw your mom today, too, Christian. She was very reassuring. And she's a Mariners fan!"

"She's not crazy about fishing, though."

"Don't know many women who are, eh?" Ray's smile is weary. He needs to rest.

"I'll see you tomorrow, okay?" Ana kisses his forehead, and there's a trace of sadness in her voice.

Hell. Why is she sad? "Come." I hold out my hand. Is she tired? Maybe what she needs is an early night.

ANA WAS QUIET IN the car and quiet when we got home, and now she's just chasing her food around her plate with her fork, taciturn and distracted. My anxiety has climbed to DEFCON 1.

"Damn it! Ana, will you tell me what's wrong?" I push my empty plate away. "Please. You're driving me crazy."

She turns apprehensive eyes to mine.

"I'm pregnant."

What? I stare at her as a frisson of disbelief skitters down my spine, and for some unknown reason, I'm suddenly at the door of the skydiving plane, hanging over the world without a parachute, about to leap out.

Into the air.

Into nothing.

"What?" I don't recognize my voice.

"I'm pregnant."

That's what I thought you said.

But I thought we took care of this.

"How?"

She tilts her head to one side and raises a brow.

Fuck. Anger like I've never felt before erupts inside me. "Your shot?" I snarl. "Did you forget your shot?"

She just stares at me, eyes glassy, as if she's looking right through me, and says nothing.

I don't want kids.

Not yet.

Not now. Panic knots in my chest and tightens around my throat, feeding my fury. "Christ, Ana!" I bang my fist on the table and stand. "You have one thing, one thing to remember. Shit! I don't fucking believe it. How could you be so stupid?"

She closes her eyes, then stares down at her fingers. "I'm sorry," she whispers.

"Sorry? Fuck!" *A child. What do I do with a child?*

"I know the timing's not very good."

"Not very good!" My bellow echoes around the room. "We've known each other five fucking minutes! I wanted to show you the fucking world and now... Fuck! Diapers and vomit and shit—!" I close my eyes.

You won't love me anymore.

"Did you forget? Tell me. Or did you do this on purpose?"

"No." Her word is a quiet rush of denial.

"I thought we'd agreed on this!" And I don't give a fuck who can hear me.

She cringes, folding in on herself. "I know. We had. I'm sorry."

"This is why! This is why I like control—so shit like this doesn't come along and fuck everything up!"

"Christian, please don't shout at me."

Fuck.

I'll be displaced.

She starts to cry.

Don't you dare, Ana. "Don't start with waterworks now! Fuck." I run a hand through my hair, trying to comprehend this colossal fuckup. "You think I'm ready to be a father?" My voice cracks on the last word.

She turns tear-filled eyes to me. "I know neither one of us is ready for this," she mumbles, "but I think you'll make a wonderful father. We'll figure it out."

"How the fuck do you know!" My voice clamors around the room. "Tell me how!"

She opens her mouth, and closes it again as tears stream down her face.

And there it is—her regret.

Regret that's writ large in every feature of her face. Regret that she's saddled with me.

I can't bear it.

My fury is drowning me.

"Oh, fuck this!" I rage at the world and back away, holding up my hands in defeat.

I cannot do this—

I'm out of here.

Grabbing my jacket, I storm out of the room, slamming the foyer door. Frantically, I stab the call button, and even though the elevator is on our floor the doors take far too fucking long to open.

A child?

A fucking child?

I step into the elevator, but in my head I'm underneath a kitchen table, in a shambolic, grimy, neglected hovel, waiting for him to find me.

There you are, you little shit.

Hell and damnation.

Fuck, no.

On the ground floor, I slam through the main doors out of Escala and onto the sidewalk. I drag in a lungful of fresh fall air, but it does little to assuage the anger and fear that surge in equal measure through my veins. I need to get away. Instinctively, I turn right and start walking, barely noticing that it's stopped raining.

I walk.

And walk.

In a daze.

Concentrating on the simple act of placing one foot in front of the other.

Blotting out all other thoughts.

Except one.

How could she do this to me?

How?

How can I love a child?

I've only just learned to love her.

When I look up, I'm at Flynn's office. There's no way he's going to be here. The door doesn't shift—it's locked. I call him but get his voice mail. I don't leave a message. I can't trust myself.

Jamming my hands into the pockets of my jacket and ignoring the commuters on the streets, I trudge on.

Aimless.

When I look up, Elena is locking up the salon, shrouded in her usual black attire. We gaze at each other; she's on one side of the glass, I'm on the other. She unlocks and opens the door.

"Hello, Christian. You look like shit."

I stare at her, not knowing what to say.

"Are you coming in?"

I shake my head and step back.

Grey, what are you doing?

Somewhere deep in my subconscious an alarm is sounding.

I ignore it.

Elena sighs and taps a scarlet nail against scarlet lips, her silver ring catching the evening light. "Shall we go for a drink?"

"Yes."

"The Mile High?"

"No. Somewhere less crowded."

"I see." She tries and fails to hide her surprise. "Okay."

"There's a bar around the corner."

"I know the one. It's a quiet place. Let me grab my purse."

Standing on the sidewalk while I wait for her, I feel numb.

I've just walked out on my pregnant wife.

But right now I'm too mad at her to care.

Grey, what are you doing?

I shake the disquieting voice from my head, and Elena steps out of her salon, locks the door, and with a slight nod of her head indicates right. I jam my hands farther into my pockets and together we walk the rest of the block, around the corner, and into the bar.

It's had a considerable makeover since I was last here—it's no longer a dive, but an upscale watering hole, all paneled wood and plush velvet seating. Elena was right—it is quiet except for Billie Holiday's soft, melancholic voice over the sound system.

Apt.

We slide into a booth, and Elena signals for the waitress.

"Good evening, my name's Sunny. What can I get you folks?"

"I'd like a glass of your Willamette pinot noir," Elena says.

"A bottle," I order, without looking at the waitress. Elena's eyebrows rise a fraction, but she maintains her familiar air of cool detachment. Maybe that's why I'm here; that's what I'm looking for— cool detachment personified.

"Coming right up." The young woman leaves us.

"So, all is not well in the world of Christian Grey," Elena observes. "I knew I'd see you again." Her eyes are fixed on mine and I don't know what to say. "Like that, is it?" Elena fills the silence between us. "Did you get my text?"

"On my wedding day?"

"Yes."

"I did. I deleted it."

"Christian, I can feel your enmity from here. It's coming off you in waves. But you wouldn't be here if I was the enemy."

I blow out a breath and sit back in the booth.

"Why are you here?" she asks, not unreasonably.

Fuck. "I don't know." Could I sound any more sullen?

"She's left you?"

"Don't." I give her a glacial stare.

I don't want to talk about Ana.

Elena purses her lips as the waitress returns. We both sit back and watch as she uncorks our wine and pours a sample into my glass. "I'm sure it's fine." I wave in Elena's direction and the waitress fills each of our glasses in turn.

"Enjoy," she says brightly, leaving us with the bottle.

Elena reaches for her glass and raises it. "To old friends." She smirks and takes a sip.

I snort, feeling some of my tension leave my shoulders. "Old friends." I raise my glass and gulp down a few mouthfuls of wine, not tasting it. Elena frowns and presses her lips together but says nothing, her eyes not leaving mine.

I sigh. She wants me to fill the silence. I'm going to have to say something. "How's the business?"

"Good. It was generous of you to gift it to me. Thank you for that."

"It was the least I could do."

She glances down at her glass as the silence between us expands.

Eventually, she breaks it. "As you're here, I think I should apologize for how I behaved at your parents' house."

Well, this is a surprise. It's not like Mrs. Lincoln to apologize for anything. Her mantra has always been "never apologize, never explain."

"I said several things that I regret," she adds quietly.

"We both did, Elena. It's in the past."

I offer her more wine, but she declines—her glass is still half full, while mine is empty. I pour myself another.

She sighs. "My social circle is considerably diminished. I miss your mother. It hurts that she won't see me."

"It's probably not a good idea for you to get in contact with her."

"I know. I understand. I never meant for her to overhear us. Grace was always most fearsome when it came to protecting her brood." She looks wistful for a moment. "We shared some good times, though. Your mother knows how to party."

"I don't wish to know that."

Elena laughs. "You've always placed her on such a pedestal."

"I'm not here to talk about my mother."

"What are you here to talk about, Christian?" She cocks her head to the side and runs a scarlet nail around the rim of her glass, icy blue eyes on mine.

I shake my head and take another long draft of the pinot.

"Has she left you?"

"No!" I snap. If anything, it was *me* who walked out.

What kind of man walks out on his pregnant wife?

Hell. Maybe my father was right.

His words come back to haunt me. *It's about you. You living up to your responsibilities. You being a trustworthy and decent human being. You being husband material.*

Maybe I'm not husband material.

I shake off the thought as Elena gazes at me, and I know she's trying to work out what's wrong. "You miss it? The lifestyle? Is that it? The little woman not giving you what you want?"

Fuck you, Elena.

I don't have to listen to her bullshit.

I start to slide out of the booth.

"Christian. Don't go. I'm sorry." She reaches for my hand, then changes her mind, so her outstretched hand becomes a fist on the table. "Please. Don't go," she pleads.

Two apologies from Mrs. Lincoln in such a short time.

I settle back in my seat. Warier.

"I'm sorry," she says once more, for emphasis. Then tries a different tack. "How is Anastasia?"

"She's good," I answer, eventually, and hope that I haven't given anything away.

Elena narrows her eyes; she doesn't believe me.

I exhale and confess. "She wants children."

"Ah," Elena says, as if she's solved the riddle of the Sphinx. "This shouldn't be a surprise to you. Though I will say she's a little young to be producing your spawn."

"Spawn?" I scoff, because she's said the last word with such malicious invective. Elena's never wanted children. I suspect she doesn't have a maternal bone in her body.

"Baby Grey," she muses. "That *will* put an end to your predilections." She looks amused. "Or maybe they've come to an end already."

I scowl at her. "Elena. Shut up. I'm not here to discuss my sex life with you." I drain my glass and pour more wine for us both, finishing the bottle. The pinot noir is beginning to work its magic. I'm already feeling hazy around the edges. It's not a sensation I normally enjoy, but right now, I welcome the oblivion that beckons from the bottom of my glass. I signal the waitress for another bottle.

"Has she done something specific to upset you? I haven't seen you drink like this in years." Elena sounds most disapproving. But I don't give a fuck.

"How's Isaac?" I ask, to move the focus to her lover and away from my wife. My marriage is none of her business.

She half smiles and folds her arms. "Okay. I get it. You really don't want to talk." She pauses, and I know she's waiting for me to spill my guts. But my secrets are mine. Not hers.

"Isaac is fine," she continues, finally. "Thank you for asking. In fact, we're really good at the moment." She launches into a tale of their latest sexual escapade, but to what end, I don't know. I half listen and half let the wine carry me away.

"So, is it the business? Is that your issue?" she asks when I don't react.

"No, it's going great. I bought a shipyard."

She nods, impressed, I think, and I refill both our glasses from the latest bottle, and give her a rundown of what I've been doing at work: the solar-powered tablet, the fiber-optic business takeover, Geolumara, and of course the shipyard.

"You've been busy."

"Always."

"So, you're talkative about your business, but not your wife."

"And?" *Is this a problem?*

"I knew you'd come back," she whispers.

What?

"Why are you drinking so much?"

"Because I'm thirsty." *And I want to forget how I behaved two hours ago.*

She regards me through half-closed eyes. "Thirsty?" she breathes. "How thirsty?" She leans in and reaches over, taking my hand. I tense as her fingers slide under my palm, and beneath the cuffs of my jacket and shirt. Her fingernails digging into my flesh over my pulse. "Maybe I could make you feel better? I'm sure you miss it." Her breath is stale, not sweet like Ana's. Her hand tightens around my wrist, and from nowhere the darkness circles my chest and starts spiraling into my throat. It's a feeling I haven't experienced for a while, and now it's back, amplified, echoing through my body and screaming for release.

"What are you doing?" I squeeze the words out.

It's tightening its hold on me.

Don't touch me.

This was how it was.

Always.

Me fighting my fear as she laid her hands on me.

"Don't touch me." I withdraw my hand from hers.

She pales and frowns, her eyes on mine. "Isn't this what you want?"

"No!"

"That's not why you're here?"

"No, Elena. No. I haven't thought about you like that for years." I shake my head, wondering how she could have so badly misread my intentions, but my thoughts aren't as clear as they should be. "I love my wife," I whisper.

Ana.

Elena studies me, her formerly pale cheeks reddening with wine or embarrassment or both. She frowns and looks down at the table. "I'm sorry," she mutters.

Apology number three.

My cup runneth over.

"I don't know...what came over me." She laughs—but her laughter is loud, forced. "I have to go." She gathers her purse. "Christian, I wish you and your wife well." She stops and looks me squarely in the eye. "I miss you, though. More than you know."

"Good-bye, Elena."

"The way you say that has a finality about it."

I don't answer her.

She nods. "It would be difficult. I get it. I'm glad you came to see me. I think we've cleared the air."

Have we? Cleared the air about what? Us? There is no us.

"Good-bye, Mrs. Lincoln." I know it's the last time I'll ever say these words to her.

She nods. "Good luck, Christian Grey." She slides out of the booth. "It was good to see you. I hope whatever it is that's bothering you sorts itself out. I'm sure it will. If it's about being a dad, you'll do great." She tosses her sleek hair over her shoulder and exits the bar without a backward glance, leaving me with a half-empty bottle of pinot noir and an uneasy feeling of guilt.

I want to go home.

To Ana.

Shit.

I put my head in my hands. Ana will be mad as hell when I get home.

Grabbing the bottle and my glass, I head toward the bar to settle my tab. There's a stool free, so I sit down and replenish my glass.

Waste not, want not.

I nurse my drink. Slowly.

Hell. I hate it when Ana's mad at me. If I go home now, I may say something else I'll regret. Besides, I've had too much to drink, and I don't think Ana's ever seen me drunk. Of course, I've seen *her* drunk—that first night I slept with her at The Heathman, and the night of her bachelorette party...

Her words float through my slow, intoxicated brain.

Are you going to punish me?

Punish you?

For getting so drunk. A punishment fuck. You can do anything you want to me.

Stop. Grey.

I wonder when she got pregnant.

On our honeymoon? In our bed? In the Red Room?

Fuck...

Junior.

We'll need a fucking minivan.

Will he have Ana's blue eyes? My temper? *Shit.* My glass is empty. I refill it, finishing the bottle.

There will be hell to pay if Ana ever finds out I've had a drink with Elena. She loathes Elena.

Christian—if that were your son, how would you feel?

Oh, Ana, Ana, Ana.

I don't want to think about that.

Not now. It's too raw and too painful.

I need oblivion.

I want to forget who I am, and how I've behaved.

The way I used to...before...everything.

Before Mrs. Robinson.

The barman looks my way.

"Bourbon, please."

W e're here." The driver turns and flashes me a wide big-toothed grin.

"Wha?" I'm in a car… A cab. My face is pressed against cool glass. My head is spinning. *Shit.* Closing one eye, I squint up at the building we're parked outside. The brass lantern beckons bright in the darkness.

"Escala?" the driver says.

"Oh. Yeah." From my inside pocket I fumble for my wallet and paw through the notes. I hand one to the cabdriver and hope it's enough.

"Wow! Thanks!"

I open the car door and fall onto the sidewalk.

"Fuck."

"You okay?" he calls.

"Yeah." I lay there for a second, staring up at the night sky, waiting for the world to stop spinning. It's clear and there are a few stars shining down, winking at me. It's peaceful.

I'm lying on the sidewalk.

Get up, Grey.

A man looms over me, blotting out the light from the lantern, and for a moment a chill grips my heart. "Here." He offers me his hand.

Oh, he's here to help… Cab guy? Maybe. He hauls me to my feet.

"One too many, eh?"

"Yeah. More than one. I think." I make a half-assed attempt to brush myself down, and the driver climbs back into his car. Turning around, I start to sway and use forward momentum to stagger into the building and over to the elevator. I'll be okay if I can just get to bed. The elevator doors open and I stumble inside. I punch in the code… the elevator doesn't move.

I try again.

Nothing.

Hell.

One more time.

I close one eye and jab at the buttons. That does the trick! The doors slide shut and the elevator hums, indicating some movement on its part... Wait, no—everything is moving. I lean against the wall and close my eyes to stop the spinning. The ping sounds. I'm here! I open my eyes and stumble out into the foyer.

Fuck. I bump into something.

Who the hell moved the foyer table?

"Shit!" Placing my hands on the table, I steady myself, but it fucking moves again, the scraping sound grating on what's left of my nerves.

"Shit!" I make it to the double doors.

"Christian, are you okay?"

I look up, and there she is, dressed like a goddess on the silver screen.

Ana. My own Aphrodite. My wife. My heart fills with love and light. She's so beautiful. "Mrs. Grey." The doorjamb holds me up. "Oh, you look mighty fine, Anastashia."

Suddenly she's closer and I have to squint to bring her into focus.

"Where have you been?" She sounds worried.

Oh, no. I mustn't tell her. She'll be mad as hell. I bring my fingers to my lips. "Shh!"

"I think you'd better come to bed."

Bed. With Ana. There is nowhere I would rather be. "With you." I give her my best smile, but she's frowning.

"Let me help you to bed. Lean on me." She wraps her arm around my middle, and I lean against her, catching the scent of her hair.

Nectar. "You are very beautiful, Ana."

"Christian, walk! I am going to put you to bed."

She's so bossy! But I want her happy. "Okay." We move. Together. Down the corridor. One slow step at a time. And then we're in our bedroom. "Bed." It is a most welcome sight.

"Yes, bed," Ana says. Her face is a blur. But it's still lovely. I hold her to me.

"Join me."

"Christian, I think you need some sleep."

Oh, no. "And so it begins. I've heard about this."

"Heard about what?"

"Babies mean no sex."

"I'm sure that's not true. Otherwise we'd all come from one-child families."

Mrs. Grey has an answer for everything, with her smart mouth. "You're funny."

"You're drunk."

"Yes." *Very.*

To forget.

There you are, you little shit.

"Come on, Christian," Ana says. Gentle, compassionate Ana. "Let's get you into bed."

Suddenly I am on the bed.

It's so comfortable.

I should just stay here.

She stands over me, dressed in silk or satin, as tempting as Eve herself. I hold my arms out to her. "Join me."

"Let's get you undressed first."

Hmm… Naked. With Ana. "Now you're talking."

"Sit up. Let me take your jacket off."

"The room is spinning."

"Christian. Sit up!"

I smile up at her. "Mrs. Grey, you are a bossy little thing."

"Yes. Do as you're told and sit up." She places her hands on her hips. She's trying to look stern…I think. But she just looks lovely.

My wife.

My beloved wife.

Slowly, I wrestle with the bed, to sit up.

I win.

She grabs my tie.

And I think she's trying to undress me. She's close. So close. I drink in her unique scent. "You smell good."

"You smell of hard liquor."

"Yes. Bour. Bon." Oh shit—the room is a carousel again. To keep myself anchored to the bed, I rest my hands on Ana, and the spinning slows. Her nightgown is warm and soft, augmenting her body heat. "I like the feel of this fabric on you, Anastay-shia. You should always be in satin or silk."

Of course. It's not just her now. I jerk her closer. I want to talk to Junior. We need to set some ground rules. "And we have an invader in here. You're going to keep me awake, aren't you?"

Ana's hands are in my hair. I raise my face up to her. My Madonna. Mother of my child. And in that moment, I tell her my darkest fear. "You'll choose him over me."

"Christian, you don't know what you're talking about. Don't be ridiculous—I am not choosing anyone over anyone. And he might be a she."

"A she. Oh God."

A girl?

A baby girl?

No. The room won't stop spinning and I fall back on the bed…

Baby Mia, with her shock of dark hair and watchful dark eyes. Ana holds her. There's a light breeze on my face. It's cooling in the sunshine. We're in the orchard. Ana's face radiates with love as she smiles down at Mia, then aims sad eyes to me. She walks away, not turning back to look, as I stand watching her. She doesn't look back. She continues and disappears into the garage at The Heathman. She doesn't look back. Every sinew, every bone, every atom of my marrow is aching. *No.* I want to call out. But I can't speak. I have no words. I'm curled on the floor. Bound. Gagged. Aching. Everywhere. The clip of red heeled stilettos echoes off the flagstones. *So, you got drunk. Again.* Elena's wearing a strap-on and wielding a long, thin cane. No. No. This will be hard to take. *I'm sorry. I didn't say you could speak.* Her tone is clipped. Formal. I brace myself. Digging deep. She trails the cane down my spine, and suddenly it disappears from my skin, offering me a brief respite before she strikes me across my back. I take a

deep breath as I embrace its fiery bite across my skin. She
pokes the tip of the cane at my skull. Pain radiates through
my head. The door crashes open and his bulk fills the frame.
Elena screams. And screams. And screams. The sound
splitting my head in two. He's here. And he hits me, a good
left hook to my jaw, and my skull explodes with pain. *Shit*.

My eyes crack open, and light slices through my brain like a scal-
pel. I shut them immediately. *Fuck*. My head—my throbbing, aching
head.

What the hell?

I'm lying on top of the bed, cold and stiff.

Dressed?

Why? I open my eyes again, slowly this time, allowing the day-
light to creep in. I'm home.

What happened? I struggle to remember, but something, a mis-
deed maybe, is chafing on my conscience.

Grey. What did you do?

Slowly, my mind draws back the curtains on last night, revealing
some of my transgressions.

Drinking.

A keg full.

I sit up, too quickly—my head swims and bile rises in my throat. I
force it down while I rub my temples, racking what's left of my brain
to recall what happened. Vague images of the previous evening flash
fuzzy and malformed through my mind. Red wine and bourbon?

What was I thinking?

The baby. Fuck.

I lift my head to check on Ana, but she's not here, and it's obvious
she didn't sleep in this bed last night.

Where is she?

I take stock of myself. No injuries, but I'm still in yesterday's
clothes, and I stink.

Hell. Did I drive Ana away?

What time is it? I glance at the clock and it's 7:05 a.m. Shakily, I
get to my feet, which are bare. I don't remember removing my socks.

I rub my forehead.

Where is my wife? Unease yawns in my gut, accompanied by a burning sense of guilt.

Damn, what did I do?

My phone is on the nightstand; I pick it up and stagger to the bathroom. Ana's not there. Nor is she in the spare room.

Mrs. Jones is in the kitchen. She gives me a cursory glance, then returns to her work. Ana is nowhere to be seen. "Good morning, Gail. Ana?"

"I haven't seen her, sir." Her tone is arctic. Mrs. Jones is pissed.

At me?

Why?

Ignoring her, I check the library. Nothing.

My unease blooms.

Studiously avoiding Gail's frosty gaze, I head back through the living room to check my study and the TV room. Ana is not in there either.

Fuck.

In spite of feeling like shit, I hurry back through the living room, bolt upstairs, and check both of the guest rooms. *No Ana.*

She's gone. She's fucking gone. I dash downstairs, ignoring the stabbing at my temples, and burst into Taylor's office. He looks up, surprised, I think.

"Ana?"

His face is impassive. "I haven't seen her, sir."

"For fuck's sake, we have how many security personnel here? Where the fuck is my wife?" I explode, and my head pounds. I close my eyes as Taylor's face pales.

Shit. Get a grip, Grey.

"Did she go out?" I ask, in as measured a tone as I can manage.

"There's nothing in the log, sir."

"I can't find her." I'm at a loss.

He casts his eyes over the CCTV monitors. "All the vehicles are accounted for. And no one can get in."

I blanch as I grasp his meaning. Has she been kidnapped?

Taylor notices my expression. "No one can get in, sir," he repeats for emphasis.

"Leila Williams and Jack Hyde got in!" I snap.

"Miss Williams had a key, and Ryan let Hyde in," Taylor counters. "I'll check the apartment, Mr. Grey."

I nod and follow him out into the hallway.

She wouldn't leave. Would she? I rack my addled, aching brain and recall a vision of Ana—from last night, I think—dressed in the softest satin, fragrant and beautiful, smiling down at me. Taylor heads off to our bedroom, no doubt to look there, and I don't stop him. I might have missed something.

My phone!

I could call her.

Wait. There's a text from her, in very shouty capitals.

> **ANA**
> WOULD YOU LIKE MRS. LINCOLN
> TO JOIN US WHEN WE EVENTUALLY
> DISCUSS THIS TEXT SHE SENT
> YOU? IT WILL SAVE YOU RUNNING
> TO HER AFTERWARD.
> YOUR WIFE
>
> > **FORWARDED: ELENA**
> > It was good to see you. I understand now.
> > Don't fret. You'll make a wonderful father.

Oh, shit.

Ana's been reading my texts.

When?

How dare she?

Anger flares inside me. I press call, and Ana's phone rings, and rings. And fucking rings. Eventually it diverts to voice mail. "Where the hell are you?" I snarl into my BlackBerry, furious that she's been reading my texts, furious that she knows about Elena, furious *with* Elena—but most of all, I'm furious at myself and at the clawing fear that threatens to choke me. She's missing.

Ana, where the fuck are you? Perhaps she's left me.

Where would she go? *Kate.* Of course. I call Kavanagh.

"Hello." Kate answers after several rings, her voice thick with sleep.

"It's Christian."

"Christian? What is it? Is Ana okay?" Kate is fully awake and instantly adopts her familiar badgering tone, which I do not need right now.

"She's not with you?" I ask.

"No. Should she be?"

"No. Don't worry. Go back to sleep."

"Chris—" I hang up.

My head is pounding and my wife is missing. This is hell. I'm in hell. I try Ana's phone and again it diverts to voice mail. I storm into the kitchen where Gail is making coffee. "Can you get me some Advil, please?" I'm as gracious as a man with a missing wife can be. She stifles a smile.

Is she smiling because I'm suffering?

I scowl at her as she wordlessly places a container of Advil on the counter and turns to fill a glass of water, leaving me to struggle with the childproof lid. Eventually, I manage to pry two tablets from the plastic tub as stony-faced Mrs. Jones places water in front of me.

Glaring at her, I tip both pills into my mouth, but she turns back to the stove. I take a sip.

Hell. The water is lukewarm; it tastes awful.

I glower at her; she's done this on purpose. Slamming the glass down on the counter, I turn and stomp back upstairs to look for Ana, hoping that the capsules will settle the storm in my head.

Taylor is emerging from what was the submissives' room. He looks grim. I try the playroom door. It's locked, but in my frustration, I rattle it anyway just to make sure, and bellow Ana's name down the corridor. Immediately I regret raising my voice, as pain lances through my head.

"Any luck?" I ask Taylor.

"No, sir. I've checked the gym, and roused Sawyer and Ryan. They're searching the staff quarters."

"Good. We need a plan."

"We'll meet downstairs."

Back in the kitchen, we're joined by Sawyer and Ryan; Ryan looks like he's had less sleep than me.

"Mrs. Grey is missing," I growl at them. "Sawyer, check the CCTV footage and see if you can track her movements. Ryan, Taylor, let's search the apartment again."

All of them suddenly look shocked—their eyes wide, their mouths dropping open.

What?

A movement from the corner of my eye catches my attention.

It's Ana.

Thank Christ. She's here. For a moment my relief is overwhelming, but as Ana stands and surveys us, I see she's cool and distant, her eyes wide, but with telltale dark circles beneath. She's wrapped in a duvet—small, pale, and utterly beautiful.

And mad as hell.

As I drink her in, a sense of foreboding creeps up my spine, raising all the hair on the back of my head. She squares her narrow shoulders, raises her chin in that stubborn way she does, and completely ignoring me, addresses Luke. "Sawyer, I'll be ready to leave in about twenty minutes." She tightens the duvet around her, keeping her chin high.

Oh, Ana. I'm just so glad she's still here. *She hasn't left me.*

"Would you like some breakfast, Mrs. Grey?" Gail asks, in such a sweet, solicitous tone that I turn to look at her in surprise. Her eyes slide to me, as frigid as ever.

Ana shakes her head. "I'm not hungry, thank you." Her voice is soft and clear, but her expression's implacable. Is she not eating in order to punish me? Is that what this is? But now is not the time for that argument.

"Where were you?" I ask, bemused. Behind me there's a sudden burst of activity as my staff make themselves scarce. I ignore them, as does Ana. She turns and heads toward our bedroom.

"Ana! Answer me!"

Don't fucking ignore me!

I follow in her stately wake down the hallway, into our suite, until she turns into our bathroom, shuts the door, and locks it.

Shit!

"Ana!" I thump on the door, then try the handle. "Ana, open the damned door."

Why is she doing this? Because I walked out last night? Because I saw Elena?

"Go away!" she shouts over the sound of gushing water from the shower.

"I'm not going anywhere!"

"Suit yourself."

"Ana, please." I rattle the door once more in an effort to express my anger, but I feel nothing except impotent rage. How dare she lock the door? It takes all my self-control not to break it down, but given her attitude, and my headache, that probably wouldn't be a wise choice.

Why is she so mad?

She's mad?

After the ten-fingered, ten-toed bombshell she dropped on me?

Or is it because I got drunk?

Deep down I know the problem.

Elena. Why couldn't Mrs. Lincoln keep her thoughts to herself?

I knew it was a mistake to see her.

I knew it in the bar.

This is a fuckup, Grey.

Well, as my mother always likes to say, it takes two to tango. Wives get mad at their husbands all the time. Don't they? This is normal, surely. I scowl at the locked door.

What can I do?

Find your happy place. Flynn's words invade my thoughts as I lean against the wall.

Well, my happy place is not fucking standing here.

My happy place is in the shower.

But I don't have a choice.

My head is thumping. At least the sound of the rushing water from the shower is less painful than my shouting. Otherwise, it's all quiet. I contemplate going to have a shower myself, in the spare room. But she might duck out on me. Sighing, I run my hand through my hair, reconciled to waiting for Mrs. Grey.

Again.

Like I always do.

My mind drifts to the previous evening. To Elena. What did we talk about? As I try to remember, my sense of unease returns. What did we discuss? My business. Yes. Her business. Isaac. The fact that Ana wants kids. I didn't actually tell Elena that Ana was pregnant. Did I?

No. *Thank Christ.*

Spawn. I snort. That's the term Elena used.

And she apologized. Now, that is a first.

What else did we talk about? There's something hovering at the edge of my consciousness. Damn. *Why did I get so drunk?* I loathe being out of control. I loathe drunks.

A darker memory surfaces—not from last night, one that I try to bury. That man. The crack whore's fucking pimp, drunk on cheap liquor and whatever he could jack into his system and the crack whore's system.

Fuck.

This is not my happy place. A cold sweat breaks out over my skin as I recall the stench emanating from his unwashed body, and from the Camel cigarette jammed between his teeth. I take a deep, long breath to quell my rising panic.

It's in the past, Grey.

Stay calm.

The door clicks and I open my eyes to see Mrs. Anastasia Grey, wrapped in two towels, emerge from the bathroom. She strides right past me as if I'm invisible and disappears into the closet. I follow her and stand on the threshold, watching as she ever-so-casually selects her outfit for the day.

"Are you ignoring me?" The disbelief is evident in my voice.

"Perceptive, aren't you?" she mutters, as if I'm some kind of afterthought.

I watch her. Helpless. *What do I do?*

Her clothes are in her hands as she waltzes toward me and halts, finally looking me in the eye, a "get out of my way, asshole" expression on her face. I really am in deep shit. I've never seen her this mad, except maybe that time she threw a hairbrush at me on the *Fair Lady.* I step out of her way, when really all I want to do is grab her, press her against the wall, and kiss her—kiss her senseless. Then bury myself inside her. But I follow her like a fucking lapdog into the bedroom and stand in the doorway as she saunters over to her chest of drawers. How can she be so nonchalant?

Look at me! I will her.

She loosens the towel that's cloaked around her body and drops it to the floor. My dick stirs in response, making me angrier. Christ, she's beautiful; her flawless skin, the soft flare of her hips, the swell of her behind, and her long, long legs that I want wrapped around me. Her body shows no sign of the invader yet. Christ, I have no idea how pregnant she is.

Shit. I put Junior out of my mind.

How long will it take me to get her into bed?

Grey, no—keep it together.

She's still ignoring me. "Why are you doing this?" I try to hide the desperation in my voice.

"Why do you think?" She fishes some lingerie out of a drawer.

"Ana—" My breath catches in my throat as she bends and tugs on her panties, wiggling her fine, fine ass. She's doing this on purpose. And in spite of my aching head, and my filthy mood, I want to fuck her. *Now.* Just to make sure we're okay. My growing erection concurs.

"Go ask your Mrs. Robinson. I'm sure she'll have an explanation for you." She rifles through her drawer, dismissing me, as if I'm some fucking lackey.

As I thought, it's Elena.

What did you expect, Grey?

"Ana, I've told you before, she's not my—"

"I don't want to hear it, Christian." Ana holds up her hand. "The time for talking was yesterday, but instead you decided to rant, and get drunk with the woman who abused you for years. Give her a call. I'm sure she'll be more than willing to listen to you now."

What?

Ana chooses a bra—the black lacy one—and slides it on and fastens it. I stride farther into the room and place my hands on my hips, glaring at her. She's crossed a line.

"Why were you snooping on me?" I can't believe she went through my texts.

"That's not the point, Christian," she hisses. "Fact is, the going gets tough, and you run to her."

"It wasn't like that—"

"I'm not interested!" She stalks over to the bed while I gaze at her. Lost. She's so cold. *Who is this woman?*

Sitting down, she stretches out a long, shapely leg, points her toes, and slowly eases one thigh-high up over her skin. My mouth goes from parched to desert as I watch her hands glide up her leg.

"Where were you?" It's the only coherent sentence I can form. Ignoring me, she pulls on the other thigh-high with the same slow, sensual ease. Then she stands, turns away from me, and bends over to towel-dry her hair, her back in a perfect curve. It takes every remaining shred of my self-control not to grab her and toss her onto the bed. She stands up straight again, flicking her thick, wet mane of chestnut hair, so it cascades down her back below her bra line.

"Answer me," I murmur. But she merely stalks back to the chest of drawers, picks up her hair dryer, and switches it on, wielding it like a weapon. The noise grates on my frayed nerves, unraveling them further.

What do I do when my wife ignores me?

I'm at a loss.

She rakes her fingers through her hair as she dries it and I fist my hands to stop myself from reaching out to her. I'm desperate to touch her and end this nonsense. But the memory of her hissing at me with such venom after the belting in the playroom comes to mind.

You are one fucked-up son of a bitch.

I pale. I don't want a repeat of that.

Ever.

I watch her, wordless and mesmerized. It was only a few days ago that she let me dry her hair. She finishes with a flourish, her hair a riotous crown of chestnut streaked with red and gold that tumbles down over her shoulders. She *is* doing this on purpose. The thought revives my anger.

"Where were you?" I whisper.

"What do you care?"

"Ana, stop this. Now."

She shrugs, like she doesn't care, and my blood boils. I move quickly toward her, unsure what I'm going to do, but she whirls to face me like an avenging angel. "Don't touch me," she snarls through clenched teeth, and I'm catapulted back to that moment in my playroom when she left.

It's sobering.

"Where were you?" I clench my fists to stop my hands from shaking.

"I wasn't out getting drunk with my ex." Her eyes blaze with righteous indignation. "Did you sleep with her?"

It's like she's punched me in the face.

I gasp. "What? No!" *How could she think that? Sleep with Elena?* "You think I'd cheat on you?" Christ, she thinks so little of me. A knot twists in my gut, and a memory, lost in a mist of red wine and bourbon, stirs.

"You did," Ana continues. "By taking our very private life and spilling your spineless guts to that woman."

"Spineless. That's what you think?" Jesus, I thought I'd fucked up, but this is so much worse than I'd feared.

"Christian, I saw the text. That's what I know."

"That text was not meant for you!"

"Well, fact is I saw it when your BlackBerry fell out of your jacket, while I was undressing you because you were too drunk to undress yourself. Do you have any idea how much you've hurt me by going to see that woman?" She doesn't pause for breath. "Do you remember last night when you came home? Remember what you said?"

Hell. No. *What did I say last night?* I was just mad at you, Ana. Shocked by your revelation. I want to say it, but I can't find the words.

"Well, you were right. I do choose this defenseless baby over you."

My world grinds to an abrupt halt.

What does that mean?

"That's what any loving parent does. That's what your mother should have done for you. And I'm sorry that she didn't—because we wouldn't be having this conversation right now if she had. But you're an adult now. You need to grow up and smell the fucking coffee, and stop behaving like a petulant adolescent." She's on a roll.

I frown, and gape at her in all her glory. She's naked except for sensational underwear, her hair a mahogany cloud spilling down to her breasts, dark eyes wide and desolate. The anger and hurt roll off her in waves, and in spite of all that, she's stunning, and I am utterly lost. "You may not be happy about this baby," she exclaims. "I'm not ecstatic, given the timing and your less-than-lukewarm reception to this new life, this flesh of your flesh. But you can either do this with me, or I'll do it on my own. The decision is yours. While you wallow in your pit of self-pity and self-loathing I'm going to work. And when I return, I'll be moving my belongings to the room upstairs."

She's moving out. She's leaving.

She *is* choosing the baby over me.

Panic overwhelms me. It's like a knife in my guts.

"Now, if you'll excuse me, I'd like to finish getting dressed."

My scalp prickles as I edge toward the abyss. *She's leaving.* I step back. "Is that what you want?" My voice is a shocked whisper.

Her wounded eyes are impossibly wide as she scrutinizes me. "I don't know what I want anymore," she says quietly, and turning back to the mirror she smooths some face cream over her cheeks.

"You don't want me?" There's no oxygen in the room.

"I'm still here, aren't I?" she says, as she opens and applies her mascara.

How can she be so cold?

"You've thought about leaving." The abyss opens and yawns in front of me.

"When one's husband prefers the company of his ex-mistress, it's usually not a good sign." Her disdain drips from every word and pushes me closer to the abyss. Pursing her lips, she dabs on some lip gloss oh-so-fucking casually while I'm poised on the edge of this awful precipice.

She reaches for her boots, strides to the bed, and sits down. I watch her, completely at a loss. She pulls them on and stands to face me, her hands on her hips, her expression aloof.

Fuck.

In her boots and lingerie, her hair wild, she's a woman to tame.

A Dom's wet dream.

My wet dream.

My only dream.

I want her. I want her to tell me that she loves me. The way I love her.

Seduce her, Grey.

It's my only weapon.

"I know what you're doing here," I murmur, pitching my voice lower.

"Do you?" Her voice cracks. Is that a chink in her armor? Hope flares briefly in my gut.

She feels.

I can do this. I step forward, but she steps back and holds up her hands, palms toward me. "Don't even think about it, Grey." Her words are bullets aimed at my heart.

"You're my wife," I murmur.

"I'm the pregnant woman you abandoned yesterday, and if you touch me I will scream the place down."

What the fuck? No!

"You'd scream?"

"Bloody murder."

This is too much! Or—does she want to play? Maybe that's it— that's what she wants. "No one would hear you," I murmur.

"Are you trying to frighten me?"

What? No. Never. I back away. "That wasn't my intention."

I'm in free-fall.

Tell her. Just come clean, Grey.

And tell her what—that Elena reached for me, her intention clear? *I don't think so.*

"I had a drink with someone I used to be close to. We cleared the air. I'm not going to see her again." *Believe me, please. Ana.*

"You sought her out?"

"Not at first. I tried to see Flynn. But...I found myself at the salon."

Ana's eyes narrow, fury smoldering in their depths. "And you expect me to believe you're not going to see her again?" She raises her voice. "What about the next time I step across some imaginary line? This is the same argument we have over and over again. Like we're on some Ixion's wheel. If I fuck up again, are you going to run back to her?"

It's not like that! "I am not going to see her again. She finally understands how I feel."

Elena saw me recoil. She knows I don't want her.

"What does that mean?"

If I tell her Elena made a pass at me, Ana will go into meltdown. *Shit. Why the fuck did you go to see her, Grey?*

I gaze at my furious, beautiful wife. What can I say?

"Why can you talk to her and not to me?" Ana whispers.

No. It's not like that. You don't understand. She was my only friend.

"I was mad at you. Like I am now." The words come in a desperate rush.

"You don't say," Ana shouts. "Well, *I* am mad at you right now. Mad at you for being so cold and callous yesterday, when I needed you. Mad at you for saying I got knocked up deliberately when I didn't. Mad at you for betraying me."

I didn't!

"I should have kept better track of my shots," she continues, quieter. "But I didn't do it on purpose. This pregnancy is a shock to me, too. It could be that the shot failed."

You're shocked! I'm shocked, too.

We're not ready for a baby.

I'm not ready for a baby.

"You really fucked up yesterday," she whispers. "I've had a lot to deal with over the last few weeks."

I fucked up? What about you? Cornered again, I lash out. "You really fucked up three weeks ago. Or whenever you forgot your shot."

"Well, God forbid I should be perfect like you."

Touché, Anastasia. "This is quite a performance, Mrs. Grey."

"Well, I'm glad that even knocked up I'm entertaining."

Fuck this! "I need a shower," I grit between my teeth.

"And I've provided enough of a floor show."

"It's a mighty fine floor show," I whisper, stepping forward. One more try. She steps back. *No dice.*

"Don't."

"I hate that you won't let me touch you."

"Ironic, huh?"

I gasp as her words slice through me. Who knew she could be such a...bitch? My sweet Ana, hurt and aching, unleashing her claws. Is this what I've driven her to?

This is getting us nowhere.

"We haven't resolved much, have we?" My voice is bleak and flat. I don't know what else to say; I have failed to turn her around.

"I'd say not. Except that I'm moving out of this bedroom."

So...she's not leaving me. I grasp on to this hope as I hang over the abyss.

One more pitch, Grey. This is your marriage.

"She doesn't mean anything to me," I whisper. *Not like you do.*

"Except when you need her."

"I don't need her. I need you."

"You didn't yesterday. That woman is a hard limit for me, Christian."

"She's out of my life."

"I wish I could believe you."

"For fuck's sake, Ana."

"Please let me get dressed."

Sighing, I run my hand through my hair. What can I do? She won't let me touch her. She's too mad. I have to regroup and come up with a different strategy. And right now, I need to put some distance between us, before I do something I'll regret. "I'll see you this evening." I storm out and into the bathroom, shutting the door behind me. Like her, I lock it, for the first time ever, protecting myself. Ana has the power to wound me like no other. Standing against the door, I tip my head back and close my eyes.

I have really fucked up. The last time I really fucked up she left me.

"You don't want me?"

"I'm still here, aren't I?"

I clutch on to that hope. Right now I need a shower to wash last night's stink off me.

The water is blistering, the way I like it. I tilt my face into the stream, welcoming its stinging heat as it douses me.

Christ, I'm confused. Nothing is simple where Ana is concerned;

I should know that by now. She's mad because I shouted at her and left, and she's mad because I saw Elena.

That woman is a hard limit for me, Christian.

Elena has been a thorn in Ana's side from the beginning. And now, because of that careless fucking text, she's a thorn in mine. Last night should have put an end to it. All of it. But she had to send that text.

Elena's words haunt me. *Maybe I could make you feel better? I'm sure you miss it.*

I shudder at the memory.

Shit, what a mess.

WHEN I EMERGE FROM the bathroom, Ana's gone. I'm not sure if I'm relieved or disappointed.

Disappointed.

With a heavy heart, I dress, choosing my favorite tie as a talisman for the day. It's brought me luck before.

In the kitchen, Mrs. Jones is still emitting glacial disapproval. It's irritating and chastening at the same time. However, she's prepared a substantial fried breakfast for me.

"Thank you," I mutter. Her only reply is a tight smile. I suspect she heard Ana and me fighting last night.

Grey, you were shouting.

Everyone heard you.

Shit.

I STARE OUT OF the car window as Taylor drives through the morning rush-hour traffic. Ana didn't even say good-bye; she just fucking left, with Sawyer. "Taylor, tell Sawyer I want him to stick to Mrs. Grey like glue. I need to know if she's eating."

"Yes, sir." His words are clipped. Even Taylor is frosty this morning.

I wonder if Ana will follow through with her threat to move upstairs.

I hope not.

She fucks up her contraception, saddling us with a child before we're ready, before we've done anything—and *I'm* in the fucking doghouse? I don't even know how pregnant she is. I resolve to call Dr. Greene when I get to the office. Maybe she can shed some light on how my wife came to miss her shot.

My phone buzzes, and immediately my heart starts pounding. *Ana?* No, it's Ros.

"Grey," I snap.

"You're bright and breezy this morning, Christian."

"What is it, Ros?" I snap again.

She pauses for a nanosecond, then she's all business. "Hansell from the shipyard wants a meeting. And Senator Blandino, too."

Damn. The unions and the politicians. *Could this day get any better?*

"They have wind of the Taiwan deal already?"

"So it would seem, and they want to talk."

"Okay, this afternoon. Set it up. I want you and Samir there, too."

"Will do, Christian."

"That's all?"

"Yes."

"Good." I hang up.

What am I going to do about my wife? Truth is, I'm still smarting from angry Anastasia. Who knew she had such gumption? I don't think anyone's bawled me out like that since...forever. Apart from my mother *and* father—at my own birthday party, no less. And that was because of fucking Elena, as well. I snort at the irony. Yeah, fucking Elena.

I shake my head in disgust. Why did I seek her out? Why?

The Advil has kicked in, and Mrs. Jones's fried breakfast has helped. I feel almost human, but miserable...utterly miserable.

What is Ana doing now? I picture her in her tiny office, wearing her purple dress. Perhaps she's sent me an e-mail. I scramble for my phone, but there's nothing.

Is she thinking about me like I'm thinking about her? I hope so. I want to be in her thoughts, always.

Taylor pulls up outside GEH, and I brace myself for a long day.

"GOOD MORNING, MR. GREY." Andrea smiles as I step out of the elevator, but her smile fades when she sees my expression.

"Get me Dr. Greene on the line and tell Sarah to bring me some coffee."

"Yes, sir."

"After I've finished with Greene, I need to talk to Flynn. Then you can bring in my schedule for the day. Has Ros spoken to you about Hansell and Blandino?"

"Yes."

"Good."

"Dr. Flynn left for a conference in New York early this morning."

Fuck! "I forgot. See if he can find a moment for me on the phone."

"Will do. The flat screen you requested for Mr. Steele will be installed this afternoon."

"And the additional PT?"

"That will start tomorrow."

"Okay. Put Dr. Greene through when you have her." I don't wait for an answer, but stalk into my office and sit down, under the watchful gaze of my wife. I let out a long, slow breath, wondering if her photographer friend ever witnessed her the way she was this morning. From Aphrodite to Athena, goddess of war—a scolding, angry, alluring Athena.

My phone buzzes. "I have Dr. Greene for you."

"Thanks, Andrea. Dr. Greene?"

"Mr. Grey, what can I do for you?"

"I thought the shot was a reliable form of contraceptive," I hiss. There's a prolonged silence on the other end of the line. "Dr. Greene?"

"Mr. Grey, no form of contraception is one hundred percent effective. That would be abstinence, or sterilization for yourself or your wife." Her tone is icy. "I can send you some literature if you'd like to read up on it."

I sigh. "No. That won't be necessary."

"What can I do for you, Mr. Grey?"

"I would like to know how pregnant my wife is."

"Can't Mrs. Grey tell you that herself?"

What is this? Just answer the question!

"I'm asking you, Dr. Greene. That's what I pay you for."

"My patient is Mrs. Grey. I suggest you talk to your wife, and she can give you the details. Is there anything else you need?"

My temper reaches boiling point.

Take a deep breath, Grey.

"Please," I ask through gritted teeth.

"Mr. Grey. Talk to your wife. Good day." She hangs up, and I glare at the phone, expecting it to shrivel to ashes under my gaze; some bedside manner she has.

There's a knock at my door and Sarah appears with my coffee. "Thanks," I mutter, trying to rein in my fury at the goddamned, officious, unhelpful so-called doctor. "Ask Andrea to come in—I want to go through my schedule."

Sarah dashes out and I stare at monochrome Ana on my wall.

Even your doctor is pissed at me.

MISERY IS MY CONSTANT companion, all the way through my meetings, my lunch, and my kickboxing session with Bastille.

"You look like a wet weekend, Grey."

"I feel it."

"Let's see if we can turn that frown upside down."

Really?

I knock him on his ass twice; he deserves to go down for that comment alone.

BY 4:30 I'VE HEARD nothing from my wife, not even an angry hectoring e-mail liberally sprinkled with shouty capitals. Sawyer has reported in to let me know that she had a bagel for lunch. That's something. I have fifteen minutes before showtime with Brad Hansell, the head of the shipbuilders' union, and Senator Blandino. This is going to be a tough meeting. I'm briefed but I can't focus; instead, I'm sitting here staring at my computer, willing an e-mail to arrive from my wife. I can't believe I've heard nothing from Ana all day. Nothing.

I don't like this. I don't like being the object of her anger. I put my head in my hands. Maybe…maybe I should apologize. What did Flynn say? *It's better to concede the battle to win the war.*

And deep down, I know I've fucked up. But I'd hoped that she would have forgiven me by now.

I type out an e-mail.

From: Christian Grey
Subject: I'm Sorry
Date: September 14 2011 16:45
To: Anastasia Grey

I'm Sorry. I'm Sorry. I'm Sorry. I'm Sorry. I'm Sorry. I'm Sorry.
I'm Sorry. I'm Sorry. I'm Sorry. I'm Sorry. I'm Sorry. I'm Sorry.
I'm Sorry. I'm Sorry. I'm Sorry. I'm Sorry. I'm Sorry. I'm Sorry.
I'm Sorry. I'm Sorry. I'm Sorry. I'm Sorry. I'm Sorry. I'm Sorry.
I'm Sorry. I'm Sorry. I'm Sorry. I'm Sorry. I'm Sorry. I'm Sorry.
I fucked up. Please forgive me.

Christian Grey
CEO & Penitent Husband, Grey Enterprises Holdings Inc.

I don't want to go home to face her anger again. I want her smiles,
her laughter, and her love. I gaze up at her smiling face in the photo.
I want her to look at me like she does in this portrait. I return to the
e-mail, wondering whether to hit send. This meeting could go on for
a while. I call Mrs. Jones.

"Mr. Grey."

"I may not be home for dinner. Please make sure Mrs. Grey eats."

"Yes, sir."

"Cook her something nice."

"I will."

"Thank you, Gail." I hang up and delete the e-mail—it's not
going to be enough. I could try jewelry. Flowers? My phone buzzes.

"Yes, Andrea."

"Mr. Hansell and Senator Blandino are here with their teams."

"Call Ros and Samir to join us."

"Yes, sir."

This will be a fight about layoffs. I grit my teeth. Sometimes I
hate my job.

BLANDINO IS APPEALING FOR calm. "These are our economic
realities in 2011," she says to Hansell, who sits red-faced on the other
side of my boardroom table.

I just want to go home. But we're not finished here.

My phone buzzes, and my heart rate spikes. It's my wife. "Excuse me." I rise from the table, feeling seven pairs of eyes on me as I exit the room.

She's called. I'm almost giddy with relief—my heart feels like it will escape my chest. "Ana!"

"Hi." It's so good to hear her voice.

"Hi."

I can't think what else to say, but I want to beg her to stop being mad at me.

Please don't be mad. I'm sorry.

"Are you coming home?" she asks.

"Later."

"Are you in the office?"

I frown. "Yes. Where did you expect me to be?"

"I'll let you go."

What? But— There's so much I want to say, but neither of us speaks. The silence is a chasm between us and I have a boardroom of people locked in crisis talks waiting for me.

"Good night, Ana." *I love you.*

"Good night, Christian." I hang up before she can, thinking about all those times we've stayed on the line and neither of us hangs up. I couldn't bear to hear her end the call first. I stare despondently at my phone. At least she asked if I was coming home. Perhaps she misses me. Or she's checking up on me. Either way. She cares. Maybe. A small ember of hope glows deep in my heart. I need to wrap this meeting up and get home to my wife.

IT'S LATE WHEN WE agree on a potential compromise. With hindsight, I see that confrontation with the union was inevitable, but it's been good for all sides to air their grievances. Samir and Ros will now take the negotiations from here and hammer out a deal. Compared to the battle I'm facing at home, this wasn't so bad. Ros was an impressive negotiator, and I've persuaded her to go to Taiwan tomorrow evening without me.

"Okay, Christian. I'll go. But they'll really want you there."

"I'll find time. Later this month."

Her lips tighten, but she says nothing.

I can't tell her that I don't want to leave Ana when she's not even talking to me. Deep down, I know it's because I'm petrified my wife might not be there when I return.

THE APARTMENT IS DARK when I get home; Ana must be in bed. I head into our bedroom, and my heart sinks when I find she's not there. Stifling my panic, I head upstairs. In the dim light from the hallway, I make out her form curled up beneath the duvet in her old bedroom.

Old bedroom?

It's hardly that; she's slept in it, what, twice?

She looks so small. I flick the dimmer switch on to see her better, but keep the lights low, and carry the armchair over so I can sit down and gaze at her. Her skin is pale, translucent, almost. She's been crying; her eyelids and lips are swollen. My heart freefalls through my body with despair.

Oh, baby—I'm sorry.

I know how soft her lips are to kiss when she's been crying…when I make her cry. I want to climb in beside her, to pull her into my arms and hold her, but she's asleep, and she needs her sleep, especially now.

I settle into the chair and match my breathing to Ana's. The rhythm soothes me, that and my proximity to her. For the first time since I woke up this morning I feel a little calmer. The last time I sat and watched her sleep was when Hyde broke into our apartment; she'd been out with Kate. I was mad as hell then.

Why do I spend so much time mad at my wife?

I love her.

Even though she never does as she's told.

That's why.

God grant me the serenity to accept the things I cannot change;
The courage to change the things I can;
And the wisdom to know the difference.

I grimace as Dr Flynn's oft-quoted serenity prayer pops into my head: a prayer for alcoholics and fucked-up businessmen. I check my watch, though I know it's far too late to call him in New York. I'll try him tomorrow. I can discuss my impending fatherhood with him.

I shake my head.

Me, a dad?

What could I possibly offer a child? I undo my tie and the top button of my shirt as I lean back. I suppose there's the material wealth. At least he won't go hungry. No—not on my fucking watch. Not my child. She says she'll do this on her own. How could she? She's too...and I want to say *fragile*, because sometimes she looks fragile, but she's not. She's the strongest woman I know, stronger even than Grace.

Gazing at her as she lies here, sleeping the sleep of the innocent, I realize what an asshole I was yesterday. She's never backed down from a challenge, ever. She was hurt by what I said and what I did. I see that now. She knew I'd overreact when she told me about the baby.

She knows me better than anyone.

Did she find out before we were in Portland? I don't think so; she would have told me. She must have found out yesterday. And when she told me, everything turned to shit. My fear took over.

How am I going to make it up to her?

"I'm sorry, Ana. Forgive me," I whisper. "You scared the living shit out of me yesterday." Leaning forward, I kiss her forehead.

She stirs and frowns. "Christian," she murmurs, her voice wistful and full of longing. The hope kindled by her earlier call ignites into a fire.

"I'm here," I whisper.

But she turns over, sighs, and falls back into a deep slumber. I'm so tempted to strip down and join her, but I don't think I'd be welcome. "I love you, Anastasia Grey. I'll see you in the morning."

Damn. No, I won't.

I have to fly to Portland and see the finance committee at WSU in Vancouver. That means leaving early.

I place my favorite tie beside her on the pillow so she'll know I've been here. As I do, I recall the first time I tied her hands. The thought travels straight to my cock.

I wore it to tease her at her graduation.

I wore it at our wedding.

I'm a sentimental fool. "Tomorrow, baby," I whisper. "Sleep well."

I forgo the piano, even though I want to play. I don't want to wake her. But as I head alone into our bedroom, I'm more hopeful. She whispered my name.

Yes. There's hope for us yet.

Don't give up on me, Ana.

Thursday, September 15, 2011

It's 5:30 in the morning and I'm in the gym, pounding away on the treadmill. Sleep eluded me last night, and when I did drift off, I was haunted by my dreams:

Ana disappearing into the garage at The Heathman without looking back at me.

Ana an enraged siren, holding a thin cane, eyes blazing, wearing nothing but expensive lingerie and leather boots, her angry words like barbs.

Ana lying unmoving on a sticky green rug.

I shake off that last image and run harder, pushing my body to its limits. I don't want to feel anything except the pain of my bursting lungs and aching legs. With Bloomberg's rolling business news on the TV and "Pump It" in my ears, I blot out the world... I blot out thoughts of my wife, sleeping soundly two rooms away from me.

Dream of me, Ana. Miss me.

In the shower while I hose off my workout sweat, I contemplate waking her just to say good-bye. I fly to Portland in *Charlie Tango* this morning, and I'd like a sweet smile to take with me.

Let her sleep, Grey.

And given how pissed she is at me, there's no guarantee of a sweet smile.

Mrs. Jones is still giving me the cold shoulder, but I grill her anyway. "Did Ana eat last night?"

"She did." Mrs. Jones's attention is on the omelet she's preparing for me. I think that's all the information I'm going to get this morning. I sip my coffee and sulk, feeling fifty shades of miserable.

In the car on the way to Boeing Field I write an e-mail to Ana.

Keep it factual, Grey.

From: Christian Grey
Subject: Portland
Date: September 15 2011 06:45
To: Anastasia Grey

Ana,
I am flying down to Portland today.
I have some business to conclude with WSU.
I thought you would want to know.

Christian Grey
CEO, Grey Enterprises Holdings, Inc.

But I know my real intention in sending an e-mail isn't to inform her…but to get a response.

I live in hope.

Stephan is on hand to fly us down to Portland. After my sleepless night, I'm dog-tired. If I fall asleep, I'll be more comfortable in the rear, so for the first time ever, I offer Taylor the front passenger seat, remove my jacket, and take a back seat in *Charlie Tango*. I leaf through the notes I have for the meeting, and once I've done that, I lean back and close my eyes.

Ana is running through the meadow at the new house. She's laughing as I chase her. I'm laughing, too. I catch her and pull her down into the long grass. She giggles and I kiss her. Her lips are soft, because she's been crying. No. Don't cry. Baby, don't cry. Please don't cry. She closes her eyes. She sleeps. She won't wake. Ana! *Ana!* She's lying on a thread worn rug. Pale. Unmoving. Ana. Wake up. *Ana!*

Gasping, I wake, and I'm momentarily disoriented. Wait—I'm in *Charlie Tango*, and we've just landed in Portland. The rotors are still spinning, and Stephan is talking to the tower. I rub my face to rouse myself and unbuckle my harness.

Taylor opens his door and steps out onto the helipad while I don my jacket, careful not to snag the cable of my headphones.

"Thanks, Stephan," I say over the cans.

"No problem, Mr. Grey."

"We should be back around one this afternoon."

"We'll be ready and waiting." He frowns, his concern evident in the creases across his brow, while Taylor, head down, opens my door

Shit. I hope that concern is not directed at me. I remove my headphones and clamber out to join Taylor. It's a crisp morning, brighter than Seattle, but with a brisk breeze that carries the scent of fall. There's no sign of Joe, the old-timer who's normally here to oversee arrivals and departures. Maybe it's too early in the day, or he's not slated to work this morning...or it's an omen or some shit.

For fuck's sake, Grey. Pull yourself together.

Our driver is waiting outside the helipad building. Taylor opens the door of the Escalade and I slide in, then he takes the passenger seat up front.

With my bad dream about Ana still in mind, I call Sawyer.

"Mr. Grey."

"Luke. Stay close to Mrs. Grey today."

"Will do, sir."

"Is she having breakfast?" I keep my voice low as I'm a little embarrassed to be asking. But I want to know she's okay.

"I believe so, sir. We're leaving in about fifteen minutes for the office."

"Good. Thanks." I hang up and stare morosely out the window at the Willamette River. Its metallic gray waters look chilly as we cross over the Steel Bridge. I shudder. This is hell. I need to talk to Ana. We can't go on like this.

I have one option that might work.

Apologize, Grey.

Yeah. It's my only option.

Because I behaved like an asshole.

Ana's words come back to me: *You need to grow up and smell the fucking coffee, and stop behaving like a petulant adolescent.*

Fuck. She's not wrong.

Now is not the time. I have to help the WSU Environmental Science Department nail additional funding from the USDA. It's vital to progress the work that Professor Gravett and her team are undertaking in soil technology. Her work is reaping huge benefits in our test sites in Ghana. This is a game changer. Soil could be a key initiative not only in feeding the planet and alleviating food insecurity and poverty, but also through carbon sequestration reversing climate change. From my briefcase I pull out my notes and scan them once more.

THE MEETING HAS BEEN a resounding success—we've secured an additional million dollars from the USDA. It appears that feeding the world is quite high on the federal government's agenda, too. With the gratitude of Professors Choudury and Gravett ringing in my ears, Taylor and I head back to Portland. I check my phone, but there's no word from my wife—not even a snarky response to my e-mail. It's depressing. I'm anxious to get home and find some way to smooth her ruffled feathers…if I can.

Maybe a meal out?

A movie?

Soaring?

Sailing?

Sex?

What can I do?

I miss her.

The Escalade parks outside the helipad building, as Taylor makes a call.

"Sawyer, I read your text," he murmurs, and he has my full attention.

Text? Is Ana okay?

He frowns as he listens. "Copy." Taylor's eyes meet mine. "I see. Hold on," he says to Luke, then addresses me. "Mrs. Grey is feeling unwell. Sawyer is taking her back to the apartment."

"Is it serious?"

"No reason to think so."

"Okay. We'll fly straight to Escala."

"Yes, sir. Sawyer, we're leaving shortly. We'll divert directly to Escala, land there."

"Keep her safe!" I shout, loud enough for Sawyer to hear me.

"You heard Mr. Grey. Text me if the situation changes." Taylor hangs up.

With a renewed sense of urgency, Taylor and I enter the building, and I'm pleased that the elevator is waiting for us.

I hope Ana's okay...and the baby.

Maybe I should call my mom, ask her to go over and check on Ana. Or Dr. Greene—though I'm not sure she'd take my call. It will take us an hour to get home, and I can't wait that long; I try my mother, but there's no phone signal—we're in the elevator. I can't call Ana, either.

Surely if it were serious she'd have called me?

Damn. I have no idea, given she's not talking to me.

The elevator doors open, *Charlie Tango* is where we left her, and Stephan is waiting at the controls.

To hell with this. I'm going to fly her. I can direct my attention to the flight, rather than dwell on what's happening at Escala.

I hope Ana goes to bed. *Our bed.*

Stephan steps down from the cockpit to greet us.

"Stephan, hi. I'd like to fly her home. We need a new course, for Escala."

"Yes, sir." He opens the pilot's door for me, and I think he's surprised by the change in my attitude. I climb aboard, buckle up, and begin the final preflight checks.

"All checks done?" I ask Stephan as he takes the seat beside me.

"Just the transponder."

"Oh, yes. I see. I need to get home to my wife. Taylor, you strapped in?"

"Yes, sir." His disembodied voice is loud and clear in my cans. I radio the tower, and they're ready for us.

"Right, gentlemen, let's get home." Pulling back the collective, I float *Charlie Tango* smoothly into the sky and head for Seattle.

As we cut through the air at speed, I know I've made the right decision to pilot. I have to focus on keeping us airborne, but deep down, my anxiety continues to gnaw at my insides. I hope Ana's okay.

We touch down right on schedule at 2:30.

"Good flying, Mr. Grey," Stephan says.

"Enjoy taking her back to Boeing Field."

"Will do." He grins.

I unbuckle my harness, switch on my phone, and follow Taylor out onto Escala's rooftop. Taylor frowns down at his phone. I halt as he listens to a message.

"It's from Sawyer. Mrs. Grey is at the bank." Taylor raises his voice to be heard over the wind that whips around us on the roof.

What? I thought she was ill. What the fuck is she doing at the bank?

"Sawyer followed her there. She tried to give him the slip."

Anxiety spirals into my chest, tightening around my heart. My rebooted phone beeps and vibrates with a flood of alerts. There's a text from Andrea, sent four minutes ago, and a couple of missed calls from my bank, and one from Welch.

What the fuck?

> **ANDREA**
> Troy Whelan at your bank needs
> to speak with you urgently.

I have Whelan on speed dial. He picks up immediately.

"Whelan, it's Christian Grey. What's going on?" I shout over the rush of the wind.

"Mr. Grey, good afternoon. Um, your wife is here requesting to withdraw five million dollars."

What?

My blood turns to ice.

"Five million?" I can't quite believe what he's said.

What does she need five million for?

Fuck. She's leaving me.

My world crashes and burns, a cavern of despair opening at my feet.

"Yes, sir. As you know, under current banking legislation I can't cash five million."

"Yes, of course." I'm in shock, teetering on the brink of the abyss. "Let me talk to Mrs. Grey." I sound robotic.

"Certainly, sir. If you'll hold for a minute."

This is agony. I head to shelter out of the wind, beside the elevator doors, and stand quietly waiting to hear from my wife…dreading to hear from my wife.

She's going. She's leaving me.

What am I going to do without her? The phone clicks and my panic overwhelms me.

"Hi." Ana's voice is breathy and high-pitched.

"You're leaving me?" The words are out before I can stop them.

"No!" she rasps, and it sounds like an agonized appeal.

Oh, thank fuck. But my relief is short-lived.

"Yes," she whispers, as if she's just made her decision.

What!

"Ana, I—" I don't know what to say. I want to beg her to stay.

"Christian, please. Don't."

"You're going?" *You're really going.*

"Yes."

No! No! NO! I free-fall, tumbling down into the abyss. Falling. Falling. Falling. Reaching out, I splay my hand on the wall to support myself. The pain is visceral.

Don't leave me.

Shit, was this always going to happen? Did she ever love me?

Was it my fucking money?

"But why the cash? Was it always the money?" Tell me it wasn't the money. Please. The pain is indescribable.

"No!" She sounds emphatic.

Do I believe her?

Is it because I saw Elena? For God's sake! And in this moment, I don't think I could loathe Elena more. I breathe deep, trying to get a handle on my thoughts.

"Is five million enough?" *How will I live without Ana?*

"Yes."

"And the baby?" *She'll take our baby away?* The knife twists in my soul.

"I'll take care of the baby."

"This is what you want?"

"Yes." Her voice is barely audible. But I hear her. The pain is crippling. She wants me off the phone—I can tell. She wants it done. She wants away from *me*.

"Take it all," I whisper.

"Christian," she sobs. "It's for you. For your family. Please. Don't."

I can't stand this.

"Take it all, Anastasia," I snarl and tilt my head back and silently howl at the gray sky above me.

"Christian—" Her desperation is laced through every syllable of my name. I can't bear to hear her.

"I'll always love you," I murmur, because it's true. They're the last words of a condemned man. I hang up and take a deep, steadying breath, feeling hollow...nothing more than a husk.

I told her that once.

In a shower.

And then I told her I loved her.

"Mr. Grey?" Taylor's trying to attract my attention. Ignoring him, I call Whelan again.

"Troy Whelan."

"It's Christian Grey. Give my wife the money. Whatever she wants."

"Mr. Grey, I can't—"

"I know you hold the reserve for the Pacific Northwest. Just transfer it from the main holding account. Or liquidate some of my assets. I don't care. Give her the money."

"Mr. Grey, this is highly irregular."

"Just fucking do it, Whelan. Find a way, or I'll close all the accounts and move GEH's business elsewhere. Understand?"

He's silent on the other end of the phone.

"We'll sort the fucking paperwork out later," I add, in a more conciliatory tone.

"Yes, Mr. Grey."

"Just give her whatever she wants."

"Yes, Mr. Grey." I hang up.

I want to cry. I want to break down here on the roof and weep. But I can't. I close my eyes and wish that I were here on my own.

"Mr. Grey." Taylor's voice cuts through my pain.

I turn to face him, and he blanches. "What?" I snarl.

"Hyde has been granted bail. He's free."

I glare at him. *What fresh hell is this?*

Hyde is free? *How?* I thought we'd dealt with that.

Taylor and I eyeball each other, wondering, *What the hell?*

"*You're leaving me?*"

"*No!*"

"*It's for you. For your family. Please. Don't.*"

"Ana!" I whisper. "She's trying to withdraw five million dollars."

Taylor's eyes widen. "Shit!" he says.

We reach the same conclusion at the same instant. Whatever the hell she's doing, deep down I know it has something to do with that fucker Hyde. I punch the elevator button, as my utter despair congeals into fear. Fear for my wife. "Where's Sawyer?"

"He's at the bank. He tracked her car." We leap into the elevator and I jab the button for the garage as *Charlie Tango's* rotors start again. It's deafening.

"You have the car keys?" I shout to Taylor as the doors close.

"Yes, sir."

"Let's get to the bank. Do we know where Hyde is?"

"No. I'll text Welch."

"He left a message. Shit—it must have been the news about Hyde."

The elevator takes forever to descend to the garage. What is Ana playing at? Why can't she tell me if she's in trouble? Fear wraps around my heart and my gut, strangling me from the inside. What could be worse than Ana leaving me? The distressing picture from my earlier dream slips into my head, drawing on older—much older—disturbing memories: a woman lifeless on the floor. I screw my eyes shut.

No. Please. No.

"We'll find her," Taylor says with grim determination.

"We have to."

"I'll track her cell," he states.

At last the doors open and Taylor tosses me his Q7 keys. He wants me to drive?

Get a grip, Grey. You have to get your wife out of this mess.

Perhaps that fucker is blackmailing her.

We climb into the car and I switch on the ignition. The tires scream as I reverse out of the space and speed up to the garage entrance, only to wait agonizing seconds for the barrier to rise. "Come on. Come on. Come on. Come on!"

Barely clearing the barrier, we roar out onto the street in the direction of the bank.

Taylor puts his phone on the dash, waiting for a signal, cursing impatiently under his breath.

"She's still at the bank," he says eventually.

"Good."

The traffic is heavier than I expected. It's frustrating.

Come on, come on, come *on*!

Why does Ana do this? Keep this shit to herself? Doesn't she trust me?

I think about my behavior over the last couple of days.

Okay, it hasn't been exemplary, by any means, but she takes all this crap on her shoulders. Why can't she ask for help?

"Ana Grey," I shout into the phone's Bluetooth system. After a few moments her phone starts to ring, and ring, and ring…then it goes to voice mail. My heart sinks.

"Hi, you've reached Ana. I can't take your call right now, but please leave a message after the beep, and I'll call you right back."

Christ!

"Ana! What the fuck is going on?" I yell. It feels good to yell. "I'm coming to get you. Call me. Talk to me." I hang up.

"She's still at the bank," Taylor says.

"Sawyer's still there?"

"Yes, sir."

"Call Sawyer!" I shout into the hands-free, and moments later his cell is ringing.

"Mr. Grey?"

"Where's Ana?"

"She's just turned around and gone back into one of the offices."

"Go get her."

"Sir, I'm armed. I can't go through the detectors. I'm standing by the entrance watching Anast—Mrs. Grey, and looking very suspicious. If I go back to the car to stow my gun, I may lose her."

Fucking firearms.

"How the hell did she give you the slip?"

"She's a very resourceful woman, Mr. Grey." He sounds like he's speaking through gritted teeth, and I recognize his frustration. It makes me feel slightly more sympathetic to him; she drives me crazy, too.

"I want a thorough briefing when we have her back. Jack Hyde has been granted bail, and both Taylor and I have a hunch that Ana's actions have something to do with him."

"Shit!" Luke says.

"Exactly. We're about five minutes away. Don't let her go again, Sawyer."

"Sir."

I hang up.

Taylor and I sit in silence as I weave through traffic.

What are you up to, Anastasia Grey?

What am I going to do to you when I get you back?

Various scenarios cross my mind. I shift in my seat.

For fuck's sake, Grey. Now is not the time.

Taylor startles me. "She's on the move."

"What?" My heart jump-starts as adrenaline courses through my body.

"She's heading south, on Second."

"Call Sawyer!" I shout. Moments later, his cell rings again.

"Mr. Grey," he answers immediately.

"She's on the move!"

"What? She hasn't come out through the main entrance." He sounds confused.

"She's heading south on Second," Taylor interjects.

"I'm on it. I'll call from the car." Sawyer is obviously running. "She's not in her car. It's still here."

"Hell!" I shout.

"Still heading south on Second," Taylor says. "Wait. She's turned left onto Yesler."

We pass my bank. There's no point stopping. "That's three blocks?" I ask him.

"Yes, sir."

For the billionth time I thank God Taylor's with me. He knows this city like the back of his hand—which is odd, given he's from some rural town in the middle of nowhere in Texas.

Three minutes later, we're heading east on Yesler.

"She's still on Yesler," Taylor growls, eyes glued to his phone. "She's turned south. Onto Twenty-Third. That's eight blocks from here."

"I'm right behind you," Sawyer pipes up through the hands-free.

"Stay close. I'm going to try and dodge through this traffic." I glance at Taylor. "I wish you were driving."

"You're doing fine, sir."

Where the fuck is she going? And who with?

We're silent for several minutes. I focus on the road, while Taylor occasionally calls out directions. We head south, then east again, now through mainly residential streets.

"She's turned south down Thirtieth."

We follow for a few blocks, then turn east.

"It's stopped. South Day Street. Two more blocks."

Dread sits heavy and caustic in my stomach as I race through the back streets.

Three minutes later, I swing onto South Day Street.

"Slow down," Taylor orders, surprising me, but I do as he says. "She's here somewhere." He leans forward, and we scan each side of the road. There is a row of derelict buildings on my side.

"Fuck!" There's a potholed parking lot where a woman is standing with her hands in the air beside a black Dodge. *The Dodge!* I wrench the wheel and swing into the parking lot, and there she is—

On the ground. Unmoving. Eyes closed.

Ana. My Ana… No! Everything moves in slow motion as all the air is sucked from my lungs. My worst fear realized. Here. Now.

Taylor is out of the car before I've screeched to a halt. I follow him, leaving the engine running.

"Ana!" I shout. *Please, God. Please, God. Please, God.*

She is lifeless on the concrete. In front of her, that fucker Hyde is rolling on the ground, screaming in agony as he clutches his upper leg. Blood seeps through his fingers. The woman steps back, keeping her hands in the air as Taylor draws his gun.

But it's Ana who has my whole attention. She's lying unmoving on the cold, hard ground.

No!

This is what I've dreaded since I met her. This moment. I kneel beside her, terrified to touch her. Taylor picks up the gun lying beside her and orders the woman to lie facedown on the ground. "Don't shoot me, don't shoot me," she gibbers.

Shit! That's Elizabeth Morgan, from SIP.

How the hell is she involved in this clusterfuck?

Sawyer is suddenly with us. He draws his gun on Elizabeth and stands guard over her.

Hyde screams in agony. "Help me! Help me! The bitch shot me!" We ignore him.

Taylor bends and checks the pulse point beneath Ana's jaw.

"She's alive. Strong pulse," he says. *Thank God.* Then he barks at Sawyer, "Call 911 now. Ambulance and police."

Sawyer reaches for his phone, while Taylor quickly and gently runs his hands over Ana, checking for injuries.

"I don't think she's bleeding."

"Can I touch her?"

"She may have broken something. Best leave it to the paramedics."

Oh no. My wife. My girl. My beautiful girl.

I stroke her hair and gently tuck a strand behind her ear. She looks like she's asleep, though she has a red mark on her face. *Did he fucking hit you? Did he do this to you?*

Now my attention turns to Hyde, who's still fucking screaming. A fresh shot of adrenaline-fueled rage streaks through my bloodstream.

The fucker. He put his hands on my wife, and she shot him.

My God, Ana shot him.

I stand and move so I tower over him as he writhes on the ground. And before I know what I'm doing, I lean on the Dodge, draw back my leg, and kick him with all my might in his stomach, hard. Twice. Three times, with all my weight behind each kick.

He screams.

"You do this to my wife, you fucker?" I bellow my rage and kick him again. He drags his hands up to protect his stomach, and I stamp with all my weight on the seeping wound on his thigh. He screams again—a different, louder, feral cry of agony. Leaning down, I grab the lapels of his jacket and bounce his head off the ground. Once. Twice. His eyes are wide and wild with fear as he grips my hands, smearing his blood on me.

"I'm going to fucking kill you, you twisted, sick motherfucker!"

From the far end of the tunnel, I hear voices. "Mr. Grey! Mr. Grey! Christian! Christian, stop!" It's Taylor. He and Sawyer are pulling me away—pulling me off the vermin that is Hyde. Taylor grabs me by both shoulders and shakes me.

"Christian! Stop! Now!" He shakes me once more.

I blink at him and shrug him off.

Don't touch me!

Taylor puts himself between Hyde and me, watching me like I'm unhinged, lethal and ready to strike. I take a breath while the murderous red mist clears.

"I'm okay," I whisper.

"Look after your wife, sir." Taylor's tone is emphatic.

I nod. And glance once more at the fucker on the ground. He's rocking gently, sniveling like the weasel-turd he is and clutching his thigh. He's pissed himself, disgusting fuck. "Let him bleed to death," I mutter to Taylor, and turn away.

I kneel beside Ana and lean down to hear her breathing, but I hear nothing. Panic swamps me once more. "Is she still breathing?" I glance up at Taylor.

"Look at her chest, rising and falling." Taylor leans down again and checks her pulse. "Still strong."

Oh, Ana. What were you thinking? What about the baby?

Tears prick my eyes. I loathe this feeling of helplessness. I want to fold her into my arms and sob into her hair—but I can't touch her. This is agony. Where is the fucking ambulance?

"The girl. The girl." Elizabeth suddenly pipes up.

What girl? We all turn to look at her, prone on the ground.

"Inside," she says. "There. That building." She points with her chin.

Is this a trick?

I hear Taylor's quiet command. "Sawyer, check inside."

In the distance, sirens wail. *Thank God!*

"Taylor!" When I turn, Sawyer is standing in the doorway. "They have Miss Grey in here."

"Stay here, Christian!" Taylor raises a finger in warning.

Mia? My baby sister? Fear blooms in my gut. *What has that fucker done to my sister?* I watch, paralyzed, as Taylor disappears into the building, Sawyer regarding him from the doorway.

"It's for you. For your family. Please. Don't…"

And what Ana said all becomes clear. I stare down at her, and I know in this moment that she could have been murdered by the sick fuck. Bile rises in my throat, and time suspends, until Taylor emerges from the building. "She's okay, I think. She's drugged. Asleep. No obvious signs of injury or assault. She's fully clothed. I don't want to move her. We'll let the paramedics do that."

"Mia?" I ask, not quite believing the awfulness of this situation.

He nods. His mouth set in a grim line.

The sirens are louder.

What the fuck was Hyde planning to do to my sister? He's still whimpering like a wounded dog, quieter now, and I suspect he's lost a lot of blood. I don't give a shit. I want to kill him, slowly, painfully—but two ambulances, two police patrol vehicles, and a fire truck pull up in blaze of flashing lights and a cacophony of sirens, shattering the peace of the neighborhood, and saving Hyde's skin.

I'M IN A WAKING nightmare, sitting between Mia and Ana in the ambulance as we speed through Seattle. My head is in my hands, my heart is in my mouth, as I pray for both of them. I'm not a religious man, but right now I'd do anything, even plead with God, to know that my wife, our baby, and my sister are okay.

"Vital signs are good, Mr. Grey, for both your wife and your sister," the paramedic says, his dark eyes full of compassion.

"My wife's pregnant."

The paramedic looks down at Ana. "Sir, there are no obvious signs of bleeding."

I pale, knowing that he's trying to reassure me, but it's not working. "Why is she still unconscious?" My voice is a whisper.

"The doctors should be able to determine that when we arrive."

Mia stirs, mumbling incoherently. She's coming around. It's obvious she's been drugged. But at least she's calm. I grasp her hand and squeeze. "It's okay, Mia. We're here."

She mumbles something, but still hasn't opened her eyes, but she squeezes my hand in return and relaxes back into what I hope is sleep.

My sister, my wife, my unborn child. I should have killed Hyde when I had the chance. Impotent rage curdles in my stomach once more and I screw up my eyes, trying to dispel it. I want to weep. I want to howl to release this pain, but I can't.

Hell. I'm wrung out. The last words I exchanged with Ana...

"You're leaving me?"

"No!"

"It's for you. For your family. Please. Don't."

I told her I would always love her. At least I did that.

Please wake up, Ana.

Nagging me, deep down, is concern for the baby. Was Ana really ill, or did she make that up? This...stress, fuck. It can't be good for him.

Junior. Is he okay?

Finally, we reach the ER, and I'm immediately sidelined as the paramedics swing into action.

Mom and Dad are there, waiting. They rush to the gurney carrying my sleeping or unconscious sister. Grace takes one look at Mia and tears spring to her eyes. She takes her hand. "I love you, baby," she wails, as the paramedics whisk Mia toward the double doors where Dad can't follow. He stands aside and watches as Mom follows them through into the ER triage.

A nurse and doctor take Ana's gurney.

"Careful with my wife. She's pregnant." My voice is hoarse and hushed with worry.

"We'll take good care of her," the attending says. I release Ana's hand, and they wheel her through after Mia.

Carrick joins me, ashen-faced, looking every inch his age.

We stare at each other. "Dad," I whisper, my voice cracking.

"Oh, son." Carrick opens his arms and for the first time in my life I step into them, and he holds me. I swallow my welling emotion and grip his jacket, beyond grateful for his quiet strength, his reassuring presence, his familiar scent, but most of all his love. "It's going to be okay, son. They're both going to be okay."

"They're going to be okay," I repeat like a mantra, while my throat burns with my suppressed anguish. "They're going to be okay."

But he doesn't know that for sure.

I just pray it's true.

I pull back, suddenly conscious that we're two grown men hugging at the entrance of the ER. Carrick smiles and squeezes my shoulder. "Let's go to the waiting room. You can tell me what's happened, and we can get you cleaned up."

"Sure." I nod and look down at my hands. Shit! They're still stained with that cocksucker's blood.

ANA IS PALE, EXCEPT for the bruise on her cheek where the motherfucker must have hit her. Her eyes are closed as if she's merely asleep, but she's still unconscious. She looks heartbreakingly young and small. Numerous tubes wind into and out of her body. My heart clenches and twists in fear, but Dr. Bartley is calm as she looks down at my broken wife.

"Her ribs are bruised, Mr. Grey, and she has a hairline fracture to her skull, but her vital signs are stable and strong."

"Why is she still unconscious?"

"Mrs. Grey has had a major contusion to her head. But her brain activity is normal, and she has no cerebral swelling. She'll wake when she's ready. Just give her some time."

"And the baby?" I whisper.

"The baby's fine, Mr. Grey."

"Oh, thank God." Relief crashes through me like a cyclone.

Thank God.

"Mr. Grey. Do you have any further questions?"

"Can she hear me?"

Dr. Bartley's smile is benign. "Who knows? If she can, I'm sure she'd love to hear your voice."

I'm not so sure. She'll be mad. I thought she was leaving me.

"My colleague Dr. Singh will look in on your wife later."

"Thank you," I mutter, and she leaves.

Pulling up a chair I sit down beside Ana. Tenderly I take her hand, glad to find it's warm. I squeeze it gently, hoping to rouse her. "Wake up, baby, please," I whisper. "Be mad at me, but be awake, please." Leaning forward, I brush my lips against her knuckles. "I'm sorry. Sorry for everything. Please wake up."

Please. I love you.

I cup her hand in both of mine and press my forehead to my fingers and pray.

Please, God. Please. Bring my wife back to me.

ANA SLEEPS, HER ROOM shrouded in darkness, save for the pool of light from her bedside lamp and the faint illumination from beneath the door. Using my jacket as a blanket, I doze in my chair, fighting sleep. I want to be awake when she comes back to me.

The door opens, rousing me, and Grace enters. "Hello, darling," she whispers, her face pale—devoid of makeup. She looks as tired and drained as I feel.

"Mom." I'm too weary to stand.

"I'm just checking in, as I'm leaving to get some sleep. Carrick is here to watch over Mia."

"How is she?"

"She's okay. Angry. Still suffering from the effects of the drugs. Trying to sleep. Ana?"

"No change."

Grace picks up Ana's medical chart from the end of her bed and scans the notes. Her eyes widen and she gasps. "She's pregnant!"

I nod, too shattered and anxious to do anything else.

"Oh, Christian, that's wonderful news. Congratulations." She steps forward and grasps my shoulder.

"Thanks, Mom. It's early days." *I think.*

"I understand. Couples usually announce at twelve weeks. Darling, you're exhausted. Go home and sleep."

I shake my head. "I'll sleep when Ana wakes."

She presses her lips together but doesn't comment, and bending down she kisses my head. "She'll wake, Christian. Just give her a little time. Try and get some sleep."

"Bye, Mom."

She ruffles my hair. "I'll see you in the morning." She exits as quietly as she arrived, leaving me more bereft than ever.

Just to torture myself, and also to stay awake, I replay my misdemeanors of the last couple of days.

I've been an asshole.

About the baby.

Seeing Elena.

Not apologizing.

And to cap it all, I believed Ana…believed her when she said she was leaving me.

My eyes droop, and my head drops forward, jolting me awake.

Fuck.

I gaze at my wife, willing her to open her eyes.

Ana. Please. Come back to me. "And then I can apologize. Properly. Please, baby." Taking her hand, I bring it to my lips once more and kiss each knuckle. "I miss you."

Leaning back, I close my eyes, just for a second.

I wake a moment later. *Shit.* How long have I slept? I check my watch—nearly three hours. Glancing over at my wife, I see she's still slumbering peacefully.

Except she's not asleep. She's unconscious.

"Come back to me, baby," I whisper.

"Christian."

"Dad! You startled me."

"Sorry." Carrick emerges from the shadows.

"How long have you been standing there?"

"Not long. I didn't want to wake you. The nurse was just here checking Ana's vitals. It's all good." He stares down at my wife. "Grace tells me she's carrying my grandchild." His eyes shine in reverence as he gazes at Ana.

"Yes. She is."

"Congratulations, son."

I give him a bleak smile. "She put the child and herself at risk." I shiver, and don't know if it's because the night air is cooler or because Ana could so easily be dead.

Carrick presses his lips together, his expression grave, then turns his attention to me. "You're exhausted. You should go home and rest."

"I'm not leaving her."

"Christian, you should sleep."

"No, Dad. I want to be here when she wakes up."

"I'll sit with her. It's the least I can do after she saved my daughter."

"How's Mia?"

"She's asleep. She was groggy, scared, and angry. It'll be a few hours before the Rohypnol is completely out of her system."

"Christ." *Hyde is a sick, twisted, cocksucking son of a bitch.*

"I know. I'm feeling seven kinds of foolish for relenting on her security. You warned me, but Mia is so stubborn. If it wasn't for Ana here..."

"We all thought Hyde was out of the picture. And my crazy, stupid wife—why didn't she tell me?" My unshed tears scald my throat.

"Christian, calm down," he says, gently moving toward me. "Ana's a remarkable young woman. She was incredibly brave."

"Brave and headstrong and stubborn and stupid." My voice breaks on the last word as I fight to contain my emotion.

But what would have happened to Mia, if not for Ana?

This is so confusing. I place my head in my hands, conflicted.

"Hey." Dad rests his hand on my shoulder. I welcome his comforting touch. "Don't be so hard on her, or yourself, son. I'd better get back to your mom. It's after three in the morning, Christian. You really should try to sleep."

"I thought Mom went home."

Carrick blows out a breath in frustration. "She couldn't leave Mia. She's stubborn, like you. Congratulations again on the baby. That's some good news, in all this mess."

I feel the blood drain from my head—I'll never be as good a father as Carrick.

"Hey," he says gently. "You've got this."

And because I'm weary and despondent, I'm annoyed that he's diagnosed my anxiety so precisely.

Perceptive, Dad.

"You'll make a great father, Christian. Stop worrying. You have several months to get used to the idea." He pats my shoulder again. "I'll be back later this morning."

"Good night, Dad." I watch him quietly close the door.

A great father, eh?

I put my head in my hands.

Right now, I just want my wife back. I don't want to think about the baby.

I stand and stretch. It's late. I'm stiff and sore and heartsick with worry.

Why won't she wake up? Bending, I kiss her cheek. Her skin is soft and reassuringly warm against my lips.

"Wake up, baby," I whisper. "I need you."

"GOOD MORNING, MR. GREY."

What? Again I'm startled from my doze as the nurse opens the curtains, letting the golden fall light invade the room. It's the older nurse—I can't remember her name. "I'm going to check your wife's IV fluids."

"Sure," I mumble. "Do I need to leave?"

"It's up to you."

"I'll stretch my legs." Feeling like shit, I get up, and with a last glance at my wife, I stagger out into the corridor. Maybe I can find some coffee.

TAYLOR ARRIVES AROUND 8:30 with my phone charger and some breakfast (courtesy of Mrs. Jones). I wonder if it's a peace offering from her. One peek into the brown paper bag confirms that it is: two ham-and-cheese croissants. They smell divine. And I have a thermos of proper coffee. "Please thank Gail for me."

"Will do. How is Mrs. Grey?" He looks toward Ana, his concern obvious in the tight line of his jaw.

"All signs are good. We're just waiting for her to wake up. I can't believe we spent last weekend at OHSU, and this weekend we're at Northwest."

Taylor nods sympathetically.

"You may as well stay and update me here. I don't want to leave her side." I offer him the seat beside me. While I eat my breakfast, he recounts all that happened after the ambulances left the crime scene.

"...and the police have recovered Mrs. Grey's cell phone."

"Oh."

"She placed it in one of the duffel bags with the cash."

"Really?" I glance at my sleeping wife. That's genius. "We were following the money?"

"Indeed," Taylor responds, and it's obvious he's impressed with Ana's ingenuity. "The police have the cash."

It's the first time I've thought about the five million dollars.

"Will we get it back?"

"Eventually, sir."

I roll my eyes. It's the least of my problems. "I'll get Welch onto the police and let him liaise with them for the return of the money."

"Hyde is here, being patched up. He's under police guard," Taylor says.

"I wish she'd finished him off."

Taylor holds his counsel, and I remember him wrestling me off Hyde while I was beating that fucker to a pulp. I can't decide if Taylor's actions were a good thing or not.

Hell. If he hadn't, I'd be in a police cell now.

"Detective Clark would like a word with you at some point." Taylor wisely changes the subject as I take a bite of the second croissant.

"Now is not the time."

"Ryan has collected Mrs. Grey's car. Apart from a parking ticket, it's all good." His smile is wry. "Sawyer's mad he let her get away."

"I'm sure."

"There are photographers camped outside the hospital."

Hell.

My phone buzzes. It's Ray. *Shit.*

"Ray. Good morning."

"I need to see Annie."

Ray has heard about Ana's heroics, courtesy of the media, and now insists on seeing her. As he's the only man in the world who intimidates me, I cannot say no.

I dispatch Taylor, and thirty minutes later Ray's sitting at the end of her bed in his wheelchair.

"Annie," he whispers as I wheel him in closer to her bed. "What was she thinking?" he says, his voice hoarse. He's shaved and is wearing loose shorts and a shirt, so in spite of the broken leg and bruising, he looks more like himself.

"I don't know, Ray. We'll have to wait for her to wake up before we can ask her."

"If you don't take her across your knee, I sure as hell will. What the hell was she thinking?" He's more adamant this time.

"Trust me, Ray, I just might do that." *If she'll let me.* I clutch her hand while Ray shakes his head.

"She shot him, you know."

His mouth drops open. "The kidnapper?"

"Yes."

"Well, I'll be damned."

"Thanks for teaching her how to use a gun. Maybe you can teach me to shoot one day."

"Christian, I'd be honored." We both gaze at my headstrong, reckless, brave wife. Each of us nursing our own fearful thoughts while Ana remains unconscious.

"Let me know when she wakes up."

"Will do, Ray."

"I'll call Carla," he mutters.

"I'd appreciate it. Thanks."

He kisses Ana's hand, his eyes glistening with tears, and I have to look away.

When he leaves, I call the office, then Welch, who is in Detroit, following a lead on Hyde. He can't believe Hyde found someone to post bail. Finding out who and why they did is next on his agenda. He's going to call his contact at the Seattle Police Department to ascertain what they know.

I pace back and forth in front of the window to shake off my fatigue as I talk on the phone and watch my wife. She sleeps through my calls, she sleeps through the frequent arrival of flowers from our family and friends—so by mid-afternoon her room resembles a florist's, and she sleeps through their calls inquiring about her well-being.

Everyone loves Ana.

What's not to love? I brush her soft, translucent cheek with my knuckles, fighting the urge to cry. "Baby, wake up. Please. Wake up and be mad at me again. Anything. Hate me...whatever. Just wake up. Please."

I sit beside her and wait.

Kate barges into the room without knocking.

"Kate. Hi."

She nods a greeting and strides straight to Ana's bed and takes her hand. "How is she?"

I'm too tired for this. "Unconscious."

"Ana! Ana! Wake up," Kate barks.

For fuck's sake. The tenacious Ms. Kavanagh is here. "I've tried, Kate. I've been assured that she'll wake in her own time."

Kate presses her lips together. "She doesn't have the sense that she was born with."

I can't argue with that.

She turns to me. "How are you holding up?"

Her inquiry into my well-being is a surprise. "I'm fine. Anxious. Tired."

She nods. "You look it. You two make up?"

I sigh. "Not exactly. When she wakes..." I trail off.

Weirdly, Kate seems to accept this, and doesn't give me a hard time. "So, what happened? How did she end up here?" She folds her arms, and because it looks like I won't get rid of her any other way, I give her the executive summary of Hyde's kidnapping of my sister and Ana's heroic but utterly foolhardy rescue.

"Shit!" Kate says when I finish. "What the hell was she thinking? She's supposed to be the smart one."

"Yeah."

"You know, Christian—she loves you very much."

"I know. She wouldn't be here like this if she didn't." I clench my jaw in self-loathing for doubting her.

"Tell her I was here."

"I will."

"Hope you get some sleep." She gives Ana a last glance and squeeze of her hand, and then she's gone.

Thank God.

A KNOCK ON THE door wakes me, and Detective Clark appears. He's the last person I want to see. I don't want to share my wife with anyone, not when she's like this.

"Sorry to disturb you. I was hoping there might be a chance to talk to Mrs. Grey."

"Detective, as you can see, my wife is in no state to answer any of your questions." I stand to greet him, feeling like shit. I just want this man to go.

Fortunately, his visit is brief but informative. He tells me that

Elizabeth Morgan is cooperating fully with the police. It seems Hyde had compromising videos of her, so he was able to coerce her into helping him. It was Morgan who lured Mia out at the gym.

"Hyde's a twisted son of a bitch," mutters Clark. "He has a serious grudge against your father, and you."

"Do you know why?"

"Not yet. I'll be back when Mrs. Grey wakes. She's safe here. We have Hyde handcuffed to the bed, under police guard 24/7. He's not going anywhere."

"That's reassuring. Will we get our money back?"

Clark frowns.

"The ransom."

He smiles, briefly. "Eventually, Mr. Grey."

"That's reassuring."

"I'll leave you to rest," he says.

"Thank you."

I grimace at Detective Clark's back as he closes the door.

Hyde is here, somewhere in this hospital, because my wife put a bullet in him.

Anger surges through me again.

I could find him and finish the job.

He's under guard, Grey. I hope to God he's incarcerated for a very long time.

Dr. Bartley returns. "How are you doing, Mr. Grey?"

"I'm fine. It's my wife I'm concerned about."

"Well, I'm here to take a look at her."

I stand back and let her do her checks.

"Why hasn't she woken?" I ask.

"It's a good question. I would have expected her to by now. What she's been through was traumatic, though, so maybe she needs a little more down time to process it all. Was she under any other stress?" Dr. Bartley gives me a direct look and I flush, guiltily.

"Well, um…the pregnancy?" I keep my answer vague.

"I have an idea that may bring her around, but it might take a while to see if it works. Besides, I'm not happy catheterizing pregnant women for a long period of time. It runs the risk of UTI."

"Okay, sure. Do I need to leave?"

"It's up to you."

"I'll go fetch some coffee."

Out in the corridor, my phone buzzes. It's John Flynn.

"Christian. I heard about Ana. How is she?"

I sigh and give him the bullet-point summary. "She's expected to wake at any time. It's just—"

"I know. This must be hard on you. I'm sure she's in capable hands. I got a missed call from you the other day. I was at my son's parent-teacher conference."

Ah. The night of my transgressions. It would have been great if he'd answered the phone.

"We'll talk next week?" Flynn asks.

"Yes."

"If you need me, I'm here."

"Thanks, John."

"HELLO, DARLING." GRACE ARRIVES during the evening carrying a small cooler bag.

"Mom."

She hugs me briefly, then scrutinizes my face, her eyes full of concern. "When did you last eat?"

I gaze at her blankly while I try to remember. "Breakfast?"

"Oh, Christian, it's after eight. You must be famished." She strokes my cheek. "I've brought macaroni and cheese. I made it for you."

I'm so tired that the burning in my throat moves to my eyes. "Thanks," I whisper, and in spite of the fact that my wife has still not surfaced, I'm hungry.

No. I'm fucking starving.

"I'll go heat this up. The nurses' kitchen has a microwave. I'll be a couple of minutes."

My mother makes the best mac and cheese in America—better even than Gail's. When she returns, the room fills with its mouthwatering aroma and we sit side by side, and she chats aimlessly while we watch my beautiful wife, who stubbornly refuses to wake.

"We took Mia home late this morning. Carrick's with her."

"How is she?" I ask.

"Christian! Don't talk with your mouth full."

"Sorry," I mumble, with my mouth full—and she laughs. For the first time in forever, my lips lift in a reluctant smile.

"That's better." Grace's eyes glow with maternal love, and I have to confess I feel more hopeful with her here. I finish the last forkful and place my plate on the floor, too tired to move any farther.

"That was delicious. Thanks, Mom."

"My pleasure, darling. She's very brave, your wife."

"Stupid," I mutter.

"Christian!"

"She is."

Grace's eyes narrow and she regards me speculatively. "What is it?"

"What do you mean?"

"Something's up. I mean, something other than Ana lying here unconscious and you being exhausted."

How does she know?

Grace says nothing, her penetrating gaze doing all the talking. Silence fills the room, broken only by the hum of the machine monitoring Ana's blood pressure.

Fuck.

Interfering woman.

It's no good—I crack under her scrutiny, like I always do. "We had a fight."

"A fight?"

"Yes. Before all this happened. We weren't talking."

"What do you mean, you weren't talking? What did you do?"

"Mom—" *Why does she automatically assume it was my fault?*

"Christian! What did you do?"

I swallow, and my throat burns with unshed tears, exhaustion, and anxiety. "I was so angry."

"Hey." Grace takes my hand. "Angry with Ana? Why, what did she do?"

"She didn't do anything."

"I don't understand."

"The baby. It was a shock. I stormed out."

Mom grasps my hand, and suddenly I'm overcome with an urge to confess all. "I saw Elena," I whisper, and shame washes over me like a riptide. My mother's eyes widen, and she releases my hand.

"What do you mean, 'saw'?" she hisses, emphasizing the last word with such scorn that it rocks me. *Did you sleep with her?* I recall Ana's question from…when, yesterday? The day before?

First Ana, now my mother!

"Nothing like that! Fuck, Mom!"

"Don't curse at me, Christian. What was I supposed to think?"

"We just talked. And I got drunk."

"Drunk? Shit!"

"Mom! Don't *you* curse! It sounds wrong."

She presses her lips together. "You are the only one of my children that makes me use such vulgar language. You told me you would cut all ties." Her glare is loaded with censure.

"I know. But seeing her finally put it all in perspective for me. You know, with the child. For the first time I felt…uncomfortable. More than uncomfortable. What we did. It was wrong."

"What *she* did, darling. You were a child!" She purses her lips again and then sighs. "Christian, children will do that to you. They make you look at the world in a different light."

"She finally got the message. I think. And so did I. I'm done with her. I hurt Ana." Shame douses me once more.

"We always hurt the ones we love, darling. You'll have to tell her you're sorry. And mean it, and give her time."

"She said she was leaving me."

"Did you believe her?"

"At first, yes."

"Darling, you always believe the worst of everyone, including yourself. You always have. Ana loves you very much, and it's obvious you love her."

"She was mad at me."

"I'm sure she was. I'm pretty mad at you right now. I think you can only be truly mad at someone you really love."

"I thought about it, and she's shown me over and over how much she loves me, to the point of putting her own life in danger."

"Yes, she has, darling."

"Oh, Mom, why won't she wake up?" Suddenly, it's all too much. The lump in my throat swells, choking me, and I'm overwhelmed— the fight, Ana leaving, nearly dying, Hyde, Mia—*fuck*...and though I've tried to hold back my tears, I can't. "I nearly lost her." The words are strangled and barely audible as I voice my worst fear, and the dam breaks.

"Oh, Christian," Mom gasps. She wraps her arms around me as I break down, and for the first time in my life, I weep in my mother's arms: for my wife, my broken wife, and for myself, and the asshole I've been.

Hell. Hell. Hell.

Grace rocks me to and fro, kissing my hair and crooning soft words as she lets me cry. "It's going to be okay, Christian. It's going to be okay."

She holds me. Tight. And I don't want her to let go.

Mom.

The first woman to save me.

I SIT UP AND wipe my face, and find she's crying, too.

"For fuck's sake, Mom, stop crying."

Her tears turn to smiles. She hands me a tissue from her purse and takes one for herself. Reaching up, she caresses my face. "It's taken twenty-four years for you to let me hold you like this," she says sadly.

"I know, Mom."

"Better late than never." She pats my face, and I give her a watery smile.

"I'm glad we talked."

"Me, too, darling. I'm always here." She looks at me with nothing but love, and she grins with a hint of glee. "I can't believe I'm going to be a grandmother!"

IT'S DARKER. LATER. I don't know what time, and I'm too exhausted to look. Ana lies in her own private world.

"Oh, baby, please come back to me. I'm sorry. Sorry for everything.

Just wake up. I miss you. I love you." I kiss her knuckles and rest my head on my arms, on her bed.

IT'S A SOFT TOUCH, fingers running through my hair, and in this dream, I revel in her touch. *Shit.* I wake instantly and sit up. Ana is gazing at me with big, beautiful blue eyes. Joy bursts in my heart. I have never been so pleased to see those eyes as I am now.

"Hi," she croaks, her voice hoarse.

"Oh, Ana." *Oh, thank God, thank God, thank God.* I grasp her hand and hold her palm to my face so she's caressing me.

"I need to use the bathroom," she whispers.

"Okay."

Ana tries to sit up.

"Ana, stay still. I'll call a nurse." Standing, I reach for the buzzer at her bedside.

"Please," she whispers. "I need to get up."

"Will you do as you're told for once?" I snap.

"I really need to pee," she rasps.

The nurse arrives, and she's pleased to see Ana's finally conscious. "Mrs. Grey, welcome back. I'll let Dr. Bartley know you're awake." She makes her way to Ana's bedside. "My name is Nora. Do you know where you are?" Her blue eyes twinkle kindly.

"Yes. Hospital. I need to pee."

"I'll fetch a bedpan," Nurse Nora offers

Ana screws up her face in revulsion. "Please. I want to get up."

"Mrs. Grey—" Nora is not convinced.

"Please."

"Ana," I warn as she struggles to sit up.

"Mr. Grey, I am sure Mrs. Grey would like some privacy." Nora raises an eyebrow, and from her tone I know she's dismissing me.

In your dreams, sweetheart. "I'm not going anywhere."

"Christian, please—" Ana grasps my hand, and I give hers a squeeze, beyond grateful that she's back. "Please," she says once more.

Shit.

"Fine!" I run my hand over my scalp, frustrated that she wants to be rid of me already. "You have two minutes," I snap at Nurse

Nora. I lean down and kiss my wife's forehead and storm out of the room.

I pace the corridor.

Ana doesn't want me anywhere near her.

Perhaps she's can't stand the sight of me.

I wouldn't blame her.

Fuck. I can't bear this.

I storm back into the room as Nora is helping Ana out of bed.

"Let me take her," I say.

"Mr. Grey, I can manage," Nurse Nora scolds, giving me an icy look.

"Damn it, she's my wife. I'll take her." I move her IV stand out my way.

"Mr. Grey!" Nora chastises me, but I ignore her and carefully place my arms around and under my wife and lift her.

Ana wraps her arms around my neck, and I carry her into the adjacent bathroom. Nurse Nora follows, pushing the IV stand.

"Mrs. Grey, you're too light." I set Ana on her feet, keeping one hand on her so she doesn't fall. She seems a little unsteady. I flip on the light and Ana staggers.

Hell! "Sit, before you fall." I don't let go of her. Gingerly, she does as she's told, and once she's seated, I release her.

"Go." She waves me out.

"No. Just pee, Ana."

"I can't, not with you here." She peers up, beseeching me with wide, dark eyes.

"You might fall."

"Mr. Grey!" Nora is not happy, but we both ignore her.

"Please," Ana says.

Fuck. Get a grip, Grey.

"I'll stand outside, door open." I step outside with Nora while she glares at me.

"Turn around, please," Ana says, and I want to smile. We've done all manner of things to each other but this is a hard limit for her? I roll my eyes, but do as she asks.

Nora mutters something under her breath and I think I catch

the word *interfering* but I'm too relieved that Ana's woken up to let it bother me.

After a minute or two, Ana pipes up that she's done. I scoop her into my arms once more, and I'm thrilled when she curls her arms around me. I bury my nose in her hair, but I'm alarmed to find that she doesn't smell of Ana—she smells of chemicals and hospitals and fucking trauma. But I don't care. She's back. "Oh, I've missed you, Mrs. Grey," I whisper, and I lay her back on her bed, Nurse Nora trailing behind me with the IV, a scowling chaperone.

"If you've quite finished, Mr. Grey, I'd like to check over Mrs. Grey now." Nurse Nora is hatchet-faced when mad.

I stand back and hold up my hands in surrender. "She's all yours."

Nora huffs, unimpressed, but she smiles at Ana. "How do you feel?"

"Sore and thirsty. Very thirsty."

"I'll fetch you some water once I've checked your vitals and Dr. Bartley has examined you." She reaches for a blood pressure cuff and wraps it around Ana's upper arm while I watch. Ana's eyes stay on me. She frowns.

What is it?

Does she want me to leave?

Grey, you must look a sight.

I sit down on the edge of the bed, out of Nora's reach. "How are you feeling?" I ask Ana.

"Confused. Achy. Hungry."

"Hungry?"

She nods.

"What do you want to eat?"

"Anything. Soup."

"Mr. Grey, you'll need the doctor's approval before Mrs. Grey can eat."

Nora and I are not on the same wavelength. I pull my phone from my pocket and call Taylor.

"Mr. Grey."

"Ana wants chicken soup."

"I'm delighted to hear that, sir." I know he's smiling. "Gail's gone to her sister's, but I'll call the Olympic Hotel—they'll still have room service at this time."

"Good."

"I'll be right there."

"Thank you." I hang up.

Nora looks grimmer than ever. But I don't care.

"Taylor?" Ana asks.

I nod.

"Your blood pressure is normal, Mrs. Grey. I'll fetch the doctor." Nora removes the cuff and, without so much as another word, stalks out of the room, radiating disapproval at me.

"I think you made Nurse Nora mad."

"I have that effect on women." I smirk at Ana, and she laughs, but stops abruptly, her face stricken, as she clutches her side. "Yes, you do," she says, gently.

"Oh, Ana, I love to hear you laugh." *But not if it pains you.*

Nora returns with a pitcher of water and Ana and I fall silent, gazing at each other as she pours a glass. "Small sips now," Nora warns.

"Yes, ma'am." Ana takes a sip and closes her eyes for a moment. When she opens them, she looks directly at me. "Mia?"

"She's safe. Thanks to you."

"They did have her?"

"Yes."

"How did they get her?"

"Elizabeth Morgan."

"No!"

I nod. "She picked her up at Mia's gym."

Ana frowns, as if she can't quite comprehend the magnitude of Morgan's and Hyde's treachery.

"I'll fill you in on the details later. Mia is fine, all things considered. She was drugged. She's groggy now and shaken up, but by some miracle she wasn't harmed." My anger flares once more; Ana put herself and Junior in jeopardy. "What you did"—I drag my fingers through my hair, choosing my words carefully, and trying to hang on to my temper—"was incredibly brave and incredibly stupid. You could have been killed."

"I didn't know what else to do," she whispers, and glances down at her fingers.

"You could have told me!"

"He said he'd kill her if I told anyone. I couldn't take that risk."

I close my eyes as I imagine the most awful outcome. *No Mia. No Ana.* "I have died a thousand deaths since Thursday." My voice is hoarse.

"What day is it?"

"It's almost Saturday." I check my watch. "You've been unconscious for more than twenty-four hours."

"And Jack, and Elizabeth?"

"In police custody. Although Hyde is here under guard. They had to remove the bullet you left in him." Once more I wish she'd ended him. "I don't know where in this hospital he is, fortunately, or I'd probably kill him myself."

Ana's eyes grow wide, and she shudders, her fear evident as her shoulders tense and tears prick her eyes.

"Hey." I move forward, taking the glass from her hand, placing it on the nightstand, and gently folding her into my arms. "You're safe now."

"Christian, I'm so sorry." She starts to cry.

No. Ana. You're safe. "Hush." I stroke her hair and let her weep.

"What I said. I was never going to leave you."

"Hush, baby, I know."

"You do?" She pulls away and studies me through her tears.

"I worked it out. Eventually. Honestly, Ana, what were you thinking?"

She places her head on my shoulder. "You took me by surprise. When we spoke at the bank. Thinking I was leaving you. I thought you knew me better. I've said to you over and over I would never leave."

Slowly, I blow out a breath. "But after the appalling way I've behaved—" I tighten my arms around her. "I thought for a short time that I'd lost you."

"No, Christian. Never. I didn't want you to interfere and put Mia's life in danger."

Interfere!

"How did you work it out?" she asks.

I tuck her hair behind her ear. "I'd just touched down in Seattle when the bank called. Last I'd heard, you were ill and going home."

"So, you were in Portland when Sawyer called you from the car?"

"We were just about to take off. I was worried about you."

"You were?"

"Of course I was." I skim her lower lip with my thumb. "I spend my life worrying about you. You know that."

This earns me a half smile. That's something. "Jack called me at the office," she says, her eyes wide once more. "He gave me two hours to get the money." She shrugs. "I had to leave, and it just seemed the best excuse."

Fucking Hyde. "And you gave Sawyer the slip. He's mad at you, as well," I mutter.

"As well?"

"As well as me."

She raises her hand, her fingertips once more caressing my face. Closing my eyes, I lean in to her touch, savoring the feel of her fingers skating over my stubble. "Don't be mad at me. Please," she whispers.

"I am so mad at you. What you did was monumentally stupid. Bordering on insane."

"I told you, I didn't know what else to do."

"You don't seem to have any regard for your personal safety. And it's not just you now."

But before she or I can say anything further, the door opens and Dr. Bartley strides in. "Good evening, Mrs. Grey. I'm Dr. Bartley."

I give her a nod and step away so she has room to examine my wife. While she's doing that, I call Dad to let him know that Ana is awake.

"Oh, that's great news, son." He pauses, and I know he's listening to Grace. "Your mother says to apologize."

"I'll do that, Dad."

"Why? What's happened?" Carrick sounds confused.

"It's a long story."

"Okay. Give Ana our love. We'll come see her tomorrow."

I call Carla to give her the good news.

"Thank you, Christian!" she sobs through her tears.

Next, Kavanagh. "Thank God," Kate says. "And I hope you two have made up."

"Yeah," I mutter, though it's none of her fucking business. "I've got to call Ray."

"Okay," Kate says. "And tell Ana no more chasing kidnappers."

"Will do."

Ray is so relieved, he's silent for several seconds while he gathers himself. Eventually he says, "I appreciate the call, Christian. Tell Annie I love her."

"Will do, Ray."

When I finish my call to my father-in-law, Dr. Bartley is prodding my wife's ribs. Ana winces. "These are bruised, not cracked or broken. You were very lucky, Mrs. Grey."

Ana glances at me. "Foolhardy," I mouth.

I'm still fucking angry with you, Ana.

"I'll prescribe some painkillers. You'll need them for this, and for the headache you must have. But all's looking as it should, Mrs. Grey. I suggest you get some sleep. Depending on how you feel in the morning, we may let you go home. My colleague Dr. Singh will be attending you then."

"Thank you."

A loud knock, and Taylor enters carrying a hefty box from the Fairmont Olympic.

"Food?" Dr. Bartley says, surprised.

"Mrs. Grey is hungry," I inform her. "This is chicken soup."

"Soup will be fine, just the broth. Nothing heavy." She looks pointedly at both of us, then exits the room with Nurse Nora.

There's a wheeled tray in the corner. I maneuver it over to Ana, and Taylor places the box on it. "Welcome back, Mrs. Grey," he says with a fond smile.

"Hello, Taylor. Thank you."

"You're most welcome, ma'am—" He stops, and I glance up at him as I unpack the box. I think he wants to say more. Perhaps to scold Ana? I wouldn't blame him, but he just smiles at her.

In addition to the thermos with soup, there's a small basket of bread rolls, a linen napkin, a china bowl, and a silver spoon.

"This is great, Taylor," Ana says.

"Will that be all?" Taylor asks.

"Yes, thanks," I say. He can go back to bed. "Taylor, thank you."

"Anything else I can get you, Mrs. Grey?"

She looks at me and arches a brow. "Just some clean clothes for Christian."

Taylor glances at me and smiles. "Yes, ma'am."

What? I check my shirt. I've not spilled anything down it.

But I haven't washed or shaved for days.

I must look like shit.

"How long have you been wearing that shirt?" Ana asks.

"Since Thursday morning." I give her an apologetic shrug and Taylor leaves us. "Taylor's real pissed at you, too," I add, and unscrew the lid of the thermos to pour the soup into the bowl.

Ana dives in with an eagerness I've never seen before. At the first mouthful she closes her eyes as if in ecstasy.

"Good?" I perch on the bed once more.

She nods enthusiastically and takes another spoonful, then pauses to wipe her mouth on a linen napkin. "Tell me what happened—after you realized what was going on."

"Oh, Ana, it's good to see you eat."

"I'm hungry. Tell me."

I frown, trying to remember the order in which everything happened. "Well, after the bank called, and I thought my world had completely fallen apart—"

Ana stops and gazes at me, looking lost.

"Don't stop eating, or I'll stop talking." I sound far sterner than I intend. She flattens her lips, but continues to eat. "Anyway, shortly after you and I had finished our conversation, Taylor informed me that Hyde had been granted bail. How, I don't know; I thought we'd managed to thwart any attempts at bail. But that gave me a moment to think about what you'd said, and I knew something was seriously wrong."

"It was never about the money," she snaps, suddenly raising her voice. "How could you even think that? It's never been about your fucking money!"

Whoa! "Mind your language," I exclaim. "Calm down and eat."

She glares at me, eyes blazing with anger.

"Ana."

"That hurt me more than anything, Christian," she whispers. "Almost as much as you seeing that woman."

Shit. I close my eyes, as my remorse returns full-blown. "I know." I sigh. "And I'm sorry. More than you know. Please, eat. While your soup is still hot." My tone is contrite and gentle. I owe her that.

She picks up her spoon, and I blow out a breath of relief.

"Go on," Ana encourages me, between bites of soft bread roll.

"We didn't know Mia was missing. I thought maybe he was blackmailing you or something. I called you back, but you didn't answer." I scowl, remembering how impotent I felt. "I left you a message and then called Sawyer. Taylor started tracking your cell. I knew you were at the bank, so we headed straight there."

"I don't know how Sawyer found me. Was he tracking my cell, too?"

"The Saab is fitted with a tracking device. All our cars are. By the time we got near the bank, you were already on the move, and we followed. Why are you smiling?"

"On some level I knew you'd be stalking me."

"And that is amusing because?"

"Jack had instructed me to get rid of my cell. So I borrowed Whelan's cell, and that's the one I threw away. I put mine into one of the duffel bags so you could track your money."

I sigh. "Our money, Ana. Eat."

Once again, I'm amazed by her cool head and quick thinking, but I merely watch as she wipes the last piece of bread around the bowl and pops it into her mouth. "Finished."

"Good girl."

There's a knock on the door and Nurse Nora enters once more, carrying a small paper cup. "Pain relief," Nora announces, while I pack the detritus from Ana's meal back into the box from the Olympic.

"Is this okay to take? You know, with the baby?"

"Yes, Mrs. Grey." She hands Ana the pills and a fresh glass of water. "It's Tylenol—it's fine; it won't affect the baby."

Ana swallows the tablet, yawns, and blinks sleepily.

"You ought to rest, Mrs. Grey." Nurse Nora looks pointedly at me. I nod. *Yes. She should.*

"You're going?" Ana exclaims with a look of alarm.

I snort. "If you think for one moment I'm going to let you out of my sight, Mrs. Grey, you are very much mistaken."

Nora gives me a withering look as she adjusts Ana's pillows so Ana can lie down. "Good night, Mrs. Grey," she says, and with one last censorious glance at me she leaves.

"I don't think Nurse Nora approves of me." I look down at my wife. Awake. Present. Fed. And my relief is overwhelming, but I'm utterly drained and bone-weary. I don't think I've ever felt so tired in my life.

"You need rest, too, Christian. Go home. You look exhausted."

"I'm not leaving you. I'll doze in this armchair." I can ease up on my vigil for a little while.

She scowls, then smiles as if she's had a mischievous idea and shifts over. "Sleep with me."

What! No way! "No. I can't."

"Why not?"

"I don't want to hurt you."

"You won't hurt me. Please, Christian."

"You have an IV."

"Christian. Please."

It's so tempting. I shouldn't...but I can hold her, and my urge to hold her supersedes my common sense.

"Please." She lifts the blankets, inviting me into her bed.

"Fuck it." I slip out of my shoes and socks and climb into my wife's bed, facing her. Gently, I put an arm around her, and she lays her head on my chest.

Oh. The. Feel. Of. Her.

Ana.

I kiss her hair. "I don't think Nurse Nora will be very happy with this arrangement."

Ana giggles and stops abruptly. "Don't make me laugh. It hurts."

"Oh, but I love that sound." *And I love you, Ana. With all my heart.* "I'm sorry, baby. So, so sorry." I kiss her once more and inhale her scent. I catch a trace of my Ana. She's there, beneath the chemicals.

My wife. My beautiful wife.

She rests her hand on my heart, and I place my hand on hers and close my eyes.

"Why did you go see that woman?"

"Oh, Ana," I groan. "You want to discuss that now? Can't we drop this? I regret it, okay?"

"I need to know."

"I'll tell you tomorrow," I mutter, too tired to be pissed about her question. "Oh, and Detective Clark wants to talk to you. Just routine. Now go to sleep." I kiss her hair again.

"Do we know why Jack was doing all this?"

"Hmm…" I murmur as sleep beckons, hard and fast. And after hours and hours of worry, regret, and exhaustion, I submit, and fall into a deep, dreamless slumber.

Ana is out cold. I can't wake her. *Wake up, Ana. Wake up.*
Elena struts over to sit down beside me. She's naked but for
long, tight leather gloves that stop just above her elbows. And
her black stilettos with red soles. She takes my hand. *No.*
Her fingers clasp my thigh. *No. Don't touch me. No more.*
Only Ana. Her eyes blaze in anger, but the fire in them
dies. Defeated, she stands. Clothed now in black. *Good-bye,*
Christian. She flips her hair to the side and stalks to the door
without looking back. I turn. Ana is awake, smiling at me. *Join*
me. Sleep with me. Stay with me. My heart soars. Her words
bring me joy. She caresses my cheek. *Stay with me. Please.* She
begs. How can I resist? She loves me. She does. And I love her.

When I wake, it takes me a moment to remember that I'm in Ana's
hospital bed. She slumbers at my side, facing me, her head on the
pillow. Eyes closed, lips parted, her cheek pale except for the faint
purple blemish from Hyde's cruel blow. The sight of it twists my gut
in anger.

Don't dwell, Grey.

She's here. She's safe.

I blink the sleep from my eyes, feeling rested but grimy. I'm in
dire need of a shower, a shave, and clean clothes. My watch says 6:20
a.m. I have time. Now that Ana's back in the world of the living, I
don't mind leaving her for a little while. With any luck, she'll continue to sleep until I return. Carefully, so as not to wake her, I slide
out of bed and slip on my shoes. I brush my lips to her forehead in
the semblance of a kiss, then grab my phone, charger, and jacket and
tiptoe out of the room as if I'm fleeing a crime scene.

I'm doing the walk of shame.

The thought amuses me.

We're married, for fuck's sake.

Fortunately, Nora and her colleagues are not at the nurses' station, so my escape is unnoticed.

It's my lucky day—there's a cab waiting at the entrance of the hospital, and no photographers. And because it's early, I make good time to Escala. By the time the elevator doors open to the penthouse, my mood is buoyant.

Taylor is in the foyer, on his way out. He steps back, mouth open, surprised to see me, but he recovers quickly. "Mr. Grey. Welcome back."

"Good morning, Taylor."

"I would have picked you up—I was bringing you a change of clothes as per Mrs. Grey's instructions, and *The Seattle Times*." He brandishes a leather duffel.

"It's fine. I need a shower. We'll head back when I'm done."

"Yes, sir. I'll ask Sawyer to join us."

"We'll pick up some breakfast for her on the way."

He nods.

THE STEAMING WATER CASCADES over me.

Washing away my sins.

Damn. After all that I've done, I wish it were that simple. And to cap it off, Ana wants to know everything about my discussion with Elena. What the hell am I going to tell her?

The truth, Grey.

She's not going to like it. But I owe her that, especially considering my recent awful behavior. My effervescent humor fizzles and dies. While I shave, I contemplate the asshole who stares back at me in the mirror.

You owe her more than that.

After all that Ana's done for you.

She saved your sister.

She saved YOU.

I close my eyes.

It's true. This woman has disarmed me at every turn. She's broken through all my barriers, cracked me wide open, and shined her light inside. She doesn't take any of my shit. She's driven out my darkness like the warrior she is—and offered me hope because she loves me. I know it.

And she's carrying my child.

Fuck. *A child.*

The gray-eyed asshole stares back at me, bewildered.

She's done all of this for the simple reason that she loves me, and because she's a decent human.

And how do I treat her?

Badly doesn't cover it, Grey.

Her words haunt me. *I do choose this defenseless baby over you. That's what any loving parent does. That's what your mother should have done for you. And I'm sorry that she didn't—because we wouldn't be having this conversation right now if she had. But you're an adult now. You need to grow up and smell the fucking coffee, and stop behaving like a petulant adolescent.*

And I thought she was leaving me.

I wipe my face.

Make this right, Grey.

ON THE WAY TO the hospital, we stop and Taylor hurries into the café that he phoned for takeout. He returns with what looks like a breakfast feast for Ana; I hope she's hungry. Sawyer pulls up at the entrance to the hospital, but when I climb out of the car, I'm ambushed by a couple of photographers, who start snapping away.

"How's your wife, Mr. Grey?"

"Mr. Grey, will you be pressing charges?"

I ignore the assholes and dart inside the lobby. Taylor follows, carrying Ana's breakfast.

We head to the nurses' kitchen on Ana's ward, where we lay out her breakfast on a tray. Damn, why didn't I bring a small vase, and I could steal a flower from one of the many bouquets she's received. It would go some way toward an apology.

"Sir," says Taylor, as I lift the loaded tray, "before she left, Gail made Mrs. Grey's favorite chicken stew, if I need to bring that in later for lunch, sir."

"Good to know. I'm hoping I can take her home this morning."

Taylor nods his affirmation and pushes open the door to Ana's room to let me in, and I'm hoping for a warm welcome.

She's gone.

Shit.

"Ana!" I shout as my heart catapults into overdrive.

"I'm in the bathroom!"

Oh, thank God.

Taylor bursts through the door, as alarmed as I was. "We're good," I reassure him, and he steps out again, presumably to sit in the corridor. I place the food on Ana's rolling tray and wait, again, for Mrs. Grey…patiently, this time. A moment later she appears and rewards me with a broad grin—I'm relieved to see her up and about.

"Good morning, Mrs. Grey. I have your breakfast."

She climbs into bed, while I pull the tray on wheels over toward her and lift the cover. One wide-eyed, grateful glance from Ana is all the confirmation I need as she gulps down the orange juice and starts on the oatmeal. I sit on the edge of her bed, taking vicarious pleasure in her enjoyment as she eats. Not only is she ravenous, but there's some color in her cheeks. She's on the mend. "What?" she asks, with her mouth full.

"I like to watch you eat. How are you feeling?"

"Better."

"I've never seen you eat like this."

She looks up, her expression serious. "It's because I'm pregnant, Christian."

I snort. "If I knew getting you knocked up was going to make you eat, I might have done it earlier." My smartass remark is an effort to distract her from a serious conversation that I'm not ready to have.

I don't know how I feel about this yet.

"Christian Grey!" She drops the spoon in her oatmeal.

"Don't stop eating."

"Christian, we need to talk about this."

"What's there to say? We're going to be parents." I shrug, hoping she'll change the subject.

Ana's not impressed. She pushes the tray aside, crawls down the bed, and takes my hands in hers. I sit staring at her, paralyzed. "You're scared. I get it," she says gently, pinning me with deep blue eyes. "I am, too. That's normal."

I'm aware that I'm holding my breath.

How can I love a child?

I've only just learned to love you.

"What kind of father could I possibly be?" I whisper, forcing the words through my tightening throat.

"Oh, Christian." My name's almost a sob, and it twists my heart. "One that tries his best. That's all any of us can do."

"Ana—I don't know if I can."

"Of course you can. You're loving, you're fun, you're strong, you'll set boundaries. Our child will want for nothing." Her eyes widen, imploring me.

Ana. It's just so soon...

Is there room in my heart for someone else?

Is there room in your heart for both of us?

She continues, "Yes, it would have been ideal to have waited. To have longer, just the two of us. But we'll be three of us, and we'll all grow up together. We'll be a family. Our own family. And your child will love you unconditionally, like I do." Tears pool in her eyes and slowly trickle down her cheeks.

"Oh, Ana." I gasp while keeping my own tears lodged in my throat. "I thought I'd lost you. Then I thought I'd lost you again. Seeing you lying on the ground, pale and cold and unconscious—it was all my worst fears realized. And now here you are—brave and strong, giving me hope. Loving me...after all that I've done."

"Yes, I do love you, Christian, desperately. I always will."

Reaching up, I take her head in my hands and gently wipe away her tears with my thumbs. "I love you, too." I draw her lips to mine and kiss her, beyond grateful that she's still here and whole. Grateful that she's mine. "I'll try to be a good father."

"You'll try, and you'll succeed. And let's face it: you don't have much choice in the matter, because Blip and I are not going anywhere."

"Blip?"

"Blip."

Blip. "I had the name Junior in my head."

"Junior it is, then."

"But I like Blip." I kiss her again, tentatively teasing her lips—and it's a match to dry kindling. My reaction immediate. Innate.

No. I pull away. "Much as I'd like to kiss you all day, your breakfast is getting cold." Ana's eyes shine the color of a summer sky. She's amused, I think. "Eat," I insist.

She shuffles back into bed and I push the tray in front of her. A barrier between us. She starts on the pancakes with enthusiasm. "You know," she says between mouthfuls, "Blip might be a girl."

Christ. I run my hand through my hair. "Two women, eh?"

"Do you have a preference?"

"Preference?"

"Boy or girl."

"Healthy will do." *Jesus. A girl? Who looks like Ana?* "Eat," I snap.

"I'm eating, I'm eating. Jeez, keep your hair on, Grey."

I move off the bed and take a seat in the armchair beside her, cheered that we've finally broached the subject of…Blip.

Blip.

Yeah. I like the name.

I reach for the newspaper.

Shit! Ana is on the front page. "You made the papers again, Mrs. Grey." Inside, I'm seething. Why can't they leave us alone? *Fucking press.*

"Again?"

"The hacks are just rehashing yesterday's story, but it seems factually accurate. You want to read it?"

She shakes her head. "Read it to me. I'm eating."

Anything to keep you eating, wife.

I read the article out loud as Ana tucks into her breakfast. She doesn't comment on what's been written, but asks me to read more. "I like listening to you."

Her words warm my soul.

She finishes her breakfast, sits back, and listens as I continue, but we're interrupted by a knock on the door. My spirits sink when Detective Clark shambles in. "Mr. Grey, Mrs. Grey. Am I interrupting?"

"Yes," I snap. He's the last person I want to see.

Clark ignores me, which sets my teeth on edge, the arrogant asshole. "Glad to see you're awake, Mrs. Grey," he says. "I need to ask you a few questions about Thursday afternoon. Just routine. Is now a convenient time?"

"Sure," Ana mumbles, but she looks wary.

"My wife should be resting."

"I'll be brief, Mr. Grey. And it means I'll be out of your hair sooner rather than later." He has a point. Giving Ana an apologetic look, reluctantly I stand and offer him my chair, then perch on the other side of her bed and take Ana's hand. I listen quietly as Clark lets my wife tell her side of Hyde's kidnapping and extortion horror story; the words are at odds with her soft, sweet voice. Occasionally, I tighten my grip on her hand as I rein in my anger, and I'm relieved when it's over. Ana's done well to remember so many details.

"That's great, Mrs. Grey." Clark seems pleased.

"I wish you'd aimed higher," I mutter.

"Might have done womankind a service if Mrs. Grey had," he agrees.

Ana's puzzled look skims from Clark to me. She doesn't know what we're talking about, but I'm not going to explain that right now.

"Thank you, Mrs. Grey. That's all for now." Clark shifts in his seat, ready to leave.

"You won't let him out again, will you?" Ana flinches, visibly at the thought.

"I don't think he'll make bail this time, ma'am."

"Do we know who posted his bail?" I ask.

"No, sir. It was confidential."

I'll chase Welch for an update to see if he's found Hyde's benefactor. Clark rises to leave just as Dr. Singh and two interns enter the room, and I follow the detective out, taking Ana's tray with me.

"Good day, Mr. Grey," Clark says, saluting me, then walks on up the corridor.

Taylor rises from his chair outside Ana's room and follows me into the nurses' kitchen, where I deposit the tray. "Sir, I'll take care of that."

"Thanks." I leave him to wash up and return to Ana's room, where I hang back while Dr. Singh completes her examination.

"You're good. I think you can go home," she says, with a pleasant smile to Ana.

Thank God.

"Mrs. Grey, you'll have to watch for worsening headaches and blurry vision. If that occurs, you must return to the hospital immediately."

Ana nods, beaming, clearly as grateful as I am that she's being discharged.

"Dr. Singh, can I have a word?"

"Of course."

We step into the corridor, and I'm relieved that Taylor is still away from his station on the chair outside. "My wife... Um—"

"Yes, Mr. Grey?"

"Her injuries... Will they stop us..."

Dr. Singh frowns.

"Sexual act—"

She interrupts me, finally understanding my gist. "Yes, Mr. Grey, that's fine." She smiles and adds in a quieter tone, "Provided your wife is...you know. Willing."

I give her a broad smile.

"What was all that about?" Ana asks as I close the door.

"Sex!" I give her a wicked grin.

Ana colors. "And?"

"You're good to go."

Ana can't hide her amusement. "I have a headache." Her teasing smirk makes me doubt if she's being entirely truthful.

"I know. You'll be off-limits for a while. I was just checking."

She frowns, and if I'm interpreting her look correctly, I'd say she's disappointed. Nurse Nora bustles into the room, and after a haughty glance at me, she removes Ana's IV.

Ana thanks her and Nora exits. I smile as she leaves. I don't begrudge her at all; she's taken good care of my wife. I resolve to make a substantial donation to the hospital staff appreciation fund.

"Shall I take you home?" I turn to Ana.

"I'd like to see Ray first."

Grey, of course, she wants to see her dad! "Sure."

"Does he know about the baby?"

"I thought you'd want to be the one to tell him. I haven't told your mom, either."

"Thank you."

"My mom knows. She saw your chart. I told my dad, but no one else. Mom said couples normally wait for twelve weeks or so to be sure." I shrug. This is her decision.

"I'm not sure I'm ready to tell Ray."

That's probably a good idea. "I should warn you, he's mad as hell. Said I should spank you."

Ana's mouth drops open. It's such a gratifying response, I laugh. "I told him I'd be only too willing to oblige."

"You didn't!" Ana gapes at me, but her eyes shine with amusement.

Will this ever get old?

Shocking my wife?

I'm glad I still can.

I wink at her. "Here, Taylor brought you some clean clothes. I'll help you dress."

RAY IS QUIETLY OVERJOYED to see his daughter. It shows in his eyes, unmasked for a moment when he sets them on Ana—fear, relief, love, and anger are all reflected in their dark depths. I beat a hasty retreat, knowing he's going to reprimand Ana as she deserves to be reprimanded. Taylor is waiting outside by her door. "Sir, there are still photographers outside the main entrance."

"Find a back way out, and have Sawyer meet us there with the car."

"Will do." He strides off, and I reach for my phone to call Welch.

"Mr. Grey," he answers.

"Welch. Any news?"

"Yes. I'm waiting to board my plane. Let me find a quiet corner." There's rustling, and I hear a muffled airline departure announcement—but not to Seattle. "Right," he grunts. "I have uncovered some information about Hyde. I'll bring that to you. I'd rather you see it in person than have me go through it over the phone."

"Can't you tell me now?"

"I'd rather not. It's a little public here, and this is not a secure line."

What the hell could it be?

"Also, the police discovered several USB sticks in Hyde's apartment during their fingertip search. Sex tapes. All of them. With his old assistants. With Morgan. It's some pretty heavy stuff."

Fuck. My scalp crawls.

"My guess is he used the footage to buy their silence, and also to blackmail Morgan." Welch's gruff voice drives the point home.

I knew about Morgan—but his former assistants?

Thank God I stopped Ana from going to New York with him.

"They'll probably charge him with that, too," Welch continues. "But they're still building their case."

"I see. Any word on who posted bail yet?'

"Nothing certain. But I'll get into that when I'm back."

"What time can I expect you?"

"I'll be there around five p.m."

"See you then." I hang up and wonder what he's found that connects me to Hyde.

ANA IS SUBDUED AS we head down to the rear entrance of the hospital. I think she's been chastened by the reunion with her father, and even though I'm with her dad all the way on this, a very small part of me feels sorry for her. I would not like to be on the receiving end of Raymond Steele's ire.

Once in the car, Ana calls her mother. "Hi, Mom…" Her voice is husky with controlled emotion; Carla, on the other hand, I can hear through the phone as she sobs and wails.

"Mom!"

Ana doesn't stand a chance. Her eyes fill, and I reach over to take her hand and give her a supportive squeeze, brushing my thumb over her knuckles. But I tune their conversation out as my thoughts turn to Welch and what he might have discovered. I'm irritated that he didn't give me a clue over the phone.

Do I even want to know?

I stare out of the window and wonder.

"What's wrong?" Ana asks, and I realize she's finished her call with her mom.

"Welch wants to see me."

"Welch? Why?"

"He's found something out about that fucker Hyde." My lips form a snarl around his name. I loathe the man with every fiber of my being. *Loathe* is not strong enough. *Hate* is not strong enough. I detest him and everything he's done. Ana is still looking at me expectantly. "He didn't want to tell me on the phone."

"Oh."

"He's coming here this afternoon from Detroit."

"You think he's found a connection?"

I nod.

"What do you think it is?"

"I have no idea." It's frustrating, but I shelve the thought, as right now, I need to concentrate on my wife.

"GLAD TO BE HOME?" I ask Ana, as we step into the elevator at Escala.

"Yes." Ana's reply is pin-drop quiet, and I watch as the blood slowly drains from her face. She raises glazed eyes to me and starts to tremble.

Hell. It's finally hitting her.

She's traumatized.

"Hey—" I gather her into my arms. "You're home. You're safe." I kiss her hair, thankful that she smells more like Ana, without the synthetic tang of drugs and disinfectant.

"Oh, Christian." A sob bubbles up through her lips, and she starts to weep.

"Hush, now." I cradle her head against my chest, wanting to chase away the hurt and fear. She must have been holding all this emotion inside.

For my benefit?

I hope not.

I hate to see her cry—but I understand the need right now.

Let it all out, baby. I'm here.

When the elevator doors slide open, I lift her into my arms, and she clings to me, sobbing still, each sound a lesion in my heart. I carry her through the foyer, down the corridor, and into our en suite, where I deposit her on the white chair as if she's made of glass. "Bath?"

Ana shakes her head, then winces.

Shit. Her head aches.

"Shower?"

She nods, tears still streaming down her face. The sight claws at my soul, and I suck in a breath to contain my warring emotions—rage at Hyde, and fury at myself for letting this happen. I switch on the shower, and when I turn back, Ana's rocking slowly, keening into her hands. "Hey." I kneel at her feet and cover each of her hands in mine, easing them away from her tearstained cheeks. I cradle her face, and she blinks away her tears as we gaze into each other's eyes. "You're safe. You both are," I murmur.

Her grief wells in her eyes once more and renders me helpless. "Stop, now. I can't bear it when you cry." My voice is hoarse; my words are honest yet woefully inadequate against the tide of her anguish. I wipe her cheeks once more with my thumbs, but it's a losing battle. Her tears still flow.

"I'm sorry, Christian. Just sorry for everything. For making you worry, for risking everything—for the things I said."

"Hush, baby, please." I kiss her forehead. "I'm sorry. It takes two to tango, Ana." I try a crooked smile to cheer her. "Well, that's what my mom always says. I said things and did things I'm not proud of."

My words come back to haunt me.

This is why I like control.

So shit like this doesn't come along and fuck everything up!

Shame burns like a pyre in my chest. *Grey, this is not helping.*

"Let's get you undressed."

Ana wipes her nose with the back of her hand, and the raw gesture endears her to me even more. I kiss her forehead, because I need her to know that I love her, no matter what she does. Taking her hand, I support her as she staggers to her feet, and quickly undress her, taking particular care as I tug her T-shirt over her head. I guide her to the shower and open the door, where we pause as I strip out of my clothing. When I'm naked, I take her hand again and we both step in.

Beneath the waterfall of steaming water, I hold her hard and tight against me.

I never want to let her go.

She continues to cry, her tears washed away by the cascade flowing over us. I rock her gently from side to side, the rhythm soothing me and, I hope, Ana.

I'm rocking my child, too...inside her.

Whoa. That's a strange thought.

I kiss her hair, so grateful that she's back home with me, when I'd feared...

Shit. Don't go there, Grey.

All of a sudden, I hear a loud sniff, and Ana steps out of my arms. She seems to have stopped crying.

"Better?"

She nods, her eyes clear.

"Good. Let me look at you."

Her brow furrows, and I hope she won't stop me as I need to see for myself what that asshole prick has done to my wife. Taking her hand, I turn it over. My gaze travels from the graze on her wrist to the abrasion at her elbow, to the large fist-sized bruise on her shoulder. The sight of these marks infuriates me, igniting the embers of my earlier anger at Hyde. I bend to kiss each scrape and bruise, planting the barest of kisses at each site. Grabbing the washcloth and shower gel from the rack, I soap the cloth, inhaling the sweet fragrance of jasmine. "Turn around."

Ana does as she's told and, knowing she's fragile and wounded, I wash her arms, neck, shoulders, and back, as tenderly as I'm able. Absorbed in the task, I keep my touch light. She doesn't complain, and the tension in her shoulders eases little by little as I wash them. I turn her so I have a clearer view of the bruise on her hip; my fingers skate over the livid purple mark. She winces.

Motherfucker.

"It doesn't hurt," Ana says quietly, and I raise my head to meet her brilliant gaze.

I don't believe her.

"I want to kill him. I nearly did." The rage I felt, when Hyde was on the ground, burns deep inside my soul.

I should have kicked him to a pulp.

To shield Ana from my murderous thoughts, I concentrate on the washcloth and soap it again with shower gel. I bathe her body once more—her sides and her behind, and I kneel at her feet and wash her legs. I pause at the bruise on her knee, lean in and brush my lips against it before moving on to soap her feet. Her fingers tangle in my hair, distracting me from my task. When I look up, her expression is raw and tender, and it twists my heart. Standing, I trace the bruise at her ribs with my fingertips, the sight stoking my fury once more, but I dampen it down. It's not helping either of us.

"Oh, baby." I push the words past the anguish in my throat.

"I'm okay." Her fingers weave into my hair again, and she pulls my head down and kisses me. Soft. Sweet. I hold myself back. She's hurt. But her tongue teases me, and the fire flares once more, blazing through my body in a different way.

"No," I whisper against her lips, and pull back. "Let's get you clean."

Ana regards me through her lashes, that way she does, and her eyes flick down to my growing erection, then back to my eyes. She pouts, so prettily, and the mood between us lightens immediately. Grinning, like the clown I am, I kiss her quickly. "Clean. Not dirty."

"I like dirty."

"Me, too, Mrs. Grey. But not now, not here." I grab the shampoo and squirt some into my hands. Using only my fingertips, I gently wash her hair, remembering how gentle she was when she last washed mine, and how cherished I felt then.

After I've rinsed out the suds, I switch off the shower and exit, taking her with me. I cloak her in a warm towel, wrap one around my own waist, and hand her a towel for her hair. "Here." She can judge how vigorous to be—she's the one with a hairline fracture in her skull. My lighter mood takes a nose dive.

That asshole.

"I still don't understand why Elizabeth was involved with Jack." Ana intrudes on my dark thoughts.

"I do," I offer.

She peers at me, and I'm expecting a question, but she seems to lose her train of thought as her eyes study me...all of me.

Mrs. Grey! I smirk. "Enjoying the view?"

"How do you know?"

"That you're enjoying the view?"

"No." She sounds exasperated. "About Elizabeth."

I sigh. "Detective Clark hinted at it."

Ana's brows knit together and her gaze goads me, demanding more information.

"Hyde had videos. Videos of all of them. On several USB flash drives. Videos of him fucking her, and fucking all his PAs."

Her mouth drops open.

"Exactly. Blackmail material. He likes it rough."

So do I. Fuck.

Christ.

Self-disgust sweeps over me like an avenging angel.

"Don't," Ana interrupts, the word like the crack of a whip.

"Don't what?"

"You aren't anything like him."

How did she guess?

"You're not." Ana's tone is insistent.

Oh, but, Ana, I am. "We're cut from the same cloth."

"No you're not!" Ana's fervent denial silences me. "His dad died in a brawl in a bar. His mother drank herself into oblivion. He was in and out of foster homes as a kid, in and out of trouble, too—mainly boosting cars. Spent time in juvie." My God, she's remembered everything I told her on the plane to Aspen and she doesn't stop—she's on a roll. "You both have troubled pasts, and you were both born in Detroit. That's it, Christian." She fists her hands and places them on her hips.

She's trying to intimidate me, dressed only in a towel.

It's not going to work.

Because I know who I am.

But I don't want to rile her. Now is not the time for an argument. It's not good for her or the baby. "Ana, your faith in me is touching, especially in light of the last few days. We'll know more when Welch is here."

"Christian—"

Bending, I plant a swift kiss on her lips to end the discussion. "Enough." Her expression is sullen. "And don't pout," I add. "Come. Let me dry your hair."

She presses her lips together, but to my relief, she drops the subject. I lead her into the bedroom, then head into the closet, where I dress quickly, dragging on jeans and a T-shirt. I grab a pair of her sweatpants and one of my T-shirts for her.

While she slips on the clothes, I plug in the hair dryer, sit down on the bed, and gesture to her to join me. Ana perches between my legs and I start to brush through her wet hair.

I love combing out her hair.

It's so soothing.

Soon, the only sound in our bedroom is the high-pitched whine of the hair dryer. Ana's shoulders slump as she relaxes against me, and she's quiet for a while.

"So, did Clark tell you anything else while I was unconscious?" Her words drag me from my absorbing task.

"Not that I recall."

"I heard a few of your conversations."

"Did you?" I stop brushing.

"Yes. My dad, your dad, Detective Clark, your mom."

"And Kate?"

"Kate was there?"

"Briefly, yes. She's mad at you, too."

She jerks around. "Stop with the 'Everyone is mad at Ana' crap, okay?" Her tone is as high-pitched as the hair dryer.

"Just telling you the truth." I shrug.

I'm still a little mad at you myself, Ana.

"Yes, it was reckless, but you know—your sister was in danger."

"Yes. She was," I murmur, as a bleak morbid fantasy of what could have happened plays out once more in my head.

Disarmed with a simple truth. Ana, you humble me at every turn.

I switch off the hair dryer and grasp her chin, gazing into clear but vibrant eyes, eyes I could drown in.

No. I'm not mad.

I'm in awe of my brave, brave woman.

She had the courage to save Mia.

"Thank you." The words are inadequate. "But no more reckless-ness. Because next time, I will spank the living shit out of you."

She sucks in a breath. "You wouldn't!"

Oh, baby. My palm is twitching right now. "I would." I can't hold back my smug smile. "I have your stepfather's permission."

Ana's pupils dilate, and her lips part.

And it's there between us, that electricity that crackles invisibly—I feel it everywhere, and I know she does, too.

Ana. No.

Suddenly, she launches herself at me.

Fuck! Ana!

I catch her and twist so that we fall together on the bed, Ana in my arms.

But her face crumples in pain, and she gasps.

"Behave!" I growl, my tone harsher than I intend.

"Sorry." She caresses my cheek and I take her hand and kiss her palm.

"Honestly, Ana, you really have no regard for your own safety." I lift the hem of her T-shirt and rest my fingertips on her belly.

A thrill of the unknown sharpens all my senses.

There is life. Here. Inside her.

What did she say? *Flesh of my flesh.*

Our child.

"It's not just you anymore," I whisper, and skate my fingers across her taut, warm skin. Ana tenses beneath me, dragging air into her lungs. I know that sound. My eyes move to hers, and I lose myself in their fathomless blue depths.

It's Ana's desire. I feel it, too.

Our special alchemy.

But it's impossible. She's hurt. Reluctantly, I lift my fingertips from her skin, tug down her T-shirt, then tuck a stray lock of hair behind her ear, because I still need to touch her. But I can't give her what we both want. "No," I breathe.

Ana's face falls, her expression forlorn.

"Don't look at me like that. I've seen the bruises. And the answer's no." I kiss her forehead and she squirms beside me.

"Christian," she moans, needling me.

"No. Get into bed." I sit up to remove myself from temptation.

"Bed?" She looks crestfallen.

"You need rest."

"I need you." The whine has gone, leaving only a husky come-on in her voice.

Closing my eyes, I shake my head at her audacity and my desire.

She's hurt. I open my eyes and glare at her. "Just do as you're told, Ana."

"Okay," she mutters, with an exaggerated pout that immediately lifts my spirits and makes me want to laugh.

"I'll bring you some lunch."

"You're going to cook?" She blinks, incredulous.

"I'm going to heat something up. Mrs. Jones has been busy."

"Christian, I'll do it. I'm fine. Jeez, I want sex—I can certainly cook." She struggles to sit up but winces.

Damn it! Ana!

"Bed!" I point at the pillow, all carnal thoughts banished.

"Join me." She makes one last-ditch attempt.

I don't know what's gotten into her.

Not you recently, Grey.

"Ana, get into bed. Now." I scowl.

She answers with a scowl of her own, stands, and drops her sweatpants to the floor in a dramatic gesture. In spite of her glower, she looks lovely. I hide my smile, and part of me is beyond pleased that she still wants me, after all that's transpired over the last few days.

She loves me.

I draw back the duvet. "You heard Dr. Singh. She said rest."

Still pouting, Ana complies, sliding into bed and folding her arms, conveying her frustration. I want to laugh, but I don't think my mirth would be well received.

"Stay," I order, and with the memory of her beautiful, sour face, I hurry into the kitchen to find the fabled chicken stew Taylor mentioned this morning.

IT'S GOOD TO SEE Ana wolfing down Mrs. Jones's cooking. I sit cross-legged in the middle of the bed, watching her as I devour my lunch. It's delicious, and nourishing, too—perfect for Ana.

"That was very well heated." She smacks her lips, looking replete and a little drowsy. I beam at her, feeling pleased. I managed not to burn myself this time—so, yeah, it was!

"You look tired." I place my bowl on her tray and, standing, take both from her.

"I am," she admits.

"Good. Sleep." I kiss her quickly. "I have some work I need to do. I'll do it in here, if that's okay with you."

She nods and closes her eyes, and seconds later she's out.

ROS HAS SENT ME a preliminary report of her visit to Taiwan. She reassures me that while it was the right decision for her to go, I'll still need to travel there myself, and soon. It's strange reading her quick summary. It's been days since I thought about my business, my company, the shipyard, or even the world at large—I've lost track of time. My attention has been solely concentrated on my wife. I glance over at her. She's still fast asleep.

I read through my other e-mails, and there's a detailed earnings projection on Geolumara, and a remarkably upbeat e-mail from Hassan at GEH Fiber-Optics—morale there is up since my visit and business is going well. My trip to see them was worth it.

Taylor's gentle tap at the door disturbs my reading. "Welch is here, sir."

I can barely hear him, he's speaking so softly. I nod and, with another quick check on my sleeping beauty, follow him out to the living room.

Welch is standing and admiring the view from the window. He's grasping a large manilla envelope.

Showtime, Grey.

"Welch."

He turns. "Mr. Grey."

"Shall we head into my study?"

I LISTEN TO ANA'S breathing as I watch her, timing each of my breaths to hers. In. Out. In. Out. Focusing on her means that I don't have to focus on the photographs Welch has left with me.

Why didn't Carrick and Grace tell me?

I lived with Jackson Hyde!

How did I not know this?

My thoughts have been racing, searching through all the nooks and crannies of my troubled mind, trying to shine a light in the shadows, but I've found nothing. My foster care experience is hidden in the murky depths of the past.

I cannot remember any of it. A chunk of my life. Gone. No. Not gone. *Erased.*

In its place is a dark, gaping hole of nothing but uncertainty.

It's deeply unsettling. Surely I should remember…*something*?

Ana stirs. Her eyes flicker open and find mine.

Thank God.

"What's wrong?" She blanches, and she sits up, her face strained by her concern.

"Welch has just left."

"And?"

"I lived with the fucker." The words are barely audible.

"Lived? With Jack?"

Swallowing down my agitation, I nod.

"You're related?" Ana's shock is palpable.

"No. Good God, no."

Frowning, she moves over and tugs back the duvet; it's an invitation to join her. I don't hesitate. I need her—to anchor me to the now and to help me make sense of this alarming news and this huge gap in my memory.

Right now, I'm untethered.

From everything.

Kicking off my shoes and clutching the photographs, I slip in beside her and drape an arm over her upper thighs as I lay my head in her lap. Slowly she trails her fingers through my hair; the gesture is comforting, and it calms my troubled soul. "I don't understand," she says.

Closing my eyes, I picture Welch and recall the throaty rasp of his voice as he briefed me. I repeat his words for Ana, editorializing a little. "After I was found with the crack whore, before I went to live with Carrick and Grace, I was in the care of the state of Michigan. I lived in a foster home." I pause and take a gulp of air. "But I can't remember anything about that time."

Ana's hand stops and rests on my head. "For how long?"

"Two months or so. I have no recollection."

"Have you spoken to your mom and dad about it?"

"No."

"Perhaps you should. Maybe they could fill in the blanks."

I tighten my hold on Ana, my life raft. "Here." I pass her the photographs. I've been poring over them in the hope that they might stir a dormant memory that's buried deep. The first depicts a scrubby little house with a cheery, yellow front door. The second shows an ordinary working-class couple, and their three scrawny, unremarkable children—plus Jackson Hyde as an eight-year-old, and...me. I'm four years old, a small scrap of humanity, with wild, haunted eyes and threadbare clothes, clutching a filthy blanket. It's obvious that the four-year-old is severely malnourished—no wonder I'm always nagging Ana to eat.

"This is you," Ana gasps, and stifles a sob.

"That's me." My voice is bleak; right now, I've no words of comfort left for her.

I've got nothing. I'm numb.

I stare out at the dusk. The sky is streaked in pale pink and orange that heralds the coming darkness. A darkness that claims me as one of its own.

A husk of a man once more. Hollowed and empty.

I'm missing time. Missing a part of myself that I didn't even know existed.

And I don't understand why.

I'm scared to know why.

What happened to me back then? How could I have forgotten it all?

I cling to the residual anger that simmers beneath the surface. It's aimed at Carrick and Grace.

Why the fuck didn't they tell me?

I close my eyes. I don't want the darkness. I've lived in it too long. I want the light that Ana brings.

"Welch brought these photos?" she asks.

"Yes. I don't remember any of this."

"Remember being with foster parents? Why should you? Christian, it was a long time ago. Is this what's worrying you?"

"I remember other things, from before and after. When I met my mom and dad. But this… It's like there's a huge chasm."

"Is Jack in this picture?"

"Yes, he's the older kid."

Ana's silent for a moment, and I hug her harder.

"When Jack called to tell me he had Mia," she murmurs, "he said if things had been different, it could have been him."

Revulsion shudders through me. "That fucker!"

"You think he did all this because the Greys adopted you instead of him?"

"Who knows? I don't give a fuck about him."

"Perhaps he knew we were seeing each other when I went for that job interview. Perhaps he planned to seduce me all along." Ana's dread echoes in her voice.

"I don't think so. The searches he did on my family didn't start until a week or so after you began your job at SIP. Barney knows the exact dates. And, Ana, he fucked all his assistants and taped them."

Ana's quiet, and I wonder what she's thinking.

About Hyde? About me?

I could have ended up like Hyde if I hadn't been adopted.

Is she comparing me to him?

Fuck. I am like Hyde. A monster. Is that what she sees?

That we're the same?

What a repulsive thought.

"Christian, I think you should talk to your mom and dad." She squirms, and I release her legs, but she shuffles down into the bed so we're facing each other.

"Let me call them," she offers in a tender whisper. I shake my head. "Please," she pleads. Her expression is as compassionate and sincere as ever. Her eyes brimming with love.

Perhaps she's not comparing me to Hyde.

Should I call my parents? Maybe they can offer the missing pieces on these fragments of my past. They're bound to remember, surely.

"I'll call them," I murmur.

"Good. We can go see them together, or you can go. Whichever you prefer."

"No. They can come here."

"Why?"

"I don't want you going anywhere."

"Christian, I'm up for a car journey."

"No." I give her a lopsided smile. "Anyway, it's Saturday night; they're probably at some function."

"Call them. This news has obviously upset you. They might be able to shed some light." Ana's words are stirring. As I gaze into her eyes, there's no judgment there, only her love shining through the cracks into my darkness.

"Okay." I'll play it her way. I pick up the bedside phone and call my parents' home. Ana snuggles up to me while I wait for an answer.

"Christian." Carrick's voice has never been more welcome.

They're home! "Dad!" I can't hide my surprise.

"Great to hear from you, son. How's Ana?"

"Ana's good. We're home. Welch has just left. He found out the connection."

"Connection? With what? With who? Hyde?"

"The foster home in Detroit."

Carrick is silent on the other end of the phone.

"I don't remember any of that." My voice wavers as my shame and simmering anger surface, a poisonous cocktail. Ana hugs me tighter.

"Christian. Why should you? It was long ago. But your mother and I can fill in the gaps, I'm sure."

"Yeah?" I hate the hope in my voice.

"We'll come over. Now, if you like?"

"You will?" I can scarcely believe it.

"Of course. I'll bring some paperwork from that time with me. We'll be there soon. It will be good to see Ana, too."

Paperwork?

"Great." I hang up and regard Ana's curious expression. "They're on their way." I still can't hide my surprise.

I ask my parents for help…and they come running.

"Good. I should get dressed," Ana says.

I tighten my hold on her. "Don't go."

"Okay." She bathes me in a loving smile, and she snuggles once more into my side.

ANA AND I STAND arm in arm in the doorway of the living room to welcome my parents. My mother lights up when she sees Ana, her joy and gratitude obvious to each of us. Reluctantly, I release my wife into my mother's embrace. "Ana, Ana, darling Ana," she says, and I have to strain to hear her. "Saving two of my children. How can I ever thank you?"

Yep. Mom's right. She's saved me, too.

Dad hugs Ana, his eyes shining with paternal affection. He kisses her forehead. From behind them Mia, whom I wasn't expecting, appears and pulls Ana into a fierce hug.

"Thank you for saving me from those assholes!"

Ana winces.

"Mia! Careful! She's in pain." My shout startles everyone.

Of course. They brought Mia because Mom doesn't want to let her out of her sight. She was drugged and kidnapped only a few days ago. My irritation at my baby sister evaporates.

"Oh! Sorry," she says goofily.

"I'm good," Ana says, giving Mia a tight smile.

Mia barrels over to me and curls her arm around me. "Don't be so grumpy!" she scolds me quietly.

I scowl at her and she pouts playfully at me.

Damn. I hug her tightly to my side.

Thank God she's okay.

My mother joins us, and I hand her the photographs from Welch. Grace examines the picture of the family. She sucks in a breath and covers her mouth. Dad joins us and winds his arm around her shoulders as he also scrutinizes the family picture.

"Oh, darling." Grace reaches up and places her palm against my cheek, her eyes stricken with shock and dismay.

Why? Did she not want me to know about this?

Taylor interrupts us. "Mr. Grey, Miss Kavanagh, her brother, and your brother are coming up, sir."

What the hell? "Thank you, Taylor."

"I called Elliot and told him we were coming over," Mia pipes up. "It's a welcome-home party."

Mom and Dad share an exasperated look. Ana's glance is sympathetic. "We'd better get some food together. Mia, will you give me a hand?"

"Oh, I'd love to." She grabs Ana's hand and they head over into the kitchen area.

Mom and Dad follow me into my study, and I offer them each a seat in front of my desk. I lean back against it, suddenly aware that this is how my father would perch in his study as I stood in front of him while he lectured me about my latest misdemeanor. The tables have been well and truly turned, and the irony is not lost on me. I need answers and they're here—so presumably they're willing to shed some light on this dark chapter in my life. I mask my anger and gaze at both of them expectantly.

Grace is the first to speak, her voice clear and authoritative, her doctor's voice. "This photograph, these are the Colliers. They were your foster parents. You had to go to them once your biological mother died, because under state law we had to wait to see if you had any relatives who would claim you."

Oh.

Her voice drops. "We had to wait for you. It was agonizing. Two whole months." She closes her eyes, as if reliving the pain. It's sobering. My anger melts away as my breath catches in my throat. I cough to hide my emotion.

"In the picture." I gesture to the photograph Grace is holding. "The boy with red hair. That's Jack Hyde."

Carrick leans in and they examine the photograph together. "I don't remember him," my father muses.

Mom shakes her head, a forlorn look on her face. "No, me, neither. We only had eyes for you, Christian."

"Were... Were they kind?" I ask haltingly, my voice a shadow. "The Colliers?"

Grace's eyes fill with tears. "Oh, darling. They were wonderful. Mrs. Collier doted on you."

Silently, I blow out a breath of relief. "I wondered. I couldn't remember."

Grace's eyes widen with understanding. She reaches out and grips my hand, hazel eyes beseeching mine. "Christian, you were a traumatized child. You wouldn't or couldn't speak. You were skin and bone. I can't even imagine the horrors you endured in your early life. But that ended with the Colliers." She squeezes my hand, willing me to believe her. "They were good people."

"I wish I could remember them," I whisper.

She stands and takes my hand. "There's no reason why you should. It felt like forever for us, because we wanted you so badly, but it was only two months. We'd already been approved to adopt, thank goodness. Otherwise, the process could have been longer."

"Here," Carrick says. "It must be harrowing not knowing, but I have a few things from that time for you. Maybe they might help you remember." From inside his jacket he produces a large envelope. I sit down at my desk, steel myself, and open it. Inside I find a résumé for Mr. and Mrs. Collier and details about their family, a daughter and two sons. Several letters, and two drawings…my drawings?

I gaze down at them, and my scalp tingles with a sense of wonder.

Both pictures are in crayon. They're a scrawled child's view of a house with a yellow door. There are stick figures: two adults, five siblings.

The sun shines over them all. Huge. Bright.

The second picture is similar, but all the children are holding what look like sugar cones with ice cream.

It appears happy enough.

"We had reports on you every week from them. And we visited. Every weekend."

"Why didn't you tell me?"

Grace and Carrick exchange a look.

"It never came up, son." Carrick's jaw tightens, his voice quiet with remorse, I think, as he shrugs. "We wanted you to forget, about all…" He trails off.

I nod. *I get it.*

Forget about my life with the crack whore.

Forget about her pimp.

Forget about my life before them.

I don't blame them. I'd like to forget.

Why would anyone want to remember that?

"I hope this helps with some of your questions," he says.

"It does. I'm glad I called you. It was Ana's idea."

Carrick smiles. "She's one brave woman, Christian." He glances once more at Grace. She nods, and it looks like she's giving him permission. He hands me another envelope.

With a puzzled look at both of them, I open it. Inside is a birth certificate.

STATE OF MICHIGAN

CERTIFICATE OF LIVE BIRTH

121-83-757899	June 29, 1983
STATE FILE NUMBER	DATE FILED

Kristian Pusztai
CHILD'S NAME (FIRST, MIDDLE, LAST, SUFFIX)

June 18, 1983	Male	Detroit, Wayne County
DATE OF BIRTH	GENDER	CHILD'S BIRTHPLACE

Életke Pusztai	19	Budapest, Hungary
MOTHER'S NAME BEFORE FIRST MARRIED	MOTHER'S AGE	MOTHER'S BIRTHPLACE

Unknown	Unknown	Unknown
FATHER'S NAME	FATHER'S AGE	FATHER'S BIRTHPLACE

I hereby certify that the above is a true and correct representation of the birth facts on file with the Division for Vital Records, Michigan Department of Community Health.

Kristian! A tremor runs up my spine. *My name!*

And the crack whore! *She has a name.*

From nowhere I hear her pimp asshole shouting. "Ella!"

Ella…short for Életke.

His usual epithet was *bitch*.

I shake off the thought.

"Why are you giving this to me now?" My voice is hoarse as I gaze at my parents.

"I found it with the letters and the drawings. In Mrs. Collier's letters she calls you Christian with a *K*. So, if you wondered…" My mother's voice trails off.

"Why did you change the spelling?"

"Because you are a gift. To us. From God."

I stare at her. Stupefied. *A gift? Me?* All the shit I gave the two people standing in front of me, and this is what they think?

"We felt we owed Him. You've always been a gift, Christian," Carrick murmurs.

Tears pinch the back of my eyes and I take a deep breath.

A gift.

"Children are a gift. Always." Grace's maternal adoration is plain in her glistening eyes, and I know what she's left unsaid—that I'll find this out for myself, in a few months. Leaning over, she smooths my hair off my forehead. I return her smile and, standing, pull her into my arms.

"Thanks, Mom."

"You're welcome, son."

Carrick hugs us both.

I close my eyes, and fighting back my tears, I accept it.

Unconditional love.

From my parents.

As it should be.

Enough. I pull away. "I'll read the letters later." My voice is gruff with emotion.

"Okay."

"We should get back to the others," I mutter.

"Have you remembered anything?" Carrick asks.

I shake my head.

"Maybe you will, maybe you won't, but don't sweat it, son. You have us. You have your family. And like your mother says, the Colliers were good people." Gently, he squeezes my arm, his warmth and affection radiating through my body.

We head back into the main living room, but I'm moving in slow motion, disconnected from my reality, my head ready to explode with all these revelations. I scan the room for Ana; she's standing with Elliot and Kate at the kitchen counter, eating some canapés.

From somewhere deep in my brain, the part that stores my earliest memories, comes a fragment—a vision of a family gathered around a wooden table. Laughing. Teasing. Eating…macaroni and cheese.

The Colliers.

I'm distracted from my reminiscence by the sight of Ana with a flute of pink champagne in her hand.

Junior!

I move to take the alcohol from her, but Kate steps into my path. "Kate." I acknowledge her.

"Christian," she responds, in her usual abrupt way.

"Your meds, Mrs. Grey?" My tone is a warning as I stare at the glass in Ana's hand, trying not to give anything away. But Ana narrows her eyes and raises her chin in defiance. Grace collects a full flute from Elliot, walks up to Ana, and whispers something in her ear. They exchange a furtive smile, and they clink glasses.

Mom! I grimace at both of them. But they ignore me.

"Hotshot!" Elliot claps me on the back and hands me a glass.

"Bro." I keep my eyes on Ana as Elliot and I take a seat on the couch.

"Jesus, you must have been worried sick."

"Yeah."

"Glad that asshole is finally caught. His ass is on its way to jail."

"Yeah."

Elliot frowns. "You missed a great game."

"Game?"

He wants to talk baseball? Is he trying to distract me? He's pissed the Mariners lost to the Rangers today, but I find it difficult to concentrate on what he's saying—my attention is locked on Ana. Carrick joins Ana, and Grace kisses him on the cheek, then moves to sit with Mia and Ethan—who are looking mighty cozy on the couch—leaving Ana to talk to Dad.

My father and my wife enjoy a lively whispered conversation.

What are they talking about? Me?

"You're not listening to a word I'm saying, asshole." Elliot pulls me back into our conversation.

"Sure. The Rangers."

He punches my arm. "You get a pass," he says. "You've had a tough few days. You know, you two should come see your house."

"Yeah. I'd like that. Ana and I were planning to and then all hell broke loose."

"Ana and Mia. Fuck." Elliot's expression is grim. "Glad your wife took that asshole down."

I nod.

"Hi, Christian." Ethan joins us and I'm grateful for the interruption.

"Watch the game?" Elliot asks, and they fall into a debate about Beltré hitting a homer against the Mariners. I tune them out as Ana comes toward us.

"It's great to see everyone," she says to Carrick, as she sits next to me.

"One sip," I scold her under my breath. *And you've had that. I take the glass from her hand.*

"Yes, Sir." She flutters her eyelashes, her eyes darkening and suddenly full of promise. My body stirs in response, and I ignore it.

Jesus. We're in company.

I wind my arm around her shoulders and shoot her a quick look.

Behave, Ana.

ANA IS CURLED UP in bed, watching me as I strip. "My parents think you walk on water." I toss my T-shirt onto the chair.

"Good thing you know differently."

"Oh, I don't know."

"Did they fill in the gaps for you?"

"Some. I lived with the Colliers for two months while Mom and Dad waited for the paperwork. They were already approved for adoption because of Elliot, but the wait's required by law, to see if I had any living relatives who wanted to claim me."

"How do you feel about that?"

"About having no living relatives?" *Relieved!* "Fuck that. If they were anything like the crack whore." I shake my head.

Thank God for Mom and Dad.

They were—*are*—a gift to me.

I don my pajama pants and climb into bed, cuddling up to my wife, beyond grateful that she's here with me. She inclines her head, her expression warm, but I know she's expecting me to say more. "It's coming back to me," I muse.

Mac and cheese…yeah.

"I remember the food. Mrs. Collier could cook. And at least we know now why that fucker is so hung up on my family." A hazy memory surfaces.

Wait—didn't she use to sit by my bed?

She's tucking me into a small cot bed and holding a book. "Fuck!"

"What?"

"It makes sense now!"

"What?"

"Baby Bird. Mrs. Collier used to call me Baby Bird."

Ana's looks puzzled. "That makes sense?"

"The note. The ransom note that fucker left. It went something like 'Do you know who I am? Because I know who you are, Baby Bird.'"

Ana still looks confused.

"It's from a kid's book. The Colliers had it. It was called *Are You My Mother?* Shit." I imagine the cover in my mind's eye: the little bird and the sad, old dog. "I loved that book. Mrs. Collier used to read it to me. Christ. He knew. That fucker knew."

Though I have no memory of him…thank God.

"Will you tell the police?"

"Yes. I will. Christ knows what Clark will do with that information."

I exhale. They're here, in my brain, the missing memories. It's a relief. And once more I'm grateful that my parents came to see me this evening. They've dislodged whatever was holding these recollections back.

Ana smiles, relieved for me, I think. But enough of my fucked-up history. I owe Ana an explanation. But where to start? She might be too tired; she's worked hard to entertain my family. "Thank you for this evening."

"For what?"

"Catering for my family at a moment's notice."

"Don't thank me, thank Mia. And Mrs. Jones. She keeps the pantry well stocked."

Ana! Take a compliment. She's such an exasperating woman sometimes, but I let it go. "How are you feeling, Mrs. Grey?"

"Good. How are you feeling?"

"I'm fine."

Ana's eyes light up, and her fingers dance over my belly.

I laugh and grab her hand. "Oh, no. Don't get any ideas."

Her lips purse in disappointment, and she stares up at me through her lashes again. "Ana, Ana, Ana, what am I going to do with you?" I kiss her hair.

"I have some ideas." She wriggles beside me and stops suddenly, her face scrunched in pain.

Ana! You're hurt.

She smiles quickly, to reassure me.

"Baby, you've been through enough. Besides, I have a bedtime story for you."

She looks up, expectant.

"You wanted to know..." I close my eyes and swallow, as my mind drifts back to my adolescence.

I'm fifteen again.

"Picture this: an adolescent boy looking to earn some extra money so he can continue his secret drinking habit." I open my eyes, but I can still see myself as I was back then: a tall but scrawny teen, in cut-off shorts, with a shock of copper hair and a belligerent fuck-off attitude.

That was me.

Hell.

I shift onto my side so Ana and I are lying facing each other. Her eyes are wide, and full of questions. I take a deep breath. "So, I was in the backyard at the Lincolns', clearing some rubble and trash from the extension Mr. Lincoln had just added to their place."

Closing my eyes again, I'm there once more. The scent of summer flowers hangs thick in the air. Insects buzz and I swat them away. The heat from the midday sun is beating down on me, so much so that I strip off my T-shirt. And there's Elena. Wearing the lowest-cut dress I've ever seen—it barely sheathes her body.

When I chance a look at Ana, she's still staring at me, hanging on my every word. "It was a hot summer day. I was working hard." I chuckle, remembering this was probably one of the few days I ever did any manual labor. "It was backbreaking work, shifting that rubble. I was on my own, and Ele—Mrs. Lincoln appeared out of nowhere and brought me some lemonade. We exchanged small talk, and I made some smartass remark—and she slapped me. She slapped me so hard." My hand moves automatically to my cheek as I remember the unfamiliar sting. No one had ever slapped me like that.

My eyes are here, boy. Mrs. Lincoln points two fingers at her face.

She caught me staring at her tits.

Well. You couldn't miss them.

Fuck.

I was hard. Instantly. To bursting.

Mrs. Lincoln's gaze drifts to my pants.

Fuck. My boner! It's humiliating.

Like that, do you? she drawls, scarlet lips lifting in a sexy smile.

I think I'm gonna come in my pants.

"But then she kissed me. And when she finished, she slapped me again."

Her mouth is hot. Wet. Strong. Everything I ever wet-dreamed about.

"I'd never been kissed before or hit like that."

Ana gasps.

Fuck. "Do you want to hear this?"

Ana stares, round-eyed, and her words rush out in a breathless whisper. "Only if you want to tell me."

"I'm trying to give you some context."

She nods, but she looks like she's seen a fucking ghost, and I hesitate. Should I continue? I look deeply into her startled eyes, and all

I see are more questions. She's hungry for information; she's always hungry for more.

I roll onto my back and stare at the ceiling and continue my sorry tale. "Well, naturally, I was confused and angry...and horny as hell. I mean, a hot older woman comes on to you like that."

It was the first time I'd ever been kissed.

Ever. It was heaven. And hell, too.

"She went back into the house, leaving me in the backyard. She acted as if nothing had happened. I was at a total loss." *I wanted to rub one out right there. But, of course, I couldn't.* "So I went back to work, loading the rubble into the dumpster. When I left that evening, she asked me to come back the next day. She didn't mention what had happened. The next day I went back. I couldn't wait to see her again." I'm whispering, as if I were in the confessional. "She didn't touch me when she kissed me." *Only my face, where she grabbed me. It was a revelation.*

I turn to face Ana. "You have to understand—my life was hell on earth. I was a walking hard-on, fifteen years old, tall for my age, hormones raging. The girls at school—"

They were interested.

And so was I...but I couldn't bear to be touched.

I fought everyone off.

And pushed everyone away with my rage.

"I was angry, so fucking angry at everyone, at myself, my folks. I had no friends. My therapist at the time was a total asshole. My folks, they kept me on a tight leash; they didn't understand." I gaze at the ceiling, thinking how solicitous Carrick and Grace had been this evening.

"I just couldn't bear anyone touching me. I couldn't. Couldn't bear anyone near me. I used to fight. Fuck, did I fight. I got into some godawful brawls. I was expelled from a couple of schools. But it was a way to let off steam. To tolerate some kind of physical contact." I clench my fists, remembering one particular brawl.

Wilde. That asshole. Picking on smaller kids.

"Well, you get the idea. And when she kissed me, she only grabbed my face. She didn't touch me."

It was such a relief.

To finally experience that kind of contact.

And it was so fucking exciting.

My life changed in that moment.

Everything changed.

"Well, the next day I went back to the house, not knowing what to expect. And I'll spare you the gory details, but there was more of the same."

I could whip a savage like you into shape. Elena's drawl echoes in my mind.

Savage? *She knows!*

She sees me.

The bad seed.

"And that's how our relationship started." Shaking off the memory, I turn to face Ana once more. "And you know something, Ana? My world came into focus. Sharp and clear. Everything. It was exactly what I needed. She was a breath of fresh air. Making the decisions, taking all that shit away from me, letting me breathe. And even when it was over, my world stayed in focus, because of her. And it stayed that way...until I met you." Suddenly a flood of emotion wells inside me, almost engulfing me.

Ana.

My love.

Reaching up, I smooth a stray tendril of her hair behind her ear, because I want—no, *need*—to touch her. "You turned my world on its head." Suddenly, I see her pale, sad face, leaving me as the elevator doors close. "My world was ordered, calm, and controlled, then you came into my life with your smart mouth, your innocence, your beauty, and your quiet temerity and everything before you was just dull, empty, mediocre. It was nothing."

Ana sucks in a breath.

"I fell in love," I whisper, and strum my knuckles across her cheek.

"So did I," she responds, and I feel her breath on my face.

"I know."

"You do?"

"Yes."

You're still here with me, listening to this sorry, disturbing story. You saved me.

Her face breaks into a shy smile. "Finally," she murmurs.

"And it's put everything into perspective for me. When I was younger, Elena was the center of my world. There was nothing I wouldn't do for her. And she did a lot for me. She stopped my drinking. Made me work hard at school. You know, she gave me a coping mechanism I hadn't had before, allowed me to experience things that I never thought I could."

"Touch," Ana asks.

"After a fashion."

Ana's brows pucker together, and her eyes are full of new questions. I have no choice but to tell her. "If you grow up with a wholly negative self-image, thinking you're some kind of reject, an unlovable savage, you think you deserve to be beaten." I pause, gauging her reaction. "Ana, it's much easier to wear your pain on the outside."

It's much harder on the inside.

I don't dwell on that thought. "She channeled my anger. Mostly inward—I realize that now. Dr. Flynn's been on and on about this, for some time. It was only recently that I saw our relationship for what it was. You know, on my birthday."

Ana grimaces.

"For her that side of our relationship was about sex and control, and a lonely woman finding some kind of comfort with her boy toy."

"But you like control," she says.

"Yes. I do. I always will, Ana. It's who I am. I surrendered it for a brief while. Let someone make all my decisions for me. I couldn't do it myself—I wasn't in a fit state. But through my submission to her, I found myself, and found the strength to take charge of my life. Take control and make my own decisions."

"Become a Dom?"

"Yes."

"Your decision?"

"Yes."

"Dropping out of Harvard?"

"My decision, and it was the best decision I ever made. Until I met you."

"Me?"

"Yes. The best decision I ever made was marrying you." I smile at her.

"Not starting your company?" she whispers.

I shake my head.

"Not learning to fly?"

No, baby. "You." I stroke her cheek once more, marveling at its softness. "She knew."

"She knew what?"

"That I was head over heels in love with you. She encouraged me to go down to Georgia to see you, and I'm glad she did. She thought you'd freak out and leave. Which you did."

Ana blinks, and the color drains from her cheeks.

"She thought I needed all the trappings of the lifestyle I enjoyed."

"The Dom?"

Yes. "It enabled me to keep everyone at arm's length, gave me control, and kept me detached, or so I thought. I'm sure you've worked out why."

"Your birth mom?"

"I didn't want to be hurt again. And then you left me." I see the elevator doors closing on Ana once more, and I remember sitting on my foyer floor for what seemed like hours. "And I was a mess." I take a deep breath. "I've avoided intimacy for so long—I don't know how to do this."

"You're doing fine." She sculpts my lips with her finger, and I press a kiss to her fingertip as we gaze at each other. And as ever, I'm drowning in her blue eyes. "Do you miss it?" she asks.

"Miss it?"

"That lifestyle."

"Yes, I do."

From her look, I'm not sure she believes me. "But only insofar as I miss the control it brings. And, frankly, your stupid stunt"—I halt—"that saved my sister."

You mad. Bad. Beautiful woman. "That's how I know."

"Know?" She frowns.

"Really know that you love me."

"You do?"

"Yes. Because you risked so much. For me. For my family."

Her frown deepens, and I can't resist. Reaching over, I skim over her brow with my fingertip. "You have a *v* here when you frown. It's very soft to kiss." Her expression lightens. "I can behave so badly, and yet you're still here," I murmur.

"Why are you surprised I'm still here? I told you I wasn't going to leave you."

"Because of the way I behaved when you told me you were pregnant." Of its own accord, my finger traces her brow and down her cheek. "You were right. I am an adolescent."

She purses her lips. Contrite. "Christian, I said some awful things."

I place my finger over her mouth.

"Hush. I deserved to hear them. Besides, this is my bedtime story." I roll onto my back again. "When you told me you were pregnant—" I stop, fighting my shame and trying to find the words. "I'd thought it would be just you and me for a while. I'd considered children, but only in the abstract. I had this vague idea we'd have a child sometime in the future. You're still so young, and I know you're quietly ambitious. Well, you pulled the rug out from under me. Christ, was that unexpected. Never in a million years, when I asked you what was wrong, did I expect you to be pregnant." I sigh, disgusted at myself. "I was so mad. Mad at you. Mad at myself. Mad at everyone. And it took me back, that feeling of nothing being in my control. I had to get out. I went to see Flynn, but he was at some school parents' evening."

I glance at her as I arch a brow, hoping that she sees the funny side of that. And of course, she does.

"Ironic," she says and we both smirk.

"So I walked and walked and walked, and I just found myself at the salon. Elena was leaving. She was surprised to see me. And, truth be told, I was surprised to find myself there. She could tell I was mad and asked me if I wanted a drink. We went to a quiet bar I know and had a bottle of wine. She apologized for the way she behaved the last time she saw us. She's hurt that my mom will have nothing to do with her anymore—it's narrowed her social circle—but she understands. We talked about the business, which is doing fine, in spite of the recession… I mentioned that you wanted kids."

"I thought you let her know I was pregnant."

"No, I didn't."

"Why didn't you tell me that?"

I shrug. "I never got the chance." *You were too angry.*

"Yes, you did."

"I couldn't find you the next morning, Ana. And when I did, you were so mad at me."

"I was."

"Anyway, at some point in the evening—about halfway through the second bottle—she leaned over to touch me. And I froze." I throw my arm over my eyes. I'm mortified.

Spit it out, Grey.

"She saw that I recoiled from her. It shocked both of us."

Ana tugs at my arm, so I turn and gaze at her.

I'm sorry, baby.

"What?" Ana asks.

I swallow, trying to fight the awkwardness. "She made a pass at me."

Ana's face transforms. She's appalled. And mad. Again.

Fuck.

"It was a moment, suspended in time," I continue hastily. "She saw my expression, and she realized how far she'd crossed the line. I said no, I haven't thought of her like that for years, and besides"—I swallow again, my voice soft—"I love you. I told her I love my wife."

Ana stares at me. Silent.

Oh, my love, what are you thinking? I stumble on. "She backed right off. Apologized again, made it seem like a joke. I mean, she said she's happy with Isaac and with the business and she doesn't bear either of us any ill will. She said she missed my friendship, but she could see that my life was with you now. And how awkward that was, given what happened the last time we were all in the same room. I couldn't have agreed with her more. We said our good-byes—our final good-byes. I said I wouldn't see her again, and she went on her way."

"Did you kiss?"

"No!" *Good God no.* "I couldn't bear to be that close to her. I was miserable. I wanted to come home to you. But I knew I'd behaved badly. I stayed and finished the bottle, then started on the bourbon. While I was drinking, I remembered your saying to me some time ago, *'If that was my son...'* And I got to thinking about Junior, and about how Elena and I started. And it made me feel...uncomfortable. I'd never thought of it like that before."

"That's it?" Ana breathes.

"Pretty much."

"Oh."

"Oh?"

"It's over?"

"Yes. It's been over since I laid eyes on you. I finally realized it that night, and so did she."

"I'm sorry," she says.

"What for?"

"Being so angry the next day."

"Baby, I understand angry."

Angry is my middle name.

I sigh. "You see, Ana, I want you to myself. I don't want to share you. What we have, I've never had before. I want to be the center of your universe, for a while at least."

"You are," she objects. "That's not going to change."

"Ana," I whisper gently, with a resigned smile. "That's just not true. How can it be?"

Tears well in her eyes.

"Shit—don't cry, Ana. Please, don't cry." I lay my hand on her cheek.

"I'm sorry." Her lip trembles, and I brush my thumb over it as my heart swells.

"No, Ana, no. Don't be sorry. You'll have someone else to love as well. And you're right. That's how it should be."

"Blip will love you, too. You'll be the center of Blip's—Junior's world. Children love their parents unconditionally, Christian."

I feel the blood drain from my face.

"That's how they come into the world," Ana continues, her passion clear. "Programmed to love. All babies, even you. Think about that children's book you liked when you were small. You still wanted your mom. You loved her."

Ella.

Hey, Maggot. Let's find your cars.

I'm on the edge of a dark maelstrom.

Teetering over it.

I fist my hand beneath my chin as I gaze at my beautiful wife, floundering for something to say as I fight the current to swim away from the pain. "No," I whisper.

Ana's tears spill down her cheeks. "Yes. You did. Of course you did. It wasn't an option. That's why you're so hurt."

All the air has left the room and my body.

I'm being sucked down.

"That's why you're able to love me," she says. "Forgive her. She had her own world of pain to deal with. She was a shitty mother, and you loved her."

I'm lost in the vortex. It's choking me.

Hey, Maggot. Shall we bake a cake?

Mommy smiles and ruffles my hair.

Here you go. Mommy gives me a brush.

She smiles down at me. Mommy is pretty.

She has long hair. She's singing. Happy.

There you go, Grey.

There *were* happy times…"I used to brush her hair. She was pretty."

"One look at you and no one would doubt that."

"She was a shitty mother."

Ana nods, her tearful eyes brimming with compassion.

I close my eyes and confess. "I'm scared I'll be a shitty father."

Ana's fingers skim over my face, reassuring me. "Christian, do you think for one minute I'd let you be a shitty father?"

I open my eyes and stare at her.

And there it is…the Anastasia Steele glint.

So aptly named.

My warrior, fighting for me, with me, against me…for our child.

She takes my breath away.

I grin. In awe. "No, I don't think you would." I stroke her face. "God, you're strong, Mrs. Grey. I love you so much." I kiss her forehead. "I didn't know I could."

"Oh, Christian," she whispers.

"Now, that's the end of your bedtime story."

"That's some story."

"How's your head?"

"My head?"

"Does it hurt?"

"No."

"Good. I think you should sleep now."

Ana is not convinced.

"Sleep," I exclaim. "You need it."

"I have one question," Ana says.

"Oh? What?"

"Why have you suddenly become all…forthcoming, for want of a better word? You're telling me all this, when getting information out of you is normally a pretty harrowing and trying experience."

"It is?"

"You know it is."

"Why am I being forthcoming? I can't say. Seeing you practically dead on the cold concrete, maybe." I flinch, remembering Ana on the ground outside that derelict warehouse where Hyde was holding my sister. It's traumatic so I turn my thoughts in a happier direction, to Junior. "The fact I'm going to be a father. I don't know. You said you wanted to know, and I don't want Elena to come between us. She can't. She's the past, and I've said that to you so many times."

"If she hadn't made a pass at you, would you still be friends?" Ana asks.

"That's more than one question."

"Sorry. You don't have to tell me." She blushes, and it's good to see some color in her cheeks. "You've already volunteered more than I ever thought you would."

"No, I don't think so, but she's felt like unfinished business since my birthday. She stepped over the line, and I'm done. Please, believe me. I'm not going to see her again. You said she's a hard limit for you. That's a term I understand."

Ana smiles. "Good night, Christian. Thank you for the enlightening bedtime story." She leans over and touches her lips to mine, her tongue teasing me. My body ignites, and I pull away.

"Don't. I am desperate to make love to you," I whisper through my desire.

"Then do."

"No, you need to rest, and it's late. Go to sleep." I switch off the bedside light and we're surrounded by the darkness.

"I love you unconditionally, Christian," Ana whispers, as she snuggles up to me.

"I know," I whisper, bathing in her light.

You…and my parents.

Unconditionally.

I t's almost midnight. Apart from some exercise, I've enjoyed a quiet day with my wife; our only excursion has been to see Ray, who is definitely on the mend. Other than that, I've insisted that Ana stay in bed and rest. She's acquiesced but has been reading a couple of manuscripts, and no amount of cajoling on my part could persuade her otherwise.

Mrs. Jones has returned from her sister's, and this evening she prepared a hearty three-course meal for the two of us. She seems as anxious for Ana's well-being as I am.

Ana fell asleep just after ten.

I've caught up on work, and now I'm poring over the notes that Mrs. Collier wrote to my mother and father while I was in her care. She has a neat and tidy hand, and her words spark small reminiscences that cast light into the dark corners of my memory.

Kristian won't let me wash him, but he does know how to wash himself. It has taken two baths to get him clean and I've had to teach him how to wash his hair. He will not tolerate us touching him at all.

Kristian had a better day today. He still refuses to talk. We don't know if he can or if he's unable. He has a temper, though. The other kids are quite scared of him.

Kristian still doesn't let any of us touch him. He has a meltdown if we do.

Kristian is hungry. He has a huge appetite for such a skinny little kid. His favorites are pasta and ice cream.

Our daughter, Phoebe, has taken a shine to Kristian. She dotes on him, and he's tolerating her attention. She sits and draws with him. I don't think he's had a great deal of experience drawing.

Where Phoebe goes, Kristian will follow.

Today Kristian had a meltdown. He does not like to be parted from his blanket. But it's filthy. I let him sit and watch it in the washing machine. This seemed to be the only thing that calmed him down.

The memories flare and flicker to the surface in fits and starts, but it's the feeling of being overwhelmed that resonates most with me. I was in a strange place, with a strange family—it must have been horribly bewildering. No wonder I chose to forget that time. But, having read through the notes, I know I didn't come to any harm there and I do remember Phoebe. She would sing to me. Silly songs. She was kind and especially sweet to me.

I'm grateful that my parents kept these letters. They remind me just how far removed I am from that frightened little boy. I am not him anymore. He no longer exists.

I contemplate sharing these with Ana, then remember her reaction to the photographs. Her sorrow as she gazed at that starved, neglected child. And they'd remind of her that asshole Hyde…and how much he and I have in common.

To hell with that.

She's had enough to contend with over the last few days.

I tuck the letters, drawings, and the photographs into a manilla folder marked KRISTIAN and file them safely away in my filing cabinet for another day. Maybe when she's fully recovered. Besides, I need to talk this through with Flynn, and I should do that before I share them with Ana. She's my wife, not my therapist.

I lock the filing cabinet and check the time.

It's late, and Ana is dozing when I slip into bed and pull her into my arms. She mumbles something unintelligible while I breathe in her soothing scent and close my eyes.

My dream catcher.

A na is curled up beside me, still out for the count. It's 7:16 a.m. I'm normally up earlier, but the last few days have taken a toll on me, too. It could also be the workout I did yesterday. Not only did I go for a run, but I did two circuits of the gym and an hour's hard rowing. I smile at the ceiling while I contemplate going for another run this morning. I have all this excess energy.

Perhaps I should let Ana have her wicked way with me.

The thought is appealing.

Fuck.

Too appealing.

Taking a deep breath, I bring my wayward body to heel, grab my phone, and ease myself out of bed. Maybe I'll come back when she's awake. Right now, I'm hungry.

"Good morning, Mr. Grey." Gail is in the kitchen; if she's surprised that I'm still in my pajamas, she doesn't give anything away. She moves straight to the Gaggia to make my coffee.

"Good morning, Mrs. Jones."

"How's Mrs. Grey this morning?"

"Still asleep."

She nods with a satisfied smile. "What can I get you?"

"An omelet. Please."

"Bacon, mushroom, and cheese?"

"Sounds great." She slides over a cup of freshly brewed coffee.

I start leafing through *The Seattle Times*, glad that my wife isn't on the front page, and wonder what Ana and I will do today, when I spot the real estate section.

Of course!

"Gail." I get her attention once more. "Depending on how Ana's feeling, I thought we might go out to the new house later. Could you rustle up a picnic for us?"

"It would be a pleasure, sir. I'll ask Taylor to take it down to the R8 when it's ready."

"Thank you."

I call Andrea to inform her I'm not coming into the office and ask her to reschedule any of today's meetings. She's unfazed. "Yes, Mr. Grey. How is Mrs. Grey?" she asks tentatively.

"Much improved. Thank you."

"That's good to hear."

"I'll be on my cell today, if you need me."

MY OMELET IS EVERYTHING that I hoped it would be. I am happily eating when I look up. Ana has appeared in the doorway. She looks well rested; the bruise on her cheek has faded but she's fully dressed, as if she's going out somewhere. She's wearing a skirt that borders on indecent—she's all legs and high fuck-me heels. I lose my train of thought.

"Good morning, Mrs. Grey. Going somewhere?" I'm hoarse.

"Work." She throws me a smile that illuminates the room.

I scoff at her audacity. "I don't think so. Dr. Singh said a week off."

"Christian, I'm not spending the day lounging in bed on my own." She flashes me a quick, heated look, which I feel in all the right places. "So, I may as well go to work. Good morning, Gail."

"Mrs. Grey." Mrs. Jones flattens her lips, attempting to hide her amusement. "Would you like some breakfast?"

"Please."

"Granola?"

"I'd prefer scrambled eggs with whole-wheat toast."

"Very good, Mrs. Grey," Gail replies, with a broad grin.

"Ana, you are not going to work." I'm amused that she thinks she should.

"But—"

"No. It's simple. Don't argue." *I'm your boss's boss, and the answer is no.*

She narrows her eyes, but her glare becomes a frown as she scrutinizes my attire. "Are you going to work?"

I shake my head and glance down at my pajama pants. "No."

"It is Monday, right?"

I grin. "Last time I looked."

"Are you playing hooky?" From her tone, I think she's intrigued and slightly incredulous.

"I'm not leaving you here on your own to get into trouble. And Dr. Singh said it would be a week before you could go back to work. Remember?"

She sits down on the barstool beside me, her skirt riding up higher, exposing her upper thighs, and I lose my train of thought... again. "You look good," I murmur, and she crosses her legs. "Very good. Especially here." I cannot resist running my finger across the exposed skin between her stocking tops and the hem of her skirt. "This skirt is very short," I murmur.

I can't keep my eyes off your legs, Mrs. Grey.

I'm not sure I approve.

"Is it? I hadn't noticed." Ana waves a nonchalant hand.

Yanking my gaze away from her legs, I look her in the eye. Her cheeks color; she's such a hopeless liar. "Really, Mrs. Grey?" I raise a brow. "I'm not sure this look is suitable for the workplace."

"Well, since I'm not going to work, that's a moot point," she says stiffly.

"Moot?"

"Moot," she mouths, and I hide my smile.

There's *that* word again. I take another bite of my omelet. "I have a better idea."

"You do?"

My eyes meet hers, and suddenly it's there, that look I know so well—her desire responding to mine. The air between us sparks with our own special electricity.

She inhales and I whisper, reeling her in, "We can go see how Elliot's getting on with the house."

A momentary flash of disappointment crosses her face, but then she smiles at my teasing. "I'd love to."

"Good."

"Don't you have to work?"

"No. Ros is back from Taiwan. That all went well. Today, everything's fine."

There are certain advantages to being your own boss.

"I thought you were going to Taiwan."

"Ana, you were in the hospital." *There was no way I was leaving you.*

"Oh."

"Yeah—oh. So today I'm spending some quality time with my wife." I take a sip of Mrs. Jones's great coffee.

"Quality time?" Ana's yearning threads through each syllable.

Oh, baby.

Gail places Ana's scrambled eggs in front of her. "Quality time," I murmur.

Ana's eyes dart from my lips to her breakfast. And her breakfast wins.

Damn. Thwarted by scrambled eggs.

"It's good to see you eat," I murmur, and pushing my plate aside, I step off my barstool and kiss Ana's hair. "I'm going to shower."

"Um…can I come and scrub your back?" she asks through a mouthful of breakfast.

"No. Eat."

I stride off to the bathroom, feeling her eyes on me. As I exit, I strip off my shirt, and I don't know if it's to tempt her to join me in the shower or not. Keeping my hands off her is getting harder and harder in more ways than one.

Grey, grow up.

ANA HAS INSISTED THAT we go visit Ray first, but we don't stay long. Mr. Rodriguez is with him, watching a British soccer match from yesterday—Manchester United vs. Chelsea. Manchester United is two goals up, which seems to please Mr. Rodriguez enormously, judging by his cheer.

I sigh. Try as I might, I don't care for soccer.

Ana takes pity on me and lets Ray know that we're off.

Thank heavens.

I SIT BACK AND relax as we cruise in my R8 to the new house. I'm excited to see the destruction that Elliot has wrought, and hopefully the beginnings of what our home will be.

Ana has changed her sky-high heels for more sensible flats; she's tapping her feet to a Crosby, Stills & Nash song that blares over the Audi's sound system, looking happy to be out and about. Two days of enforced bed rest has been good for her. She has color in her cheeks, and a soft, sweet smile for me when I glance at her, and she seems to have set aside her recent, horrific encounter with the evil Hyde.

I push him out of my mind.

Don't go there, Grey.

I want to preserve my good mood.

Since I unburdened my soul a couple of nights ago, I've felt happier. I had no idea that spilling my guts to my wife would have such a beneficial effect. I don't know if it's because I've finally laid the ghost of Elena Lincoln to rest, or if it's because my parents have provided me with some of the missing pieces from the incomplete puzzle that was my former life, but my heart is lighter somehow—freer, even—but tethered, and as steadfast as ever, to the beautiful woman beside me.

Ana knows me.

She refracts my darkness and turns it to brilliant light.

I shake my head at my fanciful thoughts.

Flowery, Grey.

She's still here, in spite of all that I've done.

The warmth of her love spreads through my veins.

Reaching over, I squeeze her leg, then trail my fingers over her exposed flesh above her thigh-high, relishing the feel of her skin. "I'm glad you didn't change."

Ana covers my hand with her own. "Are you going to continue to tease me?"

I didn't know that's what I was doing.

But, hey, I'll play. "Maybe."

"Why?"

"Because I can." I beam at her.

"Two can play that game," she whispers.

I move my fingers up her inner thigh. "Bring it on, Mrs. Grey."

She takes my hand and places it on my knee. "Well, you can keep your hands to yourself," she says primly.

"As you wish, Mrs. Grey."

I cannot hide my smile. I love playful Ana.

Ha. I love Ana. Period.

STOPPING AT THE GATES to our house, I press the entry code into the keypad. The metal gates swing slowly open, creaking a protest at being disturbed. They need replacing, and we'll get around to it eventually. Speeding along the driveway, I wish I'd taken the top down on the car. The tall grass in the meadow is golden beneath the September sun, and the trees lining the drive are all decked in the colors of the coming fall. The Sound in the distance is a brilliant blue. It's idyllic.

And it's ours.

As the lane meanders around a wide curve, the house appears, surrounded by a number of Elliot's construction trucks. It's hidden behind scaffolding, and several of Elliot's crew are at work on the roof. I park outside the portico, switch off the engine, and turn to Ana. "Let's go find Elliot." I'm buzzing to see what he's accomplished so far.

"Is he here?"

"I hope so. I'm paying him enough."

She laughs and we both exit the car.

"Yo, bro!" I hear Elliot shout, but I can't see him.

"Up here!" I scan the roofline, grateful that I'm wearing aviators against the glare of the sun, and there he is, waving at us. His grin rivals the Cheshire Cat's. "About time we saw you here. Stay where you are. I'll be right down."

I reach out to Ana, and she takes my hand, and while we wait, we study the exterior of what will be our home. It's bigger than I remember.

Plenty of room for our child.

My wayward thought surprises me.

Finally, Elliot appears at the front door caked in grime but still wearing his broad grin. He's clearly over the moon that we're here. "Hey, bro." He pumps my hand like he's trying to drag water from the deepest well. "And how are you, little lady?" He grabs Ana and swings her around.

"Better, thanks," she says, laughing, a little embarrassed, I think.

Dude! Quit manhandling my wife! Her ribs are bruised!

He sets her down and I scowl at him.

Asshole.

But he ignores me—no one is raining on his parade today. "Let's head over to the site office. You'll need one of these." He slaps the hard hat perched on his head.

ELLIOT GIVES US A thorough tour of the house, or what's left of it—it's almost a shell. Meticulously he explains the work in progress, and how long each stage is going to take. When he's in his element like this, he's so engaging. Both Ana and I listen, rapt.

The back wall at the rear has disappeared. This is where Gia Matteo's glass wall will be, and the view is spectacular. There are a few sails out on the Sound, and I'm tempted to go down to *The Grace* after our visit here. But that's not such a good idea, given Ana's recent injuries. She's still recovering and needs to take it easy.

"Hopefully we'll be finished by Christmas," Elliot declares.

"Next year," I interject. *There is no way we'll be in by Christmas.*

"We'll see. With a fair wind it's doable."

In the kitchen, he concludes our tour. "I'll leave you two to roam. Be careful. This is a building site."

"Sure. Thanks, Elliot."

My brother gives us a cheery wave and heads up the covered staircase to join his construction crew, back on the roof. I take Ana's hand. "Happy?"

Ana gives me a dazzling smile. "Very. I love it. You?"

"Ditto."

"Good. I was thinking of the pepper pictures in here." Ana points to one of the walls.

I nod in agreement. "I want to put up José's portraits of you in this house. You need to decide where they should go."

Her cheeks stain that delicious shade of pink. "Somewhere I won't see them often."

"Don't be like that." I brush my thumb across her bottom lip. "They're my favorite pictures. I love the one in my office."

"I have no idea why." She pouts and kisses the pad of my thumb.

"Worse things to do than look at your beautiful smiling face all day. Hungry?"

"Hungry for what?" She peers at me with the come-hither look that I know so well.

Oh, baby. I can only take so much of this.

"Food, Mrs. Grey." I kiss her quickly.

She pouts and sighs. "Yes. These days I'm always hungry."

"The three of us can have a picnic."

"Three of us? Is someone joining us?"

I drop my head to one side.

Forgotten someone, Ana? "In about seven or eight months," I murmur.

She grins goofily at me… *Yeah. Him.*

"I thought you might like to eat alfresco," I suggest, casually.

"In the meadow?"

I nod.

"Sure." Ana lights up. And I feel ten feet tall for thinking of bringing a picnic. We have so much space and privacy here.

"This will be a great place to raise a family." I gaze down at my wife.

Junior will be happy here.

The meadow as his backyard.

I reach out and spread my hand over her belly. Ana's breath hitches and she places her hand on mine.

"It's hard to believe," I whisper.

"I know. Oh—here, I have evidence. A picture."

"You do? Baby's first smile?"

From her wallet she produces a black-and-white image on shiny paper and hands it to me. "See?" she says.

The grainy photograph is mostly gray. But in the middle, there's a small, dark void, and within that, there's a tiny anomaly, anchored to the gray, but visible against the darkness. "Oh, blip," I breathe in wonder. "Yeah, I see."

Our blip. Wow. Our tiny human. Baby Grey.

And I'm surprised by a momentary pang of regret, that I missed this moment with Ana.

"Your child," she whispers.

"Our child," I correct her.

"First of many."

"Many?" *What?*

"At least two." Ana sounds hopeful.

"Two?" *Shit!* "Can we just take this one child at a time?"

She smiles up at me fondly. "Sure."

I take her hand, and together we walk back through the house and out the front door.

It's such a beautiful afternoon. The scents of the Sound, the meadow grass, and flowers hang in the air. My beautiful wife is by my side. It's heaven. And soon there will be three of us. "When are you going to tell your folks?" I ask.

"Soon. I thought about telling Ray this morning, but Mr. Rodriguez was there." Ana shrugs.

I nod. *I get it, Ana.*

Lifting the hood of the R8, I gather up the wicker picnic basket and the tartan blanket that Ana bought from Harrods in London. "Come." Hand in hand, we stroll into the meadow. When we're far enough from the house, I release her, and together we spread the blanket on the ground. I settle down beside her, shrug off my jacket, and slip off my shoes and socks. I take a moment to just breathe, taking in a lungful of fresh air. We're shielded by the long grass, away from the world, truly in our own bubble. As Ana opens the picnic basket to inspect all the goodies that Mrs. Jones has provided, my phone vibrates.

Shit.

It's Ros.

"...**THANK YOU FOR ANSWERING** my question, and glad to hear that Ana is on the mend," Ros says over the phone.

"You're welcome." It's the second time she's called and the third call I've had since we started our picnic.

"You shouldn't be so indispensable."

I laugh. "You flatter me."

Ana is lying beside me, half listening to my side of the conversation. Her brow puckers at my last remark.

"You should take a couple of days off," I tell Ros. "After all, you spent most of the weekend traveling back from Taiwan."

"That's a great idea. I may take Thursday and Friday, if that's okay with you."

"Sure, Ros, go for it."

"Will do. Thanks, Christian. Good-bye."

I toss my phone down, and resting my hands on my raised knees, I regard my wife. She's lying beside me on our blanket, gazing up with a dreamy expression. Reaching over, I pluck another strawberry from what's left of Mrs. Jones's excellent picnic and trace it along Ana's mouth. She parts her lips, and the tip of her tongue toys with the strawberry, then sucks it into her warm, wet mouth.

I feel it in my groin. "Tasty?" I whisper.

"Very."

"Had enough?"

"Of strawberries, yes." Her tone is low.

Ana, no one can see us here.

Grey, behave.

I grin. *Enough.* I change the subject. "Mrs. Jones packs a mighty fine picnic."

"That she does."

God, I miss my wife—all of her. I lie down, gently resting my head on her belly, and close my eyes, trying not to think of all the things I'd like to do to her right now. Her fingers caress my hair.

Oh, this is bliss.

My BlackBerry starts buzzing again.

Shit. It's Welch. What does he want?

I answer, a little grumpy at the interruption. "Welch."

"Mr. Grey. I have an update. It was Eric Lincoln of Lincoln Timber who paid Hyde's bail."

Fuck.

That motherfucking asshole.

I sit up. My senses switch to high alert as my anger takes hold.

"I'd like to place him under watch, unless you have any objection."

"24/7," I snarl in agreement.

How dare Lincoln get involved with Hyde?

This is a declaration of war.

"Will do. I don't know what else he might have planned, or how the two of them are connected. But I'll find out."

"Thanks." He hangs up, and I can barely contain my fury. Gripping my phone, I realize *now* is the moment for payback. My plans were laid long ago, and as the saying goes, revenge is a dish best served cold. I give Ana a cool smile and call Ros.

"Christian. I thought you were enjoying your day off?"

I kneel up—*I'm not calling for chitchat.*

"Ros, how much stock do we own in Lincoln Timber?"

"Let me just check." She's all business. "We hold sixty-six percent between all the shell companies."

Excellent.

"So, consolidate the shares into GEH, then fire the board."

"All of them? Has something happened?"

"Except the CEO."

"Christian, that doesn't make sense."

"I don't give a fuck."

She gasps. "There'll be no company left. What can the CEO do? If you want to liquidate this company, this isn't the way."

"I hear you, just do it," I growl, keeping a lid on my anger.

She sighs, sounding resigned. "They're your shares." She's not going to argue further.

"Thank you," I reply, feeling a little calmer.

"I'll get Marco on it."

"Keep me informed."

When I hang up, Ana is wide-eyed. "What's happened?" she whispers.

"Linc."

"Linc? Elena's ex?"

"The same. He's the one who posted Hyde's bail."

Ana's mouth drops open in shock. "Well—he'll look like an idiot," she says, dismayed. "I mean, Hyde committed another crime while out on bail."

As ever, Ana has a smart response. "Fair point well made, Mrs. Grey."

"What did you just do?" She kneels up to face me.

"I fucked him over."

She shivers. "Um, that seems a little impulsive."

"I'm an in-the-moment kind of guy."

"I'm aware of that."

"I've had this plan in my back pocket for a while," I explain.

A hostile takeover.

"Oh?" Ana tilts her head, her gaze demanding answers. I debate whether to tell her.

Hell, she knows everything about Elena anyway. I take a deep breath and shoot her a warning look. *This is rough, Ana.* "Several years back, when I was twenty-one, Linc beat his wife to a pulp. He broke her jaw, her left arm, and four of her ribs because she was fucking me. And now I learn he posted bail for a man who tried to kill me, kidnap my sister, and fracture my wife's skull. I've had enough. I think it's pay-back time." My mind drifts to that awful moment when he beat me, too—I thought he'd dislocated my jaw. My hand moves to my chin as I recall the disturbing incident. I lost consciousness for a few minutes and it was enough time for him to do his worst to Elena.

And I did nothing. I was too shocked...too dazed.

Damn. *Grey, stop. Now.*

Ana's face is pale. "Fair point well made, Mr. Grey," she says.

"Ana, this is what I do. I'm not usually motivated by revenge, but I cannot let him get away with this. What he did to Elena—well, she should have pressed charges, but she didn't. That was her preroga-tive." My jaw tenses. "But he's seriously crossed the line with Hyde. Linc's made this personal by going after my family. I'm going to crush him, break up his company right under his nose, and sell the pieces to the highest bidder. I'm going to bankrupt him."

Ana gasps.

"Besides," I add, trying to lighten the tone, "we'll make good money out of the deal."

She blinks several times, and I wonder if she's seeing me in a whole new light. *Not a good one.*

Shit. "I didn't mean to frighten you."

"You didn't," she whispers.

I arch a brow. Does she mean that? Or is she trying to make me feel better?

"You just took me by surprise," Ana concedes.

I cup her face in my hands and brush my lips against hers.

I'm not sorry, Ana. "I will do anything to keep you safe. Keep my family safe. Keep this little one safe." I place my hand on her belly, and Ana's breath hitches.

Her eyes meet mine, and in their blue depths, her desire is smoldering, calling to me.

Fuck.

I want her.

She's so enticing. I slip my fingers a little lower, brushing her sex through her clothes with the tips of my fingers, teasing her.

Ana pounces, grabbing my head, entwining her fingers in my hair and tugging my lips to hers. I gasp in surprise, and her tongue is instantly in my mouth.

Desire, hot and heavy, travels at light speed all the way to the end of my cock.

Damn, I'm hard.

I groan and return her kiss, my tongue tangling with hers.

It's been so long.

The taste of her, the feel of her. She's everything. "Ana," I breathe in longing against her lips. I'm bewitched, my hands moving undirected over her beautiful behind to the hem of her skirt and the soft flesh of the thighs.

Thank all that is holy for this short skirt!

Her hands start to unbutton my shirt, as ever all fingers and thumbs.

And for a moment her fumbling fingers distract me.

"Whoa, Ana—stop." With enormous restraint, I pull back and grab her hands.

"No," she cries, distraught, and her teeth clamp over my lower lip. "No." She's insistent, darkening blue eyes staring at me with longing. She releases me. "I want you."

Ana! You're hurt!

My body agrees with Ana.

"Please, I need you." It's a heartfelt plea.

Oh, fuck.

I'm done. I concede, overcome by her ardor and my need. I groan, and my mouth finds hers, kissing her and tasting her once more. Cradling her head, I run my hand down her body to her waist, and gently ease her onto her back and stretch out beside her.

We kiss.

And kiss.

Lips and tongues locked.

Reacquainting ourselves with each other.

When I come up for air, I stare down into eyes dazed with passion. "You are so beautiful, Mrs. Grey."

Her fingers strum my face. "So are you, Mr. Grey. Inside and out."

Oh, I'm not sure that's true.

Her fingers trace the line of my brow. "Don't frown," she whispers. "You are to me, even when you're angry."

She says the sweetest things. I moan and kiss her once more and revel in her response, her body rising to meet mine. "I've missed you." My words are inadequate and no match for the feelings behind them.

She is the world to me.

I skim my teeth over her jaw.

"I've missed you, too. Oh, Christian."

Her passion spurs me on. I run my lips along her throat, leaving soft, wet kisses in their wake, and I unbutton her shirt and tug it open to kiss the soft swell of her breasts.

Sweet Jesus, they're bigger!

Already.

Mm. "Your body's changing," I murmur in appreciation, and rub my thumb over her bra, coaxing her nipple awake until it's begging for my lips. "I like…"

Did I say that out loud?

I don't know. I don't care. I'm just so enamored of my wife. I nuzzle her breast with my nose and my tongue through the white gossamer of her bra. As her nipple strains for release, I use my teeth to drag down the cup, freeing her breast. Her nipple puckers in the gentle breeze, and I draw it slowly into my mouth and suck hard.

"Ah!" Ana groans, then flinches beneath me.

Fuck! Her ribs!

I stop, immediately. "Ana!" *Damn.* "This is what I'm talking about. Your lack of self-preservation. I don't want to hurt you."

Desperate, blazing eyes meet mine. "No! Don't stop," she whimpers. "Please."

Shit. My whole body is screaming don't stop.

But—

Hell!

"Here." Carefully, I lift her and shift so she's sitting astride me, and my hands travel smoothly up her legs to the tops of her thigh-highs.

She is one helluva sight. Her hair falling toward me, eyes soft and full of desire, her breast free. "There. That's better, and I can enjoy the view." I hook my finger into the other bra cup, drag it down so that I have both of her breasts to enjoy. As I take them in my hands, Ana groans and throws her head back, pushing them farther into my palms.

Oh, baby.

I tug and tease each of her nipples, and they lengthen further beneath my touch until she cries out. I want her mouth; I sit up so we're nose to nose and kiss her, my tongue and my fingers teasing and tantalizing her.

Ana's fingers are at my shirt again, scrambling to undo the remaining buttons, and she's kissing me back with such fervor that I'm sure either one or both of us will combust. There's a desperation in her kiss. "Hey—" Gently, I grasp her head and ease back. "There's no rush. Take it slow. I want to savor you."

"Christian, it's been so long." She's breathless.

I know. But you're hurt. Let's not be hasty.

"Slow." And that's not a request. I press my lips to the right corner of her mouth "Slow." The left corner. "Slow, baby." I suck her bottom lip into my mouth. "Let's take this slow." Cradling her head, I continue to kiss her, my tongue subduing hers, hers enticing mine. She glides her fingers across my face, my chin, my throat, and starts on my shirt buttons once more. She tugs my shirt apart, her fingers caressing my chest, then pushing me down so that I'm prostrate beneath her.

She gazes down at me and squirms over my groin.

I push up my hips to enjoy the friction against my eager dick.

Ana watches me, her lips parted as she traces my mouth with the tips of her fingers. She moves on, her fingers skimming over my jaw, down my neck, and to the base of my throat. Leaning down, her tender kisses trail where her fingers have been, grazing my jaw and my throat. I surrender to the sensation, closing my eyes and reclining my head with a moan. Her tongue continues its journey, down my sternum, across my chest, where she stops to kiss a couple of my scars.

Ana.

I want to bury myself deep inside her. Grasping her hips, I meet her dark eyes with a dark look of my own. "You want this? Here?" My voice is husky with need.

"Yes," she murmurs, and dips her head once more, her lips and tongue teasing my nipple. She tugs it gently.

"Oh, Ana," I breathe in awe as pleasure spikes through my body. I circle her waist, lift her clear, and quickly unbutton my jeans, open my fly, and push down my underwear so my cock springs free. I sit her down once more and she grinds against me.

Ah. I need to be inside her. Running my hands up her thighs, I pause at the top of her thigh-highs. I circle my thumbs against her warm flesh and move my hands further up, so I brush the damp seeping through her lace panties.

Ana gasps.

"I hope you're not attached to your underwear," I whisper, and my fingers slide inside her panties, touching her.

Damn. She's soaking.

Ready for me.

I force my thumbs through the fabric and the material rips apart. *Yes!*

I move my hands to her upper thighs and let my thumbs brush against her clitoris as I tighten my ass, searching for some friction against my cock. She slides over me. "I can feel how wet you are."

You fucking goddess, Ana.

Sitting up, so we're eye to eye once more, I wrap my arm around her waist and rub my nose to hers. "We're going to take this slow, Mrs. Grey. I want to feel all of you." And before she can argue with me, I lift her again, and gently lower her onto me and fill her, languidly. I close my eyes and relish each delicious inch of her.

She's bliss.

"Ah!" Ana moans, and grasps my arms. She tries to lift up, eager to begin, but I hold her in place and open my eyes again.

"All of me," I murmur, and tilt my pelvis up, claiming all of her.

Ana lets out a strangled moan and throws her head back.

"Let me hear you," I whisper. And she tries to rise again. "No— don't move, just feel." Her eyes spring open, and her mouth is agape in a fixed gasp of pleasure. She gazes at me, barely breathing, it seems. I drive into her once more, but hold her still. She groans while I bend my head to kiss her throat. "This is my favorite place. Buried in you," I whisper to the pulse under her ear.

"Please, move," she begs.

But I want to tease her.

Take it slow.

So she doesn't hurt herself.

"Slow, Mrs. Grey." I flex my ass one more, pushing into her, and she caresses my face and kisses me. Her tongue consuming me.

"Love me. Please, Christian."

My resolve crumbles, and I skim her jaw with my teeth. "Go."

I'm all yours, Ana.

She pushes me to the ground, and she starts to move, up and down. Fast, a little frantic. Taking all I have to give.

Oh God.

I grab her hands and complement her wild pace. Pushing up, again and again. Relishing the feel of her, enjoying the view, my wife, the blue sky behind her in the outdoors. "Oh, Ana." I groan, surrendering completely to her rhythm. I close my eyes and move my hands up her thighs once more, to that precious point between them. There, I press both thumbs against her clitoris, and she cries out, exploding around me, in a gasping, rolling climax that tips me over the edge.

"Ana!" I cry as I succumb to my own heady orgasm.

WHEN I OPEN MY eyes, she's sprawled over me.

I cloak her in my arms, and we lie together. Still joined.

I've missed this.

Her hand is over my heart as it slows to its normal rhythm.

It's weird. Not long ago I couldn't have tolerated her hands on me.

Now, I crave her touch.

She kisses my chest.

And I kiss her hair. "Better?" I ask.

She raises her head, her grin reflecting mine.

"Much. You?"

I'm just grateful that she's here and whole and still with me, after everything that's happened. "I've missed you, Mrs. Grey."

"Me, too."

"No more heroics, eh?"

"No," she breathes.

"You should always talk to me," I insist in a soft voice.

"Back at you, Grey."

"Fair point well made. I'll try." I kiss her again, smirking. She's not taking any of my shit, as usual.

"I think we're going to be happy here," Ana says.

"Yep. You, me, and Blip. How do you feel, incidentally?"

"Fine. Relaxed. Happy."

"Good."

"You?"

"Yeah, all those things." *Deliriously happy, Ana.*

She peers at me.

"What?" I ask.

"You know, you're very bossy when we have sex."

Oh. "Are you complaining?"

"No," she says emphatically. "I'm just wondering. You said you missed it."

And I wonder what she means for a moment.

Control? I need that. The playroom? *What we do in there?* A vision of her shackled to the four-poster, the Tallis ringing through the room, comes to mind. Or maybe the cross and a riding crop…the brown leather one. My memories go on and on, seducing me.

"Sometimes," I whisper.

Yeah. Sometimes I miss it.

She smiles. "Well, we'll have to see what we can do about that." She drops a kiss on my lips.

Oh. That sounds interesting.

"I like to play, too," she says, and peeks shyly up at me.

Well. Well. Well. This perfect day just got a whole lot better.

"You know, I'd really like to test your limits," I whisper.

"My limits for what?"

"Pleasure."

"Oh, I think I'd like that."

"Well, maybe when we get home." I hug her gently, marveling at how much she means to me.

How much I love her.

Who knew I could fall so desperately and completely in love?

Flynn is at a loss for words.

This might be a first.

I've given him an executive summary of all that has transpired since our last session. "So that's why you came looking for me," he mutters.

"Yes."

He shakes his head in disbelief. "Well, first things first. How's Ana?"

"She's good. On the mend. Desperate to get back to work."

"No PTSD?"

"I don't think so. But it might be too early to tell."

"I can recommend someone, if she needs a therapist." He stops and taps his lip with his index finger. "Shall we take this in stages? Let's start with the pregnancy, and your reaction."

"Not my proudest moment." I stare past him at a space on the wall, embarrassed to look him in the eye.

"No," he agrees, far too readily. "How are you feeling about it now?"

Sighing, I lean forward and rest my elbows on my knees. "Resigned. Excited. Scared. In about equal measure. I would have preferred if we'd waited. But now that Junior is on his way...well." I shrug.

Flynn's expression is sympathetic, I think. "You don't truly learn what unconditional love is until you have a child."

"That's what Ana says. But I've only just learned to love her..." I trail off, unwilling to voice the rest of my thought.

"How can you love someone else, too?" Flynn finishes the sentence for me.

My smile is bleak.

"Christian, knowing your extraordinary need to protect and provide for those who are close to you, those you love, there's no doubt in my mind that you have an innate capacity to love your own child."

"I hope you're right."

John allows himself a small smile. "We'll see. You'll find out in a few months. How are you feeling about Mrs. Lincoln?"

"As if that chapter's closed."

Flynn nods.

"I think it helps that I told Ana everything. How it all began and how it all ended. It feels complete."

"Sounds like it. Any regrets?"

I blow out a breath. "Telling Ana? No. None. Severing my relationship with Elena… Yes. No…"

John purses his lips and I add quickly, "I know you don't agree. I know what Elena and I did was wrong…what she did was wrong. Her behavior was predatory—I understand that now, but I don't wholly regret it. How can I? I've always believed she was what I needed at the time. She taught me so much."

He sighs. "She took advantage of a vulnerable adolescent, Christian. You can't dodge that truth."

I stare at him.

He's not wrong.

But I'm not prepared to admit that…yet.

"Give me time," I state quietly.

He nods. "No doubt we'll keep coming back to this, so let's give you some time and we can dig into that again when you're ready." He blows out a breath. "I'd like to ask you about the conversation with your parents with regard to your foster placement. How that felt?"

"Strange, for several reasons."

"Please, elaborate."

"First of all, I was stunned they were so quick to respond to my call for help."

"Have they not done that before?"

"Well, yes, they have. My mom was really helpful with Ray, when he was in an accident."

"But that's different. She's a doctor."

"Yeah. I'm not sure I've ever asked them about something so personal before. I think I gave up trying a long time ago. As you know, in my teens, I had a difficult relationship with both of them. And they were so disappointed and disapproving after I dropped out of Harvard."

Flynn nods. "But as a parent you always think you know what's best for your child. It's a lesson worth remembering. Dropping out obviously did you no harm."

"But the other evening when they came over, they were more than helpful. They brought all that stuff with them." I point to the manilla folder that Flynn has already leafed through. He reaches for the photograph of the Collier family and their two foster children.

"And that's Hyde?" He indicates the truculent red-haired boy.

I nod.

"And you. The smallest kid."

"Yes."

"It must have been very unsettling for you, not to remember this time."

"It was."

"Do you remember more now?"

"Yes. I think it was my mother's reassurance, that I came to no harm in the foster family's care, that was the most comforting. It enabled me to let the memories in. Before then, my imagination went wild. I was scared to remember. You know...when you don't know."

"Yes. I understand. You believe her?"

"Yes. The recollections I do have are all good."

"And what of Kristian Pusztai?"

I sigh. "He's no more."

Flynn's brow creases. "Are you sure?"

I scoff. "No. But I think it's time I grew up and left him behind. My wife told me in no uncertain terms that I need to grow up and smell the fucking coffee."

Flynn snorts. "Did she, now? Have you told her? About this?" He holds up my birth certificate.

"No."

"Why?"

I shrug. "She knows me as Christian Grey."

John considers my response. "That child is part of you."

"I know. But I want to keep him to myself for a little while longer. Get used to him."

"Will you tell her?"

"One day. Sure."

"You've only known about him for a few days. I think you're entitled to keep him to yourself for as long as you want, Christian. Learn to love him. Forgive him. It's in your power to do so."

I gasp as the full weight of Flynn's words blindside me.

Forgive him.

"What did he do that requires forgiveness?" I whisper.

John smiles at me, kindly. "He survived."

I'm frozen. Staring at him.

"And his poor mother didn't. You might want to direct some of your forgiveness at her, too."

I gaze at him for what feels like minutes, then I glance at the clock. "Okay." I blow out a breath, relieved we're done. "As ever, you've given me a great deal to think about."

"Good. That's my job. We still have so much to discuss, but I'm sorry, we're out of time."

"We're getting there, surely?" I ask.

Flynn's grin is amicable. "Slowly. Now we're at this point, your attachment issues alone could fill a year."

I laugh. "I know."

"But you're beginning to open up to your wife. Making yourself vulnerable. These are giant steps."

I nod, feeling like I got an A in therapy. "I think so."

"I'll see you next time. And congratulations, Christian."

I frown. *What?*

"The baby." Flynn grins.

"Oh, yes. Junior. Thank you."

IT'S DUSK, A GOLDEN pink light filling the room. My hands in the pockets of my pants, I stare out at the Seattle skyline toward the Sound and smile—from my ivory tower, as Ana would say. And I would correct her and tell her it's *our* ivory tower.

She was animated and talkative at dinner, happy to be work-ing. After our meal she returned to her lair—well, the library—to sort through query letters that she had messengered over from SIP. Perhaps she should go into the office tomorrow. I think she's well enough.

My mind shifts to my conversation with Flynn.

Forgive him.

Forgive her.

Perhaps it's time. I've spent so long loathing the crack whore, I'm not sure I can move on from those feelings, but Ana was passionate in her defense… *Forgive her. She had her own world of pain to deal with. She was a shitty mother, and you loved her.*

My shrink and my wife are of one accord. Perhaps I should listen to them.

Idly I walk to the piano, sit down, and start to play Debussy's "Arabesque No. 1." A piece I haven't played in forever. As the upbeat, evocative melody echoes through the room, I disappear into the music.

My phone buzzes, interrupting the second Arabesque.

I have an e-mail from my wife.

From: Anastasia Grey
Subject: My Husband's Pleasure
Date: September 21 2011 20:45
To: Christian Grey

Sir
I await your instructions.
Yours always
Mrs. G x

I stare at it in anticipation as desire wakes my body.

Ana wants to play.

Best not to keep a lady waiting.

I type a response.

From: Christian Grey
Subject: My Husband's Pleasure <—— love this title, baby
Date: September 21 2011 20:48
To: Anastasia Grey

Mrs. G
I'm intrigued. I'll come find you.
Be ready.

Christian Grey
Anticipative CEO, Grey Enterprises Holdings, Inc.

She can't be in the playroom—I'd have noticed her moving to the upper floor. I open the bedroom door, and here she is, kneeling at the entrance—eyes downcast, wearing a pale blue camisole and panties, and nothing else. On the bed she's laid out my Dom jeans.

My heart lurches into overdrive as I gaze at her, drinking in every detail: her parted lips, her long lashes, her hair curling in luscious waves below her breasts. Her breathing's accelerated; she's excited. My beautiful girl is offering herself to me, wholly. Again.

Last time we were in the playroom, she safe-worded on me.

And yet she trusts me enough to go again.

What did I do to deserve her?

She's still healing, Grey.

Fuck.

But she's dropped enough hints these last few days.

We'll have to see what we can do about that.

And suddenly a barrage of visions of Ana in the playroom fill my mind.

That first time.

Her nervousness.

My excitement.

Damn. She wants this…so do I. I reach for my jeans and, turning, head into the closet to change. As I strip, I think of what we could do. We'll take it easy…*easy sweet.*

But I'm going to drive her wild.

A frisson of pure excitement runs down my spine to my dick.

Bring it on, Mrs. Grey.

I return to the bedroom and she's still kneeling at the door. "So, you want to play?"

"Yes."

Oh, Ana. You can do better than that.

When I don't respond, she looks up at me and registers my annoyed frown.

"Yes what?" I whisper.

"Yes, Sir," she says quickly.

"Good girl." I stroke her hair. "I think we'd better get you upstairs now." Offering my hand, I help her to her feet, and together we walk to the stairs and up to the playroom.

Outside the door, I bend down and kiss her, then grasp her hair and tip her head back so I can drown in the depths of her eyes. "You know, you're topping from the bottom," I murmur against her lips. But then, she's been doing that since I met her.

She owns me, body and soul.

"What?" she breathes.

"Don't worry. I'll live with it."

Until death do us part, Anastasia Grey.

Because I love you.

More than life itself.

And I know you love me.

I run my nose down her jaw, filling my senses with her sweet scent. I nibble her ear. "Once inside, kneel, like I've shown you."

"Yes, Sir."

Ana peers at me through her lashes, and I don't miss her I-so-own-you smile.

It makes me smile, too.

Because it's true.

She is my everything.

And I'm hers...always.

Now, let's have some fun...

Epilogue

I lie perfectly still, drinking in the sight of my gorgeous wife lying beside me. Early morning light streams through the gap in the curtains, gilding Ana's hair and revealing the adoring glow in her face. She doesn't know I'm awake yet, as she's busy breastfeeding our son—smiling down, murmuring quiet words of love to him, and stroking his soft, plump cheek.

It's a stirring scene.

Ana has a fathomless well of love to give. To him. To me.

She shows me how it should be, and that it's okay to feel this thrill, this passion for someone so small. This flesh of my flesh.

Ted.

My boy.

I'm besotted, with both of them.

She peeks up to check on me, and I'm caught mid-ogle. Her face erupts into an enormous smile. "Good morning, Mr. Grey. Enjoying the view?" She cocks an eyebrow, amused.

"Very much, Mrs. Grey." Leaning up on my elbow, I press a tender kiss to her waiting lips, and another on the coppery down atop Ted's head. Closing my eyes, I breathe in his scent; after Ana's, it's the sweetest fragrance in the world.

"He smells so good."

"That's because I changed his diaper ten minutes ago."

I grimace, then smile.

Rather you than me!

Ana grins but rolls her eyes, knowing full well what I'm thinking. Teddy ignores us, his eyes closed, his hand splayed over the swell of Ana's breast. He's too busy enjoying breakfast.

Lucky boy.

He's a very lucky boy. He sleeps with us.

That was a battle I was never going to win. And while it has some-what curtailed our bedroom activity at night, it's reassuring to know he's so close when we sleep. It's ironic to think that until I met Ana, I'd never slept with anyone, and now there are two people in my bed.

"Did he wake last night?"

"Not since I fed him at midnight." She strokes his cheek once more and croons. "You slept all night, little man." He pats her breast in response, staring up at her with eyes the same shade as hers, and with a look I know only too well.

Complete adoration.

Yep, Teddy and I suffer from the same fixation.

He closes his eyes and his suckling slows and stops.

She strokes his cheek, then delicately slides her finger into his mouth so he releases her nipple. "That's breakfast done," she whis-pers. "I'll put him in his crib."

"I'll do it." Today is a special day. Sitting up, I gently scoop him into my arms, enjoying his warmth and weight against my chest. I kiss his head once more and, holding him close, carry him next door to his room, *where he should be sleeping*. Miraculously, he stays asleep as I lay him down in his crib and cover him with his cotton blan-ket. Gazing down at him, I'm lost in an overwhelming swell of emo-tion. It hits me now and then—an immense tidal wave of love that washes over and through me. This tiny human has invaded my heart, ensnared it, and trashed all my defenses. Flynn was right: I love him unconditionally.

I shiver, because this feeling still frightens me, and scan his room. It's painted like an apple orchard, and one day, I hope to teach him how to grow sweet red apples from a bitter green apple tree with the help of his namesake, Grandpa Theodore. Switching on the baby monitor, I grab the receiver and take it back to our bedroom.

Ana is fast asleep.

Damn. I never wished her a happy anniversary.

For a moment I contemplate waking her, but deep down I know that wouldn't be fair. Ana is tired most of the time; sleep is prized over everything. Hopefully, now that Ted's nearly three months old, she'll get more rest.

I miss her.

Feeling a pang of regret that I know is completely selfish, I stride into the closet to change into my running gear.

I scroll through the songs on my phone and find one that Ana must have uploaded. It brings a smile to my lips.

With Rihanna's "We Found Love" blaring through my earbuds, I set off for a run down Fourth Avenue. It's early, and the streets are relatively empty, except for the occasional dog walker, and refrigerated trucks delivering to the local restaurants, and early-shift personnel heading to work. My mind empties as I concentrate on finding my rhythm and setting a long run pace. I'm heading northwest, the sun is shining, the trees are in full leaf, and I feel I could run forever. All is right in my world.

An idea occurs to me.

I decide on a nostalgia tour and set my sights on Ana's old apartment, where Kate and Ethan live.

For old times' sake.

Their living arrangements will change shortly; Kate and Elliot are getting married this coming weekend. As soon as Kate found out Ana was pregnant, and her due date, she changed all their plans so that Ana could still be her matron of honor. That woman is as determined as ever—I hope Elliot knows what he's doing.

His bachelor party was epic, far more gregarious than mine. But that's Elliot. And what happens in Cabo San Lucas stays there. And even though as best man it was my responsibility to organize the whole shebang, I spent those few days missing my wife and son. But then, I'm not the party animal—Elliot is—and he had fun. That was the point.

As I round the corner onto Vine Street, I'm reminded of my desperate runs during the dark days when Ana left me.

Damn. I was crazy then.

Crazy in love, Grey.

And I didn't even know it.

Approaching my stalker's hide, I contemplate pausing there, but dismiss the idea. Those dark days are far behind me. And I don't want to be away from Ana for too long.

I turn left at the corner onto Western Avenue, my mind drifting to all that's happened since Ana and I tied the knot—on this day, last year. Of course, the biggest change was the dramatic arrival of Theodore Raymond Grey on May 2, who now rules our hearts and our domain.

God, I love my boy.

Even though I now have to compete with him for my wife's attention.

I do choose this defenseless baby over you. That's what any loving parent does.

Damn right, Ana.

Her words still sting, but they resonate with me now. It's hard, surrendering her to someone else. I wouldn't do it for anyone but him.

And to see her care for him!

She loves him so much. She'll do anything for him.

I know that my birth mother, to some degree, must have done the same for me. I wouldn't have survived to age four otherwise. It makes me feel a little more kindly toward Ella…just.

In a way, I envy Ted; he has such an advocate in his mother. She'll fight for him. Always. That's why he's in our bed.

While I'm breastfeeding him, he's here with us. Deal with it, Christian.

My girl does not back down.

And, of course, he has *me*.

I'll do everything in my power to keep him safe.

That fucker Hyde is locked up. The trial was a painful but necessary evil—he was convicted of aggravated kidnapping, arson, extortion, and sabotage and sentenced to thirty years. Not long enough, in my opinion, but at least he's out of our lives and where he deserves to be—behind bars.

Lincoln is bankrupt and currently on remand for felony fraud charges. I hope he, too, rots in jail. Revenge is indeed a most satisfying dish.

Enough, Grey.

I direct my thoughts back to my family as I run through Pike Place Market. I love this time of the morning here: the florists setting up their colorful displays, the fishmongers icing their fresh catch, and the grocers arranging their fruits and vegetables—it's such a vibrant, bustling part of the city, and so much easier to navigate this early, without the tourists in the way.

Next weekend's wedding will be held at Eamon Kavanagh's Medina residence. I still have to write my speech, and much to Kate's irritation, I've refused to give her editorial approval.

She's such a control freak.

I don't know how Elliot puts up with her.

Ana and Mia are both part of the bridal party—Ana as matron of honor and Mia as bridesmaid. I hope it's not going to be too awkward with Ethan.

I shake my head. *He's just not that into you, Mia.*

I continue on and pick up my pace on Stewart Street, running toward Escala.

Running home.

Well, to one of our homes.

We divide our time between our two residences—Escala during the week and the Big House, as Ana calls it, on the weekends. So far, it's working well.

As I reach the main entrance, I check my time. Not bad.

In the elevator I catch my breath and, as I'm alone, stretch out.

Mrs. Jones is busy in the kitchen as I walk past on my way to my bedroom. I check in on Ted and find that he's still fast asleep, his chest rising and falling.

Damn, but I love it when he sleeps.

Hope, his nanny, should be up and with him shortly.

Ana is still out for the count, too.

I strip down in the closet, dumping my sweaty clothes in the laundry basket, then head into the shower.

The hot water douses me, washing off all the sweat from my run. I'm lost in my thoughts as I soap my hair when I hear the sound of the shower door open. Ana snakes her arms around me and kisses my back, pressing her body against mine.

My day just got a whole lot better.

I make to move, but Ana tightens her arms and splays her hands on my chest. "No," she says, between kisses on my back. "I want to hold you here. Properly."

We stand quietly, together, until I can bear it no more. Turning around, I pull her into my arms, enjoying the softness and warmth of her body against mine. She raises her lips to me, her eyes darkening.

"Good morning, Mrs. Grey. Happy anniversary."

"Happy anniversary, Christian." Her voice is husky, laced with desire.

I touch my lips to hers and my body comes alive. As does Ana. She moans as she kisses me back, opening her mouth and granting me access to her tongue, which greets mine with heightened fervor. We kiss, tongues tangling and tussling together, pouring what must be a week's worth of frustration into each other as she runs her hands up my back, over my shoulders, and into my hair, pushing me against the cold tiles.

Breathless, she nips my jaw to my ear. "I've missed you," she murmurs above the rush of the shower.

Fuck.

Her words pour gasoline on the fire. My erection is harder and fuller, pressing against her. Wanting her. My fingers are in her wet hair, angling her lips to mine, while I take more from her mouth.

I'd expected maybe some gentle lovemaking, the way we have recently.

But not this.

Ana is lit and greedy. Her teeth scrape along my stubbled jawline. Her fingers tug at my hair as my hands move to her behind, pressing her to me. She squirms against me, finding some friction, her intent clear.

"Ana? Here?" I gasp.

"Yes. I'm not made of glass, Christian." She's emphatic as she kisses the line of my clavicle, her hands now roaming down my back to my ass. She squeezes hard, and then her hand is on me.

"Fuck," I whisper through clenched teeth.

"I've missed this." She wraps her fingers around my cock and starts to move her hand up and down, her mouth on mine once more.

I pull back to gaze at her; her eyes are dazed with passion. Her hand tightens around me, and I watch and clench my ass with each move, thrusting into her hand.

She licks her lips.

Oh, no. To hell with this.

I want inside her.

She said she's not made of glass.

I lift her. "Wrap your legs around me, baby." She complies, with a surprising agility.

That must be her sessions with Bastille.

And her lust.

I turn, resting her back against the tiles.

"You're so beautiful," I whisper, and slowly ease into her.

She tips her head up against the wall and cries out.

The sound travels to the end of my dick.

And I start to move.

Hard. Fast.

Her heels press into my butt. Spurring me on. Her arms wrap around my neck, cradling me as I drive myself into her. Over and over. Her breathing accelerates, becoming louder and harsher in my ear as she climbs.

"Yes. Yes," she whispers, and I don't know if it's a plea or a promise.

Ana.

My love.

Suddenly she cries out as her orgasm consumes her, and I let go, following her over the edge, coming inside my wife and calling her name.

When I'm sane again, I'm leaning against her, holding both of us up. Ana unhitches her legs and slides them down my body so that we're both standing together in the shower.

I press my forehead to hers.

And together we catch our breath.

Holding each other beneath the stream of hot water.

Ana tilts her head up, cups the back of my neck, and brushes her lips against mine. Gentle. Sweet. "I needed that," she says.

I laugh. "Me, too, baby!" My lips are on hers once more, but this time in thanks.

"Can we enjoy part two in bed?" Her eyes are still smoldering.

"But…work?"

Ana shakes her head. "I've taken the day off. I want to spend it in bed with you. We'll never have this first again, and I want to celebrate our anniversary, doing what we do best."

I beam down at her, feeling all the love in the world. "Mrs. Grey. Your wish is my command." Lifting her into my arms, I carry her back to bed and lay her down, both of us soaking wet.

ANA IS DOZING, FACEDOWN and naked on our bed. I kiss her shoulder and get up. In our closet, I drag on some sweatpants and a T-shirt and go in search of food. I check in on Teddy and find Hope with him, changing his diaper.

"Good morning, Mr. Grey." She has a sweet drawl, betraying her southern roots.

"Good morning, Hope."

Hope minds Teddy when Ana's at work and lives upstairs with the rest of the staff.

She's in her early forties. Never married. Never had kids. I'm sure there's a story there that Ana will unearth one day. Ana has a knack for getting people to talk.

She did it with me.

Hope has been with us for three months, and so far, it's working well. Ana had insisted on someone older—a career nanny, because Ana's so young. *I want someone I can learn from. My mom lives too far away, and your mom is so busy.*

Hope does not approve of Ted sleeping in our bed.

As much as I love him, I'm with Hope on this, but Ana will not be swayed.

Hope kisses Teddy's belly and he chortles with glee.

It's a beautiful sound.

"I'll leave you to it," I tell Hope.

Mrs. Jones is at the stove. "Good morning, Gail."

"Ah! Mr. Grey. Good morning. Happy anniversary."

"Thank you. I'd like to take Ana breakfast in bed."

"Lovely idea. What would the two of you like?"

"Pancakes, bacon. Blueberries. Coffee."

"Coming right up. It'll be about twenty minutes."

"Great." I amble into my study to fetch the first of my anniversary presents for Ana. The second one, an eternity ring—a symbol of my eternal love—I'll give to her over dinner this evening. I open my desk drawer to check that the red box with her ring is still there, but my eyes stray to the photograph of Ella Pusztai adorned by a silver frame that's now tucked away in my drawer. Ana liberated the snap from my childhood bedroom and had it enlarged and placed in the frame as a gift for my last birthday, but no matter how often I open the drawer, the sight of my birth mother catches me unawares.

You still wanted your mom. You loved her.

My wife is nothing if not persistent. She also found Ella's final resting place and we'll go one day…I think. Maybe I'll find out more about her then, and maybe after that, she'll earn a place on my shelf.

You might want to direct some of your forgiveness at her.

I'm working on it, John. I'm working on it.

Enough, Grey.

I close the drawer and retrieve the first present I'm going to give Ana this morning. I hope she likes it. Placing the gift on my desk, I check the time. It's 8:30. Andrea should be at her desk. My wife has decided to stay home, and so will I. Picking up the phone, I press call.

"Good morning, Mr. Grey."

"Good morning, Andrea. Cancel all my meetings today. I'm taking the day off."

There's a slight pause and a small gasp before she replies, "Yes, sir."

"And don't call me. At all."

"Er…sure. I mean, yes."

I laugh. "Thank you. Tell Ros, too. Whatever it is can wait until tomorrow."

She laughs. "Will do, Mr. Grey. Enjoy your day." That's two of us in a good mood.

ANA IS DOZING WHEN I bring in her tray—the sheet loosely wrapped around her body, so I'm treated to the spectacular view that is my wife. Her hair is tousled from our earlier lovemaking and spreads across the pillows in a lush sprawl. She has one arm raised over her head, one breast and one shapely leg partly exposed. The morning light caresses her body, as if she's been captured by a Grand Master himself. A Titian, or a Velázquez maybe.

Aphrodite.

My goddess.

She's lost weight since Ted's birth, and I know she wants to lose more, but to me, she's as lovely as ever.

The rattle of our coffee cups rouses her, and she rewards me with a breathtaking smile. "Breakfast in bed? You really are spoiling me."

I place the tray on the bed and take my place beside her.

"A feast!" She claps her hand. "I'm famished!" She tucks into her pancakes and bacon.

"You'll have to thank Mrs. Jones for this. I can't take any credit."

"I will," she mumbles, mouth full.

We eat in a companionable silence, enjoying the nearness of each other.

It's a curious feeling.

This utter contentment.

I've only ever felt it with Ana.

And I allow myself a moment to reflect on my extraordinary good fortune.

I have a loving, smart, gorgeous wife.

A beautiful son, who is at present being entertained by Hope.

My business is in good hands. All the companies we've bought over the past few years are highly profitable. The solar tablet is a huge success, and we're creating new technology around it, specifically for the developing world.

Sitting here, with my wife, eating pancakes, is about as good as it gets.

Once I finish, I put my plate down. "I have something for you, which I can take credit for." From beside the bed, I hold up the gift-wrapped package.

"Oh!" Ana grabs a napkin and wipes her hands while I place her empty plate on the tray and push it out of the way.

"Here."

She gives me a quizzical look as I hand her the broad, heavy, oblong package.

"It's our paper anniversary. That's your only clue."

She grins and starts carefully unwrapping the paper, trying not to tear it. Inside is a large leather binder. Ana bites her lip as she unlatches the strap holding it shut and lifts the cover. She gasps, her hand flying to her mouth. Beneath the cover is a black-and-white still of Ana and Ted: she's smiling down at him, and he's gazing up at her in adoration. The light is perfect, illuminating both of them in a warm, loving glow. I took it a couple of weeks ago, specifically for this series of ledger-sized prints, and it reminds me of the Virgin in the small shrine in St. James's cathedral in Seattle. "This is lovely," Ana breathes, her voice ringing with awe.

I'm proud of these stills. My intention is to hang them in place of some of the Madonnas in the foyer. In the next one, she's holding Ted and looking at me, her eyes alight with amusement, and something a little darker…something for me. I love this picture.

There are four prints with Ana and Teddy—and then the last one.

She gasps again. It's me and Ted, in a selfie. He's in my arms, all dimples and baby fat, curled against my naked chest, fast asleep while I gaze into the camera. "Oh, Christian, this is fabulous. I love it." Ana turns to me, tears in her eyes. "My two favorite men, in one exquisite capture."

"They both love you, very much."

"And I love you!" She closes the book and sets it aside carefully and pounces on me, rattling the cups and plates. "You *are* the three wishes from Aladdin's lamp, the state lottery, and the cure for cancer rolled into one!"

I laugh and brush my fingers down her cheek. "No, Ana. You are."

ACKNOWLEDGMENTS

Thanks to:

Dominique Raccah and all the dedicated team at Sourcebooks, for welcoming me into my new home with such warmth and enthusiasm, and for doing such a fabulous job on this book.

My editor, Anne Messitte, for once more steering me with such grace through the mayhem that is Christian Grey.

Kathleen Blandino, for the beta read and for wrangling my website. Ruth Clampett, for the beta read and for your gracious, constant encouragement. Debra Anastasia, for the writing sprints and words of encouragement—we got there in the end! Crissy Maier, for advice on police procedure. And Amy Brosey for all her hard work on the manuscript.

Becca, Bee, Belinda, Britt, Jada, Jill, Kellie, Kelly, Leis, Liz, Nora, Rachel, QT, and Taylor—ladies, you are all amazing and such a safe place. Thank you also for the Americanisms. You constantly remind me that we belong to four great nations divided by a common language. Who knew that a buttonhole is called a boutonnière?

Vanessa, Emma, Zoya, Crissy—for being such wonderful friends and social media advocates.

To all the wonderfully supportive book bloggers out there, of which there are too many to mention! I see you and thank you for all that you do for me and the author community.

Philippa and all the social media allies who amplify and support. Thank you so much.

The Bunker 3.0 ladies, you rock.

And to all my book-world friends for being a constant source of inspiration and support. You know who you are; I only hope that we can get to see each other sometime soon.

Julie McQueen, for all the off-site help and all that you do for me and mine.

Val Hoskins. My agent. My friend. You are a wonderful woman to have in my corner. Thank you for everything.

Niall Leonard, thank you for the initial edit, cups of tea, fud, steadfast support, and most of all your love.

And to my two beautiful boys—my love for you overwhelms me sometimes. You are my joy. Thank you for being such wonderful, supportive young men. (And, Minor, thank you for all the help on the poker game!)

And to my readers, thank you for waiting.
This book took much longer than I intended,
but I hope you enjoyed it.
It was for you.
Thank you for all that you've done for me.

ABOUT E L JAMES

E L James is an incurable romantic and a self-confessed fangirl. After twenty-five years of working in television, she decided to pursue a childhood dream and write stories that readers could take to their hearts. The result was the controversial and sensuous romance *Fifty Shades of Grey* and its two sequels, *Fifty Shades Darker* and *Fifty Shades Freed*. In 2015, she published the #1 bestseller *Grey*, the story of *Fifty Shades of Grey* from the perspective of Christian Grey, and in 2017, the chart-topping *Darker*, the second part of the Fifty Shades story from Christian's point of view. She followed with the #1 *New York Times* bestseller *The Mister* in 2019. Her books have been published in fifty languages and have sold more than 165 million copies worldwide.

E L James has been recognized as one of *Time* magazine's Most Influential People in the World and *Publishers Weekly*'s Person of the Year. *Fifty Shades of Grey* stayed on the *New York Times* bestseller list for 133 consecutive weeks. *Fifty Shades Freed* won the Goodreads Choice Award (2012), and *Fifty Shades of Grey* was selected as one of the 100 Great Reads, as voted by readers, in PBS's The Great American Read (2018). *Darker* was longlisted for the 2019 International DUBLIN Literary Award.

She was a producer on each of the three Fifty Shades movies, which made more than a billion dollars at the box office. The third installment, *Fifty Shades Freed*, won the People's Choice Award for Drama in 2018. E L James is blessed with two wonderful sons and lives with her husband, the novelist and screenwriter Niall Leonard, and their West Highland terriers in the leafy suburbs of West London.

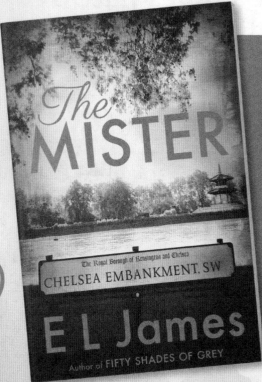

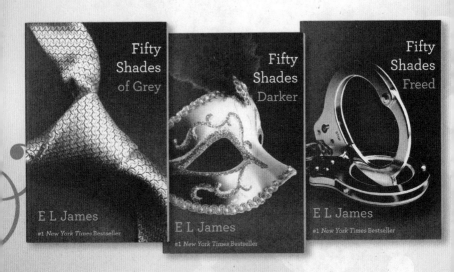

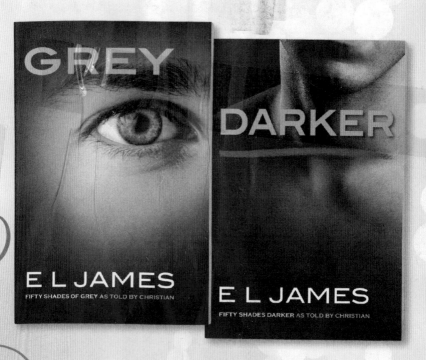

See yourself *in*

Bloom

every story is a celebration.

Visit **bloombooks.com**
for more information about

E L JAMES

and more of your favorite authors!

 bloombooks   @read_bloom   @read_bloom   read_bloom

 Bloom books